## Additional Comments about *River of Red Gold*

🔳 Exceptional in the genre of C............................... st paints a
world of nature and civilizat............................... y and big-
otry on the California frontie...............................
.......................... ciation of
.......................... y Colleges

🔳 [West] tells the story of a Donner Party survivor set against the excitement of the California gold rush. This beautifully written, haunting story is a must-read for Donner buffs and for those who like a good tale well told. —Reno Gazette-Journal

🔳 California's history has been presented in a lustrous haze of land conquered and people tamed. These notions and more are challenged in River of Red Gold. —California Geology Magazine

🔳 A wonderful blending of dramatic history and insightful imagination. A delightful, rewarding read ... gives voices to people that in the traditional Western stories have been silent. West is a scholar who can write popular fiction. Not many scholars can do that.
—Richard W. Etulain, Center for the American West, University of New Mexico

🔳 Alive and bursting with excitement. —The Sacramento Bee

🔳 I didn't want it to end, and when it did, the world looked different—the grass, the trees, everything. —Lydia Gascon Samaniego

🔳 Excellent and soul-stirring saga—three dimensional characters ... profoundly immersing the reader.
—Laurie Mcgonagill, teacher, California history

🔳 Insightful multicultural perspective ... a wonderful analysis of power. ...enchants the most reluctant reader.
—Deborah Moreno, California History Instructor, Folsom Lake College

🔳 I have never, never, ever read such a delightful book. I've read zillions of great novels over the years, but this is the best.
—Gail Hannan, California History Instructor

### Frequently repeated comments:

🔳 Awesome research!

🔳 I've read it before, but am reading it again.

🔳 A side of the Donner Party story I hadn't heard before.

# River of
# Red Gold

# River of
# Red Gold

## A History Novel

*Naida West*

Rancho Murieta, California

ISBN: 978-0-9653487-5-1

Interior design by Pete Masterson, Æonix Publishing Group, www.aeonix.com
Cover by Karen Phillips, Phillips Covers, www.phillipscovers.com
Cover photos by Tom Myers, www.TomMyersPhotography.com
Photo of his great, great grandmother's watch by Rick Grimshaw

Published by Bridge House Books
P.O. Box 809
Rancho Murieta, California 95683
www.bridgehousebooks.com

Printed in the United States of America

# Author's Note

This book started when I was digging in my garden, expanding it to move the climbing beans away from the squash. My shovel stopped on a layer of hard clay into which small flat stones had been pressed. Struggling to dig through it I was surprised to find a straight edge and a right-angle corner. Then I understood. This was once the floor of a cabin facing the barely discernible old road angling down across our front pasture. For years on this remnant of a once-large ranch at the start of the Sierra foothills, we had been finding rusty square nails and other bits of the past. The rock wall around the lawn of our old farmhouse contains petrified wood, gold-bearing quartz, and a purple-obsidian core from which arrowheads had been flaked. While installing a water line, my husband found pieces of hand-blown bottles that had probably been disposed of down an outhouse, a once common practice. The former owners had told us that in the 1940s their turkeys had unearthed a stash of gold coins while scratching and fluffing holes in the dirt to lie in and cool themselves. One day a man from the East Coast knocked on our door and asked if we had found the grave of Perry McCoon. At the time I'd never heard of him, but I knew that the bones of a story lay all around us, and I decided to dig them up.

I interviewed descendants of local pioneers. In particular I am thankful to Ellen Cothrin Rosa, who maintains a large family collection of historical papers passed down through her mother, Kitty Sheldon Cothrin. From her I learned that a young survivor of the Donner Party had moved to this place a few weeks after her 1847 rescue from the snowbound mountains. Next I went to the helpful staffs of the History Section of the California State Library and the Sacramento County Archives and Museum Collection. I read every published and unpublished work available at that time and put puzzle pieces together until I had my own Mother Lode, a story far more dramatic and significant than I had imagined.

I could have written this as straight history (if any history is straight), but I wanted to share it with a broader audience, the more so at this 150th anniversary of the Donner Party and the upcoming 150th anniversaries of the Gold Rush and California Admission to the Union. I wanted people from all walks of life to know what I have learned. The tools of fiction allowed me to flesh out historically sketchy characters and convey emotional and spiritual sides of the story.

My five years of research and writing were buoyed by walks along the Cosumnes River, which hurries down through the boulders before stilling itself in quiet stretches and spreading out on the Sacramento Valley floodplain. Many evenings I stood near the river where the air is fragrant with moss, lupine, peppermint, and other herbs. Deer and coyotes stepped out to look at me. I ran my fingers over the smooth inner surfaces of mortar rocks where native women had pounded acorns into meal, and I began to feel that I was not alone among the oaks and cottonwoods. No sudden revelation this, but a growing awareness and a welcoming feeling. The history of this place ran deeper than words in diaries and letters. I expanded my research.

Anthropologist Jerald Johnson of Sacramento State University was generous with his time. I am also indebted to many other scholars, including James A. Bennyhoff, Malcolm Margolin, Albert Hurtado, James Rawls, S. F. Cook, R. F. Heizer, who have written of the destruction of the California Indians and their durability. I am grateful to the Miwok people who shared with me the dignity and expansiveness of their culture. For that side of the story I used the voice of magical realism, which comes to literature from south of the border, ultimately the native peoples. I make no claim that it is the authentic voice of the individuals who walked this land before me, but I believe their descendants will understand when I say it is what I heard when I listened.

For the Donner side of the story I owe thanks to George Stewart *(Ordeal by Hunger)* and Joseph King *(Winter of Entrapment: A New Look at the Donner Party)*. As a child, I listened to my father, Arthur L. Smith, a spellbinding storyteller and admirer of fellow-Idahoan Vardis Fisher, author of the Donner Party novel *The Mothers: An American Saga of Courage (1943)*. Never had I imagined that I would later live in a place where a survivor had lived. The memoir of Eliza Donner Houghton, written 65 years after that tragedy, provided many fascinating details. Only four years old at the time, she consulted with her sister Elitha, who was ten years older. From that source I took the description of Perry McCoon's adobe cabin and the ancestral home of the native people who worked on his ranch—not much changed from the place I often visit a bit upriver from my house. From Elitha comes the description of the hornet-grub excursion. I am also grateful to Elitha's descendants and the descendants of her neighbors for sharing their insights into her quiet strength.

Finally, without Bill Geyer, my tirelessly interested husband and a California historian in his own right, this book could not have come to fruition. I also wish to thank the writers who helped me hone the craft—Cleo Kocol, Louise Crawford, Jay MacLarty, Liz Crain and Gene Munger—Ruth Younger for English editing and Araceli Collazo for Spanish. Sloughhouse pioneer-descendant Janis Blawat James ably assisted with production. And I cannot leave out my "Go!" coach, Bud Gardner.

All errors and liberties with language are my own.

## FACT AND FICTION

Whereas in most historical fiction a fabricated plot and fictional characters are imposed upon an historical setting, I have used real events as story guideposts. The book moves from documented event to documented event, and the names of the characters are unchanged. In most historical novels, conflicts between the needs of storytelling and historical facts are resolved in favor of fiction, but I veered toward history. I filled in the gaps between the exciting, shocking, and at times almost unbelievable events, providing motivation and connective tissue. María (also "Indian Mary" and "Mary") and Pedro Valdez were sketchy in diaries and oral history, so I all but created them. While their presence brushes history with a fictional gloss, to omit them because they left no papers and others recorded only a few of their actions would have perpetuated a greater fiction: that the gold rush was about men of European and North American origin. I hope this book inspires readers to reflect upon the connection between the land and those who walk upon it, the influence of gold in our lives, and the extent to which the past lives in the present.

Readers interested in the details of fact and fiction should read the Endnotes.

Naida West, August 1996
Rancho Murieta

## FIFTH PRINTING NOTE

During the years since this novel was first published (August 1996), thousands of readers have gifted me with praise and appreciation. Some of them also shared information from their family collections. A few times I revised the Endnotes of upcoming printings to reflect those contributions. In this fifth printing, 3rd edition, I have for the first time, altered some of the main text, as well as the Endnotes, to reflect new information. Details of the Donner Party are continually being updated by Kristin Johnson, who first published *Unfortunate Emigrants: Narratives of the Donner Party* in July 1996. Since then Johnson, an academic librarian, has maintained a reader-friendly website, *New Light on the Donner Party,* which operates as a clearing house for existing and new research by interested parties, and also discusses how she separates myth from fact, given the many contradictory voices. This new edition of my novel contains a number of changes attributable to that outstanding resource.

Naida West, June 2013

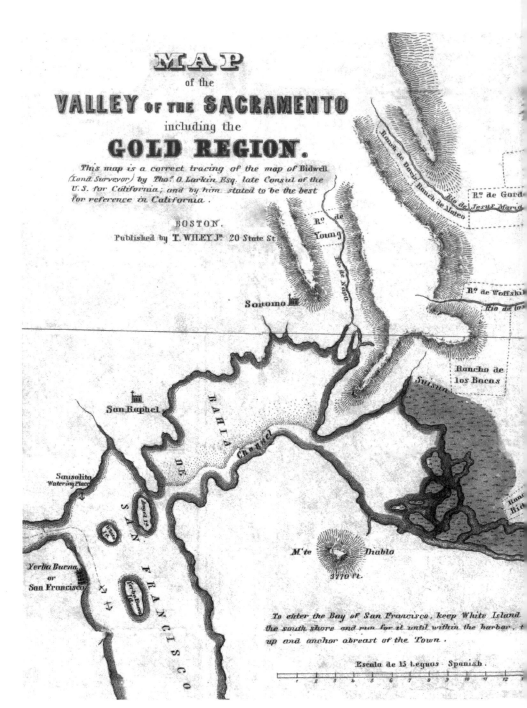

This portion of a rare map is the earliest to show California's gold region. Published by an act of Congress in 1848. It is a tracing of an earlier map by John Bidwell. The instructions to sea captains refer to a rocky island covered with white bird quano, now known by its Spanish name, Alcatraz, meaning pelican. "Tulares" indicates

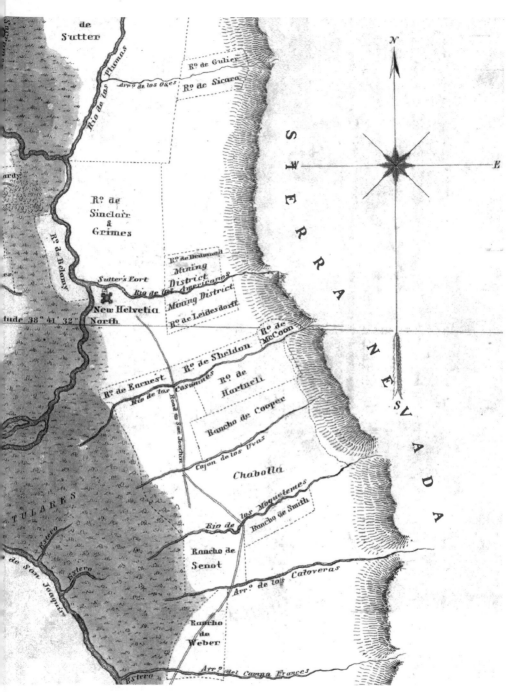

marshland. "Ro de" means Rancho of. On the east, the Sierra Nevada mountains were unmapped as of 1848. On the far west, the narrow neck of water entering the San Francisco Bay was called "The Golden Gate." Minor spelling corrections have been made for the sake of clarity.

AMERICAN RIVER

(Folsom)

Rancho de Leidesdorff

REGION OF
RANCHO SACAYAK
&
RANCHO OMUCHUMNE

Road to Sutter's Fort
(Hwy 16)

(Grant Line Road)

Rancho Omuchumne

DEER CREEK

COSUMNES RIVER

(Dillard Road)

N
W        E
S

① Daylor's Store          ⑥ Michigan Bar
② Omuchumne Village       ⑦ Bridge House
③ Slough House            ⑧ Grizzly Hair's Vill
④ Sheldon's Mill Ranch    ⑨ Cook's Bar
⑤ McCoon's Adobe          ⑩ Katesville

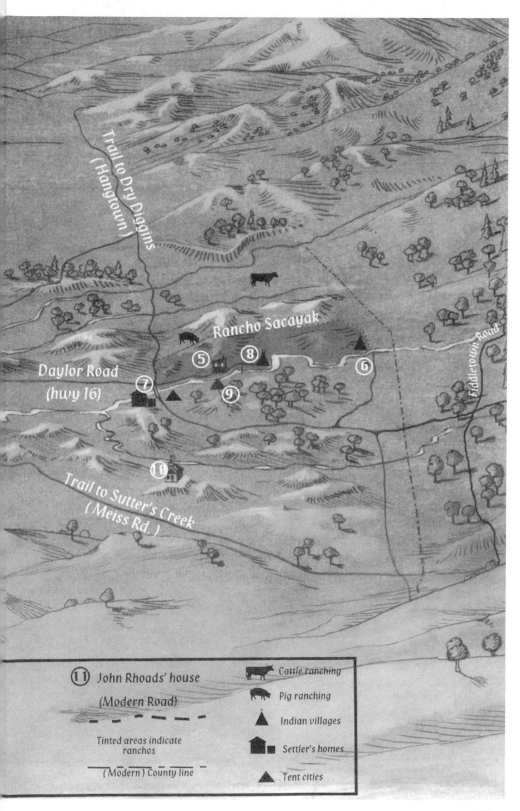

Trail to Dry Diggins
(Hangtown)

Rancho Sacayak

Daylor Road
(hwy 16)

⑤    ⑧    ▲
⑦  ▲  ㊉      ⑥
     ⑨

Fiddletown Road

Trail to Sutter's Creek
(Meiss Rd.)

⑩

⑪ John Rhoads' house        🐄 Cattle ranching

(Modern Road)               🐖 Pig ranching

- - - - - -                 ▲ Indian villages

Tinted areas indicate       ■ Settler's homes
ranchos

——— (Modern) County line —— ▲ Tent cities

# I

## Pedro and María

**HOWCHIA SPEAKS:**

Once I was Eagle Woman. Now I am an oak tree.

When I walked these paths the nights came often and life in the village hurled past like the river in the time of early flowers. When I died I should have gone to the happy land, but I looked back, unable to turn away from the home place I loved. Thus my spirit lingers. But I did not choose to inhabit a being so long-lived or to stand overlooking the dancehouse—a hollow in the earth now, overgrown with high grass—where the outpourings of our human hearts once rent the sky and the mysteries of the universe were felt so deeply. Through the soil of human time my roots suckle the rotted acorn husks and bones of my people. My trunk is sculpted and broad, and even while it bleaches in the sun, my taproot, far below, sips from a pool of wet sand as eternal as the river.

An occasional vehicle parks here, and the new people picnic on the river beach. The laughter of children in the water pleases me and I think how I played there as a child, as did my little son and his daughter after him. But the new people leave at dark. They miss the orange moon rising over the eastern hill and layers and layers of sparkling stars. They miss the music of owls and the urgent drum of frog calls, and the rustling of night animals.

In the quiet time I fathom all that happened here.

Next time I die I shall look forward and walk the pathway of ghosts, for now I yearn for the cheer and dances of the spirit world. Before an evening fire I shall tell the stories and my people will exchange sly smiles when they hear that despite the melancholy teachings and sober striving of the new people, many of them would like to live much as we did. For the spirits that live in the boulders and the river and the plants and animals are beginning to touch them too.

Out of the heat waves over the tired grass comes Old Man Coyote. He seems to float, a dirt-brown shag on high slender legs, trotting his rounds, head cocked a little askew. He stops beneath my branches.

I greet him the old way. "Where are you going?"

"Just ate a cat over there." He flips his head toward the gigantic houses. "That pampered sack of lard didn't even have claws. Heh heh. They'll blame Hel-eh-jah, Moutain Lion. I'll rest for a while and then trot over to Stan's ranch and check on the lambs."

A familiar glint lights his eye. "Maybe I'll sneak inside his helicopter and wait 'til he's hovering over the hills trying to find me. Then I'll howl in his ear. Woo-ooo woo-woo!"

Coyote never stops scheming.

"My ancestors came to this river," I say, "and life was much the same for a long time. Then in only a few seasons everything changed."

"Uh-uh-uh," he warns in a rising tone. "You're looking back again." He loves to mock me for breaking the custom of my people, who tried to look forward.

"I'll bet you miss the big times," I tease back.

"Those dancing clowns trying to be me? That was the best part. Woo-oo-oo!"

"Have you ever stopped to think, Old Man, that at the slightest whim the new people could bulldoze me and exterminate you? We exist in their obliviousness."

He turns in a circle and plops down in my shade, his pink tongue draped thinly over the humps of his incisors. "They can't kill me."

A smile tickles up my bark. "You made us to be like you, Coyote, optimistic and inquisitive. Sometimes I wonder, don't you? What would have happened if the Spaniards had learned of the gold, or if they had stopped the North Americans from—"

"If if if," he sniffs.

I laugh, for he is right, and it is good to laugh. The twists and turns of Condor dreams—the events of the world—cannot be predicted, though many have tried. "Have you heard?" I tease, "Some people say Condor is dead."

He jumps up feigning terror, looking all around, but then plops down again. "Ground Squirrel is still chasing his wife," he says. "Blue Heron is on the riverbank hunting as always, and you still tell good stories."

A breeze rattles my leaves, unsettling the ghosts of the past, and I see again the man named Pedro Valdez.

# 1

## SUTTER'S FORT, SUMMER 1844

The night was warm, and within the fort's adobe walls a candle cast a restless halo on the ceiling. Pedro lay naked on his rawhide cot, ankles crossed, fingers moving over the ancient helmet on his chest, down the holy cross of the nose and eyebrows. The earthy fox-den smell seemed particularly strong, and it conjured up a disturbing memory of the house of Pedro's childhood, in the small pueblo of San José. It had been dark there too.

The wooden latch had rattled. Pedro and his brothers bolted up in their bed. Mother rose to her feet as the door creaked open, the spinning-wool tumbling from her lap.

Father, Old Pepe, stood in the candlelight—home at last. About his loins he wore only a vine of wilted leaves. His hair was long now, and white as his beard. His hooded eyes avoided the stares of the family as he crossed the room to the bed he shared with Mamma. Smears of blood marked his footsteps on the hard clay floor.

His voice rasped high, the pride gone out of it. "I found much gold," he said, "but the Indians took it. Again. Threw it away. Flung it into a thorn thicket." He looked down, muttering until the words all but vanished. "The devils stole my helmet too. And my horse, and my clothes."

Ashamed, the old man had walked forty leagues across the big valley. To Pedro that now seemed an eon ago, and yet the memory still gave him a sick feeling.

By a miracle of the Virgin the helmet had been found among the ashes along the Stanislaus River after the Indian uprisings of 1829. Pedro ran a thumb over the rough spot in the metal where a spike had broken off. He'd been very young when Old Pepe told him and his brothers about the heroic ancestor who had worn the helmet while riding with El Cid Campeador. In the fabled olden days El Cid and his freedom fighters had liberated Spain from the Moors and pushed them back across the sea. They saved Europe for Christ. Their manly deeds rang down the centuries, and now the helmet lay in Pedro's hands, passed down from Valdez to Valdez in an unbroken chain of military service to the Crown of Spain. Dazzling Spain, powerful colonizer of continents.

Spain ran in Pedro's blood. Grandfather Valdez had sailed the Atlantic to serve in New Spain, Mexico now. Father, Pepe, had come north to the remote garrison on the Bay of San Francisco to pacify Indians in the regions served by the northern missions. He'd been thirteen years old, a bastard son, his mother an Indian. Hence he'd remained an enlisted man all his life. Only a man of pure blood advanced in military rank. The helmet had been Old Pepe's sole inheritance, and yet no prouder or more loyal soldier ever served the Spanish Crown. Before gold drove him mad. Ay madre, Pedro sighed, it took a proud man to go insane, a man with too big a dream.

Dreamers had clawed for gold in the coastal hills and valleys for sixty years, and every time excitement flared the ore proved of little or no value. During Pedro's lifetime men had stopped looking. All but Old Pepe. With a mad twinkle in his eye he declared, "I am the only one looking far enough to the east." People made the crazy sign by their temples. Children pointed to Pedro's ragged pantaloons and taunted, "See how grandly he dresses! His father has a big gold mine."

The laughter still rang in Pedro's mind. He crossed his other ankle. Any fool could see that the Indians of Upper California lived in hovels and wore shell beads. If they'd had gold, some of them would be drinking from golden chalices and wearing golden ornaments. A man had to be crazy to think gold abounded where tens of thousands of Indians lived in poverty, a people acquainted with every rock in their land. Grudgingly, sadly, Pedro had agreed with the town. Old Pepe had gone soft in the head. Recently he'd begun to understand that it was this disloyalty to his father that made him feel sick. It ran against the grain of Spanish pride.

Yet those bloody footprints held no attraction for Pedro. Like his father, he too had left home very young, signing for military duty when he was fourteen. A revolution had rocked Mexico, barely felt on this northern frontier, yet it proved to be a quake with lasting tremors. In eighteen years Pedro had served an emperor of doubtful character, more than one shadowy general, a junta, and "the people" of Mexico. It was hard to keep track. Now he served under Captain John Sutter, a naturalized Mexican citizen who had no ties at all to Spain. As justice of the peace, Sutter controlled the vast interior valley. In the five years since Pedro helped lay the Captain's first adobe brick in this uncharted land, he'd done his share of pacifying Indians.

"Mother of God," he said aloud, spreading his hands over the solid curve of the steel. In a way it represented his soul, his destiny, but the helmet wasn't enough. At thirty-three, a man had to think beyond barracks and mess meals, especially a man of mixed blood. Terreno burned in his imagination. Land. A sweep of it peppered with cattle and worked by Pedro's own skilled vaqueros. Land gave a man a bit of nobility. Someday when he saw the right place he would apply to the governor, who sometimes rewarded soldiers with land grants. But being of mixed blood, Pedro also needed a strong letter of recommendation from his superior officer, Captain John Sutter.

Wrapping the helmet in the old sarape, Pedro replaced it beneath the cot and puffed out the candle. As the wick smoke scented the warm air, he thought about tomorrow, when he would ride up the Cosumnes River. Captain Sutter was reaching farther east for native laborers and militiamen, illness having decimated the Indians of the big valley. Pedro would ride to where the first foothills mounded toward the Sierra Nevada, the Snowy Range.

He turned on his side to his sleeping position. Tomorrow he'd do some trick riding. Indians loved it. It loosened them for talk.

❦

María Howchia pushed her basket of acorn meal into the scooped-out sand where the river would leach out the bitterness. The village dogs began to bark.

She stood up to listen, the tattoo of womanhood new on her chin, her hair singed straight across her brows and shoulders. Squealing children added to the din, and then she heard the pounding of horse hooves. She headed toward the excitement. The u-machas and dancehouse were a blur as she ran, and her amulet bounced between her budding breasts. She rounded the berry brambles, crossed the dry streambed, and stopped in her tracks.

A fully clothed man stood upright on a galloping horse, one boot before the other. His bent knees flexed with the running gait, and he flew like a bird—arms wide, white sleeves billowing. His hat, attached to his neck by strings, sailed behind his head. He circled the field where ti-kel was played and then galloped toward her out of a gilded dust cloud, his reddish hair flaming in the low sun. Gooseflesh rippled down her limbs.

The gathering umne, the People, gaped as the flying rider crouched to retrieve the reins, which had lain loose across the horse's neck. He stopped the horse and sprang to the ground, arms upraised, smiling at his admirers. His glance met hers and a spark of magic shot through her.

She moved between her parents, touched the arm of Father, Grizzly Hair, and asked, "Is he a black hat?" The hat the stranger returned to his head was indeed black with a red band. It had the same stiff brim Father had described as the mark of the enemy Español warriors who lived near the western sea.

Father, hy-apo of the umne and a man of knowledge, stood tall and powerful. Sunlight caught the polished bones in his earlobes and the broad planes of his face, and his topknot made him look even taller—the long hair gathered in rabbit-skin lacing so it stood like a tree on his head, spilling over the top in a plume. She saw agitation beneath his practiced calm. Not answering, he stepped toward the stranger and asked in Spanish, "Where do you come from and where are you going?"

The umne crept forward to hear, María Howchia among them.

The stranger squared his shoulders, lifted his chin—a thin line of trimmed hair sketching a square jaw—and spoke in Spanish slowly enough to be understood.

"I come from the establishment of Capitán Don Juan Sutter, from his hacienda on the River of the Americans. It would please me to talk with you."

She noticed that Father's name for the big river to the north was also used by the Españoles. But that wasn't on the western sea. It was only a half-day's walk to the north.

"He flew like a bird," she said quietly into Mother's ear. The man's hair had glints of red like the red-tailed hawk. *Proud Hawk* she named him in her mind.

The stranger removed the wood-framed saddle, the straps from the horse's head, and a puzzling metal thing from its mouth. Then he and Grizzly Hair walked toward the village center. She and the umne followed. Important talk would come. Father and the stranger sat opposite each another in the village clearing, and María Howchia found a place among the umne near enough to hear. Dogs sat down beside their people-friends.

"Capitán Juan," the stranger began, addressing Father by the name the mission long-robes had given him. *"Mañana yo me voy al establecimiento del Capitán Sutter. El necesita más trabajadores...* "As he talked he held himself with dignity, which indicated he came from honorable people and his demeanor honored Father—not what she expected from a black hat, if that's what he was.

Most of his Spanish rolled past her as she examined his face—the slight hawk-like curve of his nose, the trim mustache. His gaze swept across her as he talked, and briefly their eyes met. Strange eyes, the color of an evening pond fractured as when pebbles are dropped and ripples cross from different directions. Penetrating eyes that invited her. She realized she was holding her breath.

She knew enough Spanish to understand that he was urging the umne to go to Captain Sutter's place.

Clearly suspicious, Father talked of fair trade. However María Howchia's older brother Crying Fox listened with enthusiasm, as did many other young people.

Later Proud Hawk joined the family fire, stretching his legs out and placing one square-toed boot across the other. As María helped her mother Etumu prepare supper, she stole glances at him and his black hat, which lay on the ground beside him. On its red band was a mark that resembled the track of a crippled turkey. When he looked into her eyes, another spark of magic sizzled through her.

She'd been reaching into the fire with the blue-oak tongs, picking up the red-hot cooking stone, when his power weakened her grip and she dropped the stone into the nu-pah, splashing the uncooked acorn porridge on her legs and feet. Mother scowled. Grizzly Hair shot her a silent question. Embarrassed, she dashed under the shade porch of the family u-macha and made her way down into its comforting darkness.

There she stayed, listening to the talk of Father and Proud Hawk. Soon she heard the distant singing of Grandmother Dishi returning from her shell-drilling place near the river. The old feet knew the trail and her outstretched hands kept her from bumping into things. Giving her time to arrive, María peeked out the entrance of the u-macha and saw Crying Fox seated next to Proud Hawk. They made room for Grandmother.

Mother's movements seemed stiff and unfriendly as she offered salad with ant vinegar to Proud Hawk. He ate that and strips of roasted ground squirrel, but refused the nu-pah, the mainstay of the umne. As the night shadows darkened and the fire brightened, María Howchia began to feel foolish to have run away, but it would draw attention to her foolishness if she returned, so she stayed in the u-macha.

Everyone around the fire ate in silence now, and the howling of several coyotes sounded like laughter directed at her. Eventually Proud Hawk stood up and yawned in an exaggerated manner. With a nod to each member of the family and a glance around the village to all the other people seated around their dying fires, everyone covertly watching him, he walked toward the field where he had performed and the grazing horses spent the nights. Father and Crying Fox, and the other men of the umne retired to the sweathouse for the night. She knew they would talk about the Español.

Alive with strange feelings, she left Grandmother already snoring on her mat and went back outside to help Mother gather the cooking baskets and bank the fire. Not wanting to ask Mother a rude question about why she'd been unfriendly toward the visitor, María Howchia said, "The black hats don't capture people for work at the missions anymore." The war at the time of her birth had achieved that victory.

Etumu's eyes widened, and in the light of the glowing embers her normally peaceful face had a fierce expression. Her words stung like wasps. "They can never be trusted."

Mother never spoke of the long-ago battles. Something awful must have happened. Scooping cold ashes over the smoldering firewood, María asked, "Why does Proud Hawk want us to go to Captain Sutter's place?"

"Proud Hawk?"

María's face and ears heated.

Mother finally answered. "He wants men and women to collect grass seed."

"But that's women's work!"

"Capitán Sutter expects men to gather too."

Pondering this amazing statement she asked, "Is Capitán Sutter a long robe?"

"Talk to your father about those things." Etumu went to her sleeping place on the porch of the u-macha. Father and Crying Fox went to the sweathouse. The dog curled up beside Mother. María Howchia lay down on her mat an arm's length away, too excited to close her eyes. Gazing through the porch roof, a loose weave of willow branches, she located the first campfire of an Immortal twinkling high above the world. She listened to the river-baby spirits singing in subtle harmony while a chorus of crickets kept time in unexpected rhythm. Inhaling the fragrance of the night moisture on dry grasses near and far, she wasn't spooked at all by the who-who of an owl close by. Things were different now. The war against the black hats was long ago. She decided to speak to Crying Fox after the sleep, and together they would convince their parents it was safe for them to go to Captain Sutter's place.

It wasn't long before all the campfires of the Immortals glittered and winked in the sky, the brighter with Mother Moon still in her eastern house. The mat whispered as María Howchia sat up and rose to her feet.

"Where are you going?" Mother was not asleep!

"To pass water."

"Don't go to the black hat. He will hurt you." Patient, soft-spoken Etumu never gave orders. She taught by example.

"He is our guest, Mother, and he is polite." Actually he shouldn't have looked into María Howchia's eyes quite so long, but she knew he meant no harm.

Etumu's tone was flat and final. "Black hats are cruel."

María persisted, though such behavior was frowned upon. "I think he is too young to have fought in the war. Besides, the world has changed since then. I heard his music and it was good."

Silence.

Irritated at Mother's old ways, she left the porch, intending only to peek at the man from a distance and see whether he slept like normal people. She stepped quietly across the loose pebbles of Berry Creek and up the bank to the open field. The pale spot that was his shirt came into view. A horse nickered.

Silently she drew nearer, listening for sleeping sounds, but the drumbeat of her heart covered all sound—river, frogs, crickets. His magic pulled her. She craved more of it. She couldn't stop herself. A twig cracked beneath her heel.

"*Que va?*" The deep and resonant voice of a man-singer.

"*Yo,*" she said. Thin and weak.

The pale shirt moved. He sat up and thumped the ground beside him. "*Ven.*"

That meant come. Her heart drummed ever louder as she stepped toward him, pulled like Mouse when he couldn't resist the magic of O-se-mai-ti, Grizzly Bear. Like a sleepwalker she arrived next to the man, thrilled by scents of leather, aromatic smoke, and man-musk.

Knees weakening, she lowered herself beside him. She lay on her side facing him, her neck and face burning with excitement and naughtiness.

Proud Hawk lay with his head on his big saddle, and he lightly cupped her high shoulder with a warm and gentle hand. The hand slowly moved down to her waist where it rested in the curve, leaving a fiery pathway on her skin. She could hardly breathe.

"*Indita mía,*" he said softly, his smoky breath connecting them in the warm night. That meant, my little Indian girl.

She reached over and touched the surprising softness of skin next to the bristly line of hair along his jaw. "Is Captain Sutter's place a mission?" she asked.

"*No, Indita mía, es un castillo, un presidio, un pueblo.*"

Presidio! That was the home of the black hats, even more dangerous than a mission.

"It is more of a pueblo," he continued, "a village where people make things and grow wheat and raise cattle." His hand retraced the glowing pathway up her side and down again, stealing her breath as it went. "Would you like to go there with me?" Resonant, low, musical.

Her heart leapt and she almost exclaimed *Ho!* But a wet nose startled her—mother's dog, who always stayed near her mistress. The dog was now sniffing Proud Hawk.

The man's hand remained on the swell of her hip, but he called quietly, "Hola."

"We are only talking," María Howchia added in the tongue of umne. "The man is kind."

Spanish rolled from his mouth. "Your daughter is safe. She goes to her house now."

Gently he nudged her away while saying loud enough for Etumu to hear, "I came here to make friends. Go now, Amapolita. I have no wish to upset your family."

Amapola was the Spanish name for the golden poppy that bloomed in the season of second grass. He had named her Little Poppy.

# 2

After the pretty Indita left, Pedro lay studying the stars that salted the black sky. He never tired of matching the constellations with stories he'd been told, some from old Spain, some from his Indian grandmother. Far and near, coyotes howled, a sleepy sound in the warm night.

It came to him that this was the perfect place for his rancho. Like the other villages on his ride up the River of the Cosumne it had plenty of Indians to work for him, but here at the start of the foothills the land had a manly feel. He would build his house on a rise overlooking the river. In the summer when he sat on his veranda, climbing roses on the pillars would perfume the air and Indias would be in the cookhouse preparing tortillas and tamales. His shy Spanish wife would sit beside him in high comb and mantilla. His clothing would be imported from Mexico, silver brads down his slim trousers to the bleached cotton that belled out. His bolero would be beautifully embroidered with colorful thread. Having him as their teacher, his vaqueros would excel. He'd be a leading citizen of Alta California, Sutter's respected neighbor, General Vallejo's friend, and a loyal retainer of the governor in Monterey. Men would come to his hacienda to discuss important matters.

Soon he was dreaming.

When he awoke the pretty Indita stood at his feet as naked as Eve but for a sparse skirt of cattail leaves. Surrounding her were the bare children of the village, black eyes sparkling. Birds chattered and whistled from the thickets along the river, and dawn tinted everything rosy. Invigorated by the freshness he sprang to his feet and spread his fists wide, stretching. Mingled with the scent of dewy grass was the faint, peachy scent of the Indita.

She said in Spanish, "I'm going to Captain Sutter's place with you."

The Captain liked young girls. "I think you should stay home," he said, realizing that his decision about this place had changed the tune he'd sung to her last night.

"But before the sleep you said—"

"Show me the place for swimming."

She eyed him, then turned to lead, her firm little buttocks shifting, her hair singed off just above tender shoulders. He followed her scent cloud. Children grabbed both his hands and trotted beside him, smiling up like he was a god. *Patrón*, he corrected in his mind. He remembered the poppy-petal feel of her skin. Yes, the Capitán would surely take her, and Pedro didn't want her used by him or the scoundrels his distillery attracted. She should stay here and soon he would be her patrón. At the thought he felt a sudden tightness in the prickly wool of his pants. One good thing about clothing was that it hid this condition. Yet the men in these villages went about entirely naked. Ay madre!

He followed her through the village where naked and near-naked people smiled at him. Some were spooning their fingers into baskets of congealed acorn porridge.

The Indita walked straight into the water with the children, and they all swam like tadpoles. Indians were jokingly said to be amphibious. Brown faces grinned at him from the moving water, wide where the river spread out after coursing around two sides of a small island. With her hair slicked back the girl looked as young as the others. On shore, Captain Juan gazed at the rising sun in the way of Indian chiefs, while the men and women of his tribe came down the path from their little pointed houses, wading into the river.

He wanted to be a part of this communal bathing. Not the normal behavior of a patrón, but he sensed it would serve as a link today. Water was sacred to Indians. Stripping quickly he waded in and paddled out through warm water to where it was deep and cooler. He was relieving himself when the chief, finished with the sun salutation, joined his people in the river. The Amapolita swam to Pedro.

He asked, "What do you call this ranchería?"

"Ranchería," she answered with a teasing grin.

Of course it was an Indian home. "I mean what name? *Comó se llama?*"

As she bobbed in the water a crease appeared between her perfectly shaped brows. "No name."

He'd heard this before. Some Indians didn't name their villages, yet they named every boulder and hill. "Come with me," he said, beckoning with his head.

He swam to shore and led her up the bank to where they could see the face of a large granite boulder. He knew that in springtime the river would roar over it, and that's why the giant rock was smooth and rounded. Gesturing, he asked, "What do you call that?"

She seemed puzzled, and then said a bit uncertainly, "Sacayak?"

Sacayak, he repeated. *Rancho Sacayak*. "What does it mean?"

A huge smile bunched her cheeks, teeth dazzling. With two quick steps, she skimmed into the water and swam away. Amphibians indeed.

Later in the day he thought of that boulder as he nudged Chocolate up the path with seven Indians—three walking ahead, four behind. Sacayak seemed to mean something secret to these people. All the better. On the little hill near that granite boulder he would build his house, and on a warm day the riffles of the river would freshen the air of his veranda.

The Indita's parents had opposed her coming with him. Very well. She and her brother had stayed at home. The five young men who did come walked with quivers slung over their shoulders and bows in their hands. The two young Indias carried their huge conical baskets on their backs secured by thongs around their foreheads, in the way of their women. The older men of the village had stayed at home, keeping the horses—no doubt stolen from missions and ranches. But Indians on foot wouldn't slow Pedro. They had the amazing ability to trot all day, and besides, today he was taking his time. On the way back to the fort he would collect Indians from the other villages that he'd visited coming upstream. Trick riding was the key.

At the top of the first hill, he sat his horse and looked back at the brown people in the open meadow, still watching. As he waved to them he pondered a mystery. Here at the start of the foothills the natives were naked and harmless as Adam and Eve. In the Big Valley the half-clothed Horse-thief Indians, mission fugitives for the most part, plagued the rancheros in the coastal valleys, yet they rarely killed people. But on the coast, where people of all races hid beneath clothing, a man had to watch his back. When Captain Sutter sent Indian children to work at the establishments of his coastal creditors, to help allay his mounting debts, he specified that they not be quartered with Indians who'd been in missions. Otherwise they'd return to him after the specified amount of time spoiled by the attitudes of rebels.

Captain Juan was the biggest of the Indians below, a strapping man well over six feet, not counting his topknot. Beside him stood the lovely little poppy. A chief's daughter often became the mistress of the señor, but for now the excitement coursing through Pedro was for the land. He would need to draw a map of the place and ask Captain Sutter to write a letter of recommendation to Governor Micheltorena stating that he, Pedro, was of good character and had acquitted himself well in his work. It would take time for the paperwork to creak through the Mexican government, so he must start immediately. The prospect of Rancho Sacayak greatly improved his outlook toward the future.

He memorized the layout for the map. Below on his right the River of the Cosumne wound its way through the low hills. Sufficient water remained in the river even now, at the end of the long dry summer. He had examined the clay chinking on the conical huts and found it to be of fine adobe quality.

Bien. The fertile soil in the meadow where he impressed them with his riding would nourish his corn and beans. Native grapevines festooned the trees along the river. Blackberries and good herbs abounded.

Exhilarated, he galloped downhill and up the next hill, catching up with the Indians. Riding at a walk again, the image of the Indita came to him, sweet and innocent in the forward way of the unspoiled natives. He was pleased with the way he'd handled himself. A love song sprang to his lips and he sang with mournful gusto.

> *El tormento de amor que me abraza*
> *En mi pecho no encuentro consuelo.*
>
> *The torment of love that grips me*
> *In my bosom cannot be consoled.*
>
> ....

After Proud Hawk rode away, María Howchia looked at the dusty willows and sun-baked boulders and felt trapped in a world too small. Pounding acorns at the chaw-se, the outcroppings of mortar rocks, she noticed Crying Fox's crimped lips as he straightened arrows nearby.

She suspected that he too was thinking about leaving against Father's wishes. Crying Fox's best friends had gone. Her friends Blue Star and Burns Fingers had gone too. Women were the best gatherers and Proud Hawk had said he wanted gatherers. He had invited her to his home to help.

She recalled the gray eyes, the proud bearing and musky scent. Her skin remembered his touch. She could think of nothing else.

At the family's supper fire Grizzly Hair spoke loud enough for all the umne to hear. "Kadeema's people, who live on the River of the Americans," he gestured toward the north, "no longer work for Captain Sutter. So he sent his scout here. Our people should not do what others refuse to do." Clearly it upset him that so many young people had gone.

Etumu's basket-weave cap bobbed up and down in emphatic agreement. Her black eyes flashed at María Howchia as she said, "The black hats do not purify themselves. People who go to the place of the black hats will lose their strength."

María Howchia had little appetite, although the steaming basket held her favorite bulbs. She sat against the earthen collar of the house among her father's wilted tobacco plants and felt equally limp. Grizzly Hair and Etumu meant to protect their children, yet they were wrong to keep looking toward the past. The black hats hadn't captured people for a long time, and Captain Sutter wasn't to be feared. He just wanted seed pickers.

She said, "I heard that Kadeema's people left Captain Sutter's fort because they were sick for their home place."

Crying Fox added in vigorous voice. "That's true. That's why they left. But we wouldn't be homesick. We would return after the harvest. Captain Sutter pays fine goods for trabajo." That was Spanish, meaning everyone doing whatever was ordered, all at the same time. The tongue of the umne had no such word. Father had learned about work at the mission.

"The Español wants to befriend us," María Howchia reminded her parents. "He wouldn't invite us to his place if it were dangerous."

Suddenly Crying Fox stood up, squared his shoulders and pointed to the west. "After the sleep I will go to Captain Sutter's place."

María Howchia held her breath. This could be seen as disrespectful to Father.

Grizzly Hair didn't move, his forearms remained on his knees, a juicy duck thigh dangling in one hand. Four drips fell. Looking at nobody in particular his voice came as flat as his expression. "Every man must find his own way."

Etumu stood up, scowling, disapproving.

For the first time in her life María Howchia didn't care whether she upset her mother. "A woman must find her own way too," she announced. "I will go with Crying Fox."

Grizzly Hair gave the duck thigh to Etumu's dog, pushed to his feet, and walked toward the west path, possibly heading for his power place. Seeing this, Etumu left Grandmother Dishi fumbling with her food and went down inside the u-macha.

María exchanged a glance with Crying Fox. They had defeated their parents, but it brought no pleasure.

⁂

Pedro squinted into the setting sun. Only a few varas remained between him and the fort. He had collected sixteen Indians from the villages. Better than expected. Grouped by village, they trotted along behind. Sutter's five-league square New Helvetia stretched alongside the American River down to where it joined the wide Sacramento. The place was more than a rancho, actually a fledgling town. Someday, Pedro mused, Rancho Sacayak would be such a place, but without the bad men Sutter attracted. And without the squalor of San José with its four to five hundred people, including renegade mission Indians and filthy mahalas servicing the cholos from Mexico—an ant heap of drunkenness and broken spirits. Señor del Cielo, no. One or more of Pedro's three brothers probably remained on the family plot in San José, a mere square vara as all town allotments were. Not enough land for four brothers to earn a living. Never did Pedro want to return.

He recalled how the shame of his father had pushed him to excel at horsemanship. He'd won contests and a measure of respect. Now he sank back in the saddle resting his hands on the big round Sinaloa horn, rocking with the gait. The heat, thanks be to God, was departing with the sun. He could feel his military life fading with it. Rancho Sacayak was the bright, happy thing.

Chocolate whinnied as they neared the fort, now dark against the red sunset, the distant air smoky due to Indian grass-burning. The remaining corner of the high adobe wall appeared to have been finished in the week since he'd left—a massive structure in an oak grassland. Está bien. He could assign the adobe makers to the harvest.

Indians and Kanakas came running, calling, "Viene el Señor Valdez!" The Captain's pack of bulldogs rushed at him, barking—English dogs the Captain acquired in the Sandwich Islands. Pedro beckoned the new Indians, who hung back timidly. Perhaps they were afraid of the guards with bayonets pointed upward, or the cannons they stood beside.

Returning the salute, Pedro sat tall as he rode through the big gate. The new Indians followed, their heads pivoting in every direction. The grain-soup aroma of pi-no-le reminded him of his stomach. He'd have Señor Daylor put a beefsteak on the grill. Bill Daylor refused to cook California food, a disappointing aspect of Sutter's Fort, but the Englishman made good leavened bread.

Pedro tied Chocolate to the stair rail, heard footsteps, and turned. He found himself looking straight into Perry McCoon's lopsided grin, with that maddening dimple digging a hole in one cheek!

"Looks like the greaser's back, and about time it tis," the bastard drawled.

Another reason Pedro wanted a rancho. McCoon and his ilk. The Captain had made it clear that Pedro would lose his rank and be sent back to Monterey if he took the bait of the English-speaking men who worked here. Fortunately, not all of them were as bad as McCoon. Pedro moved to mount the stairs.

McCoon planted a boot on the first stair, his blue eyes sparking with mean humor. He had recently oiled the perfect wave of dark hair on his forehead, over a nose so straight it could have been planed. The cabrón was vain, a lady's man North Americans called him. Worst of all, he flattered himself to think he was Pedro's equal on a horse. Pedro was considering changing the shape of that nose when Sutter emerged on the landing above, arching his brows in delight to see the new Indians.

"Esteemed Capitán," Pedro said with a salute, "these strong young Indians are ready to serve you." Ay, ay ay, he needed to keep a tight rein on his anger. Sutter was the only man in the great valley whose recommendations for land grants influenced the governor.

Smiling with approval, Sutter bobbed his head toward the soup troughs. "Tell dem to eat. And Lieutenant Valdez, come to my room ven you haff eaten."

McCoon removed his foot.

# 3

After the sleep María Howchia stepped from the river and brushed dry with her tuft of wing-feathers. Father stood at the edge of the sandy beach as he did each morning, facing the sun as it rose, absorbing power. He hadn't spoken yet. Never had his eyes seemed as rocklike as when he'd looked at her before the sleep. She forced back tears at the memory, but returned to the u-macha to pack.

Inside the dim u-macha she saw the curve of Mother's back on her mat. Quietly reaching into the rafters María untied her large burden basket, the bottom of it containing acorns that she'd taken from the family silo before the sleep. No doubt food would be at hand in the fort, but to be safe she would carry the staple of life.

On top of the acorns she placed her folded deerskin mantle. Then her cloth skirt. She must look her best for any big time that might be held. She added the family's old cooking basket and her bone awl for coiling redbud. She might need to make a basket. She picked up her small stone mortar. It was heavy for travel, but the fort might not have a grinding place. She lifted the mantle and placed the stone beneath it, and then set her seed beater and seed cradle on top.

Her rabbit-skin blanket lay on her mat, unneeded in this warm weather. On such a long journey it might be damaged. But if she left it here, she'd have to return before cold weather.

She scowled, wondering how long she would be gone.

Crying Fox intended to return home after Sutter's seeds were stored, before the time of rain. But she might need more time to win her man. And even if he agreed to marry her, she couldn't be sure he would return with her to live in the u-macha with her parents for the proper time while they decided if he'd make a good husband. She hoped he would. If so she wouldn't need to carry the blanket now. But Father said other peoples didn't follow custom. Maybe Proud Hawk would ask her to stay at his house. Maybe he already had a good blanket and hers wouldn't be needed. In the mission, married men slept with their wives every night, having no sweathouse. Maybe it was the same at the fort.

Never had she felt so frozen in indecision.

As she stared at the blanket it seemed to cry out not to be left behind. Dogs might come in and shred it while she was gone. She saw herself making it—the care with which she'd rolled the pelts, fur side out, sewed the soft tubes end to end into long hollow ropes, and then wove the fur-tubes over and under. The blanket spoke of suitors who had brought the rabbit pelts, including the man Father hoped she would marry. But she had rejected them all, waiting for a special man. Only respected married women had as many pelts. The blanket meant she was attractive to men. It spoke of all the warm glances and coupling at the two big times since she'd become a woman. In the time of cold rain she'd snuggled under the rabbit fur, tucking the silkiness around her, and drifted into pleasant dreams.

Etumu turned over and looked at María. "You are going then." A hurt tone.

María nodded over the big round opening of her gathering basket. If she took the blanket, Mother would think she didn't intend to return. The sudden dimming of the light made her look at the doorway.

"Are you coming?" It was Crying Fox standing on the porch looking down the ramp. He'd been waiting with his full quiver across his chest.

Tears of frustration welled. How could a blanket do this to her? Making it so hard to leave home?

"Want me to go without you?" Crying Fox asked.

She looked at her older brother, recalling her bravado before the sleep. But then she remembered Proud Hawk's hand on her back, and said, "I'm coming."

She folded and placed her rabbit-skin blanket in the basket, leaned the big basket against the wall while she jammed her grass-weave skullcap on her head, and then paused. Father had said the women of the Españoles wore cloth skirts. Perhaps she should wear hers for the journey. No. She must protect it for the big times. Then a new thought. Captain Sutter paid in cloth for the collection of grass seed. Soon she could make herself a new skirt. Hurriedly she dug under the blanket, feeling for the length of striped muslin, pulled it out, and tied the skirt around her hips. Now she wouldn't appear old-fashioned to Proud Hawk.

The sudden return of light told her Crying Fox was leaving. She slipped the deer thong around the basket, bent her knees, rump to the basket, placed the thong across her forehead and stood up with a little jerk to center the weight. At the doorway she turned toward Mother and said, "I will return."

Etumu said nothing. This was the way of the umne, quickly so as not to bring tears. She knew Mother would think of her each day, as she would think of Mother. Outside, she nearly bumped into Father. His long wet hair was plastered to his shoulders. He stood beside the house, less imposing without his topknot. Greatly relieved, she saw no anger in him. His eyes spoke of pain and love.

"Daughter. You are young, and the men at Sutter's place have no understanding of polite behavior."

"Soon I will have fourteen años," she reminded him. He had taught her to count birthdays like the mission people did. But despite being adult she felt the fright of a fledgling leaving the nest. She was leaving the protection of this man of knowledge, going to a man who might send her back to the umne.

The square-shouldered back of Crying Fox crossing Berry Creek beckoned. She trotted after him, pulled by the magic of Proud Hawk.

Following Crying Fox on the tamped trail, she felt stronger in her purpose with each step, for she could see the recent tracks of *his* horse. She could still hear him saying, Indita mía. This was no dream. He was her man, unlike any other. She had lain awake in a fever of wanting him.

Walking ahead, Crying Fox seemed absorbed in thought. She caught up behind his bunching calves and strong buttocks, the delicate heron bones swinging in his earlobes.

"Why didn't you bring your horse?" she asked.

"Father said it might be stolen from the fort."

"Who would steal it?"

"Raiders. Maybe Sick Rat and Gabriel. Maybe Maximo's men."

"I don't think Sick Rat would steal your horse." Gabriel's men sold stolen horses to Americanos at the Lake of the Tulares at the southern end of the great valley. That was terribly far away. Sick Rat hadn't returned home after the war, but remained with the horse thieves.

Crying Fox's feet landed perfectly on their sides, rolling flat to push off. "Raiders round them up in the night," he said.

Would she be safe in such a place? She felt safe with her brother and hoped Proud Hawk would protect her at the fort. She wanted to talk about him, but once when they were children, Crying Fox had said to her, "Don't talk until you have thought four times about what you are saying." That had embarrassed her and she'd never forgotten it.

She asked, "Am I pretty?"

In stride, Crying Fox turned his head just enough to reveal a half-smile.

Pleased, she resumed thinking about Proud Hawk. More than four times she had thought about marrying him, but she couldn't bring herself to mention it to Crying Fox. He might assume an Español was an inappropriate man for her. In age, Proud Hawk was between her and her parents, so very unlike old Jacksnipe Song, with his saggy neck and worn teeth. Her man could stand on the back of a running horse!

Crying Fox kept a determined pace. They rested at the Omuchumne village, politely accepting food and learning more about Captain Sutter. People said he possessed power, and he and his fighting men had killed whole villages on the southern river where the Mokelumne lived—killed them with guns and a wheeled cannon. Father had told of such guns.

Omuch said, "Captain Sutter ordered his men to cut off Rafero's head. They left it on a iron spike on the gate. Birds ate it. The empty skull hung there for two long-dries." The big eyes of the Omuchumne matched the horror creeping through María Howchia.

Later, walking behind Crying Fox, fear niggled her stomach, but Proud Hawk's magic beckoned through it. The river had turned south and left them.

They were now on the fainter trail heading westward over flat oak grasslands. The dry grass on either side of the trail stood to their shoulders, some of it over her head. The sun was hotter away from the river. Perspiration stung the chafed places where the basket rubbed her back and shoulders.

All day they walked at a fast pace. At last Crying Fox stopped and pointed. She followed his finger to something in the distance, black against the blazing low sun. The fort of Captain Sutter. The size of it made her uneasy and she turned to look but couldn't see the comforting green line of vegetation that marked her river. They walked onward.

The sun was low when they began passing cattle and sheep, animals Father had described. Men in hip wraps sat alongside a field of high, strong-looking grass gone to seed. One of those men jumped up to scare a flock of birds away. "These must be the seeds we are to collect," said Crying Fox.

Suddenly, several dogs barked and bounded toward them. Demon dogs with horribly flat faces and huge loose lips, maybe shape-changers! Just when she expected to be eaten alive by whatever monsters they really were, Crying Fox lunged toward them screaming like a cougar and waving his arms. The smooth brown demons stood at bay and allowed him to walk past, though they barked and surely saw the telltale waver in his gait. With her stomach in a hard knot María caught up to her brave brother. On her heels, the barking demons followed all the way to the immense wall of the fort. Weakened by fear, she felt calmer when the dogs trotted to a man standing beside a cannon. Panting, they sat at his feet with strings of slobber sliding off their lolling tongues.

Two men fully clothed in identical dark blue clothing held guns fitted with long knives, which they pointed skyward as they stood at the closed gate. Such weapons could easily cut off heads, but the posture of the men conveyed no threat. María looked up at a little roof made of overlapping scales that reminded her of the scales of snakes. The roof covered a tower where two of the fort walls met. From two little openings beneath that roof jutted the snouts of two more cannons. The gigantic gate was held together by iron straps and decorated with iron spikes along its top—no human head she was glad to see. One of the men in blue spoke in a strange tongue.

Crying Fox answered in slow, practiced Spanish, "*Nosotros venir a trabajar.*" We come to work.

The guard looked at Crying Fox's charmstone, the fused cluster of elongated blue crystals that he wore around his neck. Brought home long ago by Father returning from the coastal mountains, no one had seen anything like it. "*Bonita,*" the guard said nodding at it. Then in the tongue of The People he asked, "Are you Mokelumne?"

María's heart jumped. She stepped back, ready to run into the approaching night. The umne of Mokel had made Captain Sutter angry enough to kill whole villages! She and Crying Fox must never be confused with them.

"No," Crying Fox quickly replied. "From the people of Captain Juan. To speak to Señor Valdez."

With a nod towards each other, the guards leaned their long-knifed guns against the cannon each was guarding and pushed open the heavy gate, waving Crying Fox and María through it.

Inside, a man in loose brown clothing and a bush of hair on his face led them across a yard, which was littered with strange things. María caught sight of grown men with light brown hair. She smelled unwashed bodies, shaved wood, leather, and good grains cooking. They arrived at a tall adobe house with stairs leading upward. Off to one side lay a hollowed-out trunk of a sycamore tree, containing some kind of soup. Normal looking people kneeled along the trough, dipping their spooned hands into it and quietly eating supper. They all looked up at Crying Fox and María as they followed the lead man up the house-hugging stairs.

At the landing the bushy-faced man rapped loudly on hollow wood. A wooden door swung open, and there stood Proud Hawk! Not an arm's length away. His aromas enveloped her and she could hardly draw breath. But his expression wasn't friendly. He scowled to see her. Only now did she fully face the reality that he had changed his mind about wanting her. She had remembered the feel of his hand on her skin and kept reminding herself of his original desire to have her come to his place. She'd been blinded by her desire and had done a stupid thing. Now he was clearly sorry to see her.

While she was wishing to become invisible and run away, Crying Fox said, "Venimos a trabajar. We came to work."

A furrow deepened between Proud Hawk's eyes. "From the ranchería of Capitán Juan," he said in a tone tinged with exasperation.

From deep inside the cornered room came a man's voice speaking in an alien tongue. Proud Hawk answered in a strange tongue. Briefly, the unseen man spoke again.

Proud Hawk signaled them to step across a level board floor and look into a smaller, adjoining room from which emanated a disgusting rancid odor mingled with the smell of cooked meat.

In the alcove sat what appeared to be a man, though he could have been a demon. He wore dark clothing with glittering buttons reflecting the light of two candles before him on a table. Staring at María with large, nearly white eyes, like the eyes of some snakes, he had a very pale face and hair the color of rotten straw—short on top, bristling down the length of his cheeks and disappearing under a hairless chin. The tip of his pink nose slightly overhung a remarkable mustache, darker than the hair on his head and pointed outward like sideways bobcat ears. His nostrils were unnaturally long. The ugly man gripped a knife and a forked implement, both pointing upward, on either side of a plate of food before him. Along the wall behind him were piles of boxes, baskets, and rolled blankets. A long gun with no knife leaned in the corner.

Proud Hawk swept his black hat toward the man and said, "El Capitán Don Juan Sutter."

The man continued to stare at María Howchia from the tops of his white eyes. Then he put down his implements, picked up a cloth, dabbed at his bobcat ears as if training them to grow sideways, and glanced up and down her length, lingering on her breasts. Perhaps he noticed that she was a woman, her chin properly tattooed. He said something in a strange tongue.

Proud Hawk replied, and then scowled and spoke slowly to María Howchia. "He wants to take you to his bed. Do you want to make amor with him?"

"No" she said—wanting to say, *I came here to you.* But the Spanish was too difficult.

Captain Sutter scraped his chair back and came around the table, half a head shorter than Proud Hawk. Proud Hawk spoke to him, and the two stared at one and exchanged more talk. Meanwhile, Crying Fox was whispering into María's ear, "The Captain is hy-apo, headman of this place. He wants to couple with you." He was telling her she should do it to be polite.

Proud Hawk turned toward them, his back to Sutter. "I told him you are the children of Captain Juan and your father would be angry if he takes you to bed. But the Captain says your father should be honored to please him." Jerking his chin toward the door, he whispered quickly in Spanish, *"Salir de aqui! Ahorita!"*

She was trying to translate that in her head when Captain Sutter spat terrible sounds at Proud Hawk, who breathed audibly.

Crying Fox spoke up, "Maybe she make amor with the captain." His face conveyed growing alarm.

Seeing that, María jangled with fear down to her toes. Captain Sutter could shoot them and cut off their heads. Maybe he was telling Proud Hawk to do it now. She saw with clarity the confusion in the Español's face. He lacked power before Captain Sutter.

She turned to run but Sutter's hand closed on her upper arm. He pointed at the door and yelled at Proud Hawk and Crying Fox, *"Herous!"*

She hated the defeated look on Proud Hawk's face as he followed Crying Fox to the door, backing more than walking. The door shut behind them.

For an instant she faced the Captain's horrific eyes, one looking slightly inward. And then she squirmed to break free. To no avail. With surprising strength for a small man he pulled her to the far end of the alcove, to a raised platform of blankets lit by the candles on the table. A second long gun stood in the corner.

She tried to face her death.

He pulled down her skirt, let it drop to the floor, put his hands on her breasts and stared into her eyes. Maybe he wouldn't kill her after all. The thought staved off a wave of darkness.

A rabbit-toothed smile parted his lips as he pushed her back to sit on the blankets. Breathing rapidly in her fear, she told herself this was only a man, not a demon spirit. She saw by the swelling in his trousers that he wanted to couple. Maybe afterwards he'd let her go.

The boots beside the bed, too near her nose, emitted a putrid odor like the pink-slime mushroom. A sharper smell slammed into her as he threw off his jacket and raised his arms to pull his shirt over his head, revealing bushy underarms. Smells couldn't escape here. Doors and windows were tightly closed. The house had no smoke hole. He dropped his trousers and stepped out of them—the pale fur of his legs haloed brightly in the candlelight, his arousal pushing out the thin cloth of short gray pants. He lifted a leg and pulled a foot-covering from one white foot, and then the other. The nauseating pink stench hit her harder, though she tried not to breathe. He draped the foot coverings over the boots. Did he never bathe? She stood up, suddenly needing fresh air like life itself.

"*Nein mädchen.*" He seized her upper arms and shoved her down on the bed, then stepped from his short pants, his man's part flipping free, nearly in her face. The end of it was encrusted with a yellow cheesy rot and the stench gagged her. Swallowing back a heave she pointed at it and managed to get out the Spanish, "No quiero." Gagging again, she lurched to her feet.

"No, mine chile." He slapped her hard across the cheek and mouth. It threw her back on the bed so suddenly she hardly knew what had happened.

She sat up, putting a hand over her stinging mouth. The room spun. Never had she been intentionally struck before. She'd heard of it only once— a mother slapping an extremely disrespectful child. Her lip pulsed with the beat of her heart and she feared he'd hit her again. She felt like a moth in the hands of a cruel child.

He grasped her shoulders, put his face down nose to nose with her and said, "Ya, dat iss goot." With those intense sounds a stink blasted from his mouth like decaying vegetation from stagnant water—a fulsome black-green reek. Even in shadow with candles at his back, she saw the terrible white eyes. Her stomach lurched again. She tasted bile, swallowed hard and tried to keep her stomach down. Surely he'd kill her if she vomited on his floor.

He laid himself beside her, pushing her back so their heads sank into a puffy square thing that threw off a new stench—brown and rancid, as if generations of sick mice had sweated and died there. This, she realized, was the underlying smell of his house. He rose up on an elbow and groped between her thighs with a harsh finger, and then shoved it inside her, the nail scratching. She jerked away.

He rolled his white weight upon her, squeezing out the last good air. His knees parted her thighs. She wrenched her head from side to side but could not escape the rot of his mouth or the biting stench of his underarms as he pinned her hands down. His man's part searched, trying to probe. She could feel its sticky pathway on her thighs.

A sudden wooden bang reverberated, and a tendril of good air found its way to her, followed by rapid footsteps. The door had opened. A silhouette loomed, a woman by her angry voice, a woman with the long hair of a man. She picked up a boot and pounded Captain Sutter with it. He rolled away, fending off blows while speaking in soothing tones. But the woman was quick and fierce. As they grappled, María scooted off the bed.

She ran fast, scooping up her skirt and burden basket as she flew out the open door and down the stairs.

It was nearly dark. The clean aroma of dry grass washed over her, but fear and confusion pursued her. What would Captain Sutter do when the struggle inside was over? The courtyard was deserted, Crying Fox nowhere in sight. Candlelight glowed in many little square windows around the inside of the adobe wall. As she stepped off the last step, a strange clanging noise stopped her. She held her breath. It clanged repeatedly in cadence as a man's voice called out in an alien tongue, "*Twenty bells and all's well.*" She saw a dark figure moving around the interior of the fort, in silhouette when he passed the windows. "*Twenty bells and all's well,*" he called and clanged—again and again.

Hunting for her no doubt. Announcing the hunt to others. She had angered the headman. Behind her eyes she saw her head on a gate spike as a warning to others, and she crept beneath the shadowy staircase, trying to see whether the gate was open or closed. She couldn't tell. She needed to hide and when it was darker make a dash for the gate, hoping it would be open.

"Ven!" A forced whisper. A smell of smoke and leather. It was Proud Hawk! He put his head close to hers and said in Spanish, "Tonight you sleep in the ranchería."

She had no idea where that was, but she could hear that his kindness had returned. She had no choice but to trust him.

# 4

The next morning Pedro was on his way back through the gate, having assigned the Indians to the fields, when trouble broke out in the fort yard. Bill Daylor, the tall, broad-shouldered cook, stood cornered by three Indians and Captain Sutter. Pedro hurried to Sutter's side.

"Bill Daylor iss a traitor," the captain sputtered. "Trow him in jail, in chains!"

"What has he done?" Pedro asked. Señor Daylor had blood on his apron but that was normal for a cook. He stood hatless, legs braced, the white expanse of his forehead gleaming in the morning sun as he glared at the captain.

"He hass made sex with Manu-iki." Drawing a noseful of air the Captain added, "In da cookhouse! Now go, fetch twenty strong mens."

Right there in the cookhouse! Amazed, Pedro trotted to the field for more Indians and Kanakas. With every step came a growing realization that he likely bore some responsibility for this. He'd been congratulating himself on how well it had worked to send Manu-iki to the Captain's room last night, but now he believed Manu-iki had seduced the cook to get revenge on Sutter for that girl, for all the young Indian girls. Lately the constant gossip of the Indian and Kanaka women was Sutter's role in the death of a five-year-old who'd visited his room. And now Bill Daylor could be paying the price for Pedro's interference, and his luring the Indita here. Ay, ay, ay! Life in the fort was one excitement after another, followed by incessant gossip in at least three languages. This time it was cutting too close to him. He needed to get away. How peaceful life would be on Ranch Sakayak!

Soon twenty Indians and Kanakas surrounded Daylor, and Pedro was helping Luis and another man from the foundry drag heavy chains across the courtyard.

"Just ye try'n taik me, ye bloody bastards," Daylor snarled through his large English nose, apparently unimpressed by the reinforcements.

Daylor had arrived in California walking the plank. As the ships cook, he'd argued on behalf of the unhappy crew, who wanted to linger in Monterey, ostensibly to take on more water and fresh meat. The real reasons, Pedro knew, were the pretty señoritas and the lush countryside that beckoned after months aboard those floating prisons. The brig was sailing out of the huge harbor while Daylor was still arguing, insisting they turn back. English ship captains didn't like to be contradicted. Daylor was the only one to go ashore and he would have drowned except for the help of Jared Sheldon, who happened to hear his cries. That had been two years ago, and now Daylor was hunched forward ready to fight, blue eyes throwing daggers at another captain.

A hush hung over the courtyard. Carpenters, tanners and candle makers peered from doorways around the wall. Indian women and children watched, and Señor Lienhard was scribbling in his journal, as Pedro had seen him do on other entertaining occasions. Manu-iki stood by the oven with her cowrie shell necklace deep between her golden breasts. She knew her power over men.

Sutter clenched his fists and hopped for emphasis. "Hit him, hit him. *Verdammt.*" Normally he behaved like a gentleman officer. Pedro reminded himself that women could make the captain a little loco.

Two Indians and Kanaka Henry rushed forward, but the Englishman knocked them back like a bear swatting hornets. Kanaka Henry, the big mayordomo of the Islanders, avoided Sutter's accusing stare and got up to try again.

It was hard to believe sometimes, that Manu-iki, Sutter's favorite lover, was Kanaka Henry's wife and had been since Sutter brought the Kanakas from the Islands. Pedro knew that if he had a wife and Captain Sutter made her his lover, Pedro would kill him. Never mind rank. But to fight another man at Sutter's order, and for this reason—ay madre! Sometimes he couldn't fathom the Kanakas. It would be comical if it weren't so dangerous.

A hefty Indian dashed at Daylor. The cook's fist thunked into his face and the Indian fell back, cradling his head.

Daylor growled, "John Sutter, so help me if ye don't call off yer lackeys, I'll kill you, I will."

Now Sutter wouldn't sleep well while Daylor still breathed. Daylor was known to be a fierce fighter and he didn't make threats lightly. Pedro hoped he wouldn't be asked to hang him. A few feet away dangled the end of an oak limb where a number of condemned Indians had died kicking.

Sutter shook his fists. *"Donnerwetter, Gott im Himmel!* Nay nay nay, idiots! At da zame time! Togezer! Run at him all at da zame time!"

Kanaka Henry translated that into Island talk, Pedro into Spanish for the Indians, and twenty men closed ranks on the fighting cook. "Ya ya, iss goot," Sutter encouraged as they stepped forward.

Daylor dove at Kanaka Henry's knees. Kanaka Henry collapsed and all the Indians and Kanakas piled on top. Underneath and out of sight, Daylor erupted, living up to his fighting reputation. Naked limbs and torsos thrashed and heaved atop his volcanic force. Dust enveloped the pile of writhing men as knees and feet scrambled for leverage and arms flailed for holds.

Manu-iki laid a smug glance on Captain Sutter and he seemed to ignore her.

The heap of men gradually stilled. Indians regained their feet and backed away. When he could get near enough, Pedro knelt beside Señor Daylor, who lay spread-eagled beneath the large frame of Kanaka Henry, Indians kneeling along his legs.

Clapping him in wrist- and ankle-irons, Pedro whispered in Daylor's ear, "I am sorry, señor."

"Wrap him in chains," Sutter bellowed.

"He cannot get away now, Capitán. I don't think we have the need for—"

"Lieutenant Valdez, wrap dot man in chains from his neck unto his foot. He iss a dangerous fellow."

"Sí, Capitán." He helped Daylor to his feet and turned him around and around as Luis fed out the chain. Men in the shops snickered. Indians laughed outright, and it did look funny—a tall iron sausage with a head on top.

"Ya ya, iss goot," said Sutter with satisfaction.

Luis passed the lock through the links and handed the key to Pedro.

"Lieutenant Valdez," Sutter said in a tone deepened by his restored dignity, "lock dot bastard in the calaboose." He flashed Daylor a triumphant look. "Tomorrow, send him wit a big escort to Monterey. The Governor iss to be told dot he, William Daylor, iss a bad disturber of the peace. He iss to be deported far away."

"Sí, Capitán."

Sutter's pale blue eyes flashed in the morning sun as he glared at the cook. "You goat! I hope day trow you on da same ship and next time you to da bottom sink!" He whirled and started up the stairs, but then turned and announced to the whole fort: "All mens, back to vorking."

Men ducked back into their shops.

Pedro made eye contact with Daylor. "If you would please be so good as to walk, señor?" He nodded with his sombrero toward the jail.

Daylor growled, "Not goin to that hellhole, I ent."

Sutter's boots thumped back down the wooden stairs and his shrill voice knifed from behind. "Goot, I kill you now." He grabbed Pedro's gun and reached for the powder bag.

Softly Pedro said to Daylor, "Señor, por favor walk." No one would question Captain Sutter killing a cook in this wilderness. He was pouring in the powder.

Daylor, a much taller man, looked down at Sutter and must have read the pent-up violence. The pistol lock clicked, and then to Pedro's relief Daylor took two tiny steps toward the gun tower, weighed down and hobbled by the clanking chains. Sutter jammed the gun into Pedro's hands and left, thumping up the stairs.

Gun in hand, Pedro inched across the hushed courtyard behind the cook.

Jared Sheldon had been watching from the door of the carpentry shop. Now this man from the state of Vermont put down his adz and stepped forward to accompany them to the jail. His chiseled face and steady hazel eyes always made Pedro think of an intelligent wolf. He didn't say much but was usually on the side of reason. Pedro knew he'd be level-headed even with his best friend in chains.

"Bill," Sheldon said quietly, "don't worry. I'm going to Monterey tomorrow about my rancho papers. I'll explain to the Governor and he'll let you go." A free contractor, Sheldon's time was his own, and he'd helped rebuild the Customs House in Monterey. The Governor owed him.

Daylor and Sheldon, equally tall and lean, exchanged a look. Sheldon had fished Daylor from Monterey Bay and later brought him to Sutter's Fort. Sheldon would save his friend again.

With a nod, Pedro turned back to his captive. "Señor Daylor, por favor, enter."

At last, Daylor crossed the threshold and Sheldon returned to the carpentry shop. Obviously neither of them blamed Pedro.

It was dark inside, even with the outer door open. Excavated beneath the spiral stairwell that led to the cannon ports above, the jail reeked of stale urine. Pedro inserted the big key into the lock of the inner chamber and stepped back as the iron-barred door squealed open.

Daylor's jaw worked. "I vowed to meself I'd die before gittin locked up again."

"Go, señor, por favor." He kept his voice gentle.

Finally Bill Daylor shuffled inside the cell in his swaddling of chains. Some of the runaway sailors and flea-bitten trappers who hung around Sutter were cheats to the bottom of their souls. Some treated Pedro like an outsider in his own country. But Daylor and Sheldon treated him with respect.

He swung the barred door shut. The clank echoed up the gun turret. In the light from the outer door, Daylor, a strong man made helpless, looked out over his chains at Pedro. Anyone could sneak in and fling a knife through the bars. Sutter wouldn't—he was neither a devious nor a violent man at heart—but impulsive men lived around the fort and some of them looked for a chance to do the Captain a favor, so with the babble of tongues nourishing misunderstandings, anything was possible. The outer door had no lock.

"Do not worry, señor," Pedro said, "I will sleep here tonight, and ride with you in the morning. You will be safe."

"Why would you care?"

"You are a good man." He lowered his voice. "Captain Sutter, he is a little bit crazy about the women, no?" He cut his reassuring smile short. With the light at his back he'd be nothing but a black shape in a sombrero. "If I can help in Monterey, without embarrassing Captain Sutter, I will."

Daylor's throaty, emotional tone surprised Pedro. "Thankee mait. I understands your position." Then his jauntiness returned.

"Ah but Manu-iki loves me manly body, she does. And she the fairest female to walk the earth."

❧

All day María Howchia worked in the field. Much of the time her seed beater wouldn't dislodge the barbed seed-heads like it did the grasses at home, so she twisted them off with her hands. Blue Star did the same beside her. In the hot sun they stepped steadily and rhythmically as their mothers had taught them, tossing the filled seed-cradles over their shoulders into their burden baskets. The barbs hurt their hands. María wiped sweat from her eyes and looked across the plain where a line of green marked the River of the Americans. How she wished to be there sucking in a long drink of water!

Pausing to look at her red, swollen hands, Blue Star declared, "I'm going to dump my load." She glanced enviously at the men swinging huge metal hoops at the wheat, better tools for this kind of grain. "Will you go with me?"

"Ho!" María had had enough. Their baskets were only half full and she and Blue Star had gathered only four loads today, but her hands told her to quit. Tomorrow they'd be as sore as Blue Star's, who had been working here one day more than María.

The memory of Captain Sutter's body barged into her mind again—all day it kept happening and María couldn't make it stop. She ached for the home place, but Crying Fox didn't want to leave, and a woman couldn't travel that far alone. She had trapped herself.

As they started back through the field toward the high walls, the report of a gun stopped them. One of the men who scared birds was running toward them, leaping over stubble with his gun, his red headband flapping behind his head with his long hair.

"No. You work until I fire my gun two times," he said, arriving. He spoke in the tongue of The People, no doubt one of the Cosumne who worked for Captain Sutter. María had been a guest of those people last night.

"Our hands hurt," María Howchia explained. "We need to quit now." She showed him her palms, as did Blue Star.

He stepped back and aimed down the barrel of his gun, his long hair flanking the stock. He moved his aim to Blue Star.

Shocked, María sucked air and Blue Star cowered beside her.

The man pointed the gun back and forth between them. "I'll shoot you if you leave," he said. "Pick seeds until your baskets are full, and keep filling them until you hear the two shots at the end of the day."

The sun was low when María Howchia heard the gunshot signal. She and Blue Star joined about three twenties of pickers dumping their loads on the seed hill in the large adobe corral. She could hardly wait to jump in the river. A bit jittery from hunger and thirst, she hurried along the path—hands throbbing, throat prickly with chaff, soul wounded.

In the shade of the giant trees, the big river surged toward the setting sun. With a running dive she entered its cool embrace and found herself in a deep pool teeming with seed pickers. After a brisk underwater swim, she surfaced, cupping water and sucking it down. Turning on her back, she floated on the watery bed in the slow but powerful current. Cottonwoods and enormous oaks stretched toward the branches of their friends on the other side of this wide river, almost bridging it. Why would the trees here be so much bigger than at the home place? So many things she didn't understand. Why hadn't she found the right moment to tell Blue Star about Captain Sutter?

Her stomach growled. Supper would be ready when they returned to the fort. The morning gruel had been too thin, but the bread tasted wonderful. Maybe she would get more of it tonight. Strangely, however, it was the thick, oily goodness of nu-pah that came to mind. People didn't make nu-pah here. She had her mortar rock, but no time to grind and leech acorns.

She swam to shore. Men and women stepped from the water, whisking themselves dry with feather tassels like the one she'd accidentally left in the home place. She joined the women who were wringing out the cloth skirts they'd worn all day.

Tying her skirt back on, María asked a tall woman, "Who cooks while all these women are gathering seeds?"

"On most days Señor Daylo and Manu-iki and their helpers cook, but now Daylo is locked up in the calaboose, so Manu-iki is in charge." She started up the path.

Manu-iki was the fierce woman who'd beat Captain Sutter over the head with a boot.

Blue Star stepped out of the river with water sheeting from her. "Ah, that felt good!" Water sprayed as she whipped her head from side to side. Then she joined María and others on the path through the high thicket, heading back toward the fort.

When the two of them caught up with the tall woman, María asked if Manu-iki was Captain Sutter's wife.

"She is his woman. She is also Kanaka Henry's woman."

María and Blue Star exchanged a surprised look. Sometimes a man had more than one wife, but no woman had two husbands!

Just ahead, a man said over his shoulder, "Captain Sutter couples with many young women, girls too." Reaching for a clump of grapes from a vine cascading from the trees he popped a few in his mouth.

Girls! With her stomach growling María reached up and also plucked a cluster of ripe grapes—sweet, with crunchy seeds. "What does he do if a woman runs away?"

"They don't run away," the informative woman replied. "It insults the Captain if a woman resists. And sometimes he gives them nice presents from the store if they make him happy. One young woman ran away though. They tracked her down and locked her in the calabozo. The Captain meant to have her whipped the next morning, but her brother helped her escape again. Sutter had him hung by the neck in the courtyard. He died."

A shiver ran through María as the tall woman continued. "In the time of second grass the Captain took a tiny little girl to his bed, and later she died. We think the coupling tore her up and evil things found their way into her blood. Our doctor couldn't drive them out with his powers. We are all sad. That was my sister's child. Captain Sutter said is wasn't his fault."

"He smells bad," was all María could muster as she imagined the suffering of that little child.

One of the women following close behind joined the conversation. "They all smell bad, all the men with pale skin. You'll get used to it." She added, "We know you went to his bed."

Blue Star's glance conveyed hurt feelings, not being told about this. "Don't they ever bathe?" María asked no one in particular.

Wet heads wagged and someone said, "The Captain believes a crust of dirt protects him and gives him power."

Mother had warned about impurity in this place. Proud Hawk didn't smell bad, and he'd bathed at the home place. She felt like she'd blundered into a den of rattlesnakes. She wanted to go home, but a guard would likely shoot her, and if she went a different way they'd track her down. She dared not ask Crying Fox to help her escape or he'd be hung.

She asked, "Why does Captain Sutter want a woman who doesn't want him?"

The tall woman shrugged. "Nobody understands him. People bet on what he'll do next." She smiled over her shoulder like a sympathetic auntie.

María had done this to herself and somehow she must get herself out. She hoped Señor Valdez wouldn't tell her to go to Captain Sutter again, as he did last night. Just the thought of it made her skin crawl. Coupling wasn't supposed to feel bad. She'd never heard of a woman being forced. Except … maybe *that* happened to Mother during the war, when María Howchia was a baby. If so, this would explain why Etumu hated the Españoles so much.

A cool breeze cut past her wet skin, chilling her, now that the sun had gone to his western house. It was Acorn Time at the home place. The People would be playing games, singing, dancing, and having a good time.

# 5

That night, making sure the pretty Indita was safely hidden in the huts of the Indians outside the fort wall, Pedro closed the outside door of the jail behind him. He removed his sombrero and sat down leaning against the wall, his gun over his lap. The stench was as thick and pervasive as the night was black.

They sat like that for a while, Daylor behind the bars in the dark, Pedro outside the cell.

"I thought we were going to Monterey today," Daylor said. "Or am I supposed to rot to death in here?"

Pedro sighed. "The Captain put it off until tomorrow, and he won't give me leave to accompany you. But I'm sure Jared Sheldon will set you free."

"Well, I 'ope you're right. He's a man of his word, and the Gov'nor owes him. I'll bet me boots 'e gets his papers this time. When I gits meself free I'll set me sails for Rancho Omuchumne, far from John Sutter."

Pedro recalled that fertile stretch of land where the River of the Cosumne turned southward, not a league from the Rancho Sacayak of his dreams. "A good place, señor," he said, "if you can clear it of berry brambles." A creek ran parallel to the river, creating a fertile, green strip of land, but it was choked with briars.

Daylor began talking about the time he'd tracked Sutter's stolen horses and found them grazing in the bottomland near the Omuchumne village, a story another man had told Pedro, but he wanted to hear it from Daylor. Daylor and Sheldon had ridden together to see the place. They made a deal that the Indios would be their vaqueros, and agreed between themselves to split the land. Sheldon would petition the Governor for the land and give Daylor half of it in exchange for Daylor's work clearing brambles, building corrals, and holding the land until Sheldon was ready to work it full time. A talented millwright, he now worked for the padres in Mission San José and Russians near Fort Ross, as well as Sutter.

Something scurried across Pedro's boot. He jerked his leg back. "I'd like to get some land too," he said.

"I didn't peg you for a farmer."

*Peg.* Strange English words kept cropping up, but Pedro understood the meaning. In English, farmers meant rancheros, men who worked the land and herded stock, and Daylor, like most men around the fort, saw Pedro only as a soldier.

"I've been with Captain Sutter five years now," Pedro explained, "and it's time I had a rancho in this beautiful land." He'd been a good officer for Sutter. Enlisted man in the beginning, he never would have risen above corporal, but one day the Captain had simply started calling him Lieutenant, and Pedro wasn't about to argue. Captain Sutter was a law unto himself. Ay, ay, and now Pedro would walk on eggshells to keep the Indita from him.

Daylor grunted. Straw rustled, chains rattled.

Silence fell between them, Pedro sitting in the dark thinking of Rancho Sacayak, and the need for Sutter's letter of recommendation. He thought back over the years, when he'd first seen Captain Sutter in Monterey. The Swiss had emerged like an emperor from the Commander's headquarters. As he strode up the revelry yard his blue jacket bristled with brass and red ribbons. The fringe on his gold epaulets swayed, the white plumes flounced on his tricorn, and his fancy scabbard glinted in the sun. Every soldier had been impressed by his deportment. Even now, knowing the Captain's weaknesses, Pedro admired the man, one who often alluded to his military leadership in the French Army. But something about that puzzled Pedro. Daylor was English, he might know.

"Why would a French military captain establish himself in this uncivilized frontier?"

"I'd say he's runnin," Daylor said, chains clinking as he adjusted himself. The joke was that every man at the fort was running from something. But surely not Sutter, with all his connections in the European courts. "Really?"

"At's me guess," said Daylor. "Eatin me alive, the damned critters is. Have ye measured the size o' them that hops about in here?"

Pedro grunted agreement and shifted to his other hip, recalling the speech that changed his life. The Monterey Commandant had introduced Captain Sutter as a naturalized Mexican citizen who would soon be granted five square leagues of land at the confluence of two large rivers. He asked for volunteers to serve with Sutter. The mission was to pacify the frontier, the Horse-thief Indians in particular. The Commander explained that Captain Sutter was the new justice of the peace of the entire interior region, and the Governor would pay close attention to his successes. "Men, this is an opportunity."

Pedro beat five other soldiers to the line. Sutter accepted all six, and within a few months the buildings of this fort were well underway. Not much later Sutter stocked his land with cattle loaned by Don Ygnacio Martinez, and tools, guns and furnishings from the Russians, also on credit. Pedro had quickly become the Captain's right-hand man. Now he hoped he hadn't performed his duties so well as to make himself indispensable.

He had drawn his map and needed the Captain to write that letter.

Morning. Seven bells. Pedro mustered the militia on the parade ground, now nearly eighty Indians, and marched them in two straight columns under the red, white and green Mexican flag. Sutter waited in his dress uniform on the stair landing. Among the women and girls watching from the shade of the big oak was the pretty Indita from Captain Juan's ranchería. She had looked at Pedro strangely last evening, but she had successfully evaded Captain Sutter the last two nights. Manu-iki had occupied the Captain's bed.

"Company halt," Pedro called.

The Indians returned his salute. The new men learned quickly, enjoying the military ritual as much as he did. He employed every flourish he'd ever seen in Presidio Monterey.

As Sutter came down his stairs Pedro stepped back to let the Captain inspect his men—some naked, some in shirts but no pants, others in tattered mission loin cloths made of wool. Most of the Kanakas and the best of the Indians were absent, escorting Bill Daylor to Monterey.

"Lieutenant Valdez."

Pedro snapped his heels, "Sí Capitán."

"As I told you before, General Maríano Vallejo comes to us late in this day. Ve giff him a formal welcome. Trousers and shirts must be on the new Indians. Find some in da Russian crates."

"Sí, Capitán." Pedro saluted.

Sutter saluted back, pivoted, and mounted the steps.

"At ease," Pedro said, and then explained the day's work. Each Indian was to cut wheat until eleven bells. More cowhide bags were ready in the leather shop. At eleven bells all Indians were to dump their grain, police the grounds, and put on as many clothes as they had. "Report to the token room if you need pants or shirts."

"Dismissed," he called. As men dispersed and women secured their head thongs, balancing the big conical baskets on their backs, he went to the Indita. "Momentito," he said laying a hand on her soft little arm.

Her wet hair was tidy from her morning swim and her breasts tilted up toward him, but her large black eyes had developed the glazed look of her people when they didn't want to be friendly.

"It is good you are staying out of the Capitán's sight," he said quietly.

He detected a tremor in her lower lip as she glanced at him.

Just then the door of the big house swung open. Captain Sutter stepped out on his landing, and the pretty Indita hurried to the gate with the big basket hiding her shapely backside.

She was doing her part.

# 6

General Maríano Guadalupe Vallejo and three men went up the stairs with Captain Sutter. Pedro dismissed the militia, which had looked remarkably respectable. Now they crowded before the door of the armory to hand in their guns. When that was done, Pedro mounted the stairs. He had been asked to attend the meeting.

"Hello Pedro," said a North American voice.

He turned to see John Bidwell and Pablo Gutiérrez hauling saddles through the gate. Dusty from the trail, they worked at Sutter's north ranch, Upper Farm. Sutter called it *hoch,* which meant upper in German. Pedro knew they expected to petition for land on opposites sides of the Bear River.

"Are there batéas at the fort that we could use?" Pablo asked.

Pedro shook his head. As far as he knew, there were none. In Mexico those wide wooden bowls with carved ridges were used for panning gold. Maybe these two had found a few flakes of it. If so, they wouldn't be the only ones. In the last few months he'd heard of an informal system whereby raw gold was exchanged in San Francisco for negotiable Mexican gold pieces, every link in the chain keeping quiet, the lynchpin being Captain Sutter. Pedro wasn't supposed to know, but he felt sure this was just one more sad dream of riches based on tiny amounts of gold. Hoping Bidwell and Gutiérrez wouldn't lose their senses over it like his father had, he watched them lay their saddles under the oak and head for the stairs of the big house.

"I'll have John order some," Bidwell said in a cheery tone.

Pedro held up the palm of his hand. "Sorry but the Captain is occupied with important matters. You've had a long ride, Please help yourselves to any food you can find in the cookhouse. We'll talk later."

Disappointment showed in their faces as the two retreated, trying to talk with one another, Gutiérrez in poor English, Bidwell in poor Spanish.

Pedro opened the door, the meeting not yet started. At the elegant Russian table sat General Vallejo, the General's three men, and Sutter's closest confidant John Sinclair, who had known him in the Sandwich Islands and joined him in California. In the alcove, the Captain's backside bobbed around as he rifled through a pile of things behind his desk-table. Vallejo's uniform looked a bit shiny but distinguished, and Pedro felt a thrill of pride to meet this grandest of his countrymen. He took off his hat and swept it toward the floor before seating himself on the opposite side of the table.

As they waited for the Captain, the General talked pleasantly of the journey from his Sonoma rancho and the launch ride across the Sacramento River. Dark mutton-chop sideburns flanked his round white face, which appeared to be too young for a man of his experience. Pedro and the General's three men gave each other mutual nods as they were introduced.

On previous occasions when General Vallejo visited New Helvetia, Pedro had wished to speak to him. Now he had the opportunity.

"I owe you a personal debt of thanks, esteemed General," he said.

Vallejo tilted his head in puzzlement. "How so?"

"You had my father's helmet returned to me."

Vallejo pursed his lips. "I don't seem to recall…"

"In 1829, Estanislao's rebellion, after the last batt…"

"Ah, yes. Now I remember. Umm. Let's see, Fifteen years ago. It was remarkable finding that ancient relic in a field of ashes. It must be precious to your family."

"Sí, General. It was worn by my ancestor in the Holy Wars."

Vallejo widened his eyes and nodded in appreciation. "Did you fight in the Estanislao Rebellion? Or, no. I think you were too young."

"I was young, but I fought and got a shoulder wound. Nothing serious."

Vallejo's smile was friendly. "We were both young."

Sutter emerged from the alcove in his military jacket, bringing a writing plume, a bottle of ink, and paper. Bowing formally to the General, he seated himself at the head of the table and asked Vallejo about the progress of his farming activities. The General spoke in vague terms about his new buildings and of Chief Solano's success as majordomo, recruiting and managing the native labor crews. He asked Captain Sutter about New Helvetia. Sutter replied in equally vague terms about his crops and other enterprises, including his profitable salmon-packing business on the Sacramento River. Despite the fact that everyone present came to the meeting well aware of all the mentioned activities, this polite exchange consumed about half an hour. Everyone also knew that both men were stocking military fortresses in their separate fiefdoms. Pedro translated for Sutter when necessary

Disagreement began to emerge.

General Vallejo agreed with Captain Sutter that Upper California must rid itself of the criminal depredations of the cholo soldiers acquired by Governor Micheltorena from the jails of Mexico. "But Captain Sutter," he elevated the arcs of his dark brows, "I draw your attention to an important fact. The cholos are leaving."

He paused as Pedro translated, and then continued, "Twelve days ago Governor Micheltorena ordered that they be sent back to Mexico. All Californios were notified. I have begun implementation at my rancho. Surely as a Mexican citizen you also received the order, but my Indian runner informs me that you continue to amass soldiers. The alarm is finished, Capitán. It is over. The cholos are going home. No need for your big militia."

Sutter lowered his head and his eyes floated to the tops of white seas. "Den for vhat reason is General Castro collecting troops in San José, hmm? And wit cholo soldiers?" He didn't wait for an answer. "Iss perfectly clear the agreement iss soon broken and war is afoot." Sutter's expression changed to pity. "Perhaps your information iss, mm, un-fresh?"

That could have been taken as an insult, but Vallejo didn't flinch. "Captain Sutter, I sorrow for my country, which, I'm sure you have no need to be reminded, is your country too. You have written certain letters, and I have seen your enlarged militia. Rumors fly quickly up and down California that you sympathize with the foreign invaders from the United States—an unauthorized and armed invasion."

Pedro recalled the bedraggled and starving men of Lt. John Frémont's expedition, who had been crazy enough to traverse the snowy Sierra in winter—men hoping to capture California for the United States.

"General Vallejo," Captain Sutter said, "I giff dem every kindness, as you yourself would. Please, say to your Californio friends dat my generosity not be misunderstood. Mexico iss my country. I hold no favor for the United States."

The furrow between Vallejo's brows remained. "I am happy to hear that. And now another problem. If you fight General Castro, you do yourself harm." He glanced at the ceiling before continuing.

"I came here determined to make you understand. No matter what Governor Micheltorena has told you, war will endanger our mutual dreams of the future of Upper California, yours and mine. Please, Capitán, do not let old troubles between us color your understanding. I come today open and clean of grudges. For the sake of our country, I implore you, go back to your farming and stay away from warfare."

Like stepping from stone to stone in a fast river, Pedro selected his words. He couldn't simply blurt out what he thought had been implied. He might be wrong, and the reputations of two prominent Californios—Castro and Vallejo—were at stake.

He stuck to the literal translation. Sutter repeated his determination to support Governor Micheltorena against Castro, the rebel general, in war if necessary. Vallejo approached his request from new angles until the light faded at the windows and it was hard to see the faces. Later, Pedro thought, he'd share his hunch with Sutter. Then misunderstandings could be repaired by letter. That was the Captain's way.

Sutter pushed back, scraping his chair noisily on the plank floor, and bowed. "Esteemed General, I would be honored if you and your men would partake of our humble supper." He rang his cowbell twice—his signal for the servants to set places. Playing host was his strength.

General Vallejo took his tricorn from the table, pressed it to his belly and returned the bow. "The honor is ours, esteemed Capitán."

Rising, bowing all around the table, Pedro realized he wouldn't get a chance to speak to Sutter alone until tomorrow. Meanwhile the matter of his own rancho churned in his mind.

Outside, the sky was still light though the days were getting shorter. A stiff breeze came from the southwest. As Pedro descended the stairs he saw the Indians crowding before his room, waiting for the day's tokens.

He crossed the courtyard and moved through the Indians, who stepped back politely. Unlocking the door, he lit the two candles on the overhead iron wheel and waved the people into the warm room. He pulled the box of tin tokens from under his bed and began handing them out, staring intently at each face, assuring himself that the Indian had actually worked this day. They threaded the tokens through their neck thongs to jingle with the other tokens. On Saturday they would redeem them for the brightly striped cloth they all loved, and the equally desired colored beads from Italy.

Halfway through the line, he looked up to see the daughter of Captain Juan offering her reddened palm. Her downcast lashes lay on her soft, brown cheeks.

"Hola," he said.

She looked away, so very different from when they'd first met.

He slipped her an extra token and whispered, "Do not forget to stay out of the Captain's sight."

She dipped her head and walked away.

The next morning, after an evening of drinking with Captain Sutter, the Vallejo party galloped away toward the Sacramento River. Pedro signaled the Indians flanking the road to fire their guns in the air, a gesture of respect.

Once, twice, twenty times, as the visitors shrank into the dust and distance.

Dismissing the men, Pedro headed for the big house, reviewing what he would say to Sutter. First the nuances of Spanish diplomacy, then Rancho Sacayak. His carefully drawn map was in his vest pocket.

John Bidwell and Pablo Gutiérrez met him at the base of the stairs.

"Buenos días," Pedro said. "Did you order the batéas?"

"Not yet," Bidwell said. "We came to ask the Captain to order two of them, to be sent on the next boat up the Yuba River."

"Have you found gold?"

"We believe so."

Captain Sutter flung open his door and called down, "Oh, yust da men I look for." He hurried down the stairs, saying to Bidwell, "Good day, Johann, I am heppy you be here."

Bidwell removed his hat and was about to speak when Sutter shouted over their heads, "Jared, Perry, fife minutes we meet upstairs." *Jared Sheldon and Perry McCoon!*

"Go up," Sutter said eyeing Pedro, Pablo, and John Bidwell. "I need talk with all of you, and now I send for John Sinclair and others."

Watching Sutter hurry across the grounds toward the guard station, Pedro felt the sting of frustration. Would he ever get the Captain's attention? Inside the parlor room, ink, plume and notebook remained on the table from the day before. He seated himself opposite McCoon and stared at a flaw in the adobe wall.

In Monterey he'd often been assigned to hunt disloyal ship jumpers like McCoon, scum who hid until their short-handed captains were forced to sail without them. Yet Captain Sutter made no distinctions. He treated all English- and German-speaking men like gentlemen, no matter how dishonorable they were. It grated.

Jared Sheldon came in and took a seat, nodding at Pedro, then McCoon, his wolf eyes taking in everything. Pedro realized that the three of them were all in their mid-thirties, at the peak of their manhood—as was Bill Daylor. He admired Sheldon more than any other North American. As a young man he'd been left to die on the Santa Fe Trail by a trading company that promised him passage in exchange for work. They laid him on the desert floor like bad beef when he fell ill, and drove off without him. Without food or water, Sheldon survived until Indians rescued and doctored him in their village. He learned their language and rode with them, hearing about Mexico. Next, he rode to Mexico and built water-powered mills, a trade he'd learned in Vermont. By then he was fluent in Spanish and one Indian language. Next he rode north to the little village of Los Angeles where he worked for another millwright, but had to escape into the San Gabriel Mountains when trouble arose. He stayed with renegade mission indians about a year. Ultimately he rode to Monterey and worked for the Governor of Alta California, whom he now considered a friend.

Pedro hadn't followed the banter between Sheldon and McCoon, something about the calf headcount—it was whispered that McCoon branded far more than his allotted share of calves in exchange for his vaquero work for Sutter—and now Sheldon said to McCoon, "You're so full of shit, you wouldn't know the truth if it harpooned you."

McCoon's blue eyes sparked for a second, but he whisked a leather flask from his sheepskin vest, uncorked and raised it. "And I suppose ye never rode with the Horse-thief Indians." He gave Sheldon a dimpled grin before taking a swallow.

Color drained from Sheldon. Men didn't say that to his face. His story was that he'd run from the law rather than be arrested for his employer's debts. He told anyone who asked that he'd lived in the mountains with the mission fugitives, learning their language, but never participated in their horse raids. Pedro hoped Sheldon would knock the bastard flat on the floor. Instead, he directed his steely gaze out the window.

McCoon reached over an empty chair and nudged Sheldon with the flask. "Jared, 'ere's to the good times. All speed."

Sheldon considered that for a noticeable length of time, but then took a swig and handed the flask back. Once again Pedro found himself thinking that if the Captain shut down his distillery, the worst scum would vacate the fort.

McCoon smirked at Pedro as he deliberately inserted the cork and pocketed the liquor, not offering any.

The door banged open and Sutter came in with Sinclair, Bidwell, a French trapper, three Germans including the cooper, and Pablo Gutiérrez. Sutter nested his rump in his captain's chair at the head of the table and began. "My good men, our friend General Maríano Vallejo says he will not fight on behalf of our esteemed Governor Micheltorena. And more, he makes the fool of me for doing so." He tapped a forefinger on the table.

The men around the table exchanged looks and Pedro groaned inwardly.

"Mine Indians tell me of General Castro's activities. He iss preparing three-hunnert soldiers to march from Los Angeles to Monterey. We must go and support Governor Micheltorena against dat army. If not, one day Castro comes marching here to fight, and ya, iss better we fight in the south and not on my rancho. We wait not, as General Vallejo advises. You men, I need you to collect American trappers. They be goot shooters. We march as one army against the rebels."

He turned to Pablo Gutiérrez. "You and the other men who want land with my recommendation and so fort, you will fight with us. Not so?"

Pablo shifted on his crate and nodded assent, despite his gold discovery.

Pedro, who very much wanted a rancho nevertheless said, "Captain

Sutter, I believe General Vallejo was trying to tell us something important about General Castro. I think we should consider his counsel and not march to war until we understand that better."

A lost-boy look flitted briefly across Sutter's eyes, replaced by indignity and then the squint of a wise man. "Loyalty stems from da land, Lieutenant," he said in a teacherly tone, "and land binds men to der country. If I want to know who be the leaders of my country, I look who granted my land. The Mexican government hass giff me New Helvetia. My loyalty I owe to Mexico and der governor. You who want land be just zo in my debt. Ya? You march wit me. I order you to make our militia much bigger."

Having spoken boldly, Pedro dared not push it further. A hunch was only a hunch, and his lot was with Captain Sutter.

"Lieutenant Valdez is a goot officer," Sutter added, to Pedro's embarrassment, "And now, if each man speak his mind, please, hmm?" The Captain glanced around the table twirling his mustache, his pale eyes glittering.

"The Captain's right," said John Sinclair, owner of Rancho Del Paso across the river. "We owe the government loyalty. I can get more Indians and riflemen to march with us."

John Bidwell, a reasonable man who'd been with Sutter for several years, agreed. "I'll bring the Indians and some Frenchmen from Hock Farm." He managed Sutter's farm on the Yuba River. English speakers couldn't say *hoch* with a German catch in the throat. Neither could Pedro. So people pronounced the northern rancho "hock."

Jared Sheldon glanced around the table at each participant. "I don't 'spose I can hold my hand out for a land grant and stand by while Castro fights the Governor. Count me in, but if we're in a fight, I'm in it to win." His jaw was flint.

Sutter stopped twirling his mustache. "The governor's cholos fight with us, fight like cornered dogs, so they not go back to the calabooses of Mexico." His lips turned up slightly, like the painted figure of San Joaquín in San José's mission church. "I giff you my word, we win. When iss finish, alla us win rewards." He smiled in pained sympathy. "General Vallejo iss an unhappy chile. He dreams of ruling upper California. He fears dat his hands get dirty in war." He snorted softly. "I listen not to him."

"Ve fight," said a German, and another nodded his agreement.

"And you, Señor McCoon?" Sutter inquired.

All eyes turned to the slouching bastard grinning a one-sided dimple. "I'll kiss the arses of the powers that be," he said.

Sutter slapped the table with both hands. "Ach zo! Iss ended. Pablo, ride fast to Monterey. Talk to the Californios along the way. Tell dem to join us on the march. And giff to Governor Micheltorena a letter." He opened his portfolio and scratched out a short message, dipping his plume twice. Waving the paper dry, he folded the letter and presented it to Pablo. "I write dat we march to defend our Mexican government." A pleased smile smoothed the Captain's countenance.

Pushing his chair back he stood up, looking intently at each man he addressed. "Perry, go nort to San Rafael and bring American trappers. Careful. Vallejo hass spies. Jared and John," he said, turning to Sheldon and Sinclair, "help me recruit settlers and trappers. We need marksmen. Pedro, keep training our Indians and the new ones brought in. I'll dispatch a message to the Moquelumne." He smiled warmly around the table.

As the men donned their hats and stood to leave, Pedro pressed forward to speak privately with the Captain. Bidwell got there first. With the look of a preoccupied man, Sutter listened briefly and waved at Bidwell, showing he wasn't interested in batéas. He motioned all to leave except for Pablo Gutiérrez.

As Pedro went out the door he saw Pablo remove a false sole from his boot, insert Sutter's letter, and stamp down. He'd have a long ride to Monterey before he could return to the hills and look for gold on the Río de los Osos, Bear River.

If General Vallejo had been sincere in his advice, it was too late. The die was cast. And Pedro knew better than trouble Sutter about a recommendation at this time.

# 7

María Howchia waited with Blue Star among the milling people. Guards held back the crowd, but she could see through the partially open gate that Manu-iki was pulling a long wooden paddle from a dome oven while her helpers poured buckets of pi-no-le into the eating troughs. At the end of Manu-iki's paddle a loaf of bread steamed in the cool morning air. María hoped to learn how to make that marvelous bread.

Two men in loincloths stepped into the big yard, one clanging a bell, the other making a drum purr like a bobcat kitten—the eating signal. The gate was pushed open and María moved through it with all the people, many of them the Cosumne, the People of Salmon, from a place where the rivers joined on their way to the western sea. She had learned their story before sleeping in one of their u-machas.

Blue Star joked, "I think my hand is too swollen to eat."

María glanced at her own swollen hands as she knelt before a trough. Crying Fox found a place opposite them, kneeling. His blue crystal charmstone reflected morning sunlight as he watched the bread quickly disappear, passed from hand to hand down the trough, each person tearing off a piece. Hungrily, he scooped the gruel, then licked his fingers and studied his swollen hand.

About two twenties of people knelt along the trough, and about as many prepared to eat at the other hollowed log. María scooped up the thin soup, one of a flurry of hands moving up and down the trough churning gruel to mouths. The level of soup lowered as though draining through holes in the bottom.

Manu-iki approached Crying Fox from behind. Large breasts and no chin tattoo, a freakish sight, a girl in a woman's full body. She tapped him on the shoulder, offering another loaf of bread. He spun around, taking it, blushing. Manu-iki smiled warmly at him before she sauntered away, and he watched the motion under her tightly tied skirt as he tore off a hunk of bread and, like a sleepwalker, passed the loaf across to María.

Hadn't he seen what happened to Señor Daylor? María had told him that Manu-iki had been the cause. Sinking her teeth into the delicious bread, she feared that he was under that child-woman's spell. Now Manu-iki was back at the dome-oven pinching off a nub of dough and handing it to her pale-skinned daughter. The child popped it in her mouth and chewed while Manu-iki slapped a dough ball back and forth in her hands, stretched it over itself, and laid it carefully in a basket.

María watched with her head high to see over the people on the other side, hoping to learn the secret of the light bread. Bending forward, Manu-iki pushed the paddle into the oven, her shell necklaces and long hair playing about her wrists. María's scalp prickled.

She looked at the big house, and to her horror locked eyes with Captain Sutter! He'd been watching her from his landing. Quickly she drew down so Crying Fox's head screened her.

But it was too late. "Lieutenant Valdez," Sutter called.

Almost immediately Pedro Valdez came around the big house from where he and other Españoles ate their meals. She dared not look as the Captain spoke to him, their talk covered by the slurping around her. When he returned to the other side of the big house, she sat numbly. The gruel vanished before her. The bell sounded, and she lined up with the others to hear the man she'd followed to this place speak to the Indians. But fear blocked her ears, and later she went out the gate with the others on their way to the fields.

A hand touched her elbow.

She startled, whirled around. But it was only Señor Valdez. He lifted one of her swollen hands and said, "You can make yourself a good cutter from a split willow."

He looked to Blue Star and Crying Fox, who were with her. "Go to the river and cut willows, split them lengthwise and tie them to make hoops. Bring one for her."

As they left, his gray eyes searched hers and he spoke softly. "Captain Sutter wants you to go to him after supper."

She couldn't control the squeak in her voice. "I didn't stay out of his sight."

"I am sorry, but he says you are the prettiest Indian girl in his establishment."

She didn't correct him for calling her a girl, and no happiness came from being called pretty.

"You can go home," he whispered. "I will help you."

Hope flamed. But she must go alone. She couldn't ask Crying Fox to accompany her or he might be hung. If she left now she could get home before dark, before the bad spirit Bohemkulla could scramble her brains. But how would Señor Valdez arrange it? And when could she go?

The hoof-beats of many horses sounded, coming toward them.

Pedro Valdez glanced around as if to assure himself he wasn't being overheard. "Captain Sutter will be angry," he said. "He doesn't want Indians to leave during the harvest. Especially you." He raised his voice to be heard over the approaching horses. "If you are asked, por favor, say nothing of our talk, of my help." Beneath his sombrero his face, framed by dark curls glinting reddish in the sunlight, appeared kindly and well meaning. She didn't want Captain Sutter to kill him either, for helping her.

"I will say nothing," she said. Now that he'd lost his magic she could easily leave him. But on this grassy plain she'd be visible in daylight.

The horses, maybe twenty, were being herded by Indian vaqueros into the corral where she had poured the contents of her burden basket so many times. Over the din of the horses and yipping men she yelled to be heard. "When can I leave?"

With his hands on his waist sash he watched the vaqueros close the gate, its poles serving as small windows through which she glimpsed neighing horses running around in the high-walled adobe corral.

"Pick wheat with all the others this morning," he said still looking at the horses. "Then when the pickers move to the south field, stay below the uncut grain on the edge of the field. Keep low and make sure no one sees you going east. I have a spy, so be careful, por favor."

She knew she must trust him. "Maybe you can come to my place later and visit us," she blurted over the whooping vaqueros. She hadn't thought about that four times.

They watched the horses run up and over the hill of wheat—sliding, scrambling, neighing, wheeling back toward the opposite wall. The vaqueros trilled their tongues in falsetto and loud-clapped to frighten the horses back again. Most of the time the horses' ears were all she could see above the wall as they stampeded back and forth, skidding on the grain.

"I will come to the ranchería of your people. Hasta la vista, Amapolita."

Señor Valdez strode toward the corral.

Suddenly María's rabbit-skin blanket came to mind. "Wait," she called, following him. He turned.

"My blanket is in the house of the Cos-umne. Will you bring it when you come?" She couldn't go back near the fort, where Sutter lurked.

A smile softened his face. "The pleasure would be mine."

For a moment she didn't recognize the man who came through the fort gate and stood looking at her and Señor Valdez. But when he pushed the sombrero back on his head, she saw with a shock that it was Captain Sutter. Never had she seen him in such a hat, and in trousers with straps over his shoulders. Heart pounding, she pivoted, positioned her basket, and walked swiftly up the path between the stubble fields.

Dread drove her toward the harvesters in the uncut field. She knew Proud Hawk would be telling Captain Sutter that she'd go to him after supper, and she feared that he would want her now.

Pedro stood at the gate with Captain Sutter, watching the vaqueros run the horses over the wheat. In an hour a thousand bushels would be threshed. Then, on the first windy day, he'd have the Indians start the winnowing, the shoveling of wheat and chaff into the wind so that the chaff blew over the wall. Then the Indians would bag the grain and sew the leather closed.

Captain Sutter yelled over the noise, "I see dot you haff talk with the muchacha."

Pedro avoided the twinkling eyes. "She will come to you." The lie came out just a little rough.

"Ach ya, iss goot." Sutter's cheerful tone continued despite the unhappy words that followed. "This year we haff wheat enough for our needs only. Pity."

Translation: *nothing for the Russians.* Each autumn the Russians sailed to San Francisco to collect payments in grain, and every year Sutter paid them fewer fenegas than promised, a remarkable feat of diplomacy. Not that the harvest was small. It increased annually as the labor force increased. But every year more men had to be paid for cutting wood in the mountains, spearing and packing salmon in barrels that had to be coopered, building extra corrals, and for many more activities. Suppliers had to be paid too, for importing all manner of goods from Mexico, New England and Japan. In addition, Indians had big appetites. Much of the wheat profit went back into them. The enormity of Sutter's debts secured by promises of fenegas of wheat was beyond what an ordinary man could conceive. And now the Russians would receive nothing. How the Captain managed it mystified Pedro. He half-expected the Czar to reclaim New Helvetia and all the Russian goods.

Sutter yelled over the din, "After the harvest, we plant dopple so much again." Delight lit his features as he watched the vaqueros whip the horses into frenzies on the spread-out wheat, much of the chaff already powdered into dust.

"Capitán, por favor, I need a word wi…" The dust made him cough.

"Yes, mine son. Come with." The Captain turned and walked through the fort gate.

Silently rehearsing his speech about Rancho Sacayak, Pedro followed. But as they neared the big house Perry McCoon came from the kitchen with a hand up. "John," he said, "I needs to palaver."

When had the bastard returned from San Rafael? Had he even gone? His dark hair was clasped neatly at the nape of his neck, his boots blackened and shiny.

Sutter smiled from Pedro to McCoon. "You two want talk. Both come with." There was spring in his step as he mounted the stairs ahead of them. Perhaps thinking about the pretty Indita. Ay madre, Pedro was in treacherous waters. And he wasn't about to mention Rancho Sacayak in McCoon's presence.

"Capitán," he said, "if you please I'd like a moment alone with you, por favor."

Sutter turned and looked down at the two of them. McCoon could have been made of syrup. His body melted into the railing and a smile poured across his face. His blue eyes twinkled, challenging Pedro before he said to Sutter, "The greaser's hidin something, me thinks."

Pedro kept his face blank.

"Perry," Sutter said, looking at McCoon as though he were a child who'd forgotten his manners, "you must not call mine officer dot name. Understand? I not haff dat at mine establishment." He glanced at the sun as he motioned them inside.

Pedro felt like he'd been stepped on by a horse, but he kept his pride, seating himself on a polished Russian chair opposite McCoon. He would listen to what that bastard had to say, and then think up something to tell Sutter.

Sutter folded his hands on the table, donned his judicial expression, and as Pedro expected, looked at McCoon first. "Ach zo, vhat bring you here?"

"I've been talking to Jared about the piece of land he's got a petition for. I'd like to try my own hand at farming. Thought you could help me along. There's a bonny piece east of Jared's." Pedro maintained a calm demeanor despite realizing that the land McCoon was referring to was near Rancho Sacayak.

McCoon continued, "I'd like to see if farming's to me likin. Talk is, you're looking for a hog farm. Let me breed your hogs, and I'll bring pork to the fort fresh on the hoof." Captain Sutter queried, "Far away? Vhat? Ten kilometers?"

"More. Me thinks the farther a hog farm, the better." He grinned at Sutter with a dimple boring into his cheek. "A half league or so upstream of Jared's. North side of the river. Help us both, it would. Ye'll git half me crop o' pigs. Just start me off with two brave lookin sows and a boar from Hock Farm, and we'll both prosper."

A half league upstream of Sheldon's. North side of the river. That described Pedro's rancho!

Sutter was saying, "Perry, you be a sailor, not a farmer."

"Ye've seen me ride a horse. Better'n any man alive, ent it so?"

Disgusted at that, Pedro cleared his throat. But Captain Sutter was nodding. "Ach zo. Iss true."

Damned Englishman! He knew the Captain was no judge of riding, and so ignorant about horses he didn't know a jenny from a stallion. Pedro fought to contain himself.

"Help run yer cows too, I will, 'til I gets me paipers. And what red-blooded man could turn his back on the beauteous brown lasses such as grace that fine land?"

Pedro searched his mind for the English word *lasses* as McCoon continued. "I wants me own pick o' the crop, if you gits my drift. An' fer that, a man figures t' get mor'n twenty miles outside your range, all due respect sir." He chuckled, dimples in both cheeks.

Sutter threw back his head and laughed, Pedro still puzzling over *lasses*. Sutter bobbed his head up and down. "Ya ya, iss goot. I want dat my friends to settle all sides of New Helvetia. We be strong together. I write today a letter to Johann Bidwell dat he giff you two zows and a boar. And he tell Adolph Brüheim to drive the hogs in mine oxcart to dat place on the River of the Cosumney. We see how farming likes you, hmm? Ya ya." Smiling, he smoothed his mustache back from its part.

At the start of the hills. North of the river! Mother of God, this was a joke of Coyote, as his old India Grandmother would say. Just when a man thought he knew where he was going, something like this!

"And you Lieutenant? Can I help you, hmm?"

Skimming mentally over possible ruses, Pedro quickly settled on: "Capitán Sutter, our soldiers are excellent as you see each day, but we need more men if we mean to fight a war." He told him he'd like to ride farther up the Cosumney for Indians. He didn't say he'd use that opportunity to find another place. Except even then McCoon'd be the nearest neighbor. Damned bad luck!

"Ya ya. More men." Sutter scowled in thought. "Go on the morning." He then rang his cowbell, slapped the table, scraped his chair on the plank floor and stood up. "Iss not every day I make all mens happy, hmm?" He smiled with pleasure from Pedro to McCoon.

Summoned, Manu-iki came through the door and stood waiting for instructions. At the sight of her ripe breasts, Pedro recalled the meaning of *lass*—one of many English words for girl or woman. McCoon would go after the pretty Indita and exercise the traditional right of the señor.

# 8

The air was chill, the path dark as María Howchia hurried toward the home place. She tried to watch her footing, but the crescent moon gave little light. Rattlesnakes liked to lie on a path absorbing stored warmth. Hel-le-ja, cougar, and grizzly bears roamed at night. But mostly she worried about Bohemkulla, the evil spirit who prowled at night seeking to scramble the brains of travelers.

She had run most of the way and was close to home. It had been dark ever since she'd left Omuch's village. She had accepted their food, but hadn't wanted to stay for the sleep. Now she wished she'd stayed. Exhausted, she hurried as fast as she could, stubbed her toe on a root, and almost cried out.

The night was alive. Owls screamed throughout the oak forest. Straining to see into the shadowy trees, she heard deer moving in the dry grass. Sometimes skunks ambled before her on the narrow path, but so far no spirit had wailed. Maybe Bohemkulla could overtake people without their knowing. People said it had happened to Grandmother Dishi. Never had María felt so alone and small. But at least she wasn't in Captain Sutter's house, and soon she'd be home. That kept her going.

The moon was higher now, and the path became familiar. She went down the gully where the little creek joined the river, and then climbed the last hill. With a sigh of relief she saw the red glow of the sweathouse through the trees, a distant triangle of pinewood with plenty of cracks. Father would be inside.

A deep rumble moved the roots of her hair. She stopped, looked toward the boulders on her right, and saw a pair of green eyes reflected in the moonlight. Too high above the ground to be a skunk. Heart racing, she stepped slowly off the path and felt with her feet for a rock while letting her burden basket slip to the ground. She felt fallen sticks and branches but no rocks. Four-legged hunters like cougars enjoyed the chase, so she must not run.

She grabbed a stick and hurled it at the eyes. They disappeared, but then reappeared a short distance away. Nearby another pair of eyes glinted at her. She whirled to look behind her. Two more pairs of eyes. Wolves! How long had they been following her? They knew that a woman carried no weapon.

*Don't run.* She needed a big stick. On this tree-canopied hilltop limbs fell in the wind, but people collected them for firewood. *Don't let them smell fear.* But surely it was too late. Any animal would smell this much fear. One set of eyes moved toward her. Scrambling around for a weapon she screamed with all her might, "Father, Father!" If the men weren't talking in the sweathouse they would hear.

The grass swished, coming at her. She dodged, whirled, caught the odor of wolf. She found a fallen tree limb, lifted it. It was huge and too heavy but she managed to swing it as she moved her back against the tree for protection.

*I must be fierce.*

A snarl came from the side. She whirled, every hair on her body tingling. Out of her mouth came the most hideous and inhuman noise she could make. Courage and anger coursed through her. *Bad wolves to attack a human!* She yelled for Father, swinging from side to side in great swoops.

A heavy animal landed on her, knocked her to the ground. She twisted, jammed the branch into its jaws just in time. She felt a spray of saliva, smelled bad breath as she shoved. Hind paws shifted back and forth over her groin, digging in for balance. Fore claws cut her from chest to neck as the wolf fought the branch. *How dare you jump at my throat!* Focusing all her anger, she forced the branch hard into that open mouth and screamed again for Father.

Teeth clamped on her ankle and yanked her. The wolf wanted to drag her away so that Father and the men couldn't find her! Anger mounted to blind fury and she kicked with her free foot, gouging a toe into the other animal's eye as she struggled against the wolf on top. *I'll show you how strong people are!*

The top wolf jerked free of the branch. She rolled to the side and swung hard at the spot she'd vacated. A thunk and a yipping squeal. Her leg was free. She jumped to her feet. Her return swing pounding another wolf. Growls and snarls continued to surround her as she swung the limb fast as she could, back and forth. Solid hits made ribs boom, followed by squeals of pain. How many wolves? She couldn't tell. Swinging blindly, she saw firebrands moving up the hill toward her. "Father," she yelled, "Here I am!"

The wolves saw the men too. They rustled away in the dry grass.

Lit by torchlight, Grizzly Hair, Jacksnipe Song and several others came to her. She lost strength, dropped the branch. It was all she could do to stay upright. Although she was supposed to maintain a period of pretending not to see anyone, she put her arms around Father's thick middle and stood on quivering legs, hugging him.

He held her and petted her hair, also ignoring custom. Closing her eyes she melted into the safety of his warm power.

❧

The next morning, after Etumu applied more salve to her lacerated ankle, María Howchia limped beside Grizzly Hair as he went to check his rabbit snares. Relieved not to be injured worse, she kept pace and he slowed to accommodate her, but her tongue felt heavy, and she could not speak of Captain Sutter.

Father didn't ask. Bending over to wring the neck of a cottontail he then straightened up and sang a wisp of a song to send the spirit on its way. Many men sang only to the spirits of larger animals, but Father wasn't like other men. He was a man of knowledge.

The plume of his topknot shaded his face as he reset the snare. They walked together down the trail. The walnut trees had turned golden and the ground was soft with the slim yellow leaves. She bent down and tossed the round black nuts into her burden basket. Walnut paste balls would taste good with rabbit stew.

"You were brave, daughter," he said, startling her. It was the first he'd spoken since the sleep—keeping a semblance of tradition. But she didn't feel brave. She felt foolish for having expected Proud Hawk to become her husband, and ashamed of everything that happened in Captain Sutter's house.

Grizzly Hair sat down against a sturdy alder, a water tree that put its roots into the riverbank. He patted the ground beside him. When María was seated next to him, the burden basket upright on the other side of the tree, he said, "You remind me of your mother's sister."

Oak Gall was the auntie whose name was rarely mentioned—speaking the names of deceased relatives invited dangerous ghosts.

"I wish I knew more about her," María said, craving a long story to take her mind off Captain Sutter and his place.

"She was brave." He sat watching a red-tailed hawk flying over the brown hillside on the other side of the river. "She went to the mission with me. Running Quail's eldest son also went. Just we three. Everyone else was afraid to go."

María Howchia waited to hear more.

"People told me not to go. Even my mother. She said the danger was great. Your grandparents told their daughter not to go with me. I did too. I wanted her to stay at the home place and wait for my return. We planned to be married. I wanted her parents to like me."

He seemed to be finished.

María had always noticed a coolness between him and Etumu's parents, her grandfather and grandmother. "But you learned things at the mission," she prompted. Everyone respected him for his knowledge of the Españoles. He and the old woman he brought back, old María, had taught the People to speak Spanish. And some of the children, including María, had been given Spanish names.

He brought his knees up and rested his forearms on them, hands hanging loose. "Yes, I learned things." He watched the hawk and then said, "Clarity comes when fear is defeated."

María tried to imagine the fears he must have had, going to Mission San José when none of the People had been there. "All three of you risked a lot to go to the mission."

He nodded almost imperceptibly. "I was afraid harm would come to your auntie."

"And it did," María recalled.

"Sometimes fear is well founded, but sometimes we fear small things, like looking foolish to our friends. Defeating these fears helps us *see, and such* clarity is the first step on the pathway to knowledge."

"By *see* you mean more than look."

"Yes. Can you *see* now what was hidden before you went to the fort?"

"I know more about Captain Sutter." It came out low.

He glanced briefly at her and then gazed past the bushes and the boulder through the denuding trees, where the river lazed past.

"He makes men and women do his bidding," she said. "He tells other men to wrap his enemy in iron chains and the chained man lives in a bad place behind iron bars. Sometimes Captain Sutter tells a man to hang his enemies by their necks with rope until they die. Or he has their heads cut off and put on iron spikes for everyone to see."

His expression didn't change.

She looked up through fringes of yellow leaves against the blue sky, still disappointed about Captain Sutter's control over Pedro Valdez, and continued, "Captain Sutter is hy-apo, but not like you. Here each person decides whether to marry or hunt or make a basket, or…" A catch in her throat stopped her from adding, *with whom to couple.*

Tenderly he patted her knee. "You are so very young," he said as if to himself. Then he was teaching again. "Maybe you *saw* a different kind of power."

"Señor Sutter couples with other men's wives, and girls." She wished her voice wouldn't shake. "He forces them."

Silence fell between them as she wondered again about Mother during the war. Then she thought about Father's wisdom and how everyone came to him for advice. But now his knowledge was aimed at her. The honor of that gave her the strength to ask, "Do you think I could become a doctor?" *A woman of knowledge.*

His hand reached around her and came to rest on her shoulder. "I think you're brave enough. And I believe you have the potential for strong power."

This thrilled her. It straightened her back and steadied her voice. Few in this world were capable of linking with the power of the universe. The steps would be frightening, everyone knew that. But with Father's guidance she might convince old Bear Claw, of the Yal-umne, to teach her medicine. Grandmother Howchia had been a singing doctor. María Howchia would follow Eagle Woman's tracks. She realized that she had indeed been brave. She had defeated her fear of leaving the home place. She had faced Captain Sutter alone. She had even defeated bad wolves. "What must I do to become a woman of knowledge?"

"What do you fear the most?"

She shivered, knowing where this was leading. "Captain Sutter's power."

"That is your enemy."

"Must I defeat him to be a woman of power?"

"Yes."

She doubted she had that much courage.

"You're thinking it will be difficult. But it will be easier than the next step on the pathway to knowledge. After you have defeated Captain Sutter and gained new clarity, you must defeat the clarity. That will be your new enemy. Each step of the way, the enemy becomes stronger, more devious, and more difficult to conquer. But you must keep finding and defeating your new enemies. Few people can do that."

"I don't understand. How can clarity can be my enemy?"

After a thinking pause he said, "Fear is straightforward. You know what you're afraid of. But clarity is sly. It refreshes you, lulls you, leads you to believe you know more than you do. That makes it a stronger enemy." He gazed into the distance. "The warrior sees clearly and believes to the bottom of his stomach that the peace chiefs are wrong. That makes him a good fighter. The long robe sees clearly and believes in his stomach that the teachers of other peoples are wrong. That makes him a good teacher. But the warrior and the long robe can never become men of power unless they triumph over their clarity." He paused.

"That boulder." He pointed at one the size of the family u-macha, splotched by circles of overlapping grey lichen. "Does it appear to be strong and eternal?"

"Yes."

"Some day it will be sand. You cannot know that unless you *see* it. It's like removing your hands from your eyes." He cupped his hands at the sides of her head making a vision tunnel, and then removed them. "You thought you were seeing everything, but you were not."

"What is my next enemy, after clarity?"

"The respect people give you. People come like hummingbirds to nectar, asking for advice. People who *see* gain respect and can easily influence others. Respect becomes the strongest enemy of all. Few can defeat it. But you must, if you are to become a woman of knowledge."

This was almost too much to comprehend. She went back to the beginning. "How can I defeat my clarity about Captain Sutter's power?"

"Each person finds a different path. If I tried to tell you, I would be wrong."

He stood, looking down at her with worry lines around his eyes, and she knew he would rather she lived like any other woman, pounding acorns, cooking, marrying, and having babies. But she also knew he'd help her along the treacherous pathway to knowledge if he could.

She positioned her head thong and the burden basket for the walk home.

# 9

It was the middle of the big time, the third day of the Salmon Festival. María Howchia's ankle, hands and skin gouges were recovering well, and her energy had returned, but in the place where dreams are born her spirit felt different. Last night she'd watched couples walk toward the hills after the dance, but she didn't want to do that. Quietly she had lain on her mat inside the u-macha thinking about Captain Sutter, his bad smells, and how he controlled other men. She missed nothing about that place except Blue Star, and had all but forgotten Pedro Valdez.

Now, she was running hard up the ti-kel field surrounded by about forty players, all of their poles pointed upward. The teams were well matched, and it felt good to be lost in such vigorous fun. Cousin Quail Song intercepted the scrotum, as it was jokingly called, and raced for the goalpost whirling the two balls in a softened otter-skin bag around his pole. She ran after him to protect him from the other team, now converging from all sides, all trying their best to hook the scrotum with their poles.

A man passed her, fast enough to catch Quail Song. She grabbed his arm. He yanked hard to get rid of her. Her feet slipped. She hung on, gritting her teeth as she skidded along the ground behind him, pole dragging. Another man hit from the side and both men fell on her, knocking her wind out. When the air came back she tried to laugh. The crowd's roar told her that Quail Song had made a goal.

She'd been running from one goal line to the other for half a day. Now, weak from thirst, she disentangled her legs from other arms and legs and slowly regained her feet. She gave her staff to a man on the sideline and headed for the river.

The screams of the game pursued her as she passed through the village and down the path to the bathing place. Young mothers on the beach were hanging split salmon on the drying racks while toddlers played in the sand. The river was too warm on María's ankles and knees, and not much cooler on her thighs. She fell forward, sinking until she felt the roots of her hair moving underwater. Soon the spirits would send rain—Turtle Claw had beseeched them—and she looked forward to colder water. Salmon creased the surface now, the faithful red-fleshed sojourners who offered themselves in abundance to the umne. They made the People rich.

Underwater, stroking along the bottom, she opened her eyes to see the slack-jawed salmon, and then popped up near the island and pushed back her hair. Sun sparkled across the wrinkled blue water—this blue only in salmon time. Treading water she stilled herself and caught the purifying smell of peppermint. A deep-voiced roar came from the playing field and then it was quiet again, except for a clown bird knocking on hollow wood. Her spirit floated as easily as her legs. The bright river narrowed downstream, held in by water-sculpted boulders, which were shaded by alder branches at her family's fishing hole. She was glad to be home.

The branches thrashed. A sombrero and pale shirt pushed through the thicket. She blinked. No one at the festival wore long pants and a shirt. Had Pedro Valdez come to return her things? The man came to the water's edge, which was partly hidden from her location, and she knew by the sling of the hip—one boot on an outcropping, long gun in his hand—it was not Pedro. And too slender for Captain Sutter. The hat darkened his face, but she sensed she had seen this man before.

Looking her way, he slowly sat down on a rock, gun over knees. She felt his eyes, and her skin prickled with fright, but she continued to tread water, watching him. No doubt he had seen the ti-kel game, and hadn't caused trouble there. As she faced him her fear dissolved into curiosity, and she decided to go closer. She slipped into the current kicking downstream, carried by the water, stroking only a few times. The bottom came up rapidly. Big rocks met her knees and she found footing.

The stranger had deep blue eyes, as if holes had been bored in his head and the sky came through. Looking calmly from those eyes he watched as she stood up with water sheeting from her body, and he smiled in a lopsided way, causing a dimple to appear in his cheek. She thought she remembered him from the fort, but if he'd come to capture her, he didn't act like it. He was a handsome man in his prime, with a perfectly straight nose. However he smelled very bad.

"*Hello, pretty lass,*" he said in a strange tongue.

Hearing friendliness, she stepped closer, a light breeze prickling her wet skin.

He patted the boulder beside him, smiling an invitation.

She remained standing. "Where are you going?" she asked in Spanish.

He opened his hands like he was sorry he couldn't understand.

"You come to our Cos festival?"

He shrugged again and said, "*No palaver.*"

He didn't speak Spanish.

He placed his gun in the bushes behind him and turned a teasing smile upon her. "*Palaver poco,*" he said, and she understood the word for little.

"*Bonita,*" he said. Spanish for pretty. He brushed his gaze down her length, and she marveled at his long black lashes curving upward. Unlike other Americans, he had no bush of hair on his face. The clean lines showed. His brown hair, tied at the nape of his neck, made a wavy tail down his pale shirt. He dazzled her with his smile.

"*Wot's the nime o' this plaice?*" he said, gesturing up the river.

How odd that people could make such sounds!

He needed a bath. In the spirit of the festival, she laughed, grabbed his hand, and pulled him up on his feet.

He lurched and caught himself. "Wait a minute," he said, throwing his hat on his gun. He sat down and yanked off his boots and placed his misshapen, bone-white feet in the water.

She pulled him up again, but he stopped and undid the square of buttons at his front, letting his pants drop, then tugged his shirt over his head—the stench not unlike Captain Sutter's. He then tossed everything over his boots and gun. The skin below his neck was white as Coyote Man in his ash-paint, with patches of dark hair under his arms, on his chest and around his man's part. Hair grew on his legs too, like on Captain Sutter, but on this man it was black against white. It looked preposterous, clown-like, and she couldn't hold back a giggle. Wrinkling her nose at the bad smell, she pulled him toward deeper water. He came haltingly, picking his way from submerged rock to submerged rock. She tugged him upstream against the current, now to his knees, and laughed to see a man walking like a teetering baby holding its mother's hand. His attention never left his footing.

In deeper water where the bathing pool spread before them, she tugged his hand. But this time, bracing his feet on a rock, he shook his head in solid refusal. He looked so precarious and acted so serious, she couldn't stop laughing. He was a very good clown.

On shore, toddlers watched from between the racks of drying salmon. He feigned fear. Of babies! Truly a funny man. But she knew how to get the better of him. She dogpaddled around his rock while he slowly turned with mincing steps and looked at her with questions in his blue eyes. She suddenly realized with a fresh seizure of giggles, that he didn't know what she was about to do. Any of the home men would know.

She gave him a mighty shove, pushing him into water over his head and then plunged on top and held him under. He thrashed and grabbed at her, but she held on, sputtering laughter. She began to think he knew this game after all. He wasn't really trying to get to the surface. Sometimes men pretended to struggle in water fights as a way of showing they liked a woman. She hooked an arm around his chin and swam strongly, towing him face down under water against the current. He thrashed ineffectively. She couldn't help but smile the whole distance. Soon he would be clean.

By the time she pulled him through the braided current to the calm place where she'd first seen him, he had assumed a limp posture and she admired the length of time he could hold his breath. The young men of the umne competed to see who could hold their breath the longest. This man was as good as the best of them. She tensed for a surprise move, a sudden burst out of the water with both hands pushing her head down in retaliation. She knew that trick.

But then her smile faded as another possibility began to dawn on her.

She pulled his head up. Half-moons of blue showed above large white orbs. She stared. He wasn't pretending! Holding his chin above water she swam hard for the shore.

Cousin-sisters gathered around as she dragged the man up on the sand. Little children pointed and laughed at his furry chest. With help, she heaved him to his stomach, head to the side, and pressed sharply between his shoulders, trying to force water from him. "Run. Get my father!" she said to no one in particular as she pushed rhythmically on the white man's back.

One of the girls took off running toward the playing field as the cheers of another goal rocked the air. The wait seemed long. Beside her, a big-eyed boy baby asked, "He sick?"

"Drowning," she said between pushes. "I thought we were playing."

"He no play."

At last Father came and knelt over the white man, heaving him to his side. The motion triggered an explosion of coughing and vomiting, and María exhaled in relief.

The strange man struggled to rise, but got only as far as his hands and knees. On all fours he hung his head, swung it from side to side like a bear, coughing and coughing.

"He will live," said Father. "Where did he come from?"

She spoke loud enough to be heard above the coughing and a burst of cheers from the field. "I don't know, but he must have come from Captain Sutter's place." She knew by his dress.

The dripping man coughed a fine mist, and then became still. He rotated his head, looked at her with narrowed blue eyes, and said, *"You bitch!"*

She was so happy to hear him speak that it didn't matter what the strange sounds meant." *Sky Eyes,* she named him in her mind.

The little boy squatted, craned his neck and peered at the man from underneath. With a rigid finger the man poked the child hard in the chest, making him cry and run to his mother.

Puzzled by the meanness, María Howchia watched the man struggle to his feet and walk haltingly down the river trail, his white buttocks blotched with patches of dark sand.

❧

María Howchia and the women were steaming poison oak and other greens for the feast when word came that Sky Eyes had been joined by another pale-skinned man. This new stranger drove a wagon that contained animals that no one had seen before. Supper could wait. She joined about four-twenties of people hurrying up and down the hilly trail, all excited to see the newcomer and his strange animals.

Where the grassland sloped more gently toward the river, she saw Sky Eyes and a man with a bushy yellowish-red beard. A curtain of pale hair curled about his shoulders. Downwind, even at this distance, she picked up his bad odor. At the fort she'd seen oxen like the one that tossed his horned head, but what were the animals dancing inside the high-walled cart?

The two white men spoke loudly as though having trouble understanding each other. She stepped close to one of the wagon wheels, a slice of an oak trunk skewered by a pole that connected to an identical wheel on the other side of the cart. She looked through the woven-saplings of the cart walls. Three sparsely haired animals snuffled and grunted inside. All had round flat noses and short, coiled tails. Horn-like teeth jutted from the largest.

When the white men stopped talking, Grizzly Hair, who stood in the crowd of festively decorated people, pointed to the animals and said, "Puercos." She knew he'd seen them at the mission.

Grizzly Hair greeted Yellow Beard. "De donde viene y a donde va?" Where do you come from and where are you going?

Yellow Beard said haltingly, "Yo … vívo … Aquí. El tambien." He nodded at Sky Eyes.

They had come here to live! María looked at the assembled people, all milling around for better views of the men and animals. Many understood Spanish. Maybe they were thinking, as she did, that it would be fun to have such interesting neighbors.

Lockl, headman of one of the visiting peoples, spoke to Grizzly Hair, but just then a puerca squealed louder than a hurt child. The heavy animals shoved each other around, causing the cart to rock violently. People began to laugh so hard that some of them collapsed on the ground and held their sides.

When the noise and laughter abated Lockl asked, "Did they bring the puercos for you?"

"I don't know," Grizzly Hair replied.

A gift would be proper, María thought, since the strangers expected to live in the umne's hunting grounds.

Looking at the people, Yellow Beard spoke in halting Spanish. "We want a cerca for the puercos. You Indians make fence." He pantomimed the cutting and piling of oak limbs around a large area.

While this was going on, Sky Eyes became visibly upset, his face twisting into a frown. He yelled alien words at Yellow Beard. Yellow Beard stopped pantomiming and shouted back. Sky Eyes became so enraged that he shoved his supposed friend. Recovering his balance Yellow Beard ran at Sky Eyes and shoved back. With raised fist he yelled again.

The spectators gaped with amazement and hidden humor. Children looked at their parents with questioning eyes, knowing a public display of anger was a sure sign of weakness. María Howchia covered her mouth so as not to add to the muffled explosions of laughter around her. This was difficult at this time of merriment and so very soon after the puercos had squealed and pushed each other.

To recover her calm, she watched the lowering sun cast its glow over the world—the oaks, the people, the hillside of bleached grasses, boulders, and the river snaking past with fat ducks afloat. Crimson grape leaves blazed among the yellows and browns of the trees. Salmon Time also brought the black-throated geese. An impressive V of them winged and gabbled overhead. A cock quail called ki-ka-go, ki-ka-go, sharp cries that soothed, a constant of life in the home place. At last the white men stopped arguing.

Yellow Beard furrowed his brow and spoke to Grizzly Hair, obviously thinking between words. "Adobes. Indians fabrican una cerca de adobes." They were to make a fence of mud bricks, like the ones at Sutter's Fort.

Grizzly Hair spoke in Spanish to the blue-eyed men. "Soon the sun he goes down. After the sleep we make the adobes." He translated for those who had not understood, and then said to Yellow Beard, "We have fiesta now, fandango. You come. Bring puercos. They watch from the carreta."

People smiled and moved about, talking about what had occurred. María Howchia felt happy anticipation, and not just for the coming feast and dance. The world was changing. No longer did the home place seem small. Exotic men and animals had come. Father was encouraging the changes, and Captain Sutter's powers, father said, did not extend to the home place.

Lifted by exuberance, she and her cousin-sisters raced back toward the village. As she passed the cart that Yellow Beard drove—whipping the ox with a leather strap, his boots and buttocks braced against the woven willows—she realized that every bird and animal had fled from the unearthly screech of the wheels. This too made her laugh and run faster.

Sky Eyes rode past the runners on a horse with large brown and white spots, looking at María. She could tell he thought she was pretty. He puzzled her though. He hadn't seemed a bit amused, as many men would have been, to be nearly drowned by a playful woman. Was he really that weak? Unable to swim, or laugh at himself? Surely not. Different people had different ways. That explained it.

She hoped to see his dimpled smile again, wanted to make friends with him. Maybe he would teach her his strange tongue, one of the languages spoken at Captain Sutter's place. That would help her face Captain Sutter. As she was thinking this, something slowed her feet. She looked back over her shoulder.

Back up the trail a horseman watched from a hilltop, a dark shape in the low and bloated sun. She knew by the proud bearing as he sat in the saddle that it was Pedro Valdez.

# 10

Shadows on the circular wall loomed as María Howchia danced with the Sumne and the visiting peoples around the ceremonial fire. Many feet patted the earth to the heartbeat of the log drum, and Turtle Claw chanted in the ancient language to help conjure up the spirits.

He raised his arms and began to sing the most powerful spirit of all into the dancehouse. The log drum throbbed more slowly. Goose bumps pricked her scalp. She and the other dancers made their way across the pine boughs to join the spectators. She sat with her family on the purifying branches. Everyone waited for the enactment of first things. An infant whimpered and the small fire crackled, but those were the only sounds.

Then the great spirit-bird representing the power of the universe entered to the whooshing sound of many surprised people sucking air. Towering over Turtle Claw, he walked on long skinny legs, chest out, fully extending his enormous black wings. He strutted around the fire, turning this way and that to show the white undersides, the long tendrils of his big head-feathers trembling. The huge shadow of Molok darkened the entire wall and ceiling, and when the shadow fell on María, a tremor shot through her. She was glad she had scrubbed herself very clean, glad all the people had. Such power could kill. But with the proper purification, the strong could absorb a little of the power.

Big brother of Raven flapped his wings and then seemed to fly around the circle, bounding and landing. Meanwhile Turtle Claw chanted the story of the beginning of earth. Coyote Man, white and ashy, entered from the smoke hole and hung by his knees poking fun at Condor Impersonator. Only Coyote could do that. Then, after a few jokes about Turtle Claw and Grizzly Hair, Coyote Man jumped before the fire and he and Turtle Claw enacted the creation story—Turtle bringing mud from the depths of the endless gray sea to the light above, Raven molding it into land, and Coyote planting raven feathers here and there on the land where they would become the many peoples of the earth. Three women singers embellished the chants of the chorus, their polished voices weaving high and low through the story.

Pedro had come, he told himself, to collect more Indians for Sutter's militia and return the Indita's belongings. But he also came tracking Perry McCoon. And it was just as he had feared—the Englishman was here on the very land that Pedro wanted.

Now Pedro stood uncomfortably near McCoon and the German named Brüheim, the three watching the bright entrance to the roundhouse about thirty yards away. Captain Juan's daughter was inside among the packed Indians, maybe a hundred and fifty, all focused on a dancer with a tall headdress and cloaked entirely in black feathers. McCoon seemed a little less obnoxious than usual, clearly absorbed by the theater inside the roundhouse. So was Pedro.

An Indian on stilts was walking and hopping around the fire, occasionally opening the wings of his costume, each wing long as a man. The wings were intact. The costume had been made from the skin of an actual condor.

"Blow me down," McCoon exclaimed. "If that ent the damndest thing."

Grandmother María, who'd been born on the lower Río de los Cosumnes, had told Pedro that the condor was sacred to her people, and sometimes when he was riding and a condor glided overhead, he understood why. A thrill of fear would momentarily stop his heart as the sudden shadow swept over him, like a mouse must feel beneath an eagle. Afterward, as the condor flew away, turning its head back and forth on its hunt over the grasslands, he felt the miracle that anything that big could fly. No wonder Indians revered the great bird.

McCoon and Brüheim went to the doorway and stood blocking Pedro's view. To see better, Pedro followed. In the steamy smoke of the doorway he saw the source of the relentless beat, an Indian stomping on a hollow log. It unified the low chant and the dance of the condor. Hidden within a black-feathered costume, the tall Indian performer, made taller by an elaborate headdress, opened and closed the huge wings by manipulating unseen strings as he pranced on stilts around the central fire. In the firelight, the eyes of the seated Indians glinted around the round wall. Four massive oak trunks defined the central structure and supported the enormous ceiling beams, now shimmering with streamers of iridescent turkey feathers. Another performer, in whitened skin, dashed around howling. This would be Coyote, who signified everything confusing and chaotic in life. Indian humor revolved around him. Indians laughed hardest when somebody was caught in a trap of his own making.

McCoon tilted his head for Brüheim to follow him inside.

"Don't go in there," Pedro said. They ignored him.

The Indians closest to the door looked at them like invading bears. They picked up pine branches and brandished them, but most of the people were too intent upon the ceremony to give it any attention.

"You'll set them against us," Pedro said in a voice to be heard over the drum and the chanting. Before the dance, several Indians had agreed to go to war with Sutter and he didn't want them to change their minds. He wouldn't have thought McCoon would want to antagonize his future hog herders either.

"Ent hurtin nothin." McCoon said as he and Brüheim continued to push inside. The Indians shoved branches in their faces. The two crossed their arms in defense, McCoon snickering. Brüheim finally backed out. A few minutes later, fending off pine branches, McCoon yelled, "All right, all right. 'Ave it your way, 'eathens." He ran out giggling and jumping in an exaggerated fashion, hands crossed behind, like a child escaping a mother's whipping.

McCoon sat down, took the leather flask from his vest, downed a swig, and handed it to the German. "Those niggers'll conjure up the Devil, they will."

Pedro joined the others on the rise where they'd been originally, but didn't sit down. "They want the condor spirit to be good to them," he told the others.

"Aff-breed like you oughta know."

The now-distant firelight caught McCoon's perfect teeth, his unfriendly grin.

Standing a bit downhill, Pedro doled it out low and measured, "Sometimes I think, Señor McCoon, that you would like to fight me." He'd promised Sutter he wouldn't take the bait, but he was a hair's breadth from his limit and twenty miles from the fort.

McCoon took the flask from Brüheim, swallowed twice, wiped his mouth and drawled as he looked at Pedro, "Ashamed o' yer nigger blood, methinks."

Pedro ground his nails into his fists. "Both my grandfathers were outstanding officers who served the King of Spain. My mother's father was Don Pedro Fages, a nobleman and governor of Upper California." It didn't change those truths that both of his grandmothers were Indians and his father a bastard. He let his pride speak, "I am Spanish, señor." His back was straight and he used the polite address to satisfy himself, not the English cur.

"All the same," McCoon drawled in a bored tone, "Greasers."

Pent-up rage exploded in Pedro's arm and he rammed his fist into the source of that word. Half amazed, he felt flesh slide beneath his knuckles and heard the hollow sound of McCoon's head hitting the ground.

Breathing hard, he glared at the writhing worm of a man.

Brüheim, now on his feet, grabbed Pedro from behind and yanked his elbows together.

As Pedro struggled to throw him off, McCoon got to his knees and snarled, "You filthy, rotten piece o' shit!"

Brüheim yelled, "Schtop! Both of you!" Pedro jerked, but the German hung on.

McCoon was on his feet, tonguing his lip out. In the orange firelight from the doorway of the roundhouse, his handsome features were twisted and ugly, his lip bloodied. He pulled back his arm.

Pedro jerked free just as the fist slammed him. Something snapped. Pain seared past his right ear and up through the top of his skull. He stumbled on the slope of the hill and caught his balance. His vision doubled and then swam back into focus as he steadied himself. McCoon was braced to strike again.

Pedro was faster. His knuckles found McCoon's teeth a second time. He heard a crack and felt something give. McCoon reeled and fell.

Agony pulsed through Pedro's head. His jaw was frozen. His knuckles hurt as he stood over the lump on the dirt, watched it start to get up again.

This time Brüheim grabbed McCoon when he got to his knees, and pinned his elbows behind as he had done Pedro's. "Herr Lieutenant Valdez. *Bitte*, please. Enough. No more. Do not hit him again. I beg of you."

McCoon looked spent, dazed, and very bloody. A tooth dangled in his open mouth.

Pedro's stomach rose. From the sight of the blood or the pain in his face, he wasn't sure. Still, if the disgracer of God hadn't been immobilized, he felt sure he'd have silenced that tongue forever.

He stepped into the shadows. The throb of the hollow log and the wails and yells from the roundhouse mixed badly with the throb in his head. Brüheim's spitting words came through it. "He iss officer on Captain Sutter's dragoons." *Admonishing McCoon.*

Pedro unclenched his sore knuckles, placed the heel of his hand against his face, and pushed. With a rip of pain, his jaw popped back into alignment. Instantly he felt better, carefully opening and closing his mouth.

The German continued, "—and you be my partner, needing Herr Sutter's goot vill."

Pedro figured McCoon had Sutter's good will in any case. It hadn't even made a difference when Sutter discovered that McCoon had been stealing from him. And of course the bastard would tell the captain that Pedro had attacked him without provocation.

Something large darkened the roundhouse doorway—Condor Man bent forward and backlit by the fire. He was leaving. Behind him came the whitened Indian playing the part of Coyote. Their footsteps receded into the moonless night. A pig squealed from the cart and all around the real coyotes warbled and howled.

Abruptly the drumming stopped. McCoon addressed Brüheim as though Pedro were not present. "I'll show that greaser who's the best on a horse!"

Pedro smiled in the dark at this call for a showdown on horseback. He had delivered two good blows to McCoon's one, and nobody, but nobody within the wide sphere of Sutter's authority was better on a horse than Pedro Valdez. The light dimmed as Indians crowded out the door of the dance house, speaking softly to one another.

"Tomorrow we will ride to see who is the best," Pedro said, noticing the daughter of Captain Juan with firelight glowing behind her curvy all-but-naked figure.

McCoon growled, "We'll ride when *I* say, not before."

"As you wish." Pedro's velvet tone. "Any time you say, señor."

Satisfied that McCoon wouldn't enjoy the night, Pedro approached the Indita from behind. It was dark and she was surrounded by Indians, so he followed just far enough behind to keep her in sight. The sky twinkled like a field of diamonds giving a little light. She and another girl headed toward the river. "Hola," he called and the girls turned. He sensed rather than saw the one with skin like a poppy petal.

"Señorita, may I speak to you a moment?" The faint scent of peaches made him stir. Indian girls were known to be a mix of innocence and lust and he envisioned her small up-tilted breasts. She said nothing.

"I brought your blanket and mortar stone. I'll bring them to your house." Crickets chorused all around, and the sounds of joking and splashing came from the river.

"Gracias, señor. Put them inside." The girl seemed anxious to leave him.

He had hoped she'd be more receptive. He wouldn't force himself on a girl, and it made him ache to realize Indians were doing it all around him. They did it in front of their families and had few qualms, especially after round-house ceremonies. "Are you going swimming?"

"Sí. You come and swim too?" Her voice had a vanilla tone of maturity.

Hope swelled in him. "Yes." If that's how it started, he'd bare himself in the night air and swim.

"Come." She turned away with her friend and walked quickly and quietly ahead of him. He followed her scent cloud as she waded into the river. Stopping to undress, he feared he'd lose her among the splash and laughter of many swimmers. He'd expected the men to go to the sweathouse, but no, they were out there fooling around with the women. At first the water warmed his calves. He waded to his chest where his lower legs were cold. Indians darted past. Black heads and arms wove chaotic patterns, a crazy quilt of ripples and a bubbling of strange talk.

The rocky bottom fell away sharply. With games being played around him, he dogpaddled into the midst of the Indians, hoping to find the girl. He sensed that she saw him, saw that he swam poorly, and that he couldn't find her. He treaded water. Water lapped in his eyes. He knew he wouldn't know the chief's daughter from a snaggle-toothed hag. Out of his element he accidentally gulped water and coughed. She wasn't helping. That was clear. He paddled back to the sandy beach. What was he thinking!

Onshore, he stood holding his pants, letting his feet dry a bit before stepping into them. A breeze had picked up and his lusty feeling had shriveled. He saw himself in his mind's eye, a shivering stranger among people who didn't feel the cold.

If only McCoon would disappear! Maybe the bastard would catch valley fever and die, or drink himself to death. He headed for his horse. The girl's things were in the pack behind his saddle. Leaving Chocolate hobbled on the playing field near the creek, he groped his way back to the huts, remembering which one was Captain Juan's.

At the entrance the vanilla voice gave him a pleasant shock.

"Gracias." She accepted her blanket and mortar stone.

"For nothing." He reached through the dark, explored with his fingers until he recognized an upper arm, damp and cool. She didn't flinch. He moved his palm across to a handful of resilient breast with a nub of nipple.

She stepped back and said in bad Spanish, "You speak for Captain Sutter."

He wanted to tell her about the hard words Sutter had thrown at him the night she left the fort, and how he had lied about knowing the whereabouts of her village, but said only, "I think you know that I don't always follow his orders."

In truth he knew that his service at the fort was about over. It didn't matter that Sutter seemed to have forgiven him and had sent him on this trip to procure more Indians for the war. The Captain's willingness to back down and go back to business had always puzzled him. In this case it was fortuitous. Pedro would continue as Sutter's lieutenant for now, or he'd never get title to any rancho.

The older woman spoke in the dark. He remembered her, a woman with slit eyes, about Pedro's age. She shifted into broken Spanish. "My daughter no talk to black hat. *Vaya* away from house. Go from ranchería. Go or I bring man. He make you go."

The girl said something, perhaps in protest. Then it was quiet except for a few soft voices in the dark as other people moved about the neighboring huts.

Swallowing disappointment and wishing he'd latched onto another young woman—all were occupied now—Pedro wouldn't antagonize the chief's wife. "I go, señora."

The Indita asked, "You go to Captain Sutter's place?"

"First I'm going up the river."

"You come back?"

"Yes."

"To live in the house with the blue-eye man?"

Her vulnerability clutched at his gut. "Perry McCoon," he said, "is a bad man. And you, señorita, should stay away from him. I would never live with him." He bowed formally in the dark. "Señora, I go. Good night."

The next day Pedro found a good-sized village of natives and a nice place for a rancho. The river had cut a steep and rocky gorge as it tumbled down the Sierra foothills, and in the midst of the granite ridges nestled a substantial grassland in the rolling hills. He could grow a field of corn and squash there. Unfortunately, however, the natives turned out to be less friendly. They recognized his clothing as Spanish and wanted nothing to do with him. Furthermore, they didn't understand enough Spanish for him to explain that he worked for John Sutter. The meeting was tense and short—he didn't really need to bring in more militia recruits. He rode eastward, mulling over the fact that none of the people he'd just encountered had been at the Salmon

Festival in Captain Juan's ranchería. In Alta California the native peoples normally partied with friends and relatives up and down their home rivers. They took turns playing host. This meant that something of a tribal boundary existed between Captain Juan's place and the nearest upstream neighbors. But the worst aspect of that place, as a possible rancho for Pedro, was its nearness to McCoon.

Pedro explored farther upstream, but the higher he climbed the rougher the terrain became. Slate boulders stood on end all over the landscape, half-buried in the soil, or rather half-excavated by the rains of centuries, and in various stages of fracturing, like pages of stone books. All that broken, sharp-edged, disintegrating slate made poor cattle-grazing. He also learned as he rode up the Sierra foothills that the next village was farther away from civilization than he ever wished to live. He turned back and spent another night camping near Captain Juan's place.

Proud Hawk had ridden back to the fort. That was good, María Howchia said to herself. He belonged there.

The weather had turned cloudy, and cool. "This is not a good season for making adobes," she told Sings-with-Frogs, a young man about her age. "The rains will spoil them." She had seen a melting adobe house just outside the wall of Captain Sutter's place.

He smiled. "But this is fun."

Most of María's friends thought so too. She laughed to feel the soft mud between her toes. All around her, people talked and sang as they stomped dry grass into the wet clay. Some of them hauled water from the river; others brought baskets of clay or scooped the sticky adobe into the forms that Yellow Beard had laid out beside the mud pit. Adobe-making had become a game, a part of the big time, and the corral for the puercos was to be located here at tai yokkel.

The white men were setting up camp. While Yellow Beard talked broken Spanish with three young boys who were helping them, Sky Eyes stood near the adobe pit watching María. He looked like he'd fallen on his face. He was badly bruised and his dimple wasn't to be seen.

"I'm going with Señor Valdez to fight a war," said Sings-with-Frogs, stepping beside her so that his foot slid beside hers beneath the mud.

"But you didn't go to the fort with him."

"My cousins and I will leave after the big time. Señor Valdez can wait for us. They won't be leaving the fort for ten sleeps." He looked proud.

She knew those men had talked about going. Long ago nearly everyone had gone to fight the black hats, women as well as men. This time it seemed more of a game. No one mentioned danger. "Are any of the other men going with you?"

"Only two or three." He pivoted as he stamped, brushing his thigh against hers. His man's part had begun to swell.

By their amused expressions, she knew her friends had seen it too. A strong gust of wind swept up from the river, blowing her hair into her eyes. She caught her cap just before it sailed away.

Sings-with-Frogs bent forward, scooped clay and slathered it down her body. The cold made her gasp. She glanced at her friends, speaking to them head to head. Seeing the gleam of willingness in their eyes, she pushed him into the mud. They piled on while he sputtered and flailed.

Laughing, María sat on him and held him down. When she looked up, sky blue eyes were still watching. The white man's swollen lips bent into the ghost of a smile, but no dimple dug into his cheek. A tooth was missing. Something bad had happened.

The tussle in the mud continued without her as she got up to smile at Sky Eyes. He interested her, and his puercos interested her. She wanted to know why had he brought them here. She hoped he would teach her about Captain Sutter's power. Pedro Valdez had warned her against Sky Eyes, but that didn't matter to a woman going down her own trail.

❧

Salmon Time ended. Sleeping inside the house now, María Howchia listened to the rain on the steeply pitched slabs of the u-macha. It gathered in the little ditches that diverted it from running through the u-machas. Often during long rainy nights she thought of Crying Fox, who had not returned to the home place. Blue Star had come back, however, telling the People that Crying Fox had been sent to the eastern mountains, along with other men, to help some travelers bring their wagons from the Snowy Mountains. Perhaps he'd stayed at the fort after the wheat harvest because of Manu-iki, and that explained why he'd been sent away on a dangerous journey.

As predicted, the rain melted the adobes of the puerco corral. She often went there to help place brush along the slouching walls. The two white men also needed women to tie bundles of cattail leaves for the roof of their adobe house, to keep the rain off the walls. Whenever she came near him, Sky Eyes smiled at her.

Twice he followed her home, and she hid from him. But she grew more and more intrigued, and wondered what he and Yellow Beard argued about. Then Sky Eyes went away from his new house, leaving Yellow Beard alone with the puercos.

One day she was tearing herself a new ceremonial skirt from the bolt of cloth Father had brought from a horse raid near the coast, when Etumu entered the u-macha, sat beside her, and said in a strange tone, "Our acorns will be gone before the next acorn time."

María Howchia lowered the cloth. This had never happened before. The cha'ka held up to a three year's supply. Oo-lah must be served at ceremonies, and nu-pah was eaten every day. It wasn't possible to live without acorns.

"You were gone during the harvest," Mother said, "so we couldn't gather enough."

Shamed that she'd been gone, and shamed that she had let her mother do so much acorn grinding, María Howchia set the cloth aside and went outside, cringing as cold water struck her shoulders and ran down her back. She would see for herself.

The cylindrical cha'ka of woven vines stood like a sentinel about twenty paces from the u-macha. From her earliest memories it had held the most important food, a promise of something to eat, a knowledge so deep she'd never given it a second thought. The floor of the storehouse was raised on legs to discourage ground animals, and a small peaked roof higher than Father's head kept out the tree squirrels.

She glanced through veils of rain at the other cha'kas, wondering if they were full. If so, her family could trade cloth for the acorns of others. She parted the vines at face height. No acorns. She restored the opening and parted the vines at a lower level—again and again. The level was just above her knees, almost the bottom of the silo, but the acorn harvest was many moons away.

Grizzly Hair came through the rain shouldering a soaked goose. Seeing her at the cha'ka, his eyes registered something, and she knew he'd talked to Etumu about the acorns.

"Father, I'm sorry. I should have stayed and helped gather." She had gone to the fort in the middle of the harvest. Mother always warned that squirrels and woodpeckers would have them all in five sleeps if the people didn't gather them first. It was true.

Rivulets of rain ran down Grizzly Hair's cheeks, and his wet hair clung to his shoulders and chest, "The blue-eyed men take our food for the puercos," he said as he swung the goose from his shoulder to the ground, indicating that she should take it.

Later, while plucking the goose, she heard Father talking Spanish outside the u-macha. She looked outside and saw Yellow Beard, a man who spoke worse Spanish than most of the umne. The man's heavy blue cloak was soaked and she couldn't see his face beneath his pulled-down hat. He held a bucket in his hand. People peered from their doorways.

"No mas bellotas," Grizzly Hair said, emphasizing each syllable in a loud voice. No more acorns.

Yellow Beard went to Turtle Claw's cha'ka, parted the vines and poured a bucketful. At their doorway the doctor and his wife looked at one another but didn't stop the white man, who waded Berry Creek and headed up the path to tai-yokkel with a full bucket.

Grizzly Hair spoke quietly with Turtle Claw, and then returned to the u-macha. He lay down on his mat and closed his eyes.

Rain continued to pelt the village, and María Howchia struggled to blow the cooking fire to life in the center of the u-macha. She wished for a sunny day and worried about Crying Fox up in the eastern mountains. She also wondered where Sky Eyes was, and what he and Yellow Beard would do when all the people refused to share their acorns with the puercos.

Grizzly Hair spoke without opening his eyes.

"Very soon we will have a new kind of big time."

"What kind?" María asked.

"First Puerco."

# 11

**JANUARY 3, 1845**

At eight bells, a mist bordering on rain darkened the morning. Chocolate pranced nervously as the snare drums began to roll. "Steady boy," Pedro said, patting the neck of his first-rate stallion, the likes of which ought to be leading the company.

Meanwhile, ludicrous on his jenny, Captain Sutter exited the gate of his parade ground. Pedro closed his eyes and took a deep breath. He was Sutter's lieutenant. He would serve honorably. But, opening his eyes, he knew that when General Castro saw his opponent on that she-ass, he wouldn't be able to shoot straight for laughing. The captain's military finery and ostrich-plumed tricorn made it the more ridiculous.

Waiting with Pedro were the three remaining soldiers from Monterey Presidio who had come with him four years ago. Their blue waistcoats and lighter blue trousers were worn and frayed like his, the number four faded but still visible on their red hatbands. However they sat their macho horses well. This was the trained part of the cavalry, riding to the first war since the battle of 1829 against Estanislao and his renegade Indians. Alongside these horsemen, Pedro felt the spirit of his ancestors warming his veins.

The Indian drummers delivered a snappy rat-a-tat-tat beneath the whipping red, white and green banner, and the sky threatened the storm of the decade. "Easy boy," Pedro crooned. The bigger part of the cavalry, the riflemen, left next—some of them spurring their horses rudely past Captain Sutter as they strapped their mounts, laughing and whooping. These trappers and adventurers, which included Perry McCoon, were disloyal men who cared only about themselves. They came from five or six different countries, mostly the United States. Pedro had a bet with Jared Sheldon that less than twenty riflemen would report. Sheldon had more faith. Why, Pedro didn't know. Each autumn Sutter begged the Russians to wait for their payment until the winter beaver came in, but every spring the trappers turned up their hands helplessly and claimed the harvest had been unaccountably poor. If the captain didn't know they cut deals with the northern fur companies, he was blind and deaf. Why didn't he stop supplying these freeloaders? Pedro counted hats—beaver-tailed, stained and slouching leather, skull-hugging woolen knit—fifteen, sixteen, seventeen. Sheldon owed him three plugs of tobacco.

Seven immigrants from the Stephens-Townsend-Murphy Party rode with the riflemen—men who had just crossed the Sierra Nevada with wagons and women, the first ever to do so. Luis and Salvador, the latter the brother of the pretty Indita, had helped guide the last of them safely down the mountains and then joined the militia. The immigrant soldiers were thin, but they carried fine guns. Pedro coveted the long Kentucky rifle with a fancy maple stock and its distinctive hexagonal barrel that sent balls straight and far. It made a toy of Pedro's musket.

Following the riflemen, six Kanakas fell into stride. Four wore pants and two had colorful sarongs stretched around their big haunches. Besides the French guns, they all clutched long wooden spears, the fighting tool of their native islands.

"Company march," Pedro called. The hundred and seventy Indian foot soldiers straightened their lines, five abreast, stamping their bare feet in place until the forward details moved. Pedro had transformed them into a disciplined force, dressed as well as could be expected—pieces of French uniforms taken by Russians from Napoleon's freezing army, a pair of pants here, a shirt there, an occasional French kepi. They held the French muskets on their shoulders as smartly as soldiers anywhere. Even the naked men, the new recruits, marched flawlessly out the gate, bows swinging in their left hands. The drummers closed ranks behind the marching men, delivering a steady beat. The fife player began a military air.

Chocolate danced a bit but settled into stride beside the other three stallions, who with Pedro and his countrymen brought up the rear. Lastly, after all the fighting men, came Indian vaqueros leading thirty loaded pack mules in lines of ten, and three brass field pieces. No presidio in Alta California had ever fielded a larger force. Pedro only wished some of the Californio rancheros and their horsemen had joined—Rufus Chabolla, José Amador, Antonio Suñol at the least. Word must have spread that General Vallejo was sitting this out.

Glad to be on his way, Pedro exhaled a chest full of air. It made a cloud and then vanished in the wind along with his doubts about this campaign. General Vallejo could have a hidden purpose. Things were rarely as they seemed in Spanish politics, and Pedro reminded himself he wasn't born to it. Anyway, it didn't matter. There was no turning back.

❧

The next day, with the rain coming in fits and starts, Pedro decided to find out whether Perry McCoon's hog farm was a serious enterprise. He rode past the trotting Indians and joined the Captain, who, under his bouncing feathers, looked like a pink-cheeked boy on an adventure.

"Iss goot vetter," Sutter said, eyeing a gap in the clouds. His eyes sparkled as he bumped along, the toes of his boots sticking out.

Pedro looked toward the coastal range and Devil Mountain, where Indians said Coyote came from. He'd grown up hearing tales of a murderous feathered devil who roared down that mountain. Even Spanish soldiers had vanished into thin air. The Indians looked skittish, and Pedro wasn't the only Californio surreptitiously crossing himself as the Diablo peak loomed. Ahead rode the riflemen, unconcerned about such matters.

The captain's white plume was blowing straight back. "The Governor will be happy," he said, "dot I bring militia to help him." He expected a doubling of his land grant in exchange. "You know I haff debt wit the Russians." He cut his eyes over to Pedro.

"Sí, Capitán." Perhaps they didn't seize New Helvetia because they knew it bristled with their own cannons. A Coyote joke for sure. Gathering his words, Pedro swayed casually in the saddle, letting the Captain talk.

"Soon Herr Rotcheff comes from Russia and brings wit a gentleman who studies Indians. He pays for baskets and zo fort. But now he is looking for someting very special to take back to Russia for da Czar's private collection."

From his higher mount Pedro looked down at him wondering what a czar would like."I would like dot you help me find someting. Understand? To make da Russians go away happy, hmm?"

Watching a distant rider approach, Pedro said, "I'll watch for something special."

"Gracias Lieutenant." Sutter looked toward the approaching horse, and Pedro was disgusted to recognize Perry McCoon's pinto.

McCoon turned his horse alongside the Captain and said, "Me and the other blokes'll be ridin ahead to get Dr. Marsh. Then we'll head over to the mission at a fast pace, maybe by another route." Red spots still marred McCoon's mouth where the scabs had fallen off, and he had a satisfying gap in his front teeth. He'd never set a date for a riding contest.

Dr. Marsh, the eccentric loner and doctor from the United States, owned Los Meganos land grant beneath Mount Diablo. Pedro doubted Marsh wanted to join Sutter's army, but as the ranking officer of the big valley, Sutter had the right to draft anyone in his territory. Sutter and McCoon were talking in a way that left Pedro out, and would probably continue for a while, so Pedro turned Chocolate around. He'd wait for another opportunity.

Back in the rear with the other Californios, Pedro wondered if Captain Sutter could command Marsh and McCoon and their ilk. He knew he couldn't.

Fortunately it was understood that Pedro would command only the Indians and Californios, men born in Alta California. Sutter was in charges of the English- and German-speaking men.

As Pedro held the reins, resting his hand on the big Sinaloa horn, the first large drop of rain splashed on his knuckles. He looked up. Another splashed on his forehead. Inky clouds had built up in the sky as far as he could see. Ay madre! The only good thing about this was that they had the time to swim the large caballada of horses across the San Joaquín River much more easily now than later.

☙

Drenched and restive in the shadow of Devil's Peak, they camped in torrents of rain and ate cold jerky, the riflemen gone on ahead. The next day the rain continued and Pedro stayed near the back where the Indian foot soldiers trotted. Daylight vanished quickly and rain slashed through the night.

At the end of the third day he led the Indians into Mission San José. The riflemen were sprawled drunkenly along two covered corridors, Dr. Marsh among them. Soft light emanated from a number of horn lanterns. The Captain's tent was being erected in a corridor, and a gray-robed padre moved from one door to another giving quiet orders.

Thankful to be at the mission, Pedro dumped water off his hat and shook out his soaked sarape. He was hungry for the food and wine brought by a large group of neophytes, as the mission indians were called. Later, as he munched beef and tortillas and felt the warmth of the wine spreading through his limbs, Jared Sheldon sauntered over to him with a little smile.

"You win," he said opening a hand with three plugs of tobacco. "Even with Dr. Marsh."

"Gracias, Joaquín"—Jared's Spanish name. Accepting the tobacco Pedro patted the packed earth of the corridor where he'd just eaten. "Siéntese."

Sheldon arranged his long legs, leaned back against the adobe wall, and bumped his floppy leather hat over his eyes. "I hear you're looking to git land," he said in quiet English.

"Sí."

Bill Daylor must have told him, a man who didn't want to be anywhere near Captain Sutter. Sheldon's papers had been approved and Daylor was at Rancho Omuchumne making friends with the natives and building a trading post on his half of the rancho that Sheldon had given him. He'd named it for the native people who now worked for them.

"Perry's on a stretch of land on the Cosumney River too," Sheldon said, "maybe five leagues along the north bank. How much you looking to get?"

Pedro answered in Spanish. "I haven't found a place yet." He didn't want to get into details, given that Daylor and McCoon were friends. "Besides, it'd be a waste to hunt for a place and petition, and then get killed in this war."

Meant as a joke, it quieted Sheldon for a time, during which Pedro recalled that this man didn't die easily.

From beneath the hat came more English. "You planning to hang up your soldier hat?"

"Maybe when this war's over."

"Might be a good time at that. I heard Sutter's got the go-ahead to grant land direct. You hear that?"

Though he couldn't read, Pedro had helped translate it to English for Sutter, with the help of Henry Lienhard. That's why Sutter marched when he did, after he got what he thought he was waiting for. The trouble was that Lienhard found a qualifier in the decree that Sutter didn't want to hear.

"The authority is not absolute," Pedro said in Spanish.

Sheldon lifted the side of his hat, peeked at him and dropped it. "In life nothing is absolute."

Pedro raised his voice to be heard over the raucous riflemen and the rain pelting on the corridor roof. "I think land grants will move a little faster for Captain Sutter's friends now, because of that decree, but to you, amigo, it makes no difference. Am I right?"

"Yup. Got my final papers at long last. But I wouldn't bet a weasel's ass on the rest of you gettin ground if Castro wins this war. I wager all foreigners will be exiled. Even you native Californians fighting in Sutter's army might have trouble. That's why I said, we're here to fight, and we'd better win."

Pedro looked at the black curtain of night with streaks of faintly illuminated water pouring from the gullies in the roof tiles. General Vallejo would be warm and cozy in his big house—a rancher catered to by foreigners, many of them hoping for a letter of recommendation. No matter what happened on the field of battle, Vallejo wouldn't lose. But Sutter could lose everything, and so could those who depended upon him. *A bad thought to sleep on.*

"If I were you," Sheldon said, "I'd move your grant papers right along. Last letter from Vermont, my father wrote about a man named Polk runnin' for president, hell bent to take California. He's likely to win. Maybe already did. You'd need clear title. Even then you could run into trouble."

Pedro appreciated the advice. Ay madre, everything was so complicated!

An immigrant who'd come over the Sierra Nevada a few months ago sauntered over with a bottle of mission wine and sat down next to Pedro and Jared Sheldon.

"I heard the Californios around here are joinin' up on Castro's side," he said. "That priest says so." Directing a squint at the silent padre walking the other way down the corridor, he handed Sheldon the wine.

"Wouldn't surprise me," Sheldon said lifting his hat and taking a swallow. He handed the bottle to Pedro.

The immigrant exhaled. "That don't set too good, do it?"

"Nope." Sheldon's jaw dropped in sudden sleep, his shoulders sagging.

Amused, Pedro smiled and took another swallow of good mission wine. Standing to leave, the immigrant nodded he should keep it.

Pedro was already feeling light-headed and exhausted, and now this news about Castro. The complications were swimming together as the drunken riflemen began to snore up and down the corridor. Captain Sutter came from wherever he'd been and sat down before his tent. He reached inside and pulled out writing paper.

Feeling the cold, Pedro drew his sarape around his shoulders. He watched Sutter alternately tip a flask to his lips and then pen a few words. Soon he sipped more often than he wrote. "I have angst about da fort venn I be away," he said with a glance at Pedro.

"You left a good man in charge, Capitán. Señor Reading keeps everything under control."

Sutter's tone was grave, his enunciation thick with liquor. "But can I trust dot he keep da mens from Manu-iki? I write Herr Reading to lock her safe in her room, ya. Melons, Lieutenant. Dot iss big problem."

Melons? Pedro felt his jaw drop, and snapped it shut. The mind of his superior officer was far from war, but *melons!* Forbidden fruit. It seemed un-captainlike the night before the possible first engagement with Castro, a force said to be on the inland road to Monterey.

Sutter shook his head in obvious despair. "Manu-iki want dem melons be planted, so she go outside and plant seeds, and all mens see her bent down. Hic."

Pedro caught up with his meaning, envisioning lush Manu-iki bending over.

"I write my order now, dot she have in the garden a sure place for her melons. *Ja, ganz sicher,* and she be in dat room locked up and not coming out 'til I be home again." He scratched on the paper, dipped the pen in the ink, and then looked at Pedro from the tops of his eyes. "She grow big melons, ya. And sweet. Hic."

Pedro shut his eyes. A man never knew another man's mind, especially one born in a foreign land. Maybe Sutter had a subtler mind that Pedro imagined. Or, for all he knew the Captain was planning a war strategy beyond the thought of melons. Sleep was unraveling Pedro's mind, pulling the loose threads apart.

"Ve show ya strengt," Sutter said, jerking Pedro awake. "Men join strengt. Soon we haff independent empire, you vatch." He finished folding the letter and put it in the tent.

*Independent empire.* The Captain had hinted that before, but Pedro hadn't thought he was serious. Yet empire was precisely what General Vallejo and other Californios worried Sutter was developing. However it made no sense to be getting in the middle of a civil war when he had something very different, something subversive to both sides, in mind. "I haff hear, very hush por favor, very hush," the Capitán was saying. "Ten tousand Nort Americans next year be coming." A tipsy smile parted his mustache. "Loyal to me."

Pedro looked at him in amazement. Ten thousand was beyond comprehension. No more than a couple hundred people lived in the entire crowded pueblo of San José, a few more in Yerba Buena. About twenty farmed around Sutter's Fort, the same around Sonoma. But ten thousand? That was more than all the civilized people in Upper California. He felt like he was dreaming. Sutter was supposed to keep North Americans out. "Why?" he asked, "Why are so many coming here?"

"Mormons. Hic. Farmers, goot craftsmen. Families wit children. Mormons be hard vorkers, goot people. Iss vhat I need. I write letters. I giff dem landt. Now ve see empire, a-yah." He pointed down the corridor at the trappers and sailors. "Bad men. Silence please." He tried to put his finger across his lips, but missed. "Por favor, silence about letters."

The thought of such a throng pledged to Captain Sutter banished sleep like quail flushed from a bush. Whether or not he had the authority, Sutter had the power to give land, Pedro now realized. He had built an impregnable fort and armed it well. Pedro would be seen as a traitor to his country. He needed to understand this better.

"What are Mormons?"

Sutter upended the flask, swallowed. "People of a religion dot vant no interfering from government." He wiped his sleeve across his mustache. "Mormon men haff two, tree wifes, see, maybe more. I have write dem dot California haff no care how many wifes."

The padres cared. Vallejo cared. But Sutter ruled the big valley. Marriage didn't exist for him and his trapper friends. A man simply took a woman, as many as he could handle. Sudden shouting came from the riflemen, McCoon's voice jumping out, "You bastard! Heard of cuttin a bloke a bit o' slack?"

Pedro realized that the ten thousand would claim the riverbanks for themselves. Furthermore, Sutter was easily influenced by North Americans, whom he liked better than Californios. He would listen to the Mormons. And if the United States attacked Mexico, would he and his Mormons fight against Mexico? Would Pedro? Ay, ay, ay, he would be caught in the middle. It was too much for his exhausted and wine-befuddled head.

Some of the horn lanterns had gone out. The one nearest the tent flickered wildly. Sutter sat at his tent entrance listing like a ship in high wind—eyes closed, mouth gaping. Pedro nodded to Kanaka Henry, who watched from where he lay in the corridor with the other Kanakas. The two of them got up, shoved the Captain inside his tent, and covered him with a blanket.

All night rain cascaded from the roof of the corridor and the riflemen drank themselves unconscious. Pedro sat against the wall in his sarape drifting in and out of sleep. Golden melons careened at him and ten thousand North Americans fornicated across the land.

# 12

Black paled to gray behind the cataracts from the roof. The roar of it almost covered the see-saw of snores up and down the corridor. On their haunches and ready to march, the silent Indians lined the walls. Good men. Pedro was shaking out his sarape when Captain Sutter crawled from his tent and handed him a sealed letter addressed to "Mister Reading."

Pedro handed it to his best runner and watched him speed through the rain. *Melons: important news from the front.*

Mission Indians offered platters of refried beans and tortillas. They tasted good to Pedro, but Captain Sutter covered his mouth and lurched into the rain.

Pedro finished his breakfast. Then he tented his hat with his sarape and went a polite distance from where Sutter stood in the rain looking down at his own vomit. *This is no Emperor,* he thought while waiting to discuss the day's strategy—whether to engage Castro if they saw him on the road.

Sutter wiped his chin, picked his tricorn off the ground, shook it.

"Capitán Sutter, por favor, I would like your assessment of our situation."

"Ve march now." He jammed on the tricorn on his head, feathers wet and wilted, headed for the corridor.

"Capitán," Pedro said catching up. "I would suggest we march around Castro's—"

"You tell me mine command, hmm?" He'd stopped short of the corridor and glared from the tops of his eyes. His accent was thick. "Governor Micheltorena iss come from Monterey wit his army und we march together."

Pedro hadn't been told.

Two tiny points of color appeared in Sutter's cheeks and his large eyes sparked. "You vill make as ordered, Lieutenant, and no questions. Iss clear?" He turned and walked, carefully, back to his tent.

"Sí, Capitán." The rebuke burned in Pedro's craw. He bore more responsibility than a real lieutenant, yet was treated like a common soldier. He was Sutter's highest-ranking officer, in charge of the cavalry and a hundred and seventy soldiers. He returned to his fellow Californios, nibbled breakfast and tasted resentment.

An hour later the riflemen still couldn't be roused, except for Jared Sheldon and the immigrants. Sutter paced up and down the corridor before the snoring men, alternately holding his forehead like he had a headache and then fingering the pearl hilt of his sword scabbard as if he might skewer somebody.

"Stand up, if you please," Sutter would say. "Ve march now." Pedro doubted they'd be able to shoot straight for hours.

"*Donnerwetter noch ein mal, AUFSTEHEN!*" Sutter yelled.

The riflemen didn't move. Sutter stood for a while with his hand on his sword hilt, and then approached Pedro. "Lieutenant Valdez, to the pueblo ride and tell every cantina proprietor NOT to giff my men liquor of any kind. Iss clear? No matter how much money. No liquor."

Masking his disapproval and, yes, disrespect for a military leader who resorted to such an outlandish means of gaining compliance, Pedro saluted. Within minutes Chocolate's sleek muscles expanded and contracted beneath him while Pedro's consternation boiled so hot he didn't feel the rain or the cold. Bad enough that he was heading into the cesspool of his hometown—he'd keep his hat low and hope no one would recognize him after all these years—but Virgin save us, he might as well shout in the plaza that Captain Sutter couldn't control his men, the foreigners! That would flush even more men into Castro's camp. From what the padre said this morning, Don Antonio Suñol's runner having informed him, the Californios all along the coast and in this valley were flocking to Castro to fight what they'd heard was a massive army of barbarians and armed Indians sweeping across the country. Some feared they'd be eaten alive. And Sutter expected his company to attract volunteers along the way to the southland!

The Coyote of Grandmother's stories came to mind. But Pedro wasn't laughing.

                                     ❧

Later that afternoon the last of the riflemen rode out of San José, and the townspeople who dared peep around corners crossed themselves like they'd seen the devil himself. Pedro sighed, silently vowing never again to return to the pueblo. He'd been recognized and seen as a traitor—he saw it in their eyes. Sutter requisitioned horses for the Indians, buttressing the local view of Sutter as a robber chief. People had run in every direction when the riflemen stormed into the cantinas, stealing liquor if they couldn't buy it. Pedro blanched to realize that his family would hear that he served a thief, a ludicrous thief on a jenny!

Not far out of town something was wrong. He spurred Chocolate past the Indians toward where the riflemen were stopped. A long shape dangled from an oak. Reining closer, he saw to his horror it was Pablo Gutiérrez. His head was tilted unnaturally above his stretched neck and the death smell was bad. Pablo's shredded tongue lay on his black lip. His eyes had been pecked out. Pedro looked away and moaned to himself. Pablo, disgraced in death. Images flashed—Pablo strumming his guitar, Pablo happily brandishing the title to his Bear River rancho, Pablo wanting a batéa for panning gold. Nausea churned too near to his tongue.

"Cut him down," the Captain ordered. Indians dismounted.

Pedro placed his own bandana over Pablo's face, accidentally touching the forehead. He quickly pulled away from the clammy skin. When the Indians had the body buried, he rode on, and gradually the imprint of that putrid sensation transmuted into blood lust. Tightening his grip on the reins, he looked at his musket, secure in his saddle holster at his left knee. Vengeance tasted metallic in his mouth. Pablo had done nothing wrong. He was just a messenger with a note in his shoe, and Pedro was glad to be riding to war against those who had hanged him.

General Castro deserved to die.

They were on a wide green field on the bank of the rushing Salinas River when Governor Micheltorena high-stepped into camp on a magnificent white stallion. He sat straight and still in the saddle, fine-featured with dark shoulder-length hair beneath his feathered tricorn—the picture of a noble military leader. Fortunately Sutter and his jenny had been parted for this first meeting. Pedro felt an overwhelming sense of relief to see this ally. El Cid would have looked like this on his horse. Not only did Governor Micheltorena inspire complete confidence, but he commanded a large cavalry of foreign riflemen and a hundred and fifty hungry-looking Mexican soldiers—all dismounting next to Sutter's camp. Now the combined forces would surely prevail over Castro. General Vallejo had erred in refusing to defend the Mexican government.

The Captain and the Governor met formally, stiffly bussing one another's cheeks. Proud of his Spanish heritage, Pedro met a glance from Jared Sheldon. Sheldon stepped forward with his hand out and shook the Governor's hand. "Joaquín Sheldon," he said, "It is a pleasure, your excellency. Your signature is on my land grant."

"The pleasure is mine."

The meeting was short. Micheltorena said a huge force had joined General Castro and gone south on El Camino Real, heading for the plains of the Río de los Angeles. They would pick up strength as they marched past the big ranchos and leave ambush parties along the road. Therefore Sutter and Micheltorena should go down the Big South route along the coast so as not to encounter Castro's forces.

"Except," the Governor added, "I must wait here a few days for reinforcements. So you go ahead without me. You are slower, with the field pieces. I will catch up with you."

The Indians were cooking supper. Afterwards, with Governor Micheltorena back in his own camp, Captain Sutter walked around, head high, chest out, using his pearl scabbard as a cane, repeating, "Ya, ya, ve vin, ya sure."

The next morning Pedro got up and learned that Perry McCoon and several other riflemen had skulked away in the night with Dr. Marsh. Deserters.

"They will steal my horses at mine establishment and go to Oregon," Sutter grumbled.

If only McCoon would do that!

"I think Perry will go back to the hog farm," Pedro said.

Where he would take advantage of the pretty Indita. But at least now the Captain would not vouch for the scoundrel's character when he petitioned for the rancho. Surely he wouldn't. As everyone knew, a man had to petition multiple times. Surely not.

❧

Several days later Pedro looked ahead at the sinuous line of men and pack mules. Veiled in bluish rain, they were strung out with plenty of space between them so as not to crowd each other on this dangerous stretch. The pack animals and artillery carriers had gone first. From Pedro's vantage they were tiny as they inched along the narrow ledge cut into the sea cliff. Bringing up the rear, Chocolate walked carefully along same narrow ledge those figures had trod about a half hour ago, all about two hundred feet above the angry, roaring ocean. The wiry branches of a stunted shrub plucked Pedro's sarape on his left while the exposed roots clung like hands to the sheer rock wall that towered above. Far ahead, the line of men and animals repeatedly disappeared around bends and then reappeared again.

Quick movement caught his attention. Like toys across the chasm, two pack mules toppled over the edge, turning slowly as they fell until their hooves were up, and then they disappeared into the white turbulence. Terror knifed through Pedro and he reined Chocolate to a stop. All the men stared at the frothing violence that had devoured the mules, while all along the fluted cliffs great waves crashed against the crags, and white arms of spray reached up toward the cliff trail, curled as if grabbing for more sacrifices.

Pedro looked at the footing under Chocolate's hooves. Slick, inclined toward the ocean. It had become too narrow to dismount. Across the chasm ahead the line crawled forward again, toy Indians carrying toy field pieces on their shoulders. Toy mules. He patted the horse, "Good horse," and nudged him onward.

High overhead, a hawk cried. Birds had to hunt even in the rain, but the mournful sound brought an ache of loneliness. Human life was nothing against these brooding cliffs. The military campaign shrank to toy soldiers alongside the powerful ocean stretching beyond a hundred horizons, dwarfing the cliffs, devouring them like a child's pile of sand.

Who would miss Pedro if he fell? John Sutter? A few friends at the fort? Girls he had known? Not really. His family? He hadn't kept in touch. He hadn't left a mark on the world. Unless training Indians counted. Helping to

settle the frontier—running, in his way, like so many others. A silly poem of
the trappers said it:

> Oh what was your name in the States?
> Was it Simpson or Johnson or Bates?
> Did you kill with a knife and flee for your life?
> Oh what was your name in the States?

Pedro had never committed a crime, but he felt just as footloose. At thirty-
three he should have a wife and children and his own rancho. Something to
put his roots into, like these plants that clung so fiercely to these rocks.

He came to where the mules had fallen, saw the paler rock where the ledge
was chipped away. Head down, good old Chocolate kept up his careful pace
even though his withers often brushed the rock face; and as they rounded
another bend, Pedro saw that the cliffs seemed to go on forever into a misty
distance. Truly, his horse was his best friend.

The pale blotch over the sea where the sun had been trying to brighten the
clouds faded quickly into the undifferentiated gloom that had been a horizon.

For days they traversed the sea-cliffs and camped in the barrancas, the
nameless canyons between the mountains and the sea below. The march
slowed to a crawl. The Indians carried the artillery pieces and the emptied
wagons turned on their sides, and all that those wagons would have carted
had the trail not been too narrow—cannon balls, boxes of lead ammunition,
and supplies for the company. One entire day they spent at a good campsite,
resting in the sunshine. Pedro expected Governor Micheltorena's company to
catch up, but they did not. Early the next morning a mountain lion watching
from the trees attacked a mule, and the mule had to be shot.

The sun shone that day too, and they camped in a little wash with steep
brushy sides. In the middle of the night Pedro awoke to cold water running
down his neck and through his clothing. He crawled out of his flooded tent into
a rainstorm and joined the company as they pulled up tent stakes and moved
everything up into the sloping brush above the path of a swelling torrent of
water running to the sea. Leaning on the downwind side of a tree, Pedro stood
on his feet until dawn with a horse blanket around his shoulders. His mind
circled for hours around the odd circumstances of this war, the Captain's refusal or inability to ride a normal horse, and the worry that the Governor had
met with disaster. Interspersed with those thoughts came the recurring vision
of the pretty Indita, black eyes and skin like poppy petals, and the realization
that she would be with Perry McCoon. Of course he'd take her. That's how
the frontier changed into ranchlands, the chief of the local Indians providing labor for his pioneer settler son-in-law. That's how much of Mexico was
settled. Indian workers received a percentage of the calves. In this case piglets.

Dawn chased away the rainclouds. Men of all ranks wrang out clothing and wet bedding that had been heaped in the bushes above the torrent, and spread it to dry on the tangled branches of wind-stunted oaks. Soon steam was rising from the drying materials and breakfast was being served.

After breakfast most of the riflemen lay down in the sun and returned to sleep.

The Captain shouted that the company must move, that too much time had been wasted. The riflemen refused to move or mount their horses, though Sutter ordered them to march. The Captain backed down, not leader-like. Nonetheless, Pedro was relieved to stay. Surely now, he thought, the Governor would catch up.

At day's end a heavy mist came like a shroud from the sea. A man could hardly see his hand before his face, but out of this fog came an Indian. He rounded the bend and handed a portfolio to Captain Sutter. Jared Sheldon read it in Spanish for Pedro, his cavalry, and any Indians who were interested, and into English for Sutter:

*"Esteemed Captain Sutter, please be so good as to pardon my most recent delay. I remain near the Salinas River waiting for a suitable carreta to carry me over the Big Sur mountains. My Indians have gone to Monterey to search for a wagon. Strong axles and wheels are needed and a bed for me to lie down. The conveyance must be narrow enough to be carried by the Indians on their shoulders. Regrettably I have a bad outbreak of hemorrhoids and cannot mount my horse. Please be patient. I will overtake you. Together we will defeat General Castro. Your governor and servant, M."*

El Cid with hemorrhoids!

Sutter scowled. "He wait, ya, for a carriage."

Sheldon clicked his tongue and turned away, staring out to sea.

"I send a message," Sutter said. He went to his tent, sat down in the entrance, and scratched out a letter. Handing it to the courier, he said. "Ve march ahead and attack Castro." He looked determined.

Pedro kept quiet, thinking they ought to lie low.

After two more long days on the coast trail, another Indian arrived with a message:

*"Captain Sutter, please continue into the San Luis Obispo valley, but do not attack. Wait for me. A united front is necessary. M."*

Sutter grumbled a little in German, but to Pedro's relief, announced he would wait.

❧

The trail left the cliffs and Sutter's army was surrounded by a soft green countryside of grass and coastal oaks. An old Indian vaquero dressed in Spanish attire pulled his horse alongside Pedro, mistaking him for the company leader. He had a message from the owner of the land they were riding through. Pedro led him to where Sutter sat on his jenny. The vaquero slightly raised his brows to see such a sight, but collected himself and gave forth the oral message:

General Castro was gathering strength like a tar ball rolling through feathers. He had added all the ranchers of the San Luis and Santa Barbara coast, including their armed vaqueros, and a hundred riflemen mostly from the United States. The Captain thanked him for the information and bowed a stiff and formal farewell.

Before Pedro went back to the end of the line Sutter told him, "Ve not listen to dat."

A few hours later, a runner on foot arrived with a letter from Governor Micheltorena. A suitable cart had been located; however, it would be some time before it could be brought to the Governor's camp on the Salinas River.

*Not yet on the Big Sur trail!* General Vallejo's warning rang loudly in Pedro's mind, and he saw himself in a bad comedy, a farce. When he gathered himself he spoke to Sutter: "Captain, I give you my true belief. The Governor may not intend to fight, maybe never did intend to fight, and we cannot defeat Castro's forces by ourselves."

"*Das ist kvatch!*" Sutter waved him away and struggled onto his mule.

Kvatch was a German word meaning useless nonsense.

Pedro tried hard to imagine the dignified Governor Micheltorena lying on his back while being carried by Indians along the cliff trail. That too was kvatch.

Haciendas were nestled in the rolling green hills dotted with long-horned cattle. The air was warm, but the women and old men ran inside at the approach of Sutter's militia. Up close they trembled with fear.

One wrinkled old woman in a black kerchief stood her ground at her door.

"Ve not hurt you," Sutter said. Pedro translated, adding they'd like a side of beef if it could be spared.

She captured Pedro with her gaze. "Tell Captain Sutter I do not fear his armed savages. I am too old to care when I die. Mátame!" Kill me. She held up her chin as if waiting to be shot, then added with a narrowing of eyes, "But you should know guns are trained on you."

Her bravery sapped Pedro's spirit. Castro had taken all men of fighting age. If any had been present, a man would have come to the door. He removed his hat and made a sweeping gesture of respect. "You are in no danger, gracious Doña. We are retainers of Governor Micheltorena, come to fight Castro's rebels, not to plunder."

She stood like stone. General Castro had sown his lies well. Pedro turned to the sound of a horse. An Indian in fine Spanish clothing pulled to a halt and spoke in good Spanish.

"Capitán Sutter," he said doffing his sombrero, "Don Cristóbal would be honored to host you and your officers at his table this evening."

🌿

The big house stood like a vision amid formal gardens flowering in winter. Verandas wrapped around the house on upper and lower stories, and the roof was of red tile. Don Cristóbal and his mantilla-draped lady showed Captain Sutter, Pedro and Joaquín Sheldon along a corridor of paving stones, past massive pieces of carved oak furniture, to a room with several men waiting to be seated at a long table. On one wall a big fireplace radiated cheery warmth, and quiet Indians brought platters of steaming food of the kind Pedro had been dreaming about.

Toasts were exchanged, and, as always at formal occasions, Sutter comported himself with gracious dignity. Several wine refills later, Don Cristóbal looked across the table and said, "Capitán Sutter, General Castro is Governor Micheltorena's godson." He paused for the translation, then added with a riveting look in his dark eye, "They are family. I doubt they would make war on one another. As a renowned European officer, I thought you should know."

The faces on the other side of the table betrayed the ghosts of smiles. Sheldon's wolf eyes cut from Cristóbal to Sutter, then to Pedro.

Sutter was undaunted. "Esteemed Don Cristóbal, perhaps you haff been misinformed, hmm?" He told them about Pablo Gutiérrez, but their expressions didn't change.

🌿

Sutter's army arrived in the wide green plain through which meandered the Río de los Angeles, and spent two long weeks chasing Castro. Always there were old men with hooded eyes who pointed and said Castro's men had gone "that way." Each dawn as Pedro awoke in a thrall of young grass and fragrant patches of pink, purple and yellow wildflowers, his sleepy dreams were chased away by a stronger certainty that he was an unwitting actor in a farce. He continued to express these reservations to Captain Sutter, who dismissed them as "poppycock," a word used by the immigrant riflemen. English for *kvatch*. Castro was evading them. Governor Micheltorena was nowhere to be seen. Neither ally nor foe reported for battle.

Then suddenly the Governor rode his white steed through a field of golden poppies and offered the Captain his formal apology—followed by his army, which camped by the river. Then, like magic, General Castro materialized on the opposite shore with several hundred soldiers, as many Indian retainers, and a large number of field pieces. Hugely outgunned, even with Micheltorena, Pedro hoped this *was* a farce.

In the evening he saw messengers cross the river from Castro's tent to Micheltorena's bivouac. Twice.

The campfires were banked. Pedro lay under the stars, head on his saddle, wondering if Sutter's march all over the southland had forced Castro into a fight that his honor wouldn't let him avoid. Approaching footsteps made him sit up. A voice from the past said, "I've come from General Castro's camp to talk with you, Pedro." It was Jesús, from Monterey Presidio.

Questions about family were asked and answered, then Jesús said, "Do not shoot to kill. Governor Micheltorena only needs to make a good impression before he returns to Mexico."

*Good impression!* "But he is the Governor of Alta California."

"He dislikes the office, and is anxious to get to Mexico City."

"Why this form of leave-taking?"

"Honor. He must be defeated. Your side must lose. Then he can say the right things in Mexico City. It's been worked out. Pio Pico will become governor down here, and Castro will act as governor in the north. We'll shoot over your heads. You shoot over ours."

Honor. Pedro stared at the clouds moving across the quarter moon and considered the word. What of Captain Sutter's honor? And Pedro's?

Jesús' tone was confidential. "We'll capture Captain Sutter, but don't worry. He'll be quartered in a fine house and questioned like a gentleman. He will be released, that is if he's innocent of inciting foreigners and Indians to rebel against the Mexican government."

"You were the rebels, remember?"

Jesús chuckled in his throat.

But when Pedro went to Sutter's tent to report, the Captain threw down his pen and yelled, "Iss treachery vhat you say. My riflemen to Castro go. I see dem sneaking away. Running dogs! And now I need every gun shooting straight. Ve shoot to kill. No poppycock stories!"

Many riflemen had indeed gone to Castro's side, not out of liking for him, Pedro surmised, but to join their North American trapper friends who had lured them with liquor. He'd also heard that Dr. Marsh had urged them to desert.

Pedro returned to his saddle and blanket. Did honor demand that he protect Sutter's interests against Sutter's wishes?

Joaquín Sheldon came and squatted at his side saying, "An old amigo of mine just came across the river and gave me a good chew of tobacco. They're told to fire clean over our heads. Says we're to do the same."

"Do you trust him?"

"Sí."

"Will the riflemen follow your orders if you tell them to shoot high?"

"Sí."

"Shoot high then. I'll take full responsibility."

"I s'pose," Sheldon said in English, "it wouldn't do John a hell of a lot of good to rile both sides in this friendly war." He snorted a dismissive laugh.

Pedro left on his rounds, thinking. When he looked into the world of the Mexican military elite he saw darkly and from a great distance, but it seemed that the leaders of Alta California had maneuvered a delicate balance by which the rancheros in the northern and southern halves of the territory could govern themselves without interference. And in Mexico City, where central authority over the colony was housed, it might be accepted that a split in Alta California had been forced by this rebellion, which had also forced Governor Micheltorena's resignation. In this fragile balance, Captain Sutter was more than irrelevant, he was a clumsy threat. Pedro's countrymen were asking for an equally delicate action from him, one that put his personal future in jeopardy.

# 13

In the Los Angeles valley the sun fired the tops of the encircling mountains and spread across a carpet of wildflowers and green grass as far as the eye could see. Willows and cottonwoods along the river shimmered in the dewy light, but Pedro's head ached from lack of sleep. Honor required him to speak to Sutter one last time. As he walked along the cold campfires toward the captain's tent, the Indians soldiers greeted him with their flicker of a glance and continued piling cannon balls.

An Indian retainer was attending to the brass buttons down Sutter's royal blue jacket. They stood just outside the tent, the captain's chin high, the square sideburns and mustache trimmed. Pedro forced himself to repeat, "Captain, I am convinced we should shoot high."

The chin came down and harsh German words shot out dampening Pedro's face. Sutter's face flushed as red as his upright collar, and the Indian bowed away.

Pedro kept a level tone. "I believe the Governor delayed not because of hemorrhoids, but to give Castro and Pico time to negotiate a treaty. Since then they and Micheltorena have been discussing what to do with us."

"Lieutenant Valdez," Sutter spat, gripping his sword hilt, "of all der men, I expect loyalty from you. Vhat you think Napoleon do wit such an officer hmm? Run you through for treason." He whirled away and marched up the lines, excitedly ordering the men to shoot straight. "Kill the dogs! Show you are men!"

The Indians, who spoke no English, looked to Pedro and he signaled them to fire high. Sheldon sent the same signal to the riflemen—those who hadn't already ridden for home or waded to Castro's camp.

When the first rifles and cannon boomed, Pedro knew he'd made the right decision. Castro's crack riflemen fired high. Sutter screamed at the Indians and shook his fists over his head. But they looked to Pedro, who had always been their actual commander. Cannons exploded with regularity on both sides, the balls landing harmlessly until mid-morning, when one of the Governor's pack mules dashed into the line of fire. The cannonball struck its neck and, in a fountain of spurting blood, the head toppled off. Briefly the animal stood headless, a sight Pedro knew he'd always recall whenever he thought of this so-called war.

At about noon the shooting sputtered to a stop—one month and twenty days after the march from Sutter's Fort. Casualty: one mule. Four if you counted the mountain lion attack and the mishap in Big Sur. And Pablo. Unless he'd been killed for some other reason.

Fortunately Governor Micheltorena, Castro and Pico were family. The treaty would be amicable. Land grantees beholden to Micheltorena, like Sheldon, would be unharmed. Where that left Captain Sutter, Pedro didn't know. But even if he lost his position as justice of the peace of the north, that was better than losing his skin to no purpose. Pedro felt an unexpected sorrow for the loss of his military career, the line of Valdez military men broken.

Looking over the river, he watched Captain Sutter being captured by about thirty riders in a surround. At this distance he seemed a boy in grand trappings as they herded him toward the Pico-Castro camp. The final act of the farce.

Whooping came from about a hundred foreign riflemen, who had splashed to the center of the river from both sides, raising flasks. A thought niggled Pedro, that if those men ever fought on the same side and actually cared about their cause, they would be hard to beat. And if they were joined by ten thousand… ay, ay, ay. He looked beyond them, to Sutter's escort on the green plain, hoping that Castro and Pico would satisfy themselves very soon that the Captain had never intended to turn the foreigners against Mexico or incite the Indians to riot. And maybe the Captain would realize Pedro had done the right thing in countermanding his order—a hanging offense. But he didn't fear punishment. One lesson from this campaign stood out: Sutter was all bark and no bite. He had grumbled to Pedro when the riflemen defied his direct orders and killed and roasted the rancheros' cattle. He had threatened to have them flogged and they had all but attacked him. He had backed down and actually tried to pacify them with hints of land as a reward for following his orders! Amazing that a man so lacking in military leadership had become a captain in the French army. No, he didn't fear John Sutter.

As he walked over the hill to retrieve Chocolate, the pretty Indita came to mind. The thought of her with Perry McCoon wrenched something inside him, though he didn't know why he should care this much. McCoon wouldn't flee to Oregon, as Sutter flattered himself to think. McCoon wasn't afraid of Sutter. More than likely the two would soon be friends again.

He led Chocolate back to where the gear was stowed and looked over the river from the higher vantage point. About fifty riders from the Castro-Pico camp had surrounded the Indians. About twenty more were galloping for the horses. Booty! That hadn't been mentioned as part of the shoot-high deal.

He spurred Chocolate past his fellow Californios, who were running for their horses, and galloped down to the river where the Indians were being herded across.

"Corporal," he said to Pico's man, apparently in charge, "por favor, these Indians are under my charge. I request their release into my hands."

"Sorry," he replied, "they belong to us now. Payment. We had considerable cost as you can imagine, marching all over this territory." The man flashed a smile beneath his presidio hat, number 2 on the band—San Gabriel. The naked Indians carried the three cannons on their shoulders. More booty.

Briefly Pedro thought he might be able to collect a force to ride for the Indians. But the Californios weren't sufficient force and Sutter's riflemen were drinking with the supposed enemy. Then he saw Sutter's remuda of horses being herded across too—horses needed to run alongside and spell the main mounts in case of a chase. No, it couldn't be done, so few against so many, and the ammunition and horses gone.

The three Californios rode up, turning their mounts to watch with him as the mass of men and horses headed across the grasslands.

"I guess there's nothing we can do," Pedro said swallowing a lump.

But he couldn't just ride away and allow those men to be slaves to the southerners. Their homes were in the north. "I'm not leaving until I get them back," he said. "No matter how long it takes." There would be supper talks and diplomatically dangerous strolls in gardens. Maybe he could dictate a letter to Vallejo, and get help from that quarter. The lack of casualties made everything easier.

It seemed his friends saw the fire in his spirit. Like chanting acolytes they echoed his feelings about the Indians.

"They never complained."

"They were completely loyal."

"They kept the powder dry."

Pedro's voice cracked. "They can do anything with their hands. They understand... It's their..." He struggled for the right word. Nobility? Yet in the descending comprehension that defined this ridiculous war, they had toiled at the bottom. Pedro felt as if he loved these men as much as he'd ever loved anybody, and his Indian blood made it more complex.

He rode over to Joaquín Sheldon, who sat his horse watching the departing men and animals and the celebrating riflemen. "You go ahead and return to the fort," Pedro said, "I'm staying until I get the Indians back."

"Glad to hear it. Castro and Pico oughta listen to you, after you played their game." His wolf-like gaze turned back to the prairie. "I just might have a friend or two left in Pueblo de los Angeles. I'll send messages to them. See if they can help."

Grateful, Pedro let the silence change the subject.

"Could you and Señor Daylor use a good vaquero at your rancho?"

Sheldon cocked an eyebrow. "Of yer caliber, any day. But I'd have t'pay in calves."

That suited Pedro. He could build up a herd while waiting to see who'd be appointed governor of Northern California, and whether McCoon would actually get title to Rancho Sacayak. "After I finish here," he said, "I'm working for you."

Sheldon extended a hand. "My mayordomo."

The hand was hard and dry, and Pedro felt some of the weight lift. "Maybe I'll petition for the land across the river from you."

"William Hartnell has title to that ground."

"Then I'll wait, find another piece."

"Might be a spell before Mexico City figures out who can grant land. I hear that the You Ess of A is about to declare war for Texas and California. Heard it last night from a man who oughta know."

"Would you fight for Mexico?"

"Nope. I'm through with war." Not a moment's hesitation.

"I too. I am your mayordomo." It felt exactly right.


# 14

A cold wind brought the promise of more rain.

In the darkness María Howchia felt paralyzed as she stood at the drape covering the door of Sky Eyes' house. That was odd because she'd just danced the O-se-mai-ti. The Bear dance had given her the light and easy feeling of a powerful animal. Walking up the dark path with the blue-eyed man, she'd felt that strength, but now something kept her from entering. She shivered.

Sky Eyes pushed the cowhide drape aside and hooked it there. His hand closed around her wrist and pulled her toward the doorway. She jerked back, out of his grasp. She'd been glad to see his dimple in the light of the dance fire, and had felt drawn to him, but now she didn't want to go inside his house.

With Yellow Beard gone to the fort, Sky Eyes had come alone to the festival.

He had danced, removing his shirt in the warm, smoky dancehouse. The hair on his chest made her think of a bear as she'd never thought of a bear before.

Many of the umne had watched her leave with Sky Eyes, but it was her right to choose. She didn't feel sorry for him anymore. She'd been telling people she wouldn't accept a marriage present from any man.

In the corner of his house a flare of light briefly illuminated his face and hand as he knelt touching his fire-striker to a piece of fluff, and blowing air on it. He then lit a candle with the burning twig, slowly poured melting wax from the candle into a little dish on the table, and pressed the butt of the candle into the lump of soft wax. His shadowy form turned to her.

I could run, she thought, but no. She must face her fear and learn from it. That could bring clarity.

*"Methinks it's cold ye be, lass."* Seductive sounds without meaning. He drew closer. She welcomed his odor, now that the rain had washed his clothes many times over. Cold drops of new rain came with the wind.

*"Come,"* he said reaching around her, pulling her buttock toward him. *"I needs you."* Hoarse, intense, almost a whisper.

His other hand dragged a slow finger between her legs. Pleasant lightning ran through her and she gasped. It wasn't newborn. It had been hiding during the dance and waiting as she walked up the path. She wanted him.

He took something from his back pocket, uncorked it, put it to his lips, swallowed, corked it and then closed the space between them. She didn't pull away when his lips touched hers. With his odor came a nose-flaring smell and the taste of fiery liquid. She ran her tongue around his lips.

The medicine tasted like—what? She wanted more.

He handed her the flask.

She swallowed a mouthful and coughed unexpectedly, her throat on fire.

He chuckled. *"Here, I'll feed it to you."* He took a drink and put his mouth on hers. A gust of wind stole her basket-weave cap and blew out the candle in the house, but standing against him, sipping through his lips she didn't care. She rolled the liquid in her mouth, swallowed. She wanted more—the dark magic, the spark of blue eyes, the dimple, the sharp odor, the fur on his chest.

His hand was on her again. This time it lingered and she felt herself becoming wet. Walking into her fear she entered his house. Wind swirled around her. Maybe a spirit warning.

Sky Eyes released the cowhide across the doorway, slowing the wind. He knelt to relight the candle and she saw his dimple and, as he lit the candle, his approval of her and his wanting.

He set the candle-dish on the floor beside the bed, gentled her down to sit on the blankets beside him. "Aguardiente," he said.

"Aguardiente," she repeated, learning to sip tiny amounts. Warmth spread through her belly and mixed with the other warmth. It ran to the muscles of her arms and legs, weakening them. It settled in her woman's parts and made them voracious. Her breasts grew heavy from wanting him, and with each sip her foreboding melted away.

"Perry McCoon," he said pointing to his chest.

"Perrimacoo," she repeated, pointing at him.

He pointed to her chest with a quizzical look. Pale men had no qualms about speaking their names, and she had already thrown her scruples to the wind. "María Howchia," she said, speaking her name aloud for the first time.

Moments passed and nothing bad happened. That made her feel strong and she inhaled the pungent smell of his skin along with the fire of the aguardiente. She longed for him, feeling his man part under his clothes.

"Mary," he whispered, cupping her breast, kneeling before her.

They lay slowly back, together.

"Mary," he groaned as his clothing came off and she fed him her body, her femaleness, craving his milk. When at last she had him, the shadowy corners of the room circled in a sickening rhythm and she thumped down and down to another world where her spirit was lost. There she wandered, crying where no one could console her.

In the upper world the man flopped over on his back.

When she opened her eyes, harsh light lay across the packed earth beneath the hide drape. It also invaded the room from the window-hole and hurt her head. Her tongue stuck to the roof of her mouth. Scratching itchy bumps, she realized she was lying in a filthy blanket beside a snoring man, with lice in his bedding.

She lifted the covering, stepped over him, and carefully replaced the blanket. Swallowing to keep her stomach down, she went to the door, lifted the hide and glanced back at the severely lit clutter of the room. In the corner behind the table lay a big heap of something soft and dark. Feathers? The urge to vomit gripped her. Everything about the place was bad.

Outside the door the sun was a cruel slap on her eyes. The spirits had warned her not to go inside the adobe house, yet she had done it. She had spoken her own name. An owl blinked at her from a naked oak limb and who-whoed. Bad luck. Bad luck.

Walking up the path through hillsides green with first-grass, she smelled the man all over her. Because of that, deep within and against her will, her body prepared to receive him again, even as she walked away from him in disgust.

The people were assembled before the dancehouse for the final oration of the O-se-mai-ti festival. Father's talk had begun. He was admonishing the young men to avoid arguments and exhibit patience. When he finished with that, he stood quietly on the roof of the dancehouse, the focus of every eye.

In formal tones he continued, "My son Crying Fox and all the young men who went to the white man's war are prisoners in a southern place called the Pueblo of the Good Spirits...."

Stunned, María Howchia listened as Grizzly Hair explained that they worked like men in the mission—lines of them carrying loads to large boats. They were now *esclavos*, a word not understood in the people's tongue. She couldn't imagine Crying Fox forced to carry loads. He would leave in the night.

"...Captain Sutter is a prisoner inside a big house, and Hy-apo Micheltorena left for a southern place called Mexico."

Grizzly Hair stood quietly, as if focused on some distant point. What he said next puzzled her.

"Our condor robe is gone."

The People stared at him. She glanced at Turtle Claw's impassive face. This was not new to him. Grizzly Hair continued, "Someone stole Molok's vestments." His chin fell to his chest and his hair glistened, wet from his morning swim.

María Howchia felt her breath coming shallow and rapid. People looked at one another with horror, the horror that inhabited her body. Molok's robe had been stolen. This had never happened before.

Bad luck would fall on the people, terrible luck, and death. No one would know when, or upon whom, or for how many generations. They hadn't protected their most sacred possession.

As from a dream she saw the dark and ominous pile in Perrimacoo's house. It couldn't have been the robe. Anyone who touched Molok's vestment without purification would have sickened immediately and the unleashed powers of the universe would have killed her, if not immediately then as she slept in its presence. Yet the robe was missing and bad luck stalked the land.

The acorn supply was low. Crying Fox and others were enslaved. Even Captain Sutter was imprisoned. Tragedy would spread everywhere, touch everyone. Scrambled power rained like daggers.

# 15

### SECOND GRASS CELEBRATION, HOME PLACE, 1845

Longer in the sky every day, Father Sun blessed the world with his warmth. Second grass burst into luxurious growth, overshadowing the tiny spears of first-grass, now yellow and wilted. The tall grass waved across the hillsides and shouldered against the cha'kas and u-machas. Joy in the grass glowed from the soft eyes of pregnant does as they grazed. It sang in the trilling of birds and emboldened the fingerling salmon as they arose from their pebble beds to swim the gauntlet to the sea. María Howchia liked the warmth, but the ambient jubilation failed to enter her blood—even yesterday when she danced in the roundhouse. She wanted to be one with the umne at this special time. Instead she felt like a spectator.

This was the way with people, she told herself, to forget dire predictions. The umne buried thoughts of the lost condor robe beneath dancing feet, games, feasts, laughter and coupling. But poison nauseated María, made her breasts sore and quickened her tears. She hadn't been to the woman's house for three moons. Mother said she had a baby in her blood. Father said she should marry the man who put it there.

She could not. Perrimacoo would refuse to live in her parents' house for the trial period, and she would never step inside his defiled house again, though sometimes when he insisted, she lay with him under the trees. Coupling blotted out the curse of Condor for a little while, but the insult Perrimacoo had dealt the powerful spirit was killing her. Either she must find clarity and more power, or she was doomed.

She couldn't run as fast as usual. Club in hand, she trotted across the hillside on the trampled grass playing the Yokuts game Father had taught the People when he returned from the Mission. The Omuchumne team wasn't far behind, and that kept her going. But her mind wasn't on the ball. She recalled that before the sleep Turtle Claw had looked at her stomach in a disapproving way and she had left the dance-line. She had wondered then, and still did, why a woman with a baby in her blood must be married. Great-Grandmother Dishi never remarried after the black hats killed her man. Grandmother Howchia, her namesake, had never remarried. They both brought up their children alone. *But first they were married,* a voice in her head whispered.

Father, the leader of her team, smacked the rounded burl. It flew high and long, and María Howchia ran after it, behind her three teammates. In the best of times she couldn't outrun Blue Star, who had now started running while Father was hitting.

Blue Star got to the ball first. She set her feet and swung her club. The ball sailed well and by the time it landed Grizzly Hair had covered half the distance with two other teammates on his heels. María Howchia wasn't even up to the place where he'd clubbed it.

Father was bracing himself for the next shot when something hit the back of María's head. Dizzy with pain, she grabbed her head and pushed off her woven grass cap. The ball of the Omuchumne team had struck her.

Soon the first of them was tramping around in the long grass, parting it with his club, searching for what had bounced off her head. Bad luck. She sat down to rest.

The ball was found. Five Omuchumne people raced after it. A young woman on that team glanced back at María and wrinkled her brow in sympathy. Pain still pulsing, María made out Grizzly Hair across the hill, retrieving the burl from the last hole and thrusting it triumphantly overhead. Her team had won.

Father tossed the ball to Turtle Claw's son and strode back to her. "Are you well, Daughter?" Perspiration ran down the creases of his wide cheeks after the vigorous game.

"A ball hit me."

He felt in her hair and gently probed the painful bump. "Come." He guided her with a hand between her shoulders. "Or do you need to sit here for awhile?"

"No, I can walk."

In the u-macha she shoved her polished club into the rafters beside his— making them had been a shared pleasure.

"Come with me to the sweathouse," he said.

She waited outside. Quickly he emerged with bow and quiver. She kept mum as he slung the otterskin quiver over his shoulder, legs and tail dangling. Something was afoot. Why would she, a woman, be brought on a hunt? And many other women too?

Besides that, midday was no time to hunt, yet all the home men were retrieving their bows and walking the path toward tai-yokkel. They moved as a group, clutching their bows and watching Grizzly Hair from the corners of their eyes as though this had not been done before and they needed guidance.

When everyone arrived at the corral of the puercos, Grizzly Hair opened the gate and stood back. "Today we celebrate First Puerco," he said to María Howchia.

Stunned, she looked at Perrimacoo.

Hair mussed from sleep, he stood in the doorway of his house holding back the cowhide curtain. The whites of his eyes were red like when he drank too much aguardiente. "What the bleedin fuck's going on?" he yelled.

She heard his fury but didn't understand the words.

A sow peeked out the open gate.

Barefoot, Perrimacoo half hopped over the rocks and sticks until he came to where he could see the gate. "Ye bloody savages," he yelled. "Shut that gate or I'll blast ye I will!" He tender-footed back to his house.

Grizzly Hair signaled, and about ten men stepped from the surrounding trees and boulders with their bows drawn. Weakness overcame María Howchia, for they were about to kill her man. Obviously, all the umne had known about this.

Reappearing at his door, Perrimacoo rammed something down his gun. He jerked the stock to his chin, looked down the barrel, and then, with his eyes turning to see all the arrows pointed at him, he lowered the gun. The bowmen held their aim. Bad spirits danced in María's stomach.

The sow, swollen with young, rushed to freedom trailing a string of half-grown puercos. The boar shoved his way past them and vanished into the trees.

Kneeling with his bow at the ready, Grizzly Hair let fly. Not at Perrimacoo. The arrow entered the mother pig's eye. She staggered and fell without a squeal. The only cry came from María. She had loved watching the twelve piglets nurse in two neat rows. Sometimes she and Perrimacoo watched it together. She frowned at Father, who had signaled the men to shut the gate before more pigs escaped. For the first time in her life she disapproved of what he'd done, and this made her feel like a ghost in a story.

With calm dignity Grizzly Hair knelt before the fallen pig. Her family of young puercos ambled around him, unafraid as he lifted their mother's head and yanked the bloody arrow out. Accepting a small basket from Jacksnipe Song, he tenderly poured water into the puerca's mouth and sang her spirit to the pathway of ghosts. The song floated over the loud talk of Perrimacoo, who stepped forward but stopped when the encircling men drew their bows tighter.

The song apologized for the need to kill one who had been penned, fed and taught to trust. Goose bumps pricked on María's arms to think of that. She recalled Perrimacoo's delight that both sows were about to give birth a second time in six moons.

The last word of the song faded and Grizzly Hair signaled. Four strong men tied the sow's feet to young blue oak sapling—the ties and carrying pole having been brought from the village.

"Ye filthy, bleedin 'eathens!" Perrimacoo raised his gun again.

Arrows hummed, thumped into the ground and quivered in a half-circle around his feet. As he stared at them María felt her heart bumping under her ribs. She was caught between conflicting truths—Father doing what he thought was best for the umne and Perrimacoo expecting to trade the unborn piglets for aguardiente and goods at the fort. Now they would never be born, and his face had become such a hateful glare that she had to look away. She knew he thought she'd known about this all along.

Grizzly Hair's words came low and firm. "Daughter, invite this man to First Puerco."

She turned to her man and said in a shaky voice, "He wants you come to big time. We dance First Pig."

"First Pig!" Perrimacoo screamed. "Damnation ye nigger bitch!" His eyes were big.

She swooned with fear though she couldn't understand those words.

Grizzly Hair said calmly, "Tell him his presence at the feast will honor the puerca."

When she conveyed this as best she could, Perrimacoo yelled, "Just ye tell this to the honorable pig!" Without lifting the gun or aiming, he fired.

One of the men in the circle fell clutching his foot. Blood seeped through his fingers.

Before Perrimacoo could reload, several men took the gun from him. He yelled about hell and demons and kicked at their shins, but without his boots the kicks had little effect and seemed to hurt him more.

"Daughter," Grizzly Hair said, "tell him he owes us four of the half-grown puercos in payment for the injury to this man. He signaled the men of the umne to the gate, and the other sow and half-grown pigs streamed out of the corral.

Arrows hummed. Four half-grown puercos fell as their frantic mother rushed about nosing her young ones, one after the other. However they lay kicking in the grass. María's tone was that of someone else as she explained to Perrimacoo why the animals were killed.

His face twisted into the sneer of a demon.

"I not know," she said, gesturing toward the corral.

"Like hell you didn't." He flopped around but couldn't escape the grasp of the men.

Not understanding the rush of his words, she watched the men of the umne lift the snouts of the young pigs and give them each a drink for the spirit journey.

Patiently Father said, "Tell your man we will take him to the feast." He signaled the umne to round up the escaped pigs and lock them inside the corral, adding, "The man-pig will come to the woman-pig."

About seven twenties of people sat watching the skewered piglets roasting over several fires. They gave off a sweetish smell as their skins crackled. Father had invited the related villages to the big time and everyone had come, no doubt curious about the taste of the new meat and wondering how Perrimacoo would behave.

He'd been forced to walk up the path after surrendering his gun to the umne. Now he sat on the ground staring at thin columns of smoke leaking from the earth pit where the sow was baking. Anger darkened his eyes.

To pass the time people took out black walnut shells and played gambling games. Children romped around and women pounded acorns or checked the salad greens heaped on the anthills to be sure they were sufficiently anointed with ant vinegar. People anticipated the feast with obvious glee, often murmuring with their heads together. Grizzly Hair, sitting against the big oak that lodged his mother's spirit, seemed to be lost in thought. Meanwhile the strange aroma pervaded the village.

Cloying, too sweet. Gripped with nausea, María swallowed hard, pressed a hand over her mouth, and ran to the river. There she breathed in the fragrance of her plant friends and took her time collecting her calm. Acutely she felt her separation from the umne—like a bird among squirrels. Yet she belonged nowhere else.

Later, Father Sun was in his western house and the young pigs had been eaten. Strips of sow meat were being distributed, but María wanted none of it. She tried not to see people on every side smacking their lips over the meat. She stared into the distance when Grizzly Hair ate the heart and eyeballs. People all around at last lay down holding their sides as people do when gorged. Throughout the feast Perrimacoo refused to eat.

Father laid down a rib and looked around at the many people, signaling with his eyes that he intended to speak. Everyone quieted to listen.

"Daughter, tell Perrimacoo he is welcome in our village."

She told him in English. He rolled his eyes.

"Tell him he does not know polite behavior."

She told him and he snorted rudely.

"Tell him I will teach him polite behavior."

His eyes widened.

"Tell him that when a man puts a baby in a woman's blood, he should bring her parents a gift so they can decide whether she should marry him."

Unnerved at this unexpected turn of talk in front of all the peoples, she translated it brokenly.

Perrimacoo's lips twitched. "Wot kind o' gift?"

She asked Father the question.

"Tell him the puercos taste good, and we would accept the other sow, or his horse, or four more young that were not killed today."

"Father, I do not want to marry him."

He raised his voice. "Then we can send his gift back. I'm just telling him how to behave." The twilight was darkening, but she could see well enough to know he wasn't angry, just serious in his purpose. She gave Sky Eyes the list of possible gifts.

He tried to jump to his feet but the surrounding men were quick. He twisted back and forth in their hands. "Why don't ye bloody 'eathens just kill the lot o' me 'ogs and get it over with!"

"Doesn't he want to learn good behavior?" Father asked.

Tears suddenly blurred her vision though she didn't feel sad about any particular thing. All she could do was listen to the frogs bellow in the dwindling light.

Grizzly Hair didn't demand an answer. He collected his long legs, stood like a tree and spoke in a commanding tone. "Tell Perrimacoo we are honored to have him as our neighbor, and we appreciate his puercos. They taste very good." He rubbed his stomach to show it while she tried to say that in English. "Tell the man I would be honored to receive a marriage present."

Without looking at Sky Eyes, she murmured that in the few words she knew.

"Tell him if he becomes my son-in-law and the father of my grandchild, his wants would be my wants, my home place would be his home place." She struggled to say it all, translating home place as rancho. Perrimacoo listened quietly.

"Tell him we enjoy helping him take care of the puercos. But the females have too many babies and are pregnant too soon afterwards. These oaks," he gestured all around, "provide enough for the umne and a few puercos. Each year we will have a feast such as this."

Perrimacoo's outbursts seemed to be over.

Grizzly Hair studied him in the light of the dying fires, and then picked up the gun. "Tell him I do not want his gun. It is his if we are relatives."

She repeated that as best she could.

Grizzly Hair placed the gun over his wrists and walked it to him.

Perrimacoo accepted the gun, checked its working parts, placed it on his knees and shifted his glance from side to side as if seeking an escape route.

"I am finished," Grizzly Hair said. He sat down and cut another slab of puerca meat, sprinkling it with a pinch of salty marsh-grass.

All the men were watching Sky Eyes, though they appeared not to. María felt calmer now that her man had assumed a thoughtful demeanor. She also felt proud of Father again, understanding that he must put the welfare of his people first. The puercos had been eating too many acorns. It was only fair for the umne to share the meat.

Perrimacoo said, "I will bring a marriage present."

Earlier she had thought she would return any such gift, but now it occurred to her that the way to knowledge was to marry him. Then her child would have a father, her friends and relatives would look at her approvingly, and Perrimacoo would be part of the umne. She sensed that such a life would give her more clarity.

# 16

ACORN TIME, 1846

It felt good to be replenishing the family cha'ka, and now the vine-woven silo was nearly full again. Nevertheless the baby's crying grated on María Howchia, because she couldn't do anything about it. He couldn't be hungry already. She straightened her back and looked at him across the shade of the oak where she was gathering. Weeping bitterly, he stood upright in his bikoos, laced to the neck, the bikoos lashed to a stake in the ground so he could watch the gatherers. Beside him two other laced-up infants stood in perfect peace. Their faces were tan. His was red. Dogs shared the shade with the babies, lying with muzzles draped over their paws, eyebrows alternately cocked as the eyes beneath checked back and forth, clearly wondering when she'd do something about the noise.

"He is not well," said Mother's cousin-sister. Her big haunches, breasts and stomach rippled and swayed as she whacked a branch with a long pole and then gathered the acorns that rained down.

"Have you seen illness of this kind before?" Mother asked.

The big woman swept up acorns in her seed beater and reached behind dropping them into her gathering basket, the thong cutting visibly into her woven cap. Her eyes showed the wisdom of one who was older. "Grasshopper Wing's grandchild cries like this," she said.

Grasshopper Wing had left her husband's house and gone to another man in a downstream village. Perhaps that brought bad luck. María Howchia took the long pole and sharply prodded a branch. Acorns showered her cap and rolled off her shoulders. "Can it be cured?" she asked.

"Bad luck is in the child's spirit." The big auntie shrugged her basket between her shoulders, bent under its weight, and waddled away under the load.

María Howchia winced. She'd heard that before. As she gathered nuts she mentally ticked off what she'd done right while she was pregnant—never looking out a door or backing out for fear of breech birth, never looking at Great-Grandmother Dishi for fear the baby would be born blind, never looking at a sick person or a dying animal. All the bothersome precautions she had taken, yet still the baby howled, his puffy face streaked with tears. It was the same whether she held him or not. His father must have brought this, she decided. It was part of the bad luck from Condor's robe. Her man rarely purified himself. He also took too many acorns for the puercos. Twenty-three lived in the corral, now that the remaining sow had twice more given birth, and one piglet suffocated under its mother. Twice Perrimacoo had struck María, and once chased her with a burning stick. No other man acted like that, except Captain Sutter, and she would never mention it to anyone. It was shameful. Yes, he'd brought the bad luck and the least of it was the crying baby. The stolen Condor robe could make the entire world go awry.

She sighed and bent forward, sweeping up acorns with fluid motions. She too had behaved badly. No other woman refused to enter her husband's house. With so much wrong, no wonder the baby cried. Etumu's dog got up, stretched, and barked a little into Billy's face, turning toward María as if telling her to shut him up. But he cried louder.

She closed her eyes. Yes, Molok was having a bad dream. She felt she must sit down or fall. Hurrying to Billy's side, she unlaced and bounced him on her knees.

She'd never been inside the bad house since that one night, and when she asked Perrimacoo about the condor-skin robe, he became angry and raised his fist. Now she never mentioned it. She moaned aloud—the sound lost in Billy's howl—feeling almost as sick as she'd been that morning in her man's bad luck house.

Turtle Claw crawled out of the sweathouse and squinted into the sunlight at her. "The men in the sweathouse want to sleep," he said. "They want you to take the baby away from the village for the afternoon."

Shame! The baby had disturbed the men's nap, and the doctor was upset with her. Grabbing her angry bundle, she hurried away. Passing by the entrance, she stole a glimpse of male faces frowning from the shadows. The thump of a woman pounding acorns beat time for María's rapid retreat up the east hill.

She couldn't ask the doctor to cure Billy. He'd want to be paid more goods than she had, and that wasn't all. Turtle Claw needed to be warned about the insult to Molok; she was honor-bound to warn him. Yet she endured the crying and the horror and never told anyone that her man had stolen the robe. If he knew, Turtle Claw might take drastic measures to right the insult. Maybe kill her and the baby with magic.

At the top of the hill she adjusted her head thong, breathing rapidly. Billy had apparently fallen asleep. She heard the rushing river and smelled the blue vinegar flowers blooming at the end of the long dry. She leaned down, picked a sprig and brought it to her nose. These were tough plants, their harsh scent almost too much to take in.

Shifting the cradleboard to the other arm, she headed downhill, realizing that the flower was a sign. She too was strong, and the only protection against unloosed power was one's own power.

At sunset she cooked rabbit strips over the fire while Mother prepared the greens. Perrimacoo arrived and settled himself against the family u-ma-cha, setting his leather hat on the ground and running his fingers through his wavy hair.

"Mary," he said, "tell yer daddy I needs to palaver."

Hearing that, Grizzly Hair turned toward his son-in-law.

"Mr. Brüheim's gone fer good," Perrimacoo said, "And I'm sittin in yon house like a ship becalmed. I wants yer daughter t'cook me food over there like a regular wife. In me own 'ouse." His voice elevated. "Or 'as ye forgot, it's me bleedin wife she is." His blue eyes drilled into Father, then into her as she talked for him.

Father sighed. "Daughter, he gave me the present of a fine leather hat and three little puercos to roast. We all accepted that. A woman lives in her man's house after a decent time." He stared toward the river. It was hard to deny Father's wishes after he'd made a bargain, but he didn't know about Condor's robe.

She extended him a basket of fresh nu-pah, watched him scoop it with his curved fingers. The caring lines on his face remained as he waited.

She finally said, "Staying out of that house probably saved my life, and little Billy's too." The baby cried in his cradleboard. Without her permission

Perrimacoo unlaced him, and by the time she presented him roasted rabbit on cress and two boiled quail eggs, the baby was naked and laughing on his father's knee, clutching the pale sleeve of his shirt.

"He's fat," Perrimacoo said with pleasure, standing the baby on his feet, the little toes clenched in the powdered dirt. Then his expression darkened. "I wants me answer."

The baby grinned up at María Howchia, dimples in both cheeks, chubby knees pressed together. When he smiled like this it seemed the entire world consisted of his sweet face framed by his light brown curls. She couldn't endanger him any more than he was endangered already. "My husband's house is not safe," she told Father.

He sat thinking, and then said, "A woman does not marry a man whose house is unsafe."

For a moment she couldn't reply, and when she did it felt too private. But she forced herself to say, "Sometimes a woman is sorry she married a man." It came out soft.

Father sighed. "Tell him his house is unsafe, and then think about your death." This was Father's way of reminding people to live each day with joy.

Hearing again that his house was unsafe, Perrimacoo gnashed his teeth. "Mary, ent a bleedin thing wrong with me bleedin 'ouse!" But he left.

A moon passed and the baby was bigger. Perrimacoo was proud of him. "Mary, I needs ye to come with me to New Helvetia so I can get Sutter to write me babe's nime in the big book."

The thought of Captain Sutter made her stall.

"What the hell, Mary, just say you'll go!"

Mary, as she now thought of herself, didn't want to face Sutter yet. She doubted she had more power than the last time she'd seen him. But after a time she began to reconsider. Perrimacoo would be with her, and Sutter wouldn't take her from him, a white man. This would likely make her safe. Furthermore, she wanted to see Crying Fox again; he had returned as far as Sutter's place. And she was curious about the fort now that so many Americans were there. Perry said that women and children had come over the eastern mountains in big wagons. She'd always wondered what the women looked like. Several men of the umne planned to help Perrimacoo herd the puercos, so she'd be traveling with the crowd. It might keep her man's mind off coupling. Besides, the cha'ka was full of acorns. Her parents didn't need her. She nodded that she would go.

She also wanted to see Blue Star again. Her friend had married Quapata and gone to live among the Omuchumne. Mary would be traveling through that village, and maybe Blue Star would show her the wonderful seed-grinding machine Señor Sheldon had made. Everyone was chattering about it.

### RANCHO OMUCHUMNE, OCTOBER, 1846

Pedro sat his horse, resting his forearms on the big round pommel horn. From the high ground north of Daylor's trading post he saw the sweep of the countryside—golden hills sloping down to the green bottomland of the Cosumney. Midway between him and Daylor's adobe, Quapata leaned into his horse's mane, bare heels tight, and cut a cow from the herd. Pedro had to smile. These Indians were natural vaqueros, and Quapata was the best of the young men.

About a mile downriver Pedro could just see the top of the millhouse where he bunked—on the second floor under the peaked roof between the cottonwoods. He liked the privacy of that upstairs room, and its size—larger than any place he'd lived—even if he had to share it with flour bags and a family of mice.

Ay, ay, ay, Quapata rode well. The Indian looked back over his shoulder to see if he was looking. Pedro waved encouragingly.

Sheldon and Daylor were men of their word. Life was good on Rancho Omuchumne, with no troops to drill, no sessions with Sutter on everything from soup to buttons, no prickly translations, but Pedro's enjoyment came more from what he did than what he didn't do. As surely as Quapata was whirling the rope, the patrones needed Pedro on this huge rancho. He was a good mayordomo, and he got more enjoyment from training vaqueros than he'd imagined. Working on horseback every day gave him a feeling of.... what? Maybe it was fitting into the scheme of things. He was born to this life.

Oh, no question about it, a man his age should have his own place, but Mexico City had recognized Pico as governor, and Señor Sheldon said it would take a while before it was clear how to petition for land. The United States hadn't started a war yet, and Perry McCoon was still raising hogs on Rancho Sacayak. So there was nothing to do but enjoy life. The India Tomaka was comfortable as a feather mattress. Heavy of flesh, slow moving, happy disposition, she accepted the temporary arrangement and gave him his privacy. Besides, big times gave him other opportunities. Indians held their fiestas at least once a month, days of guiltless, rollicking fun. Those Indian fandangos pumped euphoria into Pedro until he took his shirt off and sang to the moon. Even the sourest puss could laugh at himself at those fiestas. All without liquor, which Señor Daylor refused to provide.

That boy could ride! Quapata handled the horse like his brown body was a part of it. He moved in tandem with a crazed cow, zig-zagging across the hill. Wild, these long horns were. Vicious. Then Quapata whirled a nice big lasso.

The cow skidded into a turn and thundered uphill toward Pedro. Quapata came after it, closing the gap. Pedro heard the bellowing herd shy behind him, felt the ground tremble. Quapata's powerful thighs spread over the mustang's ribs as he threw the lasso, catching only one horn. The cow twisted and changed course. The rope whipped free of Quapata's hand and streamed behind the cow in the dirt.

Pedro tightened the bead under his chin and urged Chocolate toward the cow. This might require his help. Quapata let his body slip to the side, legs clamped, and reached down for the dragging rope, the cow turned again, and the boy missed the whipping, bouncing rope. Nothing was harder than this. With Chocolate loping smoothly alongside, Pedro yelled, "Míra, watch!"

He touched the horse with his spurs and overtook the cow. The trick was to keep her on a straight course, but she swerved. Again Pedro overtook her. This time the cow held course long enough for Pedro to rotate down with his leg under the horse's belly. "Steady, boy." He kept up a patter of encouragement to calm the stallion, help him tolerate the lopsided weight. No question, this was dangerous work, every time.

Face near the pounding hooves, sombrero skidding, he gritted his teeth against the flying dirt. The horse was slowing a little because of the dropped reins, and the longhorn gained. Pedro made a kissing sound. Chocolate accelerated. He stretched his right hand after the trailing rope. Debris stung his wrist and he felt the tip of the braided horsehair rope licking up and down off the dirt and bunch grass.

"Hah!" he yelled. The horse surged ahead and Pedro gripped the reata. This was the worst part, inching back into the saddle with a thousand pounds of craziness attached to your arm, but Chocolate was the best. He kept pace with the cow, and she didn't twist away.

In the saddle again Pedro spat out a mouthful of dust and tried to blink away the grit. Would this cow ever wear out? Glancing up, he saw with horror that he was heading straight for Sheldon's wheat field. The harvesting Indians seemed frozen in place as the longhorn and horse bore down on them.

He spurred. The big horse lunged ahead, cut off the cow and turned her up the path toward Daylor's adobe. At last she slowed to a trot.

Pedro breathed easier, pleased that he hadn't lost his touch. He looked back to see Quapata not far behind, face cracked in an admiring grin. Looking ahead, Pedro was astonished to see a herd of pigs with Indian herders. At the sight of the cow the pigs squealed and tried to run, but the herders raised sticks and threatened them back. Perry McCoon had to be nearby.

"Hold, boy." Pedro hopped off Chocolate and made his way along the taut rope toward the heaving, blowing cow. By the look in her eyes, she expected to get her throat cut. He was talking to her when suddenly a boar broke free and careened toward the cow. She panicked, twisted her head, and the rope slipped off her horn. Circling at a gallop she lowered her head to charge the boar.

The boar skidded sideways and then ran toward Daylor's place, preceded by its knife-like tusks. Pedro jumped on Chocolate and coiled the rope with a loop on the end. The cow veered away, but the boar kept going. Indians and Perry McCoon scattered as the boar and Pedro parted them. Then suddenly the boar was charging an Indian girl with a baby on her back. She stood there not knowing which way to run.

Pedro gauged the speed and let fly. As the macho hog ran neatly into the noose and he yanked the horse to a stop, the boar flopped to its side, hind legs kicking, tongue out.

The India stared at the animal, which was only an arm's length from her, then looked up at Pedro. Her big black eyes met his. It was Captain Juan's daughter! The pretty little poppy McCoon had taken to bed. Pedro hadn't seen her since before the farcical Micheltorena war. Her face was so beautiful now that he hardly heard the baby screaming in her arms, or noticed the reek of pig excrement.

Her expression had changed from terror to admiration—for Pedro. With a red skirt tied about her hips and clay beads tight between her full bare breasts, she was a woman now, yet young enough to have a flat stomach and a nipped in waist. His insides went soft at the sight, and it felt good. He had missed feeling that way. This was still the tender girl-woman he had wanted, and the Heavenly Señor must have enjoyed designing her. McCoon interrupted these thoughts.

"Next time, lasso both horns," McCoon said.

Pedro leveled him a look before he tossed his rope to the herders telling them to tie up the boar. Then he spurred Chocolate toward the fighting cow, which Quapata had lassoed over both horns this time and was struggling to hold onto. Pedro aimed the lasso of his spare lariat at a back hoof, tripped the cow, jumped down and whipped the rope around her kicking legs. In a few moments the animal was immobilized. Pedro noted she was pregnant and healthy, the right ear notched. Daylor's cow.

Quapata said with a grin, "Maybe I be good vaquero like you sometime." The boy untied the cow, jumped on his horse and herded her up the hill, expertly cutting back and forth.

Pedro smiled after him and led Chocolate back to the hog-tied boar. "Buenos días, Señora McCoon," he said sweeping his sombrero before the pretty India, ignoring McCoon. He spoke loud enough to be heard over the baby's crying. If it angered McCoon to see her treated like a lady, bien. She regarded him with the eyes of one who had witnessed a miracle. He'd seen that same look on her face long ago, after his riding exhibition in her village.

The pigs, flies rising from their dung, the smelliest muck in the animal kingdom, belonged to the Englishman who was hunkered down against Daylor's big cottonwood. McCoon kept his rifle over his knees, smiling enough to dimple his cheek but not enough to expose the missing tooth. "Appreciate it, I would," he drawled, "if ye'd keep the cows away from me 'ogs."

The man had no honor. "Maybe we should have our riding competition now, señor." Pedro said. It had been over a year, and Pedro struggled to hold himself in check so he wouldn't kick the rest of those teeth out.

McCoon pointed his rifle at Quapata, who was receding toward the hill. Looking idly down the sights, he muttered, "I told you, greaser, I'll name the time."

After a moment of fear, Pedro knew the bastard had done that just to unnerve him. Quapata disappeared over the brow of a hill. "Any time señor, any time." He waved pig-flies away and stared into McCoon's insolence. *Real men raised cattle.*

Meanwhile, the Indita continued looking at him like that. A sudden sorrow grabbed him, so profound and unexpected that he couldn't keep it from his face. McCoon had her and the land too. The baby made her doubly the man's wife, the way Indians thought. Pedro found it difficult to look at the weeping child, living evidence of McCoon's foul touch.

Señor Daylor pounded up on his dappled gray, his long face under a big sugar-loaf sombrero. "Well blow me down if it ain't me old maitie," he said sliding his lanky frame off the horse and looping the rein over the rail.

McCoon got up and clapped him on the back. "A wee visit on the way to the fort with me 'ogs. Why, a bloke'd mistake ye for a Mexican in that git-up."

Pedro reined Chocolate away.

"Pedro," Daylor called. Pedro turned in the saddle.

"Take that adz back to Jared, would ye?" He nodded toward a carpentry tool by the hitching rail.

"Sí señor." Without slowing he swept the tool from the ground, already planning a visit to the fort tomorrow. McCoon was headed there and Pedro wanted to see how he treated the girl when he got there.

Besides, he needed to see about getting his own land. A growing herd of cattle bore Pedro's earmark and he was restless to give them a permanent home. After he'd helped get the Indian workers home from the southland, Sutter had forgiven his insubordination, but Sutter had been stripped of his position as justice of the peace. His friend from Hawaii, John Sinclair, was now the man to talk to. Land titles were being granted again. Even that scum of a former sailor named Johnson owned title to Pablo Gutiérrez' old rancho. Pedro had wanted it, the only land the new justice of the peace had the legal authority to grant, unless the confounded rules had changed again. The land had been properly granted by the governor but the owner had died. Ay, ay, ay. Murdered to be precise. Sinclair had held an auction and accepted a hundred and fifty pesos from Johnson. Pedro's herd hadn't been big enough at that time. No importa, Pedro had enjoyed his work at Rancho Omuchumne, all the time waiting to hear whether McCoon would leave Rancho Sacayak due to the irregularity of his supposed ownership.

But now, seeing the girl again, he felt a sudden urgency he didn't entirely understand.

# 17

On the trail to Sutter's Fort, Mary couldn't stop thinking about the man she'd named Proud Hawk. He didn't live at the fort anymore, so she doubted he was still under Captain Sutter's power. Now she could hardly wait for the journey home. They would stop for a real visit at Rancho Omuchumne and she would see him again. She also wanted to see the seed-grinding mill and Blue Star, whom she had sorely missed, but mostly it was Pedro Valdez who filled her mind. The same magic as long ago had sizzled through her again, even now just thinking about him as she walked behind the pigs with her cousin-brothers.

The sun was low when they arrived at the fort. It looked different. A new adobe structure shared a wall with the wheat-winnowing corral. And another new adobe house, a long one, stood half built outside the gate. Also outside stood many big wagons, some with pale cloth stretched over big hoops. Beyond that, short-horned cattle grazed, and west of the gate there were reed houses that hadn't been there before, with horses and strangely dressed Indian people moving about. In amongst the wagons, tents had sprung up, where long-skirted women stirred pots over fires.

Children with hair of strange hues turned and looked at Mary and the puercos. They ran alongside. "They're nekked," a child shouted. "That buck's got a necklace!" said another. More children joined them, some wearing shirts and trousers, others long flowing dresses. Little girls stared at little Billy in his cradleboard.

"Hello," Mary said to them. They gaped at her in wonder that she knew an English word.

Two men wearing a new kind of blue suit stood at the gate with long guns. Perrimacoo signaled the herders to wait outside with the pigs and beckoned her to follow him into the courtyard. Walking behind, she was so intent on the changed fort that she stumbled on a rut. Americans were everywhere, some in trousers and shirts like Perrimacoo's, some in fringed buckskin. One had a face as dark as a black lizard, and the braids under his floppy leather hat were stiff and thick. Overhead, the red, white and green banner was gone, replaced by a cloth bearing something that looked like a brown pig, or bear. Everyone talked, many people standing before tables heaped with hides and other objects. They were trading.

Some of the women wore hats with big wings that tunneled their vision.

When Mary caught little glimpses of their faces, she realized that their skin varied greatly in hue—some in normal shades of brown, some pink with small brown spots, and some white as demons. The hair falling from the wing-hats ranged from black to brown, orange, yellow, gray, and white. Some were tall, some short, many of them lacking in flesh. One had a straight narrow nose like Perrimacoo's. One had a nose that looked cut-off, with too much nostril showing. A women with the beak of a fierce eagle scowled at Mary's breasts and sucked her tongue with an audible snap.

Then she was suddenly at the foot of Captain Sutter's stairs, Perrimacoo tugging her hand. She pulled it back and shrugged out of the bikoos, handing Billy to his father. "You take him," she said. It was he who wanted Billy's name marked on the captain's paper-that-talks. Billy woke up and began to fuss.

Looking at her with disgust, Perrimacoo took the baby and went up the stairs.

She dashed around the big house, out of view of the Captain's window, and nearly stumbled into a group of the new kind of blue suits. They stared impolitely. A slow smile spread across the features of one and he reached for her. She darted among strangers and ducked inside the iron-making house, which was attached to the fort wall.

Luis, a young Indian she had met before, smiled in a friendly way. Wearing only a leather loincloth, he sweated as he pumped the big bellows that blew the fire bigger, and as he pumped she asked in Spanish. "Is Salvador here?" Crying Fox's fort name.

"He went with some other men to a nearby rancho," he said. "He'll be back in time for the fandango tonight."

Sorry about that, she was peering out the small window, when she saw Manu-iki, her long black hair tied in a tail at her back, like a man's. "Are Americana women friendly?" she asked Luis, who began pounding a piece of glowing iron.

The hammer clanged. "Not to me." He had a humorous twist in his smile.

She smiled back. Then through the window she caught a glimpse of Perrimacoo on the landing of the big house—looking over the busy courtyard, probably for her. The baby was crying. She stepped out the door.

"Come to our fandango tonight, you and Salvador," Luis said from behind.

"I'd like that," she called back, already heading across Captain Sutter's parade ground.

She was almost at the bottom of the stairs when a crowd came through the gate. Through the many people she saw men helping what seemed a living skeleton walk, a skeleton in torn Americano clothing. This amazed her. How could anyone starve at acorn time?

Perrimacoo came down the stairs to her side, handing her the crying baby. Blue-suited men poured around the corner of Sutter's house to see the bony man. So many people had pressed together that she could hardly see the stick-like arms of the thin man draped over the shoulders of those who helped him walk. Around his skull face hung long brown hair that joined the huge, dark beard on his chest. She could feel bad power crackling around him, and remembered Molok's robe.

The skeleton spoke, "Please. I must speak with Mr. Sutter."

"I'm in charge here now," said a blue suit.

"This is Mr. Sutter's fort isn't it?" The man asked. "I have a letter for him from George Donner. We had hoped our families could benefit from Mr. Sutter's famous generosity. People up in the mountains are in dire need of his help."

"Who are you?" The blue suit showed not a trace of embarrassment in speaking for the actual headman of the fort.

"I am James Reed," the thin man said. "There are nearly ninety people in Donner's party back on the trail." He rolled his eyes as if searching for strength in the sky. "My wife and children were almost out of food when I left. That was weeks ago. They won't make it without supplies. You or Mr. Sutter or whoever is in charge must immediately send a pack train of food up the mountains to meet them."

The blue suit yanked up the belt of his trousers and said, "Two men come in about a week ago, to get help for that same Donner party. Stanton and McCutchen. Said you'd be dead if you be Reed. Mr. Sutter's gettin relief together now." He eyed the thin man up and down. "You musta had a bad crossing."

"Yes. I barely made it. I'd like to give this letter to Mr. Sutter. Is he here?"

The blue suit looked suspicious as he said, "The men that come in said you was involved in foul play and was exiled from the Party without provisions."

The skeleton's voice changed from thin to loud and clear, a man of pride. "Defending myself and my wife, sir. And that's no crime. I'd think a man in uniform would hold his opinion until both sides were told."

A big straw-haired man with a bushy reddish beard boomed out, "Way I recollect, you warn't about t' listen to no reason. You was too high falutin." A few Americans nodded in agreement.

James Reed took his stick arms from the shoulders of those who were helping and looked at the man who had just spoken. Fire smoldered in his sunken eyes. "If it's that cutoff you're talking about, we followed Lansford Hastings' directions."

The thin man's bones seemed to melt and men grabbed for him.

The blue suit cleared his throat. "Now let's all keep our shirts on."

The thin man raised his head. "How far did the wagon train get?"

Another Americano spoke up. "We don't know."

Captain Sutter pushed his way through the crowd. Beside the others he looked short, and he had gained flesh since María had seen him. "I am Colonel

Sutter," he said extending a hand toward James Reed. "Ve think the Donner people be in da high mountains now."

James Reed reached and grasped the captain's hand. "I am so relieved to see you, Mr. Sutter. These men said you aren't in charge here. I don't understand."

Sutter looked down in an embarrassed way, and then brought up his bare chin and bushy cheeks. "Iss mine landt." He gestured broadly. "Mine establishment. Haff you a letter for me, Mr. Reed?"

"From Mr. George Donner, a good friend of mine." Mr. Reed pulled it from his pocket. "It says he'll pay you for supplies, if you could have them sent back up the trail. Immediately, if you can, sir."

"To you, Mr. Reed, my storehouses are open. Please be so goot as to come to mine rooms, and ve talk about beds and so fort. Alzo I show you provisions ve pack for your party." He glared at the blue suits, raising their eyebrows to each other as they departed for the other side of the big house.

Mary watched Señor Reed being half-carried up Sutter's stairs. The crowd was dispersing into chattering groups when Perrimacoo headed for the gate. She trotted behind him.

"Is the blue suit the captain? I don't understand." The English had been difficult.

"Campin 'ere, they are, till the Americans figger out wot they're doin'." He reached the gate and shaded his eyes against the late sun, surveying the various wagons and tents.

"Is Captain Sutter not the headman?" she tried again.

He waved at the men of the umne, who held the pigs in check, and strode toward them.

Hurrying behind, she called, "Who is headman now?"

He whirled to her with flattened eyes. "See yon flag a'flyin?" He pointed back toward the courtyard. "Things just ent the same. Now shut yer flappin' trap, or I'll pop ye good." He raised a hand.

Molok swooped through her mind, his huge shadow darkening the world.

🐝

After supper Mary scrubbed every bit of her skin in river sand and swam into the current of the giant River of the Americans. She plucked cleansing herbs and tucked them into the bikoos. Walking back on the trail to the fort, she promised herself she would behave correctly in all things in preparation for the spirit dance. She would connect with power. Only power could stop bad luck.

Later, she laid the sleeping baby against an oak near the big ceremonial fire and joined Luis and many strangers in the dance lines, women stepping one direction, men the other. She had not yet seen Crying Fox. The strange languages of the dancers didn't matter as the fire licked high against the dark plain. She sang her own chants. She ignored the Americans who hadn't purified themselves, sitting on stools on the edges of the firelight, their children hopping and laughing alongside her. They had no idea how to speak with spirits, and that was bad, but she did her part properly, opening herself to power.

A crisp breeze carried the smell of roasting pig meat. Perrimacoo had sold all his pigs to Americanos. Now he sprawled in the shadows between the fires, drinking with his old friends. It occurred to her that aguardiente would help her forget the world and ignore the hopping Americano children. She left the dance line and went to her husband, signing that she wanted a swallow from his flask.

He handed to it her, his friends eyeing her.

The second time she left the dance line and went to the shadows for a drink of the fiery liquid, she heard a big graybeard say, "McCoon, that thar's one sweet-lookin *bolsa*." She knew the word that reduced her to her woman's part.

"At she is." Perrimacoo reached, she thought for the flask, but grabbed her skirt and pulled it off, yanking her down.

"No!" she yelled, rolling away in dirt powdered by animals and wagons. "The baby still drinks milk." She fought him, dust in her nose. Molok's powers were abroad. Things must be done right. Nursing women were not supposed to couple.

He giggled. She could almost see his tongue between his teeth when he sounded like that. "Help!" he said in a mocking tone to his friends, as he struggled to hold her. One grabbed her leg when she twisted to get away.

"I go dance!" she said.

"A reg'lar spitfire!" Perrimacoo said, fighting to pin her hands down. "Johnson, ye auld fucker, I'll give ye a poke, I will, fer a peso. Warm the bitch up." Laughter came from all the men. "I'll warm her good," said another leather shirt. "Me too," said another.

The big graybeard fell on her with his stinking beard thick in her nose and mouth. Gasping for air, she tried to heave him aside, but rough hands were spreading her thighs and holding her shoulders down. Knees crushed her hands into the dirt. Horror squeezed her heart as the man opened his trousers. He rammed her, making her breath suck inward in an inverted scream. She saw the slavering men waiting their turn, and bit her lip. The spirits hovered. Coyote laughed. She tried to focus her powers and make the men leave her alone. But she was too weak.

She choked back sound. A grown woman didn't cry.

All the next day, after washing herself in the river, removing the scent of the bad men, she hid in a secluded corner outside the fort, a place where adobes were stacked, beyond the eyes of the leather shirts. She hurt, inside and out. All her husband's friends had coupled with her. The spirits could kill her. Strong power was loose, and she couldn't stop it.

A woman with a basket of nu-pah hesitated as she rounded the corner.

She offered it in a kindly way, obviously surprised to see Mary among the stacked adobe bricks. Having refused to eat with Perrimacoo in the morning, Mary felt hunger squeezing her insides, and tried to smile in thanks. The woman sat beside her and they ate in silence, but the mush didn't fill the emptiness or quell the pain. Tears streamed down Mary's face, and she was grateful when the woman left with her basket. There was no joy in her, even with the coming of First Rain.

Through a gap in the big clay bricks she watched seven mules being loaded, tied with bulging leather bags. Then Luis came through the gate with Crying Fox and Captain Sutter. Still hidden, she crept nearer to hear the men, the baby asleep in the bikoos.

"You hang if mine mules die," Captain Sutter's voice said. "Iss clear? Even one." Her brother was in danger.

Crying Fox said, "No mule dies." He was dressed in trousers and a long-sleeved shirt, open at the chest revealing his pendant of blue crystals.

Luis added, "Big snow no come for a moon."

They were both heading to the eastern mountains!

A small Americano in a big floppy hat and worn clothing approached on a horse, pulling two other horses. Crying Fox mounted one of them. Mary forgot about being seen, forgot to be afraid of Sutter. She walked into the open.

In the tongue of the umne Crying Fox said, "My sister, you look like you saw Bohemkulla." Even with that name on his tongue, he looked almost jovial as he sat on the fine horse.

Mary shut her eyes and said. "Molok."

Some of the joke faded from his eyes.

"Big bad luck comes. You must stay here." Somehow she knew.

He dismounted and put a hand on her shoulder. "If bad power flies free, little sister, I am no safer here. Molok flies wherever he wishes."

"Don't go," she said, surprising herself with the urgent tone.

"Salvador," said the Americano, "let's git on up the trail."

Crying Fox gave her a brotherly look, patted her shoulder, and gave his horse a little kick.

She couldn't stop him.

Luis said "Adios." He and the small Americano reined their horses around and trotted up the path following Crying Fox toward the paso, ford, in the American River, each of the two Indians stringing a pair of mules, the Americano three.

She watched her brother disappear around a bend. Clouds had thickened and a light rain was falling. Night coming. No one began a journey at night. No one went to the eastern mountains in time of rain.

"Hello, *Liebchen*," said a voice. She turned. Captain Sutter was reaching for her.

# 18

It was overcast, nearly dark and somewhat chilly by the time Pedro arrived at the fort, now surrounded by canvas-topped wagons and campfires. He'd worn his sombrero from habit, not necessity. He wished he'd brought his heavy sarape too. Campfires winked beside the wagons under a darkening sky. He smelled coffee, ham and beans, cattle dung and the oniony scent of human beings. Quick motion caught his eye. An Indian woman ran through the Indian huts pursued by a man with a build like Captain Sutter. Could he be reduced to this ridiculous behavior?

Curious, Pedro nudged Chocolate through the immigrant camps, more than fifty wagons he guessed. These had to be the first of Sutter's Mormons, who were supposed to make him emperor in his own nation. But what were North American soldiers doing at the gate? He'd heard that Captain Frémont had come again, but not that there had been a takeover.

Passing beside wagons, he glanced at the immigrants, maybe ten or twelve to a campfire, all staring at him. More than one woman for each man? Yes. And swarms of children. More wagons arrived each day, he'd heard, and Sutter was letting them use his land. But not ten thousand. Not anywhere near that number.

A boy with a loose trouser strap ran toward him pointing and screaming, "Look, look, a Spaniard!"

Chocolate started to rear. As Pedro worked to control him, he was amused at the comical freckled face with brown hair slicked on either side of a center part, the boy gazing at him in admiration.

A woman with a determined gait approached, more children following. "Jonathan, you know better'n point. Now git back to yer supper. All a you! Hear?" She pointed.

They slunk away, never taking their eyes off Pedro. He smiled to himself. The boy's tone implied that these immigrants held Spaniards in esteem.

The woman said, "I'm sorry my kids got no better manners than that."

"It is nothing, señora."

An older man approached with a Kentucky ring maple rifle. He had a stocky build and thick, white hair. His pressed-together lips turned down like a horseshoe. "Thomas Rhoads is my name." He extended his hand.

Pedro reached down and squeezed leather and iron. "Honored to make your acquaintance, señor. I am Lieutenant Pedro Valdez." He nodded around at the wagons, "Are you Mormons?"

"All of us here." He gestured at a circle of ten to twelve wagons. "I am an Elder."

"Elder?" Indians used that term too.

"A church leader."

Pedro jumped from the horse and swept his sombrero before the man. "Glad to make your acquaintance, esteemed Elder. Captain Sutter told me he is expecting ten thousand Mormons." He glanced momentarily toward the Indian huts and saw the Captain trotting like a child seeking a lost playmate.

"Ten thousand?" the old man asked incredulously. His deep brown eyes crinkled and his horseshoe mouth straightened in what must have been a smile. "Well, that'd be mighty fine, but only a couple hundred came with me. You might say we're scouting. If it looks good, we might attract several thousand at that."

*All looking for land.* Time was running short. "With your permission," Pedro said, excusing himself.

He nudged Chocolate toward Sutter, cutting him off between wagons. "Good evening, Colonel Sutter." Governor Pico and Sutter had made a series of agreements, one of which was Sutter's higher rank. Still most people called him Captain.

"Ach zo, Lieutenant Valdez. Vhat brings you here?" He glanced around for the girl.

"I came for Señor Sheldon's mail and to speak to you about land." To his surprise he saw the pretty Indita peering around a hut behind Sutter's back, covering the baby's mouth, and he realized with a shock it was she Sutter was chasing. But now she revealed herself to Pedro and he felt a rush of warmth, that she trusted him to help.

Sutter was saying, "I am occupied now, Pedro." A man-to-man tone.

Pedro used the direct approach. "I noticed it was Perry McCoon's young wife you were after." Peeking from the hut, her large black eyes pleaded. He took care not to betray her location with his eyes.

Sutter raised his brows. "Iss zo? Perry McCoon hass taken my pretty little *liebchen*?" Then he laughed. "Now I know why he iss vanting der hog farm. Ha ha. And only yesterday I write in my journal dot Perry hass a son, and da mama iss Indian Mary." He pressed his lips in a closed, confidential grin that spread his mustache. "Perry giffs me a half hour wit her, ya ya." He nodded toward a group of wagons near the west wall. McCoon was perched on a wagon tongue surrounded by North Americans, mostly women, his pinto tied to the wagon.

The girl ducked out of sight, helped by the gathering darkness. The clouds hastened the fall of night. "Colonel Sutter," Pedro said, "I have an urgent matter I must discuss with you."

"Find yourself a muchacha, lieutenant. Ve talk on the morning." He whirled, searching.

McCoon was now on his horse galloping around the wagons. The fires lit his antics and the faces of his enthralled audience. As the horse reached a measured stride, McCoon slowly rose to a crouch, almost standing, arms precariously at his sides. Then he fell back into the saddle.

A cheer exploded. The Englishman had been practicing. Now he rode through the parting crowd, leaned down from the saddle and picked up a coffee pot. He righted himself, brandishing the pot aloft. A loud, collective sigh of approval rose. McCoon's smile flashed across the distance, his face clean-shaven, his perfectly waved hair clasped behind. A lady's man showing off for the ladies.

Pedro reined Chocolate back toward the fort gate, against the flow of North Americans hurrying toward the cheering. As he dismounted at the rail, the Rhoads family approached—two attractive girls, one short, one tall, following the older couple, numerous children bouncing alongside. *How many wives?* "Hola," Pedro swept his sombrero to the ground.

The boy with the hair parted in the middle said, "We're gonna see that buck-arrow do tricks. Look Dad!"

"Vaquero," Pedro corrected. But it wasn't the fractured Spanish that bothered him. It was hearing the term applied to that scum of a runaway sailor.

The Rhoads family left when a full-throated shout exploded near McCoon. As it trailed off, a small voice said, "Gracias for helping me."

He whirled to the vanilla voice. "Indita, is that you?"

"Sí, Mary."

The tenderness of the tone took him by surprise and he went to where she stood, indistinct in the shadows behind the gate. The baby seemed asleep in its cradleboard on her back. Her skin still smelled faintly of peaches. He cupped a velvety shoulder, her thick hair brushing across his knuckles. She seemed to welcome his touch. Unable to form words around his surging emotions, he put his arms around her and gentled her to him, his chin on her hair. Soft breasts yielded to his chest. He stifled a moan. "María, María, María." Oh God, what was happening?

"Señor Sutter might come," she whispered, taking his hand, pulling him along the wall. Her warm little palm shot pleasant electricity into his depths, and he never wanted to let go. In the dark overcast night no moon or stars illuminated the plain; he saw her curvy figure by the faint light of the campfires. She rounded the corner and headed up the north trail past the adobe pit, toward the river.

Then she crouched and pulled him beneath the canopy of a large oak, a curtain of low branches catching his sombrero, which he removed and ducked down. Only one campfire glowed through a rounded canvas top, and almost no light filtered inside the hanging branches. The dry grass and fallen leaves rustled beneath their feet, and his heart labored in his breast.

He half saw, half heard María remove the cradleboard, set it in the leaves, and reach for him. His insides trembled as he knelt beside her, so powerful his desire, so soft the breeze moving his hair as it came through the branches.

Also kneeling, she pulled back and said, "I must not couple. It is bad now, when the baby sucks milk. I want only to embrace you."

"Have no fear. I will hold you only." He touched her cheek and was surprised to feel tears. He traced them from her eyes to her trembling chin, and then stroked her fragrant hair.

She put her arms around him and laid her cheek in the hollow of his throat. She was small, soft, precious. If he couldn't lie with her he would fill his mind with her. She seemed little more than a child, yet had a child of her own.

"How many years do you have, Amapolita?"

"Fifteen."

A poppy just opening. An owl hooted high above them. Coyotes warbled. A screaming cheer said McCoon was still performing. Except for these bursts the night was quiet. "It honors me to hold you," he murmured into her hair. "I would hold you for a thousand years and not couple if you did not want it."

"Muchas gracias, señor."

"For nothing." He felt a shudder run through her. "I think you are unhappy. Maybe you dislike your husband looking for the attentions of the North Americans?"

"I hope he couples with them all night." Not peevish.

"But he is the father of your child."

Without removing her cheek from his throat: "I am sorry I married him."

His pulse quickened. Regardless of what lay ahead, he felt he loved this girl. At first he had thought of her in connection with securing rancho labor. Now the land didn't enter in. He knew his love for her would heighten his conflict with McCoon, but the feel of her in his arms, the velvety skin of her back, the narrowness of her waist and roundness of her hips made him dizzy with amor. And now she didn't want McCoon. It was more than he had hoped. "Let us lie together in each other's arms," he said.

She lay back, her hand warm through his shirtsleeve, pulling him down in the deep cushion of small leaves. He gathered her length to him, sorrowing that he'd left her with Captain Sutter that time long ago, and that McCoon had started his pig farm on her people's land.

She murmured into his shoulder, "I trust you, Señor Valdez."

It opened his heart. "I am honored." He stroked her petal-like skin, cupped her full breasts and ran his thumbs over the toughened nipples. "If it does not worry you, I would like to remove my shirt. Only my shirt and bolero."

"My brother says not to lie with a man, except to couple."

"What do you think, señora?"

"I want your skin next to mine."

He pushed to his knees, tossed the vest aside and drew the shirt over his head.

She was saying, "Salvador said do not talk unless the thought is there four times." She paused. "I have not thought about this four times."

"Neither have I, señora." A roar of approval came from McCoon's side of the fort.

When it subsided, she said, "Please do not name me that."

He spread out his shirt and indicated she should lie on it. "I meant it only for respect. What should I call you?" He was naked to the waist and leaning down to meet her, the soft firmness firing his loins to exquisite pain.

"Name me anything but Señora McCoon."

Luxuriating, nearly dying of sentimiento, his voice went gravelly, "María." Her warm hand explored his back, banished the cool air, heated every part of him. He moaned, "María." It was a prayer, and though his lips hadn't uttered a Hail Mary for a long time, he thrilled to the name that meant the most blessed of women. He rubbed her cheek with his nose and felt hot tears. "You cry because of me?" Señor en el Cielo, no.

"Yes."

He held his breath. "If you do not want me, I will leave."

"No!" Then she was quietly sobbing, her whole body jerking. He hugged her tightly, trembling to contain his wild passion. "I do not want to make you cry."

She was trying to stop. "I—talk later."

Ay madre, the erupting desire he felt for this girl!

❧

As the distressing roar near the fort gate surged and ebbed to the antics of her husband, Mary clung to Pedro with her ear over his thudding heart. It spoke of intimacy and trust, and she felt like a child, safe and cherished in her father's arms. She knew she would want this always. Debasement and humiliation had crept up on her unawares, long before her husband's friends forced themselves on her. She hadn't realized until now that she'd been that depleted of power. Her Spanish was too clumsy to put any of it into words.

Pedro's chest amplified his quiet, beautiful voice. "Does Mister McCoon hurt you?"

Perrimacoo hadn't injured her. Whether he hit her with his hand or with sticks she recovered. Embarrassed to be treated that way she never admitted it to friends or family. But knowing he had stolen the most sacred possession of the umne made her feel she had wronged the world, made her feel like a bad thing that ought to be slapped, and she could only stagger away from his blows with mind unfocused, trying not to care. She alone had selected this man who gave her to his dirty friends for their amusement. Last night she'd have welcomed her death, except for the baby. The magic of the man in her arms revealed all of this to her. No tongue could convey half of it.

"No need to talk if you do not want to," he half whispered, "but if McCoon hurts even a hair on your head, my little poppy, I will kill him."

This frightened her. Men didn't make idle threats. Killing brought more killing, and retribution. She must not tell Pedro that Perrimacoo struck her. But perhaps he could do one thing.

"When you talk with Captain Sutter, por favor, ask him if anyone at the fort has heard of the condor robe. Someone stole it from my people, and I want to know what happened to it."

After a moment he said, "Maybe one of your people sold it."

"No. My people would never sell our most valuable thing. That would bring bad luck. Maybe death to us all."

# 19

All night he lay with María in his arms. He slept a little toward morning, believing by then that his sentiment for her could be matched by hers for him. That changed everything. Lightly he kissed her cheek. She didn't wake. Nor did the baby. Quietly Pedro gathered his sombrero and bolero and ducked through the dangling oak limbs. Making water outside the canopy, he smelled coffee and bacon. North American women bustled around campfires, the tails of their shawls crossed over their breasts and tucked into their skirts. Clabbered clouds dulled the sunrise. Perhaps an omen of early winter—a good time for putting his life in order. At what cost he didn't know, but it didn't matter. He was determined.

He brushed dry leaves from his pants and walked toward the gate. He would speak to his former Captain, but it was early. Sutter would be asleep, so first he'd visit the shoemaker and get his boots resoled. He was at the place where the bastard had performed to an audience too ignorant to recognize real horsemanship.

A lanky woman kindling a fire stood up with the back of her hand on her forehead as she squinted at him. Beside her, a young boy stared openmouthed at Pedro's embroidered bolero.

"Pardon me, señora," he said in English, "but I wish to find the man who rode his horse here last night. I would be grateful if you tell me where he is now."

She slapped her thigh. "My land! Wouldn't a believed if I ain't 'a seed it!" She lowered her voice to a conspiratorial tone. "Don't rightly know zactly whar he went. Last I seen, that young widow Lewis was ahangin on 'im. And her man only a few weeks gone!" She rolled her eyes.

"I seen 'em." said the boy squealed. "In yonder trees." He pointed at a bunch of willows growing along a seasonal lagunita, called a slough by North Americans.

The woman was about to swat the boy with a tattered towel.

"Geemanee Ma, he wanted to know!" The boy danced around the fire, escaping the swat and flashing a grin at Pedro like he did this every day.

"Gracias," Pedro said. He backtracked to the other side of the fort, passing the oak tree where his Amapolita slept. Not far away, making sure his spurs didn't jingle, he saw McCoon's pinto tied in the thicket. That was all he needed.

🌿

"Ach zo," Sutter said scratching his side. In his nightshift, his bare toes wiggled as he stood at the door. "You be early on da morning. Come in." He gestured Pedro inside, to the table. "Sit down. I dress now."

Pedro sat down and placed his sombrero on the varnished pepperwood. He heard Sutter rustling around in his sleeping alcove, where he'd touched María. How far had he gone? The stench of long-unwashed bedclothes wafted into the outer room.

Sutter called, "You interrupt a most unfortunate moment last evening." He emerged in shirt, trousers, and boots, his hair and mustache wet-combed. Sitting opposite Pedro, he handed him a battered envelope postmarked USA. "Please giff to Mr. Sheldon." He rang his bell three times and smiled. "Vhat bring you to mine establishment after zo long a time, hmm?" He offered a flask that stood on the table.

"No, gracias." As Pedro looked into the pale, watery eyes, he wondered what Sutter now thought about the episode near the Pueblo de los Angeles. "I have two things. First, I have wanted land on the River of the Cosumne for a long time, the very piece, I am sorry to say, where Perry McCoon has the puerco rancho. Por favor, tell me if you think he will be granted title."

"I giff him already title." Sutter's expression settled somewhere between irritation and challenge. He hastily tipped the flask to his lips.

Pedro recalled the letter of authority, which he'd helped translate, the qualifying words—if the land has been properly granted, if the owner has died. He asked, "Did Pico expand your authority after the war?" Sheldon had said General Pico was now the governor of north and south California.

Sutter's cheeks turned red as he glared at Pedro. Then Manu-iki opened the door and came to the table, her golden melons as lush as ever. Sutter ordered breakfast and gazed at her with somewhat less attention than before. He watched the door close behind her and turned to Pedro. "My powers haff been sufficient before my unfortunate arrest."

Translation: no new authority. Pedro set aside the vagaries. He had waited too long to let courtesy stand in the way. "I recall that Governor Micheltorena gave you authority only to re-issue land which—"

Sutter jumped to his feet and slapped the table with both hands, the chair tipping behind his legs. "Enough. Finished."

Pedro stood up and straightened himself. "Please forgive me, Colonel

Sutter. Accept my humble apology." He would go to John Sinclair for a letter of recommendation.

The large sapphire eyes glared and the mustache quivered.

Pedro picked up his sombrero and turned to go.

Just before he reached the door, Manu-iki pushed it open with her tightly covered backside. She carried a full tray to the table—a steaming pot of coffee, cups, two plates of fried pork, fresh bread rolls, a cask of butter, and a small China ewer of milk.

The flush drained from Sutter's face and he beckoned. "Sit, Lieutenant. Eat." He poured aguardiente into a cup and topped it off with coffee."

Pedro reconsidered. Playing host brought out the best in Sutter, and one day Pedro might need the man's goodwill. If the recent past was a guide, possession could be as powerful as paper documentation. If Sutter thought he was handing out land titles, why shouldn't Pedro get one? He'd just wait to see how it turned out.

He placed his hat on the table, watched departing Manu-iki, seated himself, and spoke in a courteous tone. "Muchas gracias, esteemed Colonel. Forgive me please. I have been out of touch at Rancho Omuchumne. Perhaps you would be so good as to grant me a piece of land."

Sutter slurped his liquored coffee. "If you haff ask before summer, maybe. Now Captain John Frémont says he hass authority of the fort, and mine trappers and immigrants say they haff seize Upper California for an independent nation. They raised a new flag and arrested General Vallejo, so all iss unclear."

*General Vallejo arrested!*

Sutter continued, "But soon Captain Frémont he leaf us again and goes to Washington D.C. And so I haff again mine establishment. Den I grant land, ya." He was about to pour aguardiente into Pedro's coffee.

Pedro covered his cup. "No, gracias." Deciding not to probe into the circumstances of Frémont's actions Pedro asked, "Colonel, if you please, where is General Vallejo now?"

"In the calaboose." Sutter flicked his wrist toward the tower.

Horror lifted Pedro from his chair. "General Vallejo in the jail? Here? Now?" It was barbaric to throw a noble officer in that lice-infested place like a common soldier.

Sutter patted the air over Pedro's side of the table. "Zo unfortunate. Sit. In da beginning I entertain General Vallejo in der guest room. My bestest room." His eyes had a sorry dog look. "I haff send brandy, aguardiente, delicacies from Yerba Buena. I giff the General mine fullest hospitality. Sit please."

Pedro sat down and Sutter continued, "Captain Frémont say I not know how prisoners be treated. I say to him, I haff myself been a prisoner of General Pico. Pico knows the code of gentlemen officer treatment for prisoners."

Pedro listened to a story of how Frémont had declared Sutter incompetent to manage prisoners. He'd left a young lieutenant, an Army artist named Ned Kern, in charge of the fort while he, Frémont, went on a military expedition. Putting General Vallejo in the jail was Kern's doing. Sutter cut his meat, forked it into his mouth, talking and chewing. "Captain Frémont says to me I be arrested in mine own establishment if I walk mit the General by the river." He leaned forward. "Frémont iss *schlecht!*" With that wet word, meaning rotten in German, came a particle of food that stuck to Pedro's cheek. "He says I be hanged if the General escapes!" He took another slurp of coffee.

Surreptitiously Pedro wiped his cheek with the backs of two fingers. "Where is Captain Frémont now?"

Sutter shrugged. "Chasing after Castro. Ach, zo many troubles I haff! Iss war mit da United States in Texas, maybe California. Maybe not. I vait. Later iss clear. Ya, ya."

And so, it starts. Pedro recalled the North Americans toasting each other in the middle of the Los Angeles River. Now they would fight on the same side. The United States controlled the fort, and thus the entire interior of California. Sutter, the ranking Mexican officer apparently hadn't resisted. What would happen to Sheldon's rancho? And Vallejo's? Pedro looked across the table at the sad little man who was losing the little empire he'd named New Helvetia. Unless the Mormons…

Pedro cut his meat and spoke carefully. "I met Elder Thomas Rhoads outside. Maybe his Mormons will help you fight the North Americans and get your fort back."

Sutter ripped a roll in half and plunged it in his liquored coffee. "No. The Mormons come far, running from bad fights in Illinois." He popped the dripping bread into his mouth, chewed and shrugged. "One cannot ask dat men fight the United States Army in da moment der vagons schtop." He scowled. "*Gott im himmel,* some of dem now ride wit Captain Frémont! The son of Elder Rhoads also!" The lost-boy expression Pedro had seen on the Los Angeles plain flickered across Sutter's pale features.

As surely as he breathed Pedro knew this man had never been a European officer. Somehow he'd acquired a fancy uniform and fooled the Governor. He settled in the California wilderness to be far from those who knew him. "Colonel," Pedro selected his words so as not to offend, "One might say the United States military has occupied your fort. Do you fear they will do damage?"

"No. Lieutenant Kern iss sick, hass a bloody cough." Sutter described the pitiful condition of Frémont's men when they arrived and how Sutter himself brought them back to health with food and liquor, for the second time. Sutter's tone lifted and Pedro sensed him coming to a conclusion. "I try wit General Vallejo again. Ya ya." Smiling with his old confidence, he reached across the table with an outstretched hand.

"Está bien." Pedro shook his hand, wishing he could as easily shake the thought of Sutter with María. "There is another matter I wish to speak about."

"Ya ya." Sutter eased back into his chair, assuming the demeanor of the Justice of the Peace of the Sacramento region, his former position.

Taking a sip of coffee Pedro said, "I heard that a condor-skin robe was taken from the ranchería on the River of the Cosumney where Perry McCoon has his pig farm." The Indian strutting on stilts beneath that feather robe came to Pedro's mind, and then the memory of the sweet pain when his knuckles smashed into McCoon's perfect teeth. "Do you happen to know where the feather costume is?" Sutter made it his business to know everything about the natives.

"Ach ya. Dat I giff to da Russians. Make dem heppy. You see, a noble Russian come here, goot friend of the Czar. He belief our Indians be relatives of da primitive peoples in Siberia. He vant baskets, bows, arrows, all those tings. Da bestest iss dat feder robe. Der Czar hass big interest." An eyebrow cocked above Sutter's sly smile.

*Manipulating further delay in his payment to the Russians.*

"I heard that robe is sacred to the Indians. If you don't mind, sir, how did you find it?"

"Perry McCoon giff to me." He seemed to be assessing whether there would be a recurrence of doubt regarding his authority.

Of course, Perry. "I am curious. Have the Russians already taken it with them?"

"Ach sure. Maybe in Russia by now."

Ay madre! After a moment, in which Pedro wondered how María would take this news, he said, "Por favor, I must visit General Vallejo."

Sutter stood up saying, "I come mit."

In the parade ground dogs were fighting over kitchen scraps. North American carpenters planed boards between sawhorses, and the children of immigrants from the United States darted about. Walking with Sutter, Pedro thought he felt María's eyes on him, and it felt good. A plan was forming in his mind, but first he must see if there was anything he could do for the General.

Halfway across the yard they met Lieutenant Kern and three soldiers. Sutter was obsequious. "Your Worship," he said to Kern, "mine friend Pedro Valdez here tells me Californios be sad dot esteemed General Vallejo is by us treated as a common soldier while he is zo unfortunately detained by you."

The birdlike young man—probably ten years younger than Pedro, but a real lieutenant with a red stripe on his sleeve—said, "The opinions of this Mexican greaser, or, fer that matter the one over there, don't make no never mind to me." He jabbed his thumb at the gun tower.

Possibilities evaporated. Such rude speech about Californios was likely condoned by his commanding officer.

Atop the white pools of his eyes, the gunboats of Sutter's gaze leveled on Kern. "I am sorry to report, esteemed Lieutenant, dot our supplies be low. And now all men eat Indian gruel for breakfast, flat cornbread for dinner, and perhaps a very small taste of jerked beef for supper. The aguardiente iss gone. No wine. No whisky." He gestured toward Manu-iki, who watched and listened from the kitchen house.

"Why didn't you say nuthin before?" the slender officer said in a tone of disbelief.

"I haff hear it today only. Zo many guests! Ach zo much eating! And food for the starving Donners!" He threw out his hands helplessly. "Now, if you excuse us, I must say this bad news to our honored prisoner."

Kern's bird eyes snapped. "My men will examine the storage rooms."

The gunboats leveled again. "You not trust me, hmm? Haff I not feed you like a king? And my cooks criticize, for now ve all eat poor, hmm?"

Kern asked to speak to Sutter alone. Pedro headed for the tower, three North American soldiers trailing. He opened the door and held his breath against the stench. The light from the door revealed several figures sitting and lying in straw, one scratching under his shirt, the other clawing his beard. Vallejo's men were jailed with him. "General Vallejo?"

"Sí." A stocky shape came to the bars.

Mindful of the soldiers at his back, Pedro lowered his voice. "I am Pedro Valdez. Perhaps you remember—with the helmet? It humiliates me more than I can say to see Your Honor in this place. Somehow I will get you out and take you to Joaquín Sheldon's rancho. You will be safe there."

A warm chuckle and a conversational tone surprised him. "Of course I remember you. And the helmet. But Lieutenant, you should know that we have considered the situation and we believe our interests are well served by Upper California coming under the control of the United States." He sighed. "We must stay prisoners for a while. It can't be helped."

*What was this?* Pedro whispered, "Because they listen?" He thumbed over his shoulder.

"They speak no Spanish and I wouldn't care if they did." General Vallejo sounded like a man spreading glad tidings: "The Mexican revolution has been a grave disappointment. Each time we Californios petition for land something happens in Mexico City and the government ignores us. Not one square league of land around Sonoma has been granted in over a year, though I have sent numerous petitions. Meanwhile, the United States has just granted vast lands to its settlers in Oregon territory. In the States people rule themselves. That's what we need in Upper California. In the States, trade is wide open. We would prosper. We would receive help fighting the horse-thief Indians. Señor Valdez, I have been in touch with the United States consul in Monterey for years."

Sand shifted beneath Pedro's boots. That's why Vallejo hadn't fought

General Castro. He had bigger things in mind. "But it is an outrage for you to be in this hole."

The General chuckled. "The lice in New Helvetia are huge, it is true, and I may have little blood left, but I must wait here until Frémont and his rowdies finish terrorizing the countryside. You see, Mexico will lose without question. It is sad, but when the laws of the United States replace the tyranny of Frémont, I want no man charging me with resistance. I came peacefully. I stay peacefully. I endure the lice with fortitude."

*Mexico will lose without question.* Pedro let out a lungful of air. All ties with Old Spain would vanish. But if he couldn't rescue the General he would learn from him. "What is the meaning of the Bear Flag flying in the parade grounds?"

Vallejo snorted. "An excuse to plunder my hacienda. Frémont is encouraging those men who came to Sonoma and declared a so-called Bear Flag Republic. My guess is he humors them so they'll ride with him to fight Mexico—did you know there is resistance in the Los Angeles region? Then watch, as soon as Frémont no longer needs their rifles, he'll hoist the U.S. stars and stripes and the bear flag will be forgotten. Would you do me a favor?"

"Sí, General. Anything."

"Tell Joaquín Sheldon, Rufus Chabolla, Antonio Suñol, and all our countrymen not to resist Frémont. We Californios must be seen as friends of the United States."

"I will tell them." Pedro's mind was still reeling, but he remained focused on land, and he needed to know what the General knew. "Captain Sutter told me he issued a land grant after his release from captivity."

"Impossible! He hasn't the authority."

"That was my belief. I would like to petition for that same piece."

The General chuckled in his throat. "To whom does one send a petition? Wait amigo. We are working with the United States to assure that those who have land will keep it. Next comes the treaty. After that we'll learn what agency to petition for new land grants."

As Pedro tried to imagine the difficulties of petitioning the United States, Lieutenant Kern's voice came from behind, speaking to the waiting soldiers.

"Escort Mr. Vallejo to Mr. Sutter's guest room," he said.

Pedro smiled in the dark. Sutter had won. It was amazing what men would do for liquor and good food, and gratifying to know that he, Pedro, hadn't served six years under a complete fool. As the U.S. soldiers accompanied the prisoners out of the cell, Pedro was also amused to recall Sutter's testiness about General Vallejo's refusal to join the Micheltorena War. Now those two were on the same side. Pedro watched the portly General walk across the grounds toward the portly man who might have become an emperor. *If* ten thousand Mormons had come. *If* he'd been that breed of leader known as a European military officer. If if if. He could almost hear his Indian grandmother say, "Coyote is smiling." She had a point too, about the schemes of men.

As for Rancho Sacayak, the General had revived Pedro's hopes. No land had been granted. Perry McCoon didn't own any of it. The U.S. government would give no preference to an Englishman over a Californio, if the General's effort succeeded. In any case, when the war against the States ended, Pedro would ask Jared Sheldon for help in petitioning for the Sacayak land grant.

In the meantime it was time to take María. Never had he felt so sure about anything. She made him appreciate the Indian in him, and after last night the Spaniard in him wouldn't allow any other man to possess her.

# 20

Mary sat quietly in the doorway of the u-macha watching for Pedro. He had returned to her beneath the oak with something new and exciting in his voice. He had asked her to wait for him in this house of the Cosumne headman and his family. Then he had slowly kissed her in a gentle but passionate way that lingered on her lips even now.

Billy laughed in his bikoos as the children of the house performed silly stunts for him. The parents and mother-in-law were present too, because for reasons Mary didn't understand, little work was being done at the fort.

A horse pounded up to the gate frothing with sweat. A blue suit jumped off, tied the horse to the rail, hurriedly unlaced a saddle pack, and handed a packet to a blue suit beside the wheeled cannon. Two soldiers then disappeared through the gate. Very soon a drum rat-a-tatted like a woodpecker, the signal for people to gather. Something important had happened.

The Cosumne in their various u-machas looked outside, exchanged puzzled looks, and answered the call of the drum. Mary stayed. Proud Hawk had asked her to wait.

The Walla Wallas, a wealthy people who for many sleeps had camped beyond the wagons, were also going through the gate. Cosumne friends had told Mary that Yellow Snake, the Walla Walla headman, was here with his people to negotiate reparations for the killing of his kinsman by one of Captain Sutter's friends. If his reparations didn't satisfy them, they would make war on the fort. Now the men and women of that tribe entered the gate in supple deerskin clothing like straight-backed Immortals, the men gripping fine bows. The most amazing was Yellow Snake's daughter, who always looked like a column of bright sparkling water. The clouds had opened and the sun blazed on her shimmering form. Coils upon coils of small reflecting disks hung about her neck and descended in opulent ropes to her waist. Sprays of those little mirrors dangled from her ears to her shoulders. They looped between her braids and hung over her forehead. Columns of them blazed on her long skirt and moccasins. To look at her was to be struck in the eyes. Her beauty blinded. In the face of such wealth surely Captain Sutter would negotiate with caution.

Beyond the shining form, Mary suddenly saw Pedro beckoning.

She picked up Billy, shrugged into the straps of the bikoos, and hurried toward him with her eyes down, not about to cross glances with the leather shirts arriving on horses. She wouldn't have been able to identify all of those who forced themselves on her in the dark. Now they all looked alike under their floppy hats. Rancheros and their women rattled up in wagons, excited children jumping out. Mary walked with the crowd into the courtyard, where the Walla Wallas and Cosumne stood alongside people of different skin hues, hair color, and form of dress. Several blue suits stood facing each other at the high pole from which the bear banner hung limply.

Pedro stepped to Mary's side in shiny boots with thick new soles. His grey eyes invited her and she stood beside him, thrilled, not caring that Perrimacoo or his bad friends would see them. He took her hand, and a current of power fused them. This was fated, Molok dreaming, not for her to question. She asked, "Did Captain Sutter know about the Condor robe?"

"Later," he said with a squeeze of her hand, holding it close between them.

Captain Sutter came down his staircase with something under his arm. A broad-shouldered Americano almost blocked her view, and more people were squeezing in. Someone was yanking the rope attached to the bear banner. It squeaked and jerked down the pole. Then, after much moving about a blue suit caused a new banner to jump up the pole. Thrilled by Pedro's touch, she watched it arrive at the top—upturned faces all around. A small wind briefly opened the flag revealing stunning bright red and white stripes, with a flash of blue in a corner, and then it fell limp again.

BOOM! Her insides compressed. The earth moved and she felt it up her legs. Instinctively she grabbed Pedro's arm. The baby wailed on her back. All the babies screamed. Dogs howled and barked. Pedro's lips formed a word, but another boom sounded. "Cannons," he repeated, smiling down at her in a way that assured her all was well. She covered her ears as the booms continued. Window glass shattered and tinkled around the courtyard. Americans laughed and pointed. At last the cannon thunder stopped and she stood rubbing her ears. All the babies were crying along with Billy. Young Americano children wept into their mothers' long skirts and, smiling, the mothers patted their backs.

Captain Sutter was about to speak when a blue suit stepped forward and began to orate, blocking Sutter in a rude manner. "Ladies and gentlemen," the blue suit began, but with Billy crying at her back she heard little.

Billy continued to cry after all the other babies had stopped. All she could hear were words such as ".… President Polk… Manifest Destiny… California into the fold—sounds that had no meaning."

People cheered but also turned to stare at her and Billy. Pedro squeezed her hand, telling her not to worry. She glanced around at the assortment of peoples: Mokelumne, Wapumne, Cosumne, Ochehamne, Nisenan, Walla Walla, wagon people, women with tunnel hats and chalky skin, blue suits with shiny buttons, rancheros in boleros and sombreros, leather shirts with huge bushy beards—including one with black skin and strips of red cloth woven into his fat braids. She jerked her gaze away, recognizing two leather shirts who had coupled with her. Suddenly she saw Perrimacoo on the other side of the flagpole, standing between two Americanas, one in a yellow dress. As if feeling her eyes, he looked at her hand in Pedro's, then at Pedro. He might kill them both. Husbands had the right.

She started to unclasp her hand, but Pedro's squeeze stopped her.

"… common tongue to be English," the blue suit orated. She moved a little behind a high comb and mantilla. Her tightening stomach told her to leave this place immediately. Perrimacoo had stepped to the side to see her better and Captain Sutter was looking at her too. Americanas continued staring angrily at Billy, who kept screaming.

"People are looking," she said trying to take her hand away. She had to leave.

"Not a problem," Proud Hawk said, keeping her hand as he looked over his nose at the speaker. "Your husband is a coward."

The blue suit leveled terrible eyes at her, but continued, "… soon a star for California… flag represents that destiny. Commodore Sloat needs… We shall respond." She couldn't understand any of it, nor could she tolerate any more hateful glances.

Wrenching her hand loose she slipped through the crowd, wedging between people, nudging them aside, and never looked back. She ran out the gate and around the corner of the wall to the big oak where she and Pedro had spent the night. Fearful that Perrimacoo would follow, she crawled in behind the wide trunk and peered out from it. Perhaps Pedro would follow too, thinking Perrimacoo would kill her. And he might. Or Pedro would kill Perrimacoo if he touched her in anger. They could all die. But perhaps—she hoped—Españoles didn't follow women and crying babies.

With her stomach clenched in fear, she shrugged out of the bikoos and hugged Billy to her breast, his lashes and red face wet with tears. She must quiet him or run to hide in the riverbottom. Watching the corner of the wall, she quietly crooned him a sleeping song, and gradually the hiccoughing sobs came further apart. Dogs sniffed around the wagons. She listened for the speaker, but heard only bursts of cheering—like before the sleep in this same place. With Pedro's arms around her, she had felt warmth and peace. Much of the dread had lifted from her spirit after she confided to him about the missing robe. But now he might not want to see her again. She was Perrimacoo's woman. She could only hope she hadn't brought them all to their deaths.

No one came around the high adobe wall, and Billy fell into slumber. Through the branches with scant brown leaves she caught small glimpses of the red, white and blue banner above the high wall. The clouds were thickening. She felt moisture in the air and smelled leaves moldering on the earth. The season had changed. Beyond the fort golden grasslands stretched peacefully as far as she could see.

A roar of many voices sounded, and then the first people appeared— Americanas and their children. They climbed into wagons left standing with harnessed horses. No Perrimacoo. Maybe he didn't care about her. And Proud Hawk? Would he be angry with her for leaving as she did?

Suddenly a dark horse galloped around the wagons. She slipped the bikoos on her back and crawled to the drip line of the tree, the better to see. The rider wore a sombrero. It was Pedro! What was he doing? People jumped out of the way as his horse thundered between the wagons. He slowed, sitting the horse sideways to her. Their eyes met, and then he spurred the horse directly toward her. She stood up in the path, not knowing where this dream was going.

He didn't slow the horse, and she assumed he wanted a closer glimpse of her before leaving the fort. But with the horse upon her, hands squeezed her middle and she was whisked off the ground and placed into the saddle with the high round knob—Proud Hawk leaning into her from behind, the baby between. They tilted to the side as the horse circled and pounded back around the wagons with all the staring people.

She couldn't help but grin into the wind, thrilled at the way he had picked her up. Strangely she had no fear of Perrimacoo. Pedro had called him a coward. People pouring from the gate, returning to huts, wagons and camps, backed out of the way as the expert horseman cut through, the harnessed horses stepping fitfully about. Pedro seemed to be looking for someone, his sombrero turning this way as they bounded full tilt around the large encampment, all eyes upon them, Captain Sutter staring at them from the gate. She was in a story she'd never heard before and didn't know the ending. One thing was certain, Pedro Valdez had all his powers now.

He veered to the left, and then stopped the horse abruptly, hugging her so she didn't lurch forward.

Perrimacoo stood before them! With an arm around the waist of the Americana in the yellow-striped dress. She might have been a little older than Mary, though it was difficult to read such a pale face inside a yellow hat tunnel. Perrimacoo looked past Mary as if she were a stranger. She watched his hand, afraid he'd pull his gun on Pedro. But his arm stayed around the Americana and his shoulders remained slack, his weight slung to one hip.

"I am taking her to my house," Pedro announced to Perrimacoo in English.

The Americana turned her tunnel hat toward Perrimacoo while he looked around as if trying to figure out to whom Pedro was talking. But then he grinned in his lopsided way and said, "Hit's about time, greaser."

The woman frowned at Mary's breasts and said, "I don't understand."

Quickly Perrimacoo guided the yellow-clad woman away, murmuring to her as she looked back over her shoulder.

Confusion overtook Mary—relief that her husband hadn't pulled his gun, joy to be with the man she wanted, and anger that her man denied her as though the mother of his son were unimportant to him. With his arms on either side of her, Proud Hawk spurred the horse into a rocking gallop. She gripped the saddle horn.

They were flying up the trail heading east. When she caught her breath and felt secure with her grip on the knob, she turned partway around in the saddle and yelled to be heard over the pounding hooves, "He acted like he didn't know me." All she saw was the curve of his sombrero.

"He has another woman."

"Is that how Americans leave their women?"

"Maybe."

Hope lifted her spirit with each lunge of the big animal, the long black mane flying back toward her. Pedro squeezed her between his arms, reining the horse to a walk. They were well beyond the fort. She turned back to see it, a speck in the midst of an endless sea of grass. She loved the feel of him behind her, his warm breath on her ear, the sureness of his control over the horse.

"Can a woman of your people end her marriage and leave her husband?" he asked.

"Yes." Her heart quickened.

"How?"

"Throw his things out of the house."

He was quiet a while, and then said, "Españolas cannot do that."

"What stops them?"

"My people are married by God. In His eyes they are married for all time."

God was the Great Spirit in the sky. What power he must have! To marry people for all time! "Are you married?" It came out weak, for she feared his response.

"No."

A wondrous word! She let out her breath and laughed at a covey of quail racing up the path on tiny legs before the horse as though attempting to outrun him. At the last moment before being stepped on they lifted as one in a riotous explosion of wings, roaring into flight. The horse flinched in mild surprise.

For a long time she rocked with Pedro in silence, savoring his warmth behind her, his arms against her arms, trying not to think how the world was fracturing into a dangerous scramble of unaligned power. A woman couldn't begin a new life if bad luck prevailed. But at last she asked about the robe.

He took his time. "Captain Sutter says he sent it to Russia."

That was far away. "Can you get it back?"

"No, Amapolita mía." He put his head around the baby and nuzzled her cheek. "Please do not be unhappy with me. I would do anything else for you, but I cannot go to Russia."

Of course he couldn't. She hadn't thought about that four times. Father had said that Russia was across the western sea. Now the robe couldn't be returned except by extremely powerful magic. She shivered to think of it in a faraway place, gazed upon and touched by unpurified people. Terrible luck would plague the Russians, and Captain Sutter for handling it. She blurted out what she suspected, "Perrimacoo stole it, didn't he?"

"Yes. He gave it to Captain Sutter."

Doom would fall on the umne, who had allowed it to be stolen, and upon her, unless she could become a women of great power. For the moment, cradled between Pedro's arms, she felt like she might be able to fend off whatever was coming. Strangely, she felt lucky.

"Where is my brother?"

"He rode to the mountains with Luis and an Americano named Charlie Stanton. They are taking food to the Donner party."

She recalled the spirit warning. But nothing could be done about that, or the robe. Together with Proud Hawk and swaying with him like the sleeping babe in her bikoos, it seemed they were one person with fused powers.

"How do your people become married?" More than four times she had wondered about that.

With her heart thudding under her ribs, she watched a herd of elk flow away from them like water, bounding over the high grass, rising and falling like salmon heading upstream. Then one of his hands gave the other the braided rein and his free hand cupped her breast. Strong but gentle, his voice husky in her ear.

"Amapolita, touching you like this has married us. Understand? In God's eyes we are already married. Later a padre can say the matrimonial mass." He slid his hand down over her waist and hip and caressed her thigh as he murmured in her ear, "Now you must throw Perry McCoon's things out of his house."

Happy tears blurred her vision as she twisted around in the saddle to see him as he looked around the sleeping baby awaiting her answer. "I never lived in his house," she said. "I am your woman and we are married." Strong emotion overwhelmed her.

"María, my sweet Indita. Te quiero."

"What does te quiero mean?"

He reined the horse to a stop, jumped down and reached for her. With tears running down her face she leaned into his arms and slid down his length to stand facing him so the baby wasn't between them. He kissed her hungrily and said between more kisses, "I love you. I want you." A spot of power on his tongue gave off a puzzling metallic taste and she lost herself in it and the softness between the bristles of his mustache and trimmed beard. She wanted to kiss him like this forever but after a time her neck felt a sore from craning upward.

She turned, still in the crook of his arm, and gazed happily down the hill. They were overlooking the valley of the home river, the ancient bluffs and gentle hills channeling the river southward, and the line of white mountains in the distance stretched from the northern horizon to the southern horizon. The snow was lower than she'd ever seen it in the time of first rain. She pushed away the thought of Crying Fox up there. Here, longhorns grazed peacefully in the green lowlands and smoke from the u-machas of the Omuchumne curled up through the yellow cottonwoods. Pedro's home was beautiful, and she was eager to live here in the house of her new man. She would cook and gather for him. Her good friend Blue Star also lived here with her man Quapata. Life would be good in the bottomland.

On her back the baby cooed—an omen that this was right. And as they gazed upon the quiet scene, a rush of strength coursed through her, enlarging her in every way. With it came the profound belief that the Great Spirit with the power to marry people for all time would help align the loose power careening through the world. She would do her part by observing the rules of living and not coupling while nursing, and she was ready to pursue the pathway to knowledge and power.

María, for that's who she had become again, felt lucky.

# II

## Elitha

# 21

SIERRA NEVADA MOUNTAINS, DECEMBER 1846

Snowmelt leaked through the rotting hides laid over the canvas tent. The plink... plink... resonated in the silence of the enclosed space at least ten feet under the snow. Fourteen-year-old Elitha Donner wondered how deep under the snow their tent was now.

The icy water dripped on Pa, quiet against the tent wall. It dripped on Tamsen, Elitha's stepmother, lying next to Pa where she could feed the fire without getting out of bed. It dripped on the quilts over Frances, Georgia and tiny Ellie, huddled together for warmth and quiet at last after chattering about mashed potatoes and gravy. It dripped into the muddy pool next to the fire and between the makeshift beds, and it dripped on Mrs. Wolfinger, who lay next to the huge living pine tree on the other side of Leanna.

Leanna, Elitha's hundred-percent sister, wasn't much of a talker. She rarely complained of hunger. Her warmth under the quilts came through two sets of stockings, frocks, shawls and cloaks. Sometimes Leanna changed places with her for a time and Elitha warmed up in the middle. But Elitha was two years older and had a stronger constitution, so most of the time she lay on the outside.

Elitha often recalled the time when she and Leanna had their own blood mother, Mary Blue. She died, and not long afterward Pa married Tamsen, the schoolteacher. People said a woman in her forties was too old to be having babies one after the other, and it was true that the three little girls needed a great deal of attention, but Elitha had been eight and Leanna six when it started so they'd always helped. And Tamsen had a way of making work fun. She also taught them to paint with pigments and told them about remarkable things, including the clever ways plants spread their seeds. The children of California were lucky to be getting a school run by Tamsen Donner, with her stacks of books and vials of plant specimens. That is, if it didn't all spoil in the wagon. Elitha sighed. At least they knew where the wagons were. The poor frozen cattle would never be found.

"I wanna go up and see the sun." Ellie's baby voice.

"The sun's not out," Ma said.

"Is it night?"

"I don't think so."

The fap fap of the tent door at the bottom of the ice stairs told Elitha it was still storming above. To save their strength the family stayed in bed. Ma insisted.

It was silent again, except for the fap fap and rattle of loose boards against the tent entrance, and the plinking. Elitha spent most of her time reflecting on how life had been up to now. She figured they all did. She knew Pa felt terrible on account of their not getting through to California before snowfall. People blamed him and Mr. Reed for taking the cutoff. Senseless, they said, to chop a road through a forest when everyone knew a proven wagon road lay a little ways to the north. But they were wrong about it being Pa's fault. Every one of them agreed to leave the main trail and take Mr. Hastings' cutoff, and they'd still have gotten through if it hadn't snowed so early. Mr. Sutter's Indians said it never snowed so much in October and November. So maybe it was God's fault. But He wouldn't do that on purpose, would He? At this point her thinking always came to a dead end.

The light from the small fire lent the canvas walls a fleshy color and the flicker of shadows stayed the same day and night. And day and night the smell of moldy hides simmering on the fire kept her on the verge of nausea. There was nothing else to eat. Added to that, the chamber pot stunk something awful.

If this storm ever ended the pot could be taken up the ice stairs and dumped. The snow up top would dazzle in the sunlight and she would fill her lungs with fresh air. She'd sit on a stack of firewood the hired men had cut and dry her cloak. Sometimes when it was clear like that Ma brought up her pigments, which she'd thought to remove from the "school wagon," and she'd paint the mountains on canvas. Elitha loved to watch.

But now wind whistled down the ice-stairs and Elitha tugged the quilt around her shoulder. At least they had fire. During that one storm the wind snuffed it out and for lack of wood the family lay in blackness for what Pa figured was seven days. How he knew when a new day began mystified her. Oh how she'd shivered! It made her back sore. Staring into the black, bone-rattling cold she'd had the terrifying thought that she was already dead and this was the real hell and everyone had been mistaken about hell being hot. But then she'd stopped such foolish thinking and hugged Leanna.

Jean Baptiste had dug down to the wagon and taken out boards for the tent door, and since then the fire hadn't blown out. Elitha worried about him on account of the hired men's wigwam being so poorly made. That first night when the sleet and wind blasted and Pa decided to make camp to wait out the storm she'd wondered how the men got their lean-to up at all, after struggling so long with the family tent. She'd seen desperation in their faces when the wind stole the canvas from their stiff fingers.

She sighed. All the hired men were dead now except for Jean Baptiste. Ma had been in their tent when the first one slipped away in happy delirium. He thought he was a little boy again, warm and eating at his mother's table. Ma said the next one died like a tired child going to sleep. The third confessed that back on the plains he'd helped some other men kill Mr. Wolfinger. Ma told that to Elitha the last time they were up above sketching the mountains.

"Why did they kill him?" Elitha had asked.

"Greed," Ma said. "Mr. Wolfinger carried a lot of money in his wagon." Tamsen cocked her head at her artwork. "I think it's true that money is the root of evil." The shadows of her hood hid her sharp-boned face, but Elitha could tell she wasn't really looking at the painting. It was often so with her, as if she stared at an unseen presence. The silence of the mountains had felt painful that day, the tall pines whispering faintly in their snowy tips.

Now, a blast of wind rattled the boards at the door and Elitha turned over in bed recalling the fun of helping Ma sew ten thousand dollars of gold coins inside the apple-green quilt. They'd also stashed money behind a cunning little door built into a false side of the wagon. Besides that Pa wore a money-belt and never took it off.

*Killed Mr. Wolfinger.* The murderers were stranded with the rest of the emigrants a few miles up the trail, and they might sneak back here and steal the Donners' money too. Mightn't they? And kill everyone? Pa had figured they'd all be at Sutter's Fort by now, but no one had made it across according to Dutch Charley. Not long ago that funny little barrel-shaped German who started out working for Pa had come back with two of Mr. Reed's teamsters to see if the Donners were all right. A right neighborly thing to do, being as how the snow was so deep and they so starved. Ma fretted about having no food to share. But it occurred to Elitha now, as she lay thinking this through, that Ma could have been thinking about those teamsters when she stared over her painting. If those men could come back so could the murderers. Worse yet, they could *be* the murderers. Oh no, not Dutch Charley, Elitha corrected in her mind. He was too jolly, but those other two she wasn't sure. It was something to worry about because last summer on the prairie she'd caught a fragment of conversation as she passed by the Rhoads' family fire, big John Rhoads saying, "The Donners are wealthy people." At the time she'd felt proud. But now it was a danger. And all the gold in the world couldn't get them through to California. Only God could melt the snow.

Each day she prayed more. "Please God, make the storm stop. Help the Murphys and the others in the forward camp, and protect us from the bad men. And please God, save Jean Baptiste. He's such a good boy." Two years older than Elitha, the last of the hired men, he cut the firewood every day for the family. Half-breed though he was—people said they were unreliable—she hated to think of him alone in the hired men's tent. But Pa wouldn't hear of him staying in the family tent, and that would be immodest so all she could do was pray.

Five-year-old Georgia began to whimper again. She'd never been a healthy child. Little Ellie, a year younger, had taught her to walk. People back in Sangamon County used to tell of it with a chuckle, the younger one teaching the older.

"I'm *hun*-gry!" Georgia wailed. Elitha gritted her teeth to hear that again.

Ma was patient as always, "Georgia baby, we'll have supper soon. It's almost ready." The mess of moldy gel.

To divert her mind from the stench Elitha thought of the apple orchard on the Donner farm near Springfield. Like a fairy princess she would sit on a certain branch with the trunk for a backrest, loving the fragrance of the white and pink blossoms—the bees so busy they never thought to bother her. Overhead, a mother robin kept landing at her nest to stuff worms down the throats of her hatchlings. Warm in the dappled sunshine Elitha threw her shawl and bonnet to the ground and loosened her braids, letting her hair fall silky and black down past her shoulders. Would she ever be that warm again? Ever see green grass again?

Tears of wonder had filled her eyes on account of the beauty of the world. Everyone should sit in apple trees. But maybe some of them didn't smell springtime the way she did. Maybe they didn't have a secret engine inside that started up at snowmelt. *God gave me that memory just so's I would have it now,* she suddenly realized. And right now she'd be glad for some juicy worms to eat. She'd been like a baby bird then, with her mouth open expecting food to be brought. It seemed that Ma and the hired girl were constantly preparing meals in the big farm kitchen. She'd known without thinking that meat and potatoes would soon be on the dinner table, and hot biscuits under a cloth with butter standing full in its wooden tub, scraped across the top with a knife. Oh, how her empty belly ached and twisted!

"Ma, I'm hungry!" Little Ellie's piercing whine.

Something made a scratching sound. Elitha listened through three plinks. Perhaps a mouse. It scratched again. She raised up on an elbow and scanned the dimness. "Don't move. Everyone quiet." She'd done this before.

"Catch a mousey! Catch a mousey!" squealed little Ellie.

"Hush now." Lifting the quilt, Elitha eased down on her hands and knees in a puddle. An icy drip rolled down the back of her neck, but she didn't move. All her life she'd watched cats do this. Tiny whiskers twitched. She narrowed her eyes at a triangular face peering from an aperture in the pine boughs beneath Ma. The mouse stepped forward, sniffing in both directions, green-eyed in the firelight. Larger than the grey mice at home. Browner, with a fluffier coat. She hoped her sisters would keep quiet while the animal lost its fear. Minutes passed.

It darted toward the uncooked hide. Elitha struck lightning quick. "I got it!" The mouse bit her little finger and she cracked its neck.

She raised it by the tail for all to see.

"Hurrah, hurrah," filled the tent.

Ellie, Frances and Georgia scrambled out of bed, begging to hold it. The limp warm thing was passed around. Pa declined, so did Mrs. Wolfinger, but Tamsen took it and passed it on. Then she took the empty pot from the fire and pushed the flap and boards aside, stepping up a few ice steps for snow.

She backed in, the wind flattening the flames. Though she was no bigger than many eleven-year-olds, Tamsen's shadow was huge on the canvas. She set the pot of snow on the fire. Moving out of Ma's way, Elitha jammed a switch down the rodent's throat and then held it over the fire. The smell of burning hair momentarily covered the bad odors, and four sets of tiny toes clenched.

"Cook the parts separate," Ma advised.

The fresh mouse parts didn't need much boiling. Elitha placed the pieces on the melting snow, counting the innards as two of the eight portions. The back would make a portion, and the head, cooked a bit longer to soften the skull. "Pa, you want the liver and the lights?"

"You womenfolk take what you want, give me the rest." Even with fresh meat coming, his voice sounded tired and high. Would he ever be cheery again? His hearty haw haw used to make her think of St. Nicholas.

Mrs. Wolfinger sniffled as Elitha cut through the animal's shoulder. It was horrible about Mr. Wolfinger being murdered, and she an eighteen-year-old lady as elegant as any Elitha had ever seen whimpering at odd times like a child with a toothache. Even the little ones knew better than ask what the matter was, though in normal times that might be polite.

As Elitha watched the meat on the melting slush, she pictured Mrs. Wolfinger as she'd looked last summer strolling on a meadow with her husband, her hand resting on his elbow. Every female in the wagon train admired her ivory brooch. Herr Wolfinger touched his bowler and smiled in a distinguished fashion. Pa had maintained that people shouldn't expect him to cut down trees like a common laborer. And now Mrs. Wolfinger had nothing but the clothes she lay in, and it was more than a pity to see a grand lady thrown utterly on the hospitality of others. It wouldn't do to remind her, but Elitha decided to give her a haunch anyway, which she did so crave for herself, and worried that Mrs. Wolfinger would feel the charity.

"Let's sing," Ellie cried.

"That's a splendid idea," Tamsen said. "But first, you girls turn your heads."

She rustled in her special things and Elitha knew she was fetching her stash of flour.

"You can look now!" Sure enough, Ma sprinkled flour into the pot to thicken the broth. Her alto voice began, "Rock of Ages, cleft for—"

"No, sing 'bout the gravy," piped Ellie.

"Whatever song is that?" Ma asked.

"You know," Ellie said.

"Not unless you sing it."

The three-year-old voice faltered as she tried to hook onto a tune, but she gave up and peevishly whined, "'Bout the rose."

Elitha, watching bubbles form around the mouse parts, couldn't recall such a song.

Georgia suddenly blurted out, "Yes! Let's sing that one!" It had been the longest time since she'd said anything except *I'm hungry*.

Ma was patient as always. "Sing the first part, dear, and then we'll know it."

Georgia sang like a trumpet skipping upward. "Up from the grav-cy arose, with a mighty feeling in his ..." Her voice sagged as she came to the end of her words.

Elitha recognized the hymn. "Yes let's sing that." It had a triumphant feel.

Pa sang the verse in a scratchy voice, and everyone hushed because it sounded like a funeral.

*Low in the grave he lay, Jesus, my Savior*
*Waiting the coming day, Jesus, my Lord.*

Elitha, Ma, and the girls bounced up the happy notes of the chorus.

*Up from the grave he arose!*
*With MIGHT-y triumph o'er his foes*
*He arose the victor of the dark domain*
*And he lives forever with the saints to reign.*

Everyone shouted out the end:

*He aROSE! He aROSE!*
*Hallelujah! Christ arose!*

"Sing it again!" Ellie yelled.

And they did. This time Elitha joined Pa in the somber verse as the others lay in wait for the explosive chorus. At the end, fishing with a spoon for cooked mouse parts, Elitha felt better. Tamsen handed her the plates one by one, and she ladled the thickened broth over each portion.

Accepting her plate, Ellie asked, "Why did Jesus wait so long?"

Leanna popped a tiny morsel into her mouth and said, "He was waitin' for daylight."

"But that's a long time," Ellie said, "to be in the gravy."

Elitha was trying to figure that out when six-year-old Frances corrected in her grown-up voice, "You see, Ellie, he was way down in there aholdin' his breath and people was all sprised when he jumped up, cause he was a rose now."

Tamsen put her arm across Elitha's shoulders, shaking. Elitha had to look at her to see that it was laughter. They were on their knees beside the fire, Ma no heavier than an empty feed sack trembling in the wind. Elitha tried to imagine Jesus the way the little girls did; and though it was a sacrilege, it struck her so funny she caught Tamsen's hysterics. They hugged each other, tears streaming, Pa's hearty guffaw boomed like in old times, and though Mrs. Wolfinger, a German, probably never heard that song before, she giggled to see the others. Even the little girls laughed though they hadn't the first idea what was funny. Just when it seemed everyone would stop, someone would erupt again, and it took quite some time before the usual hush settled over the tent.

Ma removed her lightness from Elitha's shoulders, and in the quiet Elitha felt a swoosh that raised goose bumps down her arms. Something spooky had entered the tent on a wisp of wind. It disturbed the fire and sent an awful thought to her mind.

The family might never rise from this grave.

Shoving that firmly from her mind, she picked a tiny morsel from the outside edge of the heap of gray entrails and placed it on her tongue. This was the way she made food last longer. She didn't want to be finished while others were still eating. Her sisters imitated her, each trying to finish last.

Frances muttered, "Ebbreybody laughed at me."

"Because we love you," Ma said.

"No, silly!" Leanna exclaimed, "Because Jesus was in a GRAVE."

Not about to let that linger, Elitha shot back, "I just know we'll get through to California!"

"Of course we will, dear," Ma said in her teacher voice. "Why, Dutch Charley said people in the forward camp are getting ready to go out on snowshoes. They'll bring help. Mr. Reed will see to it they come for us, and he can be counted on."

"Do they have snowshoes?" Elitha asked. The Donners didn't, and she figured they'd packed just about everything anyone ever thought to take on an overland journey.

"Ward Graves is slicing oxbows and making strips of the harness leather," Tamsen explained, "to weave over the wooden frames."

Elitha let out a breath of air she hadn't known she was holding. "Then help will come." The family had a whole hide left to eat till then, and Pa's arm would get better any day now. In California they'd buy a nice farm from the Spaniards and Ma would start her school. The Murphys would visit. Spring would come, and surely California had apple trees.

# 22

Coyote enjoys the sight of fourteen people testing their clumsy snow-shoes. "They expect to escape from the mountains on those things," he observes wryly.

The death bird does not blink. "It is a hundred miles of deep snow."

Sixty malnourished emigrants also observe the spectacle. Solemn children are surprised to see grown people tumbling in the snow and laughing. Everyone senses the mounting heart of the snow-shoers. *Maybe I should go too* plays on many minds.

Uncle Ward Graves, a resourceful Illinois pioneer nearly sixty years old, lifts a snowshoe high before he plunges it forward into the snow. It was his idea to convert oxbows to snowshoes.

"He looks like my baby sister tryin to walk in Ma's shoes!" somebody says.

"Quitcher cacklin'," Uncle Ward jokes. "Here's how it's done." He high-steps on the pristine snow until one awkward device catches on the other and he pitches forward yelling a waterfall of sound. It echoes off the granite mountain that stands between the hungry camp and California. It flies back over the frozen lake and loses itself in the tall pines. Trying to regain his feet, he flops like a fish in a powder box.

*They will fail*, the spectators think, recalling how a storm raged for eight days and nights while the men worked in their dens cutting hides to ribbons and tying knots. *At least their hands had more to do than feed fires. We who stay here will become too weak to gather firewood and we will die. Unless they make it across.*

Amanda McCutchen will leave her nursing baby and walk through the snow for help. Now she trips and falls. The spectators don't smile as she struggles to regain her feet.

Salvador and Luis will go without snowshoes. The supply of oxbows was limited. They wrap their feet in cloths unneeded by the Americanos. Captain Sutter will hang them if they return without the mules, which were eaten long ago, so if they get to the lower foothills they will sneak away to Salvador's home place—Luis' home in the Delta having been vacant for thirteen long drys.

Coyote says, "The last time they tried to go for help, a blizzard whipped them back to their dens."

"They think it's different now, with the snowshoes," the bird says.

"They're gambling on the weather."

"They won't return this time." The beak snaps shut.

All the excitement of the huge wagon train as it first rumbled onto the prairie is funneled into this one thin stream of hope. *My life won't ebb away in a stinking hole,* the show-shoers tell themselves. *I will fetch help or die with the wind in my teeth.*

After nightfall the death bird lights in camp and Baylis Williams is stiff by morning. All recognize the omen but no one speaks of it. With smoke-reddened eyes, those who will stay in camp bid their farewells to those with blanket packs slung over their backs. Four departing mothers hug their bony children. "Mrs. Murphy will take care of you, precious. Be good, and remember, no matter what happens, you are my children. Don't ever forget me."

Forty-five-year-old Elizabeth Graves will care for her nursing infant, six of her other children, and Amanda McCutcheon's baby. She kisses Ward, her tower of strength, one last time.

Other wives cling to husbands.

"We'll bring help," Bill Eddy promises his Eleanor, knowing her lot is harder here with little Jimmy and the baby. He adjusts his large possibles pouch, which contains ten days' lean rations as well as a bag of bullets and his tinderbox. The best hunter of the Party, he will carry a borrowed rifle over his shoulder, expecting to kill game. His load is heavy but he is strong.

Charlie Stanton, a bachelor without family, leads across the trackless powder toward the summit, followed by the thirteen others, five without snowshoes—Dutch Charley, the two Murphy boys, and the Indians. Even those in snowshoes sink to their ankles, and the death bird hops alongside through the dazzling snow.

Having left their babies with "Ma," sisters Sarah and Harriet step into the tracks of Sarah's husband Bill Foster, Charlie Stanton, Bill Eddy, and Uncle Ward. Harriet is mourning the recent death of her bridegroom in a gun accident. Behind them trudge another set of sisters, Sarah Graves Fosdick and Mary Ann Graves, the beautiful unmarried belle of the wagon train, daughter of Uncle Ward. Joining the sisters is Amanda McCutchen, at twenty-three the oldest woman on the trek.

After a half hour, malnourished muscles ache. They all keep it a secret. Dutch Charley and the two Murphy boys bring up the rear, often breaking through to their thighs. Ahead, the line of emigrants gradually creeps away from them, lengthening as it moves up the steepening incline.

Twelve-year-old Lem Murphy stops to catch his breath and spies the dark figure of the person ahead of him about to disappear. The sun slips behind the cold mountain, erasing the surface features. Night will come and he'll be far behind. The death bird cranes his scrawny neck and pecks him on the shoulder, but the boy throws himself into the trail. The bird hops back to Dutch Charley and Lem's ten-year-old brother, both trembling with cold and weakness. They realize the folly of coming without snowshoes. The blue shadow of the mountain sweeps over them back to the smoke rising from the snow. The bird cocks his head.

The boy and Dutch Charley crave their pine-bough beds back in camp. The poking twigs and needles won't bother them, or the stench, and they'd rather die in bed than on the mountain. Dutch Charley cups his mouth toward the figure up ahead and calls, "Lemuel. Lemuel! Ve go back. You come mit us."

Lem Murphy turns, sees their beckoning arms. "I'm a-goin to Californy!" he yells back. The snow gives way and he sinks to his waist, but scrambles on-ward, not from any strength in his emaciated limbs or thumping heart, but his zeal to live, his vision of food ahead, and his promise to Ma, "I'll be back with help in two, three weeks." She and a crowd of little children are waiting. Besides, it feels so good to just get up and go!

Soon the stars glitter through the snow-shrouded pines, the sole witnesses to his struggle. His legs are dead below the knees, his arms below the elbows. The wind picks up and casts hard snow in his eyes, but he can feel the tamped and frozen trail. Ahead, others will be resting. He just needs more time to cross the same distance, that's all.

At last he sees light and crawls toward it. A fire is burning on a cross of logs and a platform of heavy pine branches. The people sit around the fire holding blankets over their heads. He squeezes in between his sisters, Sarah and Harriet, and adds his blanket to the canopy. Then he fumbles with one hand to untie his possibles pouch with the meat and sugar lumps. People reach over and pat his head, glad to see the youngest made it.

He tells them about the others going back to camp.

No one speaks.

"Wouldja look at that," Lem says, picking up his dead feet and placing them near the fire. "My arms and legs is still a-goin." They jerk and tremble.

People chortle about their cramps and shakes. Uncle Ward is striking his calves, careful not to disturb the blankets.

Charlie Stanton says, "We've already et." He means that Lem should do the same.

Lem pops a sugar lump in his mouth. After that he'll eat a string of ox meat as long as a finger. The rations have been calculated for the estimated ten days to Johnson's place on the Bear River, the first civilized place since St. Joe, Missouri.

Here's some coffee." Charlie Stanton hands Lem a tin cup. "It's a might nippy out."

"Yup. An' we didn't git fur, neither." Not even up to the summit. Cold drills through Lem's coat and blanket. He can't feel the warmth of the fire on his feet, but his wool-gloved hands are beginning to tingle around the hot cup.

"Not more'n about four miles," Stanton agrees.

All know they must travel farther than that each day to get to Johnson's ranch, as Stanton estimates the distance, and Stanton thinks the snow won't be deep down there. Besides, they believe Reed and McCutchen will be bringing up supplies. Amanda expects to meet her husband on the trail. If there is a trail.

The death bird squats to the side and folds his wings, knowing McCutchen's big frame lies abed at Sutter's Fort, malnourished beyond a quick recovery; and Reed got up too soon and tried to lead a rescue party, but the eight-day storm turned him back. The forlorn snow-shoers are the only people in these mountains.

Salvador and Luis know they can't find roots and berries under snow this deep. To them, the silence is loud. Bears and marmots sleep in snow dens. Deer and birds are far away grazing in green valleys. Only people, who imagine themselves to be clever, struggle through the frozen heights.

"What do you think?" Coyote asks. "Will they reach the Bear River?"

The bird says, "Charlie Stanton can't make it and he's the only one who knows the way."

"He's twenty-eight and looks strong, in the prime of human life."

"Wait and see." The death bird snaps.

"Lem," Charlie Stanton says from under the blanket canopy, "when I was acomin up the mountain the other way, I hung a pack saddle in a stunted tree near the summit. Mebee I can make you a pair of snowshoes from it, if I can find it tomorrow."

❧

The next day the emigrants and two Indian boys scale the wind-swept summit and then descend a short distance to find wind shelter and make another platform fire. Out of breath in the thin air, Stanton heads into the gale and locates the saddle. Later, when Lem drags in, Charlie Stanton and Uncle Ward are tying leather strips around the halved saddle frame. Soon Lem has a pair of snowshoes even odder looking than the others.

Nearly weeping for joy, he says, "Aw gee, thanks."

Wind seeks out the party and cuts through clothing as though it isn't there. Nobody sleeps. They roast their backs, then face the fire until their backs are cold, and then they turn around again. Men cut time-toughed branches from the bristle cone pines, taking turns with the hatchet. All night, blankets are retrieved from the wind and rearranged. Several times the smell of burning wool or shoe leather brings the cry, "Som'ems burnin!"

At dawn some of the gaunt people return to the summit to look one last time. In the mountainous cleavage the dawn pushes a streak of pink across the frozen lake.

"Hey look!" One of the Sarahs says, pointing. "It's their smoke!"

The ghostly link with their families spellbinds them.

Salvador nods to Charlie Stanton, meaning that they need to make tracks. Stanton doesn't move. He's waiting for his usual surge of morning strength, but for the first time in his life it fails him. "Well, we'd better git on agoin, at that," he says, slowly pushing to his feet.

The emigrants trudge down the incline toward the frozen unknown. Knees are stiff, feet already numb. Lem brings up the rear in his snowshoes, learning to use them. Their rations will last nine more days.

In midday Charlie Stanton stops and waves the line forward with his hat. His strength is gone. It fueled a thousand-mile walk across the plains, a lightning ride over the mountains to Sutter's Fort, then back with the Indians to the Meadows and up the mountains again, helping the wagons cross the Truckee River twenty-seven times. In starvation camp it kept him going for thirty days almost without food, for he refused to eat unless the Indians had a share. Now his snowshoes weigh too much for his quivering thighs. Breaking trail is hard. Bill Eddy can do it. He's strong. The sun glancing off the snow stabs his eyes, and for hours he's been biting into imaginary hunks of pork, pressing the pulp against the roof of his mouth and savoring the sweet-salt richness of it. He wonders if he's losing his mind.

When Lem catches up, Stanton feels the boy's courage like a snake feels warmth. "I'll be bringin' up the rear," he explains to Lem. "You go on ahead."

"You all right?" Lem peers into the reddened eyes of this grown man no taller than he is.

"Oh, sure. Just fixing to bring up the rear."

The death bird hops behind.

Late that night Stanton drags into camp.

For him, the following day is dark, though the others say the sun glistens on the snow like millions of diamonds. He is proud of getting a good group together, a bunch with grit. He waves the bird off, saying, "I'm takin my time, is all." A luxury now that Eddy leads.

Charlie Stanton wonders why he of all men volunteered to go for help, a thirty-five-year-old with no family to save. Only three months ago he was in the Sacramento Valley eating pork and corn bread. But he hadn't taken the time to flesh up. People needed him and hell, he could outlast anyone. Or so he'd thought.

Coyote stands sidelong, bushy tail low, smiling under the pines. "Thought you'd be the hero of the Party, didn't you?"

Stanton scowls. "Well, if I hadn't'a brung up seven mule loads-a flour and beef, half a-them woulda been dead by now. Bill Eddy, for one." He nods toward the distant line where Eddy leads. "Why, that man and his little family was about famished down there at the Meadows camp at the base of the mountains. People wasn't sharing their food."

Coyote yips, "You gave everyone the same amount when some still had cattle to eat."

Stanton isn't about to argue with an animal. He lifts a shaky leg and sets it forward. God knows, with all the bickering and concealing of food, nobody could have figured it any better. He'd doled to each family according to their number. But why be agitated over that now? What's done is done.

The yellow eyes follow his difficult progress. "It's your fault they didn't make it over the summit. You should have made them leave the Meadows sooner."

"Well hell!" he shouts, bristling at the familiar accusation, "those oxen needed to graze on the grass that was long and green down there!"

"Now the oxen are frozen solid under the snow," Coyote reminds him. "It was wasted."

Stanton almost shouts an oath, but sound carries in the thin air. Antonio, the Mexican teamster, is looking back at him. Stanton lowers his voice. "Sure, I advised 'em to rest a while. It was a gamble. And I lost by a day. We would'a made it if the damned snow had held back for just one more lousy day!" *Sweet Jesus, I need to lie down.*

Coyote trots out of sight, saying over his shoulder, "Losers always think, just one more day, one more shot, one less mile."

With closed eyes Stanton feels his way along the lumpy trail while snow heavy as anvils sticks to the webbing. Once in a while he sits down and knocks it off, heart banging on his ribs. He can't make it to Johnson's ranch, he knows, and more than likely neither can anybody else. But if they hadn't got out of camp, crazed men would be taking food from the mouths of babes.

Towards morning he crawls to the fire. "Bill Eddy," he calls in a raspy voice. "Where are you?" Across the fire the new leader lifts his head and waves. Charlie crawls over to sit beside him. After catching his breath he says, "The Indian boys don't know the way. Their people never come up here in winter, and they've only seen the trail one time. Without snow. You gotta go north to get through to Johnson's, and then go south to Sutter's Fort."

"Is there a landmark where we turn north?" Eddy asks.

"Naw, just go the way the land lies. A giant gap slopes to the northwest. Keep that in mind and follow it."

The next morning the sky is clear, but unlike the others Stanton neither pounds his muscles nor ties on his snow shoes. He sits against a big pine and pulls out his pipe and tobacco. "Lem, wouldja mind?" His voice is muffled like a creek under snow.

Lem finds a live coal and holds the burning twig to the pipe. Stanton sucks and puffs. "Thanks, son." He wishes he could see the boy's face as more than a blur. Wishes he had a son like Lem to live after him. Hell, any child at all. "You're a fine lad," he says.

"Aw shucks."

"No foolin. You got what it takes." He smiles, noticing the calming effect of the smile on his heart. He senses people standing around. "Git going!" He flicks a hand at them. "I'll catch up. Go on, git! See you at the next camp."

The blurs fade and Stanton tells the bird, "Just a little longer now." He puffs on his tobacco, deeply inhaling this last earthly pleasure.

A few minutes later, snow squeaks coming toward him.

"Who's there?"

Salvador squats, places a hand on his shoulder. "Cholie, you come." The Indian knows a few words of English.

"Gracias, but I want to sleep now." He holds his hands together, miming a pillow under his head. "Understand?"

Salvador touches Charlie's inflamed eyelids. "You, I help walk." They have journeyed far together. The others were not generous, but Charlie shared his food with Luis and him. Salvador doesn't want this friend to freeze on the trail.

"No, amigo. I want to stay here and sleep forever."

After a silence, strong hands grip his shoulders and give him a friendly shake, and then release him. Waiting for the sound of receding footsteps, Stanton hears instead a mournful song in an alien tongue. Sustained tones carry across canyons and vast spaces. The song is not of this world.

"Now spirit go happy," Salvador says when he is finished.

"Gracias. Go now. Take my tinderbox, my knife and snowshoes, and get the people to Sutter's Fort."

Salvador accepts the three items, but drops the snowshoes when out of earshot. The cloth wrappings on his freezing feet will not buffer the added pain of the crude-cut leather straps. The tinderbox containing a fire-striker and dry char cloth he slips into a shirt pocket, and then inserts the knife in the rope that keeps his baggy trousers from falling off.

The tenth morning dawns clear and cold. No rations remain in camp. The fourteen people shiver as they eat snow and wonder how much farther it is to Johnson's ranch.

Uncle Ward says, "At least the snow won't stick to the webbing today."

Coyote smiles. "They are hopeful."

The death bird does not blink.

Later, carrying the heavy footgear over their backs along with the blanket packs, the fourteen scale the second high ridge of the day. Twelve pairs of worn leather shoes dig into the snow following the bloody tracks of Salvador and Luis, whose feet have frozen, thawed and split open many times.

"Ifn we can jes git up top to see, we might figger a better way to go," Sarah Foster says.

"I sure never thought as how I could go this far," her sister Harriet replies, nearly falling back into the canyon. Sarah grabs her. This often happens when the blood leaves Harriet's head and black vertigo descends on her. She has not felt entirely well since Sarah's husband accidentally shot and killed her husband back at the Meadows.

"The men must see something," Mary Ann Ward says, pulling herself up to the top.

Tall Mr. Eddy, Sarah's husband Bill Foster, and the two Indians are looking over a long vista. Seeing the promise land? Sarah staggers toward them, buoyed by the hope of seeing green grass and smoke from Sutter's Fort. She arrives, reads dismay on the men's faces, and sees the cause—a world of mountains, wave after wave of white ridges stretching in every direction as far as can be seen.

Anger nips her in all the hungry places. She glares at the Indian guides, their cheekbones cutting sharply to big teeth overstretched with thin lips. "Which way from here?" Hearing no reply, she turns to the Mexican teamster and waits for him to translate.

Salvador and Luis point northward.

"No!" Sarah shouts in a breaking voice. She stabs her stiff fingers toward a small pinkish ball low in the sky, less visible by the minute as the clouds thicken. "That there's west, you redskin idiots! The sun sets in the west. WE'RE S'POSED TO BE GOIN' THAT WAY!"

She falls to her knees, knowing she'd be howling like a baby if she had the strength. "Bill," she says looking up at her husband, "We're out here akilling ourselves 'cause we're headed the wrong way. Do something!"

Coyote enjoys this. The winter sun sets in the southwest, opposite from the northern route, which is farther but easier. "They won't make it," he says.

The death bird's beak is shut.

Bill Eddy closes his eyes against the discord. "We're all tired," he says. "Let's make camp."

Everyone obeys this man with the hatchet and gun, though no game has been seen. Bill Foster takes the honed hatchet and cuts pine limbs while others sit picking for crumbs in the stitching of their blankets and turned-out pockets.

By the time Uncle Ward arrives, a cold wind whips the blankets, and his daughters lift the covers. He crawls in between them, facing the little fire on its rickety platform. Mary Ann touches his face. "We was afeared for you, Pa."

"I said I'd catch up." His voice is high and raspy.

"How far to Sutter's Fort?" somebody asks.

After a long silence Bill Eddy admits, "Sixty, seventy miles."

No one speaks in the presence of this terrible knowledge. Everyone knows they must eat immediately.

"But first we'll come to Johnson's ranch," says Eddy. "Sutter will have food supplies there for us."

"How far is that?" Patrick Dolan asks.

"Doan no, mebee fifty miles."

Clouds darken the dawn, and the people rise with the same hunger that kept them awake during the night. Salvador and Luis point northwest, but everyone else wants to go west. Bill Eddy recalls Charlie Stanton saying the Indians don't know the way. He straps on his snowshoes and starts down the mountain, heading west. The others follow.

With a shrug, Crying Fox–Salvador says to Luis, "Maybe they know a better way." He looks at the gorge into which the people are headed, beyond that another high mountain. "Yes," Luis replies, "they must know a better trail."

They smell the coming snow.

The first flakes fall as fleeting and innocent as an afterthought. Then the people wander in swirling whiteness. At the bottom of the canyon they crawl up the next mountain, their only purpose to keep the dark figure ahead in view, for if the chain breaks those behind will be lost.

Two days later Uncle Ward dies in the blizzard and his son-in-law Jay Fosdick fails to arrive in camp. Sarah Fosdick goes back down the trail to find him. She sits all night at his side, determined to die with her bridegroom on this, their wedding journey. She covers him with her body against wind, snow, and cold. In the morning she hears a gunshot. Jay wakes from his stupor, opens his eyes. "Eddy has shot a deer," he rasps weakly. "Now, if I can get there I will live."

Soon his breathing stops, and by the dull light of morning he freezes solid. Sarah fights her way through the blizzard, ashamed of her need for meat. It takes her all day, and when she drags herself into another early camp, no deer has been shot. It was a rabbit that got away. The flame of hope gutters to near extinction.

Bill Foster raves that he can smell bacon frying. Amanda McCutchen keeps saying she sees her husband coming through the trees, and Pat Dolan, the Irish farmer from Ohio, prays the same mumbling thing over and over. Everyone eats snow.

The next morning they dig out and realize the wind has stopped, but they can't see through the veil of falling snow. The sky is the same gray. No one wants to leave. Lem eats all the nubs of wool off his blanket. Tears warm his face as he recalls his foolish promise to Ma to be back in a couple of weeks with help.

Bill Eddy knows they are lost yet blindly leads, giving heart to the others.

Luis whispers to Salvador in the tongue of the People, "They didn't know a better trail."

Salvador nods in agreement. This morning when he discarded a blackened toe that had fallen off, he noticed Bill Foster eyeing it and giving the two of them a strange look. Since they acquired the knife and fire-striker, the Indians have made their own camp.

Long before dark the eight stop and make a fire. Bill Eddy lies back on the snow. "I'm plum tuckered," he says. "Somebody else get the firewood."

"I will," says Lem, to be a man. The ritual has changed. The leader has weakened. He must step up.

The death bird pecks at Lem's guts. Suddenly dizzy he falls on his side, but then fights to regain his feet. He swings the hatchet into the base of a pine branch, shutting his eyes against a small avalanche. The next branch is tougher, or he is weaker. The young supple pines are all under the deep snow.

He donates two boughs, and then offers the hatchet to the congregants around the place for the fire, the bowed heads resting on knees. Harriet rises and accepts the hatchet. The women are stronger now, taking turns with the men. Lem joins the circle, head down.

Branches are arranged as they are brought in. Bill Eddy, swaying on his feet, delves into the big leather pouch on his belt, throwing away every unneeded thing to lighten his load. For a long time his back is turned, but then he returns and kneels at the hearth with his fire-striker and precious shred of char cloth. Also on her knees, Mary Ann Graves cups her hands around the char-cloth, carefully placed over a loose arrangement of pine needles. Harriet puffs at the spark. One strike does it.

When the branches begin to crackle and snap and everyone inches forward to feel the miracle of warmth, the first spoken words fall gently on their ears. In her ladylike diction Mary Ann Ward says, "I think we should go back to Starving Camp—a name newly coined."

After a respectful pause, Bill Eddy says, "We've come too far. It'd be farther goin' back."

Silently Lem agrees. Others add quiet yups.

"Blessed are they that hunger," Patrick Dolan chants in his Irish accent, "for they shall be filled." His weak voice penetrates through the pops and snaps of the green fire. "We oughta kill one of us for food. Draw lots to see who."

Sarah Foster quickly says, "He's outa his head. I agree with Mary Ann. We should go back to the camp. Somebody will come up for us. Maybe Bill McCutchen." Thoughts of her two infants are pulling hard on her. Her mother wasn't well when she agreed to care for them.

"No, Pat's right," Bill Foster tells his wife. "All we need is a few days' meat and we'll get through. Let's draw lots."

"By thunder," Bill Eddy booms, "If it comes to that, two men should fight it out with knives. The winner lives. Draw lots to see who fights. That's a good deal fairer."

Lem wonders if he'd be counted as a man. He knows he couldn't win a fight against even a weakened man. Glancing at the two Indian boys at their own fire, he wonders if they would be counted as men.

Others oppose a knife fight. Only Eddy is in favor.

"Well then," says the Irishman, "let's keep on agoin' but partake of the flesh of the next man that dies. Likely me."

Everyone agrees with that plan.

Coyote chuckles, and the death bird waits unblinking.

The Mexican teamster leaves the circle to speak to the Indians behind the trees, a long stone's throw away. He tells them about what has been said.

The next morning another storm whirls in, almost obscuring the two Indians, who now lead. Bill Eddy has fallen behind after giving his gun to Bill Foster. The line stumbles forward so intent on keeping the person ahead in sight that they fail to notice their northwest direction. Bringing up the rear, Bill Eddy overtakes the Mexican teamster flailing along on his knees, having thrown away his snowshoes.

"They're tougher than I thought," Coyote remarks.

"It is always so," says the death bird.

Several hours later Antonio, the Mexican teamster, flops down next to the fire and closes his eyes. His hand falls back into the flames.

Lem lurches to pull it out.

Bill Foster stays his arm, explaining, "He's a goner."

The hand shrivels into a black fist. The aroma of cooked meat blows with the smoke, and stomachs growl in blind anticipation. But hunger must wait. Another enemy is upon them. Wind screams in their ears, pounds snow in their eyes, and steals their breath. They drag the Mexican from the circle and hunker down. A calmer feeling settles over the emigrants. Food is again in camp.

Lacking enough strong green wood to support it, the fire melts down inside a widening snow cup, providing welcome shelter from the wind. The emigrants take turns with the hatchet. In succession they climb out, chop a branch, and slide down the snow-cup, placing the branch on the fire, which is suspended above a pool of reflecting water—a miracle of beauty and life.

In her turn, Sarah Foster swings the hatchet but it flies from her numb fingers. She crawls around patting snow, trying to feel where it sank. She gives up and lies down in the snowstorm thinking how easy it would be never to rise.

The death bird hops near.

Her eyes fly open. "Lordy, my babies!" She crawls back to the fire, slides down the bank and tells the others about the hatchet. All stare at her. Bill Eddy crawls up and cuts a tip of a branch with his knife. When he returns with the small limb, the fire flares brightly over the water. Next, Pat Dolan arrives with another limb, but stumbles and falls down the bank.

Snow slides before him, snuffs out the fire. The snow-cup is black.

Above, the wind screams and the crack of frozen trees bending too far sounds like gunfire. Their feet will freeze solid in the pool of slush and water. Bill Eddy rouses the others. They flail and slip as they fight their way out of the dark pit, dragging the unconscious Lem Murphy and Pat Dolan, and the dead Antonio. Out in the wind they kneel down and dig like foxes. Then they huddle under their blankets inside the excavated hole, backs to the outside, the unconscious propped between them. The dead Mexican is within reach. The hollow clacking of teeth seems too loud. Now and then they battle to recover the tail of a flyaway blanket.

"If I live, I'm never complainin' of the heat, never again," Amanda McCutchen says.

"Pat's quit shiverin'," Harriet says. She feels his throat and pronounces him dead.

"No, listen, he's tryin' to talk," Mary Ann puts her ear to Dolan's mouth. Several others lean over to hear.

"Eat of my flesh and ye shall be saved. Eat so's ye can git help for them babes at the lake camp, Eat of my bod—" The rattle of a long breath overwhelms his effort to speak.

They roll Dolan out into the storm.

Later in the night Lem Murphy regains consciousness. He shrieks, "I'm agoin' to Californy." His legs thrash like he's running. Men and women lunge to hold him.

"Gitcher hands off me," Lem yells. "Leggo a-me!" His kicks are violent, his screams piercing. Blankets entangle his legs and whip in the wind. His sisters Harriet and Sarah kneel on his legs, and Bill Eddy grasps his hands while the others try to recover the blankets.

At last Lem becomes still and quiet. Sarah takes her brother in her arms. "He was the best of us," she sobs. In turns, the others kneel over him and hug his light bones, thinking, *We have lost our heart.*

Gently they roll him out.

In the morning, men revive the fire. Women in hooded cloaks bend over the stiff bodies, ripping knives through cloth and frozen flesh. Weeping softly, they lay out small portions. Six people fill their pockets with the meat, avoiding that from kin.

At their own fire Salvador and Luis turn their backs to the abomination. They sing to the spirits of the dead.

Bill Eddy snowshoes to a secluded place where no one can see him and falls in the snow crying for the first time since he was a child. He is appalled to know that he would be joining the man-eaters had he not discovered a sizeable cube of meat from a bear he'd hunted in November in the bottom of his possibles pouch, meat that Eleanor and the boys should be eating at Starving Camp. But she'd hid it in his pouch with a note instructing him not to eat it until his need was extreme. He'd been chewing on it for days and keeping it a secret.

With the end of the singing an unnatural silence settles.

Condor glides silently over the snow-clad mountain. Crying Fox recalls his sister's omen, which he ignored. He sings to the spirit that lives in all things, the one that makes the living cling to life beyond all expectation. Afterwards he touches Luis on the shoulder and waits a moment for him to emerge from his trance. Then he asks, "Do you see your death?"

"When I turn my head a certain way. In the corner of my eye I see the bird jump away."

I do too, but first let's live until we see grass again, and oak trees."

On the stem of a neck, the skeletal face turns toward him and the lips slide across inflamed gums—a smile, and a bargain.

𝕊

Coyote observes, "Skin and stringy meat from the bones of two starved men and a starved boy doesn't last long."

The death bird counts. "Four days, with six people eating. They were chewing the pieces all day long."

"They wasted the marrow. They could have boiled the bones all night if they had brought a pot."

"No one would have carried a pot that size." The bird's beak snaps shut.

Hunger returns to the emigrants, bleak and hard. The five women and four men, most of them under the age of twenty, continue their slow struggle through the unmarked snowfields of the wide mountain gap. Bill Eddy, at thirty, is the old man. Once again he is the leader. Strengthened by the bear meat, now gone, and proven to be the best hunter of the wagon train, he again carries the gun. However no deer tracks have been seen. And he has no faith in finding Johnson's place, but figures a river might flow out of the mountains somewhere ahead, a river where peaceable Indians could live. He ponders the fact that human meat sustained the people long enough that no one else is near death, except the Indian boys who did not eat it. Eddy will attempt to hunt a deer, though his strength is waning fast, and if that fails he must take other action—for the sake of his Eleanor and his two little boys in Starving Camp.

The Indians limp along in the tamped tracks of the emigrants. All of their toes have been left behind. They leave a trail of blood.

"I see a little black-cap bird," Salvador says to Luis, pointing to a pine branch. "What does she eat?"

"Maybe she stores food for snow-time."

"Mm. Maybe she's a spirit bird come to tell us something."

After a silence, Luis stops and points. "I think that's an oak tree."

Salvador discerns a round, translucent shape in the distance, almost hidden by the taller pines. "It is a sign," he says.

"Time to find acorns," Luis adds.

That night the two silently leave their little fire.

In the morning they kneel beneath the oak and dig like coyotes. The snow is not as deep here as it has been, and at ground level they find a few shriveled bits of bird-pecked acorns. They chew these hard black morsels, stomachs bucking at the bitterness and frozen fungus rot. Without pause, they dig for more.

A loud bang.

Luis falls. Salvador turns, looks up the barrel of a smoking gun and sees Bill Foster looking down.

# 23

LATE JANUARY, 1847

*I must go to the home place.* The sudden thought struck María Howchia as she stood at the rain-streaked window of the room she shared with Pedro—a big room above Señor Sheldon's millhouse on the bank of the river. She sensed something bad had happened. Her parents needed her. An Omuchumne runner had gone to the fort and reported back that Crying Fox and Luis had not returned from the mountains with the seven famished people from the Donner Party, to whom they had taken food. The survivors looked like living skeletons. Her parents would soon hear of it and María wanted to be with them.

Pedro was leaning back on the wall behind the bed, playing sad music on his guitar, lulling the baby to sleep. A tree hurtled down the river swift as a galloping horse, riding the big waves. The rain never seemed to stop. The elders in Omuch's place couldn't recall this much rain. Power was unleashed. Snow would be deep in the mountains. In the time of falling leaves, when Pedro brought her to this place, the lower mountains had been white too early.

Another sudden thought. *It is time to become a woman of knowledge.* For everything there was a time. She touched her amulet, which contained oam'shu, her plant spirit-helper. *Thank you, friend.* She must talk to Father about learning from Bear Claw in a neighboring village.

Pedro quit singing, the roar of rain the only sound. Then he said in a near whisper, "María, are you sorry you left Perry McCoon?"

She turned to see his fingers stilled over the strings, bare feet crossed on the bed. His eyes spoke of puzzlement and sorrow. She shook her head no, and then turned to watch another tree ride the waves—roots that had once spread over the earth now standing upright. "For three moons I have enjoyed living with you," she said. "Now I want to visit my people and learn from a doctor. But I am your woman, and I will come back to you."

His fingers strummed a haunted chord that lingered and faded in the room. "Are you worried about your parents?"

"They need me."

A board creaked, Pedro approaching. He massaged her shoulders.

"I thought maybe, since McCoon's new wife died, you would go back to him and his house. You seem unhappy."

The Americana had sickened in the adobe house. Señor Sheldon said that Perrimacoo had taken her to Sutter's place to find a doctor, but a few days later they buried her in the Fort cemetery. Her death confirmed that strong power was in the adobe house, and yet Perrimacoo didn't destroy it like a man of the umne would have. "He is no longer my man," she said. "You are." She turned, looked into his gray eyes in the way of his people, and hoped he understood the strength of that.

His hands continued to knead her shoulders. "He will want you."

She hoped not, but she would never touch that man again. She adored Pedro with the tenderness of a mother and the passion of a woman. This was a constant source of hurt between them. He honored her wish to abstain while the baby nursed, but he often crept quietly from the room in the night. She knew he went to Tomaka's hut, for the kindly woman told her, always with a report of Pedro's love for her. This made her love him more, because he respected her need to wait. Some days she laughed to see how earnestly he encouraged little Billy to eat mashed food. Maybe Bear Claw would teach her how to protect against bad luck while being a full wife.

Boots pounded up the wooden stairs. Pedro's hands left her shoulders. He opened the door and admitted a blast of wind-driven rain that hurled his sombrero from its peg on the wall. Señor Sheldon stood at the door in a flapping, wet cape, yelling to be heard above the storm. "Come to Daylor's place. Bring a shovel. The levee's breaking."

"Come in, Patron. I'll put on my boots."

As Pedro shouldered the door shut, Joaquín Sheldon removed his dripping hat and nodded a greeting to María Howchia. She picked up the awakened baby, sorry Pedro would leave so soon again. Only yesterday he'd added mud to the embankment behind Daylor's house. Soon snow in the mountains would melt and add to the torrent.

In the time it took for Pedro to stamp into his boots and pull his sarape over his head, she determined not to wait for him as she had yesterday. She shrugged into the cradleboard without bothering to change the baby's absorbent fur, and wrapped herself in her rabbitskin blanket.

"Where are you going?" Pedro asked.

"To my parents. I'll go to Señor Daylor's house with you and keep going."

Sheldon swung his wolf-like gaze between the two and said, "It's the Devil's brew out there."

María touched Pedro's shoulder, wishing to impress upon him the permanence of her love.

Leading, Pedro descended the stairs, Sheldon following. The wind stole María's breath as she closed the door on the smell of her man.

Joaquín Sheldon pointed the top of his leather hat into the storm, Pedro threw a shovel over his shoulder, and María followed. He could tell her mind was made up. For some reason he could never say no to her. Already he ached for her.

Cold rain drove through his pants and trickled inside his boots. Overhead, branches whacked together. The wheat field on his left was a choppy sea. On his right the roar of the river drowned out talk. Pedro stepped off the trail and walked between the trees where a mulch of leaves buffered the mud.

In normal winters rain came in bursts, a day or two followed by sun. Now sometimes it rained six, or eight days straight. Señor Sheldon's cattle stood on the hills marking the ancient bluffs of the Cosumnes. But as Pedro lay awake last night he'd had more than the high water on his mind.

It seemed that ever since he'd brought María to his room, he'd been waiting for a stretch of contentment. McCoon's baby seprated them. Maybe McCoon himself. He sighed. If she wanted the Englishman, he couldn't change that, though it would break his heart. If only he could love her as a real husband!

The cursed condor robe, which McCoon had stolen, also interfered. That's why she wanted to become a medicine woman, to fend off bad luck. Ay madre, Indians didn't let go of ideas once they stuck in their minds. Pedro had tried to make her forget the superstitions. On stormy mornings he told her she didn't need to bathe in the raging river. But she insisted. She even dunked the howling baby in it. She refused to eat meat unless the Omuchumne medicine man had sung to it, and she didn't want Pedro to eat it either. Sometimes he had the impression she prayed to every tree and bush. Even he had begun to think of the damned condor costume as a curse. Now she walked into the rain in what appeared to be a state of deep calm.

Pedro rounded the last bend. Daylor's adobe and the Rhoads' covered wagon came into view, water all around. A bulky man slogged through the rain, obviously on his way to the trading room, the temporary quarters of the Rhoads family. Behind the house naked Indians shoveled mud on the augmented riverbank. In a flapping oilcloth coat, Elder Thomas Rhoads worked with them. Bill Daylor shoveled in his shirtsleeves—hatless, pants rolled to his knees. Daylor looked up at them, water streaming from his long face and hair, his shirt wet as second skin. He called instructions to Quapata, and then pointed to his adobe, indicating everyone should go inside.

"I thanks ye both fer coming," Daylor said, following Sheldon, Pedro and María inside.

The chilly room smelled dank and clammy. Daylor's India gestured toward the streams of water falling into the fireplace in explanation for the lack of heat. Ceiling leaks added to the puddles on the mud floor. "I have no cooked food for you," she said in Spanish.

Pedro glanced at María as she stood against the wall holding the baby in his cradleboard. Her eyes were black pools. She was as brave as any man, but felt some supernatural thing coming at her.

Señor Daylor touched two willow chairs indicating the men should sit. "Jared, methinks it's hopeless," he said. "Even if the bloody rain stopped this minute, too much water is washin' down the hills." He nodded eastward. "It's get out or build us an ark, it tis. No point in any more shoveling."

Señor Sheldon turned his wolf stare on Daylor. "Is the young wheat gone?" Señor Rhoads had helped plant it in exchange for a chunk of Sheldon's land.

"Every plant washed away, I'm certain."

A drop of water from the ceiling fell on Sheldon's face and he wiped it away, nodding at Pedro. "We two can move a lot of dirt." He glanced at the shovels they'd left at the door.

"Jared, we're holding back a sea, and not for long. I say we go to McCoon's for a time. Hit's high and dry there, and 'e might bring a demijohn o' brandy from the fort. The Rhoadses should go back to the fort." He shrugged, the gesture of a strong man who'd done all he could.

Sheldon looked over to Pedro, "I can trust Señor Valdez with the stock."

"Sí, Patrón, I will stay with the herd." This meant he wasn't free to go with María while his employers needed him.

Three bangs sounded at the door. Daylor's India threw it open. Wind and rain pressed her black skirt between her legs as she stepped back to allow Señoritas Sarah and Catherine Rhoads to enter, shaking out their kerchiefs. Following them came Señora Rhoads, a tired-looking older woman, and the huge, drenched man Pedro had seen riding up. Lastly, Mormon Elder Rhoads entered, rolling his pantlegs down over powerful, muddy calves. Pedro stood up, as did Sheldon and Daylor.

Bowing toward Señora Rhoads, Pedro said, "I would be honored if you take my seat." Smiling her thanks, she sat and Pedro joined María at the wall. Willowy seventeen-year-old Sarah Rhoads cast a guarded look at Señor Daylor as she seated herself in the chair he'd vacated, and Catherine smiled at Señor Sheldon. A quiet smile tugged his lips. The patrones liked the daughters of the Mormon elder.

Señora Rhoads said, "This is my son, John Rhoads." She touched the stranger's thick arm. "Go ahead, son, tell them."

The young man ran a hand though his dark hair, the wet peaks of which touched the ceiling. His beard hung dark and full. "I just come from Johnson's ranch, been aworkin there," he said in a haunted tone. "Saw a terrible sight." In the pause Pedro recalled Johnson, the disgraceful sailor who had bought Pablo Gutiérrez's 22,000 acres on the River of Bears for a hundred and fifty pesos.

Señorita Catherine turned impatiently on her chair. "Tell how you tied logs together and floated down the rivers." She flashed a warm smile at Señor Sheldon.

John Rhoads said, "My little sister is right. This here valley's a lake from one end t'other. The only way I could get from Johnson's was on water. There's no footing for horses. But I had to come talk to you good men of California."

His manly features twisted with emotion as he shook his head with its thick black hair. "The most pitiful, most famished people you ever seen come down off the mountain. Skeletons is all they was. Couldn't even walk. Injuns come in half acarryin a man named Bill Eddy. Six more was back up at an Indian village, five ladies. We had to carry 'em in."

María's hand tightened on Pedro's arm, and he realized these famished people were the same ones her brother had gone to help rescue.

The big man continued, "They come from the summit, where the rest are camped, and got through only by eatin them that died." He let that hang—Pedro noting the horror in María's eyes—then pointed eastward. "Upward of eighty Americano men, women and children is starvin up there right this minute, bad off or worse'n them that come through. I'm rounding up help, and sure was hopin' you men would join us. Mr. Sutter's headin up the relief. He says to tell you he needs any flour you got left, and horses and mules. But mostly we need strong men to get up those mountains and bring down them that can still walk."

Señor Sheldon scowled and cocked his head. "Who are those people at the summit? Friends of yours?"

Elder Rhoads stepped forward, his dark eyes intense under flyaway white brows. "They're the Reed and Donner Party, part of the wagon train we come across with. They're good people but took some kinda fool cutoff. Got trapped in the early snow." His lips pressed down to make a sad horseshoe.

Pedro glanced at María and saw her inward-looking expression, her eyes not tracking. He knew she was thinking of her brother and the damned condor curse.

Across the room Señor Daylor seemed to be measuring the giant of a man, and Pedro read his thoughts: No sane man would venture into the high Sierra Nevada in this weather. Sheldon looked skeptical too.

"You say John Sutter's headin up the relief?" Sheldon tilted his head eastward. "He going up there with you?"

John Rhoads shook his shaggy head. "No. He's dryin beef and gittin supplies together. Sendin word to Yerba Buena. Part of the United States Navy's anchored there. Askin em to send volunteers, that kinda thing. Maybe you know that Englishman named McCoon he has workin for him. He's sailin supplies up to Johnson's place." Pleased to hear that, Pedro looked down at María, but saw no emotion. "They're puttin a relay team together to take packs of food up to Johnson's place and beyond, several stations."

"How many men have ye to hike up there?" Daylor asked.

"Just me, so far. That's why I'm here. To ask you."

"You're new to California," Daylor said, "and wouldn't know what kinda winter blows up in yon mountains."

John Rhoads regarded him with his deep-set eyes. "We've got winter in Illinois."

Señor Sheldon, standing before the cold fireplace, narrowed an eye. "I don't know what kinda winter they got in Illinois. I'm from Vermont. But I'm tellin you," he looked east, "it's not atall the same up there. My advice is, take a good gander at John Sutter. He's not going up. Hell no. Heada relief or whatever you call him, he knows no horse or mule can git through the snow and men can't pack enough on their backs to feed that many people. Why they'd be lucky to feed themselves, gettin all the way to the summit. It wouldn't accomplish a thing." He shook his head. "More'n likely you so-called rescuers'll starve too. It sounds hard. I don't think Sutter's leveled. This is a real bad winter, and I'd hate to see a man as brave as you lay down his life fer folks foolish enough to git stuck up there."

That was a long speech for Señor Sheldon, and Pedro sensed it was as much for the ears of Señorita Catherine as her brother. These people might not know that Sheldon had survived by stamina and cunning when he was young. A brave and wise man, he disliked foolishness.

Daylor said, "We got goods and cattle that need lookin after." He glanced at his partner. "Jared, you got any flour left?"

Sheldon raised one finger. The decision was made. The partners would donate food and stock to the relief effort, but not sacrifice their lives.

The door flew open. Quapata stepped in with water cutting trails through the mud down his body and legs. "River come now. No can stop." A hint of horror showed in his brown face.

Pedro pulled María out the door. A churning arm of mud half as high as the house was pushing around the corner. The Rhoads family rushed out to their covered wagon. Sheldon and Daylor hurried there too, to help with the oxen and horses.

Pedro and María splashed up the trail into the storm, stopping where they knew the higher bank would hold. He looked into her big black eyes. "I'm going back to the millhouse. I must stay with the cattle now, but I'll come to your ranchería when I can."

She stood tenting her head and shoulders with her rabbit blanket.

He swallowed a lump. "Will you go to McCoon's house?"

She shouted over the lashing rain, "Never! I go to the house of my father."

He warmed at the *never*. "I must fetch my things," he called over the storm and breaching river.

"Things are not important," she called back.

"My horse is important, my helmet, and my guitar. Now go Amapolita. I must hurry. And María, you were right to leave today." Grateful for the understanding in her eyes, he kissed her, tightened the bead under his chin and pointed his black hat toward Daylor's.

The swollen mud arm had advanced beneath surging brown water. Pedro broke into a run. The Rhoads oxen strained in their yokes under a cracking whip, Elder Rhoads on the buckboard yelling, "Haw, haw!" John Rhoads prodded their rumps with a pole, the brown water up to his knees. The wagon wheels moved. The Rhoads family would make it out.

It was a poor time, Pedro reflected as he splashed through rising water, for the men of Rancho Omuchumne to be asked to rescue people in the high mountains. The partners had their own battle with nature, to save all they had worked for.

# 24

Sleet cut into María Howchia's face and legs as she pushed homeward in hopes of arriving before nightfall. A bad vision slammed her—water rushing faster than a man could run, a galloping tree knocking Pedro unconscious, sweeping him downriver. Her feet stopped. *Pedro and Crying Fox could die in the same storm.*

What if it rained forever? Condor could dream that. All living things would drown. This had happened long ago, when the great valley was an ocean. Muffled under the blanket, the baby wailed and she turned from the wind to catch her breath.

She touched oam'shu and calmed herself before facing the wind again. By the time she walked up the first of the home hills, she had confronted her fear of Pedro's death. With that came clarity. If he lived, she would savor each moment. She would encourage the baby to live on food other than milk. In every way she would love her man. She would do everything to help him get the land paper he wanted, the one that allowed him in the eyes of black hats, blue suits, long robes, Americanos, leather shirts and Captain Sutter to live at the home place as Perrimacoo had.

❦

Morning dawned overcast, but not raining. A good sign. Outside the u-macha the earth smelled clean and the grass bent under heavy beads of water. Her breath made clouds and her feet sank into wet loam as she took the baby down the trail to the bathing place.

The raging brown torrent had torn away the earth nearer to the village center than she had ever seen it. Stepping up to her calves, she felt the goodness of the powerful stream and hugged the naked baby to her breast. Since the time of the Ancients her people had lived here. Every hump in the ground was familiar to her, and it warmed her to see blind Grandmother Dishi walking with confidence toward the water and singing to the river-baby spirit. María Howchia watched her bent figure step into the river's edge to bathe.

"Daughter, it is good to have you home."

María turned in the water and smiled at Father. His size was only part of his impressive presence. His eyes crinkled in a loving smile, his face framed by his long wet hair. She splashed to him and hugged his solidness with her free arm while he hugged both her and the baby. Yesterday, to honor the time spent apart, neither she nor her parents had let slip even a hint of recognition. She had crept into the house and lain on her old mat, knowing how a young bird feels when it returns to the nest. Now she was wholly back.

Grizzly Hair patted her head and dove into the torrent, stroking to the center where the two currents met around the island. His black head disappeared for a few moments, and then he swam back through the hurtling water, thick arms pulling to keep from being washed downstream. With a wide grin, he waded ashore and stood in his strength as he gazed toward Father Sun rising from his eastern house—a red glow behind the clouds. Steam rose from his torso and floated upward with his prayer.

Today she must tell him that Perrimacoo stole the Condor robe, and that she had slept in its presence. Secrets stole power. But now he was meditating, so she waded deeper and submerged, holding the baby out of the water. The cold water stung her chest and back, quickening her mind. She thanked the river spirit for purifying her of cloudy, cowardly thought, and then dunked the sputtering baby. He howled and she laughed at him, holding him by one arm as she washed his lower parts. Despite this bit of noise, he had been much calmer of late, ever since she had left Perrimacoo.

Father was still communing with the sun when she returned to the house. Mother emerged. They hugged, Etumu shorter and smaller than Howchia remembered. Her distinctive smell brought back memories of when she had seemed large and had leaned over María to show the proper way to weave a basket. It was good to be home, even with bad news. As Etumu left to bathe, María Howchia's attention was drawn to the mother oak growing in the mound. She had always liked it, growing so straight and branching in perfect symmetry, different from those on the hills, which though older were gnarled and smaller. The corky smell of damp bark drew her to the trunk, and when she touched it, calmness entered her hand. It traveled up her arm and suffused her body. Her breathing slowed. She leaned on the trunk and closed her eyes.

The tree said, *Granddaughter, you are strong. You can walk the path of a medicine woman, as I did.* It was Howchia, Father's Mother! She'd been named Eagle Woman after the black and white eagle that wintered here. No other person had been named for that powerful spirit, but Grandmother had been the singing doctor. She knew magic. It was a great honor that she had spoken to María Howchia, her namesake. Everyone assumed Eagle Woman had gone to the happy land, but here she'd been all the time! A powerful ally. María would cherish Grandmother's secret.

*❦*

Later in the day, ready to speak of the condor robe, María Howchia took a rat to the chaw'se along with a basket of leached acorn meal. Father and Mother joined her, and she could tell they had missed her. While she skinned the rat, Grizzly Hair rolled fibers on his thigh for a new fish net and Etumu, with a lap full of loose black feathers, bent the notched quill tips over a netting of twine and snapped them into place, making a new ceremonial robe for the dance doctor. Etumu asked María about Señor Sheldon's molino.

"It has big heavy stones, round and flat, that turn and rub together. You could grind a basket of acorns this fast." Setting down the rat and obsidian knife she clapped her hands. After a short time she clapped again and picked up the knife and rat. "It grinds seeds to dust that fast."

Grizzly Hair glanced up appreciatively from his fibers.

Mother paused with her feathers. "Who turns the stones?" Beneath the hair across her forehead, her infolded eyelids gave her a crisp, distinctive look.

María considered. "Remember the homeplace of the Omuchumne?"

Etumu's cap bobbed up and down.

"Remember the long tongues of yellow sandstone at the river's edge?"

"Yes of course. The Omuchumne use it for their chaw'se, and their nupah is salted with sand." She put her teeth on edge and made a gritty smile, glancing at Grizzly Hair with a look that said their home place was better.

He smiled in an agreeing way, the love between them visible. It had always been there, but now that María loved Pedro, she saw it more clearly. In no hurry to get to the upsetting subjects, she continued.

"Omuch's men carved channels in the sandstone, one to bring the river to a paddled wheel, the other to take the water back to the river. A wooden gate keeps the water out until it is needed. When the gate is lifted, water rushes in and turns the wheel, which twirls an oak pole jammed into the wheel's center. The top of the pole is fitted with wooden teeth."

Her parents paid close attention as she demonstrated with stiff fingers how the teeth interlocked with wooden cogs embedded in a log, and how that log spindle made another spindle turn, and yet another, each faster than the last. "This happens beneath the millhouse, and the fastest pole pokes up through the floor of the mill and spins the mill stone. Seeds are poured on it and a matching stone is lowered to meet it. Señor Sheldon's stones are very hard. His people have no sand in their meal."

Etumu exhaled audibly. "We need a molino." She looked at Grizzly Hair. "Make one for us."

"First I must see Señor Sheldon's poles and cogs." He added a handful of fiber to the twine on his leg and spun it up and down his thigh.

Considering Father's feelings, María Howchia spoke carefully. "A molino is not easy to make. Cutting channels through our greenstone would be more difficult than through sandstone. And the spinning logs are braced with many poles. It looks like a giant spider web under the millhouse. Señor Sheldon is very clever. He showed the Omuchumne how to make it."

"Many newcomers are clever," Grizzly Hair said. "When the next runner comes from Omuch, I'll let him know we would attend their next big time if we were invited." He acknowledged Etumu's grateful smile, and watched her flying fingers.

Then he glanced at María Howchia and said, "What else have you learned?"

*First the land paper.* She tossed the rat into the acorn meal and pressed hard with the pestle. "The men of Sutter's Fort speak on paper—fiber pounded thin as a leaf. Marks on paper talk for those who are far away. A paper says who can live at a place and who owns the earth." Under her pestle the mash turned dark and bristled with bones.

Grizzly Hair said, "When I was in the mission I saw paper with black and red marks. It told people how to play their musical instruments and what to sing. The *glav-nyi* of the Russian fort also had papers that talked." Thoughtfully he asked, "What is the meaning of owning Earth?"

"It is like owning fishhooks and baskets. The men of Sutter's Fort look to the paper to tell them which man possesses everything on that piece of earth—plants and trees and river and fish and all the animals. The paper tells that man to build a house. That is why Perrimacoo came here."

"And what of people who called it their home place since the time of the Ancients?"

"They cannot ask the newcomer to leave if he has such a paper, even if he is bad."

Father's eyes crinkled with humor. "When the men of a home place wish a stranger to leave, he will leave."

Father had made Perrimacoo stop raising puercos, but that didn't end the power of the land paper. Pedro had explained it. She repeated his words. "A man with such a paper has the right to kill anybody who bothers him. Captain Sutter and his men kill people who do not honor the paper." Cannons on wheels and racks of knife-tipped guns came to her mind.

"We are many," Father said, "and our relatives in the neighboring villages are many. Paper holds no magic for me. Any man who comes here must learn to be our friend."

María Howchia squeezed the mash and felt the prick of a bone sliver, she resumed pounding. "I want Pedro Valdez to live with us. I want him to have the land paper that gives him the right. He is my new man." Ignoring Etumu's look, she explained that Perrimacoo only pretended to have such a paper.

Attaching feathers so rapidly her fingers were a blur, Etumu said, "Pedro Valdez is a black hat."

"Not now," María said, "He is Señor Sheldon's head vaquero." She pounded with vigor. "He is my man now. I want him to be welcomed as one of the umne. I want to have his children."

Grizzly Hair's brows rose. "Have you told Perrimacoo he is no longer your man?"

"Not yet."

"He had a pale wife."

"Yes. She died."

He waited.

"Remember I said Perrimacoo's house was unsafe?"

"I remember."

She took her hand from the pestle, put it on her lap with her other hand, and looked toward the river wishing it could wash her clean of what she must say now. "He stole the condor robe."

Etumu and Grizzly Hair seemed to turn to stone.

"I slept in his house when the robe was there. I didn't know it at the time, but I saw something black and fluffy in the corner, and later I knew it had been the robe."

Etumu jumped up and ran away—feathers scattering, half-finished cape askew on the chaw'se. Saddened, María watched her run past the u-macha, her own mother terrified by her presence. Now on his feet, Grizzly Hair looked at her briefly, his eyes wide with horror but quickly changing to sorrow and sympathy.

She had more bad news. She scooped rat-acorn paste into the cooking basket and wiped the residue on the rim. "Crying Fox is still in the eastern mountains. He did not return with the skinny white people who were rescued."

Father looked toward the mountains and said, "The rains came early, like the snow in the mountains." She could tell he already knew about it.

They glanced at one another, both thinking, she knew, that everything had gone awry due to the Condor robe. Seeing his sympathy, she added, "I have not died."

Perhaps Grizzly Hair would not fear her. Her voice caught in her throat as she finished her bad message. "Molok's robe is in Russia."

He squatted down and put his head in his hands.

She let that settle before changing the subject.

"Father, it is time for me to learn from Bear Claw, but I have nothing to pay him. My spirit helper told me it is time. I believe I can help straighten the scrambled power around us. I was there without purification and have had some good luck in spite of it." This meant she had potential. "But I need someone at the highest level of knowledge to guide me."

She looked toward the river, awaiting his reply. Over many a long dry since he'd become hy-apo of the umne, men had gifted him with valuable skins and tools. She hoped he would trade some of them for her training.

Finally he said, "You are alive. Therefore you did not sleep in the presence of Molok's robe."

Certain that she had done that, she said nothing.

"Strangers saw it," Father said. "They might have stolen the Condor robe."

She tried to think back, but he remembered for her. "Yellow Beard and Pedro Valdez were here at the big time. And the unruly young men of Sek's village."

Dismayed, she said. "Pedro would never steal it."

His expression remained calm, but she knew he didn't trust Pedro. Such trust, she realized, would take time. "And what of Bear Claw?"

"I would be proud to have a medicine woman for a daughter." He laid a hand on her shoulder, displaying his lack of fear. "Go to Bear Claw. He will say what presents to bring." He turned and walked away under the ashen sky.

She watched him speak to Etumu, who had stopped on the hill where a dancehouse of the Ancients had almost completely eroded away. Was he saying the thief might have been Pedro? Or maybe he was saying that since she'd been in their house many times, they were in no more danger now than before. Or that she would become a powerful doctor who could help to protect them.

Sorrow and relief wrestled within her like the two river streams around the island. However, now that she was straight with her parents, she would go to Bear Claw's village tomorrow and begin her journey. It was a terrifying honor that Father and Grandmother Howchia both trusted her ability to become a doctor.

As she rose to take the rat mash to the outdoor hearth of the u-macha, the air around her moved and gooseflesh prickled her arms. She looked up and saw the clouds parted over the eastern mountains, revealing in the afternoon sunlight the huge snow-covered fangs of the mountains—a gleaming and treacherous smile. As a mouse knows its size against an eagle, she knew her smallness against Condor.

# 25

**FEBRUARY 19, 1847**

M en, men are coming!"

Sitting on a stack of tree limbs near the hole above the family tent, Elitha Donner and three of her younger sisters looked around to locate Jean Baptiste, the only other person up on top. It took a moment to register what he'd said, less on account of his accent than the abruptness of that shout in the silent noontime. Elitha shaded her eyes against the glare and saw the young teamster in a pine tree, excitedly pointing his hatchet.

Three-year-old Ellie cocked her head at Elitha, "Did he say men are coming?"

"I'll go see." Elitha stood up and let the black vertigo pass. Hope felt almost painful as she lifted her skirts and plunged into the powdery snow. Too much heart pumping, too much blood jumping through her veins.

Jean Baptiste yelled again, "Three men, with big packs!"

She struggled forward in the powdery snow until she saw the dark figures more clearly, coming single file across the small white meadow, as real as anything. Two of them were enormous. Not the skinny men from the forward camp! Without pause she reversed directions and hop-climbed her way back. Ellie, Georgia and Frances still sat on the branches, staring at her as she passed—large eyes in sharp little faces.

"Those men are gonna take us to California," she told them, out of breath and backing down the ice tunnel.

Halfway down she slipped and bumped to the bottom. Rubbing her smarting hipbone, she laughed at herself and called, "Ma, Pa, relief is coming! The snow-shoers got across."

Ma looked up from where she knelt, washing the purple sausage that was Pa's arm. "We are saved then," she said, sobbing and laughing simultaneously while hurrying to tie on the new bandage. "Help me clean."

The place did look a mess and smelled worse. Elitha began straightening things. Ma stuffed dirty clothing under the blankets and laid a blanket over the chamber pot.

Mrs. Wolfinger stood up from the bed, catching her heavy skirts before they slipped from her hips, hurriedly knotted the ends, and then carefully mounted the icy steps. Leanna was sitting up in bed, blinking.

Elitha kneeled beside Pa. "Did you hear? Help is coming."

He moaned.

"Pa! We're saved! Men are coming. Big men. Tall as Abraham Lincoln and twice as broad!"

"Bout time that odd duck got hisself hitched. Runnin' for gov'nor, I hear."

"Oh Pa, Pa!" It nearly made her weep. His friend from militia days had been married long enough to have two babies, as Pa well knew. He'd personally welcomed Mr. Lincoln and his wife to the farm to address a gathering of neighbors, but he was running for the General Assembly, not the State House and by now would have been elected or defeated. It worried her to see him confused like this, and now these spells were coming so often as to be normal. How could an infected arm cloud the mind? She gentled her tone. "Pa, I said men are coming to rescue us."

He cracked his eyes to slits. "Oh. I'm glad."

He added, "For you."

She caught her breath. "For you too. Don't talk like that!" She threw her arms about him, loving him more than anything.

Wincing, he shrank back.

"Oh Pa! Now I've hurt you, and you smartin' so terrible! I'm so sorry." Feeling like a clumsy ox, she turned toward the stairs, tears welling.

"Elitha lamb."

The old tone. How long since he had called her that? She turned to see his good arm reaching, his brown eyes melting her with a love she felt for him in equal measure. She knelt and clasped his good hand.

"I just wanna say, Elitha, you got the Donner blood. Good stock. Nothing can stop you. No matter what happens, just keep on agoin' down the trail."

She swallowed hard, Donner blood coursing through their clasped hands. She couldn't bear the sound of his giving up. Not the Pa she knew. He helped his dad settle the Kentucky wilderness and carved a farm out of the rank growth. Then he'd done miracles with his homestead in Illinois. Pa was a tower of strength. He kept on moving to virgin land whenever the human race got too thick, packing for California at the age of sixty-two. Neighbors said he was too old for such a journey, but he had an iron constitution. Unlike his brother Jacob, who had perished a month ago in the other tent, seemingly of despair.

"Now gitcher self on up there and see who's come." He gave her a friendly shove.

Leanna, still darkening the tunnel, crawled up the ice stairs like she was ninety. It tried Elitha's patience. By the time she followed Leanna up into the sunlight, three strangers in floppy leather hats and heavy beards stood at the entrance hole smiling at her. Jean Baptiste, short and scrawny beside them, touched one of the giants as though assuring himself they were real. Mrs. Wolfinger wiped away happy tears. Slogging across the snow from Uncle Jacob's tent came Aunt Betsy and cousins Mary and Georgie Donner, and Will Hook, a twelve-year old cousin by a former marriage. Aunt Betsy was looking to heaven and thanking God.

Elitha asked a dark-haired giant, "Are you from Sutter's Fort?" On the tamped snow around the ice stairs his thighs resembled tree trunks. He turned a pair of deep-set brown eyes on her and Elitha recognized him from back on the prairie!

"I'm John Rhoads," he said. "This here's Ole Dan Tucker." He pointed at the other huge man, this one with red hair and a red bushy beard. "That there is Mr. Moutrey."

"You were on the wagon train," Elitha said to Mr. Rhoads. He'd made the remark about the Donners' money. *Come to murder them?* The thought fled before his whiskery smile. She felt kindness in this bear of a man, and could almost see herself in his eyes, a sorry sight despite washing her face in snow each morning. Her frock and cloak were badly creased from being slept in.

Ma emerged from the hole yanking her skirts straight. In the strong sunlight she looked older than her forty-four years, and she was shorter than anyone else except the youngest girls. Her voice had a smile in it. "I'm Tamsen Donner. Are you men from heaven?"

The man with the red beard chuckled and doffed his hat. "Reasin P. Tucker, ma'am. And I'm glad to say I haven't seen heaven yet."

Timidly Georgia said, squinting at Mr. Rhoads but pointing at the red-haired man, "You said he was Old Dan Tucker. Is he the man in the song?"

The ruddy giant laughed full out, then said, "That's not my real name."

"Well, land sakes!" Ma said, "Never have visitors been more welcome." Her smile compacted her wrinkles like an accordion. "We'd be pleased if you'd come in and rest. You must be tired."

"In a minute," John Rhoads said, swinging the pack off his back. Unlacing it, he reached inside, brought out a biscuit, and placed it in Elitha's hand.

Amazed, she curled her fingers around its floury bigness, felt its hard substance, and ran her thumb along browned edges that had touched grease. Tears sprang to her eyes. Saliva shot under her tongue and her stomach knotted. She was about to break the biscuit into parts when she saw biscuits being handed to everyone else.

Will Hook and Jean Baptiste stuffed their biscuits whole in their mouths, and chewed hugely. Mrs. Wolfinger sniffed hers. Little Ellie pressed hers lovingly against her cheek. "Can we eat it?" she asked, cocking her head at Mr. Rhoads.

"Little girl, if you don't eat that blamed biscuit that I carried all this way, I think *I* will cry. Now you wouldn't want to see a grown man do that, wouldja?"

"No SIR!" Ellie pinched a nub from the bottom edge, tongued it like a frog, and grinned close-mouthed at Elitha.

Elitha put the browned edge of her biscuit between her teeth and sucked in the feathery aroma of flour. Then she bit off a nub and chewed. It stung the raw roof of her mouth, but she loved the taste of lard, baking soda, and a hint of salt, none of which she'd had since early October.

"Well, eat the goddam things!" Mr. Moutrey demanded, and then lifted his hat to Ma and Aunt Betsy. "Begging you pardon, ladies. Been a while since I seen white women."

# 26

I am the daughter of George Donner.

Elitha repeated it over and over as she put one foot before the other, careful to avoid slips on the downhill trail. Tamsen, who'd decided to stay with Pa and the three little girls, had prepared for the overland journey by packing larger sizes of shoes and clothing for all five daughters, in case no such merchandise existed in California. Elitha had argued that her feet stopped growing and she didn't need bigger shoes, but Tamsen nonetheless bought a pair of high-tops a full size too large. That turned out to be fortunate. Although the new shoes did feel clumsy and slick on the ice, they were sturdy and had room for two pairs of woolen stockings. Another stroke of luck was the weather. The route was visible. The rescuers had tramped up the mountains on trackless snow and since then no new snow had fallen to hide the trail.

From the Donner tents the rescuers had taken Elitha, Leanna and Mrs. Wolfinger, and from Aunt Betsy's tent they took nine-year-old George, Elitha's full cousin, and also Will Hook from Aunt Betsy's first marriage, a lively boy Leanna's age. The rescuers deemed those five to be the most able and willing to walk over the mountains. At eighteen, Doris Wolfinger was the oldest. That first night, the three rescuers led them six or seven miles to the forward camp where four more rescuers had been assessing the fitness of about sixty famished people. Elitha and Leanna slept in a slapped-together cabin with the big Murphy family and other people. The next morning the seven rescuers prodded everyone to hurry and say their good-byes. They feared a change in the weather. The previous night, when questioned about the snowshoe party, they had lightly mentioned blizzards and difficulty finding the way, but added that all had survived and were recovering at Sutter's Fort. They themselves, on the way up, had been lost for over a week, each carrying sixty pounds of food, but once on the correct course they notched the trees and kept an eye out for landmarks. Elitha trusted these strong young men to lead them to safety.

Mrs. Wolfinger and three other young women walked single file behind John Rhoads and his brother Dan. Elitha, Leanna, and Mary Murphy followed the women. Behind them came Virginia Reed and her mother, and then six single men and women and seventeen children. Five rescuers brought up the rear and helped the children. Around thirty people, Elitha figured. She kept trying to add up the exact number, but always confounded herself. The rescuers claimed there were seventeen children, but where was the dividing line between adults and children? Oh, and not to forget two-year-old Naomi Pike on John Rhoads' back.

Three days out, and Elitha couldn't for the life of her imagine Fort Sutter, where she and Leanna were to wait for the rest of the family. Nicer than the forts on the prairie, people said, Spanish in appearance. The rescuers said the next relief party, led by Mr. Reed, would be on its way up by now, to lead more of the stranded party to safety. At any time Elitha expected to meet them on the trail. She would remind them about her parents and half sisters six or seven miles down the trail from the lake. She kept a vigilant eye for Mr. Reed and his companions, but the dark things in the distance always turned out to be pine trees with some of the snow blown off the branches.

"Smile often," Tamsen had instructed. "Nobody likes a sourpuss. And tell people you are the daughter of George Donner." Tamsen was rightly proud of the Donner name and their nice house and well-kept place in Illinois. In California, Elitha planned to behave in a manner that spoke well of her people. She would help Tamsen establish an English-speaking school.

Now, however, the snowy mountains seemed endless. Every once in a while, Mary Murphy, walking just behind, whined that her feet hurt. Water had seeped through the cracks of her worn shoes. Leanna fell behind to walk with Will Hook and her younger cousins. Elitha turned to see them snaking through the trees. The four rescuers who'd waited at the forward camp now walked among the children, urging them to keep moving. At first all seven rescuers insisted that everyone must be able to walk; however John Rhoads made an exception for little Naomi Pike, whose eighteen-year-old mother Harriet had been in the snowshoe group. According to Mary Murphy, Harriet's sister, he'd taken pity because Harriet had lost her husband in a gun accident and wouldn't be able to abide the death of her baby in addition. *So much misfortune in the Murphy family!*

*I am the daughter of George Donner.* Tired, lightheaded, and suffering soreness around her gums and the roof of her mouth, Elitha longed to lie down in the snow. But they must find a food cache first, one of several cowhide bags stowed in the trees, safe from wolves and bears. Today, the rescuers said, they would find the first cache, and a good thing too. Shivering this morning, Elitha had lined up for rations. The rescuers handed out the usual jerky the size of a thumb and a teaspoon of flour to each person. They did that every morning and evening, but today they handed out the last of the supplies. Mr. Tucker scraped the last flour from his pack, while the little ones all around cried, "Me! Me! Me!"

"Don't worry, we'll find the cache today," John Rhoads repeated. Like a big strong St. Nicholas, he swung the blanket pack containing Naomi Pike onto his back. Elitha wondered if anyone else noticed he hadn't taken his morning rations.

Tamsen had been right. Lying in bed saved your strength, but now everyone walked all day, every day. Despite her new hightops and woolen stockings, she felt a sensation of tiny knives stabbing up her feet and legs. Her stomach churned and the pain seemed to twist her inside out. A cold sun inched across the sky, and still no cache. Never had she longed for anything as much as rounding a bend to see John Rhoads and his brother Dan removing a fat leather bag from a tree limb.

Behind, Mary Murphy released a long sigh and said, "I betcha Lem and Sarah and Harriet is down at Mr. Sutter's right now alickin' up pot roast with potatoes and gravy."

*Gravy again.* Shutting her mind to the image, Elitha said, "Lemuel was brave to go out with the snowshoers."

"What?"

She looked back. "I said, Lemuel is brave." It felt good to turn away from the sun's glare. Looking forward again, she saw John Rhoads also turn his head forward, but not soon enough to prevent her from seeing a peculiar expression on his face. He and his brother struggled as the tamped trail softened in the midday sun and their heavy bodies broke through. She felt sorry for them but glad to be moving at a reduced pace.

From behind, Mary's high voice penetrated. "I heared Lem got frostbit re-al bad."

"Well," Elitha said, "I guess we'll all be frostbit." She hadn't the strength to talk, but kept her eyes on John Rhoads' back, like a massive silhouette of a Biblical prophet breasting into the blinding light. It wasn't long before the brilliance disappeared behind a mountaintop and the snow turned bluish. The footing hardened. The cold would be bad again tonight. She could smell it settling on the pines. But if Lem Murphy could get through, in blizzards, so could she in this good weather! That gave her hope.

The trail went over and down a hill, and there stood Dan and John Rhoads staring at a tree.

Joy pushed Elitha faster. "They found it!" she called over her shoulder.

Happy sounds tinkled back down the line. Two more rescuers bounded up past her, stopping at the tree to stare with the Rhoads brothers.

Arriving, Elitha saw shreds of something dark on the snow. Uncomprehending, she looked up, but nothing unusual hung in the tree.

Dan Rhoads said, "Maybe a bear."

John Rhoads squatted, fingered a scrap and scowled. "Some'm with big teeth."

Mr. Tucker added bitterly, "Et every bit."

There was no food!

Mary and Leanna stood beside Elitha while the gaunt children arrived.

Naomi Pike wiggled out of the green blanket, which John Rhoads had put down on the snow. Mary picked up her two-year-old niece and carried her back to where Elitha slumped to her knees in the snow.

Little Naomi's voice was weak and scratchy. "Muk, muk." *Milk.*

As John Rhoads looked around him at the whimpering children, Elitha saw despair on his face. What would they do? Everyone was spent, but they must have food.

Mrs. Wolfinger pressed her palms together like a sad nun. Elitha followed her gaze to a small coral cloud above the mountain, the only color in the landscape. She appeared to be praying to it while the tall pines stood vigil in their white robes.

No food at all. The hard knowledge settled on Elitha and she recalled Pa saying, "Whatever happens, just keep on goin' down the trail." He must have known the crossing would be worse than she'd figured. Foolishly she'd thought the presence of rescuers meant an end to trouble. But they were men, not miracle workers.

Big John said to the other men, "Look yonder. There's the dead snag we used on the way up. Get out the hatchets. We'll make camp here."

Elitha sat with her head on her upright knees, listening to the grinding monster that was her stomach. She closed her eyes and silently prayed. "Please, God, if you let me get through, I will always be a good Christian." Never had she felt so weak. *How long did people live without food?*

Mary Murphy lay back on the snow with little Naomi Pike prone on her belly, the bony little face turned to the side. She didn't cry but made odd noises. Virginia Reed sat down next to her mother, Margaret, both of them obviously miserable. Virginia removed a tiny doll from her coat pocket and held it to her cheek. That seemed to calm her a bit. "My husband will be coming up the mountain any time now, with supplies," Mrs. Reed said to no one in particular.

Philippine Keseberg wept softly as she sat with little three-year-old Ada in her arms. Doris Wolfinger, though five years younger than Philippine, put an arm around her friend and spoke comforting things in German—Elitha recognized most of the words from growing up with her grandparents, Oma and Opa Donner. Meanwhile over a dozen children cried bitterly, "I wanna biscuit. Biscuit and milk! I'm HUNgry! Gimme some supper!" So much distress! And no help for it.

Elitha clapped her mittens over her ears, but could not block the wailing. It was simply too much. She couldn't give any of them what they cried for, but then she realized Leanna needed comfort too. She put an arm around her hundred-percent sister. "We'll get through, you'll see." She snuggled up to Leanna as the men built the fire. "Remember what Pa says. You can always go farther than you think you can."

Hearing that, Leanna seemed a little less wilted, and they watched the rescuers make a cross for the fire platform and pile on green pine limbs. Very soon the rescuers, the girls and young women, the men and boys trying to be men, and all the bawling, whimpering little ones sat around a popping fire that didn't warm their feet. Elitha's new shoes had become soaked, her feet numb, but she never took her shoes off for fear she'd have trouble putting them back on—chilblains, a pitfall the rescuers warned about.

John Rhoads stood up and spoke in a voice that sounded like God.

"Children, everyone, listen. In the morning four men will go ahead to the next cache. They can move a sight faster'n you can. They'll be back with food in a day or so. But you gotta keep walking so's they won't have so far to come. Understand? The farther you walk, the sooner you eat."

"Will you go with them?" Elitha asked.

To her relief, he shook his head no.

"I'm HUNgry!" a child whined, and the others joined the loud and futile chorus.

Mrs. Wolfinger leaned over and said in Elitha's ear, "Giffs a schtorm coming."

Elitha looked to where a twist of coral had been in the sky. Gray clouds now covered it. She buried her face in the hammock of her cloak between her knees and tucked her cold hands underneath. She was spent, hungrier than ever before, and she ached beyond sleepiness from so much walking. *Please God, no storm.*

❧

"What the god-damned hell!"

Elitha's eyes flew open to a pale gray sky, a rescuer pointing to the empty frame of a snowshoe dangling on a mutilated pine limb.

"You low down, rotten vermin!" the man yelled, glaring at all the people around the frozen soot where the fire had been. Elitha and everyone else looked around but saw no sign of guilt on any face.

"Which a you bastards et my snowshoe!" Red eyes glared in his hairy face.

John Rhoads placed a hand on his arm. "Hush, man. You'll get along with one shoe."

The man threw off John's hand. "I'd like as hell t' see YOU walk with one snowshoe!"

"Here, use mine." Rhoads took down his snowshoes and handed one of them to the man.

Obviously surprised, the man accepted it. "Thanks, but the thief's gotta be punished."

"That's your hunger talking," Rhoads said. "You've had three weeks of low vittels, and it makes you peevish. Some of these people'ov starved for months." His tone said, *That's enough.*

No more was said. Everyone headed down the trail thinking, Elitha assumed, about the next cache. John Rhoads, with a child over his back and only one snowshoe, had gone toward the back of the line, prodding the little ones into motion when they stopped or lay down to rest. Old Dan Tucker now led the party.

The snow stung Elitha's inflamed mouth before numbing it. She noticed more clouds in the sky and realized that this was the longest break from blizzards since that first storm stopped the wagon train in October. To the beat of another silent mantra, she helped Leanna walk over the humps of snow on the trail, *Please God, no storm.*

The younger children walked on the smooth crust outside the recessed trail. Elitha tried it. The crust held! Leanna joined her and so did Mrs. Wolfinger, Mrs. Keseberg, and Mrs. Reed, all as light as wraiths. The crust held until early afternoon, when the women stepped back into the lumpy trail. However the younger children continued to walk on the crust of snow. Behind, big John Rhoads broke through, floundering to his thigh every other step, the boot without a snowshoe, but he continued to coax the children, "Keep going! That's a good boy." Once, Elitha heard him say, "You'll get an extra lump of sugar when we get there if you walk up that rise ahead."

Every so often three-year-old Ada Keseberg grabbed her mother's knee with one arm and lifted the other, whimpering, *"Gehe mit Mutti, Mutti. Gehe mit."* She wanted to be carried. Elitha would carry Ada for a spell, but soon she had to set her down. "Ada, *du kanst ja laufen,*" she would say. You can walk. She'd imitate John Rhoads. "That's right, keep putting one foot ahead of the other. You can do it." She knew that Philippine Keseberg, a tiny woman, needed every ounce of her strength to keep herself upright and had none left to carry the child. Elitha was tall and strong like her natural mother's people, the Kickapoo, and physically mature for her age; but even she couldn't carry Ada for long. She noticed, however, that helping the rescuers do their work took her mind off her own pains and fatigue.

Ahead, the line bunched. For a moment she thought the forward rescuers had returned with food, but they'd only lit out this morning. When she caught up to the crowd she saw a man curled in the snow like a baby in bed. It took a while before John Rhoads arrived with his bundle over his shoulder.

"Mr. Denton, get up!" he ordered, pulling the frail man's arm. It only dragged the man in the snow.

Mr. Denton's dull eyes pleaded from his withered face, and his voice was faint. "I'm too tuckered out, John. Please, leave me be."

Mr. Rhoads and Mr. Tucker exchanged looks. Then Mr. Tucker's red beard ticked back and forth. "John, it's no use. He can't go on."

Ada curled up next to Mr. Denton. Several more children lay down beside him. Leanna flopped down, explaining to Elitha, "I can't go on either. I'll just rest here a little while with Mr. Denton."

That started an avalanche of children lying down.

John Rhoads used his God voice, causing Elitha to jump in her skin. "You kids git up this minute, hear? Every one of you. On your feet! OR I'LL TAN YOUR HIDES!" He looked huge and ferocious scowling that way, with legs braced and black eyes flashing.

Trembling, Leanna slowly pushed to her knees and Elitha helped her stand. The children whined as they staggered to their feet, crossing their hands over their bottoms and saying, "Don't whup me, Mr. Rhoads." All except little Ada Keseberg, who lay there as still as a rag doll.

"Git yerselves on up that trail," John pointed. "What would your folks say? To think you got no more gumption than this old man!" Elitha knew that "old man" was half as old as Pa.

The children trudged down the trail with slumped shoulders and pitiful cries, but Ada Keseberg didn't move. Mr. Rhoads swung down his green blanket, spread it and placed Ada next to Naomi Pike. Two inchworms. He slung them both over his back.

Mrs. Keseberg folded her hands as if in prayer. "Oh, *danke, danke. Danke sehr.*"

Elitha recalled the rescuers' decision before leaving the lake camp, "No child who must be carried can come." Mrs. Keseberg had offered them twenty-five dollars and a gold watch to carry Ada, but the rescuers stood firm; they needed all their strength, they said, or they too would founder and no one would make it through. It was then that John Rhoads had patted Naomi Pike's head and said, "'Cept for this one. I'll carry her. I never saw a girl so pitiful as her ma down at Johnson's place, a-crying for her baby."

Mr. Moutrey had tried to change John's mind. "Man, yer gun weighs twelve pounds!"

Rhoads drew his bushy black brows together and nothing more was said. Elitha realized he had a soft heart, though he was very strong in other ways.

"He's mean," Leanna muttered, looking over at John Rhoads while throwing an arm over Elitha's shoulders, using her as a crutch.

"Mr. Rhoads is keeping us alive," Elitha corrected. "He did it to save you. Why, Mr. Denton couldn't even gather firewood. You and all those children would'ov froze to death."

The snow was softer now, and the three rescuers sank with each step, even in the tamped trail. The monster gnawed Elitha's insides. Snow stuck to her shoes and had to be constantly knocked off. She too sank to her calves every so often. Nevertheless she supported Leanna and tried to give heart to the tired children. That helped keep her mind off her stomach and her smarting feet.

When another early camp was called, Mr. Tucker offered his snowshoe strings to be roasted, and Elitha gratefully accepted a piece of leather string. It was very tough, not having been boiled for hours like the hides back at the family tent, but it gave her mouth something to work on and a number of swallows of something like meat.

# 27

I'm afeared we ain't gonna make it," Mary Murphy said at dawn the next morning. Getting up beside Elitha, she looked like an old woman with her kerchief tied beneath her chin and her big blue eyes terribly exposed.

"Course we will." Elitha rolled onto her hands and knees, and stood up with her skirts crackling. Her backside felt petrified with the cold.

"Those four men who went ahead?" Mary said, "I'm thinkin they mayn't come back atall. What if they done et everything and gone on?" Her face wrinkled up to cry. Two days had passed since the supplies gave out and the men left.

Elitha noticed Virginia Reed listening, and knew she couldn't let Mary's supposing spread. "They'll be back. You'll see," she said.

"Besides that, we'll meet my husband," Mrs. Reed added, patting Virginia's head. "Your father will be coming up with supplies and other men."

John Rhoads was rolling the inchworms in the green blanket, and Elitha realized he'd heard what she and Mrs. Reed had said. The pain in his eyes reminded her of Pa when he saw Elitha and Leanna leaving.

"You just watch," Elitha said loud enough for everyone to hear, "Those men'll show up in a few hours. Come on! The faster we go, the sooner we meet them." She stuffed a handful of snow in her mouth and waited for it to numb the raw places, put her arm around Leanna, and walked down the trail. Mary Murphy and her younger brother Will walked behind.

Elitha recalled a time last summer when she and Mary Murphy had first become friends. They scrambled up an incline and sat on a flat boulder with their legs stretched out before them. Looking over their scuffed shoes they saw the stalled wagon train below and the men chopping and sawing the trees down so the wagons could pass through. Many of the women and girls were sitting in groups mending clothing, while Mr. and Mrs. Wolfinger strolled along the already cleared road like a royal couple, her hand on his well-clad elbow. How sweet the summer air had been! A warm sunny day with bunches of lupine and shooting stars all abloom.

"You have a big family," Elitha had said. "How many of you are there?"

"Just seven," Mary said. "Three girls, four boys. All of us is two years apart, except Sarah and Harriet. They're one year apart."

"I thought there were more."

"Mebbe you was thinking of Sarah's kids. They're like Ma's own, always around her."

"I guess that's it."

"And your father?" He was nowhere to be seen, and Elitha hoped the question wasn't too pushy.

"He died. Ma and us girls is earnin' our fare washin' clothes for the Mormons."

"What Mormons?"

"Most of us in this here wagon train is Mormons," Mary said quietly. "Now you keep that under yer hat, or Ma'll whup me go-o-od." Mary had a way of making a syllable last two or three beats.

Elitha crossed her heart. "Are you Mormon?" She glanced at Mary's head, but saw no horns poking through the wavy dark hair.

"Alla us Murphys is." She gave Elitha a sidelong grin, the cute upturn of her nose fascinatingly near her lips.

Shocked, but recognizing opportunity, Elitha continued, "You got on holy underwear?"

Mary hiked her skirt well above her buttoned shoes. Saggy gray long-johns covered her legs.

"Is that holy underwear?"

"Yup."

Elitha hadn't imagined that anything that plain would ever be called holy. "Don't you ever take them off?"

"Not never, 'less I got a leg in my clean pair at the same time." Mary flounced her skirt back over her shoes and gazed at the scene below—the bridge of her nose so low that, viewed from the side, both of her slightly bulging blue eyes could be seen at the same time. That too was fascinating and Elitha considered her to be very pretty.

"How do you take a bath?" she asked.

"One leg at a ti-ime." Slyly, the corners of Mary's lips turned up.

"Aren't you allowed to get them wet?"

"Not sposed to."

Elitha tried to imagine bathing while standing up with one leg in a tub. Below, a small breeze billowed the sleeves of Mrs. Wolfinger's creamy silk blouse and a pause in the thud of axes allowed the babble of the little brook in the meadow to be briefly heard. Elitha took a breath and punched straight into the worst of it.

"People say Mormons are cannibals."

"Folks prattle that way to make people hate us." Mary pressed her lips together like it irked her to hear that whopper again.

"You mean Mormons don't eat human flesh?"

"Course not!"

"People say Mormon men have hundreds of wives."

"I never hearda tha-a-at many."

Elitha knew she was on to something. "Would you marry a man if he already had a wife?"

Mary shook her head in denial and yet somehow conveyed the glimmer of a maybe.

"Well, isn't that what Mormon men do?"

"If they've a mi-ind, but ain't nobody can make a lady marry a man if she don't wa-a-na."

"Well, what if he married you first, then married someone else, two more? What could you do about it?"

"Nu-u-thin I guess." The pout of her lips warned Elitha she'd gone far enough.

After a pause, Elitha said, "I got a secret."

Mary's face lit up. "Cross my heart I won't te-ell." She slashed the air over her chest.

"Hope to die?"

"Burn in Hades."

"I think Lem's a looker." Maybe it wasn't enough to balance Mary's secret, but it was all she had.

Mary stared at her. "You mean my brother Lemuel?"

Elitha glanced behind them to be sure Leanna hadn't followed. "Yes, Lem."

"Well he's just a ki-i-d!"

That pricked Elitha's feelings a little. Tucking a flyaway strand of hair behind her ear she said, "Well, sisters don't see a boy the way other girls do." At twelve, Lem seemed older than Mary, who at fourteen was the same age as Elitha.

Mary scooted closer and patted her arm. "I didn't mean nuthin, honest. Lem's a good boy. Ma says he's worked like a man ever since Pa died. Landrum too."

"I'll say! Just look at them down there." Laboriously the men were axing through a forest, Lem and Landrum swinging in steady rhythm.

"I guess he's a looker," Mary allowed.

Now it was cold, and Elitha and Mary walked cautiously down the icy trail, angling across another snowy mountainside. A skitter of clouds dulled the sun. Elitha looked over her shoulder to see John Rhoads toiling behind. Now there was a real man.

Later Rhoads swung his bundle to the snow and called down the straggling line, "Make camp!" It was early, but even he had to be exhausted. No one had eaten a crumb for three days—four days for him. And everyone knew it took a lot more food to keep a big man going than ordinary people.

Mr. Tucker waved his snowshoes. "Come and get it!" Leather strings again.

John Rhoads unrolled his blanket and little Naomi Pike sat up blinking.

Mrs. Keseberg went over to the blanket and stared. John squatted down to look. They touched and prodded. A scream from Philippine Keseberg pierced the quiet of the mountains and stabbed Elitha in the heart. John snatched Ada and whisked her away as fast as he could plunge through the powdery snow. He went behind a copse of the trees, with Philippine Keseberg wailing as she plunged and struggled behind him. When they reappeared later, his arms were empty and Mrs. Keseberg shrieked at the sky, *"Du lieber Gott, nimm mich auch!"* Dear God, take me too!

Appalled now at how near to death poor little Ada had been when she made her walk, Elitha wilted down and held her face in her hands, tears wetting her mittens. Mrs. Keseberg stood hugging herself with crossed arms, rocking forward and back and wailing. She had also lost a baby at the camp, and now, Elitha imagined, she bore the guilt of insisting Ada come on this risky trek when Mr. Keseberg, who stayed in camp, could have cared for her.

Doris Wolfinger went to Philippine and held the tiny woman in her arms.

"Ma and I was feelin' sorry for that Keseberg lady," Mary Murphy whispered to Elitha between wails, "way back on the prairie… the way her husband beats her."

Elitha reconsidered. There were all kinds of people on this wagon train. Mr. Keseberg could have been a cruel caretaker of Ada, and maybe Mrs. Keseberg knew what she was doing bringing the little girl with her, risky as it was.

That night no one spoke, and no one ate. The howls of Mrs. Keseberg and the cries and whimpers of many children continued. Across the fire, John Rhoads hunched over his knees like he couldn't face anybody. Who would die next? Elitha worried that it might be Leanna, who'd never been strong and now looked sallow and more poorly than ever.

Elitha said a silent prayer, *"Please God, bring the men back with food,"* and fell into a stupor-like sleep.

The next day dawned cold and clear. Mr. Tucker said it was February 26, and he wrote a few sentences in his journal. It seemed a miracle to Elitha that her feet kept moving, frozen as they felt. All day she helped Leanna walk. At noon the rescuers roasted all the leather strings from their showshoes and divided them among the people. Roasting made the strings somewhat brittle and easier to eat.

Georgie, Elitha's nine-year-old cousin, limped slowly up the trail and over to where Elitha and Leanna sat, wiping tears off his chafed face with his coat sleeve. He shuffled on the sides of his feet as though avoiding broken glass in his shoes. He begged Elitha to allow him to take his shoes off for just a little while, but she insisted he mind the rescuers and keep them on.

"But they hurt so baaaad," he said with a twisted face." Among the younger Donner sisters and cousins, Elitha had always played the part of an assistant mother.

"Your mother would tell you the same thing," Elitha said. "My feet hurt the blazes too, but we've got to keep on going, and not think about our feet. You heard what the men said, your feet are swollen and the shoes won't go back on. You wouldn't want to walk barefoot, would you? On this ice and snow?

Sadly, he turned his head from side to side.

"You know," Elitha said with a smile and a point, "I bet the rescuers with the food bag are over that ridge over there, and we'll see them coming when we get to the top. Then in a twinkling of an eye we'll have some real dinner."

Georgie looked toward the ridge for some time and then something in his wrinkled-up face changed from hopelessness to maybe he could walk a little more and try to get that far. The slow shuffle resumed with everyone chewing leather strings and the chorus of whimpers and sobs from the children.

It seemed a miracle that after reaching the top of the ridge in mid-afternoon, Elitha won her bet. Two men came through the trees and fell back on the snow, moaning in pleasure to be off their feet. Mr.Coffeemeyer had a leather bag on his back.

Everyone circled around, and Mr. Tucker went behind Mr. Coffeemeyer to loosen the leather ties on the bag. Mr. Coffeemeyer was explaining why the other two rescuers were missing.

"Dan and Aquilla was so famished they thought it best they not eat the vittles meant for them." He made a gesture towards the women and children. "So they lit out to the Fort."

"How far didja have to go?" Mr. Tucker asked, still working on the strings.

"All the way down to Bear Valley. We been takin' turns carrying that."

John Rhoads' brows drew together. "You mean you didn't find the cache at the head of the Yuba River?"

"Eaten clean out by varmints," Mr. Coffeemeyer said. "My guess is, squirrels gnaw the ropes and the bigger varmints get to it on the ground. And John, the Second Relief wasn't at Bear Valley when we was there. They should'a been there by then." Mrs. Reed emitted a sound like an injured animal and grabbed Virginia. They sat down with their foreheads together like they were praying.

John shrugged like nothing was wrong. "You probably left before they got there. Come on people, it's dinner time." He bent over reaching into the bag, bypassing the biscuits on top, and brought up two handfuls of jerked beef. He addressed Mr. Tucker, who was older, "How much do you think for each?"

"I'd say half a biscuit and a piece of meat as big as your thumb. John, get some of this into you first, then dispense the beef. I'll do the biscuits."

Two lines formed.

"Good thing it's hi-is thumb," Mary said into Elitha's ear, both of them early in line and accepting their rations.

Cousin Will Hook took his rations and sneaked a hand into the bag, but Old Man Tucker whirled and cuffed his arm before he could pull out another biscuit. "Don't you know?" he said loud enough for all to hear, "When you've been famished your stomach shrinks. You eat too much it bloats and pops open. That'd kill you. You gotta be careful. There's plenty here. We'll stop every couple hours and have some more."

Will Hook stuck a pouty lip out and gave Mr. Tucker an evil look. Elitha was ashamed of his bad manners, even if he wasn't a genuine Donner.

"Ned," John Rhoads said looking at Mr. Coffeemeyer after all were fed, "I don't know how you got so far in three days. But you sure done a good thing."

Mr. Coffeemeyer continued to rest on the snow. "It was a hellava trek, but I wouldn't'ov traded places with you three, left with the likes of them." He cocked an eye at the children. Elitha sensed something final and bright in his tone of voice, and it seemed to signal the end of trouble. Back on the trail she became more certain of that when she heard more about what lay ahead.

Mr. Coffeemeyer was praising Mr. Sutter to Mr. Moutrey, saying the Captain was donating all the beeves, flour and sugar to feed the hungry people, and he was organizing groups of men to set up way-stations to cook food for those who were coming down. These stations were a day's walk apart, the last one a day from Johnson's ranch. "He's gittin' more men to go back to the summit too. Looks like there'll be a third and fourth relief...." He then said something so whispery that Elitha, who was directly behind him, couldn't catch, except for the word "needed."

The other rescuer who'd gone for the food bag wasn't much of a talker, but he added, "And he's sending mules up to the springs so the emigrants can ride the rest of the way." *Riding! Off of their hurting feet!*

Two days later, despite the bagged provisions being gone, hope continued to swell in Elitha. She put an arm around Leanna so they could help each other walk. Smiling at Mary Murphy just behind, who was helping her younger brother, she said. "We're gonna get through!" This time she believed it.

Then Elitha allowed her mind to drift unchecked in the direction of food for the first time since about November. She envisioned a large dinner plate of schnitzel with Grandma Donner's gravy. Sharing the gravy stood a pile of mashed potatoes with butter pooled in a crater and overflowing down the sides, and creamed snap beans with a crust of buttered crumbs folded in with chunks of pork that fell apart in the mouth. She saw herself forking through everything with abandon, and then digging into a deep apple strudel awash in sweetened clotted cream.

Before noon the next day fifteen men of the Second Relief rounded a bend, led by Mr. Reed. Mrs. Reed fell into a dead faint when she saw her husband. She hadn't seen him since he'd been exiled from the wagon train last summer. Soon she revived and the three Reeds stood hugging each other, all in tears. It was the first time Elitha had seen a grown man weep. But he had no time to waste. Learning that his children Patty and Tommy were still at the summit because the rescuers had deemed them too weak to walk, he was anxious to go save them. Elitha wedged in a few words about Ma and Pa and her three youngest sisters, but Mr. Reed made no promise to go the extra miles. He handed out nubbins of sugar cakes, saving his food cache to fuel his men up the mountains and to feed those they would rescue. Oh, how sweet that tiny piece of cake was, though it stung Elitha's raw mouth something fierce.

The following day the rescuers led the people to the source of those cakes—a small camp, the highest of three set up along the trail for the emigrants. Bread and cakes emitted mouth-watering aromas as they baked in heavy iron kettles over fires tended by two rough-looking men. The men dispensed warm bread and hot tea with sugar, along with a normal sized piece of cake. Everyone was in good spirits, but soon Will Hook, Will

Murphy, and a younger boy were rolling in pain, having gorged themselves. The rescuers forced them to drink tobacco juice that they and the mountain men spat into a cup. The boys vomited, and started to recover. However, because it was only noon and very cold, the rescuers decided not to waste a clear day, so they led the way down the icy trail while the three sick boys remained in the camp with the mountain men, awaiting Mr. Reed's Second Relief. Two days later, everyone heard from Will Murphy, Mary's ten-year-old brother, what happened to Will Hook.

It was in the evening when Will Murphy limped into the Bear Valley camp after dark. He had asked for his sister, and then arrived in the women's tent where two candles provided light. Mary Murphy, Elitha, Leanna, and Virginia Reed were about to blow out the candles and sleep on crude mattresses when they saw that Will was barefoot. Mary put a candle near his feet and it was an awful sight to see: black toes and purple, cracked, bleeding feet. His worn-out shoes hung around his neck, tied together by the laces.

"Will, your shoes!" Mary exclaimed. "And you was supposed to stay at that other camp."

Will looked too exhausted to reply. "Lemme lie down," he said, falling back on one of the beds. By now all the women and girls had gathered, except for those who were already asleep. Around each of his feet they wrapped blankets that had been provided by the men in the camp. They covered him up to the neck to stop his shivering. Somebody went out for hot tea with sugar.

"Cousins," Will said to Elitha and Leanna in a tired voice, "Will Hook is dead. I found him."

Stunned, Elitha said, "When we left he was getting better."

"It was last night. We was s'posed to be sleepin' in the tent with those men, but I woke up in the middle of the night and Will wasn't in bed. The man told me to leave him be and go back to sleep, but I went out and found him. He was on his elbows and knees in the snow—hard squeaky snow. Awful cold. The moon gave light, and I told him to come ins—"

"How come he was on his knees and elbows?" Leanna asked.

"Mebbe atryin to relieve his achin' belly. 'Cause you see, he'd gorged himself again. He was allus stealin more cake. Anyhow, I poked him and told him to come inside. I poked him again 'cause he didn't answer. He fell over on his side. Frozen stiff." Will's face scrunched up like he was about to cry. Will Hook and he had become close friends on the trek.

Horror crept along Elitha's scalp to think of Will like that.

"I couldn't sleep any more," Will Murphy continued, "so when it got light I lit out to catch up with you. I didn't like that man."

"But you took your shoes off!" Mary accused in a big-sisterly tone.

"My feet hurt somp'in bad, Sister. I took 'em off just after you left. Thought I could put 'em back on after warmin' 'em up. That there man said I'd have to stay there and die if I took them off, or walk in bare feet. So I walked in bare feet."

"Oh my poor little brother," Mary said, suddenly hugging him through the blankets.

Leanna, who all her life had played with cousin Will Hook, said, "Maybe he froze to death, and just happened to be on his knees and elbows"

"I think he gorged," Will replied. "His pockets were bulged out with wadded bread and cake. His stomach musta hurt bad."

Poor Will Hook, killed himself with food! And poor Aunt Betsy. Elitha knew she'd probably be the one to tell her dear aunt the awful news. If Auntie lived long enough to be rescued.

The melting snow had sharp lacy edges. With the regular infusion of food, Elitha's spirits lightened, when she wasn't thinking about poor Will Hook and worrying about everyone still in the mountain camps, if they were still there. With her feet and lower legs more painful every day, she looked forward to riding on a mule as much as she had looked forward to seeing Mr. Coffeemeyer with the food bag. The rescuers said they'd reach the springs today, where the mules were supposed to be waiting.

Now, as the party walked down the slopes, oak trees spread horizontal branches among the monotonously vertical pines. In a sunny place she spied a dark patch in the snow, went to it, and realized it was bare ground—wet dirt, a remembered friend, with a tatting of melting ice. In the center she saw a green fur of grass spears, like baby hair. She kneeled and laid her cheek against the cold ground and thought she heard the whir of life.

People gathered. Children stared. Rescuers smiled.

Elitha, Mary and Leanna hooked arms and the three limped along in the widening trail on throbbing feet, sometimes yelling in pain and chuckling about the yelling. Though Elitha kept thinking about Will Hook and wondering if his spirit saw her, she couldn't help the bubbling joy of knowing for sure that she would live. They passed larger and larger brown spots in the white, until the snow appeared as bedraggled and tired as they all felt.

The cries of the little ones had changed from "I'm hungry!" to "My FEET hurt!" But soon it would be over. They had broken out of the mountains. They had survived the deepest snow and the worst winter the rescuers said anyone could remember. Not even a storm could spoil it now.

Later in the day she unbuttoned her cloak and felt fresh air creep through her linsey-woolsey dress, through her petticoat, all the way down to her skin. Air was no longer an enemy. Once again she could feel spring ready to burst forth. Every hour that they walked downhill, more grass appeared, and she could hardly wait to see the first farm at the foot of the mountains—Johnson's ranch, Mrs. Reed called it. Last summer Mr. Reed had actually ridden out to visit with Mr. Hastings, who'd been in a forward wagon train. He'd learned that farms were called ranches or ranchos in California. She pictured whitewashed fences, a fine house, red barns and fashionable buggies.

"Look!" Mary pointed excitedly to a herd of mules and horses nibbling grass as if it were the most natural thing in the world. Elitha recalled poor Buttercup and all the other gaunt cows and oxen that had frozen and now lay beneath the snow, and how Jean Baptiste couldn't find them even with his metal-tipped probe. How those animals would have loved to see this grass!

Tents came into view, and men tending fires—Mule Springs this way-station was being called. She smelled sourdough bread in the dutch ovens on tripods. She let out a squeal and hugged Leanna and Mary. More men came into view, young and old, standing and staring awkwardly as if not knowing what to do with their hands.

Soon she was sitting on bare ground with Leanna, Mary, and Virginia Reed, embarrassed about being gawked at by the men. A man in buckskins staggered over to John Rhoads with a cup, but he refused it. More spirits were flowing from an oaken barrel. Some of the men collected around Mrs. Wolfinger and Mrs. Keseberg, who had stopped crying.

*Little Ada buried in snow. Cousin Will Hook buried in the snow. Mr. Denten on the snow. Wolves and bears would eat them all.*

"Will you marry me?" said a voice behind her.

Elitha turned to see a pug-nosed young man, apparently serious. "Me?"

"Uh-huh. You is the be-oootifulest sight I ever seed!" His face was a comical pout.

She suppressed a flabbergasted hoot. She hadn't combed her hair for over two weeks and knew she had soot and dirt on her face from the fires, like the other girls.

"What's your name?" he asked.

"Elitha Donner. I'm the daughter of George Donner."

"Will ya marry me, Eliza?"

"I said Eli-*THA*."

"Oh, sorry ma'am. I thought you was a lisper."

She turned to see if Mary heard that, but Mary had her own admirer, a drunken older man. Another man was sweet-talking twelve-year-old Virginia Reed, who lay in an exhausted heap. Propped up on an elbow, John Rhoads was watching. Elitha looked at the freckled face and said, "No. I won't marry you." Other men were looking at her too.

Later, to pass water in private, she spoke to John Rhoads and he made sure men didn't follow her. During the evening a cold wind swept down the mountain, and again she snuggled between Mary, Leanna, and Doris Wolfinger in a tent with other girls and women. Even there she awoke to push men's hands away and say, "Please stop waking me up."

In the morning the freckled boy removed his hat apologetically. "We don't hardly got no white girls in Californy," he said. "A looker like you won't last."

"What do you mean won't last?"

"You'll git married."

Glad when it was time to mount her mule, which she was sharing with Leanna, Elitha was relieved to see all these men would stay here and keep camp for Mr. Reed's Second Relief.

"We don't have enough gear," John Rhoads announced to the riders. "Half of you git saddles, the other half git bridles. The critters'll foller each other." He had the bearing of a leader.

Elitha reined her mule over to Mary Murphy. "I wouldn't mind marrying HIM."

"Well, he-e-e-'s already married."

Even though it was a joke and she had no intention of marrying any man until she was at least fifteen, Elitha felt a tiny twinge of disappointment. Then it dawned on her. "Is he Mormon?"

Mary pushed out a long, uphill "Uh-hu-u-uh."

"Well then, you never know who he'll marry, do you?"

Mary grinned back.

When all were mounted, John Rhoads waved them into a bunch and backed his horse so he was looking at the whole skinny, ragged crowd of riders, little children paired up with older people. He swallowed and said, "You're a brave bunch. Alla you. You done more'n I woulda thought."

He seemed to be studying his saddle horn. Everyone kept still, even the mules. When he brought up his shaggy head, moisture glistened in his eyes. "I'm tellin' yer folks what good kids you are." He kicked his mule to the front of the line and led out of camp.

Mary looked over from her mule, lips pressed in a knowing smile. "Last I heard, you was likin' Le-e-m."

Elitha nodded at John Rhoads. "Oh, I'm joshing about him." She was just relieved to be, at last, entering the fabled land called California.

# 28

## Johnson's Ranch

Rested after a night in a covered wagon, Elitha shrugged out of her cloak in the morning sun. She and Virginia Reed were watching John Rhoads stuff strips of smoked beef into cowhide bags, and she had the oddest feeling that if she didn't restrain her hand, it would reach over of its own accord and touch the man who had brought her to safety.

"Are you coming with us to Sutter's Fort, Mr. Rhoads?" Virginia asked.

"No, I'm headed back up yonder." He jerked his head toward the mountains. "No way your pa and his men could'ov brought down all those people by themselves. We're getting a Third Relief ready, with some new men that Mr. Sutter found."

Elitha felt greatly relieved that this tireless giant was going back up with plenty of help. In the Donner tents were Aunt Betsy and her younger children Solomon, Issac, Sammy, and Lewis. Add to that Tamsen, the three little half-sisters and Pa on a litter, and no telling how many more people from Starving Camp. By now, Mr. Reed and his men would be on their way down with some of those people, but which ones?

She glanced beyond John Rhoads to the velvet green hills upon which grew the black-limbed oak trees, each of then circled by wispy green fairy halos. If only, by some magic, her family could see this! California cattle grazed on the grass—cows with brown and white spots, slim hips, and horns long enough to skewer a horse. Swirls of yellow flowers streaked through the low places. Flowers! When only a few days back up the mountains, old man winter was blowing his icy breath on snow ten to twenty feet deep. The real California was more beautiful than she'd dared hope.

The visible trail from the mountains wound down through the hills into this flat land beside the Bear River, to the famous Johnson's ranch—two sad little cabins of mud brick, called adobe in California. No fences, no barn, no garden, no orchard, no buggy. Only an outdoor fire pit and drying racks hung with animal pelts. But a multitude of birds sang and whistled, cotton-tail rabbits scampered about, and ducks in the ponds and river quacked. She had gone from Christmas to Easter in two weeks.

John Rhoads looped a strap under the leather bag, his back muscles shifting beneath his red flannel shirt as he pulled and tied the strap. The smell of coffee floated across the yard, and she heard the faint sound of women's voices coming from one of the adobes. She turned to look. The scene wasn't pretty. Tumbled boxes and broken barrels littered the pocked and rutted mud of the yard. Naked Indian men strolled around as calm as you please, as did bare-breasted squaws with babies in cradleboards. A gang of naked brown children, a few with skin that looked a little white, darted between the covered wagons. She counted eight children, all laughing and babbling in an unknown language. One little boy wore trousers and a shirt. A group of leather-clad mountain men leaned against the nearer of the cabins, smoking, drinking, and telling crude jokes. They didn't lower their voices even though Elitha and Virginia were a stone's throw away. This rancho sure wasn't anything like Pa's farm.

But it was spring and she was in California, only about two days from Fort Sutter. She almost felt ashamed to feel this good while her parents and sisters suffered in the mountains. Whether left in camp or walking on the icy trail and sitting up all night, they would be suffering. Yet energy entered her pores with the sun, and her scalp tingled, it felt so clean. She had borrowed soap and a comb from Elizabeth Keyser, a sister of John Rhoads, and washed her hair in the cold river. She felt good underneath too, because a woman at Sutter's Fort had sent a package of fresh underwear for all the rescued girls and women. "Top 'o the mornin, John." A hand came down on Elitha's shoulder, and she turned to see the same Englishman who had brought supplies from Sutter's Fort on a small sailing vessel. She'd seen him asking the trappers for help unloading, and heard him joke with them. His accent fascinated her. This was the first clean-shaven man she'd seen for a long time. His hand remained on her shoulder while John Rhoads offered a howdy and the two agreed the weather was nice.

The smell of liquor wafted with the Englishman's breath. He was handsome, his straight nose right out of the pages of Tamsen's art book, the part about Greek sculpture. He wore no hat, his hair pulled back and tied with a length of brown ribbon. His blue eyes had the longest black lashes she'd ever seen on a man. They nearly lay on his tanned cheeks when he grinned at her—fringed eyes. And there was a dimple in his cheek.

He handed her an apple with a blush of orange streaks. "It's from Sutter's farm," he said, white teeth showing between shapely lips, one tooth missing.

The apple felt good in her hands and saliva shot under her tongue at the smell of it, even though she knew it would sting the sores in her mouth. She couldn't help but smile back into his eyes. Yes, they had apple trees in California, and very few white women by all accounts. What was he seeing? A tall, young brunette in a dirty wrinkled dress. Some people called her comely. At least she'd scrubbed her face this morning with soap.

"Well, eat the bleedin thing!" he ordered, his eyes crinkling irresistibly. He handed another apple to Virginia Reed and beamed at Elitha. "Me nime's Perry McCoon."

She curtsied. "I'm Elitha Donner, daughter of George Donner. I'll eat this later if you don't mind."

He smiled, his dark brows straight as sticks over those amazing blue eyes. "Expected ye'd be starved enough to eat me," he said, bringing back a puzzling joke the mountain men had giggled at, something about man-eating women being the only survivors. Now, sitting along the wall of one of the adobe cabins, these same men guffawed and slapped their thighs at what Mr. McCoon had told her. She didn't understand it, but felt embarrassed anyway.

A scream. "Elitha! Elitha!"

She turned to see Mary Murphy coming fast from the door of the other adobe, her expression distressed, her arms out. She hit Elitha running.

She steadied herself and hugged back. "Mary, whatever's the matter?"

A keening wail.

She patted Mary's back, mystified. Watching this were the mountain men, John Rhoads, the naked Indians, Perry McCoon and all the little children, white and Indian, now being joined by the skinny children from the mountains who would wait here at Johnson's for their parents to be rescued. Elitha said into Mary's ear, "Let's get off by ourselves."

She guided with an arm about Mary's waist.

Crying like her heart would break, Mary laid her head on Elitha's shoulder. They found a secluded place near the rampaging river, amid willows, budding cottonwoods and oaks.

"Oh, Elitha, Elitha," Mary sobbed. "Lem's de-ad!" Her shoulders jerked with weeping.

That galled Elitha. "No, Mary," she said sternly. "John Rhoads said all of the snowshoe party got through, and he's straight-arrow."

"They said they a-a-te him!"

Elitha's skin crawled, and now she was riled up good. "Mary, who told that horrid lie?"

Mary pushed her fingers up into her hair and rocked up and back crying, "Oh Lem, Lem!"

Some crazy mountain man must have spread that story for fun. "Who, Mary? Who said that disgusting thing?"

"Harriet," Mary sobbed.

*No. Not Harriet.* Mary's older sister had gone out with Lem in the snowshoe party. She would know. But then again, maybe Harriet had lost her mind. John Rhoads carried little Naomi all the way down the mountains and laid her in Harriet's arms, and he'd done it because, Mary had explained, "he'd never seen a girl as pitiful as that child's mother a-cryin' for her baby." Maybe a lost mind made her pitiful and she was still tetched even with her baby back in her arms.

"I think she's out'ov her head," Elitha said quietly. "Give it a little time and she'll be herself." As she patted Mary's back, the desolation returned to her—the food cache gone, the hard edge life cut when it needed to survive. At times it had seemed that Philippine Keseberg lost her mind. But the snowshoe party had endured much worse. As she tried to imagine that, she had trouble breathing and began to feel lightheaded.

Mary bawled like a little girl, inserting between sobs, "Well ifn she's crazy … then where IS Lem, and Uncle Ward? … And Sarah's husband Jay …." The rest dissolved into tears as she lowered her face into her hands, shoulders convulsing. The noisy river added to the uneasiness Elitha felt in her stomach.

Mary lifted her head, almost yelling, "Them others didn't even stop her from sa-a-yin it! She went back to bawling.

*Ate him.* Young faces peeped through the leafless willows, curious children, some of them orphans until their mothers arrived from the mountains, if ever they arrived. "I'll find out the truth," Elitha said. "I'll bet Lem and the others went on to Sutter's Fort."

Leaving Mary, she grabbed the hand of the nearest child and ordered the others to follow. They walked obediently with her as they had done on the long march. "Sit here," she said pointing to a grassy spot where Leanna lay sprawled in the sun with her eyes shut. "Now you all leave Mary in peace. Hear? Talk to Leanna if you must talk."

She pushed passed the cowhide into a low-ceilinged room that smelled of mold, earth, and coffee. Two deeply recessed windows let in light, and as her eyes adjusted she made out Mrs. Wolfinger, Mrs. Keseberg, Mrs. Reed, a young woman Elitha didn't know, Elizabeth Keyser, the bride of Mr. John-son's ranch partner, and Harriet Pike holding her Naomi—all staring at her. Elitha felt like a child trespassing in a room full of grown ladies where the air was thick with secrets. A blackened pot and dented tin cups littered the crude table, which all but filled the room. The only other furniture was a narrow bed, a humpback chest beneath one tiny window, and a stack of crates. "I've come to learn the truth about Lem Murphy," she said.

They all looked down or away, except Elizabeth Keyser, John Rhoads' sister, who had married Mr. Johnson's partner only weeks ago though she couldn't be much older than Elitha. "Take my chair," she said standing up. "You got no flesh on you." The lady of the house, she pulled up a crate for herself.

Elitha sat in a slatted chair that teetered on uneven legs or uneven floor, she couldn't tell. Sudden light washed into the room and she looked up to see Perry McCoon lifting the cowhide. She ignored him, saying to the women, "Lem isn't my kin so you don't have to save my feelings. I just want to know if he made it through." Nerves made her squeeze the apple in her pocket.

Elizabeth Keyser poured coffee and shoved a dented cup at her.

Harriet Pike, with closed eyes, let out a ghost of a moan as she rocked the bony child on the uneven chair. Her red, cracked hand looked huge on the tiny girl's pale shawl, and the others left it to Harriet to speak.

Elitha prodded, "Mr. Rhoads said all you people on snowshoes got through."

After a silence Harriet said in a detached way, "Bill Eddy made it t'here. The rest of us was fetched from an Indian village a ways up the river."

So they did make it. "Where's Lemuel?"

Suddenly a male voice roared through the doorway, "Well tar my scup-pers if it ain't Perry McCoon! Caughtcha in the henhouse, y'ole rooster!" His coarse laughter snarled as he pounded on Mr. McCoon's back.

The Englishman looked pleased.

Elizabeth Keyser quietly said, "Mr. Johnson, we women was atalkin."

Johnson dashed to her like a wild animal and grabbed her off the crate, the cups sliding and spilling from the disrupted table, and pulled her to him. "Kiss kiss fer yer man's pardner." His red lips jutted from the matted beard and she wrenched her head away just in time for his lips to press her cheek instead of her mouth. Elitha caught the sour eggs whiff of him.

Suddenly locking eyes with her, or rather one eye, the wild man with the big black beard set Elizabeth down and slowly put words together. "My my. Wouldja look at what's come down the mountain!" A black brow hiked up, the eye underneath it sweeping up and down Elitha and then Mrs. Wolfinger while the other eye looked at the wall. "No wonder yore at my door, McCoon!"

With tears shining in her eyes, Elizabeth rearranged the cups.

Mrs. Wolfinger, still regal despite her wrinkled blouse and wasted appearance, straightened her back and said, "Herr Johnson? *Nicht so?*"

"Last time I heared." The eye kept looking back at Elitha and she felt undressed by it. For a long time she had envisioned Mr. Johnson as a gentleman farmer. Instead, this was about the ugliest and rudest man she'd ever met.

In a trembling voice Elizabeth said, "Excuse me, I didn't introduce you. Mr. Johnson, this here's Mrs. Wolfinger, Mrs. Keseberg, Mrs. Reed, and Elitha Donner. They come in last night. You know Harriet and Matilda."

The German ladies bobbed their heads and said something about "*freude,*" which Elitha recalled meant glad, as in glad to meet you.

By turns, Johnson hawed and snorted like a hog, his form of laughter. "My pardner Sebastian Keyser allus said the Germans'd take over this here country." Looking around the table he roared, "Ifn he coulda kept his trousers buttoned, he mighta snatched hisself a genu-ine German female to breed with. Haw haw haw."

Elizabeth Rhoads Keyser, who apparently had been snatched instead, quietly repeated, "Mr. Johnson, we was talking." Her tears were gone and steel rang in her tone.

*How can she stand it?* She had to love Mr. Keyser a great deal to live with him here on land they apparently shared with the horrid Mr. Johnson.

Perry McCoon winked at Elitha and steered Johnson out of the room, saying to him, "I got a good story for ye." Quiet settled over the room and dust danced along the sunbeam angling over the chest from the window.

Mrs. Wolfinger said, "Elitha Donner iss a strong maiden. You can say it all to her."

Elitha braced herself.

Elizabeth Keyser inhaled with closed eyes, and then looked at Elitha. "Seven come through. The poorest bags of bones you ever saw. Bill Eddy got here first, poor man. He came and knocked on the door and I shut it right in his face afore I knew what I was about. It was like lookin at something not even human. Two naked Indians was holding him up on his feet."

*Seven.* "How many went out on snowshoes?"

"Fifteen, wasn't it, Harriet? Not counting the Indians? Or was that counting them?"

Harriet shrugged. "Here dumplin," she said, "take s'more milk." Her red-dened hand shook as it held a cup to the lips of the frightfully thin three-year-old.

*Half of them perished.*

"Elita, vhat dey not schpeak," said Mrs. Wolfinger, "iss dot the dead, the living haff eaten. Dot has needed been. Understand?" She sucked back her chin in an aristocratic manner as if everyone must accept the terrible reality that showed in her face.

"Lemuel?"

Not one woman at the table met Elitha's eyes, and the quiet one named Matilda held her face in her hands.

Harriet rocked little Naomi, her voice soft. "Sarah and I didn't touch Lem. We partook of others, not kin. Some of 'em asked to be used for food."

By the faces around her, Elitha believed she was hearing the truth, and her insides kept jiggling. "And Sarah?" The eldest of the Murphy sisters, the one married to Bill Foster.

Elizabeth Keyser answered. "All five women of the snowshoe party survived. Sarah went to Yerba Buena with Mr. Foster. Said she never want-ed to hear about the troubles of getting to California ever again. Not one word of it."

Light washed over the table, Perry McCoon entering. He touched Elitha's elbow. "Too much doom 'n gloom in here," he said. "Come and I'll show you me bonny schooner."

She stood up, pain knifing up her feet and legs. She felt unreal, and knew this moment would turn in her mind for the rest of her life. Then she remem-bered the apple. She asked Elizabeth, "Would you happen to have a knife?"

The woman of the house looked thunderstruck. "Whatever for?"

"To cut this apple." She took it from her pocket.

Mr. McCoon pulled a horn-hafted skinning knife from his belt and handed it to her.

Thanking him, she laid the apple on the table and cut it into eighths, a white juicy sunburst with apple fragrance. Pocketing the seeds—someday she would plant them—she handed back the knife, and told him she needed to talk to somebody. Reassembling the apple, she hurried across the yard.

Men had caught the horses and mules and were saddling them for the ride to Sutter's Fort. John Rhoads was still there.

"You didn't tell us the truth, Mr. Rhoads," Elitha said when no one else could hear.

"Now if I'd atold it all, who would'ov left the camp with us? More'n likely many of you'd have thought the same thing would happen again and refused to come with us. As it is, all but three of you made it, outa twenty-seven. Way I figger, that's purty darn good." He gazed up the trail. "Old California hands said it couldn't be done atall."

"But you could'ov told *me*."

He straightened to his full height. His beard lay like a dark brown blanket on his chest and his brows drew together in a scowl.

Elitha recalled that men didn't like females telling them their business. "We sure did get through," she agreed. "I guess you knew what was best." He turned back to his work, pushing leather string through holes in the mouth of a full bag.

"Will you tell my parents the truth?" she wanted to know.

"About you and Leanna being fine, yes. No more."

That made her feel better. He would treat them no different than he'd treated her. It wasn't her age. "Why did the snowshoers die, Mr. Rhoads?"

Tying off the bag, he put his thumbs in his belt and blew air through his nose. "They got lost in the storms, wandered around. Had barely enough food for ten days, but it took them over a month to get here." He squinted toward the mountains.

"You think they did wrong to eat the dead?" Cannibalism was a fearful sin, probably the worst of all, so bad God didn't even think to include it in the shalt nots.

"Not for me to say."

She gave that serious thought. Nobody knew what those people suffered. They didn't have food bags hanging in the trees, or bread and sugar cakes baked for them in special camps. Her parents and sisters might well get stranded in blizzards too. Would they eat the dead? Jean Baptiste had suggested it long ago, after he buried the other teamsters. All of this swirled in her mind. She saved the most urgent question for last.

"If Mr. Reed doesn't bring the rest of my family down, will you do it?"

John glanced at the sky the way she'd seen him do a thousand times. Clouds shrouded the mountains. "Yer ma and the three little girls," he said. "And maybe your little cousins if they can walk." He turned his deep brown eyes on her and she felt the shock of their connected gazes. "Elitha, your pa's too far gone with gangrene. You know that, don't you?"

*Gangrene.* That word hadn't been used before. Gangrene killed a person if the infected limb wasn't removed. A feeble plea came out of her, "Maybe he could be carried down to a doctor."

He shook his head. "He's a big man, even starved. You saw the trail. He can't be carried on a litter. I'm very sorry." No man could have looked more sorrowful.

This struck like a whip, although in a veiled corner of her mind she'd known it. John Rhoads had a soft heart and amazing strength, yet even he couldn't bring Pa down. She shut her eyes against the prickly tears pushing their way out. Her dear father, a generous man with many friends, a father who approved of her more than she deserved, one she had clung to after her real mother died, would die alone in the mountains. She caught her breath to think of it. Tamsen and the three little girls must be rescued, and though Tamsen loved Pa as much as any woman could love a man, she could not stay with him on his deathbed while sending her three daughters, little more than babies, on a journey with strangers that could bring them to a painful and lingering death without the comfort of their mother's arms or the arms of "Big Sister"—their name for Elitha.

Yet she managed to look at Mr. Rhoads and say, "Well I guess he'll have to stay up there then." She wanted to run and hide from Perry McCoon, who was eavesdropping, and the leather-clad men who never stopped gawking at her. But she held on to herself and said what she'd been thinking throughout the march. "You're a good man, Mr. Rhoads."

Suddenly he grasped her shoulders in his big hands. "Elitha, you're the bravest girl I ever met." She had the feeling he was about to hug her, but saw him look at the woman named Matilda, who was watching with the little white boy in trousers and shirt.

"My wife and son," John said awkwardly, answering her silent question.

Perry McCoon suddenly reappeared. "Settin sail fer Sutter's Embarcadero, I is." Suiter's he pronounced it. "Happy to take ye aboard."

Mr. Rhoads, having released her shoulders said, "That's a good offer. You'd be there in a few hours, instead of two days. And a lot easier than muleback."

She caught sight of Mary hobbling around the adobe, steered by Mr. Johnson, and felt sorry she hadn't got back to her sooner. "How many can you take?" she asked Mr. McCoon. Leanna was playing cat's cradle with some girls she'd known from the trek.

McCoon flashed his dazzling smile. "Two or three, with all the goods I'm hauling back."

"Just a minute," Elitha said, studying Mary, who looked all cried out. She accepted the apple slices Elitha gave her. In a half-whisper Elitha said, "I guess Harriet was right." Afraid of getting Mary started again, she put a protective arm around her shoulder and added gently, "Let's go to Sutter's Fort on Mr. McCoon's boat. It'll be fun."

On the other side of Mary, Mr. Johnson pulled her firmly to him. "She's a stayin right here," he said.

"You are?" Elitha asked Mary.

Mary's glistening blue eyes turned to the hills. "I'll wait here fer my ma. That way I'll see her sooner."

In the tangle of his matted beard Johnson's lips opened in a tobacco-stained, snaggletoothed smile. "Doncha worry, girlie, I'll take good care a her. We's getting married."

Astonished, Elitha searched Mary for a sign that bore it out. Like a sleep-walker she moved her head in a barely discernable nod while uttering a sound that resembled uh-uh.

"Well," said Mr. McCoon, tilting his head toward Leanna. "So I'm taikin' her and you in me skiff?"

Suddenly Elitha yearned to be gone from this place. Mary had made up her mind to stay at Johnson's ranch, and, well, that was her wish. Elitha's sharpened sitting bones hurt from bouncing on a mule for two days, and it was past time for this long journey to be over. She ached to forget the hunger and filth and snow and children saying "My FEET hurt!", and to be far from Mr. Johnson and Harriet Pike and all the ogling trappers and their coarse jokes. With Mr. McCoon, she and Leanna would float effortlessly to the rainbow's end, like Pa would have wanted them to, and there they would wait in comfort for Tamsen and the three little sisters. People said Mr. Sutter was a gracious host who set a fine table for emigrants, and obviously, Mr. McCoon was a gentleman.

# 29

Although the devastating news about Pa stabbed Elitha in the heart, she tried to soothe herself by watching birds swoop for insects just above the water. The sun's rays streamed through the budding trees that formed a loosely woven canopy over the river. With the high mast folded down, Mr. McCoon skillfully threaded the schooner through the lower branches using a back sail and a tiller.

The rising, falling river soothed her tired body as the Bear River flowed into the Feather River, and then the much wider Sacramento. "Sail now, she will," McCoon said, raising the main mast. He stood braced in the manner of a sailor, which he said he had been most of his life. While he steered with two fingers on the tiller, Elitha and Leanna sat on the deck clinging to the rail as the narrow boat skimmed the roiling brown current. The boat sailed so fast that they surpassed uprooted trees going at a good clip. Elitha's hair streamed behind, and it seemed to her they were flying to Sutter's Fort. New Helvetia, Mr. McCoon called it.

"When did you first go to sea?" she asked. Leanna appeared eager to hear that too.

"Ten years old I was when I hopped on that first brig. Came here with Cap'n Sutter nigh onto eight years ago. Sailed ever minute between, 'cept when we hove into port."

"Didn't your folks try to stop you?" Leanna asked.

"From sailin?" Seeing her nod, he snickered, shaking his head.

"Did the captain make you work hard when you were a boy?" Elitha asked.

His smile faded momentarily, then the twinkle in his eye returned. "What think ye?"

She tried to imagine life aboard a sailing vessel. Horrible tales came to mind, becalmed seas and men dying of thirst or the cat-o-nine tails. "I think they made you fetch things?"

He nodded.

"And made you clean up after everyone."

He nodded again.

"Did you like it, I mean when you were a boy?"

He chuckled like it was a private joke. "Give me hardtack and a bunk to sleep on, it did."

"Did you miss your family?"

"Well now, me daddy 'e was quick t'blow, and 'e blew hot when 'e got gin in 'im."

"He beat you?"

"Oft enough."

"Did your mother try to stop him?"

"Dead me mum was, at an early age."

"Did you sail all the seven seas?" Leanna put in.

"Aye lass. And then some." He seemed to enjoy talking into the wind, his tan, sculpted face finely lined.

"Do you remember your mother?" Elitha was thinking of her real mother.

"A wee laddie I was, but now and then when I close me eyes, I see her face a-comin." He paused. "A beauty, me daddy says she was."

Looking at him, Elitha believed that was true. "You must have lived in a seaport."

"When me mum was alivin?"

"When you signed up to be a sailor."

"Aye, if ye calls London a seaport. Me daddy and me went to London after she died. No 'ealthy plaice for man ner boy, that town." He shook his head in amused recollection. "Like to perish, we did, movin' from one room to another, then livin' on the streets." His voice took on a faraway quality as he stared into the wind. "Niver got over her dyin, me daddy. S'why he took to gin so hard, I guess." Suddenly he was cheerful again. "Hail from Illinois does ye?"

"How did you know?"

"Them wot come down before, them poor wretches, said most of the emigration came from Illinois, so I figgered ye might too. And wot might yer daddy'ov been doin there in Illinois?"

"He's a farmer. Cleared every place he owned."

"A bonny big farm did ye leave then?"

"Oh yes. Wasn't it, Leanna?" Leanna nodded enthusiastically. Neither of them had been anxious to leave the farm for the wilds of California.

"What kind of farm? Hogs? Chickens…?"

"Oh yes. And cows and corn and oats and fruit. We had big barns and silos, and an orchard. Pa sold boxed fruit to all the neighbors, and took it in to Springfield." People said George Donner had a magic touch when it came to making good on the land.

"A nice 'ouse?"

"Real nice." She thought of the upstairs room she and Leanna shared. The climbing yellow Rose of Ophir at the window gave the summer nights a beautiful fragrance.

"Yer daddy keep the farm, did he?"

"Oh no, sold a half interest to my brother before we left."

"Your brother?"

"Well, fifty-percent brother, grown now, with a family. From Pa's first family." People joked that Pa had three lives. Three wives.

"Taiks ever penny, I suppose, to provision a journey such as yours."

"Oh no. We had plenty left over."

"To get started in California?"

"For a nice place, and for Tamsen to build a school. That's my ma, my step-mother actually."

He smiled warmly and she felt a stirring inside her. She'd never seen such purely blue eyes set in a tan face framed by wavy black hair, or features so perfectly proportioned. He was a man at ease on the water and visiting with girls. He seemed to enjoy the splash of the river against the prow and the birds playing overhead.

The vistas alongside the big river reminded Elitha of the illustrated book of German folklore, *Grimm's Fairytales,* in which the goddess of spring floated in a gauzy robe, as spirits do, over the greening land. The fairy spirit wore a crown of flowers, and everything she touched with her wand bloomed and hatched and sang—eggs in a thousand nests, spotted and blue, rabbits and deer with their young, and oaks with halos of pastel green that soon would become lush and verdant. This was the paradise Pa had uprooted them to find. She could see now that he was right to do it. In the midst of so much springtime, hope bloomed in her heart that the rescuers would find a way to carry him down the mountain.

From the helm Mr. McCoon announced, "Making fifteen knots, I'd wager." He looked at Elitha. "Fancy me schooner, do ye?"

She smiled and nodded, and he explained that it had been a ship's long boat to be rowed by twelve men. For river use it had been decked over so the interior could be used as a hold. The masts had been added.

Elitha admired the way he manipulated the sails and used the wind. He made a series of changes and the boat rounded a corner, tacking back and forth across the inflowing American River, as he called it. "The westerly'll help us," he said. "But sometimes the devil himself can't sail up this river."

The enormous tree limbs on the banks limited the boat's maneuverability as they had on the Feather and Bear; but now they were sailing upriver, so Mr. McCoon had to change the boom every few minutes. Leanna curled up out of his way and napped.

Exhaustion weighed on Elitha too. She sat against the rail looking through the passing branches while the sky changed from blue to gold. A powerful longing to get to the fort's fine accommodations seized her. Mr. Hastings had told Mr. Reed, far back on the trail, that the emigrants would sleep in featherbeds. Not since mid-May of last year had she lain in such a bed. She was asleep when the boat bumped wood.

"All ashore for New Helvetia!" Mr. McCoon called, stepping to the prow. Light had faded above the towering trees—an unearthly forest.

Leanna sat up and rubbed her eyes. "Where's the fort?"

"All in good time," he said, jumping to shore to tie up the boat.

Elitha's legs felt rubbery after the long ride, and her feet hurt terribly. Chilly walking up a forested trail, she stumbled on a root and she couldn't help but let out a little yell, both her feet so tender after freezing in the mountains. Mr. McCoon caught her and pulled her to him. A little longer than necessary? He let her go, and suddenly they stepped out of the forest into a flat plain that reached to far horizons. The unleafed shapes of mammoth oaks stood scattered across it, black shapes in the twilight. Ahead stood the white-walled fort.

Approaching the structure Elitha stopped, puzzled. "We were told that California is in Mexican territory." The flag above the wall had stars and stripes.

Mr. McCoon scratched his head and replaced his hat. "Maybe it tis at that."

"But that's the United States flag."

"Young lady, it's any fool's guess wot country we're standin in." He put a hand on her back, guiding her up the trail beside the high wall. "Not so long ago I heard the British was taikin' California. Maiby done it by now, for all a bloke'd know. That'd maik me a naitive of California, now wouldn't it?" He snickered. "Wye, that flag don't mean a thing. Always bettin' to cast 'is lot with the winner, is John Suiter."

It struck Elitha that Suter was a German name, pronounced Sooter. Grandpa Donner, who spoke mostly German, had mentioned an old friend of that name. Why then did most people rhyme it with butter? This troubled Elitha because she must be polite to the leader of the fort and pronounce his name correctly.

"Ever day some bloke rides into the fort," Perry McCoon was saying, "all in a dither about the bloody war." He turned to her. "A curious lass, ye be."

Elizabeth Keyser had said a war was underway in some distant place and most of the emigrant men had gone there to fight—those who hadn't become snowbound, those who'd used the existing trail and not taken Mr. Hasting's bad cutoff and axed a road through a forest to do so. Anyway, Mr. McCoon, too, had said that almost every white man in California was fighting that war, except for a few like John Rhoads at Johnson's ranch, a few mountain men, and McCoon himself.

They rounded a corner and she saw a gate topped with spikes and flanked by cannons. Around the gate lay the dark outlines of covered wagons with the tongues down, like huge toys left by disorderly children. They would contain women and children whose men had gone to war. Beyond the wagons stood a row of square tents and beyond that a group of wigwams, all quite unworldly in the twilight.

Women and children emerged from the wagons, whispering as they followed the three of them through the gate. Elitha thought she recognized a face or two, but it had been so long since her part of the wagon train had split off from the main emigration that she couldn't recall any names.

A soldier at the gate asked, "You comin in from Johnson's?"

Mr. McCoon lifted his hat, smoothed back his hair, and announced in a voice filled with significance, "Donner girls, these two be, from the stranded wagon train."

A mutter shot through the crowd punctuated by high-pitched "oooh"s that scratched Elitha like chalk on a slate-board. Three children ran a distance away and then crept back, peering at her and Leanna as though daring to approach ghastly freaks escaping from a circus. Elitha and Leanna exchanged puzzled glances, squeezed hands, and limped onward.

A growing crowd followed them across the courtyard and watched them mount a flight of stairs. Elitha could feel eyes on her back. Inside Mr. Sutter's rooms, which weren't anywhere near as grand as expected, Perry McCoon introduced Elitha and Leanna to Lieutenant Kern, dressed in a military uniform, and to "Captain Suiter," who wore an ordinary shirt and trousers. A third man with mutton-chop sideburns sat in a chair putting down the book he'd been reading by candlelight. Captain Sutter nodded in his direction and said, "General Vallejo." The Spaniard stood, bowed formally. *"Con mucho gusto,"* he said, and returned to his book. This first genuine Californian they had seen wore a vest with colorful embroidered flowers.

Recalling what Ma had said about sad faces making no friends, Elitha smiled at everyone and answered Captain Sutter's question about luggage. "No," she said smiling, "we couldn't carry anything." She looked at Leanna standing on the sides of her shoes to keep the pressure off her toes. Her frock and shawl hung from her scarecrow's frame, and black circles underscored her weary eyes. Elitha knew she looked no better, like something the cat dragged in, Tamsen would have said. *Where were the beds?*

Captain Sutter, a man just her height with an Austrian mustache, twisted his face into the picture of pity. "Haff you girls hunger now, hmm?" Indeed, he was German.

Perry McCoon answered, "They ate on me skiff."

Elitha smiled and nodded in affirmation. *Where was the guest room?* She didn't feel up to talking. Exhaustion pulled her toward the floor, and her feet screamed with pain.

Captain Sutter's pale eyes seemed to swim as he looked at her. Then he turned and went into an alcove, lit a candle, and returned with paper, an ink-bottle, and a plume. He scratched a short note, waved the paper dry and said, "Giff to Mr. Mellus in der store." He handed it to Elitha. "He giff you supplies. Lieutenant, show dem to my new traveler house."

Relieved, she followed Lieutenant Kern to the door. But Mr. Sutter put his hand around her waist so she couldn't go out. "You are yoong to suffer zo. *Schade.*" Pity, that meant. His breath smelled of liquor.

"Thank you very much for helping us." She curtsied through her pain, and then remembered. "What is the date today, if you please?"

"March eight."

She repeated it in her mind: March eighth, eighteen forty-seven. She would remember this day, and she would also count the days until the remainder of the family arrived. With a smile she said, "Spring sure does come early here."

After another round of good-nights, Lieutenant Kern led the way through the parade grounds and out the gate, the wagon-people following—she couldn't fathom why—to a dark building that looked about a hundred feet long and ten feet wide. Rounding the end of the structure, she saw it was divided into small rooms, none of which had a shutting door or even a curtain.

Pointing through a doorway, the lieutenant said, "There you go."

"No plaice for fine young laidies such as these," Mr. McCoon objected.

"It's all we have," the young Lieutenant replied.

"I know better," Mr. McCoon shot back.

Intensely aware of the wagon-people, Elitha felt embarrassed to be causing trouble.

The lieutenant snapped, "Mr. McCoon, the rooms inside the fort are occupied by officers of the United States Military."

"This is fine," she interrupted, limping inside the tiny dark room. Leanna and Mr. McCoon followed, the onlookers remaining outside. Elitha stumbled on a loose pile of dirt, perhaps a gopher mound. "Really it is just fine," she added for McCoon. *Why are those people gawking?*

"Firepit's in the middle of the floor," Kern said. "Firewood's catch as catch can around here." The room had no window, no furniture. She forced a smile and curtsied to Kern. "Thank you ever so much, sir. We are much obliged." Hardly a featherbed, but it was good enough if everyone would just leave. She felt she could put her head on the gopher mound and sleep for a week. At least they'd have a roof over their heads, and though the temperature had dropped, it wasn't nearly as cold as what she'd become accustomed to.

"Are they man-eaters?" asked a child from the doorway.

Elitha's scalp crawled.

A large woman grabbed the boy by the ear, twisted it until he was on his toes, and ordered, "Now you say something NICE to these poor girls who are starved and frozen and all alone in this wicked world."

He screeched, "Sorry Ma, I'm sorry! Stop!" His desperate eyes shifted to Elitha and he said in a nicer tone, "Sorry ma'am." His mother liberated his ear.

*All alone in the wicked world.* These people must have assumed she and Leanna had been in the snowshoe party. Apparently everyone had heard about that. Quietly but firmly she said, "My sister and I came through with the First Relief. Our parents will get here in a week or so." People looked at her with tilted heads. She took a breath and added, "We ate no human flesh."

"Ooo-ooh," squealed a child. Others circled in playful horror, as children do, obviously not caring about the truth. Looking at Leanna's dark shape, head down, shoulders sloped, Elitha sat on the earthen floor beside her one-hundred–percent sister, very anxious to take off her shoes and give her throbbing feet more space.

Lieutenant Kern turned to leave at last, tossing back over his shoulder, "Remember, just sign for food at the store."

"Thank you sir." Elitha forced another smile, though her face could hardly do it. "Thank you for your kindness, and you too, Mr. McCoon, for bringing us down the rivers." She and Leanna would be here for a while, so there'd be time to clarify things for the onlookers. Tomorrow maybe, when she could see them. It would help, she thought, to be a little older.

Everyone left except Perry McCoon. Much as she liked him, she wished he'd go. Leanna removed her shoes and stretched out on the dirt floor despite his presence. They'd both done it on the boat, but in a small room it seemed disturbingly intimate.

"I enjoyed sailin' with ye," he said. "Hits not ever day I gits such comely company."

"Thank you ever so much, Mr. McCoon." She couldn't see him in the dark.

"Call me Perry."

She wondered if he had a wife.

Leanna began to softly snore.

Perry said, "I'll check on ye tomorrow at noon siesta. That's what they calls it 'ere. Siesta." She could feel his smile and almost see the dimples. "I'll be workin with the cows till Suiter puts up another load for me to taik to Johnson's."

Tomorrow she'd make herself more presentable.

Two days later dawned overcast, and by noon rain threatened.

Freshly shaven, Mr. McCoon again came as promised. Elitha walked with him around the fort wall, leaving Leanna in the room. Elitha's one-size-too-big shoes had helped in the mountains, but the woolen stockings had become waterlogged at times and frozen at other times. She wondered if she would ever again be able to run around like a careless child. She sat on a stack of adobe blocks, Perry sitting beside her. He surprised her by saying he owned a big spread of land.

"In California high birth has no meaning," he added with a happy crinkle in the corners of his eyes. "Me land is as big as any squire's in England."

"Oh, I thought you were working for Mr. Sutter." She pronounced it like butter.

"Being naighborly, I is. I sails where 'e needs me to go. To Johnson's and back, to San Francisco and back, to Suiter's upper ranch and back. And I'm a vaquero too, when he needs me. That's Spanish for a horseman who herds cows. Ranchers lend a 'elpin 'and in this country."

"Who's tending to your farm while you're gone?"

"Gots me fifty niggers workin' the plaice, and an overseer when he gets down from Mule Springs where 'e's maikin more money than I can pay 'im. A German naimed Adolph Brüheim."

"*Niggers?*"

"Indians."

She'd heard that before, slang for dark skin. Is your farm like this?" She opened her arms to the greening grasslands, upon which hundreds of distant animals stood in herds—cows, horses, mules, and sheep. Mr. Sutter was said to own the land as far as the eye could see and to employ many Indian riders to do the herding.

"Aye, but I got no fort, no stores, and the Captain's land is a sight bigger, a bleedin' barony, it tis."

She was feeling the first drops of rain and trying to imagine this sailor working a farm with fifty Indians, when his blue eyes turned back to her. "Would ye like to be the mistress of such a grand rancho?"

Heat flashed up her neck and ears. Not knowing whether he was proposing marriage or passing the time, she replied, "Well, I don't know. I'm going to help Tamsen, that's my stepmother. We're going to set up an English-speaking school, and I guess I'll teach in it for a while." She didn't like the way that rang back through her head—too young and silly, and off the point.

Voices were coming. They both turned and saw Mrs. Wolfinger and Mrs. Keseberg. Behind them came two men and several children. They had dismounted the mules and were limping toward the fort gate. *The first relief starting to arrive.*

"I'll get back to the cows," said Perry McCoon. "See ye laiter."

Just when he left, the sky opened up. Elitha ran to the little room to get Leanna and a broken half-barrel they'd found. They took the barrel and stood in the muddy yard of the fort holding it above their heads and watching

Mr. Sutter and Lieutenant Kern greet the emigrants in the pounding rain. Mrs. Wolfinger and Mrs. Keseberg chattered in German with Mr. Sutter. How dignified they looked bowing their heads to each other!

When Mr. Sutter talked to the men, Leanna tugged the barrel with Elitha under it toward Mrs. Wolfinger, who had smiled them a hello. "Where's Virginia and Mrs. Reed?" Leanna asked.

"Day schtay wit Sinclairs, udder side von der river."

Mrs. Sinclair was the lady who had made all the new underwear.

Leanna looked crestfallen. She and Virginia Reed had been good friends on the trek down the mountains, and Elitha knew she'd want to be near her.

"Frau Reed haff bad pain in der head," Mrs. Wolfinger explained, joining them under the barrel. "Frau Sinclair iss making good health for dem, until Herr Reed come down da mountains wit Patty and Tommy."

"Oh," Leanna said, barely audible.

"Come and see our room," Elitha suggested.

They hurried while holding the barrel over their heads like four girls in a funny Fourth of July race—even twenty-three-year-old Mrs. Keseberg. In the light from the doorway, the cooking pot Elitha had acquired in the store looked sooty and untidy in the ashes, and as the two guests stood staring into the room, Mrs. Wolfinger wore the same far-away expression Elitha had often noticed in the snowed-in Donner tent.

"Well," Leanna said, apparently reading the dismay, "I guess it's better'n being under the snow."

"Ya. Iss better," the lady replied. Maybe she was thinking about Mr. Wolfinger, or his stolen fortune, or the teamster who'd confessed to helping kill him.

"You can sleep with us," said Leanna, pointing at the wood shavings that they'd collected in their skirts from the carpentry shop.

"*Nein, danke.* Herr Sooter say Frau Kaysaberger and I in number tree sleep." She pointed toward a room two doors down.

On the second drenching day, Perry McCoon brought oranges and sat beside Elitha on the sawdust bed, now hemmed in with scrap wood that Elitha and Leanna had found. "Wish the bloody rine'd quit," he said, whacking his soaked hat on his knee.

"Spring rain brings the flowers," Elitha said cheerfully.

His other hand touched hers down in the wood shavings.

"Sure ent a pretty sight up there."

"Where?" Her heart began to pound.

"Yon mountains." His eyes turned eastward. "Snowing like the devil, tis up there."

"Snow?"

"Hard rine here means blizzards up there. Hit never fails."

That anything in this valley of spring was connected to the nightmare in the mountains had never occurred to Elitha. Leanna looked like she'd seen a ghost. Tamsen and the little girls could die, and Pa couldn't get off the litter to hunker down and keep warm beside those little pine fires. And if he lay on his back, how could so many people keep warm with the litter taking up one whole side of the fire? Deep inside that muse, she felt her hand rise and meet something soft. She looked.

Perry was kissing the back of her hand. Retrieving the hand as politely as she could, she smiled and said, "I 'spose me and my sister want to be alone now."

# 30

Elitha couldn't remember rain like this in Illinois. It was as if a demonic sky giant hurled slashing torrents at the huddled humans below. Streams from the roof eroded the corner of the building and pale rivulets of mud sloughed down into the room. It was cold inside and out. Icy water ran down her face when she went to look at the trail to the river. A pond by the wall had been transformed into an overflowing lake hopping with miniature eruptions. She asked herself questions that had only one answer. Could the rescuers keep enfeebled people walking through a blizzard? Could they find the food caches and keep to the trail? Trying to stop the shakes, she hugged herself. One thing seemed sure. They could not carry a litter.

She wished Mary Murphy were at the fort so the three of them could help each other endure the long wait. And it would have been nice if the Sinclairs had invited Elitha and Leanna to stay with them, where they'd have the company of Virginia and Mrs. Reed. Mrs. Wolfinger and Mrs. Keseberg spoke German together and spent a lot of time in Mr. Sutter's quarters. Elitha imagined that she and Leanna were seen as children, less interesting to talk to and yet too old to need help. The children Elitha had helped on the long walk had been distributed to farms being established by a few men returning from the war with Mexico. She and Leanna were alone among strangers, except for Mr. McCoon, who, she had learned, was unmarried.

It rained six continuous days and nights; and when it stopped, the goddess of spring had gone into hiding. The lake near the fort had become a river to be crossed in order to reach the main river. Snuggled close to Leanna under their cloaks, Elitha awoke to a clear sky framed by the doorway. The cold burned her toes all the way up through her insteps.

She sat up, removed her stockings and stared through breath clouds. Her feet were alabaster white, except for her toes, which had been an unnatural shade of red and now were turning even darker. Cracks showed at the joints. She hobbled to the door. Under a cloudless sky, the baby green grass dazzled with frost and the budding oaks were traced in white. How cold it must be in the mountains!

Leanna whined, "My feet hurt."

Glimpsing Mr. Mellus heading through the gate, Elitha said, "I'll get some flour and make us some flapjacks." She already had saleratus to make them light.

She pushed her feet into her shoes, biting her lip, and limped up the path, glad the store wasn't too far inside the gate. Mr. Mellus was unlocking the door—one of many along the fort's inner wall. From the hood of her cloak, she smiled her friendliest smile and followed him in. No return smile.

She pushed her hood back and surveyed the goods in his store while he shuffled things on boards laid across barrels. It smelled rich inside with so many bags of flour, jars of pickles, and crates of oranges—a luxury of California. Leather and furs were stacked beneath the window. He didn't look like he'd finish anytime soon, so she said, "If you please, I'd like four eggs and four cups of flour."

He pursed his lips toward one nostril, and ridges appeared across the wide expanse of his forehead. "How long's this sposed to go on?" he said.

"Pardon?"

"Me supplying you."

Horrified, she said, "I didn't know we were a burden," and then hurried out. Donners were taught to carry their end of a load and never to expect handouts. All she'd done was follow Mr. Sutter's instructions. Tears filled her eyes as she hobbled back to the room.

She was in the wood shavings telling Leanna when Mr. Mellus darkened the doorway. Without invitation he entered and stared down at the two of them.

Unable to meet his eyes, Elitha said, "Go ahead and take the salt and the saleratus back." She nodded at the little Mexican cloth bags against the wall. "And the pot." At least they hadn't eaten that.

"Oh for the—I'm no ogre. Just gittin blamed tired a John Sutter givin away my goods so generous like. Now THERE'S a fella who never pays up, on time or otherwise!"

"Ma'll pay what we owe when she comes."

"Look. I know you girls gotta eat and I guess John Sutter's emptied his stores to Captain Frémont and his men and the relief effort and just about everybody else in the whole gol-dern territory. I just came to say I could use some cleanin up, clothes washin, wood gatherin, that sorta thing. In exchange."

Relieved to see a way out, Elitha eagerly agreed. "We're good at tidying up and washing clothes, aren't we Leanna." She gave her the elbow.

"Yes, we do real good."

"Good. Start by going down to the river for wood. Stack it in the store by the stove. Danged if this here fort ain't picked clean. You'll git yer eggs and flour when I git my wood." He was gone.

Relieved, but feeling spent—and glad for Leanna's hug—Elitha knew that next time she'd figure things out on her own and pay no attention to Mr. Sutter's promises. "Come on," she said, "we got wood to fetch."

That afternoon Elitha's feet sent swords up her legs. She was hungry, as usual, and thinking about supper when Perry McCoon came in. He lifted his hat, smoothed his wavy hair and said, "Nobody's got through at Johnson's yet. Jes delivered goods, I did."

"Maybe they all stayed at the lake camp till that storm died down." *Please God.* But she knew that too much time had passed before the storm; they would have started.

"Maybe." His steel-blue eyes found her. "Lass, you oughta make yerself a new gown. Got fetching stuff at the store, Mellus has."

She shook her head. She was ashamed of her frock, which had once been her best, but wasn't about to buy things she didn't desperately need. It almost made her cry that she couldn't wash her dress, having nothing to wear while it dried on the rocks. "We just gotta wait till Ma gets through, that's all. And when the snow melts, they'll bring the wagon down. We've got a pile of gowns in there. And a wagon full of beautiful fabrics." *How wonderful if they could bring Pa in that wagon!* She tried to smile.

Perry reached in his pocket and pulled out a sparkling handful of blue crystals on a leather string. He dangled it and she saw that the crystals were stuck together in a sort of haphazard star, perhaps a dozen dazzling points jutting in different directions. It was a beautiful bauble that almost looked man-made. He stepped in front of where she sat and placed it around her neck.

Holding the lovely thing away from her face to admire it, she felt unsure of the propriety of accepting such a gift. But his admiring gaze prevailed. "Why thank you, Perry," she said, "It's beautiful." She stood up. "Where did you get it?"

"I traded for it at Johnson's ranch." He flashed his dimpled smile. "Glad ye likes it."

He stepped closer, his eyes narrowing to dark fringes, and before she knew what was happening, pulled her to him and pressed his lips on hers. There were prickles where he'd shaved and the smell of tobacco and the tang of liquor, but then she forgot all else except that this was her first kiss. A rush of heat took her breath away, and she didn't know what to do except hold her lips to his and keep an eye on him.

He pulled back and looked at her. "Would ye marry me, Elitha?" His eyes danced. Teasing? Happy?

"You mean it?"

He chuckled and looked at Leanna, who still sat on the sawdust bed, then back at Elitha, all the while keeping his dimpled grin. "Serious as I ever gits."

"I—I don't know. I'm waitin on the folks. I, we're going to…" She needed her parents' approval.

"I want ye on me rancho, Elitha. You and me together can civilize that wild plaice and build us a fine barony. Our babes'll 'ave land to call their own." He took her by the shoulders. "Think on it, lass." Then he was gone.

Leanna was hugging her knees, the light from the doorway emphasizing the bones of her upturned face and an odd translucence of her brown eyes, but her smile goaded. "They say he's the best looker in Californy." She struggled to her feet like an old woman and lifted the blue crystals from Elitha's chest, admiring them. Her smile was gone. "I wish I was pretty like you," she said.

"Well, you're only twelve." As though a year and a half would change anything. It was true that Leanna didn't have the large black eyes, swan neck, and high forehead that Perry praised. The heat of his kiss lingered. She felt like a leaf in a twister. What would Tamsen say? And Pa, if they got him down the mountains? She needed to talk to them about this wondrous happening.

❦

By now it was mid-March, in the late afternoon. Elitha and Leanna gathered with Mrs. Keseberg and Virginia and Mrs. Reed, and everyone else who'd come down with the First Relief. They stood in the parade grounds before Lieutenant Kern, who was about to read the names of the survivors of the Second Relief. In the early morning Perry had sailed to Johnson's ranch with supplies, because word had it that the Second Relief would soon arrive there. And now the hourly bell-ringer had just announced that Mr. McCoon had returned with the names of survivors.

Lieutenant Kern started by saying that severe storms had overtaken the Second Relief. Virginia and Mrs. Reed grabbed each other. Elitha stood in a trancelike state, holding Leanna's hand. The rest of the Donners could have been in Mr. Reed's Relief party as she had fervently beseeched God they would be. Now she hoped God had ignored her prayer. Maybe the Third Relief would be safer. The Lieutenant called out each name, waiting until the joyful shouts subsided before reading the next one. Elitha and Leanna cheered to hear that cousin Solomon Hook, fourteen-year-old brother of Will Hook, had survived. But then the lieutenant looked up and folded the paper. That was all. A mere handful survived.

The absent Donner names left a howling hole—had they stayed in the snowed-in tent? Lieutenant Kern then unfolded another piece of paper. "And now," he said, "the names of them that perished on the way."

Elitha stopped breathing, but let in air as each name rang through the silent parade grounds, followed by cries and wails. With each name her stomach tightened a notch. "Isaac Donner," he read. Aunt Betsy's five-year-old. Mr. Reed had gone to the Donner camp! The lieutenant looked up from the paper and said, "That's all."

Leanna gave a crippled little happy hop not to hear Ma, Pa and the little sisters on the perished list, but Elitha looked into her brown eyes and said, "We don't know why the rest of them didn't come through." She watched that sink in.

Lieutenant Kern turned the paper to the other side and cleared his throat and announced: "This here's a list of them that was still alive at the summit when the Second Relief left."

Elitha closed her eyes, inhaled and held her breath.

"George Donner, Tamsen Donner, and their three daughters."

*Thank you, God.* She exhaled.

"Elizabeth Donner and two of her youngest boys," the man said in a tone of finality.

Aunt Betsy was alive, but one of Elitha's cousins, either four-year-old Sammy or three-year-old Lewis, had died. Maybe it was just as well, Elitha thought, that Uncle Jacob hadn't lived to see so many of his children die. And this was not over yet.

Despite the terrible news about Aunt Betsy's child, Elitha grabbed Leanna's other hand and they jumped around in a hobbling circle of joy. Pa was alive and the family hadn't come with the Second Relief. But she didn't remind Leanna that it had been about three weeks since that news of the summit survivors was written.

MARCH 23, 1847

Perry supped with Elitha and Leanna in their room, and then left. It was evening after a warm day, but light yet. Elitha jumped in surprise—her bare shoulders exposed in her petticoat—when he stuck his head in and said they should come with him to Mr. Sutter's quarters. More from the Donner camp had been brought in. Elitha and Leanna threw their frocks back on, quickly buttoned them, gathered up their skirts and hurried out where Perry was waiting.

Jean Baptiste Trudeau, to Elitha's joy, was sitting on the bottom step, even more emaciated than when she'd last seen him. He was resting his sparse beard, not more than a few longish hairs, in his hands, elbows on knees, long tangled black hair falling about his face. At first she thought he was unwell, but as his black eyes registered recognition, a smile spread over his bony face. He stood up with an expression one sees in artwork when mortals witness heavenly beings.

"Jean Baptiste," Leanna said touching his shoulder, "you got through!" No names from the Third Relief had been announced, but it was said that they had overtaken the Second Relief, which had been slow on account of so much suffering.

Elitha felt a sisterly love for him, a boy her age. He had lived when all the other teamsters died. He had cut all the firewood, chopped the ice stairs and done a thousand things for the family. Sometimes out on the snow after cutting wood, he had laid out his sarape, rolled the three little girls in it, and swung them until they screamed with pleasure. Now, after what they'd all been through, he seemed more than a hired man. And where Jean Baptiste was, the family couldn't be far behind.

"You looking good, healthy," Jean Baptiste said, smiling from one to the other. "Many times when I come back from hunting with no animal in my hand I feel very bad, and when I no find the cow under the snow I feel very bad, and when I eat your family food I feel bad, and now I see they give you plenty food here and I am happy."

"But where's everybody else?" Elitha asked. Leaving out Pa, she continued,"Ma and Georgia and—"

"Your cousin Sol up there," he tossed a look up the stairs at Mr. Sutter's door. "Your sisters are healthy and they sleep this night at the rancho up the river. Sinclair place." He looked in that direction and looked down, his long black hair falling over his face.

"Ma and Pa?"

He didn't look up.

"Dead?" Leanna squeaked.

Not looking up he shook his head. "No. When I go they are live."

Both alive! "But where are they? Johnson's ranch?" Maybe one of the higher camps, recuperating for a few days. Maybe Bear Valley. But why was he so glum?

Still not looking up, he said, "In the wigwam."

It came like a slap, the family word for the tent—Jean Baptiste having helped so much in its construction that first night of blizzard. Ever-faithful Jean Baptiste had left his employers. But then she realized they had entrusted him with the girls. "You brought our sisters through," she said.

He never looked at them, but walked away, across the fort yard and out the gate, his feet obviously hurting. Elitha watched him go.

"'Aff-breed is he?'"

She'd almost forgotten Perry was there, and didn't like acknowledging that's what Jean Baptiste was, for she and Leanna were almost half-breeds too, though they passed as white. Leanna looked as perplexed and disturbed as Elitha felt. The little half-sisters had been brought down, but not Tamsen, and Jean Baptiste was acting like a boy caught scooping pie with a finger. With a last look after his limping figure, Elitha nodded "yes" to Perry, and they all went up the stairs and knocked on Mr. Sutter's door.

The room seemed crowded. Mr. Sutter introduced Elitha and Leanna to three bearded men with their boots off. Perry knew them all. Elitha recognized the powerful man sitting on a crate with his legs wide apart—Hiram Miller had signed on as a driver for Pa in Illinois, but then left the family in the middle of the prairie to join a faster-moving company. She also recognized Lt. Woodworth, having met him in Bear Valley cooking for the survivors. Cousin Mary Martha Donner, looking more like a battered doll than a seven-year-old girl, lay on a bed of four chairs—the backs of two serving as side rails—one of her feet wrapped in a woolen coat, the other foot shockingly black with only one toe. The red cracks in the skin wept much more than Elitha's had. Mary's little face was white as the bones underneath, which so unpleasantly shaped its contours, and she was clearly suffering, her eyes squeezed shut. Sol Hook looked about as famished, but he was half-sitting against the wall, a fuzz of new beard brown against the white of his face. "Howdy cuz," he said to her, his voice cracking in the way of fourteen-year-old boys.

"Howdy," Elitha replied, wondering if the rescuers had told him that Will, his hundred-percent brother, had died of gorging.

Perry pulled up the last chair and joined the four men. They drank from cups and watched over the rims as Elitha and Leanna knelt down beside Sol.

"We heard you came through with Mr. Reed in the Second Relief, and the blizzards gotcha."

"Yup." Both his feet were wrapped in cloth.

She didn't mention that one of his young half-brothers was reported to have died in the tent. "We saw Jean Baptiste outside and he told us Tamsen and my pa are still up there in camp, and our little sisters are at the Sinclairs."

"Yup."

Mary moaned from her makeshift bed.

Elitha wanted to ask why Jean Baptiste had behaved so strangely, but was shy about mentioning it in front of the men. Instead she said, "Is Mary going to be all right?"

Sol looked at the men.

Lt. Woodworth, who, she'd just learned, was stationed in Yerba Buena with the United States Navy—though garbed like a mountain man—cleared his throat and said, "I'm taking these two to Yerba Buena to see the ship surgeon. Fraid Mary there won't make it unless her foot's amputated. She burned it bad in a fire. It was so numb she couldn't feel it. Now Sol here," he raised his brows at him, "maybe."

With the horror of amputation ringing in her mind, Elitha asked, "Are my sisters all right?"

"Looked in fair shape to me. These two was in the worst condition."

She looked at Sol. "What about Aunt Betsy, yer ma?" Sister of Elitha's real mother.

Sol closed his eyes and wagged his head—high up on his ribbed neck. He rested it on the wall as if he needed to sleep.

Elitha pushed to her feet and asked the men, who at the moment were silent. "Were you men all with the Third Relief?"

Lt. Woodworth seemed to be the spokesman. "These two here went up," he blinked at the other rescuers. "I coordinated provisions and transportation, sent by the U.S. Navy."

She looked at Mr. Miller, realizing she'd never particularly liked him, and Pa had been disappointed in him for signing on with a faster company when the two Donner families consisted of two men over sixty with girls and many young children to look after. But it was good of the man to risk his life for others. "How were my parents when you saw them?"

Mr. Miller and Mr. Oakley exchanged a look, which made her fear that Jean Baptiste hadn't told the truth. She was trying to harden herself for what would come, when Mr. Miller said, "We heard yer dad was hangin on t'life, but Tamsen was in good condition. She decided to stay with him. We saw her at the lake camp."

*At the lake camp?* "But she sent the little girls—"

"She wouldn't come with us. See, them other men was bound and determined to git on the trail afore the next storm hit. And she was just as determined to see about your pa, if he was still among the livin. She wanted us to wait and see, as we understood it."

"So you left without her?"

"Oh, she knew we would. Asked us to take the little girls with us."

"And Jean Baptiste was there to help?"

All the men in the room, including Mr. Sutter, looked at each other. *What was it?*

Hiram Miller said, "That mongrel cut out on his duty to your ma. Insisted on coming with us."

"Did she ask him to go back to the camp with her?"

He rolled his eyes. "Think she fancied cuttin firewood herself?"

"I don't understand. Why was she there at the lake in the first place? And our sisters, if they didn't mean to—"

Lt. Woodworth cut in. "Loithy, ah, what was the name?" Perry corrected him and he continued, "Elitha, what happened up in those mountains was very complicated, and it would take too much time to explain it all now. The main thing is, your mother was in the best shape of anybody, and she'll surely be coming with the Fourth Relief, which I have arranged. John Rhoads is among them, and he's a veteran. Your little sisters should get here sometime in the morning—they stayed at the Sinclairs' tonight. Your mother should come in maybe, ah, let's see, two, three weeks. Now, we're all feeling tuckered and we need to get an early start."

She and Leanna left, but Perry stayed.

Early the next morning when Elitha and Leanna went to the pond to wash, Mrs. Wolfinger told them Lt. Woodworth's party had carried Mary and Sol to the landing at first light. Jean Baptiste had been there to help. Hoping to talk to him, Elitha left Leanna to get something to eat from the store and hurried down to the landing as fast as her smarting feet could take her, to see if Perry and the boat were still there. She saw only towering trees entwined with grapevines. And when she peered upstream into the blinding sun, she saw nothing but sparkling ripples on fast-moving water.

She sat on a patch of young grass near the water's edge thinking that if Jean Baptiste were hiding, he might eventually come from the trees. But he didn't appear. Leanna came down the trail with biscuits and oranges, and they sat peeling oranges and listening to courting birds—a cacophony of shrieking and chattering as the water lapped on the dark river sand near their shoes. Crusts of black skin had peeled off their toes, and to Elitha's great relief, new baby skin had grown underneath. Today they were supposed to clean fort rooms, air out blankets, sprinkle and sweep dirt floors, wash laundry and gather firewood. But they had the time, even with the girls coming; the days were longer now.

They gathered fallen branches and twigs and made a pile, careful not to snag their new frocks, which they'd sewn by the firelight. Elitha's bodice section was noticeably skewed at the shoulder seams. She'd never been good at sewing, hired girls having done it.

"Look!" Leanna shouted, pointing.

An Indian boat of the type Californians called a balsey appeared at the bend in the river, the point of its tule-bundle prow turned up so high she saw only a dark man with a pole standing at the back. She grabbed Leanna's hand, not sure it was the right boat until it came closer, and then three small heads popped up above the high side.

"Big sister!" the little girls yelled as the buoyant craft was poled to the landing. Frances, Georgia and Ellie. Eyes too large.

Laughing and crying at the same time, Elitha got her shoes wet catching them—birdlike beneath their soiled frocks, their hair matted—as they scrambled up and over the side of the strange craft and all but flew into her arms. Their brocade and velvet frocks were rumpled, too large, oddly cut, and hastily sewn. Tamsen had made them that winter in Illinois, thinking of the future. She had hastily cut them down for the trek down the mountains, wanting the girls to look as presentable as possible.

Six-year-old Frances said, "Ma said you was to care for us 'til she comes through."

"Yes. I know she stayed up there."

"Takin care a Pa," Georgia explained.

"He's ailin bad," Frances added, her hard little face serious beyond her years.

On the wooded path the little girls hobbled like crippled old women.

# 31

That evening after Elitha and Leanna finished their chores, they trapped Frances and Georgia and Ellie between their knees—their pelvic bones light beneath their petticoats—and gently combed as best they could through yards of hair. The girls smelled of good lye soap, and though it wasn't dark yet, their eyelids drooped even while their hair was being combed.

Smoothing the dark silky hair over the subterranean bumps, Elitha smiled into Ellie's sleepy brown eyes and said, "How old are you?"

A coy smile curved her lips. "Four?"

"That's right. You had a birthday! On the way down the mountains. And I didn't get to say, HAPPY BIRTHDAY!" With that Elitha squeezed Ellie's little bones and gave her a kiss on the cheek.

Frances said, "Now give her a spanking."

Elitha moved her arm in a slow-motion parody of four spanks. Ellie looked worried at first then pleased in a self-conscious way to be the center of attention. Then Elitha laid the three girls side by side in the wood shavings and covered them to their chins with their cloaks. Tomorrow she'd borrow some scissors and cut out the hair mats, and see about their stained frocks.

Georgia wanted a song, so Elitha and Leanna sang about Tom Pierce's old gray mare, as many verses as they could think of, and all the verses of *Old Dan Tucker*. By then it was almost dark and all the eyes were soundly shut. Quietly she and Leanna moved the warped boards they had used to hem in a bed for Ma and Pa, and pushed all the springy wood curls together so there was just one big bed, and lay down on either side of the little girls. The sharp smell of fresh wood came up around them and mosquitos zinged through the open doorway with the cool night air.

Leanna wasn't a talker, but she was awake and maybe thinking the same way as Elitha. Elitha lay staring into the dark, seeing the endless white mountains and the cold and the children left buried in the snow. It must have been hard for Tamsen to send these girls on such a terrible journey. She must have believed they'd have starved to death in the tent if she hadn't. And it *was* a miracle that no blizzard had overtaken them. God had been good to them.

Much later a high-pitched cry jerked Elitha awake, Ellie frantically screaming, "He's gonna get me!"

Elitha struggled to her knees in the shavings and hugged the tiny little girl, who was standing up. Her body trembled and her head was wet with perspiration, though the black night was chilly.

"He's coming!" she wailed into Elitha's shoulder.

"There now, you had a bad dream is all."

Frances sounded thick with sleep. "She's afeared of the scary man at Mrs. Murphy's."

Murphy's? "Now Ellie, you just lie down and I'll sing some more. Poor little thing, you had a nightmare is all."

"No!" Pitched to break glass. "He's gonna kill me!" Even her bawling trembled.

"It's not real, Ellie. There now, there's no such man. Why you three weren't even AT the Murphys' cabin."

"We was TOO!" Georgia insisted.

Elitha stopped to think. Of course, they must have stayed there with Tamsen when the Third Relief arrived. "But your ma was with you. She and Mrs. Murphy wouldn't let anyone hurt you.

"No! She wasn't there. We was there a long long time by ourselves."

"A VERY long time," Georgia agreed.

"And we was so hungry."

"And SOOO cold. They didn't have no fire."

"Frances," Elitha said to the eldest, a six-year-old not given to fanciful stories, "how did you come to stay at the Murphy cabin without Ma?"

Frances said Tamsen had paid two men a pile of gold coins to take the three girls all the way to Sutter's Fort, but when they arrived at the lake camp those men and Mr. Reed went on, leaving them at Mrs. Murphy's.

That's why they hadn't perished along with so many on the Second Relief. Greed and chicanery had saved them. "But I'd have thought Mr. Reed would have taken you with him. He was in charge of the Second Relief."

Frances said, "Mr. Reed took Patty and Tommy on ahead. That's all he took."

*His own children.*

"We was sleepin in their bed," Georgia added.

Recalling the night she'd stayed in the cabin occupied by the Murphys and Reeds—a log hut built by a party stranded at the lake the previous winter—Elitha imagined those two men going back to the Donner camp without Mr. Reed, pocketing the money, and then deciding not to tell Mr. Reed about the money. But why hadn't Mr. Reed gone back for the Donners? It was only about seven extra miles, fourteen both ways.

"Frances," Elitha asked, "do you know how much Ma paid those two men?"

"I think five hundred dollars." We saw them count it.

Greed had indeed saved the girls.

"It smelled ROTTEN," Georgia said.

Elitha had lost the thread. "Rotten?"

"Mrs. Murphy's house."

"They didn't never empty the bucket and there was dead people on the floor with big holes in 'em."

"And we was SOOO cold."

Sobs and hard sniffles followed, from all three girls.

"Cause the man what eats people don't fetch no wood," Ellie sobbed.

Elitha's scalp prickled. She heard the thud of her own heart as she stood on her knees holding Ellie. "Now, now—"

"And the old lady can't see to go out for wood."

"And she can't walk good neither."

"And a grown-up boy died, so he couldn't fetch wood neither. Mrs. Murphy cried over him when that bad man ate 'im."

People said the rescuers had found mutilated dead in the cabins, the living having eaten the dead. So that was true, and it must have frightened the girls out of their wits to see it. Gently she pushed Ellie down to sitting and said, "Now let's all forget about that and go back to sleep. Bad things happened but you're all safe now." She tried to push her little sister back into the shavings.

"No!" Ellie screamed, fighting to her feet. "That man's gonna kill me!"

Leanna spoke for the first time. "He say that to you?"

"He said it to ebbrybody. If they cried."

"And he WOULD OF too," Frances said.

"So we didn't cry none." It was Georgia's grown-up tone, but then long sobs started choking out of her like they'd been building up for years.

"You put your hand on my mouf an it HURT!" Ellie accused Georgia through her sniffles.

Elitha felt as if she was in her own nightmare. How cheerful Ma and Pa had tried to appear through their trials! They had made the little girls think being snowbound was a perfectly normal part of getting through to California. Elitha and Leanna had played their part too. These were hardly more than babies. Surely no man would threaten to kill them.

But Georgia cried like she'd never stop. Elitha knee-walked over to hug her too, one girl in each arm.

Ellie sobbed, "He's coming!"

Still lying in the sawdust, Frances said, "He's way up in the mountains, Ellie."

*What man?*

Leanna spoke softly in the dark. "DID he kill somebody?"

"No," Elitha said firmly, the black of night being a poor time to prolong this, "Now you all just go back to sleep."

But Leanna had them talking, one over the other, a waterfall not to be stopped. The story emerged. A little boy, a grandson of Mrs. Murphy, died in the bed of the bad man who had a very long beard and very long hair. He had stood over Mrs. Murphy's bed and complained of the cold and insisted he needed the boy in his bed to keep him warm, so Mrs. Murphy gave him the boy. In the morning the man said the boy had died in his sleep, and he hung the lifeless body on a nail in the wall. From time to time he got up from his bed to cut off pieces. He told the girls it was the best meat he'd ever tasted. Mrs. Murphy screamed, "You killed him. You murderer." After that she stayed in bed except when she'd slip the girls crumbs.

"She didn't want him to see we was eatin' parts of a biscuit."

"We chewed under the bedclothes."

"YOU cried," Ellie accused.

"I stuffed covers in my mouth so he couldn't hear."

Frances said in her grown-up voice, "Mrs. Murphy told us to take turns sleeping, but we was scared he would come and kill us anyhow. And eat us." All three were bawling.

Elitha quivered like her bones and everything else inside her had melted into gel. She gathered Frances up too so all three girls were in her arms, foreheads together. Leanna hugged them from the other side and after a while all five lay down in one big hugging mass. And then sometime later, still in each other's arms, the sisters fell asleep. Elitha was the last one awake, thinking *Lord in Heaven, these girls were protected from everything harsh in life, and now this!* And who was that man? One of those who killed Mr. Wolfinger? And why had Tamsen gone to the lake camp if she thought her daughters had gone on ahead?

Every night nightmares interrupted sleep. All three little girls had them. Elitha tried to soothe their fears, telling them the bad man would die in the mountains and not come to Sutter's Fort. And most likely that was true. Those left at the lake camp were too weak to walk. John Rhoads had said that over a month ago. Poor Mrs. Murphy.

"Will Ma and Pa die too?" Frances asked.

"Of course not! The rescuers say she's in the best condition of anybody."

"Don't leave us," the girls would plead when the flapjacks were eaten and she and Leanna were leaving for work. The weather was very warm now, and Mr. Mellus didn't need firewood. They'd caught him up on his washing, so now they worked for other people, often away from the fort at the new farms being settled by emigrant women, most of their men having gone to fight the Mexicans. The money they earned went for cloth, sundries and food. Food, food and more food. Every one of the five were hungry all the time.

"Don't you worry," Elitha would say, "We'll be back at the end of the day. And you know I'll never leave you." They were not alone in the wicked world. "And don't pay any mind to what those other children say. Remember, sticks and stones can break my bones but words can never hurt me. And if people look at you funny, you look straight ahead and just walk away." Since the arrival of the Third Relief, things had changed at the fort. Some of the rescuers told gruesome stories of cannibalism—though few as bad as the one the little girls had told. Women and older children sat talking in low voices around the wagon tongues, repeating the stories, exaggerating them. The children appeared to be mesmerized; women sucked in breath and turned to each other with open mouths. Whenever Elitha or Leanna or the three girls drew near, they would suddenly turn silent. Sometimes the fort seemed like the unfriendliest place in the world.

Each evening, on returning from work, Elitha would ask, "What did you do today?" Frances would recite, "We held hands wherever we went, just like you said. And Indian ladies gave us some of their mush."

"And we made the papooses laugh."

"And watched a man make a chair."

"And the Indians marched with their guns."

"And a man made a hat. And another one pounded the copper hoops."

Ellie contributed, "And the mule go round and round." Turning the grist stone. Elitha imagined they watched that often, for it was a wonder the poor animal kept going with so little prodding.

"Now you girls wear those bonnets we made you," she would say. "Or when Ma comes she'll say you look dark as Indians and then I'll be in dutch." She kissed their serious little faces and smiled the joke away. Tamsen wasn't like that. She treated even the youngest daughter as supremely sensible. She never raised a hand to them. Tamsen would know what to do about the nightmares, and Elitha waited for her like all the Christmases she'd ever known rolled up into one.

One day when she was coming back from a persnickety French woman's place—Perry gone to Yerba Buena for four weeks—thinking how she hated being a hired girl, when a hot wind stole her flyaway skirts and dust devils danced across the trail. Perhaps Pa had died, she thought, knuckling grit from her eyes. *No.* It was pure superstition that twisters meant a death had occurred. She'd been tired all day after not sleeping most of the night on account of drunken men talking in the doorway, staggering in sometimes and scaring her half to death. And the French woman had been cross all day because Elitha had cracked her crock lid in the morning. She had walked two miles under a dawn sky and was returning before sunset. Every day seemed longer—actually was. Leanna worked at another farm, and Elitha felt lonely as she milked cows, churned butter, built fires, heated water, washed clothing, stacked brush for fences and shoveled out deep-rooted grass for new gardens. She felt lonely even though she worked alongside her employers. During the long days she never forgot that in Illinois she read books while hired men and girls from less prosperous families toiled at the heavy chores. Everything in California was primitive. They didn't have pipes, so she hauled water from the river with splashing buckets banging her knees.

But soon it would be over. Tamsen would come and care for the girls, and

Elitha and Leanna wouldn't hire out any more. And with the ten thousand dollars from the secret quilt, they could pay men to build a house and school. She hoped the books in the wagon weren't ruined. Tamsen—she daren't think about Pa—would advise her about marrying Perry. After all, a girl's whole life depended on getting a good man, so this was the most important decision she would ever make.

Once she'd seen him mercilessly whipping a snubbed horse. "Beatin sense into 'im," he said with a grin, and it was true that most men believed in that. Another time she'd been surprised to find out he'd never heard of the Golden Rule. "Do unto others as you'd have them do unto you," she'd explained. "It's from the Bible." He had narrowed his eyes as if looking over the sea and said he recalled one of his shipmates saying that. Then he had smiled sidelong—his teasing expression—and said, "Do unto others afore they do unto you!" A harsh rule, Elitha thought. One that Jesus tried to change.

She knuckled more grit from her eye. To make matters worse she had her courses, which luckily Tamsen had explained back on the Platte River last summer. It was a sticky mess, and she'd been embarrassed to borrow a rag from the French woman. She couldn't imagine putting up with that the rest of her life and hiding it from a husband. God's curse on Eve, one of her friends in Illinois had called it.

Ahead, the blazing sun whitened the walls of the fort. The long adobe outside the gate looked stark white too, and she saw a few people gathered at the butt end of it where their room was. Excitement pumped into her and she gathered her skirts and broke into a halting run with the rag shifting and the devil wind blowing hair across her face.

Smoke came from the doorway, and the smell of cooking meat. Ma had to be here! Cooking supper. She pushed past several children and three women standing at the door. But only Georgia, Frances and Ellie were inside, squatting around the firepit in dirty frocks. Georgia and Frances were toasting slices of liver. Ellie had a big quivering piece in her hands and was chewing it. Blood was smeared all over her hands and arms and cheeks. She grinned up at Elitha and said, "Big Sister!" Red teeth. That's what everybody was looking at!

Elitha turned to the spectators. "What are you doing here?" They looked at her with round eyes. "Go away until you're invited!" she said.

"Cannibals!" a boy sang out, pointing at the girls.

"Go on! Git!" She reached for the blackened frying pan and made like she would throw it at him. "And don't let me see you here ever again!" With disapproving looks, mothers tugged their children away. Never before had she spoken crossly to grown people and she almost couldn't believe she'd done it.

When at last they were out of earshot, she turned to the girls, her voice unnaturally sharp. "What in heaven's name are you doing!"

Frances looked up, about to break into crying, the liver trembling at the end of her stick. "Eatin," she squeaked. Flies were all over her face, all their faces.

"Well I can see that. But where'd you get that liver?" She pointed at the meat. Leanna wasn't back yet from her work, so the only money was in Elitha's pocket.

"The man what sells meat." Ellie's chin quivered. "We was watching him cut it and he," she sniffed, "give us some."

"Cause we was HUNgry." Georgia's meat was nearly on fire.

Frances tried to sound adult. "I didn't let Georgia or Ellie play with the matches, honest Injun."

Elitha grabbed the liver from Ellie's bloody hand, jammed it on the end of the blackened switch and thrust it over the flames. "There." She wiggled it down from behind Ellie's head to get her to take it. "Now you cook it till it's good and done, you hear? Good and black!"

Ellie assumed control of the stick, her voice shaking. "Yes Big Sister." Pink tears ran through the blood and down her neck into the collar of her frock.

Elitha lay back on the shavings and forced a softer tone. "Ellie, you were eating it raw." Then, like the powerful blasts of the wind she'd battled all day, something exploded in her and demolished every bit of self-control she'd tried to hold on to. "YOU WERE EATING IT RAW!"

She knew, yes and everyone else in the whole fort knew, that some knowledgeable people claimed these girls had helped eat Uncle Jacob and the hired men. She turned away and wept into her arms. Tamsen wouldn't have let them know. The thought turned her stomach. It seemed that God had forgotten the Donners.

"Big Sister," Georgia whimpered, "What's a cannibo?"

"Hush about that!"

But then she realized that at fourteen she must set the example, and it was up to her to keep their spirits up. It was just that too much had landed on her today, and she didn't want to keep leaving them alone all day with strangers. She couldn't stand this hovel either. Tamsen would buy chairs and gas lamps for the new house and wouldn't have to sew at night by an open fire, getting ashes and dirt all over the goods. Low in her abdomen something seized up, and she gritted her teeth until it passed.

Flies hummed in lazy circles and lighted on her face. She got up on an elbow and tried to swat them, only to have them return. "Ellie," she said. All three turned to look, "I'm sorry I felt out of sorts. None of you did anything bad. Nothing bad at all."

❧

Several days later, the Donner sisters stood at dawn watching the Fourth Relief ride out—John Rhoads, five men and a string of mules trailing. Sadly, the men's previous attempt had been aborted because of snowmelt and the impossibility of getting the mules through. Elitha recognized two other men from the First Relief. In addition there was Sebastian Keyser, Elizabeth's husband from Johnson's ranch, and a man in buckskins the size of John Rhoads—Fallon le Gros people called him. He was one of the trappers who liked Mr. Sutter's distillery—a complex of barrels, pots, and pipes that made spirits.

The mules carried only a bit more food than the men needed. No caches would be hung in the trees, Lt. Kern had said, because it wasn't necessary. Only Tamsen Donner would be left living. Nevertheless, long-faced Philippine Keseberg also stood watching the men and mules depart. Her husband hadn't come down yet.

"I heard this is a salvage party," Leanna said.

"They don't want Indians getting into the wagons when the snow melts," Elitha said. The packsaddles would be filled with precious goods, so it was a blessing Ma was there to keep a sharp eye on the apple green quilt with the ten-thousand dollars, and Pa's money belt. Most of these men looked like wild men. But on the other hand, she thought as the last mule went around the bend, it seemed fair for the rescuers to be paid from what they found in the wagons. Tamsen would know how much was fair.

"Well, they're off," Leanna said with a sigh. There were fine lines around her eyes as if she were much older than her twelve years.

Frances looked up. "How many days 'til Ma and Pa git here?"

That would be asked many times, Elitha knew, and she hadn't told them how bad off Pa was. "Don't know," she answered truthfully. People said so much snow had melted that the men would reach the summit in far less time than the first reliefs. The mules might even make it the whole way up, and Pa could ride. She sent a silent prayer to God, realizing that four faces were turned to her. "About a fortnight, I guess."

Elitha told her sisters good-bye and walked down the east trail on her way to work. On either side of her the wheat was already golden and headed out—the plain flat as an ocean. She scanned the horizon, seeing a distant line of white. Cloudlike, but she knew it was the mountains. A long time ago she'd heard that thoughts could be sent through space. She closed her eyes to concentrate and tried to make her thought fly across the distance.

*Pa and Tamsen, the girls got here safely. I'm taking care of them until you get here, so don't worry. Leanna and I have to work, so we can't be with them all the time but the* Indian *ladies watch over them and they'll be all right. A man here wants to marry me, but I told him I need your permission. And Tamsen, I've seen California and you were right. They need a school here real bad. So don't you worry about anything at all. Just live, and eat what you have to. John Rhoads is coming for you, and he's a real good man.*

🌿

It was a difficult fortnight, in many ways worse than the wait beneath the snow. The family had pulled together then. But now ever more gruesome rumors about the Donner Party crackled like wildfire through the fort. The details of bodies "broken into" worsened every day. The most awful stories were about the "starved camp" where a toddler whimpered, people said, as it clung to its mother even while her chest was ripped open and her heart and liver were removed and eaten.

One day Elitha went to the outhouse and found a copy of the *California Star* folded on the seat. She read the newspaper with horrified fascination. The date was April 10—a week ago—the paper published in Yerba Buena. An article entitled "A MOST SHOCKING SCENE" told of Mary Martha Donner matter-of-factly suggesting to the families left stranded in a snow cup that they eat the dead—her younger brother being one of the first to die. The report quoted her as saying it was done all the time at the Donner tents. Then, to Elitha's horror, a terrible falsehood was printed, one that apparently referred to all the stranded immigrants:

> *Calculations were coldly made as they sat gloomily around their gloomy campfires for the next and succeeding meals... various expedients were devised to prevent the dreadful crime of murder, but they finally re-solved to kill those who had the least claim to human existence... so changed had the immigrants become that when the party sent out ar-rived with food, some of them cast it aside and seemed to prefer the putrid human flesh that still remained.*

Now the worst horrors known to humanity, cannibalism and murder, were linked with the Donner Party and the Donner name. At Elitha's ap-proach, women arranged their faces in exaggerated pity, but she saw some-thing else—a sense that females who had eaten such terrible fare had lost all claim to daintiness and femininity, all the gentle qualities that elevated them above the naturally coarser males. Mothers had apparently grown weary of telling their children to stop gawking and pointing. The three little sisters didn't understand it, and Elitha couldn't explain why they were not accepted into the little tribes of children that ran through the fort while their mothers waited for their fathers. So when a boy milked a cow and gave Ellie a cup of fresh milk, she was overjoyed just to be treated kindly.

Elitha no longer tried to contradict people. It was clear they wanted sensa-tion and perversion, not the truth. People also blamed "Captain Donner" for taking the cutoff and being too stupid to forage for food in the mountains. He was called a failure as a leader, a man who had no business coming west. The trappers called him a greenhorn, though he wasn't by a long stretch. They didn't take any account of the fact that while he was in the mountains he lay badly in-jured miles and miles from the people in the forward camp, who in any case had never paid attention to his advice. The wagon train had been a loose aggregate of families traveling together, and yet rescuers returning from the mountains,

some recruited by Lieutenant Woodworth, seemed to think Pa had commanded a disciplined army. They said openly that he bore the responsibility for all
the suffering. Most painful of all, Elitha wondered in her heart if she could
ever again proudly tell strangers that she was the daughter of George Donner.

By now, most of the survivors of the Party had dispersed across the countryside. Mary Murphy was still at Johnson's ranch, cousin Georgie Donner
still at the Sinclairs's farm, taken there, Elitha heard, so he needn't endure
this storm of lies and exaggeration. The Reed family had never stayed at the
fort, so they were spared. The Breen and Graves families from the Second
Relief rested at the fort only a few days, then went quickly to other places. So
the one other person left waiting was Philippine Keseberg, whose husband
remained at the summit—alive and a little crazy, people said, feasting on
what lay about, a man who had beaten his wife and threatened to kill and eat
Georgia, Frances and Ellie.

Perry McCoon said with a mocking expression, "Ye tender 'earts 'ave to
learn to smile at the tales. And 'ave ye thought, praps there's a bit o' truth in
'em?" He was hard to talk to.

One Sunday all five sisters were walking with Perry to see the Indian
vaqueros race their horses, when four emigrant boys came careening around
a corner and skidded to a halt. One pointed and exclaimed, "Ooo!" The boys
dug into a giggling run, pretending to be terrified.

Perry trotted after them and quickly nabbed one. He took him down kicking, removed his shoes and trousers, cackling the whole time as he dodged
the kicks, and then, still laughing, ran away with the clothes. The boy ran
close behind, covering himself and yelling, "Mister, them's my new shoes.
Please. Ma'll switch me, please mister." At the pen where Mr. Sutter's bulls
were resting in close confinement, Perry threw the shoes and trousers among
the bulls, startling a particularly mean-looking animal to its feet. It glowered
at the boy when he got there—horns as long and pointed as hay rakes and
five times as thick. All the bulls were up now, moving around and trampling
the boy's clothing into the reeking muck. The other boys left their playmate
standing outside the bullpen, bursting into tears.

Still chuckling, Perry led the way to the horse races. The little girls looked
up at him in timid admiration, but it struck Elitha that he'd been a tad bit
severe—shoes being so very dear at Mr. Sutter's bootery. But then, people
had different standards.

# 32

On April 27, seventeen days after the scavenger party headed for the mountains, the Donner sisters were eating boiled potatoes with meat gravy when a man's cough startled them and something big eclipsed the twilight. Elitha looked up to see the dark shape of a man at the doorway. John Rhoads! She felt a sting of joy. But where was Ma?

When he stopped coughing, he said in a tone lowered by a chest cold, "Elitha, I need to talk to you, in private." *Pa.* But where was Ma?

With a fist rising in her throat she got up—the other four watching—and went out the door and followed him around to the dark side of the adobe. Tamsen had to be ill and they'd taken her to Mr. Sutter's quarters. Only bad illness would keep her away while John Rhoads came with the news. She tried to get ready.

He dropped his hat on the ground and clamped his hands on her shoulders and said, "We brought in one survivor."

"My m—"

"Not yer mother. Lewis Keseberg." He turned his head, coughing, but kept holding her.

"You said you'd bring her!" She could almost hear, *Yer ma's a strong little lady. She'll live.* Everybody said she was the strongest one.

"Keseberg claims she died."

Her kneecaps melted. "Pa?"

He shook his bushy head and his brown beard from side to side. That much she had known.

"Did you see her, the—" A powerful force came up and grabbed back the word.

"We didn't see her body."

Hope rekindled. She was lost, that was all. Lost, wandering someplace. They'd missed her between the camps. "Please go back up. You've gotta find her!" Why would he believe a crazy man like Mr. Keseberg?

"Elitha." His shaggy head tilted back as if appealing to heaven. "My God, how can I say it?"

Her heart was in her ears.

"Keseberg knows she's dead. No, let me finish." He coughed and his fingers dug into her shoulders. "He killed her." It blackened the twilight and smothered all hope.

Out of the void, "He said that?"

"No."

The flame roared again, red hot with anger. "Then how do you know? You didn't even see her." He didn't know that woman. She would walk down the mountains alone if she had to, but she would come to her children. But she had to be nice. "Oh Mr. Rhoads, please go back and look for her. I just know she's alive." She was losing ground to an avalanche of wild weeping and he was coughing and they should have stayed up there and looked until they found her!

"Elitha, oh Lord," he said when he found the breath, "I wouldn't say this, except you'll hear it all. Tongues'll flap a good long spell. Now you gotta be strong and keep this from yer little sisters. But you see," it came through his teeth, "we wanted to strangle that cowardly son of a bi... that low-down excuse for a man when we figgered out what he'd done. But we all agreed, this here is to be a civilized country and we gotta stick by some kinda law. So we charged him with murder. Mr. Sutter says there'll be a trial."

"But you don't even know if she's—"

"Keseberg admitted—he ate her." He grabbed and hugged her like he could squeeze out the horror. "We saw evidence."

A high-pitched sound floated up around them and she didn't know at first that it came from her. *Ate her.* All else fell into a monstrous hole that opened in the universe, and time and space vanished down that hole along with her past and future. She stood unbreathing. Then her mind snagged on the nightmares.

"Was he in Mrs. Murphy's cabin?"

"Yup."

She pulled back, and, though the anger had gone down the hole and she was like an empty frock on a clothesline, blurted out more hope. "Then it couldn't 'ov been Tamsen. She was miles away." *Please God.*

Leanna's timid voice pricked the twilight. "That you, Mr. Rhoads?"

"She'll be a minute," he said, and when she had gone, growled out, "We found his tracks going down to your folks' tent."

MAY 5, 1847

"Corpses don't bleed," Mr. Coffeemeyer declared, his eyes finding Elitha across a courtyard full of people.

It was warm for May. She stood in the crowd that had gathered, as far back from the man on trial as she could get and still hear. She felt like a sleepwalker, drawn by horror not volition. Looking at him now she recalled the intense gratitude she'd felt for Mr. Coffeemeyer when he'd come back with the food cache. He'd seemed an angel in buckskin. He pointed a finger at Lewis Keseberg.

"You killed Tamsen Donner," he accused. "Cut her up and drained her blood and stewed her in her own pot!" A hiss went through the crowd. Women covered their mouths and exchanged horrified glances. Lewis Keseberg, a hairy skullface, sat halfway up Sutter's stairs, his sunken eyes pale in the bright day, his blond beard a pendulum moving back and forth across his dark shirt, ticking denial.

Elitha was glad she'd insisted on Leanna staying with the girls and keeping them beyond the gate. She felt dull, like a sleep-starved child trying to learn higher division. Soon the man would hang and the nightmare would be over.

John Rhoads joined Mr. Coffeemeyer, his voice heavy with chest ague. "Ned's right. Seven men surprised this sorry excuse for a man before he got his lies untangled. The motive was fresh meat. We all saw the blood in the buckets. We asked why he didn't eat the mules and cattle that was coming up outa the snowmelt. He said it was too dry." Several male voices called assent while talk buzzed around Elitha.

She closed her eyes, suddenly thinking of what Perry had told her about his being lonely out at sea when he was a boy, with his mother dead and his father so deep in drink he might as well have been dead. She felt a connection with Perry and wished he were here. She fought the hollowness that was coming up to get her and knew she must sit down immediately. But sitting, she'd see only the backs of skirts and trouser legs, and no decent girl would do that. She looked back toward the gate and thought she could sit there without drawing too much attention.

She excused her way through the crowd, a man orating about proof and evidence, and sat down leaning against a gate-post. Captain Sutter was climbing his stairs to be seen above the crowd. People with pitying expressions turned to look at her. The Captain was talking, but at this distance she understood only a few words.

"… iss not a bad man… no different dan udders… All haff eat flesh of…"

"… character assassin—" another man charged.

Fallon le Gros didn't need to climb stairs to be seen, and his voice carried farther.

"… killed her for the Donner riches," he said. "When we tightened the rope around his filthy neck, he admitted where he'd buried two hundred dollars. Claimed he didn't know where the rest was. I woulda hung him on the spot, 'cept the others wanted a trial."

Hiram Miller told the assembled people, to Elitha's amazement, that he knew for a fact that George Donner had received ten thousand dollars from the sale of his land in Springfield, Illinois. Heads bobbed and people turned to talk at each other, as though they'd known this all along.

Suddenly the hollowness sucked everything black. She put her head between her knees until she thought she could walk, and then pushed to her feet and kept her head low, hurrying out the gate, gripping her stomach to hold it down. It seemed a hundred miles to the adobe room, but she got there and gratefully flopped on the sawdust, glad the girls were gone. She pulled her cloak over her head to shut out the world. The moist warmth of her breathing mingled with the image of Keseberg's pale eyes and pendulum beard, and the pot of Tamsen's blood and... *Oh dear God.*

Even if he hanged it wouldn't erase that pot of blood.

But then, she realized with a sudden lessening of tension in her shoulders, she could marry Perry McCoon and become the mistress of a big cattle ranch. She could take her sisters away from here and try not to think of any of this ever again.

I pause in my spirit-tracking and look at Old Man Coyote, who appears to be asleep at the foot of my trunk. "That poor young woman," I say, "walked a strange trail without allies."

Coyote jerks his head up. "Oh, for crying out loud, she had all the help she needed, and talked to the God-spirit all the time."

"Her God was so far away he didn't even have a shape. And she knew nothing of catching spirit help in dreams."

"She dreamed of apple trees."

"You know very well what I mean."

Coyote smacks his muzzle to loosen a morsel of cat wedged between his teeth. "Well, I wouldn't need any magic," he says laying his chin on a paw, "if I had men breaking trail and making fires and handing out food. The only thing I wonder is why John Rhoads didn't hump her. And Perry McCoon— what was he waiting for?"

"Patience, you promiscuous old man. Anyway, I feel sorry for her."

"You're just being sentimental. Remember, the new people judge everything by their own comfort." He chuckles like he can't stop, chuckles while saying, "I like the way they wander around in their messes and can't figure a way out. It's very entertaining."

"You, of all animals call people entertaining! What about that time you insisted on bringing fire to the world? Wanted to be a hero, so you whined and schemed and wore the other animal people down until they let you carry it, against their better judgement. But you burned your fingers off short and set the whole world on fire. Why, if you hadn't found that hollow oak, you would have fried."

That wipes the smile off him, and I see him glance covertly at his paws. But Coyote never quits. The corners of his lips curl up again. "Get Perry Mc-Coon back in the story. I like him."

"You would."

# 33

JUNE 1, 1847

Dawn. Planks of the deck grew distinct. Sycamores and cottonwoods changed from dark to summer green. Elitha could now see the stubble on Perry's face, which was slack with contentment as he braced his back with his hands and stood up looking up at the thick canopy over the American River.

She was far from content as she rose from the blanket on the deck, smoothing her linsey-woolsey frock. She had sinned, and God had let her live. She had broken her solemn promise to be good. Earlier, while Perry dozed and darkness blanketed what they'd done, she'd realized she had probably committed the Unforgivable Sin. Aunt Susanna had spoken about that, shooing Elitha away when she'd been maybe six years old. In all the years that followed, nobody had given her a straight answer about exactly what the Unforgivable Sin was. It seemed to her now that the thing she'd let Perry do, being unspeakable, was it. She fastened buttons from waist to chin, realizing she could burn in hell for all eternity. Life was full of pitfalls and she shouldn't have surrendered, shouldn't have disappointed Pa. *Elitha is an obedient girl*, he used to say. Apparently not, but now all she could do was go forward and try to make it up to God and Pa, if he watched from heaven.

Her voice came quiet and smooth. "Let's go up to Sinclair's place and get married now." She pushed the last button through its loop. Sinclair was the Justice of the Peace—alcalde in California.

He raised his straight brows at her. "Now?" At her deliberate nod he chuckled, checked his trouser buttons, slipped the rope and yanked the main sail aloft. The canvas barely luffed, and he grinned as he coaxed the small craft upriver. "Now is a fine time, lass. Yes indeed it tis."

His contentment with boom and sail made her wonder why he'd left the sea. Would he be sorry one day? With a mild shock she realized such matters were now central to her life, not mere curiosities. But she liked his dream of becoming a wealthy squire, and liked what he'd said about her "learning" being what he needed to make his dream come true. It felt strange and wonderful to be fourteen and yet needed by a thirty-six-year-old man. The skiff inched upstream and she stood beside him at the tiller sailing swiftly into her new life, needing the assurance of his touch. She felt like a young animal entering a strange forest.

He craned his neck to watch the curl of green water at the prow. "Neptune's Bones, never seen it so deep in June." He pointed at the river and looked at her. "This be the ford, lass, for horses, wagons, right here. Would ye believe? We'd be shoaled up here good most years." He changed the rigging and they tacked across on the diagonal. "That's why they call Sinclair's plaice *Rancho del Paso. Paso* means crossing in Spanish."

Upriver the V of sky was a glorious orange-pink in advance of the sun. A doe jerked her head from the water while a fawn sipped at her side. Elitha inhaled the fragrance of morning and vowed she wouldn't permit, on this day, the ugly visions that had bothered her since Lewis Keseberg walked free. That was nearly a month ago. It was time to go down her trail, as she'd promised Pa. When the crying was over, that's what people did, no matter the setback—Pa had lost two wives. No matter the deaths, or ruined crops, or burned barns, whatever, people showed their grit by going forward. Heaven or hell would just have to wait. Her children would grow with the new land, from the union of a British sailor and the daughter of George Donner.

The skiff parted a forest of green cattails where hundreds of red-winged blackbirds sang like rusty gate hinges. Piloting through, Perry stepped over the rail, crouched, watched, and when they bumped land, grabbed a rope and pulled the boat to a tree. She jumped across to mud, and it occurred to her that the Reed family might still be at Sinclairs'. She'd be pleased to see Virginia again, and have them all witness her wedding.

A beaten trail led through lush growth to a low ridge. On it perched an adobe house ringed with tall blue flowers—a sort of multiplied lily that she had often admired. An outbuilding, a lean-to, and a milch cow stood to one side. Several half-clothed Indians glanced up from a little fire, their wigwams of dry rushes standing beyond.

An Indian got up and spoke Spanish, a language Perry didn't know very well. "Fetch Señor Sinclair. I wants to palaver," Perry replied.

In a short time Mr. Sinclair, who with Mr. Sutter had officiated the trial, teetered before them jamming on a boot, his dark hair mussed and his shirttail out. "You old tar," he said, casting an approving eye at Elitha, "what brings you out this early?"

"Getting married, we is. If you've a mind to 'blige us."

Mr. Sinclair, who had declared the verdict at Mr. Keseberg's trial, nodded from one to the other. "Make yourselves at home while I get respectable."

Elitha had thought she could get married without being disturbed by Sinclair's decision. A close friend of Mr. Sutter, he had ruled in favor of Keseberg, even making Mr. Coffeemeyer pay Keseberg a dollar for character defamatioin. Then life at the fort continued like nothing had happened, except that Keseberg became a fixture there, hired by Sutter, She tried very hard not to let it affect her, but it did, every day it did. Barely able to lock eyes with Sinclair, she glanced around the homey room, but saw no sign of the Reeds. Patterned carpet covered the floor and white chintz hung from glass windows, sparkling clean. A tidy fireplace had been plastered into the adobe corner. The place had a woman's touch.

"Mornin." A female voice.

She turned to see a smiling woman in a neat red-striped frock and dark hair hanging loose to her waist. "Good morning." Elitha curtsied and, almost without thinking, removed Perry's hat from his head and handed it to him. Seeing his raised eyebrows, she smiled in hopes of conveying that she hadn't meant to criticize, but men were to remove their hats indoors. She asked the woman, "Are the Reeds gone?"

"Left a week ago. Visiting the Younts over in the Napa Valley. Till they get their health back. Then I 'spose they'll go to that ground of his in San José." She made a sorrowful face. "Those poor little tykes. Never saw living children so poorly as when Patty and Tommy come down!" She brightened. "Nothing good cream didn't cure."

"I'm so glad the whole Reed family survived."

Mrs. Sinclair rearranged her face to pity. "A blessing, ain't it? You poor, poor dear."

Perry shot a dimpled grin at the woman. "Here to get hitched, we is."

Her voice jumped an octave. "So the Mister says." She pointed at the chairs and excused herself.

Elitha sank in upholstered floral print and watched Mrs. Sinclair's neat little pin-striped figure move through the bedroom, into an adjoining room, and disappear around a corner. Perry sat squirming like he was uncomfortable. On a small table between them was a glass of the same pretty blue flowers that were blooming outside. She hoped to make Perry's place this cozy—hoped they could leave the fort today and get started. Mrs. Sinclair came toward them with a tray of silver and teacups.

They drank coffee and spoke of the fine weather. Over her cup Elitha looked at the man about to become her husband—boots apart, teacup balanced on a thigh, combing his hair with his fingers. He was an enigma, a man who'd sailed the high seas then become as fine a horseman as any Spaniard. She felt the mystery of him, and pride at his wide experience.

Mr. Sinclair entered with trimmed beard and clean shirt, wielding two leather-bound volumes. "My marryin books," he said with a wink.

Mrs. Sinclair pushed the table out of the way, arranged Elitha and Perry before the fireplace, and took the flowers from the glass, shaking water from their stems, and pushed them into Elitha's hands. Mr. Sinclair gave his wife a book—*The Bible* it said in large print on the cover—and read phrases Elitha had heard before, but had paid little attention to.

She put her hand on the Bible and said in her turn, "... to love and cherish, to honor and obey, in sickness and in health, till death do us part." *Death*.

Mr. Sinclair snapped the book closed and said, "You're wed and that's my first Christian wedding as Justice of the Peace." He acted like a boy with a shiny new top.

"Neptune's bones!" Perry said, "I'm the first?"

Mr. Sinclair twisted his mouth in thought. "That time Sutter married you?

What, a year ago?" He grabbed his beard and pursed his lips, "That's right. A year ago. That was his last marrying as Justice of the Peace."

Stunned, Elitha turned to Perry, "You been married before?"

"She died."

Mr. Sinclair said, "Waitin' fer Christmas, man? Kiss the bride!"

Perry drew her into his arms and she closed her eyes. Stubble stabbed her mouth, which was slightly sore from last night, and brought the memory of a much younger Elitha sitting on Pa's lap, giggling, squirming for freedom as he playfully whiskered her. Then, in the darkness behind her treacherous eyelids, she saw the scene the rescuers had described—Pa's breast cleaved open, his heart and liver gone, his empty skull sawed wide open, but somehow his eyes, beneath the chasm, were kindly, looking at her. She pushed Perry away and turned to the fireplace.

A hand came down on her shoulder. "My dear," Mrs. Sinclair's voice said, "I hope you're not feelin' poorly on your wedding day."

"Just something in my throat." She feigned a cough and turned around to face them.

"It's the flowers, dear. Sometimes the dust of them chokes me too."

Mr. Sinclair suggested they stay for another cup of coffee. They agreed and his wife made another trip to the kitchen. Mr. Sinclair explained that Mr. Sutter was feeling "low" about Captain Frémont leaving Lieutenant Kern in charge of the fort, and appointing him, Sinclair, Justice of the Peace. "I was thinking that you ought to let him shine a little and host you a wedding feast? He enjoys such ceremony."

"A fine idea that is," Perry said.

Since the trial, Elitha had been avoiding Mr. Sutter, who had acted as advocate for Lewis Keseberg but she kept quiet. This was Perry's wedding too. Besides, she didn't entirely understand all her feelings.

Mr. Sinclair added, "The war isn't over yet. For all we know, the Mexican flag'll fly over the fort again. And if it does I'll be happy to hand this duty back to John."

Perry had a way of smiling directly into a person's eyes that could be construed as a challenge. "Me thinks Captain Sutter was a damned fine constable at that," he said.

But Mr. Sinclair only chuckled.

"See eye to eye with him pretty much, does ye?"

"John Sutter?" He smiled. "Oh sure. We're partners of a kind, ever since we left Hawaii. We've had the same dream about this country." He went to the door, signaled an Indian, and must have dispatched a runner.

The Indian runner, or rather boater, was fast. By the time Elitha and Perry docked at Sutter's Landing and hiked to the fort, people were congratulating them and women bustled around the clay ovens that resembled giant bee-hives. The little girls were not in the courtyard that she could see. Had they been afraid last night?

Feeling a mounting remorse at leaving them, she nearly collided with Mrs. Wolfinger at the foot of Sutter's stairs—Doris Wolfinger, who at the trial had called Lewis Keseberg a fine gentleman who "never tink to kill a vooman." Elitha backed up and murmured, "Sorry," then said to Perry, "I'm going to look for my sisters."

Mrs. Wolfinger tilted her head and said with a kindly smile, "Elitha, not to vorry. Frau Brunner make dem clean. You be da bride. Go up and zit!" She pointed the way. Perry, in obvious agreement, took her elbow and led her up the stairs. Mrs. Wolfinger followed with an Indian basket of flatbread rounds. Perry went into Mr. Sutter's adjoining room.

Uneasy feelings roiled within Elitha as she sat at the big table, along which Mrs. Wolfinger cheerfully distributed the bread. The worst was fearing that Lewis Keseberg would come through the door. The Man Eater, as people called him, walked around the fort appearing to bask in the notoriety, while she and her sisters watched their step and pressed into the shadows trying to avoid him. She doubted she could abide being in the same room with the repulsive man. Maybe Perry would make him leave. He understood her feel-ings about that.

She heard Perry talking and joking with Mr. Sutter, the thick odor of un-washed bedclothes wafting from the alcove. In turns, sunlight dazzled and then the room dimmed as emigrant women entered, set things on the table and left. Food aromas competed with the other smells. Bearded trappers with slicked-down hair came in, waltz-stepping comically around the women. The men smiled at Elitha. She had no idea their names, but smiled back, realizing that in a way she was the hostess. But as she sat with her hands folded in her lap, she felt reality fade into cloudiness, as if her feelings bore no relation to what was happening. Part of her wanted to run away. A light ache in her pri-vates reminded her of the night—she'd loved the feeling of being rocked on the boat, loved it when he'd said she was beautiful. His hands made her forget everything. His insistent kisses lulled her right up to the moment of shock and pain. She'd almost pushed him away, but couldn't because she needed his arms to remain around her.

People filled the chairs and pulled up crates—no Keseberg yet. She re-mained in her cloudy realm, a step back from the happy bride she'd always imagined she would be, and smiled at the Sinclairs as they entered.

A finger chucked her chin. She whirled to see Captain Sutter beaming down at her. "Perry iss a lucky fellow, hmm?" He wore his military finery, a blue jacket with gold epaulets and red trim. His chubby thighs strained the pale fabric of his tight pants, which disappeared into blackened knee-high boots. He nodded a welcome to the Sinclairs and others, and made a signal to an Indian girl. A few minutes later the girl staggered in with a demijohn and put it at the head of the table where Captain Sutter had seated himself like a king, one chair from Elitha.

Perry sat between them, his teasing smile and brandy breath pouring over her. In a blaze of sunlight a group of small people entered. When the door shut she saw an older woman in a brown frock with Leanna, Georgia, Frances and Ellie—stricken little faces above clean dresses. Ellie's chin quivered and her high voice penetrated the buzz of talk in the room. "You're not our big sister anymore!" Tears streamed from her eyes. Georgia and Frances wore serious pouts.

"Of course I am!" she said, hurrying to them. "Whatever gave you such an idea?"

The small woman with her hair pulled severely into a bun said confidentially, "I haff say you be der sister no more."

*She did this!* She searched the frightened eyes, two brown pairs, one blue pair, aware of the listeners in the room. "I shall ALWAYS be your big sister. It's just that now I am Mrs. McCoon too." She squatted and hugged each of them, their legs sticklike beneath the skirts.

Ellie murmured into her cheek. "But you're not my fambly now."

"Nonsense!" she wiped Ellie's tears on the corner of her dress, then steered the girls to three chairs beside her.

Mrs. Brunner muttered, "I vork hard *mit dieser mädele zauber zu machen.*"

*She had cleaned them.* "Thank you very much, Mrs. Brunner." Irritated at the woman but knowing she must be polite and grateful, Elitha curtsied and took her seat between Perry and Leanna, the sense of unreality mounting. Soon so many people squeezed in at the table she could scarcely move her arms. People who didn't fit sat on crates against the wall.

Captain Sutter stood at the head clearing his throat for attention. He raised a full glass. "*Prozit* to Mr. and Mrs. Perry McCoon."

With a loud scraping of chairs, all except Elitha stood and raised glasses. *Prozit* rumbled from more than thirty throats, and she tugged at Perry's trousers to make him sit down, but it was useless and no one seemed to notice him toasting himself. Then Sutter spoke in heavy accents about Perry, his "long-time friend and associate." She held a half-smile until her face hurt, and didn't understand the winking aside about rustled calves, which made old California hands laugh, and felt embarrassed to be sitting while everyone else was standing. The Captain extended his glass toward her and finished, "… a great beauty she iss, and a kind spirit alzo." Everyone looked at her as they drank their liquor, and her face burned like a hot poker.

Mr. Sutter leaned forward to jab his fork into the first piece from a sliced ham.

Perry patted her hot cheek and said, "She's shy, this one." Polite laugher.

The pink meat trembled on Sutter's fork. "And now, all eat," he commanded, sitting down. They all sat.

Elitha stared at the meat as it fell off Sutter's fork and rippled onto his plate. People smiled. A blizzard of arms and forks and spoons shot out to the dishes. Like an unbraked wagon down a mountain, images careened at her. The pot of blood. Mr. Coffeemeyer saying, *Corpses don't bleed.* She looked down and kept her gaze from the pots on the table. Tamsen's small form materialized before her, quailing before Lewis Keseberg—skeletal combatants. She couldn't look at people eating with fragments of food on their teeth, couldn't stand the peck peck of talk and forks. People had said Lewis Keseberg fed them information about how best to saw a skull, how long to simmer human brains, how much tastier human liver is than any other kind.

At last she felt again the cushioning fog of unreality, and spooned succotash and bread pudding on her plate. Handing the dishes to Leanna and the eager girls, she remembered that not long ago they had dreamed of a meal like this. Across the table the talk was German, Mrs. Wolfinger, Mr. Zins, and Mr. Kyburz all inclining their heads toward Mr. Sutter—Zins and Kyburz, like Sutter, being from Switzerland. Mrs. Brunner craned her neck over a man and joined the conversation. "Keseberger" came through the babble. Elitha exchanged a glance with Leanna, found and squeezed her hand beneath the table.

Mrs. Kelsey called: "This here's a weddin. Stop yer infernal talk 'bout the de-parted."

Heads bobbed approval. Mr. Sinclair stood up ringing his fork on his glass. "A toast to the bride," he announced. "The pluckiest girl I've ever met and so like her sainted mother, whose name will be remembered for all time." The *California Star* had praised Tamsen as a model for all women because she had stayed with her dying husband instead of saving herself. The writer never mentioned her children.

But then, Tamsen didn't expect to be murdered. And here sat Mr. Sutter and Mr. Sinclair, the old and new lawmakers, calmly eating. At least Lewis Keseberg didn't appear. People cheered and drank liquor, even the women.

Mr. Zins pinged on his cup with a fork. "I haff announcement." A short man, he stood patting the top of Doris Wolfinger's head while the talking stopped. "Dorotaya and I be married Saturday June tventy at tswelf noon," he said. "All invited." Shouts erupted. The tip of his large red nose hung down over his lips, which curved in the smile of a sickle moon. Not handsome like Mr. Wolfinger had been.

Mr. Sutter shouted over the hurrahs, "Ya and we haff feast here. All invited." He slapped the table so hard the plates jumped.

As Elitha clapped along with the crowd, it dawned on her that no inquest had been held in the matter of Mr. Wolfinger's death, despite the deathbed confession, and no one gossiped about the whereabouts of his money. With new sympathy she looked at the eighteen-year-old lady under Mr. Zins' hand—the color and flesh back in her cheeks, the ivory brooch at her throat. How wronged she must have felt! And lonely, even surrounded by the Donner family. No doubt she had vouched for Lewis Keseberg because of her friendship with Philippine Keseberg. A person needed friends. And now Doris, as people called her here, was going down her trail. It showed in her face.

"Till death does ya all part," said a trapper. Wine sloshed as glasses were raised.

People cheered and Perry lifted Elitha's hand like a prize.

# 34

She had hoped to leave immediately after the wedding breakfast, but by the time it was over, Perry had drunk too much aguardiente and fallen asleep on Mr. Sutter's floor. Later, looking a tender shade of green around the eyes, he explained he needed money to buy a wagon and team. She and Leanna handed over the coins they'd saved. Pocketing that, he said, "I need more," and went to Captain Sutter for "some Donner money."

Elitha was unclear on the details, but people said that after the rescuers were paid from the wagon booty, an account had been established for the Donner orphans, with Mr. Sutter in charge of distribution. She didn't know how much was in the account—did it include the $10,000 from the quilt? At the trial the rescuers had acted like they'd found nothing—but she knew she couldn't talk to Mr. Sutter without getting blubbery and appearing awfully young, though she was actually angry at him for helping Mr. Keseberg go free. The other thing she didn't know was whether the money was to be shared with her cousins despite the fact that Mr. Reed, a man of means, had taken the cousins into his family, and she and her sisters had nothing.

In any case, Perry had returned looking satisfied. "I'm glad you're taking care of the money," Elitha had told him. It was good to have a husband to see to these complex matters.

Now it was the next morning. Leanna scanned the adobe room and pronounced it clean. Elitha agreed. The woodshavings were neatly hemmed in and the switches laid straight by the firepit, the ashes removed. They had all pitched in, bouncing around and cheerful for the first time in a month. Their hair was braided and the carpetbag filled with their extra clothing, which Tamsen had laboriously sewn. In the bottom were Elitha's apple seeds.

Georgia dandled Tamsen's black silk stocking with the fancy gold TD embroidered at the top. Elitha knew she'd be devastated to lose this one keepsake from her mother, which she had brought down the mountains in the pocket of her cloak. Ellie held the other stocking.

"Stuff 'er in," Elitha said, pushing the carpetbag at Georgia.

She shook her head and laid the silk against her cheek, looking mournful.

"You can't hold it the whole way. We'll be six hours in the wagon."

Georgia shoved the stocking down the neck of her dress, and looked pleased.

Remembering her own sorrow, and Leanna's, when their real mother died, Elitha sympathized. "Sure it won't fall out? Here Sugar," She tightened the sash of the frock. "There. That'll help to hold it in."

Ellie, having watched this, stuffed Tamsen's other stocking down the front of her dress, then turned her back and waited for Elitha to retie her sash as well.

That done, Elitha twirled her around and squeezed her, so sweet she was with her large brown eyes and cheeks grown plumper. Tiny for her age, like Tamsen, with a mind as keen as a tack. Suddenly aware that Frances had not a stitch to remember her mother by, Elitha hugged her too and tried to revive the cheerful mood. "We're going to have such fun on Perry's farm! You'll see. There's a nice stream near the house, and you can watch him with his cattle. He's a wonderful baquéro." Sometimes she thought that word started with v.

"Is a buck-arrow a man what gits bucked off? And Indians shoot at him?"

Elitha smiled. "Ask Mr. McCoon what it means, Ellie." He would be a full-time rancher now, and, she hoped, a little happier than he'd been of late. Recalling how he'd acted last evening, she felt her smile fade.

She had gone with him to the skiff, the *Sacramento*, and he had petted the railing as though it were a living thing. "A land lubber I is, from now on."

He had laid out the blanket. Knowing what he wanted, she stepped back, uneasy about the girls. "I need to go back to the room and tell my sisters where I am," she said. "They'll fret." Like they had the night before.

He gave her a steady look. "You're married now."

"It won't take long," she said. It was a half mile, but she'd hurry.

He took her by the shoulders and his eyes glistened strangely.

"I'm sorry, I just—"

His mouth came down on hers, then he drew back just enough that his lips grazed hers as he whispered hoarsely, "Hit won't take long." Mocking what she'd just said? He was unbuttoning her frock.

"Somebody might see us." The days were long now and drops of golden light filtered through the trees, playing on the restless green water around the rocking boat. Anybody could happen upon them here at Sutter's Landing.

His fingers worked the buttons. "So what if they does? We're married now."

She had lain on the blanket feeling conspicuous with her skirt up and her bodice apart. Moaning, he moved over her, trouser flap down, and fondled her breasts. Then he pulled back and looked at her privates. Embarrassed, she squirmed, wishing he'd get it over with so she could go to her sisters.

"Ent never seen nothin to match the whiteness." He ran his hand up and down between her thighs. "Like heaven's milk they is, here in the light of day."

No doubt he'd seen the legs of every kind of dark-skinned woman from Africa to the Sandwich Islands. She felt excruciatingly uncomfortable being examined like this. "Please just—"

"Big Sist—" A small voice was smothered out. Leaves thrashed on the bank.

Shocked that the girls had followed, she pushed Perry away with strength that surprised her, threw down her dress and scrutinized the shore. All she saw were leaves. "Where are you girls?"

Perry was on his knees with his extended self visible. The four stepped shyly into view. "I told 'em we shouldn't a-come," Leanna said, looking down.

"I should'ov told you I'd be a while," Elitha said.

"Well, you got an eyeful," Perry barked, "now get the hell out of here!" They shrank back, a step at a time, Frances stumbling.

Elitha softened it. "Go on back to the room. I'll be there in a while."

When they were gone, Perry proceeded. He seemed distant, and she worried somebody else would come, and worried that she'd handled the situation badly. She didn't know much about being a wife.

Now, clasping the handles of the carpetbag and smiling at the girls, she tried to put that behind her. Things would be better at Perry's ranch. "I can't wait to get on the trail," she said.

"Me neither," they repeated one after the other as she tied their bonnets.

"Let's go to the gate," Georgia sang out.

"Yeah!"

"I'll beat you."

"No you won't."

The string of laughing girls ran out the door, their feet mostly recovered, and Elitha followed them to where Perry would come with the wagon. As the bouncy sisters darted around the young soldier at the gate, Elitha felt the sun through her frock—surprisingly hot despite the wind. It tugged at her bonnet and blew the girls' hair from their braids and bonnets—the strands she'd cut to eliminate the knotted mats.

"Don't touch the cannon," the soldier grumped.

They hunched in a circle covering guilty grins. Elitha looked up the west path, but saw no wagon, only a dust devil. *Someone died.* Many had died.

"You gonna teach me to read?" Ellie grinned.

Elitha chased after her, caught her up in her arms and growled into her neck. "Didn't I promise?" Ellie giggled a perfect arpeggio and kicked her legs in the air.

"We're going to have our own school," Georgia told the soldier, who, having made a leaning post of his gun, wiped perspiration from under a hat decorated with crossed guns.

"She's gonna be our teacher!" Pointing at Elitha.

"At Mr. McCoon's farm," said Georgia.

"And my big sisters won't go away to work no more!"

He gave them a tired look.

Glancing inside the gate, Elitha saw Lewis Keseberg coming down the stairs with Captain Sutter. She froze as they vanished into a shop. Impatience tore at her. When would Perry come? The air smelled like tinder. Then came a sound she had never heard before—like a high note singing down around them, a prickly hum within the wind. Maybe fire searing through the dry grass? She looked all around but saw no smoke. The girls stopped playing. "What is that noise?" Frances asked.

Elitha looked to the soldier, who restored the gun to his shoulder and frowned uneasily at the plains. He didn't know. Sam Kyburz drove a team of oxen past the fort, pulling a load of bulging leather bags. He smiled and lifted his hat to Elitha, apparently unconcerned about the sound. She didn't ask. Riders came and went, seemingly oblivious. Then a team of horses materialized in the dust of the west path. The girls saw it and jumped up and down, holding hands. "He's coming, he's coming!"

But the wagon's driver turned out to be a dark-skinned Indian woman wearing white woman's clothes. She pulled the team to a stop near them and hopped down to secure the team, one thick black braid swinging.

Elitha said, "Pardon me, but do you know what that noise is?"

The woman said, "Grass opens."

The eavesdropping soldier looked as perplexed as Elitha. The woman reached down beside the cannon wheel and plucked a stalk of dry grass, pointed to the papery seedpods, and then gestured around the horizons. "Open when dry."

Elitha understood. A single pop was too faint to be heard, but millions popping at the same time made this noise—surprisingly loud to be heard over the wind. She explained it to the girls, and Ellie's eyes lit up. They all bent forward, ears to the blowing pods, hands on knees, listening.

With the mystery solved, Elitha's impatience heightened. Intent on looking for a wagon, she didn't pay attention to a horse with big brown and white spots galloping toward her. Then she saw his face, pinched and hard beneath his leather hat, the dust from the hooves rapidly disappearing.

"Get aboard," he said with an expression like last evening in the boat.

"Where's the wagon?" she asked. The girls circled her like chicks.

"Can't get one now. Next time."

"We can't all fit on the horse." Her stomach felt hollow.

"Mrs. Brunner'll see after the girls, she will. I tended to it. Now get on."

He gave her a look so steely she almost couldn't speak.

"But you said—"

"I said get on!"

She felt the girls clutching her dress, heard them start to whimper.

In a vexed tone Perry yelled at a man who was strolling toward the outhouse. "Taik these girls, will ye Ned? Give 'em to the Brunner laidy when ye sees her." A man in buckskins turned, stroked his beard, ran his eyes over Leanna and said something Elitha couldn't hear over the whoosh of wind and the whine of the grass.

Looking at Perry's narrowed eyes, she wondered with a shock if he'd planned this. The thought made her feel like a scrap of paper blowing in the wind. Her fourteen years were nothing against his thirty-six. She felt weak and trembly. He could have bought a wagon; they were cheap with more having come over the mountains than people needed. This man with cruel Spanish spurs seemed a total stranger. But only yesterday she had promised before God and witnesses to obey him till death did them part. She couldn't balk at the first obstacle, no matter how much she hated leaving her sisters.

She squatted before the girls and looked into their tear-streaked faces, so recently dry and happy. But no words came. She inclined her head and they all touched foreheads.

"Oh fer Chrissake git on me bleedin 'orse."

She looked up to see his fingers close on the braided coil of rope hanging from his saddle. His ugly expression frightened her. Women and children walking by stared, pity on some of the faces, amusement on others.

Feeling a bafflement as alien as the singing grass, she stammered, "How long before we come back for them?" She saw the flicker in Leanna's eyes and knew her hundred-percent sister understood her resignation.

He dropped the lariat, left it hanging in its coil. "A few daiys."

Murmuring that they'd have to be brave and stay with Mrs. Brunner for a while, Elitha hugged the little girls one by one. Georgia collapsed crying in her arms. Ellie's brown eyes were frenzied as she flung herself at Elitha's neck, nearly knocking her down. "But you said you—" Unable to finish her sentence, Ellie hung on fiercely while Elitha tried to hug Frances. "But Grandma Brunner isn't here," Frances bawled. A desperate, last-resort argument.

At least they had a name for the woman, one that suggested familiarity and friendship. She pushed the carpetbag into Leanna's hand. Then like magic Mrs. Brunner appeared, disentangling Ellie's fingers and peeling her from Elitha's neck. The German woman corralled the weeping girls while Elitha stood stranded in their heartbroken gazes. *All alone in the wicked world.* She was leaving them after all, leaving them as their mother had done. But this was only for a few days. People traveled back and forth to the fort all the time, she told herself.

Suddenly Perry was on the ground shoving her at the horse. She put her shoe in the leather stirrup and mounted. He landed heavily behind her. Then they were galloping away. She turned back. Mrs. Brunner flapped her hand good-bye. Sad-faced Leanna stood behind the weeping girls, the devil wind whipping their skirts before them.

# 35

D amned norther!"
     It was the first thing Perry had said since leaving New Helvetia. It had been hours. Afraid if she spoke, she'd accuse him of deceiving her, Elitha watched waves moving across the ocean of golden grass and listened to its unearthly wail. *Ma said you was to care fer us till she comes through*, Frances had said when they came down from the mountains. That meant forever now. Tamsen's trust in her felt like a sacred bargain. It made tears run from her eyes, blurring the landscape mile after mile. But she never stopped countering with, *We'll fetch them in a few days.*

"Brings the bleedin 'eat, hit does."

The last time it blew like this, when she'd found her sisters roasting liver, the grass had turned brown and the fort had sweltered for a week.

Something large and dark suddenly swept toward them across the grass, faster than any earthly thing. She shrank back, heart clamped in her throat. It was nearly upon them before she realized it was a shadow. She looked up to see a giant black and white bird—a condor. She'd never seen one so close. The center of the bird looked like a black man with arms outstretched surrounded by white, the body tapering down at the tail. It was a huge bird with tremendously long black feathers at the tips soaring effortlessly on the wind. The bird glided closer in the cloudless blue, correcting, looking down at them with the ugliest head she'd ever seen—naked, blotched, pinkish—the neck swollen and loose-skinned like an old man with a goiter. Her scalp prickled and fear buzzed in her limbs as she met the bird's fierce scowl, the unblinking red eye and the bony curve of its beak.

Perry shouted, "Vamoose!" He grabbed his sidearm and fired. But the bird had already surged forward and shrank before them until it was nothing but a black spot in the sky. He stuffed the gun in his belt, grumping, "Taik calves from their mum's teats, the bleedin' bastards does."

It seemed that California had the biggest of everything—mountains, bears, trees and birds. Ahead romped a herd of about thirty antelope, peach-colored with white markings, pronghorns erect. Like the others they'd seen, these bounded away as fluid as fish in water. She saw many deer nesting in the shade of the whipping, thrashing oaks. Sometimes the horse passed so near, she could see their fur riffle in the wind. But no matter what she saw, the faces of her sisters haunted her. Had they stopped crying? The worry that Perry had planned this came at her as relentlessly as the wind, as prickly as the howling grass.

Suddenly the horse lurched off the trail at a run and she grabbed the horn to keep from bouncing off. Ahead Perry's hat was tumbling over the grass at a high speed. He spurred the horse and overtook it, maintaining a gallop beside the hat. She felt him slip and feared he'd fallen, but he swept up the hat and pulled himself up, yelling, "Hang on, lassie." Back in the saddle he jammed the hat on his head, secured the bead, and turned the horse toward the trail. A man at home in the wind, as skilled on a horse as on a boat.

A strange wind too, she thought as the horse slowed to a walk. Every north wind she'd ever heard of brought cold air. This one blasted like a blow furnace. Her lips were cracked and dry, her back wet and tight against the man she'd married—a man as alien as the wind.

They topped a rise and she was surprised to look down into a valley with a swath of green running through it. She hadn't known they'd been climbing. Far in the distance stretched the mountains—from horizon to horizon— capped in white. It felt eerie to see, with all the haze blown away, those broken, angular surfaces, and to know that she'd walked across them and her parents would remain forever in those heights.

"There be Rancho Omuchumne," he was saying. "Sheldon and Daylor's grant."

She looked at the green bottomland. "Rancho Omu—"

"Named it for the niggers, Jared did."

The horse swayed as they descended into the valley, whinnying to another horse on the slope where a dark-skinned rider sat with the cattle. The bottomland was a tangle of trees and vines and berry brambles, except for the trail on which they loped until they came to a tiny wooden cabin. A saddled horse stood outside.

"Ahoy!" Perry called, reining in. In her ear he said confidentially, "A naighbor of ours."

The door opened and out stepped a short girl about Elitha's age, maybe younger, a pink frock stretched across her plump bodice. She wasn't pretty, her nose being a little on the fleshy side, but she had a generous smile and a likeable, impish grin. The wind stole locks of her brown hair from the bun on top of her head.

"Well blow me down!" Perry said from behind, "Me eyes was set to see that man o' yours."

"He's hereabouts." The girl placed her hand on her forehead, holding back the hair.

"This 'ere's me new bride, Elitha," Perry said, clapping her on the shoulder. "That be Catherine Sheldon."

"Catey," the girl corrected with a grin.

A man stepped from mounds of berry canes as high as the house, a muddy shovel in hand. A hat shaded the hard wedge of his face but didn't diminish the power of his level gaze. "Howdy," he said. A man who was never surprised, Elitha guessed. Probably in his mid-thirties, same as Perry.

Catherine disentangled a sweating pottery gourd hanging from a rope-woven sling on the shady side of the porch and held it out for them. Her hazel eyes twinkled as she ordered, "Well neighbors, gitcher selves on down fer a drink."

The surprisingly cool water eased Elitha's throat. She couldn't get enough. It felt wonderful spilling down her bodice too, the fit still loose after these three months. Handing the gourd to Perry, she saw the teasing love Catherine sent to Mr. Sheldon, and the intimate look he returned.

Catey said, "Shame on you for not telling me we was to have neighbors." She winked at Elitha. "Come on in outa the wind."

But Perry glanced at the sun and said, "Thank 'e, but no. We'd visit a spell but we're late enough. Stopping at Daylor's too, we is." He turned to Sheldon. "Expected you'd be at yer new house up yonder." He nodded his hat at a trail cut through the thicket.

Catherine answered, "We're helpin Bill and Sally clear the slough." Sheldon seemed easy with his wife doing the talking. The same wouldn't be said of Perry, Elitha knew, though she didn't know how she knew.

Perry tilted back on his heels, "Now a man with two houses could get muddled about where his boots lie, couldn't 'e?" Catherine was taking in his dimple and the long dark lashes over his cheeks, the kind of lashes women wished they had.

Mr. Sheldon swung his gaze from Perry to Catherine and back again, lining up his lips in a hint of a smile. "No sense in tearing down this old bachelor cabin." He nodded at it. "We call it Slough House, to keep ourselves straight."

"Slough House!" Perry hawed.

Elitha wasn't sure what was funny. *Slew?*

Perry said, "A bloke'd think it were a fine inn. But slough!" He shook off another chuckle. A thing was either fine or a slough, but not both. Then she realized that therein lay the joke.

Catey said, "Just never try'n spell it!" She grinned and Elitha liked her.

Then they were on their way, waving at neighbors she looked forward to seeing again. A mile or so beyond Slough House they came to Daylor's Trading Post, a two-room adobe backed up to a riverbank and surrounded by cottonwoods. The bare earth yard was littered with green leaves, which had been torn from the trees. If it hadn't been June and hot, she would have thought autumn had come. The gale tired her.

Stepping out to greet them was a tall, broad-shouldered man with a prominent nose, lopsided smile and receding hairline—about the same age as Perry. His greeting came in Perry's accent. He looked wiry and powerful beside the willowy girl who followed him to the porch. She was maybe eighteen years old, dark hair parted in the middle and tied up in a neat bun. Elitha didn't feel the same rush of liking she'd felt for Catherine, perhaps because of Mrs. Daylor's greater age and poise.

Inside, Perry purchased flour and beans, and talked to the man. Elitha told Sarah Daylor, "I met Catey back up the trail."

"That's my little sister," Sarah said with a smile.

"Your sister! How nice you're so nigh one another."

"Yes, and Mother and Father Rhoads aren't far down the river."

"Rhoads? That's the name of the man who rescued me and my sisters." At the mention of her sisters, the sad little faces came at her and Elitha could hardly bear it.

"You mean my brothers John and Dan? They went up to rescue the Donner Party."

"Both of them came to rescue us. I'm a Donner. Came through with the First Relief." Daniel Rhoads had gone ahead to the fort while Mr. Coffeemeyer brought back the cache of much-needed food. "John's a good man," she said.

"That he is. Took in my sister-in-law's' children and brought them across to California just like they was his own. Matilda's a dear too."

Perry was counting coins into Bill Daylor's hand.

"I met your sister Elizabeth at Johnson's ranch," Elitha said, not mentioning the horrid Mr. Johnson. "Is John's place nearby?" She knew he was farming on the Cosumney, as some called the river, and she hoped he was nearby.

Sarah flapped her hand southward. "Less than a mile."

"How grand, to have family close by."

Sarah Daylor looked at her as though a question was on the tip of her tongue.

Perry and Bill Daylor were hauling bags of flour, beans and sugar to the horse and strapping them behind the saddle. Then, too soon, Perry spurred the horse and they were riding east, following the same double track, a good deal fainter now.

"Sutter's trail, this is," Perry said from behind. "His woodcutters goin' up to Piney Woods made it."

"How much farther to your place?" Layers of hills stretched before her.

"Bout six miles."

She settled back, watching the sway of their awkward shadow—horse, riders and bundles, the sun low at their backs—and worried about her sisters. The devil wind blew ceaselessly over the hum of the grass. At last Perry pointed past her bonnet and said, "Thar she be."

She followed his finger. On the brow of a hill beneath two oaks she made out a small adobe cabin, pink in the setting sun. The place looked sad and remote, with the nearest neighbor six miles away. Dark squares flanked the door, windows that would have reflected the sun had they been glazed. The cabin stared blindly down a slope that led to thick willows and cottonwoods, which had to be near a river. Strewn on the hillsides were huge boulders. It came to her that someday the house would melt into the earth without a trace, but those boulders would remain.

"Me 'ome sweet 'ome," he crooned as galloped up the slope. "Where a sailor finds 'is rest. And a good barrel of aguardiente." He threw back his head and hawed. "Me 'aunted 'ouse, it tis."

*Haunted house?* Headachy after the long day, she stored that away in her mind.

The horse stopped before a cracked hide beating at the cabin doorway. She dismounted and pushed the drape aside, peering inside. The place was dim, noticeably cooler and rank with the smell of rodent scat. In a corner she made out a tangle of dusty blankets. In the middle of the room stood an unlevel table crusty with candlewax and white bird guano. A round of a tree stump, a dusty barrel and a bucket completed the furnishings—all connected by spider webs. Denser webs choked the twin window holes, and big tits of dried mud clung to the walls and ceiling, enough nests to harbor every wasp in Illinois.

She pulled her head out and, as Perry unstrapped the bags, glanced around at the rolling landscape—the ever-present oaks, boulders frosted with gray lichens. Then it hit her. The devil wind had stopped and the hum of grass had diminished. It seemed as though the retiring sun had sapped all energy from the world. A bird called, the first she'd been able to hear all day. She caught a whiff of something familiar. Damp moss. A muddy creek bottom of a summer evening, a memory of the stream crossing the Donner farm, where she and Leanna had spent so many hours. She smelled the river.

The aromas soothed her a little, and the absence of wind. Here, far from whispers, far from Lewis Keseberg, she would find relief. In a few days she'd go back for her sisters, never mind how terribly far it had turned out to be. She set aside her doubts about Perry and told herself this was her home. "I don't see any cows," she remarked in a light tone.

"Be fetching 'em, I will," he said, hanging tack on a peg outside the door.

"But where are they now?"

The point of his jaw moved and the salt circling his lips lent him a fierce look. "Better learn this now, lassie. Me own affair, it tis, 'ow I run me rancho." His eyes punched hard as steel.

She felt slapped, and hadn't recovered when he said, "I gots me an idear."

Clamping a hand on the back of her neck, he steered her inside toward the filthy blankets.

# 36

As he was leaving the next morning, Perry pocketed a handful of glass beads. "For tamin me niggers," he said with a teasing grin. It was hard to tell when he was joking. "Now don't get near 'em," he added, "Wild as banshees, they be."

"They haven't hurt you, have they?" She knew only that they'd eaten his pigs. In Illinois, most white men had signed up for the Black Hawk War against the Kickapoo, and across the plains the cry "Indians" brought a terrified clamor for guns. But the California natives were friendly. The only Indian trouble the wagon train experienced occurred on the eastern side of the Sierra, when in the morning light the emigrants would find arrows in their cattle. This slowed the animals down until they dropped and became food for the natives. Secretly Elitha thought it was fair, because like the Indians in the Great Plains, those in California were likely to lose their hunting grounds to white people. No one ever said outright that her mother was mostly Kickapoo, but she had put two and two together.

She followed Perry out the door and watched him whistle for his horse.

"Just stay nigh to me 'ouse." With a snigger he added, "Ent about to touch ye in there."

"But Perry, I was going to wash the blankets." That meant going to the river.

He turned to her, the lines of his face softer, amused—like he wasn't worried. Then he turned and walked up the hill to meet his horse. Pondering how he could frighten her and yet be amused, she knew the Indian village was only a half mile away. If they wanted to do mischief they could have done it by now. No cowhide drape could stop them. She decided this was just his way of showing that he cared about her. She went inside for the knife and a length of split-leather strapping she'd found on the floor. Then she went down to the river to cut willows and tie the stiffer twigs together for a broom.

Seeing no Indians, she gathered a good bunch of switches and, back in the house, swept animal droppings and flattened gopher mounds. She swept down masses of spider webs and, using the bucket, scooped out a deep nest of ant eggs that she'd found when she picked up the bucket. Ants scurried all over her. Hurrying back to the river, she took off her frock and washed the ants out, submerging long enough to drown the ones in her underclothes and hair. She dressed and carried water from the river, pouring it over the floor to make the clay smooth and hard underfoot, as people did in New Helvetia.

Last, she poured water over the heaps of bird guano and scraped it from the table with a rock.

As she worked, Pa's stories came back to her, of his youth fifty-five years ago. The Kentucky Indians had been plentiful then. He admired the brave pioneer women giving birth, settling problems, and handling bloody accidents that befell their children while the men were away. With a lift of his chin he liked to finish his stories with, *You gotta be tough. Wary, but not fearful.*

It was stifling outside, her clothing already dry, but she remembered her vow never to complain of the heat again. She carried Perry's moth-eaten bedclothes to the river, rolled up her sleeves, and scrubbed them good. *What did* Indians *here do for soap?* The splashing water refreshed her. Steam rose when she stretched the blankets over boulders too hot to the touch. She let them dry all day, hoping it would fry any nits that might remain. When the sun went down, she folded the sweet-smelling blankets and felt pleased with her progress. The only setback was that a wasp had stung her hand when she'd bumped a nest with the broom.

Perry returned, tight-lipped about the Indians. He didn't seem to want to talk at all. After supper he removed his trousers and, as he called it, poked her. Despite the fact that her sisters were on her mind and he was dirty from the long day, she was glad he wanted her and she liked the feel of him against her. Afterwards she ventured, "Perry?"

"Mmm."

She decided to start with something besides the little girls. "I got stung by a wasp." She held up the back of her puffy hand. "See?"

He didn't look.

"Well, I was wondering…"

"What?"

"How do people in California clean out wasps nests?"

"Leave the sons-o-bitches be." He flopped over toward the wall.

In the presence of ladies or children, Pa had always shifted to *son-of-a-gun*. "But they're flying in and out all day and I have to watch my step."

"Leave a body alone at night, they does."

Before she could say any more, he was snoring.

As the darkness intensified, a big empty space opened inside her, in the place where Leanna used to be. She realized this was the first time they had ever been apart. In Pa's world, with children from three wives, Leanna and Elitha had been "the girls," quiet and useful, four-handed, bracketed between his two other families. Drifting toward sleep at last, she saw again the circle of half-sisters in her mind's eye, heard them crying with the wind, but she knew Leanna would do her best to care for them until Elitha came back. In a day or two. Only a day or two.

Three days later she said to Perry as he was leaving in the morning, "When we go to the fort for the girls, we should buy window glass. I saw some in Mr. Mellus' store."

He held the leather drape up in front of him in a way that caused the early sun to strike his eyes. The pupils were pinpoints. Outside, not a leaf stirred. "Warm weather we's 'avin now," he said. "No need fer window glass till fall." He dropped the hide and whistled for his horse.

"We gotta get the girls anyway," she said, following him out and feeling ever more uncomfortable with the way he put her off.

He gave her a strange look and went to Paint, his horse.

She knew her sisters were looking for her by now. It cut like a knife in her heart.

Twilight came but no Perry. She sat under the oak near the door and ate a lonely supper of salt pork and beans, leaving his portion in the pot. Afterwards she hauled it high into the tree in the rope pulley he'd made. He'd warned her never to keep food in the house, or grizzly bears would come inside looking. *Grizzly bears.* The most ferocious creatures in the world. At the fort she'd heard how they could be shot ten times and still tear a man from limb to limb.

The sun's last smudge of red and gold vanished on the brow of the hill, but the air remained very warm. In her camisole and underdrawers, she crawled on top of the prickly wool blankets, feeling her way. Then she lay listening for Paint.

The darkness thickened before her eyes. Aware of her heart thudding inside its own dark room, she felt small and fragile at the bottom of the moonless dome of night, the drape at the door no comfort. Sounds were louder in the dark. Coyotes warbled and yipped, many of them nearby. Mosquitos sang in her ears. She batted at them, wondering if Perry were injured. Lying alone on the ground somewhere.

No horse came. Only the ghostly owls landing in the branches overhead. Oo-ooo-oo. Several owls. Some in higher or lower pitches, dissonant at times. It added to her jitters. Was he dead? Something screeched above the roof. She bolted upright, heart hammering. A bird? An Indian signalling? Tentatively she lay back on the blankets. Maybe a screech owl.

A half-moon rose and traveled across the sky, invading the window through the tracery of limbs on the wall. A wolf howled nearby and she bolted up again, gooseflesh rising. Other wolves answered, hollow tones sliding upward into unearthly falsettos. She reached down, checked the tree limb she'd laid beside the bed, glad to feel its rough surface. The keen edge of the knife met her probing fingers beneath the folded blanket she used for a pillow. Did grizzly bears make warning sounds? *You gotta be tough.* Women mustn't expect to be coddled. Sometimes a man went hunting and got on a trail he had to follow. After all, Perry didn't have any cattle yet, so he wasn't like a settled farmer who could be counted on to come in at sundown.

To quiet her mind, she mimicked the owls and hoped predators would think no human was inside. Sometimes she did so well she silenced the real owls, and imagined them sitting perplexed on their branches. Then she began to think Perry had something else under his hat. Maybe he'd gone to fetch the girls! It seemed the best explanation, the only one in fact. He wanted to surprise her! And what a surprise it would be! With this thought she sank in and out of sleep, and toward morning felt cool enough to pull a light blanket over herself.

The orange sun fired the hillside when she awoke. Relieved to be in one piece, she straightened the blankets, looked around the now tidied room, and didn't know what else to do. She had no fabric to sew—not having wanted to beg Perry to buy a bolt of calico she'd seen at Daylor's trading post, not knowing at that time how many yards she'd need to make curtains. She pulled on her petticoat, frock and bonnet, tied the blue crystals around her neck, and went outside. She lowered the pulley system and ate Perry's supper from last night, thinking that if he'd gone to the fort, he wouldn't arrive before sundown today, at the earliest, or the next day if he had other business. She hardened herself to the thought of a second night alone.

Already the sun burned the backs of her hands and perspiration trickled between her breasts. She moved to the shade and watched birds busying themselves before the worst heat set in. She'd seen that yesterday. They hopped up and down vertical trunks, stabbing for insects or playing tag in the branches with no sad thoughts about the past and no fears for the future. *His eye is on the sparrow,* Tamsen used to say. About thirty quail pecked their way toward her, a muddle of fat gray creatures with baubles quivering comically before their beaks. Then in a great startled roar, they winged away.

She looked up to see what frightened them, and met cat's eyes. A gray-striped cat the size of a coyote rose from a crouch and strolled away on long striped legs, dark spots on its belly and a tail no longer than her finger. When the cat was gone, a cottontail rabbit dashed across the open space and disappeared into a tunnel of grass. She'd seen them everywhere, scampering around despite the hawks crying overhead and the cats and wolves prowling the grass. She felt herself settling into a peaceful frame of mind, not waiting, but joining the buzz of life in which all creatures, hunters and hunted, enjoyed the day for its own sake. She went down to the river to explore.

Deer clattered over the rocks at her approach. The river, not much wider than a creek by Illinois standards, moved along not too fast and not too slow. Along its banks she entered a lush, green world. Swallows dived and swooped over the sparkling water, seemingly at play, but actually hunting insects.

She removed her frock and stepped into the warm mud, moss tendrils tickling between her toes. She clutched her skirts up around her hips and waded deeper. But it was silly to keep her skirt dry, so she dropped it and it billowed. Curious fish studied her. One stood on its nose examining her enlarged, water-distorted foot. The fish didn't leave, even when she wiggled her toes. The sun pierced the water, illuminating a forest of wavy underwater plants and flashing through the blue crystals around her neck. No breeze moved the loose hair enveloping her shoulders. The bonnet protected her head from the sun, but intense heat reflected from the water's bright surface onto her face.

Not a swimmer, she stepped cautiously on the slippery submerged boulders, watching her feet. Scattered in the silt were golden scales that threw the sun's glint back at her. Too light for gold, Perry had said. Her feet stirred up tadpoles, fat heads propelled by tails darting into the muck. With heat pressing into her bonnet, the chilly water felt good inching up to her waist and torso and breasts.

She was up to her armpits, feet braced against the lazy current, when a much bigger yellow gleam caught her eye. Careful not to stir the silt, she moved toward what looked like a twist of metal, like slag she seen in the ashes of Pa's forge, except for the bright color. She touched it with her toe. It was firmly lodged in a crack between rocks. Gold? In a story Tamsen once read aloud, a boy found a pirate's treasure trove. *His heart leapt,* Tamsen had enunciated significantly. A silly thing to remember now. Even if this were gold, it was no treasure trove. Anyway, why would gold be in a river? Didn't it come from mines dug deep into the ground?

Trying to move it with her toe, she heard rocks clatter on shore and looked up to see a naked squaw. Off-balance, she put a foot downstream, afraid she'd step in over her head. But, thankfully her foot came to rest on another large boulder. She braced herself and saw that the Indian, who looked about her age, had a baby in a cradleboard. She glanced around, but no other Indians were to be seen. The young girl sat down in the shade of the willows as if to observe Eliltha. Like all Indian women in California, she wore a woven skullcap, a leather string of objects between her bare breasts and a tattoo of dotted parallel lines running down from lip to chin. From a distance it resembled a beard. Otherwise she was very pretty, in a soft brown way, and her expression was as calm as the morning.

She unlaced the cradleboard and set the baby in the sand beside her. The paleness of his skin against his mother's skin struck Elitha. He looked like one of the half-breed babies at Johnson's ranch. But Perry was the only white man around. No, she recalled. A man had been helping him raise hogs, a German named Adolph Brüheim. He'd also helped with the Relief effort, butchering at Johnson's ranch as she recalled.

The Indian girl beckoned. The yellow lump would wait. Elitha moved toward the shore. The baby squeezed sand in his fat fists and grinned at her. That grin. Those dimples. Perry was the only man in California with that smile. She filled in blanks, where he went at night and why he insisted she stay away from Indians. Was this his wife? *Dear Lord no.*

Suddenly coming at her was the talk she'd had with Mary Murphy about plural wives, and she had seen that the rough men in California had as many Indian wives as they pleased—maybe that's why the Mormons wanted to come here. Feeling like a wind-up doll, she stepped out of the water onto the hot sand.

"Hola," the girl said.

"Hello." Her petticoat plastered itself to her legs, water streaming down her body, cooling the sand as she stepped across it.

"Perrimacoo be you man?" the girl said.

*Be.* Just as Perry would use it. Lowering herself on a flat stone, she summoned her courage and said, "Yes. You too? He be your man?"

This brought a long silence. The Indian girl was looking not into her eyes, but at the blue crystals around her neck.

Wringing water from her undergarment, Elitha examined the baby, who was patting the sand, and realized that other men might well have such dimples. "What is your name?" she asked the baby's mother.

The girl gazed at the river, her eyes large black pools in which the pupils could not be defined. "Americans lose power by'm tongue," she said.

What did that mean? She noticed the girl's sitting posture, somehow dignified despite the exposure of her privates, and repeated, "What is your name?"

Her bluntly cut hair grazed her shoulders as she briefly turned full face to Elitha, then back to the river. Her expression remained calm, her hands open and quiet beside her raised knees, but she said nothing.

"My name is Elitha McCoon."

Nothing came back. The baby got up and toddled to Elitha, his brown eyes much paler than his mother's, the pupils visible. His hair was light brown. He grabbed the crystals.

In a fluid motion the girl disengaged his hand, whisked him to her lap and rubbed his fingers and palms with a bundle of leaves hanging from her neck. She intoned mournful sounds and then rushed him to the water, waded to her waist and dunked him repeatedly over his head, each time turning him a different direction. He sputtered but did not howl, as any baby Elitha had ever known would have.

The girl returned, laced him into the cradleboard and jammed it upright into the sand where he could see, but presumably not touch Elitha.

Feeling insulted, not only by that, but the girl's refusal to answer questions, Elitha studied the child beneath the sunshade built into the cradleboard. Water from his hair streamed over his face, which now stretched into a slow grin and narrowed his eyes in a way that laid his long lashes on his chubby cheeks. This was Perry's baby! Had Perry been with this girl last night? Had she come here to flaunt the child, calm as you please?

"I am daughter of Captain Juan," the naked brown girl said, with seeming pride.

Indian chieftains in California, Elitha knew, called themselves captains in imitation of Captain Sutter, and Juan was the chief of the local tribe, the one Perry said he was trying to tame. Apparently he'd tamed the daughter. Well, Elitha wasn't about to sit here and have her think she was anybody just because her father called himself a captain.

"I am the daughter of Captain George Donner," she replied with a lift of her chin. Nevertheless, she felt terribly uncomfortable talking to this bed-partner of her husband, but couldn't make herself get up and leave. There was more she needed to learn.

The girl seemed to be looking at a distant point. "Luck charm, my brother," she said, then lifted a hand to point briefly at the crystals.

Had Perry got them here instead of Johnson's, as he had claimed? A discrepancy wouldn't surprise her—she no longer expected the truth from him. She held the bauble away from her neck. "You sure?"

The girl's gaze moved over it. "My brother lucky charm. Where from?"

If it was her brother's, she'd know where it was from. "My husband gave it to me."

"Where?" the girl probed.

Had Perry stolen it? If one thing was impressed on emigrants, it was never to take Indians' belongings unless they were given. Gruesome retaliation could follow. Surely Perry knew that. "He said he got it from Johnson's ranch."

The girl gazed silently at the distance while Perry's baby looked from one to the other. Then the mother said, "Where Johnson Ranch?"

"North of here a long piece." She pointed.

More silence. Elitha took off the necklace. "Here, you can have it back."

She shied at the crystals like a horse at a snake. "Rock is power. Kill," she said, flexing her knees behind the cradleboard and shrugging it onto her back. "Perrimacoo house bad luck." She turned and started walking away.

Those were not the actions of a girl flaunting her man's attentions. But it did fit with Perry saying the Indians believed his house was haunted—a barrel of aguardiente had stood there for months without being touched. The firm brown buttocks were resolutely shifting away. "Please don't go," Elitha said. It came out before she could think

The girl turned halfway toward her, the small likeness of Perry peering around her brown shoulder.

"I'd like us to be friends." Elitha didn't know what made her say it.

A full, genuine smile shone back at her.

# 37

An hour or so later Elitha headed out to where she'd seen the yellow metal in the river. She laughed aloud. The girls would love it here and they were surely on their way, because the Indian girl had said Perry went to New Helvetia for his cattle. Surely he intended to surprise her with the girls too. She had misjudged him, and could hardly wait to see her sisters. About the Indian girl, well, things weren't a bad as she'd suspected. She'd said her man's name was Pedro.

As she searched for the nugget, Elitha reviewed the strange visit with a girl from the Stone Age, as a schoolteacher had called it. She seemed to have no guile. Elitha believed her when she'd said Perry was no longer seeing her, though she admitted the baby was his. What she didn't want to say, she didn't say at all, like her name. Talk would grow easier in time, Elitha thought, spying the sparkle beneath the moving water. And it pleased her to have an Indian friend, even one whom Perry had known carnally.

She nudged the lump up the crack between rocks and quickly grasped it between her toes, trying hard not to lose it in the murky bottom. She raised it to her hand, and sure enough, the twisted yellow metal lay heavy on her palm, as long as her hand was wide. Clearly it had been fashioned by nature. Rubbing her thumb over its slick smoothness, she stepped through the muck—miniature frogs leaping out of the way—to damp sand, wondering if it was gold, and if so, how it came to be in the river.

Part of her didn't want to show it to Perry just yet. He might laugh at her for being childish, and say this was a common rock that lay all over California. Mr. Daylor, a trader, would recognize gold. But he'd tell Perry and she didn't want to be in dutch for showing it to him first. Walking up the hill to the adobe cabin, she decided to hide it. Then after Perry arrived with the girls and the cattle and things had settled down, she'd bring it to him and ask ever so off-handedly, "You think this is gold?" If he said yes, they'd have a merry time deciding what to do with it. Maybe have jewelry made at Sheldon's forge. This was easily enough for a locket for each of her sisters.

The place she'd named "split rock" was the perfect hiding place. It was near the house—between two boulders much taller than she and as far apart as her outstretched elbows. Lichens covered the outer surfaces like tough ruffled doilies, but the inside walls were clean and nearly vertical. Indentations on one side matched the protrusions on the other—some awesome force having wedged them apart long ago. Tamsen would have known what caused that, she realized as she buried the nugget in the dirt between the rock walls. Now all that knowledge, forty-five years of studying the natural world, was lost.

The remainder of the day she explored along the river, where Captain

Juan's daughter said no harm would come to her. She found a piece of oak with a hollowed-out gnarl and put some rich damp soil in it so her apple seeds would get a good start. Then she cut armloads of cattail leaves to make mats for the girls, weaving them together the way the Indians made beds. Once in a while she saw Indians near the river, but as the hours went by, all her apprehensions disappeared. Those people lived nearby. They were as interested in her as she was in them.

The June day was long. She was beginning to think she might spend another night alone, when she felt as much as heard the distant rumble of hooves. Excitement rippled through her. They were coming! She ran down the long swale, over the muddy drainage channel, and up the hill opposite the house. Then stopped in her tracks before reaching the top.

A wide phalanx of bawling cattle appeared along the ridge, and then poured over the top and down the hill in a flowing brown and white mass. Hundreds of upturned horns bobbed in the late sun, all angled exactly the same way. It made a stunning pattern. The herd passed her at maybe fifty rods away, and she stood on one foot then the other, knowing Perry was behind. She could almost feel Frances, frail Georgia and little Ellie in her arms. And Leanna!

But when Paint topped the ridge, he had only one rider on his back. She shaded her eyes inside her bonnet and squinted into the fiery sun to be sure. Perry rode alone in the saddle. She looked toward the other two riders, waited for vision to return. They were Indians. Each alone. No sign of anyone else.

Suddenly feeling the full intensity of the heat, she closed her eyes and shut out the dust of the bawling animals thundering down the swale and trampling up the hill past the little adobe. With disappointment hurting like a whip, she felt relief that Perry didn't stop when he passed her by. She hadn't been able to raise a hand to him.

Later, as she prepared beans and salt pork, he rode from the hills back to the house, and removed the saddle from Paint. Anger seared through her disappointment, and she couldn't look up at him from the outdoor fire she was tending. "You didn't bring my sisters." *And didn't tell me you were going to New Helvetia.*

"Expect a bloke to tend sixty-five long-horns and three baby girls at the same time, do ye?" He turned toward her, the crust of dried salt around his mouth giving him a clownish look, but his steely eyes pounded her, the radiating lines around them darkened with dirt, aging him. He turned back to hobble the sweat-soaked horse.

"They could have ridden a mule tied to your saddle," she said. He'd had the money for cattle. A mule would have cost little more. Besides, he had the Donner money, didn't he?

He gave her a look like they were opponents and he was winning. "What makes ye so sure I went to Sutter's?"

She felt limp from being so upset. He looked tired. Maybe when he'd eaten and rested, they could talk. She went to the pot hanging over the fire and stirred the thickening beans.

Later, after he'd eaten and poked her, though she hadn't wanted to, she lay silent, waiting for him to speak. When it didn't seem likely he would, she brought it up again. "We'd better go after the girls tomorrow." Tomorrow would be six days.

The first owl hooted near the cabin. "We'll do it when I gits meself settled."

"Settled?"

He exhaled in a vexed way. "Now, the very minute I gits me cattle, think ye I'm about to turn meself around and go back?" He snorted and turned over. "Daft!"

Panic for the little girls mounted. Every minute they would be watching for her. She recalled that last morning at the fort, and realized she shouldn't have got on Perry's horse. She should have insisted on his getting a wagon, made him whip her if that's what it took. He might have backed down, or someone might have taken pity and helped. She hadn't persisted. Hadn't tried hard enough to keep her word to her sisters. She had been duped.

As if sensing her thought, he softened his tone. "Aw now lass, doin me best, I is. I'll git the niggers to give me one of their colts. We'll train it. Then one day soon enough we'll both ride back to the fort and fetch the little lasses." He patted her rump. "Now you just nod off. There's a good girl."

"Colt? How old is it?" It took more than a year before a colt could be ridden.

"Not foaled yet."

She couldn't stop a thin sound that came out like a wounded animal. "That's too late. We can get a wagon and—"

"Ent none out here."

Of course not out here, but he could send an Indian to New Helvetia to fetch one. The Indian girl said their young men would do almost anything for trinkets or tools. Anger flamed through her, stoked by the urgency to pass water, which she had just done, passing only a few painful drops. It was a maddening condition she'd noticed since about noon. She rose to her knees, staring down at the twilight curve of his pale skin against the dark blankets. "I promised Ma." Louder she said, "I promised my sisters I'd come for them in a few days! They're orphans, Perry." He of all people should understand that.

He leaped to his feet and grabbed her upper arms and shook her, shouting, "I'll go to the bleedin fort when I'm damned good and ready, and not a minute before! Ye hear? Now leave me sleep or I'll tan ye good, I will." His fingers dug painfully into her flesh, and in the twilight from the window his eyes appeared big and terrible. Fear crept into her anger.

He dropped her arms and flopped on the bed, hissing through his teeth. "Damned if I'll abide a scold fer a wife. Now lay yerself down and shut up."

Long minutes passed, her mind racing over being called a scold. *Elitha's an obedient girl.* She went outside to pass water. Again, only a few drops answered the urgency. The poking had worsened it. When the pain of trying subsided a little, she went back inside and lay carefully beside him, not touching. Was this condition a punishment from God? For her sin with Perry before they were married? But her thoughts returned to the way Tamsen had been happy to mother her and Leanna—women did that all the time. Why not men? But maybe sisters were seen as different from the bride's own children, and a man didn't want that responsibility. Still, he should have told her. He had led her to believe he'd accept her sisters, and then made her betray them. A hot hook of rage resurfaced. She barbed him with, "I met an Indian girl today."

His breathing stopped.

"She said her baby is yours."

He exhaled loudly. "Mary."

*Mary.* An English name. The girl had said she didn't like Perry any more, and Elitha believed her. Who could like such a man?

"Stay away from her," he said, "Or those bucks'll see you talking all friendly like, and they'll stick ye, they will, just like they do their own. Anytime of the day or night."

She weighed that, coming from a man who had deceived her, one who stuck her any time he liked.

❧

The days fell into a pattern. At dawn Perry slipped from bed, grabbed a hank of jerky and rode away to teach the Indians to use the braided ropes called lariats and tend to the cattle. He returned for siesta during the hottest part of the day, and then left when the heat lessened. They ate before dark. During the day Elitha learned useful things from Indian Mary, like where to dig the soaproot plant, which sudsed and cleaned her hair and clothing. But she rarely saw the herd of cattle anywhere near the house.

Then Indian Mary disappeared. Two weeks later Elitha saw her again and learned that she often went to another Indian village—ranchería Californians called it, where she was becoming what sounded like a witch doctor's apprentice. All this time Elitha suffered more each day whenever she passed water, and in her mind it became the pain of knowing her sisters were watching for her and she was not on her way to rescue them.

One morning she woke up and decided to make a door so she wouldn't worry about animals coming in at night. With no tools or knowledge of carpentry—not even a plan—she walked past the ranchería to the hills overlooking the river where tall gray pines leaned like drunken sailors. Pine was easier to work than oak. That much she knew, and she suspected it was the material from which the Indians made their cone-shaped huts. She hoped to find some leftover boards. She found evidence of people having taken away much of an old fallen giant. Half of it was still there. She put her foot on the loose, rotted part and pulled and yanked at it, managing to get a piece about three feet long. She was standing there thinking when she heard a noise. She turned to see two naked Indians with bones in their ears coming at her, one with a club in his hand. They were practically upon her.

Panic buzzed to her extremities, Perry's warning in her mind. *Wild as banshees.* She'd grown up hearing of Indian atrocities. But instead of braining her, they straddled the downed pine, rammed the odd-shaped "club" into a crack and pounded on it with large rocks that lay conveniently alongside. As her heart slowed, she realized that she was in their woods, watching them do the very thing she wanted to do—wedge out slabs of wood. Then she saw more Indian women and children back in the trees.

Indian Mary came to her, smiling. "How many?" She pointed at the working men.

"Two." Elitha had been teaching her English.

Mary said something guttural to the men. They straightened, smiling broadly at Elitha, and presented her with two flakes of pine, each about six feet long.

"Oh, boards, you mean." They had seen her and come to help! She pointed and repeated, "Boards." Quickly she calculated and said, "I want six."

Mary talked to the men, and they went back to work. When six boards had been wedged out, the two men carried them for her, walking at either end of the boards. Mary, with Perry's baby, walked beside Elitha. But when the adobe came into view, the men put the boards down. Mary asked, "Where build house?"

"No. I'm just making a door," she said.

Clearly disappointed, Mary spoke to the men and they left. Then she repeated what she'd said before about Perry's house being bad luck, and turned to leave. But Elitha asked her how to fasten the boards together. Soon they were down at the river at a wide sandy place where the willows stood back from the water. Mary showed her how to tease out the long thin roots of willows seeking moisture. When they had a large pile of them, Mary dug out a backwater and coiled the roots in it to soak all night.

The next day Mary showed her how to weave the pliable roots over and under the boards and tie them securely together. The result was like a giant accordion. Opened, it stood higher than the roof of the house and very uneven, but it would do. For hinges she would cut strips of the old cowhide drape, maybe tripled for strength, and nail them—when she went to Daylor's for nails—to the doorframe. For now, feeling very pleased with herself, she stood the door against the side of the adobe.

By the time she had biscuits and beans ready for supper, she was thinking about going up to the mountains to see if any bolts of cloth were left in the

Donner wagons. She wanted to make bedclothes, lace curtains, a gingham tablecloth, and frocks for the girls. Now she wished she'd gone to Mr. Sutter to find out how much had been salvaged.

In high spirits Perry rode up and jumped off Paint. He hobbled the horse then bowed to her like a country squire, accepting his filled plate. "Thankee kindly, milaidy." He sat beside her on the log by the firepit, his fringed eyes sparkling and his clean-shaven face as handsome as ever.

She said, "Let's ride up the mountains and see what's left in the wagons." She felt strong enough to view the camp now, and wanted him to share her private thoughts. Maybe it would bring back the tenderness he'd shown when he'd first learned the terrible news about Tamsen.

He threw back his head and hawed, and then eyed her like she was weak-minded. "Think them blokes what went up there didn't sniff out every ha'penny? Why, they smashed the wagons with axes, they did!" Found every nook and cranny." He tossed the remainder of the biscuit into his mouth and chewed loudly—no longer the country squire.

"I helped Tamsen sew ten thousand dollars into one of the quilts."

He choked and coughed, and a doughy projectile flew by, creasing her nose. He struggled to find his voice. "Why... didn't you say nothin?" His face was red, his eyes wet. "Keepin it from me was ye?"

"No. I mean I didn't mean to. I just, well, figured it would be a pleasant surprise if it were to be given back to me, a surprise for you. But I don't know. Maybe they'd already found it and paid the rescuers out of it," *and given it to you.* "And sometimes I thought Mr. Sutter would ask me to come to his rooms and talk about it. But then I suppose I was bothered by the trial and all..." Surely a heavy quilt jingling with gold coins would have been the first to be salvaged, but why nobody mentioned it was a mystery. However, the bolts of cloth might still be up there, some of it unspoiled. Such cloth was valuable.

Slack-jawed, he stared at her. "They was right about the money then."

Hoping to revive his happy mood, she said, "Yes. And we could make the house nicer." *For the girls.*

"Aye, that we could, lass." He stared past her.

"Will you take me then?"

He looked at her, then brought his plate to his chin and shoveled down the rest of his beans. "Like I said," he wiped his sleeve across his mouth, "I've only just come home with me cows." He reached down and patted her knee— oddly, like something was on his mind.

She knew better than to probe. After a few minutes, thinking about his reaction, every step provoking false urgency, she took the soiled tins down to the river in the last light of day. It came to her that the affliction in her privates could kill her eventually. Women died from mysterious conditions all the time, Perry's first white wife included. Looked at that way, the goods didn't matter. Who knew how much time she had? Her life was here, and she had to get it into her head that everything from the old life was gone, and a grueling ride on horseback to see the camp of starvation and death wouldn't bring it back. Perry was right.

"Lass," he said when they were in bed, "we're going to Daylor's. It's a cook-out they'll be 'avin."

"That's grand! We can see Sarah and Catherine, and buy nails for the door."

# 38

They dismounted before Mr. Sheldon's two-story millhouse—three stories if she counted the understructure down at the riverbank. The new house had the same New England look. With wooden peaks and vertical lines, the buildings could have come from Ma's picture book of Vermont. Before the millhouse stood a pair of sleepy oxen hitched to a wagon filled with big leather bags of wheat. Trying not to jiggle with urgency—she'd made Perry stop three times on the trail and had gone to Daylors' outhouse when they'd brought the nails—she looked around for Catey.

Sam Kyburz came from the millhouse, accompanied by an Indian in a loincloth. Mr. Kyburz tipped his hat and Elitha half-curtsied. He and the Indian swung bags from the wagon to their shoulders and headed for the mill-house. Then suddenly she recalled that when she'd left the fort that morning, Sam Kyburz had driven away with a full load of wheat—to be milled here, she now realized. Her sisters could ride almost all the way on the next load!

Jiggling absentmindedly and excited about the prospect, she wished Perry hadn't followed Mr. Kyburz into the mill. She wanted to talk to Mr. Kyburz alone. Just then Catherine bounded around the corner of the house, skirts hoisted, a bauble bouncing on her breast. Full of vinegar, Tamsen would have said. They hugged, the top of Catherine's bonnet fresh-smelling under Elitha's nose, then they held each other at arm's length, grinning. It was exactly as Pa had said. People on the frontier became instant friends.

"Come with me," Catey said yanking Elitha's hand. "I gotta secret to tell."

Thinking she could just as well talk to her about the girls coming out with Mr. Kyburz, she followed Catherine behind the house and tiptoed across rows of young green beans and vigorous squash. An outhouse came into view—peaked like the other buildings—and it seemed the height of civilization. Did she really need to pass water again so soon? She felt it all the time now, and when she tried to do it, the pain cut her so sharply that she put it off as long as possible. God was mortifying her with a condition she couldn't mention to a living soul.

Catherine sat down in the shade of a large tree with dense limbs and fringed leaves, a variety that Tamsen would have been able to identify. Elitha settled beside her friend on soft ground. Birds chattered overhead and Catey bunched her shoulders up around her elfish grin and said, "I'm in a family way."

Elitha opened her mouth and searched the twinkling hazel eyes. "Why, that's grand! And Mr. Sheldon seems like such a nice man."

"Oh, he is, he IS. I love him SO much!" She extended the gold watch hanging around her neck. "He gave this to me for a wedding present." She popped it open for Elitha to admire.

Elitha praised its ornate interior and, barely able to endure the urgency, asked if she could use the outhouse.

"Silly goose, go on!" Catherine gave her a friendly shove.

Dropping the wooden latch in its slot, she sat on the sanded seat. Long ago she'd heard of a disease prevalent among women of the night, females so wicked they were mentioned only in whispers. She felt sure she had their affliction. The water started. Pain knifed upward from her privates to her chin, pulsing with terrible sharpness and intensifying as the stream stopped. In the luxury of complete privacy she allowed herself to voice a moan, clenching her teeth at the ceiling while the sting throbbed on and on and eventually subsided. How wonderful an outhouse was! She hardly noticed the acrid smell in the pit or the buzzing flies. *Forgive me, Lord. Lift this punishment if you see fit.*

When she settled on the dirt beside Catherine, the urge to pass water was already agitating her again. "Good thing yer Ma is so close by," she offered, looking at Catherine's plump middle, her pink-cheeked happiness matching her frock and bonnet.

"Yup. She's real good at birthin all right."

Elitha didn't know the first thing about giving birth. When Tamsen's daughters were born, she and Leanna had been shooed outside.

Catey said, "I hope my folks stay in California."

"Why wouldn't they?"

"Well, Pa got a letter from Brigham Young—a friend of his—wrote on the trail. You see, just about all the Mormons have left for the West, and they decided to stay near the Great Salt Lake."

The trek across the salt flats came to mind and Elitha couldn't imagine anyone settling there, especially when they had daughters married to California men. But she said, "Well I sure hope they won't leave before your baby comes."

"Oh they wouldn't." Catherine wore the comfortable smile of a child who knew love and support came from all directions. "Besides, Ma hasn't got her strength back after the crossing."

It occurred to Elitha then that she might never have a baby, her condition being located where it was. More than likely she would die first. Just then, two large mushroom-shaped objects rose jerkily from the riverbank—wide straw hats of the type Spaniards called sombreros—men pushing them up as they climbed. Under one hat she recognized Mr. Sheldon. The other man wore a short black vest over a pale shirt and a red and white striped sash around the waist of his dark trousers, which split open over his boots. He looked at Elitha with interested gray eyes, his nose turned slightly down.

Mr. Sheldon touched his straw brim. "Howdy girls, Where's Perry?"

"At the millhouse with Mr. Kyburz," Elitha said.

"Wheat here already?" He gave Catherine an unmistakable look of love.

"Yup," She said.

When he started to walk away, Elitha blurted, "Mr. Sheldon, I was meaning to ask—"

He turned.

"Next time Mr. Kyburz comes, maybe he could bring my little sisters. They could ride on top of the wheat. Then we'll figure out how to get them out to our place from here."

He bobbed his sombrero and said, "I'll see to it."

"Oh, I'd be so obliged!" She felt giddy with relief. It had been so simple!

At sundown, a veil of dust and pollen gilded the air, and soon the daytime heat faded into a balmy night pulsing with crickets and frogs. Over everything floated the thrilling music of the Spaniard—the one she'd seen that afternoon.

"I love that," Elitha said to the three Rhoads women, ignoring her urgency. "What is that instrument?" It brought to mind exotic places and stories like Ali Baba and the forty thieves.

"A guitar," Sarah Daylor said, reaching over to pat Elitha's shoulder. "I'm so glad you're here. You should come visit regular."

"I'd like that."

The elder Rhoadses were here too, and John with his pregnant Matilda and a wagon load of children. Elitha felt like royalty—sitting on a log and visiting with the women while Indians served peppermint tea and tended the fire. They cooked the beans, turned half a bullock on a spit, prepared greens and watched the children, Indian and white, as they romped and toddled. Elitha's hands were free. She couldn't remember a time in all her fourteen years when she hadn't helped with supper.

Anxious to hear whether the arrangements were confirmed, she knew that Mr. Sheldon had talked to Sam Kyburz but had been busy with company ever since. Except for her affliction, she felt happier than she'd been for some time.

The men visited on the other side of the fire. Wisps of talk about ranches and cattle came through the music and the bellow of frogs and threep of crickets. Perry passed his flask, and Elitha knew by his stance that he'd be slurring his words. At the end of a musical line, a treble guitar note trilled, and then the Spaniard began to sing.

"Who is that?" she asked, enthralled by the Spanish music.

"Pedro Valdez, our mayordomo—our top vaquero," Catherine said.

That was the name of Indian Mary's husband! With heightened interest, Elitha listened.

Sarah Daylor said, "I heard your sisters are a big help to the Brunners."

*News.* "When did you hear that?"

"About a week ago. Mr. Chabolla told me when he came to mill his wheat. I mentioned that you was our new neighbor."

Elitha searched Sarah's queenly face. "How are they?" She kept her voice low.

Catherine and Mrs. Rhoads looked intrigued. Sarah said, "All I heard is Mrs. Brunner's feelin her age and with the work on the farm and all, your sisters are a big help."

Mrs. Rhoads tilted her gray head toward Perry across the fire and said, "Don't he want them with you?"

Elitha felt disloyal to be whispering about him. "Oh, we've just been too busy to fetch them," she said cheerfully. "Maybe they'll come on the next wheat wagon." She flounced her skirt and smiled at the women. "My, but it's a pretty night."

"It is at that," said Mrs. Rhoads, staring at nothing. She turned to Sarah and said, "Ever mornin' I wake up more tuckered." Elitha thought that was to be expected of the mother of nineteen living children, one who had just walked across much of the continent.

Beyond the firelight children shot tiny arrows at make-believe animals. In the dark it was hard to tell which were Rhoadses and which were Indians. Elitha asked the older Mrs. Rhoads, "Did you know Mrs. Murphy?" She figured she might, because they too had been in the wagon train hiding their Mormon religion, perhaps using the laundry services of Mrs. Murphy.

"Yes," Mrs. Rhoads said. "She hired out on the crossing. Poor thing." She shook her head.

Elitha watched an Indian woman cut a sliver of meat from the sizzling haunch and taste its doneness. "I'd sure like to know how Mary Murphy's doing," she said.

"She married Mr. Johnson," Catherine reported.

"She said she would," Elitha was sorry to say. "I think he's an awful man and I feel sorry for her."

"Yes," Catherine said, rolling her eyes. "An awful man. Like to'ov lost her mind when she learned of her ma passing. Then she up and married him at the fort."

"He abused her with his farmhands," said Mrs. Rhoads in a wavering tone that warned away further inquiry. She pursed her wrinkled lips and stared at the fire, the look of ancient wisdom in her face.

*Abused*. Elitha feared she knew the meaning of that. But farmhands? The only white men she'd seen around Johnson's looked wilder than the Indians. Poor, poor Mary!

Catherine added, "Elizabeth writes us regular. Says Mary wants to leave Mr. Johnson. And she's thinking of leaving Mr. Keyser too. Both their husbands got pickaninnies all over the place, callin 'em pa. More'n one squaw too."

Mrs. Rhoads turned her tired face to Elitha. "I'm hopin he'll move here with her, and git away from all them others." She looked ahead like she had a bad taste in her mouth.

But Elitha was thinking no girl could simply walk away from a husband. She wished she and Mary weren't separated by fifty miles. But this was a party, and she steered her thoughts to the joyful side of life—visiting instead of listening to owls and coyotes and watching Perry get drunk. "It's fine out here," she said suppressing the urge to jiggle. "You got each other, and your Indians are such a help."

At that moment she heard Perry say, "I 'ears ye be finding gold hereabouts."

He hadn't mentioned it to her, but then he often kept secrets. She had one of her own, in the split rock.

❧

Pedro fingered a series of rippling chords and watched the people around the fire react to McCoon's mention of gold. From where he played his guitar, he could hear everything and see the women's faces. Indians turning the spit made no acknowledgement. Americanas taking their ease listened. Señora McCoon—a serious girl about María's age with dark hair coiled around her ears and a pretty face except for her thinness and enormously sad eyes—brightened at the mention of gold.

Apparently Perry McCoon was just learning of it, and trying to sound casual. Señora Catherine said, "Isn't it grand! Ma keeps finding it down at their place, doncha Ma?" Before Señora Rhoads could open her mouth, Catherine added, "Pertanear ever time she washes the clothes she sees gold a-stickin' right outa the bank!"

"Not every time, dear."

The elder Señor Rhoads wiggled a thick finger toward the dark. "Mother, we're among friends. Go get the little pouch. Give our sons-in-law a gander."

Pedro rippled a chord in a different key. They were finding it down on dry creek too! He lifted his hand and let the strings vibrate. A huge orange moon was silently floating upward behind the dark trees, while nearby life crackled and hummed. The spit and snap of the roasting meat, the murmur of the Indias, the rustle of the river, the bawling of cattle wove a tapestry of sound in the warm night. Wishing María were here too, he watched McCoon.

The eyes of the cabrón glittered with an expression Pedro knew all too well. "'Ow much be ye findin then?" the Englishman asked, not hiding his drunken excitement. He widened his stance to keep from falling down.

Señor Sheldon said, "A tad bit around here."

Señora Rhoads emerged from the dark, coming from the wagon. Firelight accentuated the creases in her face as she handed a leather pouch to her husband.

McCoon hovered like a fly as the elder Rhoads loosened the string and poured the contents into his palm. He stepped to the fire and lowered his hand so the women could see, McCoon shadowing. Even at this distance Pedro saw the glitter.

McCoon asked in a cracking voice, "Where'd you git this?"

Señor Daylor answered, "Like she said, down at Dry Creek." He winked at Señora Sarah, a look of amor.

Pedro ran his fingers over the guitar, quickening the mood as the pouch—restored of its contents—passed from hand to hand. Maybe McCoon would abandon his ranch and search for gold at Dry Creek, encouraged by his wife. What a fine day that would be!

Fingering a sad melody fragment and underscoring it with a trill, he reflected that even in the presence of that gold, he felt no excitement. His fortune would come from land. Like Don Cristóbal in Santa Barbara, he would be a *gran ranchero* with a rose-perfumed patio. Ay, Californios knew how to live. Señor Sheldon was from New England. He worked too hard. A hollow beat began to interfere with Pedro's rhythm. He lifted his hand. The Indian big time was starting.

The Indias, having finished cooking, now turned up the dark path toward the drum, their children trotting behind. Pedro knew they'd dance and sing for the next three or four days. They didn't need gold to make them happy. From them the Californios had learned to fandango for days at a time. It was a good tradition.

"Cap'n Suiter know about the gold?" McCoon asked.

The elder Rhoads said, "Sure. I told him. Figgered I owed the man fer the use of the land." His mouth turned down like a horseshoe.

McCoon pressed, "That Suiter's land, is it? That far south?" *Not until the Devil dances in heaven,* Pedro knew.

Señor Rhoads turned his backside to the fire and wiggled interlocked fingers at it. "Them Mexican survey papers is the derndest I ever seen. Looked at Sutter's map myself. Couldn't make out if he owns the land he lets me farm."

McCoon's questions were coming fast. "Suiter claimin the gold, is he? Seein it comes from land 'e says is 'is own?"

The horseshoe mouth locked down. "Takes his share."

"'Ow much?" McCoon was hooked like a fish, and Pedro smiled in the dark.

Sheldon held up a hand. "That's the business of Father Rhoads." The elder Rhoads scowled at him. "S'all right, Jared. This here's a neighbor." To McCoon he said, "Takes his piece."

"Piece o' wot? Suiter wouldn't know 'ow much gold you taikes from the brook now would 'e?" He swayed and narrowed his eyes at the dour old man.

Señora Daylor straightened her back. "My pa's fair," she said. She held herself like a queen.

The Indian drum throbbed in the distance and the full moon had floated over the trees. The North Americanos were filling their plates. With his elbows akimbo, McCoon looked from face to face. "'Ow're we to keep this secret?" he demanded, "with Suiter's drunken tongue awaggin?" He sucked from his flask and wiped his sleeve across his mouth.

Pedro enjoyed the silence of the patrones.

McCoon jerked on the line, "Wye, ever bloke on the continent'll be out here minin for gold, I vow, with the cap'n writin 'is infernal letters!"

Pedro ran his thumb down a mournful chord and let it fade. Señor Daylor's melancholy tone seemed to reflect it, or perhaps he realized his friend was flopping in the wrong waters. "Lookee mait," he said, "hits up to alla us to keep our tongues tied. Sutter's doin' his part, he is. Don't worry. He won't leak it. Nor his friend who weighs the gold. Keeps quiet, Leidesdorff does."

Reflecting on that and strumming an engaging pair of chords, Pedro saw a reason why McCoon might leave the land he'd squatted on and squat in a different place—gold. As the others began eating, he played *El Tormento de Amor,* singing quietly the words that always evoked his feelings for María. The bliss of their embrace had been well worth the waiting. It was more beautiful than he had dreamed. His torment was wanting her all the time. He visited her village at every opportunity, but he had much work to do here. The patrones' cattle were multiplying, every tenth calf earmarked for Pedro. He had a good start on a herd already, but his work separated him from María even as her witch doctoring kept her from him. Ah, his bosom could not be consoled. The words precisely expressed his feelings.

But his stomach was growling. He leaned the guitar against the tree, took his knife from his sash and approached the spitted beef. As he leaned over it, considering which part to cut, McCoon said, "Maits, surprised I am ye let that greaser eat with ye."

Pedro froze.

McCoon continued, "Blab about the gold to every Spaniard on the coast, 'e will! Them niggers'll stampede all over yer rancho."

Pedro flayed a curl of meat. This was the supper feast of the patrones, and he wouldn't add violence to McCoon's repulsiveness, not in front of the señoras. But that didn't stop him from imagining how cleanly his blade would slice through McCoon's windpipe.

Señor Sheldon's clipped words came over the crickets and the distant singing Indians. "Señor Valdez is my mayordomo, and my amigo."

The cabrón persisted. "But Jared, ye can't trust his kind. I 'ear they ent even abidin by the treaty. Fightin again in Pueblo de los Angeles. I vow, this'uns no better." He swayed.

A muscle in Pedro's knife arm twitched, but he blinked a nod at Señor Sheldon meaning: Don't worry. I will not disturb the peace of the señoras at this fiesta. But he wouldn't let McCoon off entirely. He spoke softly as if to the beans he ladled to his plate. "A sailor who deserted his captain speaks of trust." Casually he wiped his knife on his thigh, and then turned his back and walked away.

Señor Daylor broke the tension. "Methinks it's time we took Mother Rhoads to 'ome." He stretched and winked at his señora, who, in the bright globe of the moon, looked like a goddess. Pedro envied him for having his woman near at hand. No longer wanting to share any part of the evening with McCoon, a coward who for more than a year had failed to name the day of their competition, he tucked his guitar under his arm, took his full plate and was about to head for his room.

Señor Sheldon got up and came toward him. In deference, Pedro waited, but he would not apologize to McCoon. Ever.

Instead Sheldon stopped at the log where Señora McCoon sat and spoke to her. "Sam Kyburz says Sutter's done milling for the year. Today was his last load. Sorry."

In the moonlight her face was white, her eyes huge and black. Her voice seemed too small for such strange beauty. "No more wagon loads will be brought out here?"

"Not this year."

On his way to his room Pedro reflected that it had not been a bad night. Pedro had delivered a couple of much-deserved blows, Perry McCoon had gold fever, and the gold he was crazy for lay three or four leagues away from Rancho Sacayak.

# 39

"Power make you *fuerte*, strong," María said to the Americana as they sat together in the shade of willow trees.

"What do you mean by that?"

Elitha had no more knowledge than a nestling bird. But her sad eyes conveyed intelligence, and María liked her. Even from a distance one could see that she had sickness in her bladder. Oam'shu, angelica root, had honored

María by visiting in a dream and telling her to make the Americana well. She would do as her plant friend directed.

"Wash," she said. "Go in water when sun come up." She pointed at the water but realized the river spirit might not cooperate. "Sing to river, she cry like baby. Sing. Make her happy, make her you friend."

Seeing confusion in the sad face, she understood the difficulty of her task. Elitha had little knowledge about health. Daily bathing and medicine tea alone were inadequate. Yet she must begin somewhere. "Come. We go to Grandmother. She make river happy." Shrugging into the bikoos with the sleeping baby, she led the way, glad to see the Americana follow.

The riverbottom widened at the family's special place, easy walking due to the smooth flat rocks the river had laid down. Here and there tufts of late poppies, redbud or lupine still bloomed. She found Great-Grandmother Dishi below the horizontal boughs of her evergreen oak, her hands resting on the drill Father had made her. The old woman's wrinkles blended with the tracery of the branches, almost hiding her. María deliberately rattled the rocks to announce their approach while beckoning the Americana.

She stepped behind Dishi and massaged her shoulders, her special greeting, which, she knew the old woman loved. The skin felt soft and loose, the white hair thick and clean, singed bluntly at the shoulders. Since she didn't carry a burden basket any more, the old woman had no need of a cap and rarely wore one. She wore nothing but the amulet around her neck.

Staring ahead with clouded eyes, she began to sing. María took Elitha's hand and held it to the old one's cheek. "She sings to river-baby spirit. You come to Grandmother and learn how to sing. Understand?"

"Is she here all the time?"

"In house at night."

Leaving Grandmother, they climbed the boulders that led up the bank, careful to watch for rattlesnakes.

Following, the Americana said, "You didn't talk to her, and she didn't talk to you."

"She no talk."

"But she sings."

"Sí. She sings."

No more questions came from this young woman brought here by Perrimacoo.

In the shade of the elderberry people, now adorned with tiny green berries, she said, "I make you medicine tea." She was about to sing when the Americana said:

"I don't think it will help. God is punishing me."

That surprised her. Was the powerful spirit of the mission, the Dios Pedro mentioned so often, an evil prankster? She tried to explain. "When you weak, evil find hole. Get in." She pointed between the woman's legs. "God there? Play tricks?"

Elitha ran a distance away and covered her face inside the tunnel hat, her long black hair veiling her cloth-covered shoulders. Her defeated posture suggested sorcery had been aimed at her. If so, the cure would call for more than bladder tea. Only Bear Claw could remove such evil, if his magic were stronger than the other scorcerer's. But first the simple remedy must be tried.

Glancing back to be sure Billy was toddling toward her, she said to Elitha, "You have enemy? Someone want God's magic to hurt you?"

Elitha dropped her hands and looked at her through wet lashes. "No. God did this for a reason. And he is not evil. You must NOT say that!" Said with strength.

*Good.* She had some power left. Then she recalled that Pedro had another word for power when it injured people. Bad power. "El Diablo," she corrected, pointing again. "I no talk good. Mebee Devil go in." She took Elitha's hand, gently tugging. "Come. We talk to Elderberry."

María sang to Elderberry, telling of Elitha's need. The Americana seemed to listen with interest. Next they went to a stand of nettle. María pointed to a tall handsome specimen and said, "He help you."

"Ooh," said Elitha making a face, "that's stinging nettle."

Quickly María edged her out of the plant's hearing. "He is proud," she whispered. "Flatter him." Seeing astonishment replace repugnance, she returned to the nettles and said in her own tongue:

"We are poor women in need of your beauty and strength. No one else will do. Won't you please give your top leaves to this young woman? Her bladder hurts." María waited until Nettle said it was all right, that he wasn't offended. She pinched off the tops of two spears and sang her thanks.

Elitha asked, "Doesn't it sting your hand?"

"I talk right to him and he no hurt me. You touch him with cloth." She pointed to Elitha's skirt.

Next, she showed the Americana how to pull a strip of bark from willow and cut a plug of oak bark. Each time she sang her songs of thanks—first in her own tongue, then in English, so Elitha could learn, for later she must do her own gathering.

In the village the Americana glanced curiously at the people who remained here at this time of day—mostly old ones and children. They looked at her politely from the sides of their eyes. María handed Billy to Etumu, selected a medium-sized cooking basket from the rafters of the u-macha, and then carried the basket down the path to the river. Elitha followed.

María laid the herbs comfortably in the shade, pleased at the Americana's attentiveness, and sang to the basket to calm its fears about holding strong herbs. She carried the basket into the current of the river, opening it to the water. Ashore again, she sang to the water, for although water was a special ally of hers, she knew she'd need to cajole it into giving itself over to the herbs for a stranger.

Elitha murmured, "I won't remember the songs."

"You forget sing?"

"I will forget the melody and the words."

That puzzled María. Until she remembered Pedro teaching her *Ave María,* Mother of God. He had insisted the chant be sung precisely on the note each time or the magic would be ruined.

María explained, "You speak from dream, quiet talk with plant people. Listen. They talk. You, me have different helpers, some plants, some animals. Good helper is good friend and maybe no need sing to friend. You sing. You listen. Understand?" She fingered her amulet, which contained pieces of her plant allies. "Helper no want same song from you and me."

Elitha looked skeptical. It would be possible, María knew, for a person without knowledge to be killed by a tree or Crying Fox' crystals. Warning her not to touch the herbs or basket, she went to the family firepit, dug some live coals, piled on tinder and spoke to the fire. When it was hot, she selected a cooking stone, placed it in the fire, and then returned to Elitha. "Sit here, in shade. We wait."

Etumu came to the river with Billy and went to the far end of the beach with the other women and children. Perhaps they all had noticed the blue crystals around the Americana's neck and feared them. Fortunately, Bear Claw's wisdom had given María considerable protection around strong power.

The rock was hot. She fetched her blue-oak tongs and lowered the stone into the sizzling water. When it boiled she added chunks of oak bark and the nettle leaves, letting them roll with the boil. Then, removing the rock after the right interval, she added the other herbs one at a time.

She gave the plant friends encouragement as they landed on the steaming brown water.

"Willow bark cures pain," Elitha said.

"Yes." María was glad the Americana knew at least one thing about plants.

"Your mint is different than ours back home."

"Which one is mint?" She liked to learn English talk.

Elitha approached a stand of peppermint at the water's edge. When it seemed she might pluck it, María stayed her hand. "Sing first, but why pick?"

"To show you."

"I look now," she said gently. "Españoles call that yerba buena."

"Yerba Buena is the name of a town."

"Yes. By ocean."

"Why is the town named Mint?"

"Españoles like." She patted her stomach. "Make quiet after much aguardiente."

When the tea cooled, María showed her how to cup her purified hand to scoop the medicine into her mouth, not upending the basket the way Pedro did. "Drink five baskets every sun. Full basket."

The big black eyes widened. She showed her stiff fingers. "That much?"

María gestured toward the river. "River run clean."

"I don't understand."

"Come." María led her to a backwater on the river, where the water was green and murky. "Water bad," she said.

"What has this to do with me?"

She pointed to Elitha's bladder. "Water slow, bad. People and salmón same. You know salmón? Fish?" Seeing her nod, she pointed first to Elitha's mouth, then down her body and between her legs. "Fast water give power. Medicine run fast and make strong." Comprehension flickered in the young woman's eyes, followed by a blush on her pale cheeks. Ashamed to learn? Surely not.

"May I take the basket of medicine home?" Elitha asked.

"Perrimacoo house?" Seeing that was exactly what the Americana had in mind, María found it difficult to remain calm, so horrifying was the thought. "House hurt medicine. Basket sad. Take and keep outside. Bad medicine come if Perrimacoo touch. Understand?"

Horse hooves sounded. María went up the bank far enough to glimpse Grizzly Hair riding alongside Perrimacoo. She went to the Americana and told her who it was.

"I don't want my husband to see me here," Elitha said.

María pointed down the river. "Go bym old grandma. You swim place be two turns of river." She told her not to spill the medicine, or bad luck would come.

Elitha smiled with strong friendship. Then she disappeared into the willows. Perhaps the medicine songs were working already. María hoped so. Grizzly Hair topped the bank, a man of power. His tone rang with it:

"Perrimacoo needs you to talk for him," he said.

"Pay ye damned 'eathens I will then!"

María repeated it in the tongue of the umne, who gathered before him, men having come from their tool-making, their snares, and Perrimacoo's cattle, and women from their gathering and pounding.

"How much?" the son of Fat Beaver wanted to know. He was a strapping young man who hoped to marry the daughter of the headman from the Walnut Grove village. A marriage present would be on his mind.

"One blue bead each day," Perrimacoo said.

María repeated that and people sat impassively.

Grizzly Hair stood. "When we take a beaver skin to Señor Daylo, he gives us three blue beads."

The sky eyes flashed around the crowd. "All right then, two bleedin beads every bleedin day. But that's all!"

Grizzly Hair walked to the back of the dancehouse and up the dirt ramp to the roof. Over the doorway he stood like an eagle on a high perch looking at the people below. His faster and quieter tone told María not to translate.

"He wants us to leave home and live in a strange place," Father said to the people "He does not say how long. He wants us to wash gravel in a stream. When we are finished we will return home with beads."

He paused and then continued, "If you stay here and trap beaver for Señor Daylo, you will earn more beads." The umne loved the home place and never wanted to leave.

Running Quail's son said, "My family will stay."

Other men repeated that. Grizzly Hair nodded at each one and instructed María to tell Perrimacoo the people would not go to Dry Creek to collect the goldenrock.

Perrimacoo elevated his pitch. "Ent I been the soul of justice? Give ye 'eathens all them beads? Don't I mark every tenth calf yours? Alright then, five beads apiece and that's final!"

Grizzly Hair walked away. One by one the families left the dancehouse, some returning to their u-machas, some to the mortar rocks, others heading up the eastern hill.

Perrimacoo's face reddened. He yelled at María, "Ye bleedin bitch! Said it wrong ye did!" He touched his gun.

Grizzly Hair turned. All the men froze.

Perrimacoo's weakness showed in his sagging shoulders. Then, clutching his gun, he jumped on his horse and disappeared up the path toward his house—where, María knew, Elitha would be by now.

"Well, if they won't work for you," Elitha said, "try the Indians between here and Daylor's ranch. Maybe they'll go."

"Daft."

"Why not?" Before they were married he had said fifty Indians worked for him. How different the reality was! They did exactly as they pleased.

"I can't, that's all." He leaned over the barrel, yanked the cork from the bung hole, and held his trembling cup beneath it. An amber drop pinged into the tin. He stepped back and kicked the barrel with such violence that it gouged out the wall, bounced back and crashed into the table legs. "Hit's their damned bloody jabber!" Flakes of adobe skittered down the wall.

Nothing she could say would help. Besides, the irritating urgency was upon her as always. She pushed open the door—which served very well—thinking she'd pass water then drink the rest of the tea, which she'd left between the two sides of the split rock.

His fingers dug into her shoulders and from behind she felt the wet words on her earlobe. "Where ye be goin then?"

Her heart raced at the tone—soft and threatening. Facing the tranquil outdoors, she murmured, "To pass water."

The fingers didn't loosen. "Every other minute ye be pissin." The P spit in her ear. "Gone long enough to meet a buck, too. Think I'm daft, do ye?"

She recoiled. "I'd die first." She meant it. Donner women didn't cheat on their husbands.

"Oh fer Chrissake, git!"

She didn't expect the shove. The toe of her shoe caught on the new threshold stone Perry had laid in an excavated hole, not quite deep enough. She fell on her hand, trying to brace the fall, and her thumb, taking most of her weight, was forced back. Pain bloomed in her hand, and her chaffed cheek, and knees stung as she lay in the dirt. A little urine burned its way out. Picking herself up, she limped toward the bigger of the two oaks, ashamed of being so clumsy—he hadn't pushed hard. She brushed embedded sand particles from her cheek as she went behind the tree and was gathering her skirt.

He was there glaring at her.

She dropped the skirt, her voice quiet and polite. "Please, I'd like to be alone." *Oh for an outhouse with a latch!*

"Makin sure ye be alone, I is." He grinned a deep dimple, steely eyes boring through her. "Go on, do it then." He placed his knuckles on his hips, elbows out.

"Please, I need privacy." She didn't want him to see her pain.

His eyes were glassy. "Stayin right 'ere, I is. Ye can bloody well do it now." He swayed with too much drink.

"I can't. With you there."

He threw his head back hawing. "Show ye, I will." He unbuttoned his trousers and flipped out his member, which, with the cloth hanging between his thighs, was framed by a square of black hair. He released a golden arc not far from where she stood, and then, holding his enlarging self with the blind eye staring at her, his tone softened. "Then again, I gots me another idear."

Pain drummed in her hand and she felt about to scream with false urgency. Yet her aunt in Illinois had said marriages were good when a wife let a man have his way. If only it didn't hurt so! Most of the pain came with the first thrusts. More would come, she knew—the longer it went on, the worse it would hurt later.

Indian Mary's advice came back to her. *You need power.* She seemed to believe weakness caused everything bad, but the amazing thing was her assumption that Elitha had a curable illness, not a killing plague visited upon her by God. As Perry pumped, she kept her injured hand out of the way and thought how casual Mary's attitude had been, even pointing to it. Her manner suggested that all Indian women knew about this—they even had a remedy! Tamsen had admired Indian medicine and Elitha's real mother, Mary Blue, had been full of medical mysteries. She resolved to give the tea every opportunity to heal her.

But as she watched the strained cords in Perry's neck, inches from her nose, she wondered again what on earth Indians meant by *power*.

# 40

Several weeks later as Perry pulled his boots on, Elitha stood scratching another neat line on the adobe wall beside the bed and called over her shoulder, "It's October 16."

"So?"

"My birthday." And she had a pounding headache, and her thumb was wrapped in a heavy Indian splint—she'd told Perry she made it herself.

He came to her. "Fifteen is it now?" His hands closed around her waist, his blue eyes sparkling.

She nodded, fearing what she thought was coming, but instead he put her over his knees, pulled up her dress, pulled down her knickers, and spanked her hard, counting. By the fifth smack her backside hurt badly, but she wouldn't cry. It also stung her pride, and he was snickering. At number fifteen, he pulled up her knickers and turned her to her feet.

"Birthday spankings are to be light," she said, hating the break in her voice.

"Won't do no good, ifn it's light." He headed out the door chuckling.

Later, her headache was so bad she decided to go out and find Indian Mary and see if she had a remedy. The frequent baskets of tea had entirely cured her of the pain in her privates.

Mary, with her baby on her back, led her to an elderberry tree that looked more like a large bush, and crawled beneath it—multiple trunks and branches fanning upward and outward into a thick canopy of soft pinnate leaves, as Tamsen called this variety. They both lay down, looking upward and inhaling the fragrance of its leaves all around them. Mary laid the bikoos to one side, the baby awake but quiet. Elitha tried to listen to the tree like Mary told her, and after a little while thought she felt the particular nature of the tree. Inhaling and appreciating it, she actually did feel her headache lifting.

"How do you make glue from soaproot?" she asked.

"Shh. Now talk to Elderberry. Maybe helper for you." Then Mary grabbed Billy and vanished through the foliage.

Perplexed, Elitha sat up and was about to call to her when Perry's bootfalls sounded on the trail. Mary, respecting Elitha's wish to keep their friendship secret, had heard it much sooner. The acuity of Indian hearing was amazing.

Elitha went to him.

Perry smiled in a jaunty, teasing way. "So there ye be, lass. Come tidy yourself. Goin on a journey, we is."

"To New Helvetia?" *To fetch the girls!* A birthday surprise.

"To Yerba Buena."

Still, New Helvetia was on the way! And a town full of whites and Spaniards would be a wonderful sight. She'd about gone wild out here. When had she last seen her hairpins? She worried her face had become browned, so often she forgot to wear her bonnet. But now she felt it stretch with a smile. "We can get my little sisters."

"We can't take them to—"

"I mean on the way back."

"We'll see, we'll see."

Yes! She wanted to jump up and down.

"Now lass, try'n guess our good fortune?" A merry dimple cratered his cheek and his blue eyes sparkled.

"What?" She couldn't imagine.

"Tell ye on the way, I will. We got to hightail it."

She trotted to keep pace with him. "Tell me now!"

"Well, seems the good citizens of Yerba Buena is feelin sorry about the plight of the Donner orphans."

"So?"

"A gift, they's givin ye."

"A gift! What?" She could hardly believe strangers were thinking of her. "Tell me what!"

"Ground."

"Ground? You mean land?"

"Tis at that."

"They're giving us land?"

"Neptune's bones they is! Drawing up streets to make a proper town and givin a whole two blocks of it to you Donner waifs. You being the eldest, I sent word you'd be there to collect the paipers."

"But what can we do with land in a town?" She was a farm girl and he already had a rancho. Topping the hill she saw Paint saddled before the adobe. She glanced from the horse to Perry, realizing he meant to leave immediately.

"It's but wet dirt now, but mark my word, smart money is on Yerba Buena, it tis. The deedin ceremony is eleven days from now, at noon. It'll take all that time to get there. So fetch the things ye need, lass."

That evening they camped in an adobe room two doors down from where she and her sisters had waited for their parents to be rescued. Mr. Sutter said the girls were nowhere near the fort. "Zey be heppy wissout you," he said.

She swallowed the pain of that, doubting it was true. Sutter said the Brunners had a farm on the other side of the river, above the Sinclairs.

"Oh please," she said to Perry, "borrow the boat. Let's go see them!" Not a day had passed that she hadn't seen their tearful faces in her mind's eye.

He looked at the sunset and shook his head. "Late, it tis, lass."

She felt her face fall. He was right. They'd be caught in the dark.

"I promise ye lass, we'll stop on the way back." He strode away with Mr. Sutter, to drink spirits, she knew. Mr. Sutter's boat would leave for Yerba Buena first thing in the morning. Outside the familiar gate she saw only a couple of broken wagons in the twilight. Most of the men had returned from the war and reunited with families on new farms. She realized that these "prairie schooners" were already relics. Life went forward.

She hunkered down in sawdust and heard the sounds of rowdy men inside the fort walls. Distant coyotes yipped mournfully, bringing back the nights she'd spent with her sisters—the weary waiting and the nightmares. Did they still wake up screaming? The coyotes brought better memories, of a time back on the farm in Illinois when she'd been safe in her family's house.

Pulling her cloak to her chin, she wondered if bad luck really came from the feather robe that Mary said Perry had stolen and stored in his house. *Leave house or maybe die*, Mary had said more than once. Elitha had been relieved to learn that his other white wife had not died in the house. Still, she had lived there with him. Bad luck was supposed to touch everybody even remotely involved with that feather robe—Perry, Captain Sutter, the Indians, the Russians who took the robe, and all who now looked at it. However, her own bad luck had happened long before she got to Perry's house, so maybe it wasn't connected.

And besides, she and her sisters had survived. Her burning pain was gone, and the citizens of Yerba Buena were giving the Donner children land. This spelled good luck, perhaps the beginning of the prosperity Pa had envisioned. If there was a curse, it wasn't on her, or, as Indian Mary would say, she had enough "power" to stop it. She would take her sisters home, to the place Indian Mary called Rancho Sacayak. She would care for them and Pa would smile down from heaven.

She didn't hear Perry stagger in and fall beside her.

✿

He left the adobe early the next morning to turn Paint into Sutter's herd where the horse would graze until their return. She rolled her hair around her ears and pinned it, put on her bonnet and packed Perry's straight razor with her extra underwear and nightshirt in the carpetbag. Then she went to

Mr. Sutter's upstairs room, where she and Perry and several other passengers were to eat their breakfast.

Over his cup of cinnamon chocolate, heavily spiked with aguardiente, Mr. Sutter said a man named Sam Brannan had brought two hundred fifty Mormons around the Horn, and they were all establishing businesses in Yerba Buena. "They be vonderful skilled peoples." She couldn't wait to see that town on the ocean bay.

After breakfast she and Perry joined the other passengers on the trail to the river. Three men walked ahead with Perry, gripping rifles. Mrs. Kelsey held a newborn babe in her ropey arms. As Elitha helped her keep her three others corralled, she reflected that this young woman had known trouble too. Five years before the Donners and Reeds arranged their expedition, Nancy Kelsey had left Kentucky pregnant with a baby in her arms, insisting on accompanying her husband wherever he'd gone. He'd gone to California with the small Bidwell Party, leaving her behind. The oxen had given out in the desert and the party abandoned all their wagons. Nancy's shoes gave out too. By the time they got to the Sierra Mountains, which they knew nothing about, having no guide, she was barefoot, big with child, and winter coming on. They scaled the trackless mountains and ate their mules, but fortunately the snow had been scarce that year.

Nancy looked hardbitten and older than her twenty-one years.

"I heard you were the one that sewed the grizzly bear on the flag," Elitha said.

"Yup." Nancy's plain frock hung straight from board-like shoulders and her small blue eyes drilled out from a face like pitted granite.

"Didn't last long, did it? California being independent."

"Nope, Martha Ann, git back here this minute!"

Red grape leaves cascaded from tall yellow and brown trees, the stunning colors reflected in the American River. The boat, called the *Sacramento*, bumped gently against the sycamore it was tied to, a tree that now dropped brown leaves the size of dinner plates all over the deck, a deck Elitha well remembered. Now the morning air had a damp chill in it.

Sutter's Indians held the boat steady while the passengers boarded. Feeling limber and happy, Elitha jumped on, anxious to see Yerba Buena and then return to collect her sisters. Sutter's Indians smiled and waved good-bye from the shore. She waved back. With a sailor's rolling gait, Perry left her and went aft to the pilot, who was swinging the small boom around, reversing directions across a wide spot in the river. When the lurching subsided and the vessel headed downstream, Elitha, in a mood to match the sunshine on the blue water, went to join Perry.

The captain turned toward her—familiar pale eyes. She stopped breathing. The wild hair and beard had been trimmed, flesh added to bone, but it was Lewis Keseberg. Loathing and nausea slammed into her. She looked at

Perry, who stood at Keseberg's side as if they were pals.

"You should have been hanged," came from her mouth almost unbidden.

Men stared.

Around the aperture in the long pale beard, the man's mouth twisted into an obscene smile, an instant of time that stretched long in Elitha's mind. She recalled a rescuer saying at the inquest that he knew for a fact Tamsen had gone to the lake camp because someone had warned her that Keseberg was planning to kill her daughters. Elitha realized she should have testified about what the little girls had told her. The man was guilty—hadn't men testified to the pot of blood? Hadn't he admitted he ate her and buried some of the gold? They should have finished what they'd started and hung him in the mountains! Instead of taking him to the fort where justice was a joke. And here he stood an arm's length away, looking saucy after getting away with cold-blooded murder.

She lunged at him, to punish him for Tamsen's sake. She felt skin give way beneath her nails, but hands grabbed her from behind and pulled her away. Keseberg was covering his wounds and looking surprised.

She battled the hands—Perry's and another man's. Her heels rattled over the deck planks as the men pulled her away. They pushed her down at the prow rail, where a pile of goods obstructed her view of the killer. Her face felt hot and she breathed like a bellows.

"What the devil! Eat loco weed, did ye?" Perry glowering down at her.

She shook so hard she couldn't speak. In her mind she saw Keseberg eating Tamsen's brains. The little Kelsey girls crowded around Perry as if for protection from *her*.

She said, "If I were a man, I'd have killed him and no one would blame me." It would be expected of a man to kill him for what he'd done to Tamsen. A man would simply move on to some other place and Alcalde Sinclair would forget all about it. People would say the cur had it coming.

Perry looked at the gawking passengers and spoke to her through his teeth, "The man was declared innocent, or has ye forgot? Now you behave proper like, hear?" He raised a stiff hand as if to strike, and then let it drop. "Thought I had me a laidy, I did." His mouth made a thin line, his eyes a mean thicket of lashes.

She sank against the rail feeling her breakfast in her throat. She wrenched herself up and tried to lean over the water. Not in time. It hit her frock and shoes. Perry looked disgusted.

A man said, "Haven't even started yet, little girl. You'll get your sea legs." He cast a secret glance to the spectators. *The ghoul.*

Perry went back to Lewis Keseberg, put his arm around his shoulder, and spoke into his ear. Rage all but asphyxiated her. Had she been able to swim, she'd have jumped over the side rather than spend another minute with either of them. Instead she avoided all eyes, thinking maybe there *was* a curse of the condor robe.

The voyage down the American River to the Sacramento seemed endless, though it probably took a half hour. At the wide brown Sacramento, they turned south. People continued to stare at her like she was crazy. Her mind boiled. Never in her life had she done anything like that, and yet what that man had gotten away with would hurt her little sisters as long as they lived. But attacking him! It was as if an uncontrollable monster lurked inside her. And the sight of Perry's arm around the offending man hurt so much she never wanted to touch him again, even if he was her husband.

"There's Sutter's Embarcadero," said a man. Logs tied together at the water's edge, backed by a slough of bulrushes and cattails. She glimpsed the trail threading east, where they might have to walk on the return trip, if sailing against the current wasn't possible. In her heart she was sailing against the current of her marriage.

"Ole Sutter oughta sell this here land fer a town," a man said, cradling his gun across bent knees.

"Naw," said another. "That's not horse sense. This here's swamped GOOD come spring."

They were losing interest in her, she was relieved to see. The boat had the benefit of a sluggish current and little breeze. Perry and Lewis Keseberg swung the boom back and forth, though Keseberg didn't need any help. With anger boiling beneath a forced calm, she sat gazing at the red grape leaves meeting their images in the water. For months she'd tried to forget about Keseberg, yet how could she? On a boat piloted by him, with a husband taking his side.

By afternoon the passengers seated on the deck had quieted and Mrs. Kelsey's youngsters slept, one in her arms and two with their heads on her lap. The men sat in a circle, including Perry, and were passing liquor back and forth.

A man in buckskin gazed up the river and said, "At this rate hit'll take a month of Sundays to git there."

"It dad-blamed better not!" said another, turning a slippery eye toward Elitha. "The cap'n might git hungry." Hard laughter erupted all around, including from Perry and Nancy.

She couldn't meet Perry's eyes. How could she live with him?

❧

After sundown the boat pulled to shore. The men took their blankets to a thicket and Elitha went on deck to try to sleep with Nancy and the children. Perry jumped on board and pulled her aside. She jerked away from his touch, and couldn't look at him.

His whisper strained, "Think ye I don't know what I'm about?"

"You knew he'd be piloting the boat."

"Now lass, think. Ye wouldn't a come, now would ye? If I'd atold of it?"

Of course not. She looked down.

"Likely as not they'd a-give the ground away to someone else," he said. The boat lurched as a man jumped on, apparently searching for something. Perry steered Elitha aft, his mouth near her ear. "'Ave me reasons fer cozyin up to the likes o' him, I does." He tapped his temple and pointed at the man. It was Keseberg!

She glared at him.

"Methinks you catch more flies with honey than vinegar."

She hated talking to him.

"Some starry night on this 'ere trip, ole Keseberg'll get drunk and tell me where he's hid the quilt." He looked at her like she should be pleased to have such a clever husband.

"I don't care about the quilt any more."

That stopped his smile.

"You think that man will tell you anything?" she seethed. "It took a noose around his neck to get him to admit to two hundred dollars."

"Like I said, honey's the better way."

For seven days the boat tacked through the widening waterway, Perry acting as a sailing tutor to Keseberg. Each night he drank with the German while Elitha, Nancy Kelsey, and the children slept on deck. Elitha felt like an actor, pretending Keseberg didn't exist. She learned that the other passengers pitied her and made it plain that they thought Perry shouldn't be associating with Keseberg in her presence. Nancy Kelsey said she would have "hauled off an give him a lick."

During the day birds filled the air—ducks, geese, cranes and herons, sometimes blotting out the sun's light. In places they blackened the water for what looked like miles, and it seemed the boat floated through a river of feathers.

"Lansford Hastings' place," a man said pointing across the water. "Calls it Montezuma."

Elitha saw a white house, the second structure of any kind she'd seen. Tiny across the broad water, it sat at the foot of rolling brown hills. The other passengers gazed with admiration, but she wondered how Hastings could live with himself, knowing that half the Donner Party had died because of his advice. Her throat tightened. Again she was being pulled into the past.

The next day the shore receded to hazy rims as the boat sailed into the widening bay. Sea birds replaced the geese and ducks. The wind that filled the sails carried a salty odor. Large brown birds with hamper-like bills flew in squadrons, diving for fish—pelicans, the men called them. She looked beyond a white island to a far shore at the foot of high peaks, clear but distant—the town of Yerba Buena.

"High-tide it tis," Perry announced to the passengers. His blue eyes looked bright, less steely, as if absorbing the color of the azure sky. He did so love to sail a boat. "That means we'll take 'er to the mole at Montgomery Street."

"A mole!" shrieked one of Mrs. Kelsey's little girls. All three jumped up and down at the prospect of the voyage's end. Adults were on their feet smiling, gripping the hand rail.

Perry helped stow the sails and pole the craft into a pile of rocks and bricks. Elitha—never allowing her eyes to rest upon Keseberg—tightened the strings of her bonnet and grabbed her carpetbag. She looked beyond a two-story building and up a brown hill was another, steeper hill. White clouds sailed rapidly over the peak dragging shadows across its flank. Long-horned cattle grazed—ant-like in the distance. Here and there among the cattle stood a shack and a stick fence containing hogs. Groves of oaks resembled old apple trees. She stepped over the rail onto the "mole"—a pile of rocks.

Water lapped the soles of her shoes, and wind whipped her skirts and nearly turned her bonnet inside out. She noticed the placard on the only brick building in sight, MELLUS & HOWARD—Mellus also being the name of the store proprietor at the fort. All other buildings in Yerba Buena seemed to be made of adobe or wood, many of the latter under construction.

The passengers said their good-byes. As Elitha walked away from the wharf with Perry, she was relieved to see that Keseberg stayed on board occupied by hiring Indians, two of whom jumped into the hold and could be seen hefting up leather bags of wheat. She breathed a little easier for the first time in over a week, though bile still burned her gullet to know that Perry had arranged for her to be in close quarters with that horrid man, for an entire week. Pa never would have done such a thing to Tamsen. He'd respected his wife.

The town of Yerba Buena looked like a picture in a book, so intense was the quality of the light. Whitewashed adobes gleamed in the fresh air. Ox carts and horse-drawn wagons creaked along intersecting roads throwing off dust tails, but the spectacular bay overwhelmed everything else. Near and far vessels with tall masts bobbed on the blue water, and flags of all colors whipped, the red, white and blue of the United States prominent among them.

"That's a three-master," Perry said, pointing to a ship. "Learned on one like that, I did." He was in a pleasant mood, as if unaware that she could barely stand to look at him. He pointed again, "There's a four-masted windjammer from the Norseland."

Hand on the back of her neck, he guided her up a well-tamped road, telling her how much he liked this town. As they passed a tent saloon that was nothing more than planks balanced on barrels, he tossed a jaunty "Ahoy!" at the proprietor, who raised a hand and shouted, "Perry!"

He pointed to the far end of the long curve of beach. "See yon shanty?" She made out a small structure. "Will Clark's place, it is. Buildin a wharf and plannin to get rich off it, that one is." He lifted his hat and scratched his head. "Last time I was here he had Kanakas divin' down under with beams. Swim like fish, them Kanakas does." He replaced his hat. "We woulda landed there if it'd been low tide."

He steered her to the porch of an unpainted wooden place with JOHANSSON HOUS painted under the peak of the roof. He knocked. Chickens clucked under the stoop. Opening the door, a Nordic giantess looked fondly at Perry. She smoothed her apron and said in Swedish sing-song, "Wouldja look at what the sea's vashed in!" Turning to Elitha she asked, "And whose pretty ting iss dot?"

"Me own wife, it tis!" Perry looked Elitha over, then grinned at the giant-ess. "You got a room? And vittels?"

"Venn you haff da money, ha ha."

"Taik me for a rascal, does ye?" His grin was angelic.

The woman rolled her eyes, turned, and beckoned them, her broad back and yellow braids leading down a short, narrow hallway. She opened a door and stepped back.

The small room was so narrow the bed nearly filled it, but it had a door with a latch, and Elitha had spied an outhouse in back. After sailing for eight days, it looked luxurious. Civilization felt good. Almost as good as the peace in her privates. She exhaled and felt her anger at Perry begin to blow out with her breath. He was only being Perry, just trying to nose whatever he could out of life when he saw the chance. She wouldn't fight him. Besides that, the people of Yerba Buena were giving her and her sisters and cousins a nice block of land. For all she knew, it might be worth something someday. That's how Pa had looked at land.

She unpacked her blue calico dress and smoothed out the wrinkles.

# 41

Salt wind made sails of Elitha's skirts and tugged her matching bonnet as she stepped across a deeply rutted road. She felt the pins tight in her hair, which she'd rolled around her ears. Walking beside her, Perry looked dapper—clean-shaven and in polished boots. He'd been cheerful since their lovemaking, the first in a long time she hadn't minded. It was late October, the sun bright—a year and two weeks since the first snowflakes had fallen on the Donners.

He steered her by the neck toward the plaza on Montgomery Street, where the stars and stripes whipped above a low adobe building with a tile roof. Men stood smoking in the packed-earth yard—not one dressed like a Spaniard, though she knew they made up most of the town's population. A man in bell-bottomed trousers slapped Perry on the back. "Wall, ifn it ent me mait from the King's naivy! This be yer little Donner girl then?"

Heads turned. Feeling conspicuous in the presence of so many strange men who doubtless believed she'd eaten human flesh, she smiled and left him with his friends. She continued across the yard where a sign proclaimed "Clay Street." Wooden forms encrusted with white dirt stood in piles beside a large mud pit. Glancing up the road at the adobe houses she realized they had been built from this clay. The street was aptly named.

A bell clanged, the kind a schoolmarm would ring. Perry came for her and steered her through the crowded doorway, people coming from every direction, and up a center aisle between the benches, upon which people sat as if in church. The buzz of talk lowered as she and Perry passed by. *They assume I'm a cannibal.* She sat demurely, folding her hands, listening to the room fill behind her.

A hulk of a man dressed like a banker banged on a table with a wooden mallet. The room quieted. He introduced himself as Sam Brannan, and then spoke in an Irish accent about the "misfortunes" and "tragedy" of the Donner Party. He praised the heroism of the rescuers, but then talked about the "victorious end of the Mexican War" and the "manifest destiny of the United States to link the continent from the Atlantic to the Pacific shores."

With shiny black hair and a topcoat of tweed, he had an Irishman's gift of gab. "Mark my words," he intoned, "California will prosper under the red, white and blue. And now, in recognition of our new status as a territory of the United States, we, the Citizens' Committee, are bestowing a new name upon this town, one that will no longer be the devil to spell and a tongue-twister to boot. Henceforth this fair city will bear the name of Saint Francis of Assisi, for whom the Spanish mission was dedicated in 1776. And a more fitting name couldn't be found, for Saint Francis it was who blessed the weary traveler." He looked down at the mallet, and then lifted his head.

"And that we all are, ladies and gentlemen, are we not? Every one of us. Weary travelers at the end of a journey. In recognition and gratitude to the Spanish friars who civilized this peninsula, the name of St. Francis will be in Spanish. So, unless I hear serious disagreement to the contrary," he struck the table so sharply Elitha jumped in her skin, "this town henceforth will be known as San Francisco."

Applause erupted, men stamped, and Brannan banged along with the noise, using the table like a drum. With his black eyes snapping, he reminded Elitha of a snake-oil salesman at a Chicago fair.

When it was quiet again, he resumed but she found it hard to listen to the names of all the citizens on the committee and the flowery language describing the thinking they had done to draw up a plat grid for the "south of Market," which was being resurrected from the mudflats. But at last he wound down and introduced a smaller man—Alcalde and Justice of the Peace of San Francisco.

Mr. Bryant, who held a scroll of paper tied with a red ribbon, beckoned Elitha. The room hushed as Perry guided her to her feet and placed her hand, tender without the splint, on his elbow. Intensely aware of being stared at by people, she remembered the Wolfingers strolling this way across a mountain meadow.

They faced Mr. Bryant and she saw the crowd for the first time—sixty or seventy people beneath a low-beamed ceiling, light angling through windows. There in the front row sat Mr. and Mrs. Reed with their children and also Mary Martha and Georgie Donner, Elitha's cousins, who had suffered such terrible frostbite. Elitha was sending little smiles to each of them when Mr. Bryant beckoned Mr. Reed to the front too.

While Mr. Bryant orated about the starvation and suffering of the Donner Party, explaining that the two large plots of ground to be granted were but small tokens from the citizens of San Francisco in view of all that suffering, Elitha suddenly remembered seeing him before—back on the prairie. This was the leader of a renegade group of single men who had worked for various emigrant families but left their employers to travel faster. Mr. Miller, one of Pa's teamsters, had deserted the family to do so. To this day, Elitha thanked God that Jean Baptiste hadn't joined that group. On the other hand, had Mr. Miller stayed to fulfill his obligation, perhaps he too would have died with the other hired men and not been available to help rescue Elitha's half-sisters in the Third Rescue. And now, Mr. Bryant, who had so vexed Pa for luring Mr. Miller away, smiled and handed Elitha a scroll with a red ribbon, "to be utilized as she thought best for herself and her younger sisters."

Applause roared all around.

Next, Mr. Bryant spoke glowingly about Mr. Reed for taking in two "Donner orphans," and gave him another scroll with a red ribbon. People stood, shouted, whistled, stamped and clapped their hands. Meanwhile Elitha wondered why Mr. Reed had not adopted Frances, Georgia and Ellie. They too were Donner orphans. So was Leanna, though at almost thirteen many would deem her to be an adult.

Smiling as though he were the object of the crowd's approval, Perry steered Elitha down the aisle and outside, and she couldn't help but think how quickly things changed. One day a man was a scoundrel, the next a hero and Alcalde and Justice of the Peace of a growing city. And what was Mr. Miller today? Perry had told her he'd been appointed guardian of the Donner money. Pa would surely turn in his grave—and he was in a grave. At the fort she'd heard that General Kearny and others had buried him properly on their way over the mountains and, though he'd been "opened up," they laid him to rest in the bedsheet Tamsen had wound him in.

In the yard men smiled and took turns congratulating Elitha. She noticed that Mr. Reed had already left. "Proud to do it," said swarthy, woolly-headed Mr. Leidesdorff, one of the leading citizens mentioned by Mr. Brannan.

She curtsied, "We are ever so grateful, sir."

Perry jabbed a thumb at him. "Would ye believe? This 'ere fancy nigger owns and masters two ships o' commerce, and now has a big rancho up along the American River."

Mr. Leidesdorff raised an eyebrow over a penetrating black eye, but perhaps heard Perry's underlying admiration. "I prefer to reside on the seashore," he said, "unless I want to go mad as a hatter. How in thunder do you tolerate that wilderness out there on the Cosumney?" His British accent sounded entirely different from Perry's.

"Workin on it, ent we lass?" Perry looked at her.

She twisted the scroll and smiled.

She met Mr. Clark, the builder of the new wharf, and Mr. Mellus' partner, Mr. Howard, after whom a street near her property was named. Three men from the U.S. Army came to meet her—William Tecumseh Sherman and Edward Ord, both stationed in Monterey, and Captain Joseph Folsom stationed in San Francisco. She also met Mr. Oakley, and he reminded her that they'd met before, at Sutter's Fort the night Jean Baptiste had come through. Too many people! She couldn't keep them straight any more and became anxious to leave.

Former sailors gathered around Perry, urging him to slake his thirst with them.

"Blow me down if that don't sound good at that!"

Two women talked quietly, looking at Elitha.

She heard but one snippet: "… Pretty thing."

Meanwhile the Reed family drove away in a double-seated carriage pulled by two sleek black horses. How lucky the Reeds were, Elitha thought, to have each other and all their goods and money. Mary Martha and Georgie were fortunate to be adopted into that family.

⁂

After Perry "stowed away" a few drinks, Elitha stood with him at a sturdy post with a paper nailed to it. Second Street, the sign said on one side, Folsom on the other. Doubtless named for Captain Folsom.

Wind riffled the grass in every direction—from the gentle curve of the beach, across the mud flats and up the hills. She saw the canvas stores of Market Street about a quarter of a mile away, and an intervening post marked Frémont Street, after Captain John Frémont, who had figured prominently in the recent war against Mexico. Running perpendicular and starting at the water, posts had been driven into the earth to mark First, Second, Third, Fourth Streets, and so on, marching in a disciplined line up the hill—lonely heralds announcing non-existing streets in a wasteland of ground squirrels and jackrabbits.

Above, seabirds cried as Elitha untied the ribbon and stretched out the scroll, turning her back to the wind. Below the fancy lettering on the paper was a grid labled: South of Howard. Mission Road connected the town with the old Spanish mission. She looked up and saw a "carreta," a peculiar California cart that Spaniards hitched to the saddle of a rider, hurtling toward the mission as if flying over the grass.

Over her shoulder Perry pointed at the inked square at Second and Folsom. "Hit's about three times as long as tis wide," he said.

"My but it's big for a town lot!" she said, squinting toward the Third Street post. "Big enough for a small farm." She couldn't imagine roads would ever appear where the ruled lines were drawn.

"Ah, but it will have stores on it someday."

"But Perry, it's not anywhere near the town."

"Some day, lass, some day." Always hoping and scheming.

At about noon the following day they stepped from the porch of the boardinghouse into a bracing fog. After a hearty bowl of mush and a mug of Swedish coffee, the grounds of which had been soaked in egg yolk, Elitha felt a dearth of sleep. Her neck and shoulders ached from sitting on a chair while Perry gambled long into the night. Unaccustomed to sleeping late, she'd roused herself and visited with the proprietress, helping with the chores while Perry slept.

"Ever time I see this place, it's sprung more houses," Perry said.

He persuaded a teamster to let them ride in his delivery wagon to the Spanish Presidio. Amid bags and bundles, they bounced along a waterfront road. Passing Clark's Point, Perry said, "They call that Broadway."

Glancing up a narrow road of that name, she saw only a few scattered huts and couldn't help but smile. She'd learned that this town was filled with optimistic men. The sun was clearing away the fog, and it was clear they were circling a peninsula, the restless bay ever on their right.

"Mrs. Johansson said people here send their wash to China," she said, exhilarated by the wind. "Do you believe that?"

Comfortable against a leather bag, Perry sucked his Mexican cigarrito and winked against the smoke, "Ent enough females to do the wash. Brannan and the boys get their shirts back neat and folded in a month or two."

"They do it then, really, send it to China?"

He nodded.

"I'd think things would get lost on such a long voyage, or the linen would get mixed up."

"Nothin gets lost on a ship, lass. All stowed neat and tidy like."

In an hour they'd passed only a few houses, then they came to a cluster of dilapidated adobe buildings. Leaving the wagon, they hiked up through aromatic evergreens to a point overlooking the Spanish buildings, and gazed across the isthmus where the ocean entered the enormous bay. The tan hills on the opposite shore looked soft and rounded. Battalions of pelicans circled the rocky island that reared up in the center of the bay, white with guano.

"Alcatraz, the Spaniards call that bird," Perry said.

She hugged herself, amazed how little warmth the sun emitted, and listened as he told of arriving at this strait with John Sutter on the ship Sutter had acquired in the Sandwich Islands. Señor Valdez had said Perry deserted his captain. When had that happened? Maybe in those distant islands.

Perry feigned the creaky voice of an old-timer. "That were in eighteen and thirty-nine." He counted on his fingers. "Eight years. My, my things has changed. I'll wager nigh four hundred souls dwells in Yerb—San Francisco now, countin the greasers, if they got souls." He laughed, and then soberly said, "Send our wash to China, we will lass. When I strikes it rich. A man can git rich in this country, if he knows what 'e's about."

# 42

Three nights later Elitha sat on the same chair in the same room where Perry had gambled every night. Only the men at the table differed. Sometimes she wondered if he was waiting for Keseberg and the *Sacramento* to return so he could travel with that awful man again. Sick at the thought and anxious to get to her sisters—the voyage could take eleven days upstream—she twisted on the chair.

Before leaving Johansson Hous, Perry had said, "Win me loot back tonight, I will."

She rotated the scroll in her hands, the ribbon worn and wrinkled—he'd asked her to bring it so he could show it off. Now she touched him on the shoulder with it, a hint that they needed to leave, to no avail. She counted twelve planks down one wall and fourteen on another, eleven at her back, and knew intimately every knothole and adz gouge. The room was cramped, her chair inches from Perry.

Opposite him sat the cabin owner, Greasy Jim, who had once been Perry's partner on the pig ranch, before Perry had cattle. The man was young and had a heavy German accent. She gathered from the jibes at the table that he'd been a butcher. Behind the table the floor sloped down to a stove, from which rancid odors wafted up with the heat. The smoke of the cigarritos gagged her. It was midnight or later and she'd been awake since early morning. She turned on one hip and rested her cheekbone on the chairback, watching the gamblers and praying for signs of quitting.

Greasy Jim raked in five piles of coins. Perry upended his flask, gulped three times, let out an ahhh, and wiped his sleeve across his mouth. Cards were slapped on the table. Perry shoved coins before him. Eventually others would collect them, as they had all night. She hoped he'd lose every cent, and quickly, so they could leave. But he won that hand. He turned to her and winked, then turned back and shuffled the deck.

She leaned forward and whispered in his ear, "I'll find the way to the boardinghouse by myself. I'm plumb tuckered." She stood up.

He twisted around, scowling, and pointed at the chair. "Sit down and wait till I'm done. Ent no time o' night for a white girl to wander alone. The greasers'll git ye." He flashed a pathetic grin around the table as if telling the men what a burden a wife was, and added, "We'll go when I gits me money back." He chuckled. They looked at him over their cards, not caring about her.

She looked down at the chair that had tortured her so long and knew she wouldn't spend one more minute on it. The Spaniards she had seen were gentlemen compared to these men. She shouldered the door open a crack. Cool air beckoned her into a fresh, misty darkness. The leather hinges creaked as she slipped outside. He hadn't even looked up. But he had seen.

The bite in the air stung her awake and her heart pounded. Gripping the scroll, she ducked behind a corner of the adjacent shack, where she could watch the cabin door, and try to think. Why had she done that? *Elitha is an obedient girl.* What would he do? Maybe she shouldn't go to the boardinghouse. He'd been drinking a lot and might hurt her. But where could she go at this time of night? *Away.*

She trotted up the road, amazed the door hadn't opened, a feeling of terror and outrage jamming her esophagus like a whole melon. Maybe, she told herself, he'd pretend her actions didn't count for anything and he'd keep playing cards. But then he'd make an excuse about being tired, and come for her.

Her legs felt free and limber, as if a mysterious force pulled her away from Perry. The road rose steeply beneath her and the fog blurred the crescent of a moon. The empty fields between the cabins grew wider. A candle flickered in a window. A horse whinnied. Her breathing grew labored as she climbed. Girls didn't do this. She sat down to rest near the iron gate of an adobe, realizing she had no plan and no reason to run from the man she had promised to obey. Gasping for breath, she shivered in the cold and damp.

"Qué pasa?" A male voice.

She jumped in her skin. She couldn't ask a Spaniard to hide her; he'd think she was a woman of the night. She pressed her back against a tree trunk and stifled her rasping breath, hoping the man would think he'd been mistaken. Moisture penetrated her frock from the grass. Her thumb throbbed. She would keep quiet, then go back to the boardinghouse—before Perry left the card game. Maybe he was glad she'd stopped pestering him. She caught a whiff of mint. Dogs barked in the distance. A drop of condensation fell on her face from an overhead limb. An owl hooted, and her breath slowed.

"Git yer arse the bloody hell over here afore I knock ye to kingdom come!"

Her heart stopped. He was across the road.

"Who goes there?" The Spaniard asked.

"A law-abiding man lookin fer 'is bleedin wife!" Perry hove from the darkness, coming at her.

She stood up stammering, "I'm sorry. I, I—"

His palm cracked against the side of her head and she fell to the ground before she knew what happened. Instinctively she covered her ear to stop the ringing pain.

"Señor, please take your woman away from my house," said the soft voice with a chuckle.

"Don't trouble yer greasy head over it!" Perry yanked her injured hand and pulled her to her knees.

She yowled involuntarily—the pain racing up her arm.

He dropped her hand. "Oh, fer Chrissake, git up!" A hard object hit her back, knocking her on all fours before she could stumble to her feet. He had kicked her. In the misty moonlight she saw him retrieve the scroll where she'd dropped it.

The whole way down the hill he never released her wrist, and never said a word. She couldn't explain to herself, much less to him, why she'd run away, so she stayed quiet. Closing the door of their room, he turned to her and said, "Let this be a lesson to ye, lass." In the faint light from the candle in the next house, she saw his balled fist coming. It rammed her solar plexus. She hit the wall and curled over onto the floor, unable to make a sound. Like a broken bellows, her lungs wouldn't work.

He fell back on the bed with his lower legs and boots hanging over the side, by her head. Gradually her air seeped back, but she suppressed the urge to gasp and breathed in the aromas of the new cedar floor. Hugging her aching stomach, still feeling the pain in her back, the ringing in her ear and the ache in her hand, she realized the only women she'd heard of who were hit by their husbands were women of bad character, from bad families. Had she fallen that low? She felt more like a trapped animal.

Maybe she was losing her mind. Attacking Keseberg, right in front of people, then running away from Perry. She had to get it into her head that she was a married woman—for better or for worse—not an undisciplined child. She had always imagined she would become a gracious farm wife. Her place was beside this man, the squire of Rancho Sacayak. Nonetheless, she stayed motionless on the floor, breathing imperceptibly, hoping he'd think he had hurt her bad. Then maybe he'd apologize.

The candle next door blinked out. The dark was profound. A cold draft blew under the door. She clenched her teeth so they wouldn't chatter. A long time went by, but no snoring came from the bed. He never moved. She'd meant to outlast him, but couldn't bear the hard floor any more. Quite sure he was awake, she got up and carefully lay down, crosswise on the bed, as far from him as she could get.

🌿

The next two days Perry was noticeably nicer, though he never mentioned what he'd done. He took the property deed "to show the blokes," and allowed her to go her own way. It felt good to look around the town alone. At mealtimes they met at the boardinghouse, and he was almost like when he'd courted her. Prowling the stores, she began to think maybe he saw her a little differently now—less like a horse or trained dog. Maybe she'd done right not to apologize any more than she had. A wife was to be obedient, but maybe there was a limit.

She admired lacquered boxes from Japan, silks and bracelets from China, checkered wool from Flanders, scissors, needles and knives from England. Mellus & Howard was truly a fine store. Leaving, she found a folded newspaper on a bench outside the door. She opened *The California Star,* Sam Brannan, Publisher, and read: "YERBA BUENA NOW SAN FRANCISCO." The front page told of the winning of the Mexican War in the town of the Angels, Pueblo de los Angeles. On page two, scattered among advertisements, articles told of the opening of new businesses by Mormon proprietors, and a few sentences about how Lansford Hastings was available to help people win title to their land. Then an editorial by Brannan gave reasons why the San Francisco Mormons should convince Brigham Young to bring the "Saints" to San Francisco. She recalled that Mr. Rhoads had failed to get them to settle the Cosumney area, but Brannan was more persuasive. Maybe he would prevail.

On the back page she didn't read the article about President Polk and General Zachary Taylor. Instead she wondered if Abraham Lincoln had won his seat in the General Assembly of Illinois. Nobody cared about that in California.

She returned the paper to the bench and walked up Market Street, passing a saloon partitioned from a shop by a length of red calico. BARBER AND HORSE DOCTOR, the placard stated. Beneath that, a smaller sign proclaimed: "New Battery Device Cures Ague." The proprietor, who had tightly bound a man into a chair, placed his boot against the patient's chest, told him to open wide, and clamped a pair of pliers on a back tooth. She hurried onward.

The next store had wooden walls and a canvas roof. The sign said: "Mr. Green, Proprietor." Inside a man pried the lid from a wooden box. Sugarcane, the same as she'd seen at Daylor's trading post, was packed inside. With a smile, Mr. Green handed her a joint. "From the Sandwich Islands," he told her.

"Thank you kindly. I'm just looking at the wares, if that's all right."

"Go right ahead, miss." He went back to his boxes.

Gnawing the cane and admiring the goods, her eye was taken by a familiar-looking young woman who entered the store. She wore a smart black jacket with matching skirt and checkered shirtwaist. She glanced away, as if a crate of oranges had suddenly seized her attention.

Moving to a better angle, Elitha realized it was Sarah Murphy Foster, one of the seven snowshoers who got through—Mary Murphy's older sister. Elitha removed the spent cane from her mouth, dropped it on the dirt floor, and approached.

Under the soft sunlight penetrating the canvas, the young woman's cheeks could have been made of white porcelain, and her jet black hair hung beneath her bonnet in springy corkscrews. *Black Irish*, Tamsen would have said. When she saw Elitha, a shadow passed across her luminous blue eyes— so like Mary's—and her voice was rough. "You're a Donner, ain't you?" She hadn't been at the ceremony.

"Yes, Elitha Donner. Aren't you Mary Murphy's sister?"

"Yup." She looked prosperous. Mr. Foster had done well here.

When nothing more came, Elitha said, "Mary and I were friends on the crossing. I'd sure like to see her again, and would be obliged if you could get word to her. I'm married to Perry McCoon now, living at his place out on the Cosumney River, past Sheldon and Daylor's place." Most people in California knew them.

Sarah didn't let on if she did. "I don't never see my sister now." Her voice was husky, her eyes veiled by her lashes. She seemed eager to leave.

Awkward in a silence screaming of the grim connection between them, Elitha ventured, "So sorry about Lem. He was a good boy."

Sarah turned away and dabbed at her eyes with a handkerchief, which she pulled from her jacket pocket.

Suddenly Elitha recalled somebody at Johnson's ranch saying that Sarah never wanted to be reminded of the crossing ever again. Wishing she could reel back her words, she said, "I'm awfully sorry. I should have known not to speak of it." Seeing no change, she put her hand on the dark fabric of Sarah's arm and added, "You did no wrong. People shouldn't judge us."

Sarah turned toward her, bright ribbons of moisture streaking the porcelain. "They judge you too?"

Elitha nodded, not caring about the misunderstanding. What did it matter? A high-combed, mantilla-draped Spanish woman was approaching the oranges. Elitha whispered, "Let's go outside." She led Sarah up the dusty road toward the boardinghouse and stopped at a stack of adobe bricks that would soon be part of a building. They sat on the bricks. Three men rode by on horses, but most of the people must have been behind walls eating their noon dinners, because the streets were quiet. Ships bobbed on the choppy water.

"Thank you for talking to me," Elitha said.

Sarah, looking intently at the blue crystals at Elitha's throat, said, "People can be downright mean." Her cheeks were drying in the wind.

"My husband gave this to me," Elitha said touching the pendant.

"I know. I got it off an Injun. Gave it to Mr. McCoon."

So, she'd met Perry at Johnson's! "Did the Indian give it to you?"

"No. He was dead."

On the prairie they had passed dead Indians left on scaffolds for the vultures. Taking objects from such corpses had been strictly forbidden because the Indians believed it would cause dangerous spirits to be visited upon Indian and white alike. Nevertheless, Lewis Keseberg had taken a buffalo robe from such a scaffold, and Mr. Reed had nearly banished him from the wagon train. All across the continent the bad blood between those two had never abated. "Where did you find the dead Indian?" Elitha asked.

"They were the guides. Don't you remember?" Sarah stood up and glared down at Elitha. It seemed the fragile bond of friendship had broken. "Mr. Stanton brought them from Mr. Sutter's fort. Or maybe you Donners was too far behind to notice."

"I didn't mean anything by it." She got up, for it was clear Sarah was leaving.

Sarah looked at her with terrible thoroughness and said, "Well, if you must know, my husband shot them. Now I never want to hear no more about it. They was about to die anyhow, and we was starvin'." She wiped an eye with her handkerchief.

"I didn't mean to pry." Deflated and more than a little horrified at this turn of events, she spotted Perry's swagger far in the distance, coming toward the boardinghouse, and absently touched the crystals at her throat. Perry said they were charmed. For good or ill she didn't know, but they had come from a dead Indian, a murdered Indian. *Killed for meat, like Tamsen.*

Anger dropped from Sarah's face as quickly as it had appeared, and a monologue spilled from her about blizzards and being lost and men freezing to death. As Perry drew near, Sarah's pace accelerated. They had kept track of the meat, she said, so nobody would eat their kin. "The Indians was grubbing for roots and acorns. I didn't want him to shoot. Harriet tried to stop him too, but he didn't pay no mind." She turned her face away as Perry arrived at the boardinghouse thirty yards away. He put his boot on the step and looked Elitha a question.

She ignored it. "Do you know where those Indians were from?"

"Well, Sutter sent them. But they was no guides atall. Didn't even speak English. Luis and Salvador their names was. Salvador means Savior in Spanish, ain't that funny?" She looked at Elitha with a blend of apology and timidity. "I'm jumpy lately. Didn't mean to be rude." She touched her arm. "You know, if it hadn't a been for that Injun meat, we'd of starved for sure. Then nobody woulda got through, would they?"

Sarah was right; Elitha too had been saved by the flesh of an Indian named Savior. Indian Mary's brother? She realized there might indeed be a connection. The blue crystals at her neck felt warm and heavy. She recalled Indian Mary's reaction when her baby had touched them, and she thought of Lewis Keseberg taking the buffalo robe off a dead Indian. He certainly hadn't purified himself. It felt like a bottomless well of confusion, no explanations fathomable. Salvador's flesh saving the Donner Party, Indian Mary healing her of an unspeakable ailment, all tangled up with condor feathers and magic crystals.

Sarah was saying, "It tasted better than white meat." A confidential tone.

That came so unexpected that Elitha couldn't hide her feeling of shock and revulsion.

Sarah stiffened. "Well, what difference does it make? It's all right if it tastes bad? Sinful if it tastes better? We done no wrong, Elitha Donner. Jes wanted to live."

Watching the Nordic proprietress come out the door to join Perry on the stoop, Elitha wasn't sure about anything any more. "I'd be grateful if you'd tell your sister I'd like her to come visit."

By then Sarah was whisking her expensive skirts up the lane.

Shaken, Elitha went to Perry, who was humbling himself before Mrs. Johansson—the backs of her hands on her waist, her color high.

He flashed her a glorious smile. "Next time I'll pay ye, I vow."

She dropped her hands to her sides. "Next time den? Shore?"

"Me solemn oath." The look on his face was a kiss, dark lashes jutting toward the big woman. Then he turned to Elitha and clucked as one would at a horse, "Hurry girl, or we'll miss the boat."

Relieved to be going at last, she dashed inside, fetched her bag and followed him at a half-trot. Then it came to her. The scroll wasn't projecting from any of his pockets. "Where's the deed?" she asked.

His silence answered.

She stopped walking. "You lost it gambling." She felt an odd sense of fate, as if she'd known all along that this would happen.

He turned to her, his face ugly. "Git to the boat, or I vow—" He stepped toward her with a raised hand.

She hurried on, humiliation and disappointment mounting with each step. She tried to sound adult, to keep what she was asking from cracking apart. "I don't see what good the paper is to those men. Their names aren't on it." *To the children of George Donner:* It was like a sacred trust. Another one.

Tight-lipped, he strode beside her. "I signed it over."

"But they gave it to me, for all of us, and I didn't sign it over." She didn't know much about property papers.

"Forget, did ye? Ye be my wife."

"I didn't know you could sign it over is all." She felt the lump hurting her esophagus again—the sense of being treated like a disobedient child. Glancing at the windswept hills of San Francisco, she told herself the land wasn't worth much anyway. It was the principle that hurt. A gawking row of frightfully unkempt men looked up at her as she passed a tent saloon.

She looked beyond, to the DICE MI NANA nosed up to the mole. A man other than Keseberg was directing the loading of goods. *Thank God.*

"Win the ground back next time, I will," Perry tossed back at her as he stepped toward the captain.

She sighed, doubting that. The scroll with the red ribbon had vanished like a dream, and maybe because of a curse. But that, she realized with a shake of her head to clear the cobwebs, was whole-hog Indian superstition. This was the nineteenth century! Tamsen had taught her the scientific method and logic syllogisms like "All wheat is grain, but all grain is not wheat." Logic was the way of the white man, of progress. If she let herself drown in superstition, she'd be lost. The Donner Party got trapped in the snow because Mr. Reed and Pa followed Lansford Hastings' untested route. Period. Half of them survived because they ate what they had to, and because of brave men like John Rhoads. Period. She had married a man whose ways were different than she'd hoped, but that happened to girls all the time and it had nothing to do with feathers and crystals. It had everything to do with making the best of things.

Soon she would be caring for her sisters under her own roof. And if Perry stopped her? Well, that wouldn't be bad luck, but something else entirely. She'd figure out then what to do about it.

# 43

Twelve days later the American River was too low to navigate upstream, so Elitha, Perry, and Joe House, the only other passenger, debarked at a collection of tied-together logs that Sutter called his Sacramento embarcadero. Earlier they had seen Keseberg piloting the boat named Sacramento toward San Francisco. Relieved to know he wouldn't be at the Fort, Elitha relaxed on the three-mile trek, a pathway heading straight east through tall dry grass and enormous oak trees. Hungrier with every step, she looked forward to a good supper at the table of Captain Sutter, who prided himself on hosting visitors.

While identifying themselves to the American guards, Elitha noticed a sheet of paper nailed to the Fort gate. The low sun provided sufficient light to read a surprising message.

NOTICE: My wife Mary Johnson, having left my bed and board, I would inform the public that I will not be accountable for any debts of her contracting after this date. William Johnson, Bear Creek. Nov. 20, 1847.

Mary Murphy had actually left Mr. Johnson! Where was she now? And who on earth had written this? Surely not that ignorant man. In confusion she glanced at Perry, who had looked at the notice only a few seconds and was now halfway up the stairs. Mr. Johnson was a friend of his, and yet Perry had seemed disinterested. Mr. House chuckled beside her, then clumped up the stairs ahead of her.

Inside, she wasn't surprised to see Mr. Johnson and a colorful assortment of men already eating, with Mr. Sutter at the head of the table. They all smelled bad, but Johnson was the worst. His beard was as long and matted as she remembered it, and his bad eye still wandered. She watched in fascinated loathing as he got up and clapped Perry on the back. Oddly, Perry said nothing about Mary leaving the man's bed.

In his turn, Mr. House said, "Looks like white women ain't 'ny easier to keep than Injuns." Men snickered and looked with open speculation at Elitha, who was seating herself. Perry seemed like a boy left out of a joke.

"The whimperin bitch," Johnson replied. "Ifn she wants a slimy Frenchman, she can have 'im."

*She left him for another man.* Perry sat down looking at Mr. Johnson as if the Oracle of Delphi were carved on the man's forehead.

Mr. House said, "You lookin to git another white woman?"

Mr. Johnson's red lips opened and a pink tongue flapped through the hole in his beard. "Them Kanaka wahinees is acallin this old tar," he said. "I'm headin to the Sandwich Isles."

"What about your ranch?" Mr. House asked.

Mr. Sutter answered by saying Sebastian Keyser was buying out the rest of the grant. Elitha watched Perry, suddenly certain that he didn't know how to read. He had lied to her about that.

Two Indian women brought more food, and the men talked endlessly about the war, the Pathfinder's latest actions, and something about General Kearny, but she was tired and barely remembered that the Pathfinder's real name was John Frémont. They speculated with liquor-loosened tongues about California becoming a slave state.

"We could get the black niggers to work our ranches."

"Hell, they cost a fortune," one of the more colorful men said. "The Injun niggers are free if a man handles it right."

"That's right," said another. "Besides, the woolly heads don't work near as hard as Injuns."

"Yeah, but you gotta figger this in. Injuns eat like horses and die like flies."

Sutter sipped his liquor and reminded them a lady was present.

Casting her the briefest of glances, a man named Zeke Merritt growled, "We shoulda had the huevos to keep ourselves free under the Bear Flag."

Perry leaned forward on his elbows. "But I'll wager the cap'n gits to be gov'nor under the stars and stripes."

Sutter blushed like a girl at the compliment, but Mr. Merritt pounded his fist on the table. "Well damnation man, he coulda been KING if we'd kept Frémont the hell outa here!"

Mr. Johnson rammed a hunk of meat into his mouth and chewed hugely, his cockeyed glance dragging over Elitha. She thought, *Good for Mary.*

"That's right," a man agreed, "Now Frémont's claiming to be governor."

"Not if he's court-martialed," came the rejoinder.

She couldn't stand a minute more. Excusing herself, she went alone to the adobe room and lay on the now-flattened wood shavings. A team of wild horses couldn't stop her from visiting her sisters in the morning, even if she had to walk there alone. With that thought, she fell asleep.

Up and up she circled, higher and higher on a mountain peak. When the wagon stopped she saw a log cabin and felt uneasy, because it appeared to be a house with no windows. The driver said he'd wait. Cautiously she opened the cabin door. The room was glowing with soft gaslight and filled with people holding crystal goblets of red wine. She realized a friendly party was underway. She saw Pa and Tamsen looking happy and healthy, visiting and smiling. Pa looked up and came toward her through the crowd, and in the link of their gazes she felt cherished. Tamsen came over and introduced Elitha all around. The people spoke to her in the manner of beloved aunts and uncles, though she'd never seen them before. Accepting a glass of wine, she said, "A pity you have no windows. It wastes a view from the mountaintop."

The murmur of talk quieted. People stepped back from a draped wall, and two women began to draw the curtains. Pa cupped her elbow in a steadying way, and she watched as a floor-to-ceiling grid of windowpanes came into view, but instead of sky and trees, she saw a solid wall of dirt. Brown earth, with tiny air spaces, as if men had recently shoveled it up against the windows. The realization hit. *The cabin is buried.* The people, including Pa and Tamsen, showed no sadness for themselves, but looked at her with kindness and commiseration.

The women drew the drapes back over the windows again, and the friendly buzz of conversation resumed. Pa turned to her, his voice deep and steady. "Elitha lamb, my only sorrow is not being able to talk to you."

She opened her eyes, Perry snoring beside her. The first gray light of dawn made a rectangle at the doorway, but she felt oddly peaceful. She had seen the other side. Life after death was different than what she'd been taught. The dead couldn't see out, but were surrounded by compassion and love, and were having a good time! She couldn't wait to tell Leanna.

Like a pastel wash over an inked scene, the peaceful feeling stayed with her through breakfast in Sutter's quarters, and afterwards. It lingered when she and Perry forded the river on Paint and headed up the trail toward Rancho del Paso, leading a borrowed horse. She could hardly believe Perry would calmly ride to the Brunner's place without excuse, without a word of protest.

Not wanting to spoil it with anything he might misconstrue, she said only, "Thank you very much, Perry."

He was so quiet she wondered if he'd heard. Then he said—his breath warm on her neck—"Elitha, I did bad to hit ye, there in Yerb—San Francisco." He cleared his throat like he had a wad of cloth stuck in it. "I shouldn'ta done it and I hopes ye don't get notions bout leavin me."

Mary Murphy had made an impression after all! The last thing Elitha had expected was an apology, yet it somehow seemed perfectly natural in the peaceful aura of the dream, and the fact that she was drawing near to her sisters—five months since she'd seen them. It seemed everything was connected but in a good way—and not by logic either. Maybe this feeling was a little bit like what Indian Mary meant by power.

"I'm not leaving you, Perry," she said, but something made her add, "Not with you saying you shouldn't have done it."

"I couldn't help meself. Hit was like a dark shade acomin over me and tellin me a man gots to beat a woman to make her... I needs ye, Elitha. You be the one wot can change this mean ole tar into a gentleman."

She knew a hidden part of him had opened and wouldn't stay open for long. And who was she to cast blame? Hadn't she felt an uncontrollable monster rear up in her and try to kill Lewis Keseberg? Some things weren't to be explained by logic. "Perry, your saying that makes me feel like we did right to get married."

"We did at that, lass," he said patting her thigh. And about losin' the paipers, I'll make it up to ye, I will. A bad run o' luck I was 'avin, is all. Never saw it so bad in all me livin days."

"Perry, I need to tell you, I'm sorry I jumped on Keseberg like I did. It must have shamed you." They were approaching a man guiding a handplow behind a mule, and she wanted to get this out. "I've been meaning to ask if Mr. Keseberg said anything about the quilt."

"Nay, sorry lass. But 'e said Fallon le Gros went back up. Turned around right after they brought Keseberg down. So 'e thinks that big bastard 'elped himself to the money. Then, not a fortnight after, General Kearny and a bunch of military men marched back through, turnin everything over. Neptune's bones, ent a chance in Hades a farthing's left anywhere thereabouts in that camp, an' those men ent daft enough to breathe a word of it either, or write it in their reports."

It looked like Daniel Rhoads ahead, but Elitha had one more thing to say. "I'll teach you to read if you like." A necessary skill for a gentleman.

She felt him release his breath—exasperated? She hoped she hadn't closed him up again. But after a moment he said, "Ent about to learn letters, Elitha. Tried before."

"But—"

"Bill Daylor can't read, and he runs his store shipshape. Now if a man can run a store without letters, 'e can run cattle." He sounded determined, and she saw that it really was Dan Rhoads they were approaching—John Rhoads' brother.

"How about signing your name? Can you do that?"

"Now I might can learn that, with a little 'elp."

"Good. We'll start there."

"Howdy," said Dan Rhoads, whoaing the mule.

"Tearin up God's green earth be ye?" Perry grinned.

Dan Rhoads smiled. "Best I can. Plantin winter wheat for Mr. Sinclair." He wiped a streak of dirt across his brow—she remembering how weakened by hunger he'd been when he'd gone on to the valley early. Now he was working to put aside money to buy land of his own, Catherine had said.

He gave directions, and in another mile they were approaching the Brunner farm. She saw a neat frame house—maybe four rooms—and fences, and realized with a pang that she would be taking the girls into far worse circumstances. Then she saw them running toward the horse.

"Big Sister, Big Sister!" they called, holding up their skirts—Georgia and Frances ahead, little Ellie trailing with a barking dog. Where was Leanna?

She slid off the moving horse and hit the ground laughing. The dog barked in her ear and she sat hugging all three girls on her lap. The dog was so noisy she couldn't ask about Leanna. Perry rode ahead to the house. She got up and enjoyed being pulled along by the bubbling, laughing girls, all neat and clean in new frocks. *Well cared for.* She couldn't answer all the questions flying at her. "Yes, silly, we have a house at the ranch. No, no children to play with, except Indians."

When she got to the house, Perry was leaning on the doorframe. She passed by him as she entered, curtseying to Mrs. Brunner and intensely aware of the indoor fireplace and adjoining rooms with wooden doors. *Much better house.* Now that the girls were standing still, she saw the healthy roses in their cheeks. "Why, you three put on flesh!" she said, "Especially you Georgia. Where's Leanna?"

The answer came from Mrs. Brunner—smaller and older than Elitha remembered, her hair drawn into a severe white-streaked bun.

"She vorks on a farm, far away." She flapped her wrist toward a framed daguerrotype on the whitewashed wall.

"Where? We'll have to get her." Leanna would be just thirteen and Elitha was anxious to introduce her to Indian Mary.

A balding man with a drooping handlebar mustache and a full gray beard stepped through the door, giving Perry what looked like a meaningful glance. "Not possible," he said. "Too far away. Frau Rotweiler needs her."

The room seemed cramped with so many people, although it was larger than Perry's entire adobe. Panic pricked her. If she didn't take them now, they'd all be working in far-flung places and excuses would be given as to why she couldn't have them. She used her motherly voice. "Now get your things and we'll all ride to the ranch." Searching each pair of eyes, two pair brown, one blue, she detected resistance.

Turning to Mrs. Brunner, she said, "I'll help them pack."

Mrs. Brunner said, "Day not vant go."

Dumbfounded at that, Elitha saw Mr. Brunner give Perry a look.

Perry said to Elitha, "Well, looks like we should be steppin' smart, lass. There's weather brewin." To Mr. Brunner he said, "I'll leave the mare with ye. Be pleased if ye'd taik er back to the cap'n."

The row of small faces before Elitha wore troubled adult expressions, but no denials came from them.

"Please, Mr. and Mrs. Brunner," she said, "I promised Ma I'd care for them. We Donners need to be together."

The girls looked up at the woman. Fearfully? Asking permission?

With a helpless shrug Mrs. Brunner opened her palms. "I not schtop dem." Peering down at the girls: "Iss so, klein mädele? Grandma schtop you?"

Georgia, Frances and Ellie exchanged glances. Then they slowly wagged their braided heads and said in practiced unison, "Nein Grandma."

Mrs. Brunner tilted her head toward Elitha, all the while holding the three with a fierce eye, "You vant go with diss one?"

"No Grandma," came the unison monotone.

Baffled, wishing to talk to each one of them alone, Elitha knelt, took Ellie's hand and said, "I've been missing you." She petted back the fine dark hair around her small face. The elf hadn't grown any taller, but was padded now. "Won't you come keep me company? I am so lonely on the ranch, with Perry out with the cows all day." She glanced at him, his arms folded, boots crossed as he leaned on the doorframe. No help there.

Mrs. Brunner nodded at Ellie. "Dot one go maybe."

Ellie nuzzled her velvet cheek against Elitha's. "I'll come with you, Big Sister."

"Oh, thank you Baby." She swallowed and blinked back tears as she hugged Ellie, then pushed her away. "Now run get your things." She saw Georgia and Frances locked in Mrs. Brunner's gaze. Afraid?

Recalling Sarah Daylor saying how much the girls helped the Brunners, she gripped Georgia's thin hand and turned to Mrs. Brunner. "Surely you can find a hired girl?" But hired girls were paid and her little sisters worked for nothing. And besides, Mr. Miller was giving the Brunners Donner money as long as the sisters lived in the house, or was supposed to be doing so. Elitha didn't trust him. She knew she shouldn't be thinking it, but she wondered whether Perry was somehow involved in a scheme with Mr. Miller, their supposed guardian, to keep the girls at the Brunners.

As she turned to him, his hand clamped on her upper arm. "We'd best be on the trail," he said. *Trial,* as he pronounced it. "Bring the young one." To the Brunners he added, "We thanks ye kindly," and pulled Elitha out the door, Ellie and the others following.

Elitha kissed Georgia and Frances, mounted the horse, and then leaned down from the big Spanish saddle and lifted Ellie by her tiny hands, one of which gripped Tamsen's silk stocking, and put the child in her lap. Frances and Georgia called good-bye as the horse plodded away from the farm. A warm tear crawled down Elitha's cheek—so many tears in the last six months! It was a wonder she had any left. She twisted around to wave, and saw Mr. and Mrs. Brunner like shadows in the window. Chickens clucked and a young pig sniffed in the dirt.

"Good-bye," Ellie sang out. Elitha hoped she'd done the right thing to separate her from the others, to take her to a house with no indoor cooking, and winter coming.

What would Pa and Tamsen say? Do your best. Hugging Ellie, who gripped the silk stocking as if her life depended on it, she swallowed the disappointment about Leanna and vowed she'd do well by Ellie. After all, most things didn't work out the way people expected. Pa didn't expect to die before getting to California. Tamsen didn't expect to be murdered, and the Citizens Committee didn't expect Perry to lose the deed.

They hadn't gone far before the sky clabbered up and wind whipped the ocean of grass. The days were short now, the air chill. Ellie whined, "My FEET hurt."

Elitha's toes hurt too, more than they should have, a legacy of the frostbite—perhaps a lifelong reminder whenever it got cold. She squeezed Ellie and said, "You'll be fine. Old Man Winter's in the air, that's all. But don't worry, it never snows in California, except in the high mountains."

# III

## Golden Dreams

# 44

Coyote stretches his forelegs until his back cracks. Hearing the approaching voices of María Howchia and Elitha, he waits, and then trots alongside.

"Do you know what this is?" Elitha reaches into her skirt pocket and shows what she found. The late-season sun blazes off a large nugget of gold.

María takes the smooth twisted shape, bites it, and says. "Españoles call it oro."

"Is it gold?"

"Hmm. Maybe English say gold."

"Maybe someone dropped it in the river and they'll come looking for it."

María smiles, thinking that's a joke.

Staying with them, Coyote hopes to sniff out something amusing.

"Does Mr. Daylor trade in gold?" Elitha asks. She looks back to check on Ellie, who enjoys playing mother to María's baby, now toddling free of his bikoos.

"Señor Daylo no trade rocks."

"Rocks! But if this is gold, I'd think Mr. Daylor would trade it for fine goods."

"Talk to Father. He sabe." She taps her temple and continues toward the village.

Elitha hesitates, unsure if she should go there, but Indian Mary is well up the trail with the nugget, so she catches up. Ellie and Billy are both young enough to see Coyote, and to understand that he is having fun and won't hurt them.

In the village María asks an older boy to find Grizzly Hair. Meanwhile Elitha looks at the home place—women taking in the afternoon sun, some sitting outside their u-machas bending feather nibs, others pounding acorns. Children laugh as they play running games around the u-machas and chak'as. Joining them, Ellie flashes a conspiratorial grin at her big sister, Perry having ordered them to stay away from the Indians. Elitha smiles back.

When Grizzly Hair emerges from the sweathouse, Elitha stares in awe of his height and girth, the bones through his topknot and the string of bear claws around his neck, each claw longer than his middle finger.

Patient despite the interruption of his nap, my son Grizzly Hair says

"Palaver," a well-known trading word, and gestures toward the sitting logs in the village center.

The two young women sit down ready for talk, while Billy and Ellie feint and dodge with the other children. Coyote, in his luxuriant cool-weather coat, finds a satisfactory spot of sunshine beneath my branches. He lies down hoping something entertaining will happen.

"Do not forget," I tell him, "my son is a cautious man."

Startled to all fours, he jerks his head around, but then realizes it is I, still here after many seasons. Indignantly he circles, wishing the spirits would stop scaring him with remarks from random bushes and trees, and plops down. "Your son is no different than the others."

I sigh, for it is true. Grizzly Hair will also become excited about trading gold. My granddaughter hands him the nugget and speaks to him in the tongue of the People. Other people arrive and seat themselves where they can hear. Small hands lightly explore the straight black hair falling from Elitha's bonnet. "It is so long!" "Like a man's," the children murmur.

Ellie dashes happily through a stand of poison oak.

Elitha feels naughty to be here, but her blood mother was Indian and she wants to have her own intercourse with her neighbors rather than hearing about them from Perry. She loves attending a pow-wow, as she thinks of it, with Captain Juan. She recalls Tamsen's tale of Delaware, a majestic chief who helped white men wage war. Captain Juan appears to be a similar grand savage, though he is naked and that to her is a disturbing condition. But the disturbance vanishes when she sees the fatherly love in his eyes for his daughter. Elitha regrets that her own father will never again look at her like that, or take his ease on a sunny autumn day, or hear a wedge of geese gabble overhead.

"What does she want with this goldenrock?" Grizzly Hair asks, turning the nugget in his hand. Before María can answer, a horse arrives. All heads turn.

Dismounting, Pedro is sorry to see Elitha McCoon here. María runs to him, petting his reddish sideburns and mustache. Powerful surges of emotion pump through him as he puts his arms around her and holds her to him.

Elitha is dismayed to see the Spaniard who traded insults with Perry, the one Perry said would tell the Spaniards on the coast about the Rhoads' gold. She is sorry she came here and wants to take the golden lump back and leave, but it is too late. It would draw more attention to the gold, if gold it is. Besides, it is likely that Perry will learn of her showing it to Mr. Valdez and the Indian workers before mentioning it to him. If it is gold, he'll be enraged. She tries to think up a falsehood to explain it.

Reluctantly, Pedro separates from his Amapolita and sweeps his hat before Elitha. "Señora McCoon," he says, "it is a pleasure to see you again." He has come to see if María's parents will accept his latest gift and warm to him. With a mien of gracious pride, he steps to his horse and returns with a

Nipponese lacquered box of bright colors. The villagers sigh approving ohs and ahs as he presents it to my son.

Grizzly Hair muses that a man generous enough to bring such expensive gifts would be unlikely to steal the Condor robe. But Etumu's expression does not yield, and a wife's opinion is important. He sets the shiny box on the ground, deciding to finish the first matter first, for Elitha is obviously uneasy. He opens his hand looking at the lump of gold and asks again why it is of interest to her.

My granddaughter sits beside Pedro and speaks Spanish for her friend. "Señora McCoon asks: Is this goldenrock, oro? And will Señor Daylo accept it in exchange for goods?"

Pedro is mildly annoyed that his fine present has elicited no comment, but he marvels at the size and shine of the nugget in Captain Juan's hand.

"Why would Señor Daylo trade anything for this?" Grizzly Hair asks, the corners of his mouth twitching into an almost perceptible smile, as one might reply to a laughable suggestion from a very young child.

Pedro is confused by the question as well as the smile. So is Elitha.

María explains in Spanish, "Elitha says oro could be traded for fine goods."

Grizzly Hair masks his surprise, and his mind flies to several mysteries. When he was young he and his friends captured a funny old black hat near the Chilumne place. They stole his clothing, horse and gun and threatened to beat him with sticks, and yet, oddly, the man stood for a long moment staring sadly after a hatful of goldenrock that they'd scattered over a mound of blackberry briars. That oddity lingered in Grizzly Hair's mind, together with the mystery of why anyone would fill a marvelous iron hat with sand and gravel. Then later, the excitable Russian ally named Egorov, whose gun was supposed to kill the cannon shooters in the war against the black hats, grabbed Etumu and deserted with her on the night before the battle. Why he did that is now clear to Grizzly Hair. He had ridden far to fetch my childhood collection of unusual goldenrocks. He stayed up all night melting and pouring liquid rock into the ball-making device, with Egorov's help, to replace the lost gun-balls. The mystery was why Egorov wanted the golden balls more than he wanted Mission Santa Barbara, which was to be his payment if the Indians won the war, and he captured Etumu in hopes she would guide him to more collections of goldenrock. He would have found none, but the three-legged bear ate him before he could try. Goldenrock was useless to the Indian peoples and too common to be treasured for its shine, at least not by adults.

Everyone awaits his answer.

If a spirit could weep, my tears would rain upon the village. The old woman, María, namesake of my granddaughter, told me long ago that my basket of goldenrock nuggets had great value, but I chose to hide that knowledge from my son, for his safety. And then I died. It had been the right decision. Now, a generation later, that knowledge endangers him.

"Ask Señor Valdez," my son says, handing the gold to Pedro. "His people know its value in the trading post better than I."

The shiny lump lies heavy in Pedro's hand, and it drops heavily into the pool of his mind, rippling outward to the shores of the known world. Old Pepe was right. Gold is all over these foothills. The ripples move two generations back, to his grandfather Don Pedro Fages looking for gold around the necks of Indians, and in their huts along the coast, never imagining that could be found inland lying where God left it. Pedro can hardly breathe for realizing that Spain lost Upper California for want of knowing what his father knew.

Coyote lets out a joyful yippity-yip.

"Hush," I say, "I can't hear."

"What is he saying?" Elitha insists, growing weary of the babble of alien tongues.

Seeing moisture in her beloved's eyes, María knows Pedro has more to say. She waits until he adds in an entranced monotone, "My father was not crazy. He only looked crazy." A tear runs down his face and he lets it run, preferring to fully express his sorrow.

Grizzly Hair is puzzled. "Oro reminds you of your father?"

"Yes. Pardon me please. He was a fine man, once." Having no reason to keep the secret from the woman he loves, or her people, Pedro offers his words like jewels. "Gold is the most valuable thing in the world. All trade is measured against it. The Spanish king would have sailed an armada of fighting men into Yerba Buena and Monterey had he known that gold was in these hills. The United States would not have California if the Españoles had known. My father knew it, but no one listened to him."

María turns to Elitha, realizing that she's being left out. "My man says gold is caro, valuable. His people want it very much."

"Of course they want it if it's gold. What I asked was, Is this gold, and what would Mr. Daylor give me for it? She is exasperated that every utterance brings forth a long pause, a stare into space, or tears. She is also distressed to have shown the gold to the Indians and the Spaniard. Her husband will beat her, and she can't think of a way out.

Coyote grins.

María translates the question, and Grizzly Hair replies in the tongue of the People. This is goldenrock. Goldenrock is oro. Its soul is dense and it can be melted. Señor Valdez will say what it can be traded for. I don't know." Looking at Pedro he adds in Spanish, "The Russians have many guns. I saw them in Ross when I was young. In a fight against the Españoles, or Mexicanos as you now call them, the Russians would win."

Pedro says, "I beg your pardon but I am sure Spain would have defeated Russia."

Elitha's frustration peaks. "I asked a question!"

María says to Pedro, "She wants to know how much Señor Daylo would give her for this gold at his trading post."

In English Pedro tells Elitha, "This is gold, worth five superior and manly horses. Maybe more."

Grizzly Hair's thoughts have roamed to the battles on Estanislao's river, the many who died from cannon balls blasting through the stockades because Egorov wasn't there to shoot the cannon shooters with the golden balls. He thinks Coyote would enjoy this joke.

"You bet," says Coyote, sitting in alert expectation.

The united Indians prevented the Españoles from coming up the rivers to capture people, Grizzly Hair muses, so they missed the gold. And to have some fun, he helped stop the funny old black hat from showing gold to the people in pueblo San José, and later the three-legged grizzly ate the Russian who would have spilled the knowledge at Fort Ross. Likely those were not the only times the knowledge about gold was blocked by accident, in consequence of some other purpose. We were lucky, he realizes. The power of the universe was with us. It saved the home place. It reminds him of the many Coyote stories in which things turn out very different than expected.

Heh heh heh heh, Coyote pants.

Elitha realizes that she could buy a team and a wagon with her gold nugget. She could drive the wagon to Sutter's Fort and collect her sisters, but Perry wouldn't want them in his small house and they wouldn't like his wrathful moods and drunken fits. Fearing a terrible beating, she decides to put the gold back in its hiding place for now, hoping no one will tell her husband about this pow-wow, at least for a while. Later, a solution might come to mind. Fleetingly she imagines escaping to San Francisco with her sisters, but she can't imagine how to do such a thing. A married woman stays with her husband.

"Where did this gold come from?" Pedro asks, showing it in his hand.

"She found it." Grizzly Hair replies, inclining his topknot toward Elitha. Mentally he is preparing his next oration. He will ask the umne to collect gold and amass large amounts of it so they can trade for guns and iron to protect themselves from dangerous intruders.

"Where did you find it?" Pedro asks Elitha in English, worried that if she found it nearby, Perry will think he owns a gold mine and will never leave.

"I'd rather not say."

Incensed, Pedro stands and holds his chin up. "It makes no difference, Señora. Gold is of no interest to me."

Curious about this Español who wants to wed his daughter, Grizzly Hair asks. "You say gold is caro, but you no hunt for it."

It is difficult for Pedro to explain why gold mining does not excite him. Sitting down, he lets the Spanish flow in a languid stream. "Captain Juan, I adore your daughter and wish to marry her. I want my cattle grazing on these hills. I want my wife and children living in my casa, my hacienda." He uses the chief's Indian name, "Yu-seh-o-se-mai-ti, I want my children to be your grandchildren. You and I together can produce thousands of cowhides. We will become rich from the lust of bulls. I will pay your men one calf for every eight born, in exchange for herding, more than McCoon pays. Besides, gold drives men crazy."

Grizzly Hair agrees with the last part. He likes Pedro and thinks maybe this man would be a helpful son-in-law. Pedro continues in Spanish:

"My father scratched for gold in the hot sun. He cooked his brains, lost his eyesight, and found much gold, enough to fill his helmet, but he came home empty handed as always. People called him mad."

Fed up with foreign gibberish, Elitha extends the palm of her hand to Pedro.

But María's attention sticks with her father, the way he leans toward Pedro with growing interest, perhaps liking him more. "What is helmet?" Grizzly Hair asks Pedro.

Placing the gold in Elitha's hand Pedro says, "It is an iron hat to protect men in war."

Elitha calls out, "Come Ellie, we're leaving." Ellie arrives out of breath. "Can I play with Billy tomorrow?" Elitha grabs her hand and hurries her away.

Quietly, Grizzly Hair says, "You are the old man's son then." He reaches across and touches a lock of hair curling beneath Pedro's hat. "Your father had a missing ear, and some of his hair was like this, robin-breast color. I lost the helmet in battle on Estanislao's River."

Connections snap together in Pedro's mind. This Indian was one of the devils that smashed old Pepe's pride and stole his prized possession. A heathen, he wore the helmet that had helped win Europe for Christ! An ocean swell lifts Pedro from tierra firma. His voice breaks as he looks at Captain Juan. "You knew my father." *The father of my beloved María is the very Indian I dreamed of dismembering.*

"Yes." Grizzly Hair says, knowing that the damage to Pedro's honor requires payback.

María gleams like sunshine after rain. The families know each other. Her Pedro will no longer be seen as an enemy black hat, and they can marry. "You knew his father!"

"I stole his helmet," Grizzly Hair says.

Her smile drops way. The families are enemies.

"Coyote played a trick on me."

Coyote lets out a happy howl. María is about to cry, and Pedro thinks maybe there is a condor curse.

Seeing the crestfallen faces, Grizzly Hair explains to Pedro, "An old woman came here and taught the People many useful things about the Españoles. She was from the home place of the Cosumne, our downstream relatives. Captain Fages and his men stole her when she was a girl. She was old by the time

I went to her house in San José to warn her when we Indians were about to start the war, and I saw the old man with a missing ear sitting in her yard. He was her husband. He was your father. The old woman was your grandmother."

Astonished, Pedro frowns at him, thinking that can't be possible. Grandmother María was captured as a child, but afterwards she lived only in Spanish settlements.

Grizzly Hair places a hand on María Howchia's shoulder and speaks in the home tongue, his voice husky with remembering. "You know the old woman, your namesake, saved my life after I escaped from the mission. She was Pedro's grandmother."

Confused, María asks, "You were her friend, but you stole her husband's helmet?"

A dim memory rises from the ashes of Pedro's past. A new recruit at the Presidio, he didn't care about the travels of his old India grandmother. But now he recalls that she did indeed go see her childhood home. Captain Juan's smile makes him hopeful again. This Indian must be, he realizes, the chief that Grandmother María spoke so highly about. It gives Pedro a strange kind of pride that the father of his little poppy was a leader in the rebellion, respected even by the Californios who fought them.

Joy surges through María. The families are friends after all. She kisses Pedro's side-whiskers, and tears dampen both their faces because her family, at last, will welcome him as a son-in-law. Pedro strokes her shoulder as he listens to Grizzly Hair.

"When I dishonored your father I didn't know him. I owe you reparaciónes. Name the goods that will return honor to your family."

Pedro hopes the older man hears the strong sentiment in his reply, "Muchas gracias, Capitán Juan. I wish to marry your daughter. Please accept my marriage present." He points to the lacquered box. "To restore my family honor, it would be good of you to make Perry McCoon leave your hunting grounds and never return."

Grizzly Hair considers. Of course he will accept Pedro as a son-in-law. He hands the lacquered box to Etumu; she smiles and nods. But making Perrimacoo leave will not be easy. The umne like to eat his calves, and he is a sure thing whereas Pedro is not. A hy-apo guides by consensus, not demands. "Son," he says, "I will think about how to make him leave and not come back."

Coyote yawns a disappointed whine.

"Do not fret, Trickster," I say, "the gold will bring plenty of strife."

"Good," he barks, trotting away.

# 45

So many redbud roots were gathered that scarcely enough remained to keep the redbud-people healthy. The days were chilly now. Women threw deerskin capes over their shoulders, talking while their bone awls flew in their fingers. They shared an excitement about the goods they would trade for the gold to be collected in these baskets. Guns would not be their only purchase. Iron pots, knives, colorful beads, hats and clothing would also be traded for gold. Skillfully they used their awls to curl the wiry roots around the guiding stays, making a new kind of basket—broad, flat and nearly watertight.

Collecting gold was not easy. Lines of young girls and boys squatted beside their mothers at the river's edge, swirling sand and water in big flat baskets. Older children dug like foxes along the riverbanks, where the elders said gold was likely to lodge after bumping down the river. Swimmers pulled it from crevices in underwater boulders. Grizzly Hair led the search for gold and orated about the need for guns.

Some of the family heads preferred to ride, rope and care for Perrimacoo's cattle. Washing sand, they said, was women's work, resembling the leaching of acorn meal.

Four Bears said, "I doubt if the golden gravel has any value."

"I agree with my brother," said Scorpion Trail. "We have tasted the calves. We know their value. I think Señor Daylo will laugh when we bring him sand and gravel."

Running Quail said, "My wife wants me to continue herding cattle. But she will wash gold. She is dreaming about the goods she can get for it."

With respected men speaking this way, it would be difficult to drive out Perrimacoo. Where was the assurance, men asked, that Señor Valdez would give them more calves than Señor McCoon? Where was the assurance, Grizzly Hair worried, that Pedro Valdez would get the land paper even if Perrimacoo went away. Above all, Grizzly Hair didn't want discord among the umne.

Each morning after sunrise purification, women and children brought their gold to the family u-macha. Etumu sat before the doorway, holding out her large boiling basket to collect it. Each day after sun salutations, Grizzly Hair inspected the level of gold in the basket. When it was full, he would take it to Señor Daylo and return with guns, iron tools, cloth, beads and more horses. Each evening, talk about these goods crackled with the supper fires. The umne were collecting more than anyone had expected.

Then rains came. Water rushed down the mountains widening the rivers and flooding the gold digging places. Little bits of goldenrock washed downstream without settling. The search stopped. "We will wait until the Second Grass Festival," Grizzly Hair announced.

🌿

María lay awake with her idea. It was entirely dark when she heard Grizzly Hair feel his way into the u-macha. He slept with the men in the sweathouse except when he wanted to couple with Mother. Sedge leaves rustled.

"Father?" María whispered.

Grizzly Hair answered, "You awake?"

"Maybe Perrimacoo would accept gold in trade for leaving."

"I have thought of that. Maybe there is a way."

Etumu moaned.

"Talk tomorrow," said Grizzly Hair in a deep voice.

In the morning they decided that the gold of the umne should be divided into three baskets: one for whatever the People wanted, one for guns, and one for reparations for Pedro's family honor. Pedro could do whatever he wanted with it, but María and Grizzly Hair assumed he would use it, somehow, to buy Perrimacoo's departure.

After the talk, María left for Rancho Omuchumne, where she would live with Pedro through the O-se-mai-ti big time.

🌿

With the help of Indian Mary's skin washes, Ellie recovered from a bad rash of poison oak. Now she whined about her feet hurting. Elitha's feet stung and ached too—morning frosts whitened the hills and a skin of ice capped the water bucket—but it wasn't nearly as cold as an ordinary Illinois winter. Oddly, the little bit of cold turned their toes as white as polished marble.

"Frostbite weakened us last winter," she explained to Ellie, who lay swaddled in her blanket. "Stay in bed. Is your blanket warm enough?" She glanced from Ellie to Perry, who sat next to Elitha at the table. She hoped he wouldn't lose patience with Ellie. In the remnant of daylight from the two small windows, Elitha could see Ellie's face, about to cry.

Rising, she patted her baby sister's hand, then limped to the window to peer through the new glass. A fast darkening sky, another rainstorm coming. It was late afternoon. She lit a candle. Bare branches of the overhanging oak tree clicked in the wind. Gusts of cold air came through the cracks in the door and underneath. The candle flickered and went out. Elitha had put off going outside to lower the food crate from the tree, and now veils of rain lashed the hillsides so thick she couldn't even see the fire pit. It would have been nice if Perry had built a fireplace inside the cabin. In the countryside of Illinois every cabin had a fireplace with a cooking rack.

"Well, I guess we won't have any hot food," she said to Perry and Ellie. She felt around for the metal box in the corner, pried it open and handed out sea crackers.

"Perry, tell us a story," Ellie begged. He often told frightening tales of his childhood in London, and of intrigue and murder in exotic ports.

"'Bout the big green sea monster," Ellie begged.

"Nay. That's folly. Go to sleep." He gulped liquor.

About an hour later it was still raining hard. Lying beside Perry with the blanket pulled to her chin, Elitha gnawed a cracker. "You're not spending much time with the Indians lately," she said.

"Ent no need now. The niggers know the whereabouts of good grass better'n I does, and wouldn't ye know. They're piling rocks along the steep banks to keep the stupid cattle from plunging to their deaths." A note of admiration rang in his liquor-slurred words.

"Well," she said to keep the conversation going, "I guess every cow that lives is one more to give birth, and they're looking for their one in ten."

"Aye, lass, that they is." He gulped and expelled air from both portals.

"This must be a paradise for cows," Elitha said. "They've got warm coats and green grass at Christmas." Despite the frosts, the grass grew six inches high in a few places. Sometimes in midday when she went to the river for water it felt like April.

He was quiet.

"You know," Elitha said, "yesterday I saw the strangest thing."

"Wha-at?" Ellie asked in a tell-me-a-story tone.

"Down at the river. I heard voices, about noon I guess it was. I looked and there was a whole line of Indian women squatting along the shore rolling baskets around in the water. Round and round." Indian Mary hadn't been among them.

"Washin their acorn mush," Perry said. "Ent ye never seen it, lass?"

"Not in those kinds of baskets."

"Do it different ways, they does." His hand groped over her in the dark.

"Ellie's awake," she whispered.

"She don't know HOW to sleep," he growled, but left Elitha alone for a while.

🌿

In the morning tears rolled down Ellie's face. "My head hurts," she whimpered. Every time she suffered bouts of missing Georgia and Frances, her head ached.

"Well you just stay in bed today. I'll get the brown paper." She'd kept the paper in which Mr. Mellus had wrapped the window glass. After soaking it in the bucket, wishing she had vinegar, she laid it over Ellie's face and patted it onto her forehead and temples. "There now, in a while it will feel better."

Ellie lay still as an Egyptian mummy. Then she murmured under the paper, "I wanna go back to Grandma Brunner's house."

It was bound to happen. Sadly Elitha sat down beside her and took Ellie's tiny hand. She rubbed its back and wished things had been different.

"Taik her back tomorrow, I will," Perry said brightly. "I has business there anyhow."

Why did that hurt so?

Ellie lifted the damp paper from her eyes and smiled at him. Then she patted Elitha's hand and said, "Don't be sad, Big Sister. I'll be warm at Grandma's.
She has an indoor fireplace."

🙥

The next morning Perry lifted Ellie into the saddle behind him, Tamsen's
silk stocking in her fist. Elitha waved through the drizzle as Paint headed
across the green hill. The black silk stocking dangled like an extra tail. She
knew Ellie wouldn't lose it, any more than a preacher would lose his Bible.

She'd done her best. To insist on Ellie staying would be selfish. Shivering,
she hobbled inside the adobe trying to avoid pressure on her toes. She felt
her breakfast loose inside her. Was the damp air making her sick? Yesterday
morning she'd felt nauseated too.

🙥

Every day Elitha expected Perry to return, expected it all day long. But
days became a week, and then two, and more. Sometimes she felt her essence drifting into the foggy wilderness. She missed Ellie, missed Leanna,
missed Tamsen and Pa, missed Indian Mary, missed Perry. Missed friends
to talk to. She longed for the safety of Perry's gun at night in case the door
would give way to a wild animal. The nausea came each morning, sometimes lingering all day. At night she pulled the covers to her chin and slept
with a club and a knife.

She lost her fear of the sneaky coyote that ate leftovers behind her back, if for
a moment she turned away from the fire pit. And one morning as she opened
the door, she saw a tawny cat the size of an enormous dog looking up at her
food crate in the tree. The big cat turned and stared at her with luminous yellow
eyes. Her heart banged wildly, but she didn't move, knowing cats liked to chase
their prey. It turned its hind end to the tree and squirted the trunk, the long
erect tail quivering, and ambled away with the tail sweeping from side to side.

She learned that she lived in the overlapping orbits and territories of many
birds and animals, such as the golden eagles that hunted for rattlesnakes and
varieties of hawks. A pair of owls, one white and one brown, stationed themselves in the overhanging oak at night, hooting in their different ways. She
began to identify individuals among the same variety by slight differences in
color and ranginess, and the notched ear of a mother cottontail. She looked
forward to late spring when long lines of baby quail toddled like fuzzy wal-
nuts after their mothers. They moved so fast they were hard to count, maybe
fifteen babies for each mother. Strangely, the feeling of loneliness seemed to
pass when she thought of herself as one of the wilderness neighbors, a privileged animal with a bigger den.

At times her mind wandered to Illinois—sausage making, quilting, cooking, sleigh rides behind Pal and Dotty all a-jingle with bells, and Fourth of
July cookouts at half-brother William's place. Here the only human contact

was Indian Mary's mother, who came with milk to curdle. Billy toddled behind his grandmother; Indian Mary had been gone for a long time. She was somewhere else learning to be a witch doctor.

"Nime Billy," the child said one day with Perry's dimpled grin. We are a strange family, Elitha thought.She went to the village and tried to ask for Mary. No one spoke English. The Indians eyed her as if waiting for her to leave so they could return to their chores, even Billy's grandmother. Feeling out of place, she walked up the faint pathway through high grass and unfolding lily-like flowers, then returned to the silent adobe.

Then she heard a horse, and before she could get outside Perry burst through the door with a sunny smile. "Hello me pretty lass!" he sang out.

She smiled, her uncombed hair hanging to her waist.

He grabbed and held her at arm's length. "Mormons be minin gold up on the American River, they is."

"That where you've been?"

"God's bones, they be haulin' it in by the sack! Every red-blooded man in the country's headed up there." He took her by the waist and lifted her in a playful circle, then set her down, staring at her middle. "Putting on flesh? Or is it a babe in the oven?"

"Oven?"

"I vow, girl, you be a simpleton. 'Avin courses, is ye?"

Her face and neck heated. The way she'd been brought up, you didn't speak of such things with a man. She'd had that only three times, one on the prairie and two last spring. "Not for a while," she murmured.

"Didn't I tell ye?" He stared at her middle. "Lass, me luck's achangin', hit is! A new babe! And riches to boot!"

"Riches?"

"Daylor and Sheldon and yours truly be drivin cattle up north. To a ranchería they call Culuma. Wye, those miners be eatin like niggers! With nothing but wild game and gold in their pockets. Just you watch, they'll pay dear for me beef. Send our wash to China, we will lass! And soon."

It didn't seem real, coming at her so fast. "When are you leaving?"

"Noon tomorrow. That Bill Daylor's a canny old tar, 'e is."

She'd be alone again. "You said you're going with Mr. Sheldon and Mr. Daylor?"

"Full in the hold and deaf to boot is ye?"

"I want to stay with Sarah or Catey while you're gone."

He narrowed his lashes at her, steel-blue piercing through. "Gone to her in-laws, Catey is, and Sally's minding the store. Just how'd ye think ye'd get there?" A teasing smile.

"Ride with one of the vaqueros, or walk."

"Climb on a horse with a nigger, would ye?"

She nodded.

"I'll not 'ave me wife prancin round with niggers and that's the last of it!"

Softly she said, "Then you take me." She waited for his rage. The certainty that she wouldn't stay alone gave her strength. She recalled that he'd become nicer after she ran away in San Francisco, and in any case she doubted he'd injure her badly. It seemed little to pay for the pleasure of company.

His voice was as flat as the line of his lips: "Wilderness making ye cross, is it?"

"I've been alone."

"That's prattle enough. Give me something to eat, then I'll poke ye like a respectable husband. 'At's all's wrong with ye."

The next day she rode behind Perry as he trotted Paint after the forty cows, the longhorns as orderly as pickets. Indian vaqueros rode at the side. It was about a third of the herd. At the junction partway to Daylor's, where the path forked north, Perry signaled. The Indians stopped the cows where they'd wait for the Rancho Omuchumne herd.

Elitha felt willful, having insisted on coming, but not sorry. He'd explained that a man had to stay on his land, in the house he built. "When I needs to be gone," he had said, "me wife stays. Then no man can say I abandoned me rancho." He remained in high spirits due to the gold and the prospect of selling the cattle, and she took the opportunity to press him.

"Don't you have papers? To prove it's yours?" Pa prized such papers.

"A letter from John Sutter, I has. Says it's mine if I builds me a 'ouse and don't abandon the land."

"I'm your placemarker then." Human bookmark.

"And a pretty one at that." No meanness there.

"But the place is so remote. I don't see who's going to come claim it the few days you expect to be gone." No white person lived anywhere nearby.

Somehow she had won the argument, and without blows.

Now, cattle and horses had their noses to the grass, and in the distance she heard the lowing of the approaching Omuchumne cattle. Perry spurred Paint to a gallop and she hung on from behind, bouncing hard against the ridge of the wood-frame saddle. Soon they skirted Sheldon and Daylor's herd, twice the size of Perry's, and reined to a stop beside Bill Daylor's dapple gray.

Mr. Daylor doffed a sweat-stained hat. "Ma'am." His brows shot up, questioning, his lips pushed over the one side of his long face.

"Mulish, she is," Perry jerked a thumb at her. "Bound and determined to stay with your Sarah. Now, maitie, if that's a bother, I'll taike 'er home and catch up with ye later."

Mr. Daylor said, "Sally might could use the company."

A hard-riding ten minutes later, Elitha slid thankfully from the horse before the adobe trading post. Perry left like a Spaniard, wheeling the horse on its hind legs, mouth open to the bit, and then thundered away at a full gallop to catch up to the herd on its way north. She hoped the cattle would bring as high a price as he expected.

# 46

"Did your ma help Catey with the baby?" Elitha asked the next morning at breakfast.

Sarah laid her fork down, and her voice cracked. "She passed on." She turned away.

Mrs. Rhoads' sallow complexion at the cookout last summer came to mind. A woman plumb tuckered. "I'm so sorry. She was a fine lady." The mother of nineteen.

Sarah turned her dark upsweep toward Elitha and dabbed at her eyes with the hem of her apron.

"Who helped with the baby?" *Who could help me?*

"Me." Sarah shook her head and sniffed. "It was bad. I don't know the first thing about birthing. Matilda came over." *John Rhoads' wife.* "She's given birth three times but never attended one. So we did what we could." She blinked away tears. "It's a miracle they both lived. Brother John drove Catey and the baby down to Brother Dan's at Mr. Sinclair's place, for her laying in."

"Well, I'm glad she's all right."

Slowly Sarah stirred the beans on her plate. "Ma's grave is lost."

"What do you mean, lost?"

She sighed as if commencing a long voyage. "Well, they don't have a doctor at New Helvetia, so when Ma got bad we thought to send her to San Francisco. I made her a bed in a wagon so she wouldn't jostle around too much, and Pa and the boys drove her to Sutter's." She sighed again. "They was loadin wheat, so they made her a bed right down in the wheat bags, under the—" she sobbed and sniffled, "the deck of the boat."

Sarah closed her eyes and shook her head." Guess they got almost as far as the Hastings house, Montezuma they call it, when Ma ..." She covered her face with her apron and her shoulders silently shook.

Elitha went to her side of the table and put a hand on her shoulder. "It hurts to lose your mother. I know. I lost two of them. My real mother and my stepmother."

"Don't rightly know why I can't git over it," Sarah sniffed, wiping her eyes on the hem of her apron again. "They buried her on the shore 'cause it was a bad warm spell—last September it was. Pa and the boys made her a marker and" —two loud sobs— "they had to go on with the wheat. They went back later, but the river had rose, and—" She cried softly now, her voice trailing almost to nothing. "The marker was plumb gone."

Elitha recalled the river as it widened into the bay, and the cries of the water birds—a lonely place. Mrs. Rhoads and Mrs. Donner and Pa were all in unmarked graves. Feeling the bond, she patted Sarah's hair. "I guess pioneers can't always visit their folks' graves." *You gotta be tough.* She steered toward the happy thing. "But I'm mighty glad Catey and the baby are doing good." She longed to see Catherine's short sassy figure as it had been before her pregnancy, and her impish smile.

Sarah looked up. "My sister's a rugged little tyke. Always was. I vow, that woulda killed me." She drew in a breath. "I'm prayin her next one comes easier."

"You in a family way yet?" Elitha hadn't told Sarah she was. In truth she wasn't sure.

"Uh-uh." Sarah got up from the table, tall and dignified like her old self. "Been married as long as Catey too—did you know our weddins was a week apart?" She took the bread pan from its nail and put it on the table. "Mr. Daylor thinks he can't have younguns."

As Elitha considered the evidence for that, Sarah put the plates in the bread pan with a cake of lye soap, took a kettle from the stove and poured steaming water over the soap and the dishes, adding a little cool water from the bucket. Ordinary actions, when you had an indoor stove.

"Now you just sit and let me do those dishes," Elitha said.

❧

Each morning the Indian woman brought milk for curdling, and Elitha made herself useful minding it on the back of the stove and making soft cheese the way the Grandma Donner taught her. Stirring, she admired the iron curlicues on the stanchions that held the warming shelf over the stove. A chimney pipe ran up through the ceiling.

Following her glance Sarah said, "That stove come outta Boston, all the way around the Horn."

"I'd sure like to have one just like it."

The next morning her stomach rode up and down as she pounded coffee beans in the stone mortar. She dashed outside with a hand over her mouth. When she came back in, Sarah looked worried, her hand poised over the crockery bowl into which she was cracking speckled quail eggs.

"I think I'm in a family way," Elitha admitted, trying to smile despite smoke rising from the frying pan—an odor that said the lard had been used too many times.

"Poor thing. Go lie down. You're white as a ghost." Sarah moved the pan to a cooler place on the stove.

The bed was comfortable, a mattress of horsehair on crossed leather straps suspended from a frame. She climbed in where she'd slept so well beside Sarah the past two nights.

"Want some eggs? Indians brought 'em in fresh yesterday."

"No thanks." The thought made her burp, a precursor of nausea. She lay perfectly still.

Slowly and quietly the door began to open on its leather hinges. Elitha stared at it, thinking the men had returned and were playing a trick by sneaking up on the house.

A large brown face in a nest of thick black hair appeared!

Too frightened to make sound, Elitha leaped from the cot and backed into the adjoining but separate trading-post room. By then a large naked man had stepped into the house with a bundle of furs on his back and his unruly hair grazing the ceiling. He smiled at Elitha.

Her heart did a flip-flop as she backed over baskets and crouched behind bags of goods. Sarah didn't seem in the least afraid. "You'll have to get used to that," she called to Elitha. "These Indians don't never knock." She motioned him into the trading room. "Mr. Daylor told 'em to just come on in." She smiled kindly at Elitha. "He won't hurt you."

Changing directions, Elitha backed into the living quarters while Sarah and the Indian went into the trading room. Elitha restored the fallen quilt and lay down on the bed watching Sarah and the Indian speak with gestures and facial expressions. She heard "savvy" and "numero," and saw them counting on their fingers. The man was no more modest about his privates than Captain Juan and his men, or the Indians at Johnson's ranch. She thought she'd never get used to them dangling out in the air without a hint of embarrassment.

Sarah added the furs to the pile in the corner, counted out glass beads and gave the man two striped blankets. When the Indian left, Elitha asked, "Why don't you make them knock?"

Giving the eggs another stir, Sarah poured them into the smoking grease on the hot part of the stove. "They think it's bad manners to pound on a door. At first they stared through the windows at me. About gave me heart failure." She pulled a plate off the shelf. "Sure you don't want any?" Elitha wiggled a hand to keep it away. "See, these California Indians aren't like the regular kind," Sarah continued. "Did you know they didn't even know how to fight a war till the white men came? Mr. Daylor says every buck among them would rather have a good meal than kill an enemy. Can you imagine?" She shook her head.

Elitha recalled that the Kickapoo were adept at avoiding war with the U.S. Army. "I like them better than the other kind," she said.

⁂

Perry's few days stretched into three weeks. Elitha soon felt at home at Daylor's place on Rancho Omuchumne. Every evening naked children came to the store for sugarcane. She loved their soft brown faces and their smiles when Sarah cut cane and handed out pieces.

"Mr. Daylor has a weakness for these little tykes," she said. "He gives 'em all the cane." They waited their turns, calmly accepting what was offered. A far-away look of sadness came into Sarah's face as she handed a stick to the last child. "It's the only reason he buys it."

Elitha wished Sarah were pregnant, instead of her.

One afternoon, as Sarah bartered with four Indians who had come from Rancho Seco, twenty miles southeast, Elitha went out to collect wild greens along Deer Creek. The aroma of peppermint hung in the late spring air, and suddenly Indian Mary was smiling at her.

"Where are you going?" Mary's unvarying first words.

Delighted to see her again, Elitha smiled at her and little Billy, now playing peek-a-boo from his mother's knee. "I'm visiting Sarah Daylor while Mr. McCoon is away. What are you doing here?"

"My man lives here."

"Oh, yes, Mr. Valdez. But sometimes you don't live here."

Indian Mary spoke to a stand of round-leafed lettuce, then pinched off some leaves and tossed them into her basket. "Live in my man's house, in millhouse," she said. "Sometime live at home place, sometime live in doctor place."

Elitha had expected she'd be a full medicine woman by now. "When will you stop going there?"

Mary had a way of going about her work while preparing her answer, and then it would come out calm and quiet, as if the listener had endless patience. "Learn of spirits all times."

Thinking about that, Elitha picked the round leaves too, one of her favorite salad greens.

"We talk later?" Indian Mary queried.

Making an appointment to talk intrigued Elitha. With anyone else she would have said, Oh, come on, tell me now. Instead she asked, "Is it about my hand?" Her thumb had mended a bit crooked, as anyone could see. She should have left the splint on.

"No. Perrimacoo."

Was she seeing him again? She searched Mary's face for a clue, but saw only a placid expression. Then she realized nothing she could do would stop Perry from seeing any Indian girl he wanted. She just didn't want to hear about it. "All right. We talk later," she said, happy to put it off. "Is that good?" She pointed at what Mary was picking.

Mary shot her a sly glance. "Put yerba buena on it."

A hearty laugh spilled out of Elitha. At Rancho Sacayak when she'd complained about the taste of this or that wild plant, Mary had advised, "Put yerba buena on it." Mint covered a world of bad taste.

Mary adjusted the band across her straw cap and straightened up with her gathering basket, to leave. She surprised Elitha with, "Tomorrow we gather. You come?" She cocked her head, friendship showing in her black eyes.

It was an honor. She'd seen the closeness of the Indian women when they went on gathering parties, but never imagined she'd be invited to join them. Tamsen would be proud of her. And her real mother, surely, would have been pleased.

In the morning Indian Mary arrived at the door with Billy. Not far behind stood the entire female population of Rancho Omuchumne, many with babies in bikooses, all equipped with oversized gathering baskets, all watching as Elitha fell into step with Mary.

The warm spring air soothed her spirit. Birds trilled, piped, whistled and twittered in thick green canopies along Deer Creek. The entire place looked like a Garden of Eden. Ahead on the path walked the Indian women, the points of their baskets reaching their knees and the wide tops yawning behind their caps. Their neatly singed hair swung just above their shoulders and their children frolicked along the trail around them. Accustomed to the sight of naked breasts, Elitha noticed the colors—skin like the red-brown clay prevalent at Rancho Sacayak, the shine of black hair contrasting with the pale straw of the baskets and caps, flashes of red and blue drill wrapping some of the women's hips, all of it winking through the lush green foliage as the line snaked ahead, clearly headed toward a destination.

Turning to see Billy falling behind, she squatted and held her arms to him. The two-year-old grinned and ran to her. He felt warm and strong and smelled clean as she hugged him, her arm under his bare bottom. A motherly feeling came over her. Perhaps, she thought, Mormon women felt this way about the children of co-wives. In a way, Indian Mary was a co-wife. Billy definitely was Perry's child. Indian Mary walked just ahead, apparently not wanting to talk about anything.

The path grew muddy. She put the little boy down, removed her shoes, tied the strings around her neck and walked on with Billy beside her. She had a busy time freeing her skirts from overhanging blackberry thorns. The short cloth skirts of the Indian women rarely snagged, but the naked women walked entirely unhampered, adept at quick moves to avoid thorny encounters. She felt overdressed.

Soon the path vanished into a marshy pond with cattails and other reeds. Staking the bikooses on high ground, the women and girls began stepping purposefully in the water, pulling up the roots of a purplish grass in their toes. They swished the clumps in the water to wash off the mud, tossed the roots in their baskets, all the while talking and laughing.

Mary put Billy near the babies, where he squatted to poke holes in the mud.

Indian Mary beckoned from shallow water choked with water plants. Elitha pulled off her frock and petticoat and waded into the muck in her camisole and underdrawers. She felt with her feet for the roots of the purplish grass. It didn't grow in masses, but was widely distributed. The women were harvesting its tiny root bulbs. As she got more efficient in bringing them up, her underdrawers became muddy, but with all the laughter and sisterly talk, she enjoyed herself even without understanding the language.

After a while the mood of the women changed. One after another they left the water and ran happily into the thicket. Elitha looked inquiringly at Mary.

"They saw a, a... What do you call this?" She made a noise like a bee and made her hands into a semblance of a winged thing.

"Fly? Bee?"

Mary inclined her head and pursed her lips. "Maybe." Brightening, she beckoned. "Come. You see. You help. First make fire."

Mary went to where two other women fanned cattail fluff on small wooden platforms which they'd brought with them. On each scorched platform they positioned wooden drills with the points down. They operated the drills by pulling twine, the same way tops twirled to the pull of a string, the same way Mary's old grandmother drilled tiny holes in freshwater clamshells. Wisps of smoke began to rise. They pushed fluff into the smoking drills and blew on it. "You, fetch little wood," Mary said.

Looking for kindling, Elitha enjoyed the giggles and squeals of the older girls sent for fuel and wondered what they intended to cook. Soon they had a fire snapping hotly, to the obvious delight of the babies who stood laced to their chins in their propped-up boards. Billy slapped pond mud. Many women began to thrust cattail heads into the flames. Then they hurried away in with their smoky torches. Not to be left behind, Elitha broke off a green cattail and held it in the flames until it smoked.

Indian Mary touched her arm. "Smoke them out," she said. "Bring sharp stick."

"Smoke what out?"

Mary shrugged like she didn't know the word for it, and headed for the trees. Elitha followed happy sounds through the thick vegetation. She saw a woman on tiptoe thrust a smoking torch into the hollow of an oak. A cloud of insects blossomed from it. The woman shrieked, ran, and circled around. Some swished their smoking torches through the buzzing cloud as others jammed torches into the hole. It seemed they were after honey. The torches drove most of the insects away, but yells and loud claps of hands on bare skin told of stings.

Then several golden-brown insects, long legs dangling, buzzed toward Elitha. Her hair stood on end. HORNETS. She ran for the water.

At the fire she glanced back and saw she'd outrun the hornets. Billy was laughing at her. A few moments later women and children came from the thicket with hands cupped together. Kneeling, they opened their hands and poured heaps of white maggots, all writhing, out where they could be skewered on the sharp switches, four and five maggots per switch. They did this as gleefully as Elitha and her sisters had once threaded popcorn for the Christmas tree. Briefly singeing the wiggly grubs over the flames, they popped them in their mouths, talking and smacking their lips, the pale flesh of the grubs visible in their teeth. They had come for hornet larvae!

Elitha's stomach pushed up against her throat and she lurched away.

Indian Mary ran to her side offering grubs. "Good," she said smacking her lips. The black-eyed maggots squirmed.

Elitha whirled away and disgorged a horrible mass of brown, lumpy pieces of pork and toast she'd had for breakfast. Indian Mary watched.

When Elitha was empty and reeling, Mary placed a hand on her abdomen. "Baby?" she asked with a motherly look.

"Maybe."

Mary smiled. "Amigas help." She nodded toward the Indian women and gave her own stomach a pat. "Baby here too."

"Oh. Is Mr. Valdez happy?" She felt like she was about to faint, but tried to be polite. Or was it Perry's baby?

"Sí," Mary said, placing a raw grub on her tongue, "Pedro's blood in me."

The world went dark. Elitha twisted away heaving. She caught herself on a tree that blocked the sight of Mary chewing those grubs. The women at the fire began to sing.

Mary asked, "Talk now?"

"Not now," Elitha croaked, staggering to where she'd left her frock. Grabbing it, she turned up the path as fast as she could go, relieved that Mary returned to the fire.

A few minutes later she felt better, walking clothed under the leafy canopy, the blooming elderberries delicately scenting the air, healing her. Behind, the singing grew fainter and she assumed the women and girls of Rancho Omuchumne had settled in for a long ugly feast.

But then, to her dismay, she heard their voices coming up from behind. She turned, thinking Please no more ugly grubs! Indian Mary trotted to catch up. "People coming," she said. Doubtless a huge pile of grubs were writhing in Mary's gathering basket.

Elitha didn't want to be within fifty feet of them. The mind picture propelled her faster but Mary kept pace, her head at a listening angle. Elitha heard nothing but birds and the chatter of approaching women and children. They walked in silence, Elitha working hard to expel the grubs from her mind though they were in a basket two feet away.

Then, in the far distance, she heard something like a strange cricket. As the minutes passed and they approached the main trail to Daylor's place, the sound intensified. Indians, Elitha realized once again, possessed acute hearing. In a minute or two she heard horse hooves and a snare drum. The others had heard it much sooner and from farther away. But what was happening? Was it Perry? Why with a drum? And why from the wrong direction? He'd be terribly angry to see her with the Indian women.

Stepping from the foliage of the less-traveled path, Elitha shaded her eyes to see up the main trail from Sutter's Fort. Dust plumed around three horsemen, one in a big white hat. From over the hill came a line of walking people, three and four abreast. When the horsemen drew nearer she recognized Mr. Sutter in a planter's hat riding a mule in the front. The other two men she didn't know, Behind them an Indian with a red bandanna around his hair was drumming as proudly as any parade master.

Indian Mary had ducked back into the thicket.

# 47

Captain Sutter said to Elitha, "Good day Mrs. McCoon." He smiled and removed his planter's hat. The other two riders touched their hats and rode on.

So astonished was she to see this procession in Rancho Omuchumne that she didn't think to ask where they were all going. Nobody used this road except Sheldon and Daylor, Indians, Perry, and occasionally Señor Pico on the way to his rancho.

By now, all the Indian women and children, except for Mary, stood staring at Mr. Sutter's Indians, maybe a hundred walking past. The men wore tattered ill-fitting pantaloons, the women cast-off clothing of female emigrants. The watching women made appreciative, sexual gestures toward the men—which embarrassed Elitha. The naked children of the local Indians ran with the strange children. Sheep and cattle trotted in fits and starts, dogs yipping at their heels.

Behind the Indians came Kanaka men and women. But so many! They looked drawn, exhausted. The men leaned on wooden spears, the women shuffling beside them with tired eyes, some holding babies in their arms. Both men and women wore hip wraps of colored cloth. The staring was mutual, the strange people giving back as much as Elitha and the Omuchumne Indian women gave. The last man, an Indian, led a long string of mules swaying beneath huge bundles. All manner of buckets, shovels, pans and axes were tied to the bindings of the bundles. The scene brought to mind the biblical story of Abraham moving his tents, servants, and animals.

Elitha ran up the line to Captain Sutter and asked, "Are you moving?"

He looked down from his mule. "Moving?"

"It looks like you're leaving the fort."

He laughed heartily. "Ve go to Jared Sheldon's, my dear. He keep us on da night. Den ve go to de suddern mines and seek goldt." He looked pleased, although weary.

"Nobody's at the mill ranch, except Mister Valdez," Elitha said. "Mister Sheldon's gone. Why don't you rest at the Daylor place? I'm staying there. Sarah and I'll get water for you, or coffee if you'd like."

"Not to vorry. Señor Valdez and I be friends. I camp at Mill Rancho. Ve all be tired. Bad happenings at the American River. Bad men."

"You mean you were at the American River with all these people?"

"Ach yah. Bad men attack mine Indians and Kanakas. Ve go where no-body find us."

"On the Cosumney River?" Would her own quiet river become crowded with strange Indians and Kanakas?

"No mine chile, first visit Omuchumne, and after ve go to Piney Voods." He started the mule up again.

She nodded as she walked alongside. "I didn't know they were finding gold south of here. Perry said the gold was mostly to the north." She recalled that Mr. Sutter had kept the Rhoads' and Sheldons' gold a secret. Perhaps he kept secrets for other emigrants as well.

He smiled wisely. "It giffs gold in Piney Voods too."

Gold is everywhere, she realized. "You have many more Kanakas now."

He nodded. "A new shiff come von der Islands. Goot heppy vorkers."

"How long will you be camping, I mean looking for gold?"

He looked down in an avuncular manner. "Mine chile, now we make holiday. Who knows how long?"

Soon the caravan arrived at the Daylor place. Sarah came around the adobe house with a basket of wash, glancing first at the drummer wiping his brow, and then staring at the multitudes behind Sutter. Curtseying with the wash, she seemed at a loss for words.

Elitha explained what she had learned.

"I'd be obliged if you'd rest here, Captain Sutter," said Sarah setting down the laundry and displaying the composure that Elitha greatly admired.

Mr. Sutter scowled. "We go first to Sheldon's. Iss not far." He waved the drummer on, and the procession continued.

Thinking that a bit rude, Elitha watched the pack mules disappear up the leafy trail. "I invited him to stay too, but I guess he didn't want to. Those poor Kanakas sure look tired."

"He and Mr. Daylor had a bad fight some years ago. There's still bad blood between 'em. I don't think he wants to be beholden to us."

Perry had told a story about Mr. Daylor fighting off Indians and Kanakas, and Mr. Sutter having him hauled in chains to Monterey. The brawl had started over a Kanaka woman. Mr. Sheldon rescued him in Monterey before he could be deported.

❧

Keeping out of sight, María hadn't lit the candle in Pedro's room. Her toe tapped in the dark as she watched the big time from the window. Indians joined in with the Kanakas, who were paired off facing each other. They sang and clacked long sticks together on the accented words.

> I HEARD, I HEARD the boss man say
> JOHN Ka-naka naka, tu-lai-ay.
> To-DAY, to-DAY is a hol-i-day
> JOHN Ka-naka naka, tu-lai-ay.
> We're BOUND, we're BOUND for Frisco Bay
> JOHN Ka-naka naka tu-lai-ay.

On John they stamped one foot then the other, on naka, naka they opened their knees and bumped them together. There were several verses.

The beat made María voracious for Pedro. She could see him sitting below with Captain Sutter in the restless shadows of the fire. She couldn't remember wanting him this much. Big times did that to women. At last the dance ended. People joked, many passing flasks. Apparently Captain Sutter's Indians acquired aguardiente freely. Some staggered. Many laughed, apparently pulling the men and women of others away from the firelight, pretending it was by accident. Hand-in-hand couples walked to the shadows. Indians and Kanakas.

At last, Pedro stood up casting a long shadow towards her. He turned from Sutter and started toward the house. Almost unable to wait she heard his boots thudding up the stairs. Then the door opened and in a wash of night air they fell together wrapped in each other's arms.

They kissed and pressed into each other. He murmured during a small break, "Captain Sutter is drunker than his Indians." He found her breast. "He asked about you."

She froze. Had he seen her on the trail this morning? Would she be hauled away? She still wasn't ready to face him.

He chuckled. "I told him you are mine." He kissed her, tonguing, then pulled back. "He said he would pay me a thousand dollars for one night with you." Pedro's eyes glistened in the firelight coming through the window.

She gasped in surprise. That much! Her people were adding pinches of gold to a large basket for Pedro, to buy Perrimacoo's land. It would take many pinches to equal a thousand dollars. "That much would tempt any man," she breathed.

"Not me." It sounded gruff, but he was Proud Hawk. He gentled her cheek to his pulsing throat. "You must know that, Amapolita." In the V of his open shirt his heart spoke to her while his breath moved the top of her hair.

Absorbing the honor of his words, her knees went weak. She had not meant to question his love for her. "Gracias," she whispered, adding "Capitán Sutter must carry many pesos."

He petted her hair. "He said he would write a note of promise for it. He expects to get a hundred times that much in gold where he's going."

"There are many women in the world. Why does he want me?"

The corners of his mouth moved in a tiny smile. "You ran away from him, Little Poppy. Some men crave what they cannot have. Besides," he kissed her forehead, "You have the face of an angel." His kisses circled her face. "And a body el Diablo would die for." His hands slid down to her buttocks and he took them in his hands.

"I am glad you want what is yours." She loosed his sash and freed the buttons.

"Por favor, my thousand dollar poppy," he murmured, "let us not wait."

# 48

Elitha heard horses coming. Yesterday Captain Sutter and his Indians and Kanakas had come through. By now they'd be on their way to Sutter's Piney Woods, where for years his men had been cutting pine for fuel and furniture. She went to the porch. The sun was high, the horses coming from the east. "Looks like the men," she called to Sarah.

The three ranchers galloped toward her—Perry, Sheldon, and Daylor. She felt sorry her visit was over. Maybe Perry would agree to stay for supper. He reined Paint to a stop and dismounted, looking weary in his two-week stubble, but grinning a deep dimple at her as he untied the saddle bundles. That and the way he moved indicated he'd sold the cattle for a high price. But what had detained them so long?

Mr. Sheldon saluted from his horse and reined up the leafy path heading back to his Mill Ranch.

"Wait!" Elitha called, gathering her skirts and running after him. He stopped and looked back at her.

"Captain Sutter came with about a hundred and fifty Indians and Kanakas. They all camped at your place last night. Probably gone by now, to the pine woods."

Mr. Sheldon's eyebrows drew together in thought. "Thanks for the warning."

Elitha heard Perry whip the girth through the loop and say, "Out mining gold now, is Suiter?"

She turned to him. "How'd you know?" Sarah and Mr. Daylor were entwined.

"I told ye, ent a man not halt or blind who ent out minin' gold," Perry said

Mr. Daylor carried his saddle to the porch rail, exchanged a look with Perry and smiled at Elitha. "You and Sally be lucky ladies." He pushed back the hat on his high white forehead.

Elitha cocked her head at him. "Why lucky?"

Perry fished down the front of his shirt and brought out his possibles-pouch. With the rabbit-skin lace still around his neck, he extended the bag toward her and said, "Go on. Take a gander."

Smelling old perspiration and liquor, Elitha pried the pouch open with her fingertips.

Held as if on a leash, Perry quipped at Daylor, "These lovelies don't know they be married to gold barons."

Elitha moved her fingers through the grainy material and brought out a nugget similar to, but much smaller than the one she'd reburied in the split rock.

"Maybe now they'll put on some flesh," Mr. Daylor said running an eye over the two of them. "We'll hire all the work done, and they can sit like queens eatin' bread and honey."

Sarah made a teasing face. "Gold barons, my eye. That there ain't near as much as my folks has found on Dry Creek."

Mr. Daylor pressed his lips together at the bottom of his long face in what passed for a smile. "Madam, what you're looking at is only the start."

Elitha handed the pouch and Perry to Sarah.

Perry went willingly, grinning comically from his leash while Sarah looked into the pouch. "We've got a pot full of it wrapped in the blankets, we has," he said. "Wye a body can pluck gold from the ground like eggs in a henhouse!" His blue eyes crinkled at her. She released him.

Excitement sparked through Elitha. She would send to San Francisco for a buggy and nice clothing, and to Boston for a cookstove like Sarah's. They must have the house rebuilt, with a fireplace and a good door, and windows that opened—a wooden house like the Sheldon's so water wouldn't seep through. And a two-seater outhouse. She would find carpenters. The Sheldons and Daylors were too busy on their rancho to direct its construction. Most men did their own building, except Perry, who didn't know how.

Mr. Daylor had his hands around the red-striped fabric of Sarah's small waist, his cheek against her dark bun. "Mrs. Daylor me love," he said, "we picked up that much in no time atall." He exuded strength, his height and broad shoulders making her small, though she was as tall as Elitha. A handsome couple, Elitha thought, and wealthy?

"Well, lass?" Perry said to Elitha. "Curious where this treasure trove is to be found, is ye?"

She had to keep reminding herself this was really happening, and not let herself ride too high. "You said you were going to the Culuma—"

"Went there, we did. Sold the cattle too for a pretty penny. But on the way back, lass, on the way back! About ten miles toward home we stopped and tried our luck in a gravel bed by a dry creek, the worst patch of nothing you ever did see. And would ye believe! These old tars hit it rich, they did!" He was like the boy in the fairytale who went out to find his fortune, but the boy in the fairytale encountered difficult tests along the road. This was easy.

"Just layin on the ground?" Sarah asked.

"Like hens' eggs," Perry said, "Learned a trick or two, we did! Throw a shovelful of sand and gravel on a blanket, hold the corners and toss it careful like. The breeze blows the light stuff away and gold stays in the blanket."

"And the place!" Mr. Daylor put in with more fervor than Elitha had ever seen in him, "Not a soul knows of it. That's the beauty. The miners are busy around Culuma, miles and miles away."

And Sutter mining in a different direction, Elitha thought.

Perry chimed in, "Deserted as a church on Monday is our dry diggins'."

Mr. Daylor headed for the outhouse, calling over his shoulder, "We're sending the Indians back for more. Ten thousand dollars a week is my guess, what they'll get out of there."

Elitha sucked in her breath. Ten thousand dollars was the savings of Pa's lifetime, and he'd been a wealthy man. Their wealth would rival the eastern bankers. Thrilled, she started thinking what to do with the money. She would write her half brother, William Donner, and tell him to send carpenters from Illinois. She could stake the crossing of the entire construction crew, and when the house was built, she'd reunite the family. The girls could help with the baby when it came. Perry's drinking might lessen a bit too, and his gambling, when he had as much money as he needed. Money makes the gentlemen, she'd been told. Oh Pa, you were right about California. If only you had lived to see this!

❧

With Billy on her lap, María listened to Señor Sheldon's fluent Spanish. Her friend Blue Star sat on one side, big Tomaka on the other. Omuch's umne circled around. Señor Sheldon's use of Indian words impressed María, and she exchanged glances with Blue Star and Tomaka. It was clear the Omuchumne admired Joaquín Sheldon. His flinty expression held firm as he spoke, and the faces of the Omuchumne, twice as numerous as María's umne, looked toward him like flowers to the sun. He had become co-headman, and Omuch didn't seem to mind.

"Except for those who stay with Señor Valdez, every man, woman and child will come with us," Señor Sheldon was saying. "It is a three-day journey on foot. Thirty miles. Women are to bring carrying baskets, blankets, mortars, knives and basket-making tools, anything you need in your daily lives. We will take more cattle with us, and leave the rest here with Señor Valdez. He will select three vaqueros to stay here and help him." Pleased that Pedro would stay, María was disappointed her friends would leave.

Nursing her baby, Blue Star whispered, "Now my people will wash gold like your people." María had confided in her but asked her to keep it a secret.

Señor Sheldon continued, "I will pay each person fifty cents for every day you work—men, women, and children."

A murmur traveled around the seated people. "A family with children will make much money," Tomaka said.

The Omuchumne were to leave home to seek gold for Joaquín Sheldon. Such a thing had never happened before. What was the foreboding María Howchia felt tickling through her?

❧

The next morning María stood beside Pedro, his clothed arm around her shoulders, Billy at her knee. Sadly she watched Tomaka walk up the trail with the Omuchumne—old people and little children among them. Billy would have no one left to play with. No big time would be celebrated until the people returned. Fortunately, Blue Star would stay with her man Quapata, but it would be lonely without the rest of their people.

She glanced at Elitha and Señora Daylor on the porch, peeling potatoes in their laps, their eyes followed the people walking away with sure, steady steps. At the front of the line, a plume of dust marked Señor Daylor's horse. Again María felt the tickle of loose power. For good or ill, one never knew, but she couldn't get rid of that feeling of approaching trouble.

Señor Sheldon waited on his nervous animal, to help the vaqueros herd more longhorns to the mines—meat on the hoof for the miners. Glad her friends had taken plenty of supplies in their carrying baskets, María was about to mention her unease to Pedro when Perrimacoo stepped between them.

"I needs to palaver, Mary. Alone."

Pedro spoke clearly and evenly, "What you say to her you can say to me." His chin was high, his embroidered bolero riding back on his shoulders.

Perrimacoo's eyes narrowed to a thicket of mean lashes. "And what if I wants to talk to her about me boy?" He jutted his jaw at Billy, who squeezed María's finger more firmly.

In measured words Pedro said, "Say what you like, but say it here, señor."

"You tellin Perry McCoon what to do, nigger?" Aguardiente fumes spewed from him.

Pedro didn't change his stance, but she sensed his readiness. Maybe it was a fight she'd felt coming.

Perrimacoo rolled his eyes skyward. "Oh, for Chrisssake, for God-damned Christallmighty sake!" His eyes came around to her.

"No comprendo," María said.

"Every other rancher in the whole dammed bleedin countryside tells 'is niggers what to do, and I've a mind to—" Snorting fumes, he steel-eyed Pedro, then turned to María. "God's bones! I wants to palaver with your daddy and needs ye to come help talk, is all."

He needed her help, like little boy wanting sugar cane. He, who had handed her to a crowd of stinking men when she needed to honor the spirits, was asking for her help—though she had another man and was doing her best to rid him from the countryside.

Pedro reminded him, "I am still waiting for you to name the day of our riding contest."

His eyes narrowed. "In good time, greaser. In good time. When we have plenty of witnesses so you can't cheat. 'Ave a big purse riding on it too, I will." He turned to María "I needs ye to palaver today, ye hear? Today!"

"You want my father's people to find gold for you, but they will not do it." Pedro didn't know her people were collecting gold for him, and this felt very awkward.

"Oh, so now you're the judge of wot my workers do! Well, no mahala tells William Perry McCoon 'is business!"

No longer able to keep her calm, she turned to leave.

His fingers dug into her upper arm.

She saw a blur, felt the blow of Pedro side-handing Perrimacoo's wrist, felt the grip loosen, and wrenched free of him.

"And your mother's a whore too," Perimacoo jeered at Pedro, blue fire sparking from his eyes. His right hand hovered over his handgun in its belt holder.

María held her breath. Pedro's gun was in his saddle holder, too far away. Quick as lightning, he pulled a knife.

Señor Sheldon stepped between them, facing Perrimacoo, hat brim to hat brim.

"Out of my road," Perrimacoo said, his handgun pointed at Señor Sheldon's middle.

The muscles of Sheldon's jaw worked a little but all else remained perfectly still. And then he spoke. "I've seen enough and I've heard enough, and I'm about fed up with your drunken antics. You're pointing that gun at my mayordomo. He's worth ten of you."

The three vaqueros who stayed to work with Pedro circled around, knives pulled from calf thongs. In a gnat's wingbeat they would fight for Joaquín Sheldon and for Pedro Valdez.

Perrimacoo's gun wilted in his hand.

Releasing her breath, María listened in relieved puzzlement as Señor Sheldon added, "And don't think I don't know where you rustled half your herd. Let's get this straight. Every one of these Indians is honest and hard-working, something you never even heard of. And if I hear of you touching a hair of Señor Valdez or that girl— "Raising an arm, he pointed at an enormous cottonwood tree without looking at it, his wolf eyes holding Perrimacoo. "I'll see you hang."

Perrimacoo looked down.

María glanced at Elitha, who watched from a distance like a sad-eyed doe. How unfortunate that he was her man! A woman wanted a man of power.

Perrimacoo holstered his gun. "Mary," he said quietly. "I'll give you an American dress if you'll talk for me."

Offering payment! She stood motionless as he went to his horse and pulled out a pale garment and dangled it by narrow straps—a once-white underdress like the one Elitha wore. He didn't look at Pedro or Señor Sheldon.

She shook her head, no. She was a medicine woman. She wanted no gift from Perrimacoo.

"What about your mum? She might like it."

Etumu would love this. No woman in the village owned an Americano garment, and they all talked about them. As wife of the headman, María thought, Mother should be wearing the best.

Etumu came from the u-macha wearing the flowing garment. She looked proud with her neck and shoulders bare and her breasts inside the cloth. The frayed hem swayed at her feet as she walked with little Billy, his chubby hand grasping Grandmother's finger. Red glass beads and shell money looked pretty with her amulet, against the white cloth. Envy showed in the eyes of the other women, and María was glad she agreed to do this.

Perrimacoo came up the path from the river after watering his horse. "Where's yer daddy?"

Before she could answer, Billy said, "Daddy."

Smiling, Perrimacoo squatted and chucked the boy's plump cheek and petted his light brown hair. "Good boy. Never forget I'm your daddy."

She kept her face a mask as she said, "My father is with his traps."

"Send for him. I'm in a hurry." His eyes stayed on his son.

She sent a boy to find the hy-apo.

Perrimacoo took Billy into his arms and said, "What's yer nime little man?"

"Nime Billy."

He laughed. "Good boy. Good boy."

Billy yanked the brim of his father's hat down over his nose.

He placed the boy into his grandmother's care and looked hard at María. "Make him learn decent English, ye hear? I wants him to say: Me nime is Billy McCoon."

She was relieved to see Grizzly Hair coming from the east hill, the bones in his ears gleaming. Two other men came with him, and happy boys trotted alongside.

Grizzly Hair seated himself on the shady side of the family u-macha. María and Perrimacoo joined him. The gathering people talked quietly among themselves, sitting in a circle close enough to hear.

Perrimacoo spoke first. "Tell your people I'll pay them fifty cents a day, each, to wash and gather gold for me. They will go where their Omuchumne friends are gathering gold." Sweat trickled past his ear, disappearing in the dark stubble of his jaw-line.

Grizzly Hair continued to gaze across the river. "Ask him if he wants us to herd his cattle or find gold in a faraway place?"

Perrimacoo raised his voice, "'Alf of the men stays here with the cattle. The other 'alf go with the women and children to the diggins." He wiped sweat from his eyes. "I'll pay fifty cents, every day, to the adults for hunting gold."

María noticed that this was different than what he'd first said—each person included children. She hoped they'd all see what kind of a man he was and would not agree to wash gold for him.

Grizzly Hair spoke the tongue of the umne. "Do you want to leave home and gather gold for fifty centavos a day?"

They lived as they pleased, voluntarily gathering gold out of respect for their headman who wanted to pay Pedro retribution for insulting Old Pepe, but they were also doing it for the goods they wanted for themselves. The umne were taking their time.

Perrimacoo looked back and forth between all of them, and then he snorted in exasperation. "God's bones! Sit there all day like a bleedin' idiot, is it?"

That wasn't meant to be translated. A bright spot of anger flared within her. How dare he speak of Father that way! Would he never learn respect? She looked at him and wanted her people to see him as she did. She translated, not glossing over his rudeness. She would risk being seen as disrespectful by repeating his bad talk, hoping if she used the right inflection they would hear her contempt. She spoke slowly, searching for words that meant "bleedin" and "idiot."

People stirred and looked at one another. They whispered, glancing at Father and then her, assuring themselves that all was well between the two. She also saw the flicker of amusement in Father's eyes.

Perrimacoo saw it too. "Now just 'old yer 'orses. What did ye say to 'em?"

"We should save gold and not work for a man like him," said Grizzly Hair. Señor Daylo will make good trades for our gold. I am a trusted trading partner."

He continued: "We should continue finding gold for Señor Valdez, my daughter's new man. He will bring his cattle and you vaqueros will earn one calf for every eight calves born. Then every day you will be helping the honorable grandson of Old María instead of a rude outsider. However, we must not let Perrimacoo know where we are finding the gold. We will say we're finding it upstream a two-day walk."

"Mary, wot's he sayin'?" Perrimacoo demanded.

Grizzly Hair continued, "The home place will be calmer if Perrimacoo leaves us. I say this although I am the grandfather of his son." People nodded in sorrow that their headman was forced to deprive his grandson of a father, but María saw that the people trusted his judgment.

Scorpion Trail signaled. At Father's nod he announced, "The hy-apo speaks well. I agree."

"Wot's e sayin?"

María showed Perrimacoo the palm of her hand while others took turns agreeing with Scorpion Trail. When all the speakers were finished she said in English. "My people gather no gold for you."

He straightened to his feet and glared at her. "Ye treacherous bitch!" He shoved her shoulder with two stiff fingers.

An arrow whirred into his hat. It sailed through the air with the hat and pinned it to a cha'ka.

He whirled to look. When he turned back fear was visible in his eyes, and his hand stayed near his gun.

Grizzly Hair raised a hand. "Daughter, tell him the next arrow will fly lower."

She said that, and Perrimacoo's eyes turned onto Grizzly Hair. Then Father's voice came calm and deep. "Tell him the men will continue to herd his cattle, but from now on, we will take two calves from every ten births." Smiles wreathed the surrounding faces.

"Two calves, is it. Me 'orse's arse!" He turned on his heel, yanked the arrow from his hat, and tramped toward his animal. Jamming the hat on his head, he vaulted into the saddle.

Everyone watched him gallop away, María feeling proud of her people and her Father.

# 49

Alone in their room over the millhouse, María told Pedro of the big basket of gold her people were saving for him. His mouth dropped open.

"It is soon full, but we will tell Perrimacoo it came from upstream, a two-day walk." She disliked telling lies because it stole power, but they could not reveal to Perrimacoo that gold could be found in the riverbottom and the hunting grounds of the People, or Perrimacoo would never leave. "Soon you can offer it in trade for Perrimacoo's land paper."

He reached out and pulled her into his arms.

Two days away from him had seemed an eternity. She nuzzled her nose into the reddish-brown hair curling on his shirt collar and grazed his neck with her lips. "Señora McCoon and I are friends. I think she can convince Perrimacoo to make the trade. She is like a young oak, frail-looking on top, but deep rooted."

"Amapolita, you make me happy. Your people make me happy. I am a fortunate man to have such a woman. My words cannot express how much I love you." His moist gray eyes looked deep into hers, their many facets an endless source of wonder.

Pedro had selected Quapata, Roberto, and Rafael to help with the herd while the rest of the Indians worked for the patrones at Dry Diggings. Keeping the grizzlies at bay with only four vaqueros was a chore, even with only four hundred head of cattle left.

But it was springtime and he felt good as he moved with Chocolate's walking gait. His blood coursed deeper, fuller, in tune with the avian melodies around him. He breathed in the sweet air and watched the golden haze of sundown over the western ridge. Making love filled him, yet emptied him, made him need more of María. Her petals were damp and firm with youth. Ah, que mujer! He had what Captain Sutter would have paid a thousand dollars for. And her people were buying McCoon's land for him! Surely he was the luckiest man alive! Don Pedro Valdez, gran ranchero. Soon. Soon!

But he must learn the rules of land ownership, now that things had settled down after the war. He'd been meaning to ask for Sheldon's help in understanding McCoon's claim to Rancho Sacayak. Possession apparently meant something. If anyone could understand it, it would be Joaquín Sheldon. He was a literate man and a North American before he became Mexican. Long ago General Vallejo had offered to help, but he was a grand man who shouldn't be bothered with the likes of Pedro. Señor Sheldon was the key.

Worth ten of you. Chuckling, he patted Chocolate's neck. If McCoon was faking his claim to the ranch, Pedro could play along as though he intended to buy it, meanwhile establishing some kind of possession. Then Sheldon could help with the papers to get title through the United States government. Of course if McCoon owned actual title and would sell it, so much the better. Maybe Señor Sheldon could pose as the buyer. How gratifying to know your employer thinks you are valuable, honest and hard-working!

Somewhere a calf bleated, the sound of pain. He touched Chocolate with his spurs and cut through the herd to a calf with a nose full of quills. Damn porcupines! They teased a baby to put its curious nose on the quills then the poor thing starved to death beside its mother's swollen udders. What a tormented way to die! Pobrecito.

Releasing his lasso from the saddle loop, he brought the baby animal to a halt, longhorns parting around him. He jumped down and trotted to the struggling, bawling animal, straddling it. Chocolate held the rope taut. The mother watched in the morose way of cows while he yanked out the painful quills and the baby screamed. With the last quill came a thought.

The gold from Captain Juan could be taken to San Francisco, as it was called now, and changed to pesos. He could claim his family had left him an inheritance. That would ensure McCoon wouldn't catch on to the fact that he was abandoning a gold mine. The bawling calf bounded after its mother, and Pedro mounted Chocolate.

*Don't think I don't know where you rustled your cattle.* Interesting. Not from Rancho Omuchumne. Pedro kept a good count on all three earmarks: Daylor's, Sheldon's and his own. Where from, then? Did the bastard have the calzones to steal from New Helvetia? His former employer. Where else?

*Worth ten of you.* He let out a whoop. The startled horse lurched, turned a big eye on him, and then resumed his dignified gait. Sometimes you had to laugh at a horse.

McCoon was paying double for Indian labor. Eighteen Omuchumne Indians working for a dollar a day would add up. Fifty cents of every dollar to Sheldon. Clever, but fair. A ranchero should be paid for the use of his laborers. Must be a big gold strike, he knew, for McCoon to agree to such terms and trot off for the diggings that fast. Dios mío, make him stay there!

His full-empty feeling buoyed him, made him feel all things were possible. The grass grew faster than the cattle could eat. No need to push the herd around. He stopped Chocolate, hooked a leg over the horn and took in the beauty of spring—purple, yellow and white flowers woven through the green. "Ay, ay!" he called to the beautiful world, and reached for his guitar in its saddle sling.

Rolling the chords of *La Primavera* in three-quarter time, he looked toward the millhouse, where María would be grinding corn. Even her terror of the condor robe seemed to be over. She hadn't talked about it for a long time.

He inhaled a lungful of delicious air and poured his soul over the countryside. *"Ya vi-e-ne la pri-ma-vera,"* Here comes the springtime. Seeing Quapata skirting the herd, he raised an arm that all was well. *"Sem-brando flor-es, ay, ay! / De mil color-es, de mil color-es"* Flowers in a thousand colors. Quapata's arm went up. Está bien. Strum, pick, pick. He embellished the lilt as his gaze swept across the expanse of bovine backs. They had their noses to the green and he had María's satin curves in his mind. *"Cantan las aves / Can-tan las aves / Repítan sus trinos suav-es."* Si-ing the birds / Si-ing the birds / Repeating their soft trills. He whistled the last refrain and the cattle looked up approvingly.

He wished he could hold María all night, but until the return of the patrones he had to get up in the dark and ride herd to spell the Indians. Three vaqueros at all times was a minimum. Ah, but the colors of dawn were like love in springtime!

I should buy a pistol, he thought, suddenly recalling McCoon's sidearm. Strangers were streaming inland from the coast, many dishonorable men. Rumors of gold had traveled far and wide.

Funny. Just when things cleared up on one side of life, the other side clouded.

# 50

María had long noticed that Elitha wore Crying Fox' blue crystals. With magic she'd strengthened herself against them. Now she felt the sun through her cap as she led Elitha up the stairs to Pedro's room, having invited her to visit. She wasn't sure how to broach the subject of Perrimacoo leaving Rancho Sacayak, but she needed to know his wife's feeling about it.

Billy fussed the instant he spied food. She sat him on the floor and reached for her basket of dried grasshoppers hanging from the rafters. "This is Pedro's house," she told Elitha, "He comes to eat when the sun is on top."

Elitha glanced around the room. Did she notice the neatness of the baskets and salmon strips in the rafters, the soaproot brushes of different sizes arranged in order on the table? Her eyes lingered on Pedro's helmet in the corner, and then slid past his black hat hanging on its peg, to his guitar on the bed.

María patted the bed, and Elitha sat there, pressing her high-laced shoes together on the floor while María stirred a handful of grasshoppers into the nu-pah and gave the basket to Billy.

"You must be lonely with your family at Rancho Sacayak and your friends mining in Dry Diggins," Elitha said.

"Sometimes I am lonely, but my man is here." Proud of her improving Americano talk, she licked her sticky hand and folded her legs beneath her at the foot of the bed, rearranging her wraparound skirt. María then went to the point of the visit.

"Where is your family?"

The sad eyes looked even sadder. "Dead, except for my four sisters."

All dead! That was horrifying. A family was a large and diverse body of people. María could have named more than two hundred relatives, and couldn't imagine them all dead. "Why they die?"

"They starved in the mountains, trying to get to California."

Crying Fox had gone there, but she must not think of him or speak of him. "Have you no more aunts and uncles and cousins?"

She shook her head. "My father and mother, my aunt and uncle, and most of my cousins died up there." She lifted her eyes eastward, then looked sadly at Billy, who was eating.

María had planned to suggest that Elitha go live with her family. "Where be other family?"

Elitha sighed long, still watching Billy. "In Illinois. My half-brother's married, with children, and my favorite aunt is there. Susanna."

"Home place be Illinois?" Seeing Elitha's nod, an idea struck. Maybe Elitha could return to Illinois and take Perrimacoo with her. "How many sleeps to Illinois?"

"Oh my! Let's see, it took six months to get from the farm to the California mountains, and another three weeks crossing over them."

More than six moons! María had always imagined the eastern sea was only a few sleeps from the other side of the mountains. One didn't walk for six moons without a very good reason. Seeing Billy dump the contents of his basket on the floor, she scooped the food back in. "Did you know of my father's ranchería before you left your home?" Perhaps its beauty had lured her to it.

Elitha looked at María with almost a smile. "No. I live there because it is my husband's land, just like you live here with your husband."

She let that settle, and said, "I saw you happy when gathering marsh nuts. But I think you are sad. No women, no family to talk your tongue."

"Catey Sheldon and Sarah Daylor are my friends. But sometimes I am lonely. When Perry is away and I'm by myself in his house." Her voice lowered to barely a whisper.

"You are Perrimacoo's wife. Say to him with strength that you want go to Illinois. Maybe he go too." Surely she'd be happier where Americanas were more numerous.

Elitha made such a bad face that María's idea stumbled to a stop. But when she followed Elitha's glance, there was Billy plastered from head to toe with grasshopper nu-pah.

Grabbing him, María said, "Come to river. I wash baby. We talk more."

Elitha followed her to the sandy spot beneath a big black walnut tree. María stepped out of her skirt. The Americana removed her shoes and stockings, bunched her long skirts above her white knees, and waded into the river on slim long-toed feet. Sunlight and shadow splotched her blue dress and tunnel hat, and her black hair hung to her waist as the water lapped around her calves.

"I think Perrimacoo sell land paper for gold," María said.

Elitha glanced up, a pretty woman except for her paleness. "You are probably right."

Ho! Politely María kept the joy from her face. "How much gold for land paper?" Pedro would want to know this. She crouched into the water, waiting as the Americana pursed her lips in thought. The friendly water tickled up María's scalp, and her hair floated around her face. She held Billy at arm's length, and let him splash like a fat muskrat. When he began to float she let him swim on his own.

Standing in the backwater beneath the overhanging tree, Elitha cocked her tunnel hat. "Why do you ask?"

"Señor Valdez wants to buy the land paper of Perrimacoo."

"Oh." The sad eyes searched hers. "You want us to leave?" She climbed to a patch of dry sand and sat down hugging her knees, face down.

"Sí." She stood upright, water pouring from her nipples, afraid she might have seemed rude. She pulled Billy from the water and joined Elitha on the bank, rocking him gently. He snuggled his wet face against her neck, ready to sleep, and she explained, "Your man and my man cannot live in same place. Señor Valdez wants Rancho Sacayak." With the charmstone blazing at her, she struggled to keep her calm.

Elitha opened the top buttons of her dress and fanned her neck where the crystals lay against her damp skin. "But Mr. Valdez has a good job here at Sheldon's rancho. Why would he want to leave?"

"He wants be ranchero like Señor Sheldon. At my home ranchería."

Absently, Elitha touched the crystals. "I see." She looked down, "I don't know how much Perry would sell the land for. But if you want, I'll ask him, and tell him Señor Valdez wants to buy it."

María smiled at her, pleased. The important things had been said. She hoped she had an ally in Elitha. Rocking Billy, she enjoyed the faint breath of air coming across the river, drying her limbs. Wood ducks, male and female, paddled into view from around an overhanging berry clump, tipping tails up in the backwater. The pleasant smells of the river always gave strength. She wondered about the silent young woman sitting beside her. How had she avoided death in the adobe house? "Maybe this give you power," she said, pointing at the charmstone.

Silence, long toes peeping from her full skirts. "I thought you said it brought bad luck," Elitha said.

So like something Pedro would say! As if power were either good or bad. "Maybe bring good luck to you, bad to me, maybe bad to you and good to me." She shrugged and looked away. It was hard to look at the crystals.

"I found out who Perry got it from."

*Crying Fox.* She must not even think his name.

"A girl. One of the emigrants. She took it off a dead Indian."

Dead penetrated. Feeling the tremor in her, Billy jerked in her arms and whimpered. She had harbored a slim hope, had ridden magically on the wings of the eagle, flown into the mountains, but hadn't located her brother. He had seemed more than lost. Her voice came ragged. "Where? The... dead Indian?"

"There were two of them."

Crying Fox had gone with Luis.

With moisture pooling in her eyes, Elitha said, "One of the women told me they were all starving and her husband must have gone out of his mind. He killed the Indians."

*Killed.* She sat Billy beside her on the bank.

Elitha continued in a grainy voice. "You see, they were all so terribly starved, and the Indians were about to die anyway. Eating that flesh saved their lives, so they got through and sent for help." She closed her eyes as if in pain.

*Eaten.* Condor flapped his wings in the maelstrom of María's mind. Nothing was safe. Almost frozen by the horror and needing to be sure, she forced herself to ask, "Names of two Indians killed by Americanos?"

"Only one man shot them." Elitha put her face in her hands and sobbed as if she understood the world's power was scrambled. Then she dabbed at her eyes with her skirt, and said, "One of their names meant Savior. I forget the Spanish for it. They were guides sent by Captain Sutter."

*Salvador.* María looked at a point of power in the southwest and unfocused her eyes, humming a melody to rub out the name, to keep from seeing her brother's face, his muscled calves, to keep from remembering Father's hope that his son would become hy-apo after him. She struggled to make herself numb to the loss gnawing a channel through her, to ignore the roaring in her head and the flood of lifelong memory threatening to wash her away. *Eaten.* He would never find the happy land and his spirit would haunt the world.

She moved outside herself, outside the pain, and felt the strangeness that the Americana seemed to feel everything just the same as she did—the abomination, the flaunting of the world's order, the flying loose of power. María had hoped her newly found power would help straighten the world. All these seasons she had struggled hard to learn Bear Claw's magic, but now—

The swirling evil ones flew up her throat and sickened her tongue and poured out her mouth. When her stomach was empty she staggered into the river, cringing under Molok like a quail in the jaws of a mountain lion. She had so little power! No matter how hard she'd tried.

Elitha followed her to the water and touched her shoulder. "It wasn't your brother, was it? Both those Indians worked for Mr. Sutter."

"Sí, my brother."

Elitha, struggling visibly to control her emotions, said, "I'm so sorry. I shouldn't have said anything. But I know how you feel. My mother was killed too and eaten. My father and aunt and uncle and cousins were all eaten after they starved."

Not looking at her, María sank into that horror. Americans ate their own kind!

Elitha looked at her with wet eyes and said, "I was told your brother and Luis never ate human flesh. They were the only ones who didn't."

They were stronger. María knew.

"The man tracked them to where they were digging for roots and acorns," Elitha continued, "they must have made it most of the way down. If it had been my brother, I would have wanted to know."

Salvador and Luis went to the bellies of the weak, to save the weak. It was backwards, power upside down. María floated upward and looked down upon two young women, and from her higher perspective she now saw that Elitha was her double, their lives intertwined, bewitched, twisted in a funnel cloud of magic. Elitha was saved because others ate the flesh of Crying Fox and Luis. All she could say was, "Power is all stirred up."

"What do you mean by that?"

"Old times, people hear talk of plants and animals. They understand the souls of rocks. They walk with spirits. Now people no hear. Only doctors hear. Americanos have no doctors." Her own voice sounded distant. "You are my other side."

"You talk in riddles. I don't understand."

"Today people no tie down power when they walk with spirits. The Ancients held the world tight. They tied power down. Now power flies free, loose, can kill you any time. No one safe. You and your people come, and you are far outside the world and strange to the spirits. You ask, what is power? In old time people say you crazy." She realized the signs were there; the earth could rise up angrily at any time and kill everyone. "Loose power mean end-time comes." She had always accepted that.

"Power means something different to my people," Elitha said.

"What you mean?"

"Men give power to other men. Captain Sutter got his power from the Mexicans."

"Man no give power. People find power, alone." She let her gaze linger on Elitha's wet eyes and realized someone must bring her brother's bones to be buried in the home place. Luis' people must be notified. "Where my brother's bones?"

"Nobody knows. They were wandering, lost."

"Americanos sing my brother spirit away?"

"What do you mean?"

They didn't sing. Faced with ignorance this profound, María stared into the distance. For all she knew her brother's soul lurked in the crystals, deadlier than a rattlesnake. But it was too late. Her bones began to shake and her vision dimmed so she couldn't see the umbels of purple brodiea beyond the green shore, couldn't hear any birds except the cawing of Molok's little brothers, mocking her weakness. She reached out to steady herself by grasping Elitha's waist, unable to stop the weakness, afraid she was being struck dead. The trembling shadows of the fringed leaves fell over them and became one and the same with María's quivering. She didn't understand the meaning of it and knew only that she and this Americana had somehow become fused. Their fates were linked. They were doubles. Both had been Perrimacoo's woman, one with his child asleep on the bank, the other with his child asleep in her body. Salvador linked them too, as did the condor robe. And Captain Sutter, who had sent Perrimacoo to live at Rancho Sacayak.

María realized her hard-won clarity had defeated her, and now it was her enemy. And she hadn't even faced Captain Sutter. She had put it off. But now she must learn to see differently. She would make preparations to face him.

Picking up Billy, María walked with Elitha back to the millhouse where Father Sun blazed too fiercely. Elitha turned and opened her hand, the blue crystals exploding into flashes of red-gold fire. "Here," she said, "this rightly belongs to you. Something to remember your brother by."

At first María shrank from the crystals that should have been burned with his body, but then she closed her fist over the hard facets of the pendant, numb to the possibility of instant death—this was the courage she needed to face Captain Sutter. She would take the charmstone home and lay it aside for the Cry that must be held.

A horse with two riders pounded toward them.

Pedro reined to a halt and helped Quapata from the saddle. Quapata's face was pinched with pain, blood streaming down his arms and dripping from his elbows as he clasped his bloody hands together.

"Help him, María," Pedro said in a tight voice, "He's lost a finger."

Teeth clenched, Quapata sank against the wall of the building.

Gently she parted the hands and looked into a surging red fountain. "Quick. Tie a cord tight around the stub. I bring medicine."

She trotted upstream where she'd seen yarrow and a stand of bone mend, flesh-healers. Quietly she explained to the plants this was the injury Pedro warned the vaqueros against—a finger left too long when the rope was wound around the saddle horn, squeezed off when the cow or bull jerked. Then she plucked the allies. To staunch blood was a small thing. The chaotic power flashing around them could kill the world.

# 51

B illy picked at Pedro's sleeve and fussed.

The curse of the condor never ends, Pedro thought, looking down at the small reminder of Perry McCoon. Half the night María had paced the room, murmuring of magic and bad luck. Devil, she called it in Spanish. Raving like a madwoman.

Now she suddenly sat up and said, "Mother will feed you."

Leaning through the shaft of sunlight angling through the window, he kissed her sleep-warm lips, stroked her hair back on her forehead and whispered, "I am sorry you suffer."

Billy wiggled between them.

"No be sorry. You do no wrong."

"I am a failure as your husband because I cannot make your troubles go away."

"They are not gnats."

He lifted her hands, skilled hands that healed, hands that made him feel like a king, hands that collected gold so he could buy Rancho Sacayak. He turned them over, kissed each palm. "Hasta luego, Indita mía. Until siesta."

Saddling Chocolate, he shook his head. He'd had to dig it out of her that Elitha thought Perry McCoon would sell the land. He'd whooped for joy, but she had barely noticed. Instead she started in about the condor robe. He was near the end of his patience when she hung her head and told how her brother had died. Mother of God! Killed like a deer. For his meat. Recalling Salvador, a bright young Indian standing straight for morning reveille, Pedro shivered.

He mounted Chocolate, crossed himself and thanked God he'd held his tongue. As the proud and virile animal loped up the trail, Pedro thought about his poor little María. Sweet soul. Trying to be a wise woman. Ay, what terrible luck, that this would happen to her brother of all people!

Sweating in the June heat, he rode to Daylor's place to replace the broken cinch ring. Daylor kept a stock of supplies and Pedro took what he needed for the ranch. The morning was still fresh and his shadow flickered through the trees. Already he smelled the straw of his sombrero wet with perspiration. It would be a blistering day.

He half expected to see Daylor's big gray at the adobe, the rancheros being overdue from the diggings. But no horse was there. Only an Indian sitting in the yard. Está bien. Señora Daylor would give him the cinch ring and record it in her book.

Drawing closer, he recognized the size and proud posture, and the hair plume of Captain Juan, his father-in-law, seated cross-legged before the porch. If he had come to trade, where were his pelts? What was he waiting for? Then Pedro saw the large, full basket shining with what appeared to be pure gold.

Realization shocked him down to his spurs. Chocolate lunged forward. Ay madre, not the gold! Señora Daylor would have seen it.

He reined to a stop before Captain Juan, majestically serene in his nakedness. The morning sun glanced off the gold and pierced Pedro's heart. The price of the land would be out of his reach now. Dismounting, he stood looking down at the Indian and his necklace of oversized bear claws.

"Where are you going?" Captain Juan asked.

Choking out the customary answer, Pedro looped his reins over the porch rail and folded his legs beneath him where Juan patted the ground. Niceties came first. Indians were even worse about that than Spaniards. Pedro asked about Etumu and all his other relations.

When all the greetings had been exchanged, Pedro took a deep breath. "Has the señora seen the basket of gold?" He nodded at the house.

"Sí."

Of course! Pedro blinked away stinging perspiration. The runner had garbled the message. Diablo! He should have gone personally to speak with Captain Juan. Now things were complicated, damnedably so. He blew out air.

His father-in-law cast him a quick look. "Runner come. Say Perrimacoo not know we give gold to you. I say good. Perrimacoo not know."

Pedro struggled to keep his face quiet. "But you showed this to the wife of his friend." The crack in his voice betrayed him. Mother of God! McCoon would do handsprings.

Captain Juan absorbed the unspoken alarm. "No," he said carefully. "I listen to runner. Gold we collect for you stay in my house. You see it first, when basket is full." He patted the side of the full round vessel. "This gold different. My people gather it for trade. I trade now. Get guns, blankets, beans." Briefly he searched Pedro's face and added, "My men want them now."

Completely garbled. Pedro feared the strain showed on his face and matched the gravel in his voice. "Now Señor McCoon will know the gold came from his land, and he will ask more in trade for it." Much more. Probably won't sell at all. Why, oh why hadn't Pedro ridden there himself?

Captain Juan remained placid. "Gold not come from land."

Hope. "Where did you get this then?" Five leagues away, he prayed, touching the gold, hot in the sun.

"In river."

"Where in the river?"

"Many places."

Pedro groaned. On McCoon's land. He ached to wrench back a week of time.

The morning sun behind Captain Juan outlined him in a brilliant halo and shadowed his already dark face.

Pedro leaned forward on his crossed legs, the tips of his fingers on his forehead, then sat straight, squinting at him. "Now Señor McCoon not want to sell land. He will search for gold in your ranchería." He remembered he hadn't been free to go, couldn't leave Sheldon's rancho for half a day with so many vaqueros gone. Anything could happen, but he still wished he'd gone to speak to Captain Juan himself. "Did you tell Señora Daylor where you found this?"

"Señora no ask."

Pedro pondered the possibility of a lie about the gold's source. Far upriver.

Captain Juan added, "She no trade for oro. She say, wait for Señor Daylo.

He come this day. He make trade. I wait." His dusky face remained calm, eyes unfocused.

Seeing the profound Indian dignity, Pedro doubted he could make him lie. Grandmother María said Indians thought lies disturbed the natural harmony of life. It was best, she said, to follow the example of straightforward animals. Coyote's treachery got him into predicaments. Anyway, McCoon wasn't likely to be fooled.

Trying to be patient, Pedro explained that more gold would be needed now to buy Rancho Sacayak. Much much more.

Not a muscle twitched in the Indian's face. The river barely whispered beyond the brambles. Pedro could feel perspiration tickling down through his sideburns.

Captain Juan's voice came low. "My people no talk of gold to Perrimacoo. No talk of it to Señora Daylo. Gold for you I give to Señor Daylo. He give it to you. He say where it come from. Maybe up river."

Pedro felt limp. "Did you get all that from the river?"

The Indian nodded. "Much gold in river." He touched the basket before him. "This oro, my people need trade now. People work long time. Two baskets more."

Pedro understood. Most of the gold was in small flakes, very tedious to separate. As majordomo for Sutter and Sheldon, Pedro knew well that it was necessary for laboring people to see their rewards. And they were collecting two baskets in addition, one to be given to Daylor for him. He laid a hand on Captain Juan's thick shoulder.

But the more gold McCoon believed came from his rancho, the less likely that he would sell at any price. Damn the bad luck! On the other hand, there was a chance this would turn out well, thanks to the hard work of Maria's people.

# 52

Gold at Rancho Sacayak! Sarah and Elitha talked of little else, and every few minutes they peered out the window to see the Indian seated beneath the cottonwood. Beside him the gold sparkled in a basket big enough to cook a good-sized pot of beans. Sarah hadn't known what to trade for so much gold. Waiting for the men, Elitha felt about to burst with excitement. Her hidden nugget hadn't been lost by some passing trapper. Gold was everywhere on Perry's land!

When at last the three trail-grimy ranchers dismounted before the adobe, Perry glanced at the big Indian, and then, as if yanked by a rope, his head jerked back, and he stared at the basket of gold. The Indian got up with it and they all went inside. Sarah explained what had happened.

"At's me gold," Perry growled at Sarah, "sure as shootin it tis! You give it to me, neighbor." Unneighborly of him, Elitha thought. The Indian stood quietly by, the gold weighing him down.

"Think fer a bloody minute, mait!" Daylor exclaimed, chopping his hand toward the Indian, "I been trading with him for four years now. Hits me livelihood. He's captain of the neighboring tribe. A relation of my workers. I canna of a sudden say I won't trade with him, and then take his gold! Merrily steal it and hand it to you!" Locked in each other's stare, the two glowered in equal measure, the grime in their crow's feet intensifying their fierceness.

Perry retorted, "Tis me own bleedin land the bloody savage got it from, and be hidin' it from me. It's mine!"

"And this me own bleedin' trading post. I runs it as I sees fit."

Elitha cringed. No matter the bad blood between Mr. Sheldon and Perry, she'd hoped the friendship between Perry and Mr. Daylor was unshakable, both having been English sailors. On the frontier neighbors had to be friends. But who was right? If Indians found gold on Mr. Daylor's ranch, would they be expected to hand it over to him? This was complicated. Maybe if Indians were paid to mine, they should give up the gold, like workers anywhere. But Perry hadn't paid Captain Juan. Still Mr. Daylor could be right. She wondered what Pa would say if he were here.

Mr. Sheldon stayed out of the quarrel, nodding Sarah and Elitha aside, telling them they'd brought home "more gold than we expected." He chewed thoughtfully on a length of sugarcane, listening to the row.

At last it was quiet and Elitha went back to the kitchen. Mr. Daylor had taken Captain Juan into the trading room, where the Indian was examining the goods. Perry stood leaning on the doorjamb, half his hat, half his shirt-back visible to her. The crusty fingers of his right hand gripped the sweat-stained shirt beneath his elbow, arms crossed, and his right boot crossed and rested on the toe. She knew that stance. Angry.

Worried that Perry's fury would spill over to her later, she lifted the cloth from the bread pan and floured her hands. From the side she could see the trading room—the Indian picking up goods. She began punching down the dough. Sarah came in with the green beans and sat down to string them where she could see the trading room too. Elitha rolled dough balls, stretched the tops smooth, pinched the bottoms, wiped them through the melting butter and snuggled the greasy orbs into the larded pan. The Indian picked out a stack of blankets. The crossed boot didn't move.

Captain Juan moved around the room selecting tools, knives, a sack of beans, a bucket of beads, she couldn't see what all. Mr. Daylor nodded assent each time the Indian raised an item. Patting the last greased dough ball, Elitha placed the rolls on the shelf above the stove, covered it with the cloth, and glanced at Sarah. Snapping beans by the feel, her gaze never left the trading room.

Elitha ventured, "Looks like it's getting nigh onto suppertime. Is Mr. Sheldon staying?" She hadn't heard his horse leave and she wanted to stay too, wanted to be near other people and not caught in the dark while riding home with Perry. But Sarah apparently didn't hear the question. It was as though the gold had cast a spell over the ranch.

Elitha ventured again, "Well, I'd best get the stove started." Wiping her hands on the sackcloth about her waist, she pushed open the heavy oak door and went outside. Hot air slapped her in the face. It was hard to breathe. The sky looked white hot, the mounded briar bushes appeared to be bleached with most of the leaves curled to their pale undersides. A mule with a packsaddle stood dozing at the porch rail, swishing at flies. Mr. Daylor must have had an Indian bring it. Poor thing, in the sun. Lately the heat intensified before sundown.

On the shady side of the adobe, where she went for wood, she saw Mr. Sheldon sitting on an uncut log chewing a joint of sugarcane. The Indian who brought the mule was there too. She smiled at the owner of Rancho Omuchumne, shy of him after the bawling-out he'd given Perry three weeks ago. The door swung open. She stepped aside.

Out came Captain Juan with a pile of blankets, two full buckets banging from each huge forearm. Mr. Daylor followed, piled with bags and boxes. They packed the mule, Sheldon coming around the corner to watch.

By the time Elitha had the fire started and was again outside for more wood, the mule was swaying up the trail under its load, led by Captain Juan. Perry squinted after him, stubble darkening his jaw, an evil gleam in his eye. Sarah and Mr. Daylor stood hip to hip, arms about each other.

Mr. Sheldon put a boot on the step and leaned on his knee. "Folks," he said, startling Elitha—it had been so long since anyone had talked—"We got a problem." He turned to Daylor. "I've sent Julio for the Rhoadses. We'll talk over supper."

Sarah smiled at Elitha. "You'll get to see Catey's baby."

Elitha was pleased by that, and glad to have more people around her. The gold had stirred up strong feelings, and Elitha was curious to hear what Mr. Sheldon would propose to do about it.

The sun sank behind the trees and the mounded berry canes, but the tension remained. Elitha could feel it when she hugged Catey Sheldon and heard her whispered account of the baby's birth, and when she smiled and chatted briefly with John Rhoads, still a bear of a man. She renewed her acquaintance with Matilda Rhoads, the luckiest woman alive, to have a husband like John, strong and wise beyond his years.

Catey's baby, named William after Mr. Daylor, lay diapered on a blanket, a tuft of dark hair standing straight up on his tiny head. He had a sweet face with eyes shut, creases underneath, pink on pink like a rose bud. Closed to the world. What would those eyes see when he grew up? Would the frontier look the same? Would Elitha live to see her own baby? You never knew. A girl had to make each day important, and she was determined not to waste a single minute mooning about things.

Blessed shade now stretched across the yard. She helped the women move barrels and boards to make an outdoor table and caught the excitement of the men's talk—Mr. Sheldon and Mr. Daylor telling John Rhoads and his father about the diggings. Perry was oddly quiet, though he'd drunk several cups of aguardiente.

"Now you just sit and rest, little sister," Sarah ordered Catherine, who stepped off the porch with napkins, butter, salt and pepper. The birth had taken some of the bounce out of her, but she rolled her eyes at her sister in a way that made Elitha smile. Still an imp.

Feeling the unreality of the day, Elitha went inside the oven-like house to check the biscuits. She lowered the stove door and the heat blew her hair back. It dried her perspiring brow. Eyes narrowed against it, she bunched her skirts to protect her hands, and carried the browned biscuits to the outdoor table. A breath of air from the river felt good. It riffled the blackberry leaves where the Rhoads children were all in a line on tiptoes, reaching through the thorns for the ripe berries.

"You kids git over here and wash now," said Matilda Rhoads, dipping water from the bucket into tin cups. One glance at their purple faces and stained teeth and she raised her voice, "My land! You look like a bunch of Indians!"

Opposite Perry, Elitha sat on a packing crate next to Catherine, who was gazing into her sleeping baby's face. Perry had washed, seemingly entranced, like he didn't know where he was. All the men were hatless and looked young with their tender white foreheads showing. Or was it the excitement that made them seem youthful despite their nearly two-score years? From the outdoor fire an Indian brought a huge half-rack of beef ribs and set it on the table.

John Rhoads said to his wife, "I've about made up my mind, Matilda. I can't stay and farm while every other man is getting rich in the mines." He turned to his father. "Pa, let's you and me ride to the American River. Send for Brother Dan." He glanced at Mr. Sheldon. "What was that Indian ranchería called? Where Marshall built the sawmill?"

"Culuma."

"What's Culuma?" A boy piped from among the children circling the table, all waiting for the adults to finish eating.

Matilda scowled. "Children are to be seen, not heard. Now you all step back three big steps."

"Yes ma'am." They stepped back.

"Culuma. Now I figure if the gold's washin down from there to those rich claims on that island, it's bound to lie aplenty in between. I say we stake a claim between. How big's a claim anyhow?" John Rhoads looked back and forth between Sheldon and Daylor.

Holding a rib, Mr. Daylor talked through his chewing. "Ent much size to it. The boys is drawin lines in the sand with their boots. They agree on the lines." He chuckled. "Why, with all the territory up there, ever man could git a claim and there'd be plenty gold left over for the King's naivy."

Perry sat still like he was scheming something in his head. Mr. Sheldon swung his eyes to the Rhoadses, father and son. "Why don't you join us at Dry Diggins?"

John answered. "Naw. Thanks anyway. You got the Indians to work for you. We don't. It'd be complicated. I think we'll do better on the American, by ourselves." He turned to his father, Mr. Thomas Rhoads. "What do you say, Pa?"

The white-haired man pushed his mouth into an upside down U, but nodded agreement.

Elitha chimed in. "Captain Sutter's up at Piney Woods. He says there's gold there too."

"At's right," John Rhoads said. "We hear from the teamsters haulin' supplies. Pertaneer every day more miners head that way."

Sheldon clipped: "Men, we need a plan."

People stopped gnawing ribs and munching corn, and turned their attention to him. By her moony expression Catherine could have been looking at a god. She breathed deeply, the watch moving up and down on the tight fabric of her bosom.

Mr. Sheldon spoke deliberately. "Way I see it, we're ranchers first and foremost. Sure I mill wheat and, Bill, you got yer trading. But it's land and cattle, hides, tallow, beef that gives us our way of life and potential for valuable land in the future. With this gold, people will come in here and it'll be another New York some day. Here's my thinking." He wiped his hands on his trousers and looked intently at each of the men. "We can't run stock without Indians. Not atall. Same at the mines. Without Indians not one of us would find a ratskin of gold. Follow? It's labor intensive."

His mouth hung thoughtfully slack before he continued. "Now Perry's Indians is diggin their own gold. Don't get me wrong, Bill, you done right to give Captain Juan that mule and all that gear. It doesn't pay to rile the Indians, cause they're all connected by marriage. But danged if I don't see trouble with a capital T galloping our way."

Matilda all but whispered, "What do you mean, Jared?"

The baby fussed and Catherine turned modestly sideways, unbuttoned her frock, and put the baby to her breast. Elitha chewed quietly so she could hear, the warm breeze lifting her damp hair and bringing the first scent of night moss from the river. Mr. Sheldon's high cheekbones and narrowed eyes gave him an intense look. "Way I see it, we gotta control our labor force. They been happy gittin every tenth calf, and now fifty cents worth of goods for mining. But what'll they do when they hear about Captain Juan takin' home that mountain of gear?" He didn't wait for a response, but turned to Mr. Daylor.

"Bill, I don't mean to tell you yer business. It just seems to me we gotta set trade standards. Git the word to Sutter and Mellus and Brannan, right down to San Francisco—all the store proprietors. Or see our workers minin' fer themselves. Follow? We couldn't even raise cattle."

Mr. Daylor scowled. "You mean make it so mining's not worth their time?" Elitha didn't quite understand.

Sheldon picked up a bone and spoke to it. "Unless they mine for us at increased wages." He gnawed on the bone. "You see another other way for us to get by out here?" His light hazel eyes conveyed pained determination. She knew he was in debt to ship captains after building his new house and furnishing it with fine things shipped around the Horn.

The table was silent, the day's light softening at last.

Perry spoke for the first time since the argument with Mr. Daylor. "So what's hard to figure? Weight the scales. Hit's done all the time, at ever port in the world. Methinks every bloak'll see the gist o' that or he'll be beggared by the 'eathens." He glanced at Mr. Sheldon, then Mr. Daylor, a little obsequiously, Elitha thought. Mr. Sheldon's wolfish stare lingered a moment on Perry before he went back to the food before him.

Mr. Daylor's tall forehead was ridged in thought. "Ye could be right, Perry."

John Rhoads sounded tentative. "Well, you ranchers do see to it the Indians have clothes and all, and horses. They're better off here than any redskins back home, thanks to you. So maybe that seems right." The elder Rhoads looked like he was still thinking.

Mr. Daylor said, "I could say I gave Captain Juan a bonus fer coming here, stead of Mellus or Brannan. A one-time thing."

Mr. Sheldon swung him a thoughtful glance.

Elitha wondered, did they mean to cheat the Indians? The table grew animated again, shadows deepened across the yard, and frogs and crickets competed with the men's excited talk about gold all through the California foothills. Something told her Captain Juan wouldn't take kindly to being treated differently at the scales. He was no ordinary redskin. Yet for all his savage dignity, white men could control his earnings. It seemed sad. But then, everyone knew Indians shouldn't have too much money, or they'd go wild with liquor. She supposed that made sense, but it still bothered her even if they didn't figure out the scales were weighted. On the other hand, Perry had to keep his ranch workers. Cattle gave him a steady income—when he didn't gamble it away. And if Mr. Sheldon's Indians stopped working for Perry at the diggings, there would be no hope of rebuilding the house—paying for the carpenters she'd sent for. But no matter how she twisted it in her mind, weighting the scales seemed like cheating. She wished Pa were here. He would know what to do.

Rising with the women to clear dishes, she suddenly thought of Indian Mary and Señor Valdez wanting to buy the ranch. Elitha had said that Perry would likely sell, but things were different now. With gold on the ranch he wouldn't need to leave home to make his fortune.

She set out plates for the children, who were scrambling for places. "Ain't 'nough biscuits left," whined a boy.

Matilda cuffed his ear. "Watch your manners!"

"S'ma'am."

Perry smoked quietly in the shadows of the porch.

# 53

María saw a glint of amusement when her cousin-sisters gathered their little ones and hurried to the round house, the village center.

Old women giggled, taking their accustomed places. "Perrimacoo is here," they said. "Perrimacoo comes to talk." Hearing the commotion, even Great-Grandmother Dishi tottered down the path, feeling her way with outstretched arms. She always enjoyed the laughter of the umne. Excited children came in packs and seated themselves under the trees close enough to hear the hy-apo. They grinned at one another, hands clasped between crossed legs, shoulders hunched to their ears like turtles. Even the panting dogs looked expectant. Grizzly Hair's sparring with Perrimacoo had become a favorite entertainment. And part of the fun was in knowing some of the men remained hidden.

Suddenly the scene struck María as hilarious and she turned her back to Perrimacoo, spitting silent laughter. He expected his bad manners to be forgotten, expected to be treated as an esteemed trader when not long ago he'd been sent home with a hole in his hat. When she was sure of her straight face, she turned back around.

Grizzly Hair was seated before the dancehouse, seemingly devoid of the humor tickling through the crowd.

Perrimacoo led with, "I wants ye to mine gold for me. But this time ye'll stay to 'ome. Do right here what ye been doing behind me back is all I'm askin, and I'll pay fifty cents a day a head." As María translated, he looked over the happy faces.

She was fairly sure Perrimacoo's new offer wouldn't sway Father or the family heads. People whispered back and forth, smiles gone from the faces, children alert. Grizzly Hair sat in quiet serenity, not a hair of his plume moving in the noon heat while, below, the river-baby spirit bubbled and cooed.

"Laid out a simple bargain, I did. Mary, tell him you people are to keep mining gold as ye've been doing and give it all to me. Good as my word, I is. Fifty cents every day, that is if I gets nice baskets full like the one yer daddy took up to Daylor's." His voice deepened to a growl. "And no more sneaking it there behind my back. Cause Daylor'll let me know real quick. We ranchers be stickin' together on this."

What did that mean?

With a straight face and a lively gleam in his eye Grizzly Hair asked, "Rancheros put on pine tar," he mimed slathering it over the face and body, "and stick together?"

Raucous laughter came from every side and María shrieked with it too, and when she finally gained control, she wiped tears and explained it to the stormy-looking Perrimacoo.

People were rocking, holding their sides. He stood before them with fists on hips, skewering her with eyes hardened to blue points. "The white men has talked," he said. "From now on you niggers don't git hardly nothin for gold you bring in. Daylor's, Sutter's, San Francisco, hits all the same at the trading posts of the white men." A slow grin spread over his face.

She translated and the laughter dwindled. Grizzly Hair sat impassively, and then said, "Tell him to sit down."

His blue eyes darted around, and he sat gingerly as if on thistles. Worried about arrows?

Grizzly Hair said, "Tell him we will make him a gold-washing basket and he can find his own gold. If he gives it all to me, I, the hy-apo pay him fifty cents a day. But if he keeps the gold he finds, I pay him nothing." People hooted with laughter, and the tiniest flicker of amusement crossed Father's lips as he paused for María's translation.

The words rolled easily from her happy tongue. Father hadn't consulted with the family heads, but from the smiles on their faces she knew it wasn't necessary. Grizzly Hair was a man of knowledge.

Perrimacoo's face reddened and he sputtered incomprehensibly. Father talked over it, "No disturbing Perrimacoo," he told the umne, "if you see him washing sand at the river." Heads nodded sagely, eyes sparkling with sly humor as she translated.

Perrimacoo jumped up and yelled, "Work for monkeys! Not in a lifetime of Sundays, ye big—" He stared into space, hands on hips, jaw working. Surprisingly, he exhaled and dropped his head, showing only the top of his soiled leather hat. Then and said, "I am finished here. Tell him, Mary."

She did. People looked crestfallen. No arrows had pinned Perrimacoo's hat.

"Walk with me to me 'orse, Mary," he said. "I gots me an idear." He looked up and down her body, but his tone was polite.

She did as asked, but only as far as could be seen by the hiding men. He narrowed an eye and said, "I 'appens to know Captain Sutter want's to see ye."

A needle of fear pricked her.

"Come with me for two days to Sutter's, and I'll give ye a hundred dollars."

She recalled what Pedro had said about a thousand dollars. "No," she said, turning toward the u-macha. She had something else in mind for her visit to Captain Sutter.

"Change yer mind, ye will," he called. She turned to see him viciously yank the horse's head around. Drawing blood with the spurs, he galloped up the trail.

As she stared after him, her good feelings drained away. Vultures played overhead, the late sun catching the white of their wing feathers. Brothers of Molok.

# 54

E litha penned a letter to her half-brother:

> July 13, 1848
> Dear Will,
> We are expecting a bundle from the stork in about 4 months, so by the time you get this I'll be a mother. I have made good friends—two sisters about my age married to men who own a big farm. Did I tell you they call farms "ranchos" in California? I have a horse now, so I can get back and forth on my own.

Something stank. She glanced at Perry, home from another week of mining, bare feet in a V over the bottom of the bed. Flies droned over him. His forehead looked too white in that gloomy corner of the room, his hat on the floor beside his limp hand, his boots tumbled where he'd left them. His belly looked concave. He was losing flesh. It seemed he was killing himself in the search for gold, but she knew he gambled away most of what he found.

Perry muttered, "Damn 'eathens." He hated paying them a dollar a day.

> If the carpenters haven't left yet, tell them not to worry

about the money for the passage. We'll pay the minute
they get here. God is rewarding John Rhoads for rescuing
the immigrants. Rhoads Diggings is proving the richest
in the territory. Perry is at the diggings most of the time
now. Seenyor…

She wanted to use Sheldon's Spanish first name and title—it seemed so
exotic, so Californian—but didn't know how to spell it. And then she'd have
to mention that the recipients of Mexican land grants were given Spanish
names, and Will would wonder why Perry didn't have one. Oh well, Will was
unlikely to think of that, or know how to spell in Spanish.

…Wakeen Sheldon and Mr. Daylor are still getting a lot
of gold, mined by their Indians. Indians are real useful
in California, and I've never heard of an uprising.

Dipping the quill she paused over the paper. There was more she couldn't
write: Sacayak Indians refusing to mine for Perry. Perry drinking more than
ever, and thinking she didn't know he buried fat little bags of gold. A world
of things she couldn't write. Like her doubts that riches would change him
and the way her stomach felt when she thought of spending the rest of her life
with him. *Till death do us part.* An ink splotch fell on the paper and spread
all over "California." She grabbed a pinch of sand, sprinkled the spot, shook
the paper, and wrote:

Your sister, Elitha.

She sighed, hoping the carpenters would come by ship. Otherwise they'd
have to wait until next May before heading across the prairie. "Finished," she
sang out.

Perry lay like a corpse.

She folded the letter, laid it on the table and went outside to fetch the
venison roast from the spit. Gay-Gay, her headstrong white mare, looked up.

Back inside, Elitha made her voice light as she cut the meat. "I bet the
newspapers in the States got wind of the gold out here, with all the emigrants
writing to home."

Silence.

"You alright?"

"I could eat a horse."

"Supper's ready."

He rolled from the bed, sat with his head in his hands, and then shuffled
to the table with glazed eyes. Thirty-eight was old.

She kept her tone cheerful. "You get good gold this week?" Some of Sheldon's Indians were still working for him at the Dry Diggins, for a dollar a day.
He'd buried a bag just before coming inside.

"Aye. But diggin' deeper now, we is, a big trench. Broke me bleedin shovel." He glanced at her over the meat. "God's bones, had to ride to the fort for a new one!" If she had known she could have sent her letter sooner.

He sawed his meat with his hunting knife and speared it with the point. "Twelve dollars, that rascal Sam Brannan asked fer it. A plain spade!" He put the meat in his mouth, chewed. "Keeps his fingernails long, that one does, to get a fat pinch."

"Pinch?"

"Pinch o' dust counts for a dollar." Chewing, he shook his head. "Fort smithy's crankin out shovels like salt at the bottom o' the sea."

She recalled the tale of the magic hand mill that never stopped grinding salt, making the sea salty. "How does the fort look now?"

Bits of food came out with the s's. "Fort Sacramento, they's callin it. Hub of the world, it tis. Men from all lands, and a colorful bunch they is. Stealing what they can't buy. Brannan's sellin supplies so fast Sutter leased him that building outside." He stabbed the air with his fork, "That one you stayed in."

She remembered the sawdust beds.

"Made doors between the rooms, they did," he said letting his fork and knife clatter on the plate. He grabbed the water bucket, tilted his head and drank, water running from both sides of his mouth and down over his shirt. "Ahhh." He poured the rest on his hair, dark points of it streaming water over his face. It would make mud under the table, and she decided to press pebbles into it to make a better floor.

How did he endure the sun? Elitha wondered. Paint was looking bony too, after trotting back and forth so many times to the diggings—thirty miles one way. Perry dropped the bucket to the floor and eyed her across the table.

"Keseberg set up a store too," he said, "Stocked it rich, 'e did. But never did give me the time of day." He grabbed a piece of gristle and gnawed viciously.

It was obvious to her where Keseberg got his money, but she was through tormenting herself with that. A hot shaft of sun came through the window glass; still it was cooler inside than out, adobe having that advantage over wood. Aloud she said, "Maybe the best kind of house would be adobe with a covering of wood inside and out to keep the rain from melting the walls and keep the dust out of the inside."

He used his knife to work a string of gristle from a back tooth.

She waited, wanting to say: I can't believe there isn't a single man in California who could build for us. But repeating that made him angry. The trouble was, the carpenters were likely to disappear into the hills the moment they set foot in California.

He grabbed another piece of dripping meat, gnawed it, spoke through a full mouth. "God's bones, the trappers from Oregon territory is swarming to the mines, and a rowdy bunch they is! Shooed 'em out of our diggings, we did."

"Did you hear anything about my stove order?" She didn't want to cook outside another rainy winter.

He shoved a whole biscuit in his mouth, stood, loosened his belt, lifted a hip and cracked a loud one. As he stepped to the bed and fell back, staring at the ceiling, a fecal cloud sickened her. "Like I said," he muttered, "clerks has left the stores in San Francisco. The bay is full o' ships. Deserted. Stacked like cordwood. Your order, that wee bit o' paper is in the pocket of some bloke up to his knees in mud. Nay, more'n likely floated out t'sea by now. Ate by a whale."

She sighed. "We live like Indians, Perry." With a king's ransom buried out back.

With startling suddenness, which made her flinch, he leaped from the bed. But instead of threatening her for what she'd said, he shoved a cup under the barrel and yanked out the cork. The amber liquid gurgled out.

He gulped half a cup and placed it on the table and, to her amazement, did a quick-stepping jig, slapping his thighs and waving his arms as he sang:

> *Oh the times was hard and the wa-a-ges low.*
> *Leave her, John-ny, leave her!*
> *But now once more asho-o-re we'll go,*
> *for it's time for us to leave her.*
> *Leave her, Johnny, leave her.*

He stopped suddenly and narrowed his eyes to dark fringes, the dimple deep in his cheek. "No ma'am, this old tar ain't totin wool atwixt his ears!"

She almost hated to ask, "What're you planning?"

He danced a quick step, slapped his thighs and placed his hands on her shoulders, all but singing, "Those trappers? Outa the Colombia River? Blokes I chased outa the diggins?"

She nodded, having no idea what had got into him. "Are they carpenters?"

He howled, and when he had recovered, said, "No. But it's rich claims they be wantin, and I gots me a sweet little idear where they can buy some." He went to the window, stared out, gulped the liquor.

"I'll show them nigger bastards. Sheldon too. Dollar a day me arse!"

"What are you going to do?"

He turned steel pointed eyes to her. "Me business, lass. Me business."

Reaching for the soap-plant bulb, she took the bucket of dishes to the river, a dread weighing her down.

❦

The red sun peeped across the hills, the air too dry for dew. Chattering, piping birds filled the morning as Perry shoved Elitha's letter into his saddle-pack. Patting the bundle, which was fat with gold bags—she'd heard him digging them up at the first light of dawn—he smiled at her, still mum about his plans.

"When you coming back?" She'd decided to stay home and train Gay-Gay.

Besides, she was getting easier about being alone. Indian Mary had taught her some tracking tricks—following small animals through the grasslands and riverbottom, learning how they spent their days. It was a cross between a puzzle and a story. Once she'd seen a young Indian boy tracking the same fox, and, smiling at him, realized this was the Indian equivalent of ABCs. And if she got too restless, she could always go to Rancho Omuchumne.

He squinted, finger-combed his dark hair and replaced his stained hat. "Few days?" He grinned. "Hell girl, you know I don't know."

At least that was honest.

He jabbed the spurs into the pinto. It jumped forward, but before it had gone three steps, he yanked on the Spanish bit and the animal sat on its tail. "Hear 'ny more about Sheldon's greaser wantin' to buy me land?"

She'd assumed Perry had lost interest. "No."

Watching him go, she frowned. He was taking a lot of gold to the fort. More than usual. And just what did he mean, showing up the Indians and Sheldon? Knowing him, it wasn't likely to come to any good.

# 55

Some men had too much land, Pedro reflected as he sat astride Chocolate watching the herd graze on land belonging to Don Guillermo Hartnell. The former Englishman owned the south side of the river—from Nueva Helvetia to the flats across from McCoon's rancho—a long series of grants on the south bank of the Cosumnes, as most Californios called it. Señor Sheldon, whose north bank holding was small by comparison, knew Señor Hartnell quite well. Said Hartnell had done paperwork for the Governor and got paid in land. Ay, ay, ay, Pedro wished he could read! It was hard to earn land by the sweat of one's brow. But he had María.

Resting his forearms on the pommel horn, he chuckled at her story about McCoon failing, again, to get the Sacayak Indians to wash gold for him. Paying Sheldon's Indians a dollar a day! It was comical, when all the man had to do was treat them with respect. He wiped his sleeve across his brow.

Dios mío, it would be nice to have the Omuchumne home again. Four vaqueros couldn't keep up with the emergencies—grizzlies on the prowl, wolves and coyotes after the calves—much less the routine chores. Pedro longed for a whole night's sleep. Besides, Indians made life pleasant. He liked their humor. María missed her women friends.

Sheldon said the Indians gathered too much gold from Dry Diggins to let them stop now. "Geniuses," he called them. They no longer winnowed it in blankets, but washed it in water they fed through a flume that they'd dug for miles and lined with wood. Indian ingenuity was as endless as the gold.

Pedro saw Quapata's black stallion approaching. Yesterday the Indian had joked: Easier to feed out rope now, though the stub of his finger was barely healed. His smile dropped. Quapata was riding low and hard.

The lathered stallion pounded up beside Chocolate. "Señor Valdez. No like hombres at Señor Daylo's. Señora no like." Quapata's face twisted with urgency.

"What men?"

"Strangers. Animal skin on head."

Walla Walla hunters wore such garb. "Indians?"

"Leather shirts. Two."

Pedro tightened the bead on his sombrero and spurred Chocolate. Quapata, who was not one to overreact, rode beside him. Pedro guarded more than cattle during the absences of the patrones. Señoras Sarah and Catherine he would defend with his life. He splashed across the shallow river, Quapata in stride, his brown heels gripping the stallion's belly. As he rode he felt the stock of his new Allen pepperbox four-shooter in his holster, reassuring himself. Gold was drawing adventurers to Sutter's camp, and they all stopped at Daylor's store.

Not wanting to alert the bad men, he signaled Quapata and jumped off Chocolate. "Wait here." Handing the reins to the Indian, he quickly pressed four balls and four packets of powder into the grooves of the stubby gun barrel, and then crept around the last bend of the trail to the adobe. Two saddle horses and a pack mule were daintily nibbling ripe blackberries in the shade of the big cottonwood—picks, shovels and tin pans strapped on their backs. He jumped to the porch, spurs jingling, and pushed open the door.

Inside the trading room Señora Daylor was backed into the corner between a barrel of beans and a pile of tumbled blankets, her gown intact and buttoned. Her eyes locked with Pedro's and he read deep gratitude.

Within an arm's reach of her, a strong-looking young man in buckskins and a wide felt hat, two turkey feathers nearly scraping the ceiling, turned cold blue eyes on him. Beside the man a rifle stood propped against a crate. A taller, thinner, older man, also in fringed buckskin, cradled his gun in his arms. The rifles were the percussion type, barrels shorter than some. But Pedro's Allen was faster and accurate enough at short range. Both men wore knife sheaths in front, horn hafts angling toward their right hands.

The younger man drawled, "My stars, the Mexican niggers is crawlin all over this here country, ain't they Daddy?"

Pedro felt his nerves tingle like when he lassoed grizzlies. He looked at the señora and asked her, "What's happening here?"

The younger man purred, "Wall whaddeya know. This here spik in a monkey suit kin talk English!" He parodied amazement as his eyes ran from Pedro's sombrero to his vest, the sash holding the four-shooter, and down to the goatskin spats over his pants.

"Were they bothering you, señora?"

Sarah swallowed and glanced from one stranger to the other. "Well, first they was lookin at the goods—"

The older man snickered.

*Wild men without principles.* Some North Americans would kill their own mothers. Pedro was glad he'd come in time. "Have they bought something?"

As she shook her head, the North Americans exchanged an amused look.

Pedro said quietly, "It is time for you to go on your way, señores."

The older man spoke for the first time, "Suh-un, peers this here greaser's fixin to throw us outa the store. Now don't that beat all." His rifle lay loose in his arms.

"Sure do, Pa. I thought the niggers'd crawled home to Mexico after they got their butts whupped." His tone was flatter, deadlier than the older man's, as if the additional generation had drained out every human quality. "Mebbe they ain't even smart as monkeys."

Sarah squeaked, "Please go."

The younger man purred, "Darlin, we'll throw the Mexican out fer ya."

"No, I mean you." Her hands moved over her apron.

The man's lips moved in a smile as his hand closed around the standing rifle. "But we ain't bought nuthin ye-et." Stepping back, flat eyes shifting to Pedro, he brought the rifle stock up to meet his trigger hand, the round dark hole coming around.

Pedro drew and fired, a flame licking across the short distance, smoldering at the edge of the hole in the buckskin shirt. The man jerked back with the impact and fell.

At the same instant Pedro threw himself at the older man's knees and heard the rifle discharge. His sombrero jumped back on his ears. Adobe flakes rained down. Sarah screamed.

The older man dropped his rifle and had his knife out before he hit the floor, Pedro on top—lengthwise over him. He held the wrist holding the knife.

The man kicked like a downed bronco. He flopped across the floor with Pedro on top. They crashed into barrels, overturning them. Glass beads spilled across the floor. Sugarcane fell on Pedro's head as he strained with his left hand to hold the man's knife hand down.

The old arms were sinewy whipcords, strong as el Diablo. With a sudden flip, the older man was on top, thrusting the knife downward, the shaft honed, shining in the light from the window.

*Cabrón!* Pedro pushed up with both hands, teeth clamped, his back pressed into something painful. The slightest release would leave him pinned through the neck. His trembling arms were about to burst when light flooded the room. Quapata, he hoped and prayed.

A brown elbow locked beneath the gray beard, jerked the man's head back in an open-mouthed grimace. Pedro seized the knife from the loosening fingers. "Gracias, señor," he said to the North American as he jumped to his feet and glanced around, breathing hard.

Sarah cowered in the corner. The man he'd shot still twitched in a widening red pool, blood jerking from the hole in the buckskin. Quapata's powerful bare legs were braced wide as he maintained the chokehold on the writhing, kicking old devil.

Pedro slipped the old man's skinning knife beneath his own sash. "Don't kill him, Pata," he said, recovering his Allen from the floor, nosing it under his sash opposite the knife. He grabbed the legs of the old man, who no longer resisted, and nodded for Quapata to help him carry him out the door.

They swung him off the porch and dropped him beside the saddle horses.

Massaging his throat, the man rasped and croaked, "Lemme git my son. I'll leave peaceable."

Pedro exchanged a look with Quapata, pulled out his Allen, turned the barrel a click, and pointed with his chin. "Pata, get the hombre."

Quapata left.

"Mount your horse," Pedro ordered.

In a minute or two, the wounded man lay across the saddle of the other horse and the old man was leading it westward toward New Helvetia, drops of blood beading in the dust of the trail.

Pedro's joints suddenly loosened. "He will die," he said to Quapata and the señora, who stood on the porch watching the retreating horses.

Quapata's black eyes flickered agreement. Sarah shut hers.

"Maybe I should have killed the old one," Pedro said.

Quapata kept his eyes on the trail. "Dead man no talk, but Señor Valdez no killer."

Sarah said, "I gotta sit down." She turned into the Daylors' living space.

Pedro watched the spot where the trail mounted the hill out from behind the trees. When the horses and mules appeared, still heading west, he went back inside the trading room. Among the beads and blankets and sugarcane were two rifles, a wide-brimmed felt hat and Pedro's sombrero with a hole through the crown. Then he saw a piece of paper in the blood.

Donning the sombrero, he carefully lifted the paper and took it outside to wipe on the fresh grass where Sarah threw out the wash water. The slanting black lines were smeared, but it was legible, had he been able to read. He blew it almost dry, folded it, and put it in his pocket.

Aware of the wide, dusty feet beside him he said, "Gracias, Pata." He embraced the powerful brown man, felt the return hug, then turned and glanced at the hill where the North Americans had disappeared. The dust had settled.

But nothing would ever be the same. Pedro had killed a white man.

# 56

In the yard of the trading post the following day Sheldon stared at Pedro as Sarah Daylor told of the shooting. Señor Daylor had stayed at the diggings with the Indians. Sheldon came quickly to the point.

"Did they shoot first?"

"The man tried. My gun is small. I pulled it faster."

He pondered that, and then turned to Sarah, asking gently, "You sure they didn't touch you?"

She smoothed her apron elevating her elegant nose, every hair now secure in her bun. "Well, no. But Jared, they would have if Mr. Valdez hadn't showed up when he did."

Sheldon nodded, overbite parted in thought. Then he dipped his head at Pedro as if to say, Good work.

Pedro reached in his pocket and gave Sheldon the scrap of paper, rusty with blood. "I found this on the floor."

Smoothing out the wrinkles, the patrón scanned, eyes swinging back and forth in the shade of his hat. When he looked up, his stubbled wedge of face was hard, his wolf eyes staring into the distance.

"What does it say, Jared," Sarah asked.

He read aloud:

> "July 15, 1848. New Helvetia.
> I, William Perry McCoon, being of sound mind, do hereby sell the following gold mining claim to the undersigned, Henry Pidd, for Two-thousand dollars ($2,000.00). The location and boundaries of said claim are depicted on the map below the signatures.
> Perry McCoon
> Henry Pidd
> Witness: Philosopher Pickett"

He handed it to Sarah and she looked at it.

When it was Pedro's turn to look at the scrawl, he studied the map, saw a circle around a place in the river. Now two men owned the land where he wanted his rancho. McCoon was selling little bits and pieces of it and keeping the grazing land.

Sheldon mounted his horse and clipped. "I won't have it."

"Señor?"

"The selling of claims."

Perhaps this was a good time to ask. Removing his sombrero and clutching it to his chest, for he had a great favor to ask, he said, "I am afraid this is a bad time, after the trouble at Señor Daylor's."

"Qué?"

"You remember I spoke to you about buying Señor McCoon's rancho?" With his dream slipping away, he was reaching out to grab its coattail.

"Sí?" The horse stepped away. Sheldon brought it back.

"Now I know that is impossible. But I was wondering if you could talk to Don Guillermo Hartnell for me. I'd like to buy the piece of his land that lies across the river from McCoon's rancho." He had the impression something was afoot between Hartnell and Sheldon. Maybe a sale, or a lease of the land across from the gristmill. Maybe land for Pedro could be discussed in those talks.

Sheldon cocked a fierce eyebrow. "Wanna be McCoon's neighbor? With the likes of the trappers coming in?"

"I want to live near Captain Juan's ranchería. The Hartnell land is flat. With good grass." Maybe the miners would leave when they learned the Indians had taken most of the gold from that part of the river.

Sheldon looked like he could eat nails. "Those Indians don't seem cooperative to me."

Pedro knew the patrón's anger wasn't directed at him. "They'll work for me, señor."

Sheldon talked through clenched teeth. "I'd sure as hell'd rather have you on Rancho Sacayak than the son-of-a-bitch that's there." His hazel eyes sparked fire. "Leading the dregs of humanity right through my place and threatening my women!"

Pedro thought of Señora Catherine and the baby, a half mile away.

Sheldon snorted as if expelling the thought of McCoon. "I'd hate to lose you, Pedro."

"Gracias, patrón." He appreciated compliments, but there came a time when a man needed to be on his own.

"I'll see what I can do. You've done a fine job. Quapata could take over here."

"Otra vez gracias, patrón." Watching Sheldon ride toward Mill Ranch, Pedro thought about the wounded North American and knew he would be dead by now. Soon more trouble would follow. The new Americanos didn't like Mexicans and didn't know the difference between Mexicans and native Californios.

A few days later Pedro saw Señor Sheldon riding toward him. "We got visitors," he said when he came close.

By the scowl Pedro knew what it was about.

"Sheriff McKinstry and that Oregon trapper."

They shared a glance. Then, signaling Quapata, Pedro rode alongside the patrón, glad he was well respected in California. McKinstry had been appointed Sheriff by the United States Army, replacing Alcalde Sinclair as justice of the peace, Sutter's bid for his old job had been ignored. Pedro didn't know McKinstry.

At the sight of the old trapper's horse, Pedro felt his blood curdle. The events of that day stayed with him like a nightmare that wouldn't fade. Dismounting, he followed Señor Sheldon to the door.

Inside the living room, Sarah Daylor was at the stove offering coffee as Pedro and Sheldon removed their hats. For a moment Pedro looked into the eyes of the man he'd wrestled with, and then shook his head at Sarah, declining the outstretched cup.

Florid-faced McKinstry, red-bearded, tin star on his shirt, nodded at Sheldon and questioned Señora Daylor. "You say you weren't attacked?" In a comical semblance of fear, his thin reddish hair stood up where his missing hat had pulled it.

Handing a steaming cup to the sheriff, she wagged her head. "But they said things." She avoided the old man's eyes, turned her elegant nose to Sheldon, nodding at two vacant chairs, meaning they should sit.

McKinstry persisted. "Mr. Pidd here says they didn't touch you atall."

"No, but—"

The old man interrupted. "Sheriff, we was aganderin at the goods as peaceable as a couple a cut jacks, when this here Mexican run in and kilt my boy. Woulda kilt me too ifn I had'na whupped im." He leveled a dead look at Pedro.

*Should have.* Señor Daylor would have broken every bone in the desgraciado's body. Pedro looked at the weathered claws in the man's lap and remembered the strength in those wrists and the close-up smell of him. A gun handle parted the long buckskin fringe in the slats of the bent-willow chair. Pedro's voice came low. "It is a lie."

He glanced at Sarah, gracefully seating herself on the side of the bed, and felt proud of protecting her honor against this filthy dog. But she was saying nothing.

McKinstry sipped coffee, cleared his throat, and rested the cup on his knee. "Jared, before this here goes any farther, I just wanna say you and Bill got a fine place, and everbody in the territory praises that gristmill a yours. With men of your caliber, Californy's bound to be a fine country."

Sheldon pursed his lips. "Thanks, Sheriff. But let's git to business. Mr. Pidd here is lying through his teeth. My mayordomo is innocent."

McKinstry glanced at Sarah, the ankles of her high-top shoes primly crossed, a cup in her lap. "With respect sir, you heard what she said. They never even touched her." His fleshy jaw quivered as he leaned down and placed his cup on the floor. He sounded like he'd rather be doing anything else. "Jared, this here man has buried his son. Now I gotta take your Spaniard to the fort for a trial." He avoided Pedro's eyes.

Sheldon clipped, "Any trial will be held right here. On my property." He trained his wolf stare on McKinstry. "You don't need one though. 'Cause my foreman was defending Mrs. Daylor and himself at the time of the shooting. It was a case of self-defense."

"Lie," the old man snarled.

Pedro tensed as Sheldon scraped his chair back and stood. McKinstry heaved his bulk between Sheldon and the old man, a palm on each chest. "Now Mr. Pidd, you didn't mean that, did you. Not that lie part." Turning to Sheldon: "Jared, he doesn't know what he's saying. Outa his head with grief." In the light that angled from the small window, beads of perspiration glistened on the sheriff's brow. His pale eyes pleaded. "We'll have the trial here if that's what you want. I can do that."

Sheldon looked at Pidd's hand, which rested on his buckskin-covered thigh near his gun, then at McKinstry. "Like I said, there's no need for a trial atall. My man is innocent."

"Sit down, Jared, please. Please." McKinstry followed Sheldon's eyes, then addressed Mr. Pidd, whose hand hadn't moved. "Hand over yer gun."

"Ain't givin it up while that murdering spick's got aholt ahis."

"Both of you," McKinstry said, "hand over your guns." He turned to Sheldon. "Tell them. Please. We'll talk this over without guns."

Sheldon, who wore his pistol and knew how to use it, looked at Pedro and nodded in the sheriff's direction. He barked at the man in buckskins, "You too."

Pedro extended the Allen. Seeing that, the old man did likewise. McKinstry took the identical guns into the adjoining room and laid them on an open bag of beans, in Pedro's line of sight. When he returned, he sat and fingered the threads of his trouser knee. "You see, Jared, there's a powerful lot of talk around the fort. We gotta have a trial."

Sheldon leaned toward him. "George, you been here in California a piece now, and you know damn well Pedro Valdez wouldn't kill unless he had to."

The Sheriff threw up his palms. "I know, I know. But you haven't seen the fort fer a spell, Jared." He nodded at the old man, whose cold eyes Pedro watched. "The whole damned place is run over now. It ain't like it used to be. You got any eye-dee how they hate Mexicans?"

"Well now," said Sheldon, clipping off whatever the old man was trying to say. "You hold a trial over that, you better haul me in too. Cause I'm a Mexican citizen."

The man in buckskins took advantage of the lull: "Ifn you don't find that thar nigger guilty a murder, at's fine with me." He jerked his stringy beard at Pedro. "Me and my friends'll take care'the sumbitch."

Ignoring that, McKinstry said, "Aw come on, Jared, you're not a Mexican the way he is." His eyes flicked at Pedro and back. Besides, with McCoon stirrin things up…" He inched forward on his chair, rolled the brim of his hat and lowered his voice confidentially: "It's all I could do to keep a whole shit load a men from riding out here with a hangin' rope. They're screamin fer his scalp." He shot a rapid glance at Pedro

The top of Pedro's head tingled. He'd heard of scalping east of the Sierra Nevada, knew North Americans favored this method of counting dead Indians.

McKinstry added, "They won't take kindly to me either, if I let him off." His face was white, freckled, his erect red hair adding visual effect to his fearful tone.

Pedro had heard all he needed to know. Not that men of Spanish descent and California birth had ever enjoyed equal respect under Captain Sutter, but Pedro had always imagined they understood his sense of honor, regardless of whether they liked him. Now his life hung by a thread because of his birth. He couldn't win a trial at the fort or anywhere else judged by such men. Señor Sheldon would need all his Indians to protect Pedro from the mob that would come, and he wouldn't dream of causing the patrón that trouble. He had no choice in what he must do.

Sheldon picked up his hat. "You do your job, George. I'll do mine. Any trial will be here, at my place. And it's my partner who's most beholden to Señor Valdez for what he did." Yellow sparks lit his eyes. Every man in the country knew of Bill Daylor's courage. The legend had grown. Now he was supposed to have whipped fifty or sixty Indians coming at him at the same time.

Beads of sweat coalesced and ran down the lawman's red face.

Fortunately, the Rancho Omuchumne partnership of Bill Daylor and Joaquín Sheldon was like a law unto itself, a separate country on account of its remoteness and the reputations of its owners. It had taken courage for the sheriff to ride out.

After the others rode away, Pedro stood with Sheldon on the porch. "I'll continue as your mayordomo, but no North American will find me." He lifted his chin. "They can come and hold their trial but without me. Even you will not find me, patrón." He sensed rather than saw Sheldon glance at his profile.

Sheldon shifted to Spanish, his voice soft. "You wouldn't be able to buy land." He paused. "I meant to speak to Señor Hartnell for you."

A man outside the law couldn't put his name on legal papers, couldn't live across the river from Perry McCoon, couldn't arm a tribe of Indians and fend off North Americans forever. Pedro sighed, his dream slipping through his fingers. But submitting to a trial was the same as admitting guilt. He'd hang for sure. Men didn't stand trial for self-defense. That was an unwritten law impressed on the heart of every man on the frontier. Apparently, Señora Daylor hadn't seen the rifle stock come up, the gun barrel swing toward Pedro the way he had seen it. Her story wouldn't silence the trumpeting for his scalp and he would never ask her to change her story. He gazed across the lush green of the river ranch.

"I'll ride to New Helvetia and sort things out," Sheldon said. "Maybe I can help get a good jury together, the Rhoads boys. Men who owe me." He avoided Pedro's eyes. Something in his face said he didn't believe he could succeed.

"Don Joaquín, muchas gracias. You do me much honor, but you must go to the Dry Diggings and check on the Indians as you planned." His heart brimmed with gratitude, but even Sheldon couldn't guarantee a favorable majority in a yard full of clamoring North Americans. And he would not dishonor his patrón by expressing such a doubt aloud.

"I got my own reasons for going," Sheldon clipped. "This McCoon thing," he swung his wolf eyes to Pedro, "sellin' claims has got to be stopped."

# 57

With María beside him Pedro lay staring at the planks of the ceiling, head pillowed by his interlaced fingers. She wanted to go to her home village. Before the lovemaking they had argued about it. Pedro knew several more North Americans had traveled the trail toward Rancho Sacayak. Quapata had warned Pedro to stay out of sight. He hated hiding. Hated feeling like an outlaw, a foreign outlaw in his own country. He'd done nothing wrong, yet his action affected everything he did. It even caused the argument with María.

The golden light no longer fell across their naked bodies. Night was coming, a warm night, Billy asleep on his mat. She lay on her side in the freshening air from the open door, a small hand under her cheek like a baby. Sweet María.

Pobrecita! An Indian runner had brought the sad news that miners had killed her three cousins, who had been searching for Salvador's body. Young men about her age. They had played together as children. Cousin-brothers Indians called them. Mother of God, the damned condor swooped around in his mind. What else explained all this bad luck?

Startling him, she opened her eyes and said, "I will be gone for six sleeps." She sat up and smoothed back her hair.

"I still don't understand why you must go."

She leaned down, grazed her lips on his forehead with breath like the summer night, her blunt-edged hair sweeping across his face. "I go."

The words pierced him. Reaching for her, gentling her breasts to his chest, her fragrant hair around his face, he was close to tears. "Stay here with me, María." It came out choked. He couldn't go to Rancho Sacayak without attracting a murderous mob.

She pulled up. "I cannot."

When she talked like that it was like trying to make the river flow backwards. He sat up and looked at her. "Among my people a man is not a man if he allows his pregnant wife to wander out into the dangerous world."

She answered in kind, the black pools of her eyes drowning him with love. "Among my people a woman who does not attend the singing of the dead is herself not worthy of burial."

"I'll go with you." Piss on the danger. "But wait until I can speak to Señor Sheldon. He might be back tomorrow." Indian funerals lasted a week. Surely a day or two wouldn't matter. It would greatly impose on the patrón—probably force him to stay home with the vaqueros—but Pedro would request the time off. He sighed, gazing at the rapidly darkening sky. He never asked for special privileges. It was as distasteful as hiding. "Wait, I will ask the patrón."

But her chin was up. "I go in the morning."

Mid-stride, she stopped, cocked her head, listened. She couldn't place the sound. A distant pop. She shifted Billy's sling to her other hip and resumed walking toward the home place. His weight and the burden basket added heat to the stifling day, and though her pregnancy would not show for some time, her breasts felt heavy. With every step she felt the weight of sadness for Crying Fox and her three cousin-brothers.

Another crack, like a sharp clap of hands, followed by a slight echo. A cottonwood tree splitting? Sometimes they grew too heavy. But she was too far from any cottonwood stream for that sound to be so loud. And it seemed unlikely that two trees would break in succession. Oaks were too wise to overburden themselves. Only strong wind broke them. She glanced at the oaks on the hills. Not a leaf stirred. Oblivious meadowlarks fluted brilliant trills in the grass, always sociable at the end of the day. She walked on.

She was closer to the home place now, Father Sun behind the hill, when she heard another pop, only louder. And another. Like the guns at Sutter's Fort, she suddenly recalled, as they would sound from a distance. She quickened her pace, ignoring Billy's moaning and his attempt to climb out. The sounds came again, ever louder. He was fussing when she reached the crest of the last hill. Heart pounding with exertion and fear, she touched her amulet and heard Angelica Root's warning: Hide. Be careful.

She put her hand over Billy's mouth and crouch-walked into a buckeye tree, brown leaves hanging low all around her. Through an opening she saw the ti-kel field far below. The sunset cast a reddish tint on the roughened dirt and seemed to hide the little depressions. No boys and girls ran on the field. Nothing moved.

She looked across the field to the green thicket that marked Berry Creek and screened the u-machas from view. Smoke from the supper fires should be rising behind the trees. Where were the voices of the people? Where were the children? The quiet chilled her. She heard only the whisper of her heart in her ears.

Something moved on the field. She blinked, trying to make it out. An ear-cracking explosion threw her off balance. Momentarily senseless with fear, she caught herself on her hands and knees and saw a familiar shape jerking on the field. Arms, legs, head! A person.

Her eyes unveiled. Slowly, as she looked around the ti-kel field she made out other human shapes, one here, one there, sprawled, motionless as the lumps and shadows upon which they lay, the color of the clay from which Coyote had made them. Some of them very small. The umne! Voices stilled. No one helping. Poison burned in her throat. Her arms and legs went limp, her body empty, except for her heart—awakened and galloping in its cage.

What was happening? Where were Father and Mother? She pressed her hand on Billy's mouth and moved quietly forward to peek through the foliage, searching for the origin of the thunderclaps. Leaves moved below her, a stone's toss down the hill. Something dark in the elderberry. A raccoon tail in the branches—dangling from a fur cap. Leather shirts! Americanos! Like the ones who tried to kill Pedro. The man with the raccoon tail stepped out of the elderberry and stood looking down at the playing field, his hide-covered foot propped on a boulder, using the long gun like a staff. Hunters.

A man's voice! She jumped in her skin. "Spose more's in the bushes?"

"Mebbe."

Two more leather shirts emerged from the foliage and stood looking over the playing field.

"Seen one hightail it over yonder." He raised an arm toward the south trail, fringe swaying. Her people were like quail to them.

Her mind screamed for Father and Mother, all the umne.

A leather shirt left, thrashing down through the brush and boulders. The others followed. Hunting. She eased onto a hip and elbow, hand pressing Billy's mouth, remembering to breathe while her heart flung itself at her throat. The leather shirts got to the playing field and walked through it, gun barrels leading. They swiveled in all directions and kicked bodies. Earth-colored bodies blending with the earth.

Spirits hovered dangerously, stealing her strength, weakening her and pounding her temples. Were Mother and Father on the field? She remained motionless.

The Americanos disappeared around the green wall at Berry Creek, heading for the village center. Slowly she released the pressure on Billy's mouth, looking into his frightened eyes, ordering him not to cry. He didn't. She patted him thankfully and reached into her burden basket for jerky. It would quiet him while she circled the field on the river side. Later she would approach the u-machas under cover of the dark and willows along the beach, to see what the hunters were doing. Maybe Father and Mother were hiding too, and she would find them.

Soundlessly she stepped down the hillside through rocks and bushes toward the mossy scent of the river, shifting her weight only when she had good footing. Twilight was rapidly fading, and she hoped the rattlers were watching for her. At this time of evening human eyes were weak.

Quietly she stepped past Grandmother Dishi's power place. Deserted. It was dark when she reached the sand of the beach. A waning piece of moon would rise later. Leaving her hand lightly over Billy's mouth as he chewed jerky, she stepped carefully across the gravel and up the incline toward the village, the path her feet knew so well. Ahead she heard harsh Americano laughter and the clatter of metal implements. Soon the crackle of a fire and through it all, the babble and coo of the river.

Her foot hit a shadow. Something big, warmer than the warm sand. She bent to touch it. Father's scent, and the acrid smell of blood. She kneeled, turned his face, brushed particles from his nose. He didn't seem to be breathing. Father! Her heart labored. Pain pinched her chest. He had power. This couldn't happen!

She took Billy from the sling, sat him aside—quiet with another piece of jerky—held her breath and lowered her lips to Father's nose and mouth, waiting for the wind of life. Something moved in the gravel and Billy squealed. She jerked up and clapped her hand over his mouth, smelling a dog in the darkness.

One of the village pets had stolen his jerky. Had the Americanos heard the cry? She waited, tensed to run. But their laughter continued. No boot crunched toward her.

Quaking in her bones she dug into her burden basket and found Billy a flat wheat cake, this time sitting him beside Father's face where she was trying to hear him breathe. She knew that when the dog returned, it wouldn't dare steal from under her. Again she lowered her lips to Father's nose. A faint stirring of air touched her lips. She waited, felt it again. Joy mingled with grief and terror as she hugged his quiet form and rested her head on his big shoulder. He must have been crawling up the path for his bow and arrows when he lost consciousness.

A gun fired. She jerked up, fear flashing to her toes. A yelp came from above. Sensing Billy gathering himself to howl, she swept him to her arms and covered his mouth just in time.

"Wahoo!" came from the village. More laughter. Then another gunshot, and another.

Terrified, she listened. No footsteps approached.

Loose souls darted around the black, silent beach. They howled in her mind, stood her hair on end and shook her bones. Yet she must hide Father. Mother, where are you? She put Billy in his sling and took Grizzly Hair by the wrists—large for her hands—and began to drag him to the willow thicket. He was a heavy man, and despite the cooling breeze over the river, perspiration stung her eyes. Mournful owls in the cottonwoods gave voice to the souls.

Her feet gave way in the noisy gravel and she listened over the pounding of her heart.

"Be damned if that thar ain't a fortune."

A night bird shrieked.

"You cut, I choose."

"Who made you boss, Wildcat?"

Their voices had covered her sounds.

She had to get Father under cover before they quieted for the night. Please don't leave, she whispered to his soul, though she knew she shouldn't ask it to linger.

Loud yells.

"... more where that come from."

"An Injun goldmine."

Her foot bumped something big and cool. Reaching through the dark, she felt a face, hair singed across the brow. Mother? No. Bikoos on the back. A cousin-sister. She groped and found the baby. Stickiness matted its hair, a hole in its skull the size of her finger. The home place was the land of the dead. Numb to the taboo, she took her cousin-sister's dead hand and dragged her out of the way so she could continue to drag Grizzly Hair. The known world was gone.

❧

Inside the thicket she probed and found two holes in Father's back, near his backbone. No exit holes. His shin was splintered. Lead balls must be removed from his body, but she had no experience carving into flesh and her obsidian knife was too broad. She would stop the bleeding and restore him as best she could. Then later get the Wapumne healer to cut out the evil.

She crawled up the path, the medicine she needed hanging from the rafters of the u-macha. The slim light of the crescent moon revealed sleeping murderers outside the family house. Four, maybe five. They snored, their upper faces white.

Gripping her blade, she stared, entranced by the thought of cutting their throats. But before she could get to all of them, they would wake and kill her. Father needed her, so did Billy. She must find healing plants in the dark.

All night she crept around the riverbank and grasslands, remembering where the plants grew, using her nose. She struggled from silent task to silent task, hampered by Billy, afraid he'd wake and cry if she left him. She cleaned Father's wounds and stopped the bleeding. She sang to Angelica, dug a root, and cut milkweed stems to twine together. She filled her watertight basket in the river, brushing every track behind her.

Splinting Father's leg with a branch and twine, she wondered if she would ever hear his voice again. Finished, she pulled the feathery willows around the three of them.

"Daughter?" His croak brought happy tears to her eyes.

She leaned to his mouth, indicating he must speak quietly.

He rasped, "Your mother. Dead."

Her spirit momentarily left her. Then a painful hole opened near her heart. A wail surged to her mouth, and she scarcely had the strength to push it back with her hands. *Mother!*

He struggled to say more.

Trembling, she lowered her mouth to his ear and whispered. "Rest, Father."

Without Mother would he want to live? She put body-mending herbs in his mouth, her whisper as shaky as her hand. "Mix this with mouth water. I cannot make tea." *Sweet Etumu.* She of quiet strength. Of deft fingers. Of bottomless pride in her man. Gone. Part of a moan escaped.

A bubbly sound came from Father, then a rasp, "Americanos."

She found his cool dry hand, held it between hers. "I know. They are in the village." She now felt like a spirit herself, hovering, disbelieving.

Weakly his hand squeezed hers. "Go." Then it went limp.

She bent forward, relieved to feel air from his nose. Go? Surely he didn't expect her to leave!

He whispered, in the voice of a child awakening from a dream, "Bad here. Go now. Far away," then went unconscious.

She cradled his big head, rocking gently, her face wet with tears. Soon the sun would come from his eastern house and the Americanos would awaken. She would not go. Could not leave Father.

He needed her. The umne needed her. Mother must be buried, and the others. She had no idea how she would do this with the murdering Americanos present. Perhaps they would leave. She would wait, healing Father by night. Oam-shu, Angelica Root, would help her know what to do.

When the first gray sky leaked through the willows, she lay on the coarse sand with Grizzly Hair at her side, Billy on the other. The willow-people hid them. She heard the whisper of small animal feet in the gravel. Then came the crunching crackling, smacking sounds of a large animal eating flesh and bone. The roots of her hair moved.

The horrible sounds continued and she couldn't stop the gruesome scenes in her mind. Billy slept beside her and Father's breathing continued, barely detectable to her lips. Dew fell, intensifying the medicinal smell of willow and the thick odor of blood.

Suddenly she remembered that Elitha and Perrimacoo had planned to return to Rancho Sacayak. Perhaps after the sleep. They would help, possibly alert the Omuchumne, many of whom were related to the dead, and Pedro would come.

Steadily the sky lightened through cracks in the willows, but morning as she had known it was gone. In none of the stories since the time of the

Ancients had anything like this happened. Here in the home place there would
be no banter, no bathing in the river, no praises to the spirits. She felt like a
rabbit alone in the universe under the cold eye of Molok.

❧

"Shee-it! These injuns'll stink up the place good by t'morra." Five Americanos moved around the beach among the gnawed bodies.

Lying loosely over Billy, a stone's toss from the bad men, María held his
mouth closed and barely breathed as she strained to see. Scorpion Trail, Singing Grass and Four Bears lay at grotesque angles, the others hidden from her
worm's-eye perspective. Any motion would be seen. She lay as still as a lizard,
narrowing her eyes to hide the whites, a color that attracted attention. All
night Father's breathing had been too shallow for sleep, but she must not go
back to him now. She would trust the plant people to help him.

A leather shirt bent over and grabbed Scorpion Trail's man's parts, sliced
them off and kicked the next body. The head lolled her direction. Sun-through-
the-Mist. The storyteller's face looked taut, shiny, resigned to his fate.

As the murderers moved among the bodies, clouds of flies rose and descended. Half the village. Other bodies lay on the field, and when seeking
herbs she had stumbled on Grasshopper Wing in the bushes just outside the
circle of houses. If the killers remembered that Father had been in the path,
they would search for him.

A leather shirt grabbed something she couldn't see, and with a ripping
sound pulled free a big white cloth. She held her breath. It was the Americana
garment that Mother had worn so proudly. Tossing it aside, he bent over and
worked with his knife.

Nausea curled up her throat. She swallowed bile. Even if the proper songs
were sung, mutilation confounded the spirits of the dead. Mother might never
find her way to the happy land.

Straightening with his trophies, the man called to the others, "Gots me
a good pair a titties." He stepped to the stand-up mortar rock, the smooth
greenstone where Mother had pounded meal all her life, and laid out the
breasts to dry in the sun.

She squeezed out the sight, tears running from her closed eyes. The bad
luck, even death that would come to her unborn child as a result of witness-
ing this shrank beside the sharpness of the larger horror, the emptiness. She
had looked forward to the closeness with Mother during the Cry, needed her
quiet strength. *This is a dream.* She blinked, tried to make the scene vanish.
But it would not. Then as she looked across the bodies, a welcome numbness
descended like fog, the murderers' movements seeming to slow, their voices
receding and unreal. Surely now this was a dream.

"Hell, just throw 'em in the river, git 'em floatin in the current." A leather
shirt tossed the long-awaited infant of Scorpion Trail and Singing Grass into

the water, the tiny backside floating in the sun-sparkled water. They reached for Singing Grass, then Etumu.

Numbly she watched as Mother and the friends of her childhood were dragged by the hair and thrown into the water. A leather shirt lifted what seemed a child, but the head lolled as he swung the body back and forth for the toss, and in the instant the face turned her way, she saw it was Old Dishi.

A witch's spell. She should have thought of that before. An unknown enemy had paid a powerful doctor to make her see what wasn't there. In reality her people were bathing and eating their nu-pah. She blinked hard and reached for the power to make the vision vanish.

Dishi splashed into the water and the river-baby opened her liquid spirit to the softness of the Old One who had sung to it for so many seasons. If this were a spell, she was powerless against it, watching as the body drifted toward a gentler resting place than this beach of carnage. She felt herself drifting with it, but caught her spirit, held it in check. She must stay strong for Father and Billy. Only power countermanded a magic spell. But if it were real—

"Looky thar. The bloat keeps 'em afloat, movin down the river."

"Naw. The biguns'll jam up like logs."

"Mebbe. Down at McCoon's place." Laughter.

"Wall, caint think of a finer roost." More laughter came and the smell of blood.

Hands clapped on leather-covered thighs. "Serve him right fer sellin us claims in a nigger nest."

A man lifted his hat and scratched his head. "Fergittin the gold is yah? Why ifn McCoon hadna—"

"That sneaky old tar done sold us these here claims fer one reason and donchew forget it. Cuz these varmints already took out the gold. Fer him! We wasn't sposed to git none." The bearded chin jutted like a weapon. "We was damn lucky to figger it out atall. Wouldna, cept fer dispatchin these here Diggers."

"Wildcat's right. Serve ole McCoon good to git stank out!" Laughter.

"Ifn he don't git t'home fer a week, won't that smell purty!" Loud guffaws. He grabbed a cousin-nephew. "Gitcher self one bout this size and see if ya can throw fur as me."

Bile welled up again. María covered Billy's eyes as he struggled to see. She shut her eyes and rested her chin on the sand, willing the vomit back down. The umne slaughtered. She and Father might be the only ones left.

⁂

When the sun had traveled west, she heard a horse. Then from the village center, a man's call. "Ahoy!"

Perrimacoo. Strange to hear his jaunty cry. Surely he would help. Billy began to say "Da—" She clapped her hand over it.

The Americanos, who had been washing sand and gravel, stood along the shore facing the village, water streaming from the baskets the women had coiled.

Perrimacoo yelled again, "Where's me herders?"

Wildcat cocked his head. "He talkin bout them thievin savages?"

The gravel crunched nearer.

"Mebbe we orter tell him how much we 'preciate buyin claims chock full of Injuns. Bought dear too." Loud enough for him to hear.

"Yeah. Injuns washin out the gold afore we could git to it."

Stepping closer, Perrimacoo shouted, "Where's me niggers?"

"Cleaned out the EN-tire nest."

"Ever one," Wildcat echoed, cocking his hairy head. "Saved ya the trouble."

A leather shirt pointed at the sand. "Come see the blood fer yerself. Thar, and thar, and thar." He looked up proudly. "Floated 'em on down to yer place." Smiles stretched the lips in their hairy beards.

An arm's length from where she lay with her chin on the sand in the edge of the willows, Perrimacoo's boots stepped by. The dark pants on his hips shifted toward the leather shirts, his handgun snug in its holster. Make them leave, she said to his mind.

He stood over Scorpion Trail's blood, then glanced around at other dark spots, squinting toward her, but not seeing. Shoot the murderers, she told him from her mind.

His voice cracked. "Ent got no right to do this."

"T'liminate varmints? On our claims? The hell we ain't!"

Wildcat added, "They'da turned on ya, sure as shootin. Jest 'ike they did them missionaries up in Oregon territory. Heared about the Whitmans? Butchered to bits with tomahawks."

"These Indians was peaceful." He sounded choked.

Wildcat widened his stance like he expected a fight, his beard jutting toward Perrimacoo. "Ain't no sech thing as a peaceful redskin. Now the sooner you Californy greenhorns larn that, the safer we'll all be. Look, we left most of the scalps for you. Send 'em on in to the agent of the You-nited States gov'ment. Pays six dollars apiece bounty. Good fer it too."

Perrimacoo shuffled back toward María, then stopped, turned toward the five leather shirts, his scratchy voice betraying his lack of power. "Me niggers was savin me gold, they was. Any you found in their shanties, hits mine. It wasn't on yer claims."

They exchanged glances, Wildcat assuming a big-eyed, innocent look. "Wye, we ain't found nuttin like at, have we boys?"

"Hell no."

"Uh-uuh. But let's show him the way outa here." The speaker dropped his basket and started toward Perrimacoo, the others following.

Swiftly Perrimacoo walked away. *Shoot them!* The thump of her heart sounded loud. Then hooves pounded away, and the Americanos laughed. And they stayed in the river, so she couldn't move.

The gray-green willow leaves fluttered against her cheek, an evening breeze coming to life. Shovels in hand, the Americanos poked around the boulders and rocks of the swimming place searching for gold. Overhead, vultures flickered in and out of her slim wedge of sight, circling. She pushed backwards through the sand to Father.

His shallow breathing hadn't changed. He was unconscious. "I cannot leave you," she whispered.

She felt the spiritual numbness begin to lift, exposing the raw surface of her mind. Every thought stung. She couldn't accept this fate. It was Molok's dream. She couldn't shake the thought of flinging herself at the men as they squatted by the river's edge with the baskets and stabbing them in the back, or when they made water. Molok was not to be mocked. She'd known that, but she had expected to be stoic when the end came. Yet her mind burned on.

She would go to Bear Claw. He had spells that killed. She would need something belonging to each leather shirt to make the magic work. That would be easy. Like infants, they made no attempt to scatter their urine. But even the thought of vengeance didn't quench the burning in the raw tissues of her soul.

She must get Pedro to avenge the murders. And yes, Pedro must help find any of her people who had fled. Together they would bury the dead. And he must help her protect the home place, for it was more than people, she realized now. It was the dancehouse, the ashes and bones of her ancestors, and spirits who lived in the boulders, and the animals and plants, and Grandmother Howchia watching from the big mother oak. Ignorant murderers had defiled everything—a defilement that started with the condor robe. Perrimacoo must go. The baskets of gold were gone, but she knew how to get a thousand dollars so Pedro could pay him to leave.

Molok's unblinking eye encompassed the world. Be quiet my soul. Accept what is.

Coyote laughed on the hill.

# 58

Bloody bastards!" Perry shouted, kicking the bucket across the room. It ricocheted off the wall in a shower of water and dry adobe flakes.

Elitha flinched. He'd been raging for an hour, ever since he came back from finding the bodies. She feared his anger would spread to her.

"Butchered a cow too. Like to skin em alive and keel haul em, I would!"

Devastated at what had happened, she kept her eyes down. She couldn't stop thinking about Indian Mary walking home yesterday. She'd seen her pass by. Was she dead too?

"Shot the babes along with the mums," he'd railed, shaking his lowered head. His head came up and he glared at her. "Have ye nuthin to say?"

"I, I—" Nothing came.

"Glad be ye Billy's dead? And now ye have no other babe before yours? That it, is it?"

"Perry, I like Billy. It's sickening what happened. I—"

"Oh shut yer blatherin trap!" He kicked the bucket to the ceiling. She flinched as it clattered down with a big chunk of dry mud. "Not a herder left to work me cattle. And every pinch of gold gone too!"

She kept her face a mask of placid concern, recalling that he was the one who invited those trappers in. "Maybe some of the Indians are hiding."

He eyed her. "Oh clever! Married to a dolt, do ye judge? Think I didn't look?" He swung his leg back for another kick. With a crash the bucket went through a window. "Now look what ye made me do!"

She stepped toward the door, planning an excuse about collecting greens. She needed time alone to absorb what had happened. She would go to the el- derberry trees, where an Indian might hide. She knew other places. And the tree where the old blind Indian grandmother sat. She reached the doorway.

He bellowed, "No ye don't!" and yanked her arm, flung her like a sack. She stumbled against the table, knocked his rifle to the floor. Her hip bone hurt.

"Fuck ye, then kill ye, their kind would."

When dark fell he slept with his pepperbox revolver on his chest. Elitha wept silent tears for the Indians. For Pa and Tamsen. For herself and the baby inside her.

⚓

María tossed a pebble through Perrimacoo's broken window, and then crouched behind the oak.

Dry grass rustled behind her. She spun toward it. In a shred of moonlight she saw the backside of a skunk waddle past. She turned back to the window. She would ask Elitha to care for Billy. Even in the bad house he couldn't be in more danger than with her. She felt for another pebble, found a piece of wood, threw it.

It thunked on the door she'd helped make. Under the brooding oaks the house looked ghostly.

The door moved, the barrel of a gun nosing it open.

She lunged behind the tree as a thunderbolt exploded. A tongue of red flame died. She stifled Billy's cry, knowing the gun would bring bad men who were a short walk away.

Perrimacoo called, "Who goes there?"

"Mary."

"Mary? Come here." He stood in the open doorway.

She approached, stopping well before him.

Elitha appeared at his side in a long white gown, dark hair to her waist. "You're alive!" she whispered excitedly. "We thought you'd been killed."

María extended Billy toward her, still covering his mouth. "Keep Billy here, por favor."

Elitha came out and took him, replacing María's hand over his mouth. "Have you been hiding?"

"Sí." She stroked Billy's cheek with the backs of her fingers. "Gracias. They will think he's yours."

Perrimacoo said, "Is Captain Juan alive?"

"Sí." When she left him, he'd been breathing.

"I needs him to help herd me cattle out of here."

"His death is near. Por favor, go tell Señor Valdez to come help." Strange that Perrimacoo was her best hope.

He scratched his head.

She heard horses. Knowing she might never see her son again, she darted into the shadows. But now, if she got caught, he wouldn't die with her.

<hr />

Before breakfast Perry uncorked the aguardiente. By mid-morning he was staggering. Elitha rocked Billy on her lap. He hadn't eaten a thing, mewling softly, saying things she didn't recognize. She mustered the nerve to speak her mind to Perry. "I think you'd better go get Mr. Valdez."

He raked his fingers through his hair, forming clumps. He lifted the cup and swallowed. "Ent goin."

She stopped rocking and looked at him. "You could get there and back with Señor Valdez in two hours. I'll mind Billy."

"Girl, I SAID no!"

What was the matter with him! Indian Mary and her father needed help.

"Put yer damned eyeballs back in. I ent riding into no nest of vipers with no..." glance darting around the room, "greaser!"

"But—"

"But nuthin. Shut yer flappin mouth!"

She stood with Billy, thinking he wouldn't hit her while she held his son. She must appeal to his vanity. "You are so good on a horse, Perry. You and Mr. Valdez could clean those men right out of here."

"Oh sure. Ride up to the five men I sold claims to and—" He bowed, made his voice sweet. "If ye please, sirs, be so good as to vacate yer claims."

"They killed our Indians, Perry. Your vaqueros!"

"So?" His eyes were black points in red mazes.

"You could send for the sheriff."

He shouted, "Daft ye be! Killin injuns ent against the law."

"Really? These were ranch workers."

"Hell no it's not against the law! But going back on a bargain is. Philosopher Pickett wrote those claims up legal-like." His hands were on his waist and he thrust his face into hers. "Read law in the states, that one did, so quit looking at me with cow eyes."

Mr. Pickett came to her mind—one of the hard drinkers at the fort. She softened her voice, trying not to rile him for fear he'd hit her despite Billy. "It's wrong to kill Indians in cold blood when they're friendly." She couldn't bear the sight of his flared nostrils—the stubborn drunkenness of him. She studied his belligerent face and suddenly knew what bothered him so. He was afraid to do the right thing. In her heart she couldn't help but think how different John Rhoads would be acting now.

She sat down on the stump stool, rocking, knowing she must fetch Señor Valdez by herself. But how? "There, there," she soothed the whimpering child, "Your mamma will come back."

Perry took another swig, glared at her, then took the cup to bed and curled around it, facing the wall.

*Not against the law to massacre Indians.* The thought cut into her like the sun fracturing through the jagged shards of window-glass, a puzzle of light reflecting over the floor and half the table. It crept slowly across the table as Perry lay silent and Billy sobbed quietly. She couldn't imagine living here without the Indians. Ranching would be impossible. She moved out of the encroaching sun and sat lightly on the edge of the bed.

He got up, stepped outside the drape and peed by the door—a disgusting habit that brought flies and acrid odor. He looked old and tired, buttoning himself. "The buggers'll kill all me cows." He uncorked the barrel and the liquid splashed into his cup.

"Wouldn't the cows run off first, being so wild and all?"

"Oh and I suppose that'd maik it better." His dream of being a country squire had died with the Indians. He was like a cornered animal, frustrated and angry.

How would she sneak out? Watching his boots, fearing a kick, she patted Billy's hair and murmured, "I'm so sorry, Perry."

With a mad glimmer in his eye, he stepped toward her, liquor breath blasting.

Eat, she thought. That's what tom turkeys did when beset by hostile males pecking and jumping on their heads. She nibbled the salt pork she'd been trying to feed Billy.

Like a turkey, Perry backed away.

"Here Billy." She put the pork to his lips. He jerked his head from it, brown eyes wet from weeping. "Poor thing," she murmured, "Hasn't eaten a thing."

"Oh fer Chrissake, he won't starve!"

Quietly she rocked to and fro. "You're right. He's only been here overnight."

Suddenly the lines of Perry's face softened. He stood looking at the wall. Then, as if they'd been playing tiddlywinks, he said, "I'll be ridin to Sutter's camp." He picked up his gun. "You go to Daylor's with Billy."

Scheming something, but she wouldn't ask. Soon Señor Valdez would be helping Indian Mary—if it wasn't too late.

# 59

The sun was at their backs but still high when Pedro and Quapata tied their horses at McCoon's vacant adobe. Pedro had suggested the Indian stay at Sheldon's ranch, but his dark face had hardened and he said, "I help. My woman's people are dead." Every inch a man.

In the dead heat beneath the canopies of lichen-encrusted oak trees, they walked up the hill between boulder outcroppings, Pedro gripping the Allen pepperbox revolver before him, stalking the disgracers of God, the stinking human trash, the cowards who killed women and infants. Quapata, arrow on bowstring, walked quickly and quietly, his full otterskin quiver slung across his back. The missing finger made no difference. He could get off a second arrow faster than Pedro could turn his chambered barrel.

Nearing the crest of the second hill, Pedro touched Quapata and nodded toward a clump of buckeye trees. They ducked under the branches and kneeled. "The North Americans are probably at the river," he said, "looking for gold." He tilted his presidio hat, pointing down the hill toward an unmarked route through the rocks. Quapata, eyes quiet as a snake's, nodded in agreement.

Maybe María would see them from wherever she was hiding. Thanks be to God she had asked Elitha to care for Billy. In McCoon's house! The instant he'd heard that, he'd known the full extent of the danger. His heart tripped at the thought of being too late. He tried to walk like the barefoot Indian, but the grass stalks were dry, the fallen leaves crisp. Everything crunched under his boots. Five men. Elitha had been sure. If he could get close enough, the Allen being accurate only at close range, he could finish two before they knew what happened. Quapata could too. That left one. Were there more? Was the old North American here? He should have sent him to hell when he had the chance.

He crouch-ran to the mounded blackberries, blinking through sweat to see the Indian houses on the other side. The call of a distant quail cut through the heat and he realized that an alert woodsman would have heard a tunnel of quail silence across the hills, would notice the screaming jays, the whistle of a ground squirrel sentinel. The old North American and his ilk hunted beaver. Men like him learned from Blackfoot and Apache. Cunning, brave, brutal.

The village was deserted, two houses torn apart for firewood. No sign of the enemy. Lying in ambush? He motioned with his gun for Quapata to circle the other way, and ran from hut to hut toward the river, noticing bedrolls and saddles. Good. They were still here. He sprinted across the open space on his way to the beach. Over the soft hiss of the river he heard a man's voice.

"Company."

He stepped behind a dense thicket of willows, kneeling to see through an opening, relieved that they had been complacent.

A gun cracked just ahead.

No ball thudded in the sand or came through the trees. Aimed for Quapata. Knee-high buckskin moccasins stepped on the path before his nose. The feet moved uncertainly, toes pointing the other way. Turning this way and that. Large feet, bigger than the old man's.

Pedro raised the Allen, pointed to where the chest would be, fired. *One.* He turned the barrel a click and jumped into the sunshine, stopping the man's forward pitch, using him as a shield as he fired at four men running at him, the old North American not among them.

Two went down, one gripping an arrow in his chest, the other diving. Two balls left. Pedro let the wounded man, who had absorbed his friend's ball, slouch before him. He turned the barrel to number three.

Something buzzed against his shoulder and he saw a sixth man eyeing him down a smoking barrel.

Firing, Pedro flung himself across the trail. A puff of dust rose where he'd been. The wounded man crawled toward him like a lizard, leading with his pistol, grimacing in pain.

Pedro turned and squeezed. *Four.* The man's mouth opened wide in his beard.

He scrambled deep into the willows, hand in pocket for four more balls and powder packets. Whirling to watch his back, willow branches in his eyes and face, he unlocked and opened the barrel with trembling fingers and stuffed the balls and packets into the grooves. Something moved in the willows. He closed the lock. It was María on her knees! Wild-eyed. She pointed at a mound shrouded in leaves, black hair showing. Captain Juan. He looked dead.

Giving her the down signal, he squirmed to the edge of the thicket. Chin on the sand, he lay searching the brow of the gravel, the water's edge. Nothing moved in the beach clearing. Where was Quapata? He felt pain in his shoulder and saw his vest torn, blood on it, a slight wound. Bugs were suddenly crawling all over his face, and arms—tiny purple iridescent beetles streaming down from the willows.

He squirmed forward, blinking beetles from his eyes.

A gun reported from behind. He whirled and saw willows thrashing. A man reloading, María out of sight. He fired. Hit the gun arm. The pistola fell to the ground. The man dropped to his knees, reaching for the gun.

He turned the barrel a click, aimed and squeezed. The man's head jerked back, the bushy beard up, a hole singed in the exposed white neck. The gun dropped. Wiping beetles from his face, Pedro pushed through the willows and saw the man was dead. He stuffed the extra gun in his sash, saw María rising from a pile of spent branches, and crawled back to the edge of the thicket.

Quapata stepped from the bushes near where the sixth man had appeared. With a bare foot he rolled a body, signaled Pedro the man was dead and pointed his stub at an injured man a short distance from away. Alive but harmless, moaning, an arrow in his side.

Pedro pointed the barrel between the man's pleading eyes and said, "Now I give you more mercy than you gave to women and children." He squeezed the trigger.

A piece of the head chipped off, pink matter oozing.

He stepped cautiously from the willows, looking around. Four men lay sprawled on the sand. Another dead in the willows. Watching the bodies, alert for gunfire from the bushes, he joined Quapata, whose next arrow was ready, and asked, "Any more?"

"One went that way." He pointed his stub past the brambles on the creek.

The first man Pedro had shot moved, touched his gun. Pedro walked over and stood over him. Too weak to lift his rifle, the man looked up, terror in his face. Like shooting a wounded horse. He fired, making a dark hole in the white forehead, and turned away.

As Quapata cut the throat of the other wounded man, María crept out of the willows, curly leaves all through her hair and terrible strain in her face. Pedro went to her and pulled her into his arms.

"Pedro. Oh Pedro. Gracias," she said into his chest.

"Amapolita mía, thanks to the Virgin I came in time."

"You are hurt," she said drawing back, looking at his shoulder.

"It is nothing. We go now, rapidamente." One man had escaped, but he would come back, possibly with others. He scanned the bushes, seeing nothing and told her to go to her father. "We'll bring horses."

He and Quapata quickly saddled one of the North American horses and a mule, and led them to the willows. María scrambled on with her carrying basket while Quapata and Pedro gently laid Captain Juan, still breathing, across the mule's saddle. He had leaf compresses on his back.

They took a circuitous route toward McCoon's cabin, far off the trail through the blue oaks, Quapata leading the mule with Captain Juan, Pedro leading the horse with María. As the animals broke sticks and kicked rocks, his heart was in his throat to see her sitting tall in the saddle. An easy target. He walked before her, swinging his four-shooter from side to side.

Ahead, a man yelped.

Quapata gave Pedro the rein and signaled him to stay with María. Positioning an arrow in his bow, the Indian crouch-ran ahead.

In a minute or two he called, "Come señor." Calm, assured voice.

Pedro led María to where Quapata stood with his drawn bow aimed at a man in a buckskin shirt and torn canvas trousers, light gray except for a large dark spot in front. He had wet himself. He was on the ground an arm's length away, clutching his wrist.

"Monster rattler got me." He made an exaggerated face of pain. "Don't mean you no harm." His eyes darted from Quapata's arrow, the point of which would drive into an eye, to Pedro's gun. "Palaver English?" His voice quavered.

"You killed the Indians."

"No. I warn't thar," he whined, "Honest." About Pedro's size, younger, silky brown beard.

"Where are your compadres."

"Don't have none." He glanced at his wrist. "I needs to suck the poison out, sir." His eyes pleaded.

Dipping his hat at Quapata, who hadn't slackened his draw, Pedro looked at the North American and said, "That Indian speaks no English and he is not happy. His relatives were murdered." He picked up the rifle and shrugged as if he couldn't do a thing about it. "Indians believe in revenge."

"Please sir, tell him I didn't kill no Injuns."

Squaring his shoulders, Pedro ordered, "Give me your other gun."

He fumbled with his good hand, tossed a four-shooter to Pedro's feet. The other hand hung limp and pink, swelling. He must have been crawling in the rocks to get bitten on the wrist. But Pedro was tired of killing, and the fear on the young face was giving him an idea. "Do me a favor, señor."

"Oh yes sir. Anything you say sir. Yes sir."

"Tell everybody you meet that a Spaniard named Joaquín will kill any North American who sets foot within five miles of this ranchería. Will you do that?"

"Oh yes seenyer." It rhymed with meaner. "Are you Wakeen?"

"Sí. And tell them my vaquero here, Tres Dedos, can shoot a tick off a coyote at half a league. Do you know what Tres Dedos means?"

"No, seenyer."

"Three Fingers."

The man looked at Quapata's maimed hand, still pulling the bowstring, and swallowed. "Yes sir. I'll tell ever man I see."

"Is that your mule?" Pedro pointed with his eyes to a grazing animal.

"Take him, seenyer."

"Gracias. Pata, no lo mate." Slowly the Indian slackened his bow.

"Oh seenyer! Thankee kindly for my life." The coward was weeping.

"De nada." For nothing.

When it was clear they hadn't been followed, Pedro sent Quapata ahead to Rancho Omuchumne, where he was sorely needed. He then rode beside María heading the same way. Progress was painfully slow because of Captain Juan's injuries and his obvious pain.

The sweet-wise aura of María, her bearing proud as she sat tall in the teeth of tragedy, her breasts swaying with the horse, her body streaked with pale dirt, made him swallow a hard lump. Mother of God! No Spanish woman could do that.

They were halfway to Rancho Omuchumne when Pedro remembered the baskets of gold. But he couldn't leave María, and couldn't ask her to turn back with him. Captain Juan was more important. Besides, what good was gold now? Even if Señor Sheldon got the land for him, the Indians were dead. And he had to be the most wanted man in the territory.

But outlaws needed gold too. He exhaled, vowing to ride back tomorrow. The man with the rattlesnake bite would probably live, and could identify him. To protect the patrón he must leave Rancho Omuchumne for good, maybe live in the wilderness. But for now María and her father needed the sanctuary of the room above the gristmill.

# 60

Dew fell heavily in the morning, two moons after the massacre. It sweetened the bleached grass before the sun rose behind the browning trees, but María moved from task to task like a cold-blooded creature, wiped clean of joy. Already she had collected herbs for Father's morning tea, and was on her way up the millhouse stairs.

Perrimacoo's brown and white horse suddenly stepped around the corner. "Where's your hair?" he said with a grin. She had singed it off to the scalp.

"My people are dead. Where are you going?"

"Came to see you."

"I am here." Standing halfway up the stairs, higher than Perrimacoo on his horse, she adjusted the burden basket and looked up to see Pedro in the window. She was anxious about every man who came to Sheldon's mill, worried about avengers coming for him.

"Elitha me wife says to me one day yer boyfriend was saving gold to buy me rancho. And I says to meself, Perry, says I, I'll go see about it."

"No more gold now." The morning after they'd arrived, Roberto had galloped in with news of a grizzly killing a cow. After tracking the animal for half a day, Pedro had gone back to the home place, but found no gold. Several new pairs of North Americans had been panning in the area, and she'd been relieved he hadn't tried to kill them, despite his threat. Before the sleep she'd made him promise not to think of the lost gold. They were already sad.

Under the leather hat Perrimacoo's eyes were blue glints in thickets of dark lashes. She turned and climbed the stairs.

"I might could make ye a bargain."

Wishing he wouldn't make her say things twice, she stopped and looked at him. "We have no gold."

His jaw shifted and his eyes took on a different cast, though his relaxed posture remained. "Come with me to Sutter's Piney Creek and you'll get rich in a few days." He smiled like a man who thought himself wise.

"You want me to couple with Captain Sutter so you could take the money. I know how much he would pay me."

"You bitch." The smile remained, insolent now.

She turned and climbed two more steps.

"All right then, you taik TWO hundred dollars a night."

She opened Pedro's door and shut it behind her.

Several mornings later barefoot footsteps sounded on the stairs. Pedro was out with the cattle. She opened the door. It was an Omuchumne man, home from Dry Diggings. His pained expression told her he knew of the murder of her people. "My people are on their way home," he said. "Today they will arrive. We will dance the Yumeh, The Cry."

He left. She turned to Father, gaunt and motionless on his mat, eyes closed. Knowing he had heard, she said, "I will go wait for my friends in their village center."

It had taken more strength than she had to stop her mind from revisiting the bloody scenes of the home place. She had begun to feel adrift, even from Pedro. It had been too quiet around Mill Ranch with all the Omuchumne away. She longed to see Blue Star, and Billy missed playing with his best friend, Shorty, people called him. Taking Billy with her, she quietly closed the door behind her.

As she walked along the path cushioned by fallen leaves, wind—the kind that might bring rain—moved across the short stubble of her hair. With the trees and vines becoming bare, the Omuchumne houses and granaries were visible from a greater distance than usual.

The empty u-machas looked forlorn with a dust devil dancing around them. Outside Blue Star's house, María put Billy down and was glad to see Blue Star there. Making the wait seem shorter, they talked about Mr. Sheldon's generosity in allowing his workers to leave for the Yumeh, the power at the old dancehouse being stronger than in the makeshift dance place at the Diggings. They also looked forward to the Yumeh, when they could think about and talk about their murdered parents and family members. Their unspeakable grief was shared yet unspoken. Meanwhile Billy and Shorty played with the leaves drifting from the oaks.

By twos and threes the Omuchumne arrived, men followed by women and children. Tomaka embraced María and Blue Star with her expression before she wrapped her big arms around her. "We are sad about your people," she said into her hair, her breath warm, her huge breasts comforting.

Hugging Tomaka in return, María blinked tears away, and felt sympathy pouring into her from the hands that rubbed her back and shoulders. Tomaka was the Omuchumne birth-helper.

Blue Star stepped back as Omuch approached and spoke to María and Blue Star:

"We are home for the Anniversary Cry," he said. "You two and your hy-apo are invited to celebrate the dance of the dead with us. We will dance in eight sleeps."

That soon. She doubted Father would be well enough. And the Omuchumne must gather and hunt for the feasts. They would weave new baskets, decorate the dancehouse, and repair the costumes. No dance was more needful of careful preparation. María and Blue Star anticipated with joy helping their friends with these tasks, and were almost glad for the rush. It would steer their minds from the river of blood.

🌿

Four sleeps later her fingers were flying over a new cooking basket when again quiet footsteps sounded on the stairs. She opened the door and saw to her great joy two cousin-brothers, Spear Thrower and Stalking Egret, neither of whom she expected to see again. She couldn't stop staring at their strong young bodies, unharmed. "You're alive," was all she could say. Then she remembered her manners and invited them in.

Grizzly Hair woke from a nap and rose on an elbow, the corners of his lips turning up in a smile. "Where are you going?" he asked politely, but his tone was high and weak. He looked much older without hair, and wrinkled skin hung loose from his upper arms.

Though their eyes betrayed deep sorrow for the loss of the People, they were clearly relieved to find María and her father. They sat on the floor beside his mat, telling how they and their wives and children had been living with the Wapumne, east from the home place. "We went back and burned the dead," said Spear-Thrower.

Grizzly Hair nodded approvingly, then looked over their heads.

"We made a platform fire and burned them and what was left of their belongings. We went downstream and found more bodies and carried them to the burn place. We sang their spirits away. We buried the ashes in the round-house mound."

Grizzly Hair exhaled, a burden visibly lifting from him. He said, "Omuch invites your families to his Anniversary Cry, beginning after the sleep."

"We will attend," said Spear-Thrower.

Stalking Egret added, "We go now to bring our women and children from the Wapumne home place."

"Are there others?"

"We are the only survivors, hy-apo."

"Where will you live?"

They exchanged a glance. Then Spear-Thrower said, "Now that we have found our esteemed headman, we will ask Omuch for permission to build houses in his village. We want to live near you."

The cousin-brothers left and Grizzly Hair closed his eyes, arms at his sides as he lay on his mat. A strong man, María realized, returning to her basket-weaving. She recalled how he had endured the cutting into his flesh. She'd been frightened watching the doctor from the southern river slash into his back, hunting for lead balls that pained him so terribly. The blood gushed, but he made no sound. The doctor pulled out one bloody ball, and said another was lodged too near his spine. It must remain. He had stitched the holes together, and she put healing herbs on the wounds.

But when she took baskets to pay the doctor, he stopped her with an up-raised palm. "I owed your father. Today I paid him."

"She didn't know of any debt." Grizzly Hair had never tossed dunning sticks into their u-machas.

"All Indian people owe your father. He was war chief against the black hats."

Now, she proudly regarded Father's unmoving face. Here lay a man of knowledge, one who had defeated many enemies. Now he was conquering more evils within his body.

❦

Eight days had passed. Pedro came in early from the range, and Grizzly Hair announced, "I will dance."

"Can you walk?" María asked. She had seen him struggle to stand.

The sunken eyes glittered with determination. Slowly he pushed up from his mat, steadying himself on a bent knee, then pulled himself to his full height. His rib cage protruded from his once-fleshy form, jutting from the concavity of his stomach. Skin hung in folds from his inner thighs and draped over his bony knees. He looked worse upright than on the bed.

Shocked by his shaking, and sensing the pain from the gun ball inside him, María put his arm over her shoulder and helped him to the door. "Come Billy," she called. Determination like this was to be encouraged.

A step at a time they descended the staircase, him towering over her,

Billy trailing. She helped them both bathe and cleanse themselves in the river, rubbing them with soaproot and cleansing herbs. She replenished the wormwood bundle hanging with Father's amulet, gave him some for his nostrils, and tied on her skirt. On the path to the Omuchumne roundhouse, people passed by them, turning to look curiously at the three as they walked, painfully slow.

Near the roundhouse the dance doctor pushed his shoulder under Grizzly Hair's other arm and helped him down the ramp through the low door to the northwest pole, where the ill would receive special strength from the ceremony. The doctor spoke to a family seated in the pine boughs. "The esteemed hy-apo of the eastern village will join you."

They moved aside, the mother holding a small boy with blistered skin, giving the post of honor to Grizzly Hair. He crossed his legs and sat impassively, eyes unfocused, preparing to receive the spirits. Blue Star and Quapata sat on María's other side, and the two friends squeezed each other's hand.

María inhaled pine scent until it tingled and cleansed her. She patted the boughs beside her to show Billy where to sit. Earth's cool breath in the dug-out roundhouse would help wash away the anguish of the last two moons. It was time to speak the names of the dead, to commune with the spirits of Crying Fox, Etumu, Dishi, Singing Grass, Scorpion Trail, Running Quail, Grasshopper Wind, Sunshine-through-the-Mist and many, many more.

As the roundhouse filled with Omuchumne, the ceremonial fire was lit between the four posts. Light from the doorway dimmed with nightfall, the orange flames leaping brighter. Spirit food was brought by the women— oo-lah, acorn soup, and peppermint tea. A buzz of conversation came from the hundred or more people seated around the wall, but Grizzly Hair never spoke.

The deep heartbeat of the drum started. In a floor-length black feather robe, Raven stepped from the shadows, hopping toward the snapping fire. The dance doctor shook his magic bundle in each of the four directions while the bird flitted around and addressed the congregation in formal, sing-song tones.

Although María had attended a Cry every year, never had the words gripped her so urgently. She embraced the spirits of her lost kin. Now she could speak, sing and wail their names, cry aloud Etumu and Grandmother Dishi and all the individual spirits. Beside her, Billy watched the dancing spirit-impersonator, his giant shadow looming on the encircling wall as he moved around the fire, facing all the people.

The dance doctor pointed his purple obsidian knife at María and others. She joined the women forming a circle outside the circle of dancing men, nearer the fire. Tomaka's rich singing to the beat of the sacred drum filled the dancehouse. Her soulful calling of the dead pulsed inside María, moving her feet as she bounced in the women's line past the men, stomping on the earth in heartbeat with the mysteries of life, shaking the dead, rousing them, bringing them back to their weeping families. The first spirits swooped. Goose bumps shivered down her spine. She barely noticed the scuffle by the door.

She glanced over there and saw Americanos trying to shove their way inside. A flash of fear. They looked drunk. Did they have guns? The people nearest the door pushed them out, and she heard laughter. She prayed the spirits would not be angry. These were white men, like so many others who had followed Captain Sutter to his southern mining camp—noisy, dirty men. But mostly friendly to Indian people.

The drum continued to move her around the fire, one foot, then the other. She felt herself blend with the song, with the man-dancers passing by, and with all the people. Then the dance doctor raised his feathered arms. The singing stopped. It was the signal for intimate remembering. She returned to Grizzly Hair.

A flute player took his place beside the drummer, opposite the door. As pairs of mourners sat facing each other at the four poles, the flautist put the instrument to his lips. The otherworldly melody soared beyond the world. She soared with it, ignoring the laughter outside the dancehouse, entering the magic.

Sitting before her on folded legs, Grizzly Hair placed his warm, dry hands on her shoulders and looked into her eyes. "Etumu," he spoke the name aloud. Gooseflesh crinkled the skin on her back and arms.

"Etumu," María repeated, searching his black eyes. She saw the depth of his loneliness. Etumu had meant everything to him, and she had called on him to notice her when she was still a girl, after her sister Oak Gall died in the mission. Mother had done countless small things to enlarge him in the village. She had always looked at him with respect. Now María saw that the love that Mother had for Father was matched by his for her. María stroked his bony chest, then wet her fingers in the streams running from his eyes, allowing her tears to flow unchecked as she too remembered Mother's face, the eye folds, the proud glances at Father. She drew Father to her, put her face against his big bony cheek, mingling tears with memories as they unlocked their everyday restraint.

Etumu's soul enveloped María and she opened herself to it like a child sucking milk.

"When do we get to the fuckin?" An Americano yelled into the dancehouse.

Fear shot through her, but Father only closed his eyes. When he opened them, they shined like damp stones in strong light. Then, quickly, his expression softened and then dimmed. He seemed to shrink as he gazed downward, shoulders slumped.

She understood. He was tired, a guest in another hy-apo's dancehouse, dependent on the generosity of others. He had no people left, except her and

Billy and the two families seated near them. He felt he should have protected the umne from the guns of men like the ones yelling into this spirit house. The ambush had been perfectly timed, when he and others were bathing before supper. The people had been shot as they emerged from the water and ran to their wounded children. Etumu would have reminded him of that, had she been living.

Proper revenge had been carried out by Pedro, a family member, but that didn't bring the umne back. She looked into Father's eyes. He locked her in his gaze, and she saw more than grief for Mother. More than grief for the people.

Etumu said: As long as any people are left, they must live where their ancestors lived. The mortar holes must be visited again. Sing to the river-baby spirit. These things will make Grizzly Hair hy-apo again.

"Thank you Mother," María murmured.

Grizzly Hair was clearly listening to Etumu's secret words for him. He gripped María's elbows as she gripped his. His eyes were deep, solemn, trusting. He and she were more than father and daughter. They were allies. Her strength was to be used for him. His strength, when it returned, would be used for her. She must get Perrimacoo away from the home place and remove his bad luck house. She would need power, and gold. It was time to go to Captain Sutter's camp. Pedro would understand.

# 61

Pedro shouted, "María, you are beyond control!"

What did that mean? She wanted him to hold her, kiss her, murmur of love.

His fists clenched at his sides. "Mother of God, think!" His eyes shot gray flashes at her, then at Billy—a frightened rabbit glancing from one to the other.

Think lingered in the wooden walls. Hadn't she spent the last two days and nights thinking? Far more than four times. His stare knifed her. Before she met Pedro, she would have said his look hurt her stomach, but he insisted that love came from the heart. If so, hers was bleeding. She didn't know exactly how, but she would match her powers against Captain Sutter's and learn his secrets. If she came home with the gold, it would be a sign. Gold would buy the home place back and placate the spirits. But she couldn't explain it in Spanish, except to say, "I go find knowledge."

"Carnal," he growled, eyes sparking fire.

She didn't know the word. Unable to bear his face, she glanced at Father on his mat. The lines of his face were sorrowful, but his sunken eyes held understanding. It took some of the ache from her heart.

Pedro opened the door. "If you go to Sutter's camp, you are a puta!" It came out like spit. "Don't expect me to rescue you." He strode away without breakfast.

She turned to Father. "The spirits told me to go."

"Then you must go. I will talk with Pedro."

⁂

She put Billy into the care of Elitha, who was staying with Señora Catherine, and then swam the river. On the opposite bank the trail led eastward. Repositioning the burden basket, she walked fast all morning. It would be a long uphill trek to Captain Sutter's Creek. She hoped to arrive before the sun entered his western house.

Walking stamped down the memories of the dead, who tried to surface in her mind. It dimmed the flashes of bloated people, once whole and dear. The thump of her feet quieted the alien voice inside her, which said at odd moments, You invited Perrimacoo to stay in the village. You made love with him and looked upon the condor robe when you were impure. You should be dead like your people. Walking helped. She was on the trail to knowledge, the only trail.

Nevertheless, the fight with Pedro lingered inside her. *Beyond control.* It meant nothing that she could understand, but the way he said it tore through her. Already weary with sorrow for her people, now she was battling her man. She had never seen him so angry. She had trusted him to understand.

Her eyes flooded and she saw everything as if under water—the parched hills wavering, the powdered trail where many horses had run. By now Pedro would be in from herding cattle, back in his room for siesta. Could Father explain it all?

Even she found it difficult to voice her love for the home place—a home spun into her thoughts and memories from the moment of birth, interwoven with the lives and spirits of the ancestors, boulders, earth, hills, river, trees, animals—and tamped into her being. She was facing her worst fears for all of that, and for her man so that he could live there freely as a ranchero.

Moisture dried on her cheeks. Bitter indignation welled in her throat as she remembered his red face and clenched fists. Amulet bouncing with her breasts, she walked rapidly, oblivious to the sun's journey above her, uncaring that she was watched by antelope and coyotes and horse-riders passing by.

A rider wearing a red shirt overtook her. Americano. She kept her eyes forward as he walked his mule alongside, watching her. The pan and shovel in his bedroll and his high boots into which his pants were tucked indicated he was a miner, no doubt headed to Sutter's camp. After a time she felt safe and wondered if he would offer her a ride. He rode on.

She had conquered fear. It was a sign. This was the way to face Sutter and his men. Some might be vicious murderers, like the old man who wanted to kill Pedro, all sucking power from Captain Sutter—hadn't Elitha said that? But María had learned magic. She would draw it to her, and by doing so prepare for the chaos of the changing world.

The heat of the long dry was lessening, and she sensed First Rain would soon come. The earth needed it. Everything was dusty, old, hot and weary. She felt the sameness of the rolling brown landscape, and for the first time her feet slowed. The gullies held no memories. The spirits were unfamiliar, silent, dry. Birds and small animals napped out of sight. She wiped gritty perspiration from her eyes, and walked on.

Walking was like the Cry, when people danced to keep their souls from flying apart. Oh, but she wanted Pedro to gallop his horse to her and hold her in his arms. She longed to see his face without anger, to feel his pride in her for undertaking this frightening journey.

But Pedro would not come.

*Puta.* A woman who received gifts in exchange for coupling. She had tried to say she sought something of greater importance, but his ears had been stuffed up. And what if a woman was a puta? Did it give a man license to be impolite? To refuse to help her? Pedro was unreasonable. All people exchanged gifts. To live in the world was to reciprocate kindness for kindness, food for care, money for work, pleasure for pay, doctoring for food. Men hunted and shared. Women gathered and shared. A woman coupled with her man when she didn't feel like it to give him pleasure, but also in exchange for the hides and meat he brought and the house he built. Wasn't every woman a puta?

So why was he angry? She knew, oh she knew! And it made her feet fly. He was blinded by jealousy. He feared she would prefer Captain Sutter. Ridiculous! And he didn't even try to defeat that fear. Pedro was like a young child who hadn't learned the first thing about life. Until he did, his vision would be clouded. *I must be patient.*

Father would make him understand. Oh, she hoped so. The sun was low at her back, Sutter's camp nearby. She could smell it.

At the crest of the hill she looked down on the largest town she had ever seen scattered among the dusty green oaks. A forest of smoke columns rose, flattened into an elliptical black disc over the narrow valley. Pale cloth houses, some round, some square—perhaps two hundred—crowded along a stream that flowed down from steep hills. In the midst of the cloth houses stood a circle of wooden u-machas, steeply pitched, and a roundhouse like the one at home. People meandered among the structures like disturbed ants. At this distance she couldn't tell if any of them were Indians.

Were the bad Americanos among them? Pedro had allowed two to survive. The one with the rattlesnake bite had seen her. They could have friends and relatives down there. The Indians who called this their home place might have been murdered, as her people were. She might be shot on sight, mistaken for one of them. Hand on her amulet, she sat on a rock to renew her strength.

Later, thanking Oam-shu, she headed downhill toward knowledge. The stench of human waste grew worse. Then came the textured aroma of boiling grains and broiling meat. She heard men's voices. Her stomach told her it was suppertime. But too many people occupied this narrow valley. Little food would be found along this muddy stream.

Approaching the first fire—Americanos by their clothes—she held her head high, gaze forward, toward where she sensed Captain Sutter would be. She felt eyes on her, heard talk and boisterous laughter. Whistles and exclamations pushed her along. She let out her breath, relieved that no guns pointed at her. Her power was strong. She saw Indians camping at the far end of the little valley, at the foot of the hills, and felt relief that they were alive. She walked tall, glad her journey was over. She was facing her worst fear, not only of Sutter but of leather shirts.

Some of the camps were unoccupied, the ground littered. Cooking pans, buckets and candles spilled from boxes and bags. Pantaloons, stockings and blankets hung from low limbs. She headed into the most crowded part of the buzzing town, drawn by Captain Sutter. Why did so many men travel without women? So far from their homes? It disturbed nature's harmony.

Aware of being followed, she turned toward the stream where men in hats squatted and swirled pans. Despite the long dry, plenty of water ran in the stream, but the bed of the stream was pitted and opaque with silt. No fish would swim here. She slogged over a hillock of mud and, from the corner of her eye, saw that men followed her, not brandishing guns. They appeared to be curious. She stopped beside a man digging a deep hole, perspiration glistening on the black hair covering most of his face.

"Where is Captain Sutter's house?"

The man's bird-like eyes moved down her length, then up, as he leaned on his muddy shovel. His beak was sharp and long. He turned to another, who sloshed dirty water back and forth in a wooden box as one might rock a baby. They spoke.

Not recognizing the talk, she started to leave.

Fingers gripped her arm. She turned.

The man had quit rocking, and he stood unbuttoning himself with his free hand. Beak Nose was grinning and babbling.

She twisted in the man's grasp, having no wish to couple with smelly strangers. "I go to Captain Sutter!" Remembering that white-skinned men shouted when they meant to be heard, she yelled, "No!" and yanked her arm but couldn't free it.

Beak Nose whipped the cloth from her hips. It fluttered to the ground in a heap of red and yellow. The men who had followed stared at it and at her, as Beak Nose yanked her to him.

From a neighboring campfire an older man rose from a pot he was stirring, and with a raised hand stepped toward Beak Nose. "Gentlemen, gentlemen. Is that necessary?"

Americano. In his middle years. Broad and solid with bushy gray beard. No hat on a thinning gray head. She felt his power. So did Beak Nose, for his grip relaxed.

More men came from their fires, forming a growing spectator circle.

She jerked free, grabbed her skirt and turned to leave.

The older Americano caught her wrist in a stronger grip. Her heart pounced. She scanned for guns in the hands of the crowding men, saw none and reached within herself for calm, for dignified expression, for the power she knew was hers.

The Americano looked at her as he gestured up and down her length with his free hand, speaking to the crowd in the oratorical tones of a headman:

"Gentlemen! Before us trembles the very wildwood flower whose existence has provoked, lo these many nights, so much skepticism of late. I implore you. Cast your eyes upon this rare dark loveliness, and you will see our princess, our Pocahontas, our own Cleopatra of the wilderness." It was Americano talk, yet only a few words sounded familiar.

He paused to survey the men, who were devouring her with their gazes. "Look beneath the mark of barbarism, which so unfortunately mars her otherwise perfect chin. My friends, she alone among the hideous females of her race is worthy of elevation upon the pedestal of Diana." His voice resonated, penetrating, but the alien talk made no sense. Did he mock her?

"Observe the rich color flashing in and out of the dusky cheeks, the natural grace and dignity of her bearing." He stood stiffly, gesturing. "Beneath the crudely cropped hair are a pair of magnificently lustrous eyes, large and black, yet soft, the kind that are prevalent in novels yet so rare in real life. Who among you has witnessed such perfection of nut-brown limb? Among females of any race?" As he ran his thumb and forefinger down her arm to her to wrist, his bulbous blue eyes stopped on her breasts, swollen with early pregnancy. "Or such graceful mounds of femininity as heave before us."

Terrified, she didn't struggle. Escape would be impossible. All eyes bored into her, rude and frightening, the crowd having attracted every man in the town. Her heart raced, told her to run. No, she said silently, and faced the men directly.

"My friends, let it not be said that this rarest of wildflowers was tarnished with frowns, that our Cleopatra of the California wilderness was ravaged by animals." Chinning his fuzzy gray beard into his ample chest, leveling his bulging blue eyes at Beak Nose and Rocker, "Or her petals bruised." He released his grip. Pedro had talked of her petals. It indicated love and respect. She breathed easier.

Cheers. Whistles. Scraps of talk came through the noise: "... Counselor's right," "Look at them heavenly curves!"

"... ifn her skin war white!"

"... Perry McCoon's mistress," a miner shouted. She'd seen him before, a man with a slightly feline face.

A man fell to his knees before her, looking up into her eyes, palms pressed together in supplication. Half the crowd kneeled, some snickering, some gazing at her with the faraway look of men communing with the spirits. A few that kneeled placed their foreheads on the ground, arms outstretched toward her muddy feet. Slowly retying the skirt around her hips, she watched the now quiet men.

Her heart stopped as a young one grabbed her. Other hands did the same and she was jostled and lifted until she sat on a platform of arms, six men carrying her. Shouts hammered her ears as her porters bumped and pushed their way through the laughing, babbling men. She shut her eyes and squeezed her amulet, beseeching oam'shu for the calm to understand what was happening so she could meet and out-magic any evil.

With a flurry of activity, men arranged barrels and boards before her. Then she was deposited on a raised platform, standing head and shoulders above the tallest. Empty bottles were brought and heaped at her feet.

The resonant voice of Counselor penetrated the din. "What is your name?"

A yell: "Squaws don't never tell their names."

She looked at the questioner, seeing no malice, and said, "Mary." It didn't matter. That was only a nickname. Besides, she had power.

A few shouts stood out from the others. "She done said som'm."

"Shut yer traps."

"Cleopatra spake."

Counselor raised his arms for quiet. Slowly the crowd hushed, front to back. He asked her to repeat the name. She did.

The men chanted: "Mary, Mary, Mary, Mary."

Looking over their heads, she knew these were not the faces of killers. Those in front kneeled as they chanted. Bottles were passed. A few Indian and Kanaka men stood quietly in the back with their women. Had Bohemkulla visited the camp and seduced the men? Her mind was functioning again. Fear hovered in the distance, ready to embrace her at the slightest invitation, but for now she glowed with power.

Something white moved at the back of the crowd. A broad white hat making its way toward the front. Under it was Captain Sutter's pink face, his red shirt tucked into brown pants, straps over his shoulders. His surprised voice came through the roar of loud talk.

"Mary, mine chile!" Sutter turned to Counselor. "Vhat goes here?" Sutter's nose was rounder and purpler than she remembered, his belly fleshier, protruding over his pantaloons. But the sight of him invited no fear. Power buzzed through her limbs.

Counselor cleared his throat. "If I may...." When the noise lessened, he continued. "We were saying, Captain, before you so kindly joined us, that this unaccompanied barbaric princess ought to have the freedom of the camp. She should choose her swain."

Men shouted approval, swiveled their hips, licentious grins on their lips—like men at the Second Grass festival, hoping to be chosen. She should choose bespoke power.

Sutter seemed confused in the midst of the laughter and excited talk. "Iss no princess. Iss one of mine Indian girls."

A roar answered, men outshouting each other, fists raised.

"He has enough."

"... ain't fair."

"Ain't MERican!"

He puffed out his chest, nearly losing his balance, and reached for her hand. "Zee iss mine."

She raised her hand out of his reach and announced to the crowd: "I trade one sleep with Captain Sutter for thousand dollars gold."

Smiles touched the men's lips. Those in front told the men behind, and when the wave of talk hit the back, even the Indians whooped with laughter. Sutter's face grew redder than the cloud on the western hilltop.

A person never knew how power would align things. Even the gold-seeking men of the camp were under her spell. She smiled inside, trusting that she would return to Pedro in four or five sleeps with knowledge, and gold.

She pushed away the memory of his face when he'd said puta, needing all her power as she accompanied Captain Sutter to his tent.

# 62

Captain Sutter lifted the canvas flap and told two Indias to bring meat and kartofeln.

They walked out, looking at María's singed hair with sympathetic expressions. In the muted light of the cloth house, blankets trailed from the bed, empty bottles littered the floor, and a metal trunk disgorged clothing. Against the far wall, two barrels supported a shelf on which lay a large open book, a heap of papers, a sombrero and two baskets. Crossing to where the slope of the canvas met her head, María saw goldenrock in the baskets.

"Today you walk far?" Sutter's voice was pleasantly quiet.

She turned. "Sí." He sat down and jammed one boot over the other, levering it off with the toe of the other. She braced herself for the stench that had sickened her five years ago.

"Eat first." His tan mustache parted like a rabbit's over big teeth. It was too dark to see his eyes.

The women—as young as María had been the first time she saw Sutter—returned with two baskets of food. After they set them down, he shooed them out and pulled plates from underneath the bed, handing one to María.

She sat on the floor against the cloth wall next to the bed, ignoring the venison and took two fleshy roots. His feet stank terribly!

He sat on the side of the bed wiggling them toward her, eating with his hands, as she did. "Iss dark," he said wiping his whiskers on his sleeve.

He leaned down and selected two empty long-necked bottles from the floor, cracked them on the trunk, detaching the bottoms, and jammed the necks into the dirt, one near her, the other on the opposite wall of the tent. He lit candles and pushed them into the bottles where the flames would be protected against wind gusts.

She watched him as carefully as he watched her, but he sang no songs nor indicated in any way that power came from the candles. She saw no hint of self-purification, heard no discourse with any object that might contain a magic ally. Equally discreet, she kept her powers secret and remained calm when he eyed her swollen breasts.

He felt beneath the bed, brought out a bottle of the candle-holder type, this one full of liquid. He cracked the neck on a crate, poured the liquid into two cups, extended one to her and said, "Trink."

She accepted the cup, but kept her eye on the half-empty bottle, which he set beside the candle. Tiny bubbles rose from nowhere inside the glass. It was magic, beautiful in the candlelight, bubbles continuously replacing themselves. Sutter was sharing his power with her!

Unafraid, she drank, thrilled by the sparkling spray on her nose and lip. But immediately her bones weakened, like when she drank aguardiente. This surprised her. If she drank more, her thoughts would weaken too. She had learned that brandy was a thief of power. So was this. Captain Sutter must believe he had power to spare. She pretended to swallow, then lowered the cup to her side away from him and poured it on the dirt. She needed all her wits to walk among the supernaturals who once populated the earth.

Sutter swallowed and gazed over his cup, lids flat across the crescents of his eyes. "Come." He patted the blankets beside him and fumbled with the buttons on his trouser flap.

Coupling would weaken him further. But she had told Pedro she wouldn't. "Trink," she said back, pouring the sparkling liquid into his cup.

He smiled. "Ya ya, iss plenty of time. The night is young. Ve finish what ve start a long time ago, nicht?"

Her shadow on the tent wall enlarged, flickered wildly and dimmed. She looked beyond the snoring figure of Captain Sutter and saw the other candle had gone out. The one near her was low in its bottleneck. Soon it too would drown in a pool of wax. The soot-blackened bottle tunneled the light, projecting it to the cloth ceiling, a circle as large as the tent, moving, breathing with the flame. Darting insects appeared on the canvas as monstrous birds swooping around in chaos. This was the world as it had become, with power flying loose and the Immortals in swift retreat. It was a time of transition, unpredictable. New animals. New people. New drinks. New plants. To survive she must reach above and beyond the boundaries of herself.

The last of the camp's revelers had quieted. Owls whooed. Shrieking night birds imitated laughing women. Captain Sutter had taken no herbs, canted no songs, wore no amulet. He said the champagne "fortified" him. That meant strength, but he had fallen to sleep after drinking one bottle.

Now he coughed like he was gagging, then rolled over and bolted to a sitting position, blinking repeatedly. "Ahhhh. Mary. You here still. Goot. I go sleeping!" He rubbed his eyes and stared at her.

She sat, quiet in her strength.

"Come." He patted the bed, branchlets and rushes beneath woolen blankets.

She rose, stepped from the low canvas to the center of the tent where she stood taller than herself, enlarging. She was Deer Woman, no longer small, no longer young. She was pregnant, not with one man's child, but the world. She was tall, old, huge of girth and hips, ponderous of breasts, heavy. She stepped toward him, flesh shuddering, feet drumming the rhythm of eternity. Men were compelled to follow no matter how they squirmed and tossed their antlers. Deer Woman enveloped all. She was the wisdom of the earth.

Sutter's eyes were like supper plates. Fear bled from his pores, stank up the tent as he sagged back on his elbows. "Mary, is it you?" A frightened whisper.

"I come to learn of your power." Her voice was round and filled with the world's harmonics.

His was thin and quavering. "I dream, ya sure. I dream now."

"Yes. Dream. I walk with you to your power place." She would enter his inner sanctum without fear, meet his spirits. She, the earth's all. "Show me the sources of your strength."

"I sleep now, ya sure."

He had no intention of displaying his power. "Then follow me," she said.

Timidly he rose, for no man can resist Deer Woman. She led him through the sleeping camp, past the camp of Indian workers, past a second camp where Don José Amador and other Españoles slept, and across the ruined creek of the world.

Morning Star beckoned. María led up the hillside, dimly lit by the thousand pricks of light from the campfires of the Immortals. Even the night animals slept. Sutter's steps were halting, stumbling in his stockings. He whined about stopping to rest but she was patient, and when they crossed a creek that talked, their feet left the ground.

Now they walked rapidly in the air, climbing mountains and traversing valleys, passing the many-branched tree of life. Captain Sutter begged to stop, but each time, she turned, showed him her awesome female flesh, and he followed.

She came to a cave in a mountainside and pulled back rocks, opening it. Inside a glowing peach light illuminated a scene of plenty. Smoke from sacred fires scented the air where hundreds of people prepared for a big time, many in feather robes and headdresses. Full baskets of delicious-smelling food were laid out over a field of tender green grass. Sutter stood open-mouthed.

She smiled at him. "Come. Meet my uncle."

He followed her up a small canyon until they came to a little u-macha beneath large shade trees. The peach light was the only indication of anything unusual. An old man sat overlooking a green meadow. His skin was soft as buckskin, his hair hanging in long gray bunches. He was age itself, eyes sparkling like polished onyx from the dim folds of his face. He engaged Captain Sutter in pleasantries, and when they were done, cocked his head, smiled slyly and asked, "You like my niece?"

Sutter, who had responded politely, seemed increasingly at ease. "She is very beautiful. But…"

"But?" The old man inclined his head curiously.

"Her feet!" Sutter looked at María's feet and stammered, "On the way here, I looked at them when she was climbing some steep rocks and her feet seemed… round, small. Pointed."

Hooves. Her magic was strong.

The old man smiled indulgently, well pleased, she knew. "Perhaps you would like to join us in a dance before we eat?" He had judged Sutter as worthy.

But she must purify herself. "Uncle, first I will bathe."

"Run along then. Captain Sutter and I will talk."

The next time she saw the captain he was dancing in a men's line, hands on the waists of the men on either side. Thunder rolled through the canyons with her approach. It rocked through her and prickled the backs of her arms as she stepped in time with the drum beat. She was light and springy.

Deer sisters came from the dance doctor's corner and pranced with her in the center of the circle, surrounded by people stomping to the drum, the rhythm of eternity. The men watched her and her sisters—all of them with enormous brown eyes and long lashes, which they batted coquettishly as they lifted their headdresses. Their hair and skin softly tan with pale spots on their cheeks. Moving suggestively, the dancing men gave María glances intended to arouse her. But she and her sisters pranced alone.

Afterwards she cleansed herself in the stream and returned to find Captain Sutter seated on the grass, feasting with the others.

"Do you want to stay here?" a woman asked him, apparently also seeing him as worthy.

He glanced around, smiling at the people. "It is very nice, but I must go back. My son comes from Switzerland. I must be at my fort vhen he arrives."

They nodded understandingly. Then before María knew what was happening she awoke with Sutter, halfway between sky and earth, their legs entangled in a thicket.

He rubbed his eyes "Where haff ve been?"

"The Land of the Immortals." She too was in awe. "Now we walk to your creek."

It seemed they had been gone a long time, at least a sleep or two, but everything in the tent was as they had left it—the rumpled blankets, champagne bottles, two baskets of gold. The coral-pink color coming through the canvas was all that remained of the land of the Immortals. And it made the tent beautiful.

Captain Sutter lay down, groaned, turned to his side and almost immediately snored. She left her skirt in the tent and went to bathe.

Emptying her mind of trivia, ignoring other Indian people doing the same, she waded to her thighs in the deepest part of the creek and turned to offer gratitude to Father Sun. Then she willed her thoughts to fly to those who had admitted her to the happy land. She was thanking them when a loud voice interrupted: "The wildwood Cleopatra! She bathes in light!"

She turned to see miners, one standing with a pan of water, the other on a knee, dipping his bucket. Tents flew open. Scuzzy-headed men in strange white clothing, tight-fitting to their wrists and ankles, peered out. They relieved themselves outside their doors and teetered across the rocks on bare white feet, beards wild, hair in clumps. Clowns. Soon she was surrounded. Some smiled, others bowed their heads before her as they had before the sleep.

"Oh beauteous creature!"

"Oh paragon of womanhood!"

"Oh fer a heavenly poke in that poon!"

That drew a shout from another, "Gitcher ugly sticker outa here!"

The first man threw up a hand to defend himself from a blow, and soon they were laughing and rolling in the mud like puppies at play.

Slipping away, she opened the flap of Sutter's tent.

He sat up. "Mary!" Scowling toward the sounds of the mock battle, he seemed surprised and befuddled.

She had spent the entire sleep with him. The sun was up and it was time to leave. She walked to the baskets of gold, waiting to be paid.

He looked from the tops of his pale eyes, underscored by puffy half-moons. "Come." He patted the bed beside him.

She reached for her skirt, began tying it around her waist. The noise outside dwindled.

"No. Komm mal. Wir machen noch verkehr." He opened his square flap, his pink man's part small and rising.

Sickened by the smell, she said, "The sleep is finished."

He stood, stepped toward her, his man's part bouncing.

She moved back.

He grabbed for her, but she slipped to the side and darted out into fresh air. Hearing his footsteps at her heels, she hurried through the camp, passing men at their breakfast fires. Some smiled and followed.

Howls, laughter and banging of metal pans told her Sutter was behind and losing ground on his tender feet.

Someone yelled in sing-song mockery, "She's tired a you."

"Peers she don't like the old goat."

"Want a young stud?"

She circled the camp and stopped at the tent next to Sutter's, where a man she recognized stood in her path.

Eyes crinkled with amusement, thumbs in his waist band, he said, "Perry McCoon's mistress, I belief." He looked her over. "Remember me? Heinrich Lienhard?" The dense brown-gray fur on his face was closely trimmed, and his nose was small. Then he smiled and she remembered the feline face, and his politeness.

"Sí. At the fort."

Counselor joined them. "Out for a morning constitutional are we?" He winked at Lienhard.

Uncomfortable with Counselor's speech, she looked toward the distance, over the men crowding around. Then she heard Sutter's gasps, watched his stricken face as he passed by into his tent.

A wall of hirsute faces smiled after him.

They belittled their captain. It had been different back at New Helvetia, where he had been feared by all men and coupled at will with their wives. Even Pedro had done his bidding. She recalled the twenty-five cannons and the racks of long guns fired by men when he raised his hand. She looked at Heinrich Lienhard and Counselor and said, "I come to learn of Captain Sutter's power."

Lienhard's whiskers moved. "Captain Sutter's power?"

Chuckles rattled through the crowd. "Power" popped out several times.

"I got more in my pinky."

"You wanna see power, darlin? Try ole Tennessee."

Counselor was talking too.

She shook her head. She couldn't hear over the disorderly talk.

Counselor held up a hand. The crowd quieted.

"Do I hear misplaced hilarity in our fair camp? Rumors that the esteemed Captain Sutter lacks manly endowment? Indeed, gentlemen, think for a moment. He hath bedded this beauteous creature all night and then ran a footrace for her in the morning. Hardly a mark of weakness, my dear fellows."

"You old men sticking together, huh?"

"Let her try me!"

Heinrich Lienhard regarded her kindly, a glint of teeth where the cat smile parted. "You men, go to your digs before Herr Sutter's Indians pick out all da gold. They work the creek now an hour."

Half the crowd drifted away, including Counselor. The remainder stood back in twos and threes, within earshot.

Ignoring them, Lienhard opened his palm toward the fire. "Join me Mary?" A pot of coffee steamed on a flat rock and a pan of simmering meat emitted the aroma of puerco. She smiled acceptance.

A man of middle years, Lienhard turned his attention to the meat, tossing the pan until all the slices were reversed. His furry chin moved as he spoke. "I too haff interest in Herr Sutter's power." He didn't laugh.

She said, "He has little strength now."

Lienhard glanced at her and cut his eyes back to the meat. "You play to his veakness."

"I do not understand."

"Females and trink are his veakness."

Drink. "Aguardiente and champagne?"

He nodded. It was as she had suspected. Thieves of power. "Where did he find his power when he had it?"

Lienhard sat beside her, looking at the meat. "His power? Mmm. Imagination and style, mein schatz. And confidence in what he can do. No fear of cost." He chuckled. "Herr Sutter was zo intent on making civilization, he tinks not at all about paying debts. Dot iss strength, and ya veakness too." He swallowed a chuckle. "Understand?"

Not really. She approached it differently. "Does he have helpers who give power?"

"Helpers? Mmm." After a moment he whispered, "He took it, my dear. Simply took authority." He lifted a brow at Sutter's open tent door and pressed a finger across his lips.

Puzzled, she lowered her voice. "Took it?" Power came after long, exacting discipline and dangerous encounters with the spirit world. Some never grasped it no matter how hard they tried. Power wasn't to be plucked like a berry from a vine.

"Ya. He pretends to be a captain." He smiled at the meat.

"Pretends?" Either a man was headman or he was not.

The smile spread. "He had imagination to fool the Mexican government." He held the pan toward her, indicating she should take a piece of meat. "He plays the big important man with confidence for the future. Men want to join it. Zo maybe he deserves his rank and land and attention." He put the pan on a warm rock.

Style. Rank. She had much to learn. Chewing the tough puerco meat, obviously dried hard before cooking, she mulled over what he'd said. In the American tongue many words meant power. Strength, authority. Imagination was new to her. Fooling others certainly was a mark of power. Still, no one could pretend to be a headman. It baffled her.

Sutter came from his tent, casting hooded glances at all the men within earshot. He lowered himself on a crate opposite María, avoiding her eyes, and poured warm coffee from the pot into a tin cup. As if it might fly away, he gripped the cup with both hands and let steam rise into his tan mustache, and he listened as Lienhard spoke in German.

They exchanged utterances, the pitch and volume rising. While Sutter was talking, Lienhard glanced at María, pointing his cat chin to a pile of biscuits in a basket, indicating she should take one.

"Zo," said Sutter, suddenly giving her a level look, "you ask after mine power." The red zigzags in the whites of his eyes looked painful as he rolled his eyes up at the men standing around them.

She nodded, unable to speak with a mouthful of Americano biscuit.

"You stay mit me. Ya. Denn you see power." He sipped.

"First, pay for sleep."

Over the cup Sutter's pale eyes locked into hers. "I owe you no-ting."

"Thousand dollar for sleep." The listening North Americans talked rapidly among themselves. She heard:

"He ain't paid up."

"We all done heared the terms."

"I'll say."

"Shore did."

"Ever man in camp."

The cat face followed the speakers, then looked at Captain Sutter's balding head and the pink tops of his cheeks as he stared at his cup.

Wishing she understood the deeper currents of English, she added: "Two thousand dollars I stay next sleep with you."

Sutter lifted his pale eyes to her. "As you perfectly goot know, I haff not pay because you… because ve…" The blue floated higher on the red and white as he scanned the listening men. His volume decreased. "Because you didn't…" His chin quivered. "I didn't…" The men stepped closer.

He was weak before her power. "You pay two sleeps," she said, "then I come at suppertime."

Coffee sloshed over the rim of Sutter's cup as he set it on the blackened dirt by the fire. He stood, hiked back his shoulders and strode into the tent. Immediately he returned like a tom turkey, chin back, breast feathers fluffed, carrying a basket of gold. Gasps came from the spectators.

"Momento," she said rising. From her carrying basket she retrieved the soft deerskin bag she'd brought for this purpose, extended it, held the sides open.

He scooped a hand into the gold, forming a careful, mounded pile, waited until it stopped sliding off, then poured it into her bag. Nine more times he did it, counting, "zwei, drei, vier, fife, sex, seeben, eight, noin, ten." From the tops of his eyes he watched the hovering men and said in a loud voice, "Tousand dollars. Paid. For last night."

"No," she said. "That was ten."

The eyebrows arched over humorless eyes. "Mine chile, one handful iss a hunnert, ten hunnerts a thousand. Und now for dis night vhat comes." He dipped his hand into the half empty basket.

Lienhard hissed, "I cannot belief!"

Sutter's hand paused. "You tink I am a poor man, hmm?" He put the gold in her bag.

"But zo much, Johannes! We yust agreed. Every flake must go to the teamster." Seeing Sutter ignore him, he spat out: "Sacrament! Nichts mehr! Ve be partners, Johann!"

Sutter made a dismissive gesture. "Not to vorry. Mine Indians and Kanakas strike big today. You see." He put the gold in her bag and said, "Fife," then scooped another handful.

Lienhard poured the remains of his coffee on the fire, where it sizzled. Then he delivered a fierce German harangue and strode to his tent.

Sutter finished the ten handfuls, speaking more to the surrounding men than to her. "Und Now!" He stood, tossing his empty basket like offal toward the tent. "Cleopatra iss mine yet another night." His chest puffed out between the suspenders, belly tight in the red sling of his shirt.

The miners exchanged awed glances as she lashed the thong around and around her fat bundle of gold, tied it, and dropped it in her carrying basket. She positioned it on her back, and the men stepped back as she passed. She would spend the day in the Indian camp resting. Because, once again, when the campfires of the Immortals pricked the sky dome, she would need all her wits.

# 63

Hooting and hollering sounded in the distance.

María opened her eyes and thought she was a child again, Crying Fox outside the u-macha playing with his friends and Etumu preparing food. She shook the bad omen from her mind. She was here, beneath the willows of Captain Sutter's creek, waking from a deep sleep. Etumu and Crying Fox were dead, along with Great-Grandmother Dishi, uncles, aunts, cousin-sisters, cousin-brothers and all their children. Father was slowly recovering.

The Immortals had sent her to this place of gold gathering. She was like Red Cloud, who long ago recovered his people after they'd been won in a game of chance and herded to the northern land of ice and snow. She would win back the home place like Red Cloud did. Her medicine was strong, and she was not finished.

It was late in the day. Shadows pointed east. A breath of air cooled her hairline. She rose and walked a few steps to check her carrying basket, which she'd stored inside the brush shelter of a friendly family working for Captain Sutter. Nisenan they called people. She crawled under the brush, reached down to the point of her basket and felt the fat doeskin bag, safe. Then, fingering her amulet and calling upon Oam-shu, she walked toward the disturbance across the creek, where miners teemed around a wagon and a pair of oxen.

She waded the stream, shading her eyes from the glare, and nodded greetings to the Indians and Kanakas who continued to wash gold along the creek. As she entered the crowd—boxes and barrels passing hand to hand over hatted heads—a man grabbed her breast and leered at her with the face of a demon, hissing with foul breath, "This handful's gotta be worth a hundred."

She pulled back in horror.

A voice: "Keep yer dirty paws offa Cleopatra!" A fist reached across her, rammed the devil-face. Bone cracked. Bright red blood spurted onto her chest. As the man fell back, two red streams from his nose soaked his black beard.

She cringed, turned toward the creek to wash. A flame-haired man pushed her out of the way and smashed his fist into the jaw of the man who had hit Devil-face. The crowd surged forward, trapping her in a chaos of yelling, shoving men. Before she knew what was happening, she felt herself picked up and moved forward as if by a many-handed centipede. From behind came grunts, hollow thuds, smashing bottles. The centipede deposited her in the wagon bed, where she watched in safety.

In a cloud of dust, fists flew, hats sailed, bottles smashed into sunbursts of glass and liquid. Hatless men rose from the ground, only to be pounded down again. Others whirled and rammed their fists into anyone within reach. Men on the outskirts pushed forward to join the fray.

Captain Sutter climbed into the wagon and stood beside her, his mien a mix of consternation and pride. In the penetrating tones of a herald, he announced to the rowdy men: "All trinks on me. Each man a full bottle!"

Men turned mid-punch. They gaped at Sutter with bloody lips. Several rose to all fours, then swayed to their feet staring. From a hundred throats a cheer rose: "Hurrah!"

"Drink to Captain Sutter!"

"A fine old gentleman."

This too was power.

But the teamster wasn't enchanted. He squinted up at Sutter through bushy brows, yelling over the din, "'At's twenty pinches apiece comin to me. And I ain't forgot the thousand you owe." Bloodied men were yanking out corks with their teeth, handing out bottles.

Sutter smiled benignly at the teamster. "Join us, mine goot man. Trink and be merry!" Loud cheers.

The teamster elbowed his way to Heinrich Lienhard, who gave him the flat look of an unhappy cat.

"To Princess Cleopatra!" somebody yelled.

"The most beautiful female!"

"To all females!"

"To beauty!"

The dirty men raised bottles, clacked them together and swilled the contents as Sutter hung his hand over her shoulder, his gaze slipping down to her breasts. He opened his mouth to speak when the teamster leaped into the wagon shouting, "I'm staying right here till I gits every pinch comin to me!"

Sutter scowled. "Mine goot sir, can you not see this iss not za time." He nodded fondly at María.

"Time my ass! I'm campin in yer damned bed till I gits paid!" Pistol raised over his head, black beard blanketing a red shirt, he jumped off the wagon and stalked through Sutter's tent door. Titters purred through the crowd, and then bursts of ribald laughter.

With a pat on María's behind, Sutter tried to imitate the jump from the wagon and caught a suspender on a peg. He dangled before falling to the dust. A roar of laughter met him as he pulled himself to his feet and followed the teamster inside.

Again María puzzled over the rude treatment of the headman. Even if Americano drink had stolen his power, he was a hy-apo. Then, glancing through the crowd, her heart stopped. A Spanish black hat. Familiar gray eyes. Severe. Eyes more wont to smiles and warmth. Eyes she thought she knew. He disappeared behind the crowd.

Drawn like a hummingbird to nectar, she turned, foot over the side, toes feeling for the protruding hub of the wheel, but strong hands stopped her.

"I go now to my man."

"I'd say yer man's got some rough comp'ny."

"He ain't a looker like you." Roaring laughter.

"No. My man is there." She pointed but saw no sign of Pedro.

A nasal voice: "We's needin s'more looks at yer beauty."

A louder voice: "Cap'ns got her all night."

"Yeah. Leastwise I git a nice long look now."

Struggle would be useless. Drawing upon her strength she returned quietly to the wagon bed and gazed at the surrounding hills. She ignored the voices and the feel of eyes boring into her. Pedro had ridden all the way from Rancho Omuchumne. If the distance were to be closed, he would come to her; if not, she must accept that.

She stood at the wagon's edge, trying to plan her night with Captain Sutter, but couldn't forget the anger in those gray eyes. *Accept.*

A sudden pounding of horse hooves. She turned to see.

Startled men leapt back. In a blur of speed a horse exploded past, Pedro standing on the saddle, whisking her into the air, the horse galloping beneath them. Frightened miners stumbled to get out of the way. At her back, Pedro's manly odor, the excitement of his strength as he sat her down before him, legs goading the surging animal.

The yelling grew fainter: "... Our Cleopatra!"

Pursuers followed. She turned to see horses behind, losing ground. Pedro's face could have been made of iron. She looked ahead. With breathless speed Chocolate galloped down a canyon filled with evergreen oak, then up the gorge and along a dry creek bed, rocks clattering.

Pedro said nothing. She had nothing to say. Her sense of being wronged mixed strangely with the pleasure of her bare back pressed to Pedro, his arms fencing her. They rode on, long after the sounds of pursuit faded. At last the horse slowed beneath a spreading oak. Pedro reined to a stop, never having spoken.

Jumping off, he paced, avoiding her eyes.

Chocolate snorted and blew. She slid down the frothing animal and stood watching Pedro. What could she say to a man who lacked understanding? Her heart went to him. He was like a spotted fawn she'd seen chased by a dog, swimming to exhaustion up the river, bleating for help, losing ground to the relentless pursuer, only to be caught on land. She wanted to hug him.

When he finally turned to her, his eyes were wild, crazed. He whirled away as if she sickened him.

An arrow to the stomach couldn't have pained her more. She closed her eyes and touched her amulet, praying for calm. *He came to me,* she reminded herself.

Choked sounds: "Any other man would beat you."

This caught her by surprise. Except for Perrimacoo and Captain Sutter, men didn't hit women.

He paced away and stood staring through the trees, one boot forward. "You must hate me." He breathed hard as if he and not the horse had been running.

Hate. A strong word, opposite from what she felt. "Te amo." It came out rich and full, for he was her life, all that was left of it.

He bent forward, placing his face in his hands, shoulders moving. The fawn bleating.

She went to him, rolling her weight from the sides of her feet so he wouldn't hear and wrench away. Softly she touched his back.

He jumped in his skin, but did not turn, or leave.

Gently she embraced the curve of his back.

He wiped his sleeve across his face and straightened, staring through the trees, allowing her to hold him, to lay her head against his shirt back.

She closed her eyes. The source of his love, his heart, spoke to her and she opened herself to it the way she listened to plants, the way she had done so often when this same heart spoke of love in the early mornings and at siesta. She pressed her ear to its muffled thumps, her hands caressing his chest through the fabric, feeling his man's nipples. She heard the low steady undertone of his heart beating for her.

His voice came through his ribcage. "Why, María?"

There was no why that he could understand. She lowered her hands to his sash, below.

He tensed.

She felt her way back to his chest, speaking to his heart. "You are my man. Te quiero."

He expelled air, his shoulders loosening.

She massaged him. "I love only you."

Slowly he lay down on the matted grass where deer had slept beneath the branches.

She went down with him.

"No," she answered.

"But you took his gold." The tightness lingered in his voice. His black hat lay beside him, the band faded to pink. He sat against the trunk of the oak with his wavy auburn hair curling around the collar of his shirt, pale and blousing around him. The sash lay in a heap where he'd dropped it.

"I did not couple with him. I hate his coupling."

The hawk nose was proud, the brows troubled. "I believe you, María. But Captain Sutter was my superior officer and you are my woman. He will think… You must give back the gold."

Kneeling before him, she studied the endless facets of his gray eyes, fractured, deeper than she could see. "I have not injured him. I owe no retribution." She wanted to understand Pedro's way of thinking.

"You deceived him."

Deceived? She didn't understand that word. "He paid me for staying a sleep with him. I did. Now, tonight, I stay the second sleep with him."

"Don't do it. Give the gold back."

It was an order. She struggled against rising anger, reminding herself this was the way he talked. As a dog barks, an egret squawks, one cannot blame them for using their tongues. If disrespect lay behind the order, it was beyond Pedro's understanding.

Leaning forward, he took her hands from her knees, held them in his. "María, María, María. I am so afraid you will be hurt. Killed. Please, give him the gold and come home with me. This afternoon." The depths of his eyes seemed to connect with the spirit world.

He wanted to protect her. This she understood. It was as he'd said before: Españoles did not allow pregnant women to walk into danger. She returned the pressure of his hands and studied the kind lines of his face between the dark sideburns, the slight curve of his hawk nose. Once again she would try to make him understand her way of thinking.

"I went to Captain Sutter's camp in full light. I walked among many strange men and was not killed, not hurt at all. My power is strong, Pedro." She returned his gaze, which was the Españolo way of talking deeply.

"You were lucky."

"Sí," she said, "I had luck." Relieved that he'd begun to understand, she said, "And I have luck now. Many seasons ago when you took me to Captain Sutter's bed" —he looked away— "I had little luck. Captain Sutter had big power. He wanted what I did not want to give. Now I have spirit helpers and much luck. I took from Captain Sutter only what he gave with his own hand." It made no sense at all to return the gold.

Pedro followed every word. His brows moved in concentration.

She added, "The gold is for you, to buy the home place." She paused. "What does deceive mean?"

He lifted her hands, closing his eyes, kissing one palm and then the other. "No importa." He looked into her eyes and his voice resonated with its normal purity of tone, the gravel gone. "Little Poppy, you must have a guardian angel on your shoulder. But do not stay with Captain Sutter tonight. Give that half of the gold back. I do not want it."

She wanted it all. Perrimacoo had recently implied he was interested in selling his land papers, as Pedro well knew. "Will you not help me remove Perrimacoo from the land?" Her voice sounded tight, and she fought to keep her expression from shattering. For so long their bond had been sealed by the desire for Pedro to live in her home place. She prayed he hadn't changed his mind.

"I am a wanted man, but I have my honor."

She frowned. He'd said this before, but it didn't explain anything. He had protected himself from a killer and took the lives of those who killed her people. Both Españoles and Americanos, he'd said, believed it was proper for those who took lives to forfeit their own. Vengeance was the way of the world. "You were brave," she said. "You restored balance. No one would prevent your buying land papers because of that."

He examined her hands, which he continued to hold, and exhaled. "I don't know. It's not certain, but whoever reads my name on a paper could come after me. No. I don't want to talk more about this now. Just promise me you will give Captain Sutter his gold—whatever he paid for tonight. Then come home with me."

He looked at her with such intensity and love that she melted. Peace with Pedro was as necessary as power. That much clarity she had gained. With bravery she had faced his anger, and learned that his love for her ran very deep. But she saw that he needed to believe that he guided her, as a mother guides a child, and that he would grow weak and angry if he felt she was beyond his guidance. Control as he put it. Therefore she would appear to be controlled by him. "Bueno," she said.

He pulled her to him, kissing her and massaging her scalp beneath her stubble of hair. "Gracias, Amapolita. I thought I would die without you."

Between kisses she murmured, "My spirit dies without you."

He stood, tucked in his shirt and said, "We go now. Soon we lose the sun." Proud Hawk.

"But you are a bandido. Maybe they shoot you."

Tying on his sash, he said, "Last time they were too busy looking at you."

Her power had saved him too. "But next time," she said, "they might see you."

He inserted the gun and knife in his sash, on opposite sides.

# 64

Pedro knew, as he cradled María's softness before him and rocked with the rhythm of the horse, that life was nothing without her. Last night he lay sleepless in the room with Captain Juan, and that bright knowledge flamed in his heart. So he'd ridden to Sutter's camp ready to die just to see her again. It was almost funny, when he thought of it that way.

But on the way he'd imagined scenes so wrenching, her with Sutter, that he considered ending her life along with his, so they would die together. Mad he was. Crazy in love. Then her denials, her sweet attentions to him. Mother of God, his poor overworked heart had climbed from the bottom of hell and soared higher than the angels of heaven. Amor!

He put his chin in her short hair, glove-tight with her. She was magic. A flower of a girl with a pull on his manhood like no woman he'd ever known. He felt the odd desire to absorb her through his belly where she would lie safe and close to his heart. She and the unborn baby were his family, his purpose in living. It surprised him, this tenderness of longing to hold the infant in his arms. And he believed everything she had said. She never lied. Helping Chocolate pick his way down the dry creek, he vowed to make a greater effort to understand her Indian ways.

"I smell a village," she said, turning to him.

"Amador's." Reining to a huge boulder, he flicked his hat back on its strings, kissed the nape of her downy neck and inhaled the peach-like aroma of her skin. Man was weak. "Wait here with Chocolate. I'll be back in a few minutes. And María?" He dismounted.

"Sí?" Ever calm, ever dignified.

He left his hand on her thigh. "Te quiero." More than he could say.

"Te amo." The vanilla voice.

She waited while Pedro borrowed clothing to disguise him from his Californio friends in Don José Amador's camp. The golden sunlight pushed long shadows up the hill, the shadow of the boulder creeping up over gullies and oaks and pines.

As Chocolate cropped the dry grass in rhythm—lip a mouthful, bite it off, chew four times, take a step, lip the next batch—she sank into thought about the gold hunters. They seemed to care only about gold and liquor. They had no respect for the spirits or their medicine man or headman. Captain Sutter's imagination worked no magic on them. Theirs was a different kind of power, the power of blackbirds lifting as one from the earth, banking, turning as one across the sun, and landing as one. Blackbirds fed in a frenzy, as did the gold hunters, and they pecked each other without remorse, yet were always ready on the slightest signal to fly together.

Chocolate ranged too far and she nudged him back to the boulder, his black eye rounding from his head, seeing her on his back. You are my man's woman, he seemed to say. I will humor you. A powerful alliance, man and horse. One of the few helpful aspects of the changing world.

She recognized Pedro immediately, striding across the dry grass, a floppy leather hat darkening his face. He wore a checkered shirt and brown trousers tucked inside his boots in the Americano manner, no sash or bolero. But his proud walk gave him away. Nevertheless, clothing disguised. From a great distance she would have recognized any of her people, before they were killed, by the nuances of their bodies. Legs, torsos and hips varied more than faces from a distance. Faces had to be seen close up to be recognized. Yet Americanos relied solely on faces. Pedro would blend with the crowd in Sutter's camp.

They climbed the ridge between Amador's camp and Sutter's Creek camp, Chocolate's strong haunches vaulting up the steep hills, and then wove a careful route down through the trees to the camp of Sutter's Indians. Pedro hobbled the horse while María greeted the men, women and children who sat around supper fires. Unable to understand their tongue, she spoke Spanish.

"Your things are safe," they said, eyes watchful.

She pulled her basket from the little house and returned to the deepening shadows of the trees where Pedro waited. They sat dividing the golden-rock into two equal amounts, half in the doeskin bag, half in the old pigskin bag she'd brought. She handed the doeskin to Pedro to tie on the horse and put the pigskin in her carrying basket, positioning the band on her woven cap. A prickly feeling of being watched made her turn around and examine the trees. Red toyon berries dotted the bushes, and a forest of reeds turning brown stood motionless at the creek. No one there.

Pedro said. "I'll be near you at all times, with my Allen." He patted the grip of his gun, jutting from his sash, and drew out his horn-handled skinning knife, giving it to her.

"I have a knife," she said. "In my basket."

"This one is better. Put it here." Carefully he tucked it inside her skirt, tying the cloth tighter around her waist. The freshly honed shaft felt cool on her hip.

"But you might need it."

"I want you to have it. Do not hesitate to use it if Sutter tries to force you and for some reason I am not there."

That struck her as funny. "You want me to return his gold but not hesitate to kill him." She smiled, having no intention of stabbing the headman of Sutter's Fort. Just look at all the trouble Pedro was in because of the necessary killing of lesser men. "I am not afraid of Captain Sutter," she said. "Aguardiente and champagne have stolen his power, and my power is good now. My husband, you are in greater danger."

"I'll take care of myself. I pray to the Virgin you won't need the knife." He studied her and said, "Use your power."

He acknowledged her! And it added to her power.

He took her hand. "One sound from you and I'll be at your side. Tell the captain you are ill and must vomit. Leave the gold in the tent and walk out to the trees behind it. I'll be there with Chocolate."

He turned in a slow half-circle, gazing intently at everything until he pointed up the hill. "Leave this place when the sun is gone from that big, dead pine tree. I'll take Chocolate around first."

The scraggly old giant had two upright spires bisected by strong light. The floor of the narrow valley where they stood was growing cool and dark more quickly than at home, yet the sun shone brightly on the mountain.

"María, I am proud of you." He swallowed. "Keep that angel on your shoulder." He kissed her mouth and left.

≋

She called on Oam-shu and gathered her calm. Wading the creek toward Sutter's Creek camp, she heard a distant violin weaving a sad melody through the twilight. In the shadow of a toyon bush she saw a coyote. He smiled at her with slanted amber eyes, tongue lolling. Coyote the Trickster. This was the gaze she'd felt earlier. She stood still until he sauntered away and she wondered about the omen. It could go either way.

"Thar she be," a miner sang out. Staring at her, he rose to his feet as she walked toward the camp. "Hel-LO DAR-lin!" He cupped his mouth and hollered to the other side of the camp, "You New York men owe me two hundred and fifty dollars!"

The violin stopped. The camp stirred, men talking and yelling all around. They watched her progress. Some groaned to see her, others slapped their thighs and whooped. "Cleopatra!" Ahead, Sutter came from his tent, the backs of his hands on his hips, waiting. Smiling.

Beneath the dark pines, Sutter's tent glowed from the candlelight within. Men crowded around as she approached, Pedro at the back beneath his leather hat. She feared only that he would draw attention to himself without cause. His Spanish honor demanded she not stay the night with Sutter, though her personal honor would have her keep a promise. Power was sapped by deception and lies, but she needed Pedro's love. She would follow his plan though it diminished her power. He didn't understand that things happened of their own accord, often turning plans against their framers. A tremor of fear passed through her as she looked squarely into Sutter's pale eyes. *Be calm.*

Liquor breath blasted. "Mary, mine chile! Goot girl." He took her by the nape of the neck and steered her through the doorway. She stood dumbfounded to see the interior, while he turned to the men outside, flapping his wrist to shoo them away.

Perrimacoo was looking at her, the last man she expected to see. An unfriendly smile hollowed out a ghost of a dimple in his cheek. He was seated at the trunk opposite the hairy teamster, each holding a fan of cards. A cloud of murky smoke hung over them, rising from cigarritos now balanced on the edge of the trunk. The teamster twisted toward her, his mouth a red "o" in the blanket of a black beard. She had forgotten about him. The young Indias she'd seen before looked at her from the opposite corner.

Perrimacoo said, "Well blow me down if it ent about time you got here, with the Captain thinkin' he'd been bamboozled." Several empty champagne bottles and one that was half full stood on the trunk. Her eyes watered from the smoke.

Sutter snaked an arm around her, his plump trousered hip against her skirted hip, fortunately not the one with the knife. "If you men be zo goot as to leaf us, hmm?" He steadied himself on her.

The "o" in the black blanket was replaced by the tip of a pink tongue and flashing white teeth. "Like I said, I ain't leaving this tent till I gits ever pinch comin to me." He turned back, slapped down his cards and looked at Perrimacoo. "Two-hundred smackers to ya. Three-hundred all told."

Perrimacoo hadn't lost his smile. "Just walked in the door, it did." He looked at her, then at Sutter. "Captain? If ye please, I'll taik me share now."

Sutter took his hand from her waist and staggered across the tent, waving the women out of the corner. "Later. Go girls. Git! Dots right." He gave Perrimacoo an intimate smile. "Now, if you please, my friends, outside a half-hour or zo. Hmm?" He tilted his head at María, his red eyes watering in the candlelight.

"Nope," said the teamster, manipulating the cards in his oversized hands. Two stacks whirred thrillingly and became one. Magic. Anything could happen.

Perrimacoo lifted a brow at her burden basket and said to Sutter. "A man's pay comes afore the delivery of goods." He seemed to know what was in it.

Heavily, Sutter grabbed her waist again. "Dot iss between you and Mary. I pay golt to Mary. What you say, liebchen?" Liquor fumes. "He iss arrange your coming? You giff him eighteen hunnert? Hmm?"

Things were twisting, but power lay in straight talk. "No. I came to give you half the gold back." She remembered she wasn't supposed to talk about it before leaving the tent. She hadn't thought it over four times.

Sutter seemed to melt, his eyes slippery. "You come to me with luff denn."

"I smells a rat, I does," said Perrimacoo. "I heard you gave the nigger bitch two thousand dollars, includin' me eighteen hundred. Now what's she tryin to pull?" He looked at her with the slant-eyed, deceitful expression of Coyote.

The teamster, who had been shutting one eye then the other as he looked between her and Sutter, thumped down the cards, drew himself up—the top of his head lifting the canvas off the teetering tent poles—and boomed: "If thar be gold in this here tent, it's mine! Ever pinch!" He glared at the basket in María's hands.

"Me gold it tis sir," said Perrimacoo looking at his cards. "I see your three hundred and double it. Six hundred to ye."

The bushy black brows writhed like caterpillars. "You gittin it off that squaw?"

Perrimacoo tilted his head at María. "Me girl she is. From me own rancho. She'll hand over ever pinch, cause she knows what's healthy." His blue stare leveled into her. "Her Spik pimp makes no never mind." Her neck prickled and he spun his words as soft as a spider weaving a web. "And you teamsters, God knows you have gold aplenty, bleedin the mines as yer wont to do. Sit man, play monte."

The teamster seemed to think it over, head high in the canvas. She wanted to slip out of Sutter's grasp and run from the tent, but his fingers dug into her arm. She dropped the big gathering basket at his feet, hoping it would distract him.

"Ve haff ya goot fortune," Sutter said, eyes riding up on the white half-moons as he looked at the tall teamster. "Mary brings me the golt, men. I say, vinner take all, but play outside? Hmm? Here take light." He released her, pulled a candled bottleneck from the dirt and extended it to Perrimacoo.

She stepped back toward the door. Perrimacoo was ignoring the candle. "First give me my gold," he said.

The teamster leaned across the trunk and grabbed Perrimacoo by his shirt and lifted him off his stump, nose to nose. His hat fell back. "Like I said, man, any gold here is mine." He held him off the ground. Sutter stared, and she stepped back again, almost at the door now.

"No no no fighting in mine tent," Sutter shrilled. "I holt da golt. You two go outside. Go!" He turned and looked at her and she froze, forcing calm into her face as if she were only politely stepping away from an argument. Never taking his eyes from her, he put the candle bottle back in the ground and without straightening up grabbed the wide mouth of her basket and jammed in his hand down to the armpit, bringing out the pigskin bundle. "Ya iss golt. For da vinner. Outside now, both you men!"

She took another step, but in an instant he was behind her with his free hand on her buttock, pushing her back in the room. "I pay big for you, lieb-chen," he said in her ear.

She would wait for a better time. The teamster, who had dropped Per-rimacoo, wrenched the pigskin bundle from Sutter's hand and hefted it up and down. He unwrapped the bag and pinched the contents, his bushy black brows wiggling with interest. She didn't breathe.

"You gave all this to a filthy mahala when you owed me?" He looked at Sutter with undisguised hatred.

Perrimacoo, down on his stool again, said softly, "Hit's mine, but yours if ye wins."

The teamster sat down and looked at him and laid the open bundle between them. He picked up the cards, divided the pile, and fluffed and ruffled them with great dexterity.

"No, outside, gentlemen. Please," Sutter said.

"Fer Crissake," the teamster growled into his wagging cigarrito, "fuck the goddamned mahala and shut up." He sucked hard on the cigarrito then jerked his chin at the bed. "Want me to take the first poke?" Smoke blasted angrily from his nose.

Looking confused, Sutter put his arm protectively around her waist. Perrimacoo upended the bottle and drained it, then lifted half the cards and set them aside. The teamster picked up the remaining cards and placed them on the first stack. She knew it was time to go.

Trying to remember exactly what Pedro had told her to say, she used the only Americano term she knew. "I go shit now." She wrenched away, the lie sucking away her power, and ran headlong out the door. The baby wouldn't be born breech, as it would have if she'd backed out, but that was the least of her worries.

She rounded the corner and ran alongside the tent, toes digging in the dirt. It was darker than she'd thought, but the candlelight coming through the canvas helped, and she saw Pedro by a pine at the back of the tent, beckoning wildly with both arms.

"Liebchen!" Sutter screamed a few steps behind.

Pedro's hand connected with hers and he ran with her, pulling her toward the horse, a solid black shape in the dark.

Heavy bootfalls crashed close on her heels. She glanced back. The dark shapes of men loomed in the light from the glowing tent, Sutter hopping, pointing, yelling to the gathering miners. "Cleopatra stolen! Kill the bastard! Men to arms!"

She tripped and fell over a log. It knocked her breath out. Pedro lifted her in his arms. She was trying to breathe when he pushed her up in the saddle.

The teamster pounced on Pedro and they fell wrestling on the ground, the horse stepping nervously.

Perrimacoo seized the bridle, growling, "You little cheat," and tried to pull her off.

She kicked but he only laughed and kept grabbing for her leg. Miners swarmed through the trees like hornets, and an ominous sound came through the noise: Droom, droom, droom-droom-droom. Bohemkulla? The Spanish Devil? Angry spirits? Her heart thumped a swift beat.

The swarm of men yanked her off the horse and held her from all directions. She saw Pedro surrounded, guns bristling. Captain Sutter pushed through the crowd with his rifle over his shoulder, marching and making the sound. "Droom, droom, droom-droom-droom." Men snickered at him, the stench of their unwashed clothing pressing in on her.

Perrimacoo, having seized the doeskin bag from the saddlebags, held it over his head and yelled, "The idol-worshipper was makin off with our gold."

"Stealin Cleopatra too!"

"Second time!"

"Don't peer to be no Mexican."

"March the rascal to light and we'll see."

Within moments they were in front of Sutter's tent, his supper fire re-kindled. Men threw branches on it and stomped crates apart, cracking slats over their knees. Fear buzzed to the extremities of María's fingers and toes and she hardly dared breathe. Facing her own death would be nothing compared with watching Pedro's.

His head was up. Proud Hawk. She tried to go to him. The men held her back.

"Hit's a Mexican all right," a man yelled.

"Hang him!"

Knowing what that meant she kicked, bit, scratched, gouged with her elbows, aimed high with the heel of her foot—and contacted whatever came within reach.

"Reglar she-devil," said a man snickering and dancing out of range.

"Spitfire!" said another.

She peeled skin down the side of a face.

"Ooo-we," he yelled, dancing back. Men wove in and out all around her, smiling, and she didn't know what they intended, but she continued to yank and kick and scratch and writhe. She reared her head back and caught one on the chin.

Captain Sutter was yelling, "No killing at mine camp. Dot man iss mine lieutenant."

*Listen to him*, she thought. He is headman. Out of breath, she paused to listen.

Perrimacoo's voice came clear, "I say flog im with is own lariat. Teach im a lesson!" She saw him in the firelight, holding the doeskin bag.

"Yeah. Teach him good."

They shoved Pedro at a young pine, face first, lashed him to the tree, a rope around his waist and neck. With a loud rip, his shirt was torn open.

"Give it to him," a man cried.

"You, teamster. You got the muscle."

"Show the monkey who won the war."

"Mebbe it's Wakeen. The one that massacred the Oregon men!"

"What's yer name?" A man jammed his gunbarrel at Pedro's face. She heard the thunk of bone. *Don't tell them*. All the men holding her were glaring at him.

"Pedro Valdez," he said clearly, and she felt her legs weaken beneath her.

"He's spik alright!"

"McCoon was right."

"Dressed up MERican!"

"Punish the Mexican or none'ov our gold'll be safe."

"Our squaws either!"

The shouts melded into an unintelligible roar, the fire coloring the men's eyes orange, as well as the lower branches of the pines around the clearing.

The teamster came back from Chocolate with Pedro's lariat, whipping it overhead. It snapped like a heavy limb breaking. Men shouted approval. Black against the firelight, the teamster looked even bigger than he was, and the men of the camp were of one heart. Her skin prickled. Blackbird men. Breathing rapidly, she searched for her calm.

"Give 'im what he deserves!"

The huge arm jerked. Crack. The braided leather curled around Pedro's back. She strained toward him, immobile in the strong hands. The leather was drawn back, but a dark stripe lingered in its place. The skin crawled on her own back.

The big arm waved and leather strap whirred and cracked again. Pedro rolled his head. Two lines crossed his skin.

She closed her eyes. She had lured him here. Crack.

A faint moan. She couldn't look.

Men cheered. "Teach im!" Crack.

"Teach im!" Crack.

Counselor's voice came over the crowd. "Gentlemen, gentlemen." She opened her eyes, saw the big old American standing near Pedro with his arms spread wide. "What crime has been committed here?"

The arm swung back. She looked away. Crack.

"Stand back sir," said a man. "We caught this here greaser ahightailin it with gold. In the dark of night."

"At's right. Pimpin fer this here mahala."

Crack. She looked. Giant bird tracks overlapped his back, his face turned away against the tree.

"Inflicting punishment outside the scales of Lady Justice," Counselor said, "hardly bespeaks of civilization."

With jarring suddenness she remembered the knife. If she had pulled it when fighting the men, she would be dead. Luck had stopped her memory. The knife was to be used with cunning. Power was shifting; she felt it inside her.

Crack. With her elbow she felt the horn haft. Counselor was babbling his strange talk: "If you can't wait for the light of day, hold a trial now. I'll be state's advocate."

Crack.

A man with a very white face jumped before the teamster. "He's right. The whuppin' oughta come after the trial." Squeezing her amulet she felt again her power. Only last night she had been Deer Woman.

The whip settled softly behind the teamster, a snake at rest in the dust. "Mebbe we don't need no trial," he growled. "Mebbe the Spik's got the idee now."

White Face said, "Sides, we got the gold."

"Whose is it?" Counselor demanded.

"Mine," said the teamster, handing the reata to White Face, who began to coil it.

*Finished*. She felt calm, ready.

"Mine," Perrimacoo said, but a man grabbed for it and the bag fell open, half-empty. All the men stared, pointed. In the firelight sprinkles of gold glittered on Perrimacoo's trousers. He hugged the bag and tried to run, but stumbled. The bag flew up in a showering arc as he went down.

"Spilt all over. Looky thar!"

The teamster dove at Perrimacoo and they wrestled on the ground.

"It's alla ours!" shouted a miner, diving to the gold.

"Yeah! Divvy it."

"It's the Merican way!" Men fell to their knees, grabbing.

A frenzy of loose power swirled and shifted, and in the maelstrom the hands left her and she stood alone. Counselor picked up a pot and banged a gunbarrel on it. But every man was scrambling for the glittering dust. Men who only moments before had been of one heart, a unison cloud of blackbirds. Now they shoved and kicked each other, grunting and snarling, "Son of a bitch!"

Swiftly and calmly she went to Pedro and slashed his bindings. He whistled, and moments later they were on Chocolate, pounding away, Pedro behind in the saddle. A few surprised shouts mingled with the roar of the fight. The horse splashed across the water and she looked back to the fire, small and bright in a black world with a writhing heap of men. No one followed.

She slumped back against Pedro, who trusted the galloping animal to see in the dark. How long could he survive with North Americans flocking into the gold camps along every stream?

His chest warmed her back, and as she narrowed her eyes to the cool night air flowing past, she vowed to stay out of danger, for that endangered him. But Coyote's warbling laughter rang out, and the forest trembled with foreboding.

# IV

*Coyote's World*

# 65

**JANUARY 1, 1849**

Now you git." Catherine shoved Elitha toward the parlor door. "Outa here!"
"I said I'm helping with the dishes!" Elitha's belly bulged but she
didn't want privileges. She loved working with the other girls, and at the moment enjoyed pushing against the warmth and giggle of her best friend. They
laughed and shrieked as the advantage shifted back and forth. Catherine's
Little Will toddled in a circle, clapping his hands but keeping a wide berth
from the table they danced around.

Sarah, queenly at the dishpan and as comfortable here as in her own
house, added to Catherine's gits: "Four hands is plenty. You're just in the road."

Catherine grabbed a hank of muslin and snapped it at Elitha's rear.

She squealed and dashed to the tallest thing in the kitchen, Sarah, then
crouched behind her and put her hands on the slender ribcage. Still not pregnant. The towel zinged around Sarah and stung Elitha's upper arm. "No fair!"
She was about to fall over laughing when pain melted her grin.

Sudsily disengaging Elitha from her waist and catching the next whipped
towel, Sarah announced: "Us two is washin' the dishes and that's that!" With
authority conferred by her almost twenty years, her blue eyes locked into
Elitha's. "You're in no condition."

Elitha blew out air as the pain subsided. She and Catherine, both of them
sixteen-year-old married women, were behaving like children. But it was fun,
more fun since .... *Better not to remember.*

Catherine triumphantly marched her into the front room past the five
men who'd been toasting the New Year around the parlor stove. Elitha smiled
meekly at the bearded faces as Catherine pushed her into the rocking chair,
shaking a finger at Mr. Sheldon. "Now don't let her git up, hear?" A warm
smile put crow's feet at his eyes.

It felt good to sit, she had to admit, even though she'd already dined like
royalty through the whole New Year dinner while Sarah and Catherine served
her and the visiting men, women and eight children. Now, embarrassed to be
the center of attention, she smoothed her apron over her frock, her buttons

a foot from closing underneath. With Perry in San Francisco speculating on something, she'd been staying with Sarah and Mr. Daylor, the three having come the mile in the Daylor wagon.

The men resumed talking about things like Mormon Island, boundless quantities of gold, and the Mormon Battalion getting a head start. She liked Mr. Daylor's cheeriness, yet felt oddly uneasy in his presence. Last evening when she excused herself to go to bed in the trading room, he looked wistfully at her belly. Speaking in Perry's quirky English-sailor fashion, he always seemed unnaturally polite when he addressed her. Maybe she didn't know how to be friends with the husband of a friend. She often found herself blushing in his presence. Easier to be a child than a woman.

The three Rhoads men couldn't have differed more, yet they were father and sons. Father Rhoads stood with his hands clasped behind his back, wiggling his fingers at the hot stove—a Biblical patriarch of blockish build, white hair, untamed brows, and a severely downturned mouth. John was bearlike even in his Sunday clothes. Every glance of his deep-set eyes brought back what they'd shared on the tramp across the mountains, and how she'd begged him to go back for Pa and Tamsen. She hadn't dreamed his strength had limits or that he'd been about to collapse from water on the lungs. Next to his dark bulk, Sarah's twin brother could have been a European nobleman, slender and blue-eyed. He didn't drink spirits, nor did Elder Rhoads, being orthodox Mormon. John drank along with his brothers-in-law.

Liquor loosened all their tongues, Misters Sheldon and Daylor in fine fettle, and then suddenly Mr. Sheldon was talking to Elitha: "I'm buying three hundred acres across the river from you and Perry. Hartnell land."

"Why?" spilled out. Most of the land around here was wild and unclaimed, and he already owned a Mexican land grant of over eighteen thousand acres.

"Cause in eighteen and forty-nine even more dinero is coming our way in the guise of hungry miners, that's why. If we're smart, we'll be ready to feed 'em more than beef. It's vegetables they need." Sheldon turned to the men, mouth partly open like he was picking up a good scent. "Every man can shoot game, but they don't know one wild plant from another. I heard of a man paying twenty pinches for a single potato. Not to cure hunger, mind you, but scurvy. Your business," he looked at Mr. Daylor, "is booming, but you haven't seen anything yet. Men'll keep swarming in from every country, and they're all suffering for want of vegetables."

Row crops didn't seem to suit a man like him. He ran more cattle than Perry ever would. Besides, Catherine would want him closer to home. "We'd be proud to put you up while you're working across the river from us," Elitha said, "but I'd'ov thought you had enough land to grow vegetables around here." His wheat grew as tall as her head.

That sounded too know-it-all, but then she saw something in the men's faces that indicated they had the same question in mind.

Mr. Sheldon looked thoughtful. "Well, Hartnell's widow came upriver last fall to see her property. We talked. I got a good price on that ground, and it doesn't have the berry-bramble problem. I found a place where I can dig and get the water to flow over that land. Elitha, I need to talk to Perry about this. Come hot weather, I'll need to dam the river. It's his ground there, on the other side."

"I'll tell Perry," Elitha said. No love was lost between those two, but now they were to be neighbors, sort of. She also realized that the brambles were much worse in Rancho Omuchumne because Deer Creek flowed parallel to the river for about fourteen miles, making a berry thicket marsh.

The door flew open. Rosy-cheeked children entered, and with them came cold air and the smell of wet wool. Señor Valdez came in last and shut the door.

Catherine dashed into the front room rounding up the children and shaking a cloth behind them. "Git along to the kitchen now. Alla you." Their chatter spilled into the parlor along with kitchen lamplight. It had grown dark, the days very short. Elitha removed the glass from the hurricane lamp on the sundries table and started to get up to light the wick, but Mr. Sheldon stopped her.

"You'll git me in trouble." He opened the stove, got a twig to burn, and lit the wick.

Señor Valdez stood in his sarape with hat in hand, his auburn hair wet and flattened. "Patrón?"

"Sí," Mr. Sheldon replied.

"The niños named the little horses."

Sheldon smiled, but the Spaniard obviously had more on his mind.

"More men at the river, patrón, swimming horses and cows across. Trouble maybe."

"They see you?"

He shook his head. "Different trouble. High water. They are having a hard time." Elitha knew he was in hiding after the killing at Daylor's store, but was he the mysterious Joaquín? Killing white men left and right? It didn't seem possible. But she never gave tongue to it because Mr. Sheldon protected the so-called Californio. It was frightful the way retaliation fired men to violent acts. The good thing was, Sarah wasn't hurt, and Indian Mary and her father were safe here in Rancho Omuchumne. This afternoon Elitha had seen the now frail Captain Juan limping up and down between the mill and this house.

Men reached for their coats. Mr. Daylor put a hand on John Rhoads' arm. "Pedro and I'll see to it, John. You'd catch yer death." Putting on his own coat, he turned to his partner. "Jared, we needs us a ferryman. I been thinking our brother-in-law Sebastian Keyser will do. He's done ferryin before." He opened the door. "It'd do us all good to get him and Elizabeth here on the Cosumney."

Sheldon said, "Maybe another improvement for eighteen-forty-nine."

As the door shut behind Mr. Valdez, joy shot through Elitha to think Elizabeth Keyser might come here to live. Then she'd have three girls to visit. The memory she had of Elizabeth at Johnson's ranch was her only pleasant memory of that place. But Mary Murphy, alone with that awful Mr. Johnson, sure would miss Elizabeth's company.

"Well now Father Rhoads," Mr. Sheldon said like a master of ceremonies, "what are you plannin' for eighteen-forty-nine?"

"I'll be headin' to Zion with the Saints."

For a moment Elitha thought the old man was dying, but then recalled that Mormons referred to the salt desert as "Zion," and they called themselves saints.

"Catey said as much," Mr. Sheldon mused, "but when you thinking to leave?"

"Brigham wrote to wait 'til the first crops is in. They can't hardly feed the people they got there now. I figger we'll cross over the route Kit Carson scouted—higher than the one the Donners got bound in—so we won't leave 'til mid-June at the least, and miss the worst of the snow. That'll get us there when crops are ripening."

Sarah's twin brother, William Rhoads, spoke for the first time since Elitha came into the room. "I was hopin you'd change your mind, Pa. With the mining so good at the diggings and all, I'd like you to stay in California and see how it pans out."

The patriarch leaned back on his heels. "Son, some things is more precious than gold. Riches are to be used in the service of the Lord." Directing his words more to his two sons-in-law, Sheldon and Daylor, he added, "Our gold'll go to the buildin' of a grand tabernacle."

Sheldon asked, "Is it true that Brigham Young wrote letters to members of the Mormon Battalion offering wages for building a town by the salt lake?"

The white head jerked down and up. "And they'll donate their gold. Mark my words. Salt Lake City will shine."

The room grew uncomfortably still, wood shifted in the stove, and a surge of wind rattled the windows. No doubt the elder Mr. Rhoads hoped all of his children and their children would accompany him to Zion. But Sarah, Catherine, and Elizabeth were married to non-Mormons, and John built a nice house about two miles down-river, so it looked like he'd stay. Brother William might be considering whether to go or stay.

The door opened and Bill Daylor stamped in, rubbing his shoulders and gritting his teeth. "Right brisk it is out there." He hung his coat on a peg and pushed in between Jared Sheldon and Father Rhoads at the stove. "Greenhorns negotiatin' the river. Got 'em acrost, we did." Whenever he came into a room, things perked up.

He turned to Mr. Sheldon. "Jared me man, ye got 'ny more ideas for forty-nine?" He grinned ruefully, "If ye don't mind spillin it to yer rancho partner."

Maybe the three hundred acres had been news to him.

In a smiling lack of hurry, Mr. Sheldon strolled to the demijohn barrel on a shelf near the kitchen door and released the amber flow into his glass. Reinserting the cork, he stuck his head in the kitchen and made a round-house gesture. Moments later Catherine was in the crook of his arm being escorted into the parlor, little Will trailing. Mr. Sheldon swept a hand toward the bent-willow chair. With an impish grin Catey plumped into it, snuggling little Will into her lap. A child holding a child. Elitha hoped she'd look older than that when her baby came.

"Folks," Mr. Sheldon announced, "Forty-eight was the best year of my life." He tousled his boy's hair. "William Chauncy here growing up strong. A loyal band of Indians bringing in gold, in surprising amounts. The mill and cattle businesses doing good. Now I'm thinkin to build a road stop, call it Slough House for fun. Add the vegetables to that, and it looks to be a right prosperous year." He smiled at Catherine. "Get us another young'un too."

Pregnant! Elitha opened her eyes and mouth at Catherine.

Crimson hit Catey's cheeks. "We're not sure yet," she said. Mr. Sheldon smiled down at his wife with a transparent look of love.

Mr. Daylor, having refilled his glass at the barrel, stood in the center of the room with shelf-like shoulders topping a tall frame. "That calls for a toast," he said. "Best wishes to me partner and his charmin' wife." Everyone raised the short-stemmed glasses, one of the Sheldon items that Elitha very much admired.

Then, with his eyes twinkling over the buttressed architecture of his nose, Mr Daylor made an announcement: "A bad year it is indeed, shapin' up for Sir John Sutter Esquire." He had the tight smile of a man hiding something jolly.

Elitha wondered why, but a severe pain called her inward. The black-eyed peas, she said to herself. Beans really, brought around the Horn. Supposed to bring luck on New Year's Day. *Just gas.*

After the silence Jared Sheldon said with sarcasm, "Well, partner mine, if you've got som'm under that overworked hat a yours, would ya tell us about it?"

Pain ebbing, Elitha saw mischief in Mr. Daylor's raised brows. "Been hatchin' it for some time, I has."

Mr. Sheldon's eyes cut to Catherine, then back to Daylor. "Think it's aged enough to let 'er out?"

Mr. Daylor glanced at his wife, now coming from the kitchen wiping her hands on her apron. Not a hair strayed from her bun despite the earlier ruckus. A flicker in their mutual gazes told Elitha the Daylors shared the secret. But Catey looked steamed. "William Daylor, I vow!" she demanded. "Tell it straight! What ARE you doin' to Mr. Sutter. We have a right to know."

Most emigrants praised John Sutter. Only old California hands knew about the bad blood between him and his former cook. Was Daylor about to take his long-awaited revenge? He was said to be the strongest man in California, violent and unstoppable, though Elitha had formed a milder opinion. Now he looked like a coyote running off with a stolen pork chop. All he said was, "The fool is nigh about to meet 'is match, he is."

Catherine rearranged her face to haughty. "You can right well stop teasin', Brother Daylor, cause I don't give a fig." She flounced toward the window, where the sky was rapidly darkening.

"As ye please." He lifted the glass to his lips, his long high cheeks streaked with color.

Catherine jumped up, sat little Will down on the chair, and stood thrusting her chin at Mr. Daylor, an amusing sight, she looking about two feet shorter. "WHO is this match for Mr. Sutter?" She glared at him then turned to her husband for help. But with his foot on a stool, his arm resting on that knee, and his lips parted in a smile, Mr. Sheldon was clearly enjoying the suspense as much as his brother-in-law.

Another pain rocked through Elitha and she leaned back in the chair, willing it to stop. No more black-eyed peas. Ever!

Mr. Daylor said, "Do you recollect all the inquiries about a loan for the vainglorious Captain Sutter?" His ranch partner brother-in-law gave him a sardonic nod.

Elitha recalled that even Perry had been approached by Sutter's son, who'd sailed from Switzerland to California. Perry called him a greenhorn tangling with smart bankers and other ruthless men starting a town on Sutter's property on the Sacramento River. So who was this match for Sutter?

"Well, I loaned him the money," Mr. Daylor announced.

"What?" barked Sheldon straightening to his full height, clearly as surprised as Elitha.

"Why?" Catherine sang out. Yes, Elitha wondered, why on would earth he of all men loan a large chunk of money to his old foe?

Said to be the richest man in California thanks to gold at Dry Diggins, the brisk store business, investments, and his half of the cattle ranch, Bill Daylor continued in his jolly manner. "Hads me a talk with young Sutter, I did, and he tells me his mum fancies sailin to California, so he's borrowing money for the fare to get her here." Still smiling, he sipped from his glass. Elitha hadn't imagined John Sutter as a family man, though he had a grown son who had come from Switzerland, and somehow she hadn't given any thought to why his wife hadn't joined him before now. It had to be ten years since he'd established the fort.

Mr. Daylor warmed to his story. "And I says to young Sutter says I, what kind of laidy might yer dear mum be then? And he says to me, Mr. Daylor says he, this woman can row her own boat. Mind ye, not in them words, but I begins to fathom Frau Sutter, and the more we jaw the more I sees a battle-ship under full sail cuttin' through the foam with all guns firin'."

Not the refined lady of a European squire, Elitha gathered.

Helplessly Mr. Daylor peaked his brows. "And I says to young Sutter says I, does yer dear mum know what lechery abounds in this California wilder-ness? 'Ave ye no care, says I, for her delicate female constitution in a locale such as this? And he looks me in the eye like a man—not a day over twenty-one—and says to me, sir says he, she'll NOT ABIDE the drunken debauchery me daddy's been wallowin' in. And I turns to Henry Lienhard, who's sitting there tuggin' young Sutter past the shoals o' the language and 'elping to ar-range the deal, and I gives him a good shake o' the hand."

With a snort of comprehension Sheldon tossed back his head belly-laughing. Then he leveled those wolfish eyes at his business partner and asked. "How much money?"

"Twelve thousand dollars, for the passage of Frau Sutter and a grown daugh-ter with a tongue to match her mum's, and a few more relations to boot—the entire lot of 'em ready to moor themselves to the so-called king of Californy. And gittin a right smart fee is Lienhard, to escort the lot to their destination."

"You ready to lose twelve thousand dollars?"

Mr. Daylor shrugged helplessly. "Wot could a bloak do? Why, not a soul in a thousand miles would loan money to poor old John Sutter, and them be-yond the less likely." His eyes sparkled. "And worth every penny it tis, partner mine. Gots me a sterling rate secured by blocks of land in what they're laying out to be the City of Sacramento." Daylor took a sip and continued. "And Herr Sutter canno' say a word to stop the deal, makin' out to 'is boy 'e's overjoyed at the approach of his dearly beloved wife who he's been missin so hard these many years." Daylor swallowed the rest of his drink and stood victorious, a man in his prime, brimming with life.

"Well, build yourself an ark," Mr. Sheldon said, "cause that town'll be un-der water." His stepped forward with his glass extended, "I'd like to make a toast." He raised his glass.

"To Johann Augustus Sutter, pioneer of California. Man of vision—Now William Daylor, put your eyeballs back in and think a minute on what he did here. Built a civilization outa nothing. Ever time somebody needed some-thing, he'd hire men to figger out how to make it. He tamed the Indians and trained 'em to work. Why this very minute he's got men making hats and barrel hoops and shingles up at the springs, ferry boats down at the water-front. He's sawing timber in Coloma, tannin hides, dryin meat, makin boots and shoes from the biggest cattle herd this country ever saw. Helped me get started, if you haven't forgot. And did it all with a gentleman's style, not to mention keeping the Mexican authorities middling content. Now this son of his comes along, and just because the boy's been taught to do sums and Sutter wants to brag on him, he hands him power of attorney. The boy sees the size of his father's debts, panics, sells the entire fort for what? Seven thousand dollars, wasn't it? Money you and I—"

"Trash heap now," Mr. Daylor put in, "a flea-infested camp for rascals thievin' their way to the mines, and ye knows damned well why Sutter gave 'is affairs to the lad. Dodging creditors. I doubt that man's ever paid off a debt in his life."

"I heard they're hauling in good rent for the fort booths, but that's not my drift, William Daylor. You are. You giving the loan. It's a damn fitting end—pardon my language ladies—to that ridiculous episode, never mind your scheming brains. John Sutter will fade from history along with his fort, and that's sad. So here's to him. For old time's sake." Sheldon lifted his glass. "Captain John Sutter, a man I'd say earned the title of gentleman."

A cockeyed smile twisted Daylor's face, but he raised his glass and drank to Mr. Sutter, Elitha was glad to see. As all the glasses clinked, the glassless Father Rhoads inserted, "He won't fade from history." Sheldon and Daylor turned to him expectantly.

"Where I come from, Mr. Sutter is praised as a friend of America. A good and generous one at that, and a benefactor of every emigrant. He was good to me and Mother Rhoads, rest her soul. Did his best try'n to get her to a doctor in San Francisco. If Latter Day Saints used spirits, I'd drink to John Sutter." The other men raised their glasses and swallowed.

In the silence that followed Elitha was inspired to contribute, "I won't forget the supplies Mr. Sutter had bought up to the different stations in the mountains."

John Rhoads added, "A lot of people wouldn't be alive to remember, but for his generosity." He looked at Elitha. "I'll go so far as to say not one of you stranded people would'ov come to safety."

"Well," Father Rhoads said, "we'd best be on our way. She's about to blow good." Out the window the sky was black and the wind pried at the eaves of the snug house.

"Fore you go, Pa," Sarah said, "We've got news too. This year we'll be hiring a shopkeeper who can do the accounts." Elitha watched Sarah move under Mr. Daylor's arm.

"By thunder, that's overdue," said her father.

Elitha wondered where the shopkeeper would sleep. Maybe the Daylors wouldn't be able to put her up for long visits after the man came. She didn't want to impose on the little Sheldon family, but with so many miners roaming the country, she also didn't want to stay home alone with Perry gone, which was often.

John Rhoads stuck his head in the kitchen, "Younguns, time to hightail it."

Children dashed into the parlor, pushing for space beneath the cloak rack. The Daylors would be leaving next, Elitha with them. Sad that the party was over, Elitha nonetheless looked forward to the bed. Lying flat might straighten out the kinks.

"Happy New Year!" everyone called. The parade of children going out the door included John Rhoads' big family, his Matilda having been too ill to come, and the younger brothers and sisters of Catherine, Sarah, Billy, and John, offspring of the elder Rhoads, who with his wife Elizabeth fathered nineteen children.

"Happy New Year!" Elitha sang out. The wind from the open door flattened the apron over her big belly. A harsh pain jabbed her. Worse than before. A moan escaped, and it was all she could do to stay on her feet.

Cloak in hand, Sarah turned and said, "You look peaked."

The Sheldons eyed her, Catey's smile gone. She put little Will down on his feet.

"It's not what you think," Elitha said.

"Well, you better lie down anyhow." Catherine took her hand and pulled her into little Will's room, Sarah following. They sat her down on the bed.

Looking up at her hovering friends, she felt foolish. "It's only gas. The baby won't come for two, three months." Little Will needed his bed. She tried to rise, but Catherine held her down.

# 66

Elitha squeezed her eyes shut as pain stole her breath. When she opened them the sisters were whispering in the corner, Mr. Sheldon a blurred shape at the doorway. Rain streaked the dark window.

She hated putting the Sheldons out and holding up the Daylors. She got to her elbows determined to go, but when Sarah and Catherine gentled her down something felt strange on her thighs, like a pan of warm water had spilled. Bringing up a wet hand and puzzling over it, Elitha felt another pang starting deep within. She held her breath and clenched her fists as it mounted. Turning from the worried faces, she lay on her side, pulled up her knees then stiffened her legs. Nothing helped.

Maybe it was happening. They knew more about this than she did. Hard behind that thought came the memory of her real mother's death. "Child-bed fever," people had whispered of Mary Blue. Indian blood in her, but she died anyway. Tamsen's screams floated back. Tamsen, the bravest woman in the world.

In the back of her mind on the dark sea where dreams formed, a horror heaved its head, something she had forced aside and refused to acknowledge. She had lived in a make-believe world telling herself it wasn't her time and somehow it never would be. And now pain and fear sailed at her with terrifying certainty, a monster looming down over her with sharp fangs and death-dealing tentacles, sucking her into a grip of total agony. Terror made boards of her legs and arms. She balled her fists and gritted her teeth, willing the monster away and the pain to subside. But it tore through her with white-hot keenness.

"… too soon," Sarah was saying. "*Something's wrong.*"

"… git brandy down her."

*God, help me!* A squeak came out as she bit her lip, determined not to scream and embarrass herself. Something's wrong.

Sarah looked down from lofty heights, a different universe. "Poor thing, she's shakin like a leaf." She laid a cool hand on Elitha's forehead.

Teeth chattering and clammy with sweat, she couldn't control her body.

Catherine put a tin cup to her lips. The fumes burned her nose and the liquid seared down her throat. "Put more wood in the stove," Catherine told Sarah. Skirts rustled from the room.

Choking on the aguardiente, Elitha couldn't say no to more wood, more heat. Fear, not cold was shaking her. The stove lid clanged, wood thumped. The monster stirred again. "Oh, no," she said, lying back with the cup, willing it away. But it muscled slowly and hard through her. She moaned and then cried out. Then, by excruciatingly slow stages, the vise loosened and she lay sweating, rigid, afraid of the next one. Too hot.

"Here, git this in you." Sarah forced more aguardiente past her clacking teeth.

But the invigorated leviathan arose again and again, its spikes grinding relentlessly through her. She couldn't take any more. Nobody could. If she was going to die, she wanted to get it over with quick.

Between attacks she opened her eyes. Rain slashed the window and wind keened around the eaves. The shadowy figures of Sarah and Catherine remained at her side. In a timid voice Catherine asked, "You all right?"

She shivered so hard her jaw felt wired shut. She couldn't say yes and was too polite to say no. Had it been like this when little Will was born? No one could know. Pain wasn't like comparing scars. She barely breathed, swallowed brandy, but the enemy welled up again and again, worse and worse each time, crushing the shame out of her.

"Outa her head," she heard—a scream lingering between the wooden walls. She saw her own terror in Sarah's hovering face, heard Sarah's whisper to Catherine, "Hope it don't go thirty-five hours, like yours."

*Thirty-five hours!* Frantic at the thought, she threw her head from side to side on the pillow, wanting out of her skin. Let me die now, God!

"You'll be fine," Catherine said.

The brandy fogged only the spaces between the attacks. A lamp was lit, her shame illuminated. Cool cloths were laid on her head. She thrashed, threw them off, screamed in crescendos, knowing that the sound passed her lips.

A child's voice: "Lady cry."

Someone at the outer door: "… don't need Indian plants."

Indian Mary's voice! A door closing. She felt the cooler, wonderful air. Soaked in sweat she tried to rise, to say that Indian Mary could help. Herbs helped.

"Never you mind, now. I sent her away."

"No I…" But the monster bit into her and she fell back into the screaming void.

⚓

She awoke to a whisper. "It was for the best."

She opened her eyes. Four squares of sunlight came through the window and blanched the bedclothes—blankets that left no more sensory impression than if they were painted on. She felt nothing. She floated. *For the best.* Catherine sat in her rocking chair beneath the daguerreotype of a fierce old woman. The chair filled the space between the bed and the door. Pink calico stretched across Catherine's shoulders as she twisted around to where Mr. Sheldon stood in the doorway, little Will in his arms. Sarah was gone.

Mr. Sheldon gave Elitha a look and stepped away. Catherine turned back, smiling weakly. "You all right?"

"Guess I lived." *Did I have a baby?*

"Oh poor, poor Elitha. It was bad." She leaned over the bed and smoothed her hair, then brought a tin cup from the floor. "Here, water will do you good."

*Was it dead? Deformed?* She wanted the water, but had no more strength than a rag doll. Catherine lifted her shoulders and head, helped her drink. She swallowed tentatively, unsure whether her insides were intact enough to ingest water. It cooled her as it went down. The mild ache in her privates she wouldn't call pain, nothing she had identified by that name would ever be pain again. Even the air felt doubtful, uncertain as the expression on Catherine's face. No baby in the room. Anxiety edged her heart like a border of crisp tatting. Maybe the whole thing had been a hideous trick, a test of her grit. "What day is it?"

Catherine's intelligent eyes studied her. "January second, eighteen-forty-nine."

She shut her eyes and breathed the fragile air, held it and exhaled. Slowly, beneath the quilt, she lifted her amazingly heavy hands from her sides to her abdomen and felt the emptiness there. The baby was supposed to relieve her loneliness. "Not a good way to start the year was it?" she dared say.

"Nope." Not a moment's hesitation.

*Dead*. She closed her eyes and saw in her mind the place of the baby's conception, the adobe, the bed by the wall, the broken window she'd tried to make Perry fix. Bad luck house, Indians called it. Cursed. "Boy or girl?"

Almost a whisper. "Boy. Never did take a breath. So tiny and all, and the birthin so—" She patted Elitha's shoulder through the quilt.

Did she want to see him? No. That would make him real. Probably buried by now anyway. She thought forward to the coming year without the child, and felt a looseness float through her sorrow, a sense of not being tied down, like she might levitate over the bed with the quilt trailing from both sides. "Perry'll be sad," she said. He genuinely cared for Billy, and she'd hoped his love for their baby would change things between them.

Catherine raised a brow and shrugged in a way that said she didn't think much of Perry. They knew he had women in San Francisco and in the floating town at Sutter's Embarcadero, and in ship-hotels where the town of Sacramento was being built. Even after he'd put in a full day of riding, his shirts gave off the essence of rose water.

"You ever wonder why you're here?" It came unbidden from her heart.

Catherine cocked her head. "With you? Here at the ranch?"

"No, in the world."

Catherine reached beneath the quilt and took Elitha's hand and squeezed it. "You poor girl. You're not alone. You know that you always got us Rhoadses, and Jared and Mr. Daylor."

It must have seemed she was fishing for friendship. She couldn't think how to undo it.

Catherine leaned over the bed. "God put every one of us here for a reason." Her eyes were a foot away yet she inhabited a different world—a respectable house with a loving husband, an adorable child, a spread of land beginning to be the center of a town.

"Tamsen, my Ma, would'ov said that. So why is she dead? And her babies living with strangers. Not going to school. Living with people who don't even speak English. People who won't even answer my lett—" Sobs erupted, racking her overworked muscles. She pulled back her hand and meant to roll over to hide the emotion, but her body was too weak. Only her head turned.

"It's natural you're upset. Get some more sleep." Gentle pats came through the quilt. Then the wooden sound of the door shutting.

Did God spare her only to watch the Donner family disintegrate? Why did He let her marry a man who lacked the respect of his neighbors? A man who frequented bad women, gambled his money, and made it hard for her to care for her sisters? Why did He make her suffer in childbed only to give her a dead baby? What was the purpose? She moaned, suddenly realizing as plain as anything that she was feeling sorry for herself. Pa would shame her. What kind of pioneer stock was she anyhow? "Catey!"

The door flew open and intense concern showed in her face—a girl who'd gone thirty-five hours. "Elitha?"

"You're the best friend I ever had. Thank you ever so much for helping me through my time."

"Course we'd all help."

Still, eighteen-forty-nine looked to be a bad year.

# 67

April 29, 1849

Covered with greenish-black mud except for the whites of her wild eyes, the mired cow bellowed and slashed out with her front hooves. Every move dug her deeper in the mud, up to her shoulders now. On the first try Roberto had settled his lasso around the far-flung horns and pulled so it slid down tight around the horn stems. Now he looked like a fisherman with a surprising catch. Clad in a loincloth with a red bandanna anchoring his long hair, he braced his muscular legs and kept the rope taut on a thousand pounds of crazed stupidity. Quapata stood waiting to help.

Pedro chided himself while knotting the end of his rope around the groove atop the windlass pole. It was past time to get the herd to safer pasture. A treacherous time, when the spring floods receded, leaving the land between the river and creek a muddy marsh. Slough they called in in English. The hot wind had browned the high ground, so the cattle turned to the green marsh grasses.

"Now?" Quapata asked, his face intent upon the situation.

"Sí." Pedro and Quapata upended the pole, slanting it away from the cow, driving the point deep with their combined weight. Then Pedro secured the free end of his reata around the base of a tough willow clump as one would anchor a tent peg. Not even a crazed cow could uproot a plant that chose to live in the path of violent floods.

Reaching for the iron bar, Pedro motioned Roberto and yelled over the trumpeting of the cow, "Está bien. Pull her out."

Within moments Roberto had the round multi-braided horsehair rope around the pole. Pedro inserted the bar between pole and rope, and the rest was easy. Roberto walked the bar around the pole, each revolution winding the rope, cinching it up. Slowly the cow would rise from the bog. "Silencio señora," Pedro told the frantic animal.

"Good work," came from behind.

Pedro turned to see Señor Sheldon sitting on his horse, reins in hand.

"Gracias, patrón, for the iron cinch." Even blue oak bent under the pressure.

"We need to talk." Trouble showed in his face as plain as the feather in his sombrero. Was Pedro the cause? Weaving through clumps of bunchgrass toward the patrón, he thought back. He'd offered to leave the rancho, but Sheldon insisted he'd be safe here. And indeed, no mob had come. Too busy mining. Even the Sheriff had gone to the mines. Strangest of all, the reputation of the vicious "Joaquín" had a way of protecting Pedro. At Daylor's store miners told chilling stories of the desperado Joaquín raiding camps, shooting men point blank, stealing their gold. Meanwhile Pedro was peacefully running cattle. Furthermore the description of the outlaw and his accomplice, "Three-fingered Jack," kept changing. Now the killer's hair was black! So was his horse, and the accomplice had become a brutal North American! Quapata, of course, was a mild Indian.

Stranger yet, Quapata's hand didn't necessarily identify him in a country where so many vaqueros had lost fingers. But the confusion went deeper. North Americans didn't count the "thumb" as a finger. To everyone else it was the first dedo, first digit. So Cuatro Dedos, a four-fingered killer rumored to be preying on the mines, had all his God-given fingers in English, but not in Spanish. In Spanish, "Three-fingered Jack" had lost two fingers. So depending on who named the bandit and who counted the fingers, Pedro had explained to María, the accomplice of Joaquín could have anywhere between three and five fingers. "Coyote," she'd said with a smile.

Now, following the patrón away from the bawling cow to where they could talk, Pedro had to smile too. He had joked that he and Quapata could stand on Daylor's Road and confess to the killings at Rancho Sacayak, and nobody would take them seriously or even care. All resemblance to "Joaquín" had vanished, and gold-seekers lost interest in what happened last month. All they cared about was rumors of "color" in this or that stream. California had become a land of strangers unbound by the normal rules of life.

Señor Sheldon turned and said, "Let's get the Indians home. Pronto. Daylor says men are pouring out of the saloons in Sacramento City, cleanin' their guns and riding for the hills."

"Coming for me?"

"No. The Indians. I want you to send word to Dry Diggins. Tell them to hurry back. And Pedro?"

Already heading for the windlass, he glanced back. "Sí?"

"The trouble is on the American River, middle and north forks. Seven white men killed, some say in retaliation for a whole village being massacred. White men are on the warpath. My guess is they'll go back to the saloons once they get their vengeance—God help the Maidu. Our Indians will have plenty of time to get home while that mob does its dirty work in the northern mines. I just don't want to take chances." His wolf eyes bored into Pedro. "Not after what happened at Rancho Sacayak."

"Comprendo, patrón." Trotting through the bunchgrass Pedro calculated. The middle fork of the American was north of Dry Diggings—Weber Creek as it was now called, after a friend of the patrones who had joined them on that first cattle drive. The town that had sprung up around the Diggings was now called Hangtown, due to a hanging there. It didn't make sense for Pedro or Quapata to go. That left Roberto or one of the two younger vaqueros.

He explained the emergency to Roberto, leaving out the part about it being a precaution. He didn't want to slow the messenger or delay the Indians' return. These were people who would hold a big time at the slightest provocation. "Want to take Chocolate?"

Roberto was running toward his mount, Quapata taking over the windlass. He yelled over his shoulder, "Gracias no. I take five horses, ride fresh. Por favor, Ramón should care for my boys." Roberto's wife and daughter and parents and grandfather were at the Diggings, but his two young sons had stayed at the rancho.

Pedro called after him, "Vaya con Dios, amigo." The Indian leaped gracefully onto his horse, slapped the haunch and turned to wave, hair flying. He would string four extra horses and cut the spent animals loose as he used them. Thirty miles. Six miles per horse.

Pedro mounted Chocolate and trotted him to Ramón and Locklock, who patrolled the edge of the herd. "Two or three days and everyone will be home," he said. "Then we'll get some sleep." The vaqueros smiled.

He had to smile too. Thanks be to God the Indians were coming home! Movement caught his eye, another vaca breaking from the herd. Wheeling, he slapped his hat on Chocolate's haunch and turned the cow so fast she flopped on her side. She scrambled to her feet and he trotted her back to the herd.

Galloping back to Quapata at the windlass, he felt pleased. It wasn't just that manpower was on its way home. María would get her midwife. For weeks she'd been adamant that every woman needed a birth-helper, and that no birth was safe without women singing in the birth house. She had asked, "Who will massage me with herbs? And pacify the spirits? And bring the baby down?" Tomaka was the Omuchumne birth-helper. Good fat Tomaka. Never had he wanted to see her as much as he did now. This morning María announced that she wanted to go to the Diggings. The Omuchumne had worked on Weber Creek for a year, so long that many women had become pregnant. They even built a birth hut. "Take me there," she had begged, her black eyes tugging at his heart. Right then and there he should have said no. But he didn't, and now she probably had her hopes up. He had agonized over it all day.

But the Omuchumne would soon be home! Perhaps tomorrow night. With a touch of bad conscience pricking him, he hoped the patrón would keep them home for good, for surely the gold was playing out. Or was that wishful thinking? Millions of pesos worth of gold had been taken from the Dry Diggings on Weber Creek.

Quapata would smile again to know his Blue Star and the two babies would soon be home. After the massacre of her family and the Cry, she'd accompanied her mother-in-law back to the Diggings. Said the rancheria was too empty, and she wanted to be with people—not frightened during the long hours that Quapata worked far from the ranchería.

He hobbled Chocolate and walked down to where Quapata was about finished winding the reata around the pole. North Americans! The bastards had lashed him for one reason: he was a native Californian. His back had healed but his pride never would. They were invading dogs. They should be punished, and he ached to do the punishing. He would go after them now, except for his duty to the patrones—ay, ay, ay the bloody scenes that teased his mind! How easy it would be to become Joaquín and step from the bushes, take their gold, slit their throats, and ride to safety on his superior horse.

But now he turned his full attention to cutting loose this bellowing beast, more dangerous now as she recovered her footing. He must judge the perfect moment as Quapata walked around the pole, the rope tightening, shortening.

# 68

Dawn was approaching in Pedro's room above the gristmill, two days after Roberto had been dispatched to bring the Omuchumne home. María lay quietly awake, glad the women would soon be back, and she urged the baby inside her to wait. All too well she recalled being outside the door while Elitha endured needless suffering. Her magic double had lacked a birth hut, pain-stopping herbs, and the proper procedures of birth. Of course her child died.

The door latch lifted. No boots had sounded on the stairs. María's soul soared. The Omuchumne were home! But no. Quapata pushed the door open and said, "Señor Daylo want you go his house."

"Is something wrong?" Pedro asked, rising on an elbow.

"Maybe." That was strong talk for Quapata.

Pedro quickly dressed, kissed the tip of María's nose, and hung his sombrero on his back. He tucked his handgun into his sash and left, boots drumming a fast descent.

Father sat up staring at nothing, intent on everything. Hair moved on the back of María's neck as she listened to the horses pounding away. In the silence she felt a rush of loose power. Beside her in bed, Billy felt it. She saw alarm in his face, and he whimpered.

Her heart beat in strange rhythms, and she could see that Father also sensed trouble. Finally she said, "I go see." "Keep Billy here." He nodded in agreement.

Pedro never wanted her to go near danger, but power guided her.

The mile to Señor Daylor's house seemed long with her big belly leading. Twinges of pain stung her groin from the pressure and speed of her steps along the river trail, a damp, narrow corridor between dormant cottonwoods and alders. Awake now, the birds sounded strident. Power crackled. Anything could happen. She feared that Pedro's anger would leach away his power and endanger him.

At a small riverbank clearing near Señor Daylo's adobe, she saw the heads and shoulders of Ramón and Locklock protruding from a deep hole, dirt flying from their shovels. Quapata stood watching at the side. She decided to watch. What did it mean that vaqueros were digging a hole early in the morning? "Where is Pedro?" she asked Quapata.

He nodded up the path toward the Daylor place.

She continued walking. If North Americans had attacked, the vaqueros would have bows and arrows, not shovels. This danger was different.

At the house she saw Señor Daylo kneeling in the yard, hammering a lid on a wooden box. Three women stood on the porch—Elitha, her little white horse still perspiring at the rail, Señora Daylo, who had her arm around the third woman, Elizabeth Keyser, the new Americana whose husband was building a house. The three pale faces looked sorrowful, Señora Keyser's eyes swollen and red. They all stared at the half-finished box as if it held awesome magic. Elizabeth's small son was nowhere to be seen. In the box, María suddenly realized.

She recoiled, knowing her baby could be born dead with her being so near to a dead person, especially a child. But then she remembered all the maimed and dead people she'd looked upon, even touched, at the home place. It didn't matter anymore. Even if she had a birth-helper, her child would likely be born dead. She calmed herself and looked around for Pedro. Not seeing him, she asked Señor Daylo if he knew where he went.

"Be back in a minute, 'e will." No fear in his voice.

Good. The loose power must be here then, swirling around the wooden box. She faced it and stayed to watch the death rite of the new people.

❧

Chocolate nudged Pedro between the shoulder blades as he peered through a small aperture in the wall of blackberry brambles. Before going farther, he needed to know whether any of the encamped North Americans could identity him as a killer. He counted eight men exactly where Señor Daylor said they'd be, a hundred and fifty yards from the adobe, about twenty-five yards from where he stood in the brambles. Still sleeping, they sprawled like logs around a cold fire, horses saddled, bedrolls packed, rifles handy—what kind he couldn't see from this distance. Some wore buckskins but the old man was not among them, nor the bastard with the rattlesnake bite. He recognized no one from Sutter's camp in the pine woods.

The Sacayak-New Helvetia trail, now called Daylor Road, intersected with the north trail just over the rise. That meant the Indians would pass by this camp on their way home. But Señor Daylor had thought these North Americans might be friendly, and had asked Pedro to inquire about their business. Sheldon and Keyser were at the Fort, Sutter having returned from his Piney Woods, and Senor Daylor had needed to go help bury the Keyser child, so that left Pedro to do this.

"Me guess is," Daylor had said, "they be resting on their way to the southern mines. Those racks they're ridin look a wee bit windbroke. See if they need horses or anything else." Raising the tufts of his brows in a semi-comical way, he had added, "Don't shoot anyone." Then he'd left to go to the grave.

Miffed at that, Pedro nonetheless had loaded his rifle and Allen pepper-box revolver. He trusted Quapata's instincts.

Now he mounted, donned his sombrero, and reined the horse around the berries and up the road, casually as if just arriving. "Hola! Can I help you?" His friendly tone. The filthy dogs had defecated on open ground, with an outhouse a stone's throw away. Some of the eight were sitting up. Others stood, leaving their rifles on the ground, oiled, reflecting sunlight.

Straight-backed, he reined the horse off the trail and approached the camp. "I am the mayordomo of the rancho of Señores Sheldon and Daylor," he said. "I would be honored to help you, if you are lost." Now he saw that the rifles were the new fast-loading kind that made his musket an antique.

One of the standing men hitched his trousers and narrowed his already small eyes in the pocked and lumpy landscape of his face. "We ain't lost."

"Perhaps you are going to the southern mines. I would be happy to assist your animals across the river."

The dead eyes didn't blink. "You call that pitiful piss trickle a river? Us Columbia men—" he ran his eyes slowly down Pedro, lingering on his leather stirrup holders "—is real men. We could walk acrost an never feel nuthin damp." Neither lashes nor brows softened the scarred face, which resembled an alligator lizard, a foot-long beast that clung to your boot and wouldn't let go when you tried to kick it away.

Pedro glanced at their skinny mounts. "Perhaps you would like to purchase new horses. We have some three-year-olds for sale." Chocolate quivered with flies, which had no doubt visited their shit piles.

"We don't buy horseflesh from Mexicans." The lizard leveled its stare. "Kill us a beef if yer so all-fired set to please. We been ridin' hard two days now."

Rage warmed the back of his neck, but Pedro kept his voice soft.

"Señores, this is Rancho Omuchumne, where guests are fed and treated well. I will speak to Señor Daylor about a bullock. But if you have no wish to buy goods or pay him a visit, you should camp at some other place. This is his property." A whole beef!

"We like it here."

"Then I must ask, señores, what is your business?"

From a man with a big nose came a nasal drawl. "Tell him, Pockface. Or I will."

Pockface shrugged. "The boys and me met up with some redskins. Up near Hangtown. We got the notion they lived hereabouts." He scratched his head with a forefinger, nudging up his stained hat. "See, we's ridin' with the biggest posse you ever seen."

"Posse?"

"Yup. We's settin out to clean out the Diggers. Mean to give 'em a right warm reception." His thin lips pulled back in a lizard grin.

Heavenly Virgin, save the Indians!

Big Nose got to his feet and extended wrinkled newsprint. "Says right here these here Diggers in Californy is the most worthless bunch of cutthroats on the entire continent. Go ahead, read." He shook the paper at Pedro.

"No, gracias." One more instant with these excuses for men and he'd pull his Allen. He turned Chocolate and said as congenially as possible, "Good-bye."

It took strength to refrain from spurring the powerful stallion, especially when he heard the thunk of leather and the exhalations of men saddling horses. In a few minutes he looked casually back and saw the mounted men facing inward, in a circle, talking. He called, "Wait here, señores, I will ask about a bullock."

Pockface cut his eyes to him and back to the riders.

Señor Daylor's yard was deserted. Pedro took the millhouse fork, heading up the narrower trail where the vaqueros had been digging the grave. Heavy vegetation flanked the path. He looked back through the trees and saw, about fifty yards back, the North Americans following! He nudged Chocolate to pick up his pace without changing his gait.

Señora Daylor had an open Bible in her hands and stood reading over the gaping grave. All other heads were bowed—Elitha McCoon, Señora Keyser and Señor Daylor. On the other side of the grave, behind a mound of dark earth stood the vaqueros, shovels in hand, and—Mother of God, María! What in heaven was she doing here? His mind had almost refused to recognize her pear-like body and trimmed black hair with the basket-weave cap.

Knowing the North Americans couldn't be far behind and wanting to appear casual in the saddle, he rode to the grave and hissed a loud whisper, "Indian killers. Hide María! Quapata. You vaqueros. Go!"

The three señoras looked at him as if he had yelled an obscenity in church.

He tilted his head back down the trail at the North Americans. "Run and hide—María, Quapata, Ramón, Locklock! Go!"

They stared like startled deer. Confused by his easy posture? His casualness?

He hesitated. Would even North Americans shoot ranch workers beneath their employer's nose? In the middle of a funeral? It was plain from the earth on the Indians and the shovels in their hands that they worked here. Besides, Señor Daylor had a reputation as a strong man. He had implied that Pedro was hot-headed. Maybe he was. If he were wrong about this it could destroy his friendship with the patrones. María crouched behind the dirt mound, her big black eyes on him.

Horses galloping! He turned to look. The riders approached three abreast through the trees, rifles in hand.

María screamed, "Run Pedro!"

"You run!" He leaned down to release the musket from its saddle holder. The Allen was worthless from a moving animal, even more so at long range.

Unarmed, Señor Daylor walked toward the oncoming riders, arms extended in a halt gesture. They didn't stop but parted and galloped around him. Shots popped.

María lay prone, legs protruding from behind the mound. Hit! The North Americans jumped from their horses for truer aim at the fleeing vaqueros, one drawing a bead on María.

Pedro leveled the big gun and pulled the trigger, but Chocolate moved and the ball drilled harmlessly through the crown of the bastard's hat. Shots exploded in quick succession. Quapata and Locklock sank to their knees. No, dear Virgin!

María was squirming toward the grave. An easy target. He aimed his Allen and fired at the man aiming at her. Missed. Turned the barrel and fired again. The killer turned his gun from María to Pedro, and María dropped, thankfully, out of sight into the grave. Pedro didn't need to think. He turned the barrel and took out his knife, a weapon in each hand, and spurred the horse hard at the man. One way or another this man was dead.

Señor Daylor, who stood in the midst of the North Americans, shouted at them, "Get the hell off my property! Stop, Pedro, don't shoot!"

Every nerve and fiber in him rebelled. It broke his concentration, changed the flow of his blood. Then he was past the man and neither of them had fired. Don't shoot! It made no sense, like a dream going nowhere.

The North Americans hugged rifle stocks to their cheeks. He turned Chocolate toward them and spurred. They jumped out of the way, their shots going wild. Horses whinnied. Women screamed.

Pockface shouted back at Daylor, "Indian slaves is gittin all the gold, Mister. Ain't Merican, Mister Mexican rancher. Ain't Merican."

Pedro sat his horse back in the trees and stuffed the wad down the barrel of his musket. This gun had aim from a short distance. *Don't shoot!* He hurried with the wad.

Big Nose was yelling, "Them's murderin redskins!"

"Not these Indians," Daylor yelled back.

Pockface stood up, looking down the grave at María, where she lay on the coffin, and raised his gun.

In a flash Chocolate was between them. Pedro leaped off as the horse trotted out of the way, and aimed the musket point blank at Pockface, who stood aiming at him.

"Put those guns away. Get off my rancho," Daylor yelled.

The desgraciado turned away and went to his horse. They all did. The cowards rode away, turning out of sight on the leafy trail. Escaping!

It was so quiet Pedro could hear his breathing. He went to María—now sitting up on the coffin—and stepped down beside her. Blood ran from her leg just above the knee and beaded on the fresh pine. The bone seemed all right. Relieved she was not more seriously wounded, he removed his shirt, tore off a strip and tied it around the wound. In a few seconds the cloth reddened.

She looked at him with that same distant look she'd had after the massacre of her people. Accepting fate. Thinking of the condor curse?

But condor feathers hadn't done this! Like a volcano, anger erupted in Pedro. White-hot hatred for North American gold-seekers swelled in his chest and threatened to explode. "I will have you taken home," he told her as gently as he could manage with a volcano erupting. He would follow the bastards and kill them. Don't shoot! What was wrong with the patrón? Had he gone mad?

"Go help the others," María said, holding the wound, blood running through her fingers. "I will heal them." She sounded utterly calm.

Silently thanking the Virgin, he stroked her hair and hoisted himself out of the grave. Señora Daylor was holding Locklock's head in her lap. As Pedro approached, she looked up and said, "Looks like a goner." She rocked the Indian boy like a baby while blood jerked from a hole in his neck.

Pedro ground his teeth. The killers would pay. Elitha, looking like she'd seen the Devil, came and kneeled down beside the Indian boy.

Pedro walked toward where Quapata lay with the scowling patrón standing over him. Just then Ramón stepped from the trees, ash-faced, shaking but unhurt, not more than thirteen años. Pedro stepped over, put an arm around the trembling boy, glad to feel him in one piece. He asked, "Where are Roberto's boys?" Five and six years old.

"Fishing I think."

"Thanks be to God."

He went to Quapata and kneeled. Blood seeped from a hole in his upper chest, too high for his heart, maybe a lung.

The patrón said. "Help me carry him to the house. Sally'll see to him." Daylor bent down, took Quapata's ankles.

Pedro put his hands beneath Quapata's shoulders, but realized the strain would pull the injury. "Wait," he said letting him settle back, "María knows the healing arts. My rafters are full of her medicines, and she is only hit in the leg. Ramón should take Quapata and María to my room." Quapata's head dropped to the side. Dead? Unconscious? Putting his ear to his chest, he was relieved to hear a steady thump. "We can put them both on Señora McCoon's horse." It was saddled and tied to the porch of the adobe.

"What's wrong with your horse?"

It took a moment to register. "Patrón, we must go and kill the cowards who shoot unarmed men and pregnant women at funerals." The man's courage was legendary and he had a fast-loading rifle in his house. They both knew every hidden passageway through the jungle-like vegetation. They could kill the vipers before they got too far.

Señor Daylor looked down his nose, his large nostrils flaring. "White men ye be talkin' about, Pedro."

"White men?" Confused, Pedro looked directly at his patrón. "We could pick them off like roaches."

"Pedro, is it a war on me rancho yer lookin to start? Think man! Men such as these is wantin' to drive us ranchers off our land. Give 'em a damned good excuse, ye will." He breathed through his nose like a winded horse. But his eyes looked kind.

"They shot my woman and the vaque—"

The warning look stopped him. Hot-headed, it said. Spaniard. As that sank in, a sick spot began to spread beneath the rage.

"Take Quapata to your room on your horse. I'll handle the white men," Daylor said, walking swiftly toward his house.

Trembling inside with the frustrated need to ride for the killers, Pedro helped Ramón lift Quapata and hang him face down over Chocolate's rump. Then they put María, with blood running from the soaked cloth, in the saddle. Pedro led the horse to the millhouse, praying that Señor Daylor was riding after the North Americans, but knowing he was a poor horseman. Thanks be to God the rest of the Omuchumne had not arrived home while the murderers camped on the trail.

White men. What difference did that make? And wasn't he white?

# 69

B ack in his room, Pedro sat on the side of the bed looking at María, her leg bound with a clean cloth that held crushed green leaves, a fringe of which poked from the sides. The ball had passed through without breaking bone or severing an artery. Quapata was in far greater danger. Numbed by her tea, which Pedro had brewed under her direction, he lay bandaged in the corner opposite from where Captain Juan sat staring at nothing.

Roiling with rage, Pedro looked into the black pools of María's eyes and said, "I cannot live here any longer."

Her face was impassive.

"I am not free here. This is not my rancho. I must be free to avenge the deaths of my friends. Understand?"

"My people are not free," she said. "Not since the pale skins came."

It caught him off guard, made him think. If he'd had his own rancho, her people would have worked for him. That was the Spanish way. She had breached an unspoken truth, something that had been niggling his mind. Ranches were established at Indian villages so Indians would work for the rancheros for little or no compensation. Their reward was supposed to be safety. Pedro recalled the difficulty of helping Captain Sutter subdue the Indians—Sutter desiring an empire with hundreds of villages in his employ. Under Sutter's orders he'd led surprise attacks against rebellious villages. Now he cringed to remember the slaughtered. When Rafero, headman of the Mokelumne, tried to avenge the death of his relatives, Sutter had ordered him hung. Pedro carried out the order and left Rafero's head to rot on the gate as a warning. Indians were not free to avenge deaths. Or to leave Sutter's fields at harvest time. And having less food stored, they became dependent on Sutter for their food. The patrones at Rancho Omuchumne never killed Indians, and they encouraged them to store their own food. Nevertheless, the pattern was the same. Every Indian in the countryside feared guns and cannons, and no doubt feared disobeying their patrones whether Spanish or North American. He was guilty too.

Back when he and Sutter first landed on the River of the Americans, Indians had outnumbered them hundreds to one. Why hadn't they banded together and fought for their freedom, like they did in 1829 against the presidios? God knew, whether or not the Spanish Commander admitted it, that the Indians crippled the missions and prevented the abduction of laborers from the valley. So why hadn't they regrouped against Sutter? Was it because the plagues of illness devastated them?

Turning to the wraithlike Captain Juan, he asked, "Why do Indians work for rancheros?"

Captain Juan raised his chin, short black hair poking out of his head at all angles. "Inyo here long time. Want see Españoles, long-horns, gun, horse, easy food. Inyo like shovel, bucket, knife, gun. When pale skins go away to home, Inyo have those thing."

Waiting for white men to leave! But with gold lying all over the place, that wouldn't happen. And what of Pedro? Why did he work for ranchers? He'd left Monterey Presidio for adventure, curiosity, hope of a land grant, the security of a position, and, sí, food and horses. Much the same reasons. But the adventure had soured. The Mexican regime was in disgrace, and no land grant was in sight. He now felt the yoke of the patronage system on his shoulders and was beginning to feel something else. The shootings hadn't outraged Señor Daylor to the same extent as Pedro. Indians were being exterminated. Would people of mixed Spanish and Indian blood be next? Did Señor Daylor consider Pedro a white man?

"When do we leave?" María asked, apparently accepting his decision.

"Not until after the baby comes and you and Quapata are well." He glanced at Quapata's sleeping face. Like a brother. He was strong. Surely he would survive.

Reaching for his sombrero and sarape, Pedro turned to Captain Juan. "Keep this gun." He gave him the Allen. "Shoot any stranger who comes up those stairs uninvited." To María he said, "I'm going to herd the cattle."

"You cannot herd them alone." She looked through him, rejecting the lie.

He went to the bed, leaned down and kissed her lips. "I may be gone all night." He patted her big belly.

"Protect the Omuchumne," she said, knowing his heart.

"Sí, Amapolita mía."

It was child's play tracking the killers. He followed the hoofprints in the damp earth, most of them continuing up the trail out of the bottomland, heading toward Sutter's Fort. But to his surprise two riders circled back toward Daylor's adobe. Pedro followed them to where they'd camped the previous night. They had picketed their horses and removed the saddles and bedrolls, planning to stay. The arrogance! He felt a bitter smile twist his lips. It would be their last camp.

Shadows were lengthening, moisture cooling the air. He stood in the same blackberry thicket as before, ready with his musket, knowing the Daylors must have seen the bastards.

Señor Daylor came into view with rifle in hand, walking toward the two men, apparently not having seen Pedro. The North Americans watched Daylor's approach, all of them with guns. Pedro braced his musket on an exceptionally sturdy cane, eyeball down the barrel, the dark nub squarely in the center of a buckskin shirt.

Señor Daylor talked in a firm and final tone, too far away to understand,

and shook his rifle at them. Talk! Pockface, unmistakably the lizard-like Pockface, stood before the patrón gesturing and wheedling. Bile rose in Pedro's throat and he swallowed against the vomit. With the sunset at his back, the barrel of his gun hidden in the berry canes and aimed at Big Nose, Pedro kept his finger on the smooth trigger.

It would be easy. The two of them could finish them, except that Daylor didn't know Pedro was here, and worse, might not want to kill the murdering bastards.

Then Daylor, que madre, walked back toward his house while the North Americans returned to their unpacking! The patrón had permitted them to stay. Now the two snakes were guests of the ranch! It was beyond comprehension.

Hot lava boiled up around Pedro's heart and his finger twitched on the trigger as he kept Big Nose in his sights. If he fired, Daylor would return, but on whose side? Never having been as close to Daylor as to Sheldon, Pedro moaned aloud and withdrew the gun. He couldn't risk shooting it out with Sheldon's best friend, partner and brother-in-law—a man whose life Sheldon had saved on more than one occasion. If only Jared Sheldon had been home! He would have exterminated the killers.

He decided to wait until the Omuchumne came down the trail—no matter how long it took. The first shot from Pockface or Big Nose would unleash him from any obligation to Daylor. Where were those Indians anyway?

It grew dark, the North Americans nursing cups around the fire.

Indians didn't travel in the dark, for fear of spooks, so Pedro settled back with his head pillowed on his arms. He stared at the brightest rash of stars he'd seen in a long time, and tried to calm his heart enough to understand. Bill Daylor was the bravest, strongest "tar" ever to set foot in Sutter's Fort, a man who had defied his sea captain and walked the plank, then had his way with Manu-iki in Sutter's kitchen. A man who had held off twenty Indians and Kanakas with his fists and ridden to Monterey in chains, only to return, a man Captain Sutter feared to this very day. Yet he allowed these murderers to camp in full view of where the innocent Omuchumne would pass by.

No, he couldn't call the man a coward. What then? A white man? One who feared losing his rancho? Daylor enjoyed the absolute, untrammeled trust and admiration of the Indians who lived here. He bought barrels of sugarcane for their children.

Where was the man's honor?

In the chill before dawn, coyotes started yipping and warbling. Pedro got to his knees, looking at the camp. Moisture had soaked through the back of his clothing. Barely enough light came from the eastern horizon to see the sleeping North Americans. His head ached with sleepless frustration and he prayed that if it came to shooting, he and the patrón would be on the same side. It was one thing to be wanted by lawless men and another to anger his employers.

He lay back, resting his eyes, unable to stop his mind. The sad excuses for men who camped here said they'd seen the Indians more than twenty-four hours ago. They should have been home long ago. Could it have been another band? A few Mexican rancheros had come north with their Indians in search of gold, so maybe—But no. He would not fool himself. Sheldon and Daylor had sent their Indians to Dry Diggings and that was the reason these vermin camped here. Lying in wait for their return! Nearly sixty unarmed people were on the trail. Sheldon had insisted they leave their bows behind to show their peacefulness, and so far they hadn't been molested. Did they know these vipers lay in wait? Is that why they were late? He'd been over and over the futility of going out to search for them in the dark. He would be more useful here, with his sights on the enemy.

His thoughts drifted to the plump brown faces of the children. Nothing was more beautiful than an Indian child smiling in that open way. They were never beaten, never yelled at. Maybe that was the secret. He tried to imagine his own child with María's magnificent eyes. He had sorted through Indian and Spanish features, moving them around like puzzle pieces, trying to imagine what his own child would look like. He couldn't wait to be a father. At thirty-seven años it was about time.

A woodpecker whickered like a woman giggling. Clown birds, the Indians called them. He got to his knees again. The sky was pinking up the Sacayak trail. With berry flowers giving off a sweet fragrance, he positioned his gun on the gnarled cane.

A door slammed. He turned to see the señora emerge from the foliage beside the adobe and walk toward the outhouse. Her dark hair swung freely over her light morning frock. She stopped for a moment, looking toward the sleeping men, and then disappeared inside. The door banged shut. When she came out, she went to the corral, opened the gate and shut it behind her. The cow bawled impatiently as she tied it to the snubbing post. Taking the bucket and stool down from the posts, she sat and hunched over the bucket, milk pinging in a rhythm that he heard fifty yards away.

Señor Daylor came rolling out in his shipboard gait to the outhouse. A tall man in long underwear and loose boots. Pedro looked east toward the junction of trails, the bright glow of the approaching sun in the aperture. No sign of people. A hundred birds had burst into song. Soon the bees would swarm over the blackberry flowers. Daylor returned to the adobe, to get his gun Pedro hoped.

Both North Americans sat up and stretched. Pockface urinated and went to the saddled horses, returning with a cooking pot. Sarah glanced at them before taking her pail of milk to the adobe. Through the burgeoning new growth of leaves Pedro saw the señora come back out and shoo chickens from straw-filled crates beside the house.

He looked eastward. A shadow moved across the bright glow of the coming sun. A deer perhaps. Then another and another moved across. A herd? No. He saw now that they were slim and upright. People!

The waiting killers pointed east. They exchanged words, grabbed their guns, and ran for their horses.

To scare them Pedro pulled the trigger and braced against the kick. The sound rang through the quiet morning. Señora Daylor screamed. He reloaded in a hurry and glanced through the aperture. The killers stood with their hands on their saddles looking in all directions, beginning to understand, he hoped, that this would not be easy.

A single black shape grew rapidly larger in the cusp of the sun. Running towards the guns of the killers. Trusting the safety of the patrón's yard! Pedro opened the lock as the two horsemen trotted across to intercept the runner. A gun popped. Theirs. His signal. Slamming the lock closed, he trained his sights on Pockface and moved the barrel with him on the galloping horse.

The Indian swerved off the trail, running a zigzagging course at full tilt. Hard at his heels the horsemen tried to aim their rifles. The Indian's legs were a blur, weaving one way and the other. It baffled their aim, as the jerking horses baffled Pedro's. The Indian passed through his sights.

He waited and fired at Big Nose. The horse screamed and fell. Que cabrón! The rider jumped free and Pedro reloaded. Pockface looked around as he galloped after the running Indian, who was nearing the corral. The shot had worried him.

Suddenly Daylor was out in the open waving his gun. "You gave your word you'd leave me Indians be! Now git, if ye likes livin."

Pedro rammed the wad down. Daylor turned and saw him for the first time, as did Pockface—slowing his horse. The Indian dove into the bushes near the adobe and Pedro was about to fire again.

But up the trail more Indians approached. Seven or eight shapes becoming larger against the rising sun. The first man had deliberately drawn attention from the others. Pedro leveled his musket at Pockface, who was wheeling his horse about thirty yards away, but as he squeezed, the horse jumped into a gallop toward the oncoming Indians and the ball grazed the back of the saddle. The horse kicked out and continued. Double cabrón!

The Indians wove in and out like the first man had, dodging the fire of the fast-loading rifles, but as Pedro jammed down his next wad, an India bent over, gripping her middle. Shot by Big Nose, who kneeled and aimed again. She staggered and fell not far from Señor Daylor's feet, and he still wasn't shooting! The gun was loose in his hand. The other Indians parted, three diving in beside Pedro, the other three zigzagging toward Daylor—Pockface galloping on their heels and trying to aim.

Daylor seemed paralyzed. Big Nose was trying to calm his excited horse, which had jumped to its feet, apparently not seriously wounded, and was attempting to mount.

Slamming his lock closed, Pedro stepped into the direct path of Pockface's galloping horse and fired at his chest. But at that instant the horse tossed his head and took the ball in the neck. Pockface catapulted off, rifle flying. The horse fell on its side, pinning the man's legs.

Pockface tried to reach for his rifle, his lizard face registering fear—the first emotion Pedro had seen on it. Pedro worked the lock ten yards from the man's head, keeping an eye on Big Nose, when Daylor stepped between them with his gunbarrel inches from the lizard skin.

"Get on down the New Helvetia Road if ye value yer ugly face," Daylor said.

Pockface squirmed free of the horse, grabbed his rifle and hat, and got to his feet. "Someday you'll thank us for cleanin' out this country of these here Diggers," he said, glancing back at Pedro. He forced an alligator smile and hooked an arm toward Big Nose, whose nervous mount approached alongside. Pockface jumped up behind the saddle.

Daylor, his gun now hanging at his side, watched the departing horse with two riders.

Stunned that he would let them go yet again, Pedro, who still had them in his sights, pulled his trigger, but not all the way. He let out the moan of a man tearing apart on a torture rack.

The double riders walked their horse past the bushes of the adobe and disappeared behind trees, on the trail to the fort. Pedro lowered his gun, both arms shaking with the need to kill.

He glanced at the Indians bleeding in the thorny blackberry patch. Dirty and haggard, like all moisture had been siphoned from them. He hardly recognized them. They looked fifteen years older than when they'd walked away three months ago—having danced their annual funeral rites. Pale dry streaks down their brown bodies had once been sweat. Never had he seen Indians in this condition. A quarter-mile run wouldn't do that. What had happened?

Señor Daylor was staring too.

Pedro glanced up wondering why the rest of the Omuchumne weren't coming down the trail. The first Indian, the one who had diverted attention from the others, walked toward him as if unsure of his footing. This was Coyote Man at the big times, Pedro knew.

Daylor asked in their language, which Pedro was also learning, "Where are the Omuchumne?" Coyote Man made a tired gesture. "Here."

"Here yes. But where are the others?"

"Dead."

Pedro's jaw dropped. Fifty or more dead? He went to the fallen girl. It was Blue Star! Quapata's wife. María's best friend! The Indians gathered around. He counted only five men and two women, including her. Seven. He felt lightheaded—the buzzing bees and shrieking birds momentarily still. No Roberto. No Tomaka. No birth helper. No Omuch. No village. No vaqueros. No smiling children. Blue Star curled in the dirt clutching her middle. Flame licked through Pedro, up around his heart like a font. His blood surged.

Coyote Man was saying in pidgin Spanish: "We run on foot. Horses fast. Americanos catch up. Stand Inyo in line, shoot. See how far one ball go in many people." He looked at the survivors. "We run. And run again."

The bloody scene exploded in Pedro's mind—children lined up. His stomach was on his tongue. A throaty Indian song came from the girl squatting by Blue Star. The death song. Coyote Man joined the singing; they all did. The naked, strangely aged people lifted Blue Star and slowly walked with her, singing the dirge. They carried her toward the big burial mound. Roberto's two little boys, who had been watching, stepped from the trees and followed the procession. Did they know they were orphans?

Pedro went to where he'd picketed Chocolate. He untied him and rode after the killers. They wouldn't get far with two men riding double. Two hearts lined up.

"No!" Daylor yelled.

"Sorry, señor." The first time in years he hadn't called him patrón.

# 70

Pedro circled ahead and found a perfect blind about a mile from Daylor's adobe, far enough away to dull the gun's report. He lay on his belly in the bushes next to the trail as it ascended from the riverbottom. The vegetation here was thinner but adequate. He braced the musket. His stillness and the branch he lay behind would conceal him.

The horse walked into view, each step bringing the killers closer into his sights. Livers being more painful than hearts, he lowered the barrel a hair, and waited with exquisite patience. They still didn't see him.

It was an easy shot now, no more than fifteen yards. He whistled, saw the startled shift of the lizard eyes to him, and braced for the recoil as he pulled the trigger. The two ejected from the saddle. A perfect shot.

He ran forward. They lay writhing. Pockface tried to raise his revolver. Pedro kicked it from his hand. Big Nose curled into a ball. By the smell he knew their bowels had loosened.

"Your mothers are whores and your fathers are cowards. You are ugly rats who kill women and children and unarmed men. You don't deserve a quick death."

Pockface, pressing his hand to his shirt with blood running through his fingers, hissed, "You fuckin filthy half-breed! Them is animals. Like you!"

Pulling his knife, Pedro knelt and told him in a soothing tone, "If I could kill you ten times over, I would." Slowly he slit the throat, silencing the flapping tongue. Realizing that Señores Sheldon and Keyser were overdue from Sacramento, and he must hide these dogs, he turned quickly to Big Nose.

Pedro's face betrayed nothing when he told Señor Daylor the two North Americans had escaped. They lay beneath a pile of brush with horror and shock stamped on their dead features. Later he and Ramón would bury them.

Awake during the night with the anger not even slightly quenched, he heard Señor Sheldon's horse in the courtyard. He got up and told him what had happened to the Omuchumne, and was glad it was dark so the patrón could not see his face when he told about Señor Daylor allowing them to escape. He turned and left Sheldon standing in the dark on the stairs of his porch.

In the morning he put on his threadbare trousers and shirt, suitable for digging a mass grave. Daylor would stay at the store, and Pedro and the Rhoads men would ride up the Wallumne trail. Quapata lay heavily bandaged on a floor mat. María was on the bed propped on her rabbit blanket. She wanted to visit the survivors of the ranchería, wanted to take herbs to Blue Star. "Por favor, take me that far," she begged him.

"Amapolita, my sweet little poppy, only a grand miracle will save your friend. She is in a sleeping death." He worried that the ranchería, deserted except for a handful of distressed people who'd run thirty miles before killers, would upset her too much. Also, he didn't want to make the Rhoads men wait after they'd been good enough to offer help with a difficult task.

But her black eyes drew him in. "On your way you will pass by the ranchería," she said. "Take me there. And pick me up when you come back from the burying."

Closing his eyes, he rolled his head to relieve a hard knot in the back of his neck. She should stay here while her leg healed, not mount and ride a horse. And she was safer here, North Americans being unlikely to look for Indians upstairs over a millhouse. Captain Juan sat against the wall with his hand on the Allen pepperbox. He would not hesitate to shoot. She was much safer here.

Why was it so hard to say no to María? A simple word. He sat on the edge of the bed and wrapped her in his arms, cradling her soft face against him. Her tears melted him. She was weeping for her people, her hard belly against him. Her relatives and friends had been slaughtered like sheep, leaving his precious flower alone in the world—pregnant and without a midwife. Indians needed their people.

Sorrow erupted from his own heart as he clung to her. Willpower could not slow the rockslide of emotion as he recalled the riotous fun the Indians had at their big times and ball games. All night he'd remembered how, as Sutter's instrument, he'd helped make them vulnerable. He squeezed her tightly, unable to halt the raw emotion. The thought of those men forced to watch the murder of their women and children hurt the most. Oh Virgin! He hadn't cried like this ever, not even as a child. He could hardly see the sunlight streaming into the room

At last his throat loosened enough to rasp, "Amapolita. I will take you there." The six Indians at the ranchería, including Ramón, would have weapons at the ready. And if the baby started to come, the three women—one Omuchumne and the two who escaped the Sacayak massacre—could help María to the birth hut. That thought helped.

Billy stared to see a grown man weep. Pedro wiped a sleeve across his face. Captain Juan was impassive, a stick man against the wall. Quapata's eyelids twitched. A good sign. Pedro blinked away the moisture, then went to the corner and picked up the helmet, dusting it in his hands. Some of God's angels bore swords and girded for battle. In the eyes of the Moorish invaders of Spain, El Cid had also been an outlaw.

His vision cleared and his heart washed itself of doubt. His destiny was to protect the survivors, and to avenge the wrongdoings against them. He returned the helmet to its corner and knelt beside Quapata, whose eyes were open.

"Amigo, I am very sorry to say that your children are dead and your wife is dying." He grabbed the hard, three-fingered hand—the right one, the left shoulder being shattered—and saw in the slits of the black eyes that Quapata had suspected the worst, or accepted fate more quickly than Pedro could.

"Almost all of your people were killed," he continued. "I go now to bury them." He squeezed the hand. "Hombre, together you and I will punish the killers."

Comprehension flickered in Quapata's eyes. A hoarse whisper cracked. "They will pay." His eyes flooded and he turned to the wall.

"Sí, we will make them pay. Make your body well, amigo, for revenge."

Hearing the strength of his own voice within the walls, Pedro lifted María from the bed so she could select herbs from the rafters, then put her over his shoulder and went out to bury the dead.

Ten yards from the line of bloating corpses, Pedro dug dirt and rocks from the long trench they'd marked off. Drenched in sweat, he leaned on his shovel for a moment, panting, when Jared Sheldon rode up to help dig. Silently, methodically he went about his work alongside Pedro. Only one day had passed since the massacre but the reek of urine, vomit, feces and decay seemed unusually toxic, so they both wore bandanas over their mouths and noses. All the gravediggers did.

About fifty vultures skirmished over the bodies, pecking out eyes and digging ragged holes. They scuffled like chickens, rising in brief flights and settling elsewhere. The constant beat of their wings was like a war drum in Pedro's soul. Missing were the corpses back at the Diggings whose skulls had been smashed with crowbars as they knelt over their baskets, doing the work they were hired to do. Unaware.

A gigantic shadow knifed across Pedro. Frightened, he looked up. It was only a condor landing. Looking two or three times the size of the other vultures, it scattered them in every direction. The low, concussive whump-whump-whump of giant wings stirred the dust as the bird lifted a small child and moved it to the top of the corpses. It seized the child's arm, violently pecked and tossed it back and forth until the arm came loose at the shoulder, then hawked it down like a robin devouring a worm.

All the gravediggers paused from their shoveling to stare, and then returned to the hard labor of chopping through rock and hardened clay. Besides the Rhoads men, two of the surviving Omuchumne men had insisted on coming back to bury family members. Being somewhat unwell from their ordeal yesterday, they had ridden in the wagon with the shovels, picks, and water gourds. All the men had been surprised to see Jared Sheldon's arrival only a few hours behind them. They knew he'd been at Sutter's Fort. The patrón had been quieter than usual.

But now, as he dug next to Pedro, he said in his flawless Spanish, muffled by the bandana, "I need to tell you something."

Pedro's heart skipped a beat. "Are they coming after me?" He didn't want to put Jared and his family at risk.

"No, not that. I doubt there'll be a trial. The law's scarce now. Sheriff's away hunting for gold. Things are not like they used to be. Everyone's a stranger, just passing through. No, Pedro, I meant to tell you, the entire Cosumne tribe is coming to live at Rancho Omuchumne."

This took Pedro very much by surprise. They were Sutter's core workforce, and had been for years. They'd walked into the fort and offered their services just when Sutter needed them the most—good vaqueros, blacksmiths, saddlers, men who'd honed their skills in Mission San José. "But Captain Sutter needs them," was all Pedro could think to say in the presence of the inert, twisted bodies of his friends.

"Well, he doesn't want them anymore."

"Is it possible?" It came out as a whisper, every part of this like a bad dream.

Sheldon slammed the cutting edge of his shovel into hard clay. "Here's what happened. They were holding one of their all-night dances. John hates that. He'd been drinking with rowdy men, probably had a hangover. In the morning the yelling and wailing kept up." Sheldon tossed his shovel-load. "He went out and told the hy-apo he wanted them off his place for good."

The scrape and clatter of shovels filled the long pause.

"Next, he burned their ranchería to the ground. I saw that and talked to them. They didn't want to go back to their old place....too many died there, bad spirits they said, so I invited them to my place. They accepted. They'll be our new ranch workers."

Digging out a new shovel-load, Pedro said in a polite way, "Pardon me, patrón, but how did you know...?" He left his question unfinished due to a sudden image of Americano killers bragging at the fort about what they'd done to the Indians.

"I had no idea about this. But we needed more vaqueros to help you. I rode home ahead of the walking Cosumne, and then you told me." He looked down, shook his head. "Don't believe I'll ever get over this. These were fine people."

"Sí."

"I'm afraid...." Sheldon chopped off that thought. "Well, let's get goin' on the next part." With his mouth a grim line, he threw his shovel to the side. The trench was long and deep enough.

Pedro took the hands or feet and Sheldon took the opposite extremities and they gently moved the corpses into the trench. The Rhoads men were already doing the same at the other end. The Indian survivors wouldn't touch the dead, so they shoveled dirt over them, one on each end.

While handling the dead, Pedro found it helpful to take his mind elsewhere. "What is Mr. Sutter doing now?" He couldn't imagine that busy man with few or no Indian workers.

Clearly Sheldon wanted to talk too, and he kept the story going while sweat dripped off their noses and they continued their work. "It's all different now," he said. "First, he has no official authority, no militia. His shops are closed. Oh there's shops there—shoes, hats, bakery, butchery, maps, everything you could think of—but he's not part of it. The fort's overrun by miners and merchants of all stripes. Sam Brannan's giving Mellus a run for his money. Then there's the embarcadero on the Sacramento—a string of merchants, lawyers, tooth pullers, iron smelters, gambling houses, brewery, you name it. Sutter is sidelined. Drinks a lot. I expect he'll go to his upper ranch so he won't keep seeing the destruction of everything he's worked for."

As they laid out the next corpse, it occurred to Pedro that Jared Sheldon had dreams similar to Sutter's, and the massacre of his workforce might foretell the end of his idea of a big town developing around his rancho. "I notice a difference every time I go to the fort," Sheldon continued. "It's more crowded, noisier, men coming in who don't know where they're headed, just to the hills. Too many of them think Indians ought to be exterminated like rats." Sheldon's words flowed out faster than Pedro had ever heard from him before. "Before I left the ranch this morning, Coyote Man told me the place was packed with dangerous spirits because of this." He jerked his head at the corpse they'd just laid in the trench. "He said the handful of survivors'll go to the hills and live like their ancestors, without horses or cows, so they can't be tracked. They're right about the danger. They're seen not as a workforce, but as vermin interfering with someone's pursuit of gold."

Evil hung in the air, personified by the greedy vultures. It was one shock after another, Pedro realized, but the coming of the Cosumne had a positive side for him. María would have friends again, and she'd feel easier about the impending birth. She spoke the same language as the Cosumne and shared a distant past, being on the same river.

With that thought, new dimensions of his future began to take shape in Pedro's mind. If Coyote Man could make a sudden change, so could he. He said to Jared Sheldon, "Sometimes a man must turn a new direction in his life."

Sheldon gave him a thoughtful look and retrieved his shovel. The two ends of the trench had met, and all the gravediggers now shoveled leftover dirt and rocks over the too-thin layer of fill. A breeze fanned the loose dirt.

The elder Rhoads, who was now working beside Pedro and Jared, wiped his brow and stepped away. "Looky yonder," he said with a sweeping gesture toward the white-capped mountains. "Snow's melting. Wagons might make it through now."

Pedro looked at the mountains, but his anguish for the Omuchumne had found its release. He needed to exhaust himself against this godforsaken earth and make his arms and back hurt. It cleared his mind. He was a warrior, back at his original profession.

Stepping alongside him, the two continuing to mound the hard dry earth on the bodies, Jared Sheldon asked, "Are you still my mayordomo?"

"Patrón, you have Olimpio now. He is the best." From the Cosumne workforce.

Sheldon closed his eyes for a moment. "Not all North Americans are bad, you know."

"That is true. You are North American." He felt the tug of their bond, the years of struggling together with the cattle, the sting of letting go.

"You know that three hundred acres I'm buying across from McCoon?"

"Sí."

"I wanted some of it for you. Maybe someday you could run cattle on it. That still holds. Never mind where you go between now and then."

"Patrón, you do me great honor. Thousand times gracias." But his destiny left no room for future plans. If he hedged now and failed to be a man, he couldn't live with himself later. "I will always be your friend. If you ever need help, you or your family, send word and I will ride to you in a moment."

Their gazes locked. "Amigos," Sheldon said. Something in the cut of his jaw said he'd never forgotten how it felt on the wrong side of the law. He'd spent years riding with outlaw Apaches of the southwestern desert, and later a year or so with the Indian fugitives from Mission San Gabriel.

"I must ask, Patrón, if María and I can stay in my room until the baby is born. Then I will take her somewhere else. It will only be a week or so."

"Naturalmente. And Pedro?

"Sí?"

"If you need anything, send word, understand?" He extended a dry, calloused hand.

They shook hands. "Maybe I have a request very soon."

"What?"

"Señora Catherine helped Elitha McCoon when her time came."

"Sí?"

"Maybe you would speak to her about helping María, if she doesn't mind, her being Indi—"

"She'll be glad to help."

# 71

A woman went alone to a birth hut. That much María Howchia remembered. She insisted on covering the distance by herself, crawling and dragging her wounded leg through the drying grass. The two surviving women of the umne waited for her. Señoras Catherine and Elitha were there to honor the birth. And women of the Cosumne who had taken her into their u-machas just outside the walls of Sutter's Fort, had arrived to help.

The tiny earth dome stood apart from the burned Omuchumne village. It nestled beneath the outspread arms of a protective oak mother. Nothing of the village had been left behind to lure bad spirits, and María thought only of what her belly promised. Glad the wait was over, she crawled through the low doorway into the dim interior.

During her pregnancy she had looked upon dead children, hence was likely to give birth to a dead child. Yet to this moment her child continued to move inside her; however another ominous portent was that her magic double, Elitha, had given birth to a dead child. A sharp pang halted her progress, but as it gradually let up, María dragged herself to the fur pallet and emptied her mind. Bad outcomes must not be envisioned in this womb of female power. She must gather her own special powers.

The fur of the mother grizzly bear felt luxurious and it retained the sweet animal scent. This too had been thoroughly washed, sprinkled with pine tea and dried in the sun. Elitha stationed herself between the two women of the

People, the wives of her cousin-brothers. Señora Catherine remained at the door, looking in.

Bent-Willow-Reflected-in-Pond, a cousin sister who had escaped death by visiting another village at the time of the killings offered María the wormwood tea mixture. Accepting the tiny basket, María swallowed. The tea would distance her from the sensations of her laboring body, but she was careful not to drink too much. She had no birth-helper to guide her, and even Bent-Willow-Reflected-in-Pond, though she'd given birth twice, was uncertain of the details and the procedures. María must give direction as best she could.

Feeling the hard pull on her insides, she was glad to have paid attention to the home-place birth helper when Billy was born. The woman had embraced her from the back, her fleshy arms covering her like a blanket. She had crooned in singsong fashion. "The baby comes. The baby comes. It is not pain but a dear little child. Do not mistake the child for pain, or the baby will fear the world. Fear is the foe. Fear is the foe. A baby comes to joy. Little child, come to the world. As I hold your mother, so you shall be held. Come fast. Come fast. We welcome you." She had crooned this as she massaged herb paste into María's abdomen and the small of her back, reminding the child to come headfirst. She hugged and rocked and crooned and circled with her hand, steadying María over the basin, which had been filled with damp loam to soften the baby's short drop to Earth Mother. María's sprit had floated above her laboring body as the women around the walls talked of happy births and sang joyful songs.

Now, at the end of a spasm, María asked for more tea. Bent-Willow-Reflected-in-Pond put the basket to her lips. She had instructed her about the herb paste, though she hadn't been entirely sure of the mixture. Tomaka's knowledge had died with her.

Bent-Willow-Reflected-in-Pond joined Hummingbird Tailfeather against the smooth, mud-plastered wall. The two sang with Broken Salmon, the only surviving woman of the Omuchumne, now that Blue Star had died. Their voices sounded uncertain, and they looked at each other for help with the words. None of them had been birth singers. María couldn't remember the songs either, but she knew that the spirits recognized good intentions. "You sing very well," she cheered them on. "Sing it again, a little louder so the baby can hear."

Elitha had removed her clothing and sprinkled herself with pine tea, but her large eyes looked confused and she stayed next to the wall. Señora Catherine, at the door, hadn't undressed, but it was good to have these Americanas present. Normally the hut wall was packed with celebrating women, but the present women would do.

She closed her eyes, opened her breathing and the mind's eye that opened her internal passageway, and let the herb people draw her beyond the mounting sensations. "Help me to the basin," she said to the women.

Quickly the three women—two from the umne and Broken Salmon—moved her to a sitting position at the edge of the pit. Broken Salmon kneeled beside María's legs, which were straight and spanning the pit. Broken Salmon massaged herb paste into her abdomen while Bent-Willow-Reflected-in-Pond hugged her from the back with thin arms, but they felt strong and good. Hummingbird Tailfeather brought more tea, and she swallowed it gratefully. The birth was peaking, the pressure almost continuous, the infant holding fast, afraid, threatening to pull her apart.

She moved outside herself and heard herself gasp, "Come to us, Little One, nothing to fear, come. Come. Now. Now. Now." The sensation split up through her core, violent, severe, no talk possible, all breath behind the infant.

"I see the head!" cried Broken Salmon.

Head first. Thank you Mother Oak. She sucked air and bore down again, "Come now." She gritted her teeth and pushed every shred of strength behind the reluctant infant.

"I've got the shoulders," Broken Salmon said excitedly.

With a sudden sense of a fish slipping through the fingers, she knew that the baby was down. The hard sensations let up. She opened her eyes, blinked back stinging sweat. Broken Salmon was on her knees reaching into the basin. Bent-Willow-Reflected-in-Pond craned her neck to see around her legs, and Hummingbird Tailfeather stood over Broken Salmon—the three woman laughing. The first smiles since....

A soft little "wa-aaa-aa." Alive! Thank you Oam'shu. Thank you, Mother Oak. Thank you Wormwood. Thank you Pine-people. Thank you Spirit that Lives in All Things. She stared at the white-sheathed, blood-streaked infant squirming in Broken Salmon's hands. No penis, a twisted blue cord trailing. Even Elitha and Catherine laughed at the baby girl as she gasped like a fish.

María reached over her knees and took the slippery little being. "I will suck out the matter." Normally this was done by the baby's grandmother. The baby was heavier than she expected, and it felt strange to place her lips, which seemed so huge, over the tiny mouth and suck out matter that had come from her own womb, and spit it to the side. The infant's eyes were wide, looking directly into hers. Oh, thank you spirits! Thank you!

The perfect little features brought tears to her eyes. What kind of changing world would this little girl see? Would death continue to come in big blasts? Or would this child live long enough to give life from the folds of these tiny labia? Five small fingers on each hand, five toes on each tiny foot. Alive despite the omens and portents. What did it mean? A new person for a new world. The baby's face twisted into a puckered cry, and María marveled at the strength of her little voice. Her joyful tears splashed down on the baby's small chest.

She cuddled her daughter to her breast, hardly aware that Bent-Willow-

Reflected-in-Pond was kneeling before her, biting through the cord. Etumu would have done that, had she lived. A child almost without relatives.

"I'll take her to the river," said Hummingbird Tailfeather.

Another task the grandmother normally performed, that and burying the afterbirth. She handed the infant to her and bore down again to expel the afterbirth, entrusting her cousin-sister with the small bundle of life whose dark hair, she noticed, had a slight reddish tint. "Bring her back," María called in jest.

Laughter erupted and she laughed through the twinge of afterbirthing. Elitha and Señora Catherine smiled too, though they couldn't know the foolish thing she had said. Of course the baby would be brought back for the four days of recuperation and spiritual cleansing. She pushed out the slick lump and laid herself back to be washed with yarrow and pine tea.

Pedro sat with Billy on the fallen trunk of an oak tree, one whose acorns the Indians had eaten maybe seventy-five years ago. He heard what seemed the soft cry of a lost fawn, but decided it was his imagination. No screams had come yet from the birth hut. He crossed himself; the worse was ahead. Then he saw a naked India hurry toward the river with something in her arms.

He stood up, peered through the scrub oak, and held his breath to listen. A soft little cry. Yes. Already! His heart vaulted. Thank you Virgin!

He grabbed Billy and rushed through the tangle of vegetation toward the river beach. The woman was up to her knees in the water dipping the infant. She turned, held a palm toward him. "No."

Was something wrong? He must see the child. He tore off his boots, told Billy to stay on the shore, and splashed out to the woman and the sound of a crying, sputtering baby.

The woman wrenched away. "No. Bad luck. Go away. Man wait four days."

Damn the Indian rules! He grabbed her shoulder and pulled her around to face him. Cradled in her arms lay a perfect baby girl crying mightily, water streaming from her auburn hair.

He stared as if paralyzed, seeing nothing amiss despite the woman's stricken face. The baby's face puckered in distress, her lower lip quivering. Her narrowed eyes seemed to blame him for the dunking. He threw back his head laughing hard and joyfully as the distressed woman waded a short distance upstream.

"Wait," he called, suddenly alarmed. "Is María all right?"

The woman, who was again dunking and rubbing the infant with water, turned and smiled. "She is well."

Thank you Virgin! Thank you God and Jesus. Thank you saints.

A name had been turning in his mind, one to fit this strong-willed infant.

Isabella. The Spanish queen who'd sent the first explorers to the new world. Yes, Isabella it would be.

Señora Sheldon approached him at the river beach, her face alight. "That was easy as pie! Golly, I guess Indians don't feel the pain as much." Her face beamed satisfaction.

Looking down into her wide smile, he said, "I will go with you to tell Señor Sheldon." It was about noon. The patrón would be coming in from the corrals.

♨

That afternoon, still in a festive mood over his daughter's birth, Pedro rode a league downstream to help the Rhoads men maneuver a barrel of gold into their wagon. He'd been away, doing careful research on the whereabouts of the murderers, but had come back for the birth of the baby. Now he pushed between John and William Rhoads, the three of them rolling the heavy barrel up a ramp to the wagon while Jared Sheldon and Father Rhoads steadied it with ropes.

"Well, Pa," John said as he muscled the barrel into place, "I reckon you'll git plenty of help unloadin' this thing at the other end." He lashed it to the side of the wagon bed.

The lips of the white-haired man straightened to a line, a smile for him. "Plan to deliver it to Brigham's doorstep," he said.

"Well, someday I'll go see that tabernacle."

"It'll be a dandy all right."

Pedro helped carry furniture from the house he'd helped build for the in-laws of the patrones. John Rhoads' little brothers and sisters scampered back and forth with boxes and bags, jumping into the wagon bed to pack them.

The old man turned to Sarah's twin. "Git yer things, Billy, and come with us."

He shook his head and smiled quietly as though the matter had been settled.

"You won't find the right kind of womenfolk around here," said the father. "You'd have your pick in Salt Lake City. More's coming in there all the time." Pedro sensed a secret pain behind the gruff exterior of the older man.

"I like it here, Pa," Billy said, checking the grease of the wagon springs on the tip of his finger.

Later, on the trail back to Sheldon's house, Pedro trotted his horse alongside the patrón's mount. "Got something to show you," Sheldon said.

At the stoop, so near and yet so far from the birth hut, Pedro couldn't help but pace back and forth while the patrón retrieved a copy of the *Placer Times* from the house. He came outside and shook out the newspaper. Pedro was still thinking about where to hunt for quail eggs, which María liked so much. The Indias would take them to her during the four days of waiting.

"First I want you to hear this front-page article about the massacre,"

Sheldon said. "I'm sure the so-called news in it was provided by one of the killers. The headline is 'White Man's Revenge.'"

Reminded of massacre and revenge, Pedro felt the joy drain from his heart. But then he listened in shocked disbelief to a short account of "an entire tribe of Indians" being gunned down in a triumphant act of patriotism. The writer congratulated himself for his part in it, saying the Indians had sneaked in to slit the throats of seven white men, after which white men from Sacramento City and many of the surrounding mining camps joined forces, spread out over the countryside, and got their revenge.

The burial scene came vividly to mind, and Pedro's heart almost refused to beat.

"That," Sheldon said, "is how most of the new immigrants feel about what happened. Keep in mind this newspaper is delivered to every mining camp in California. In San Francisco too, where mining investors read it." He gave Pedro a level look as though he knew that a secret double grave existed on his property. Then he turned to the backside of the paper.

"Mr. Daylor never learned how to write, so he dictated this to Sarah and I smoothed out a few things. It is our account of what happened. He read:

*May 12, 1849 Placer Times*
*The letter below was received at our office shortly after*
*our own prepared account had been published. In many*
*particulars it will be found to differ materially from the*
*one referred to. We readily give it a place.*

Mr. Sheldon looked over the top of the paper and said, "Mr. Daylor wrote two letters. This one he took down to the publishing office, and they printed it word for word. The other he gave to the Sheriff's office.

*"On or about the 20th ultimate, I left my rancho with a*
*party of Indians in my employ, for the mines..."*

After much wording it went on to say that in his absence, a party of armed white men attacked and killed several Indians while they were working on their knees.

*"... brains were beat out with rocks and stones. A group*
*of white men heard the 'alarm' and ran toward the spot,*
*meeting the armed party. The killers warned them to go*
*no farther because the Indians were on the warpath. Pay-*
*ing no mind, they proceeded to where they found the bod-*
*ies of the Indians, the remainder having fled. The killers*
*pursued the Indians, overtaking most of them about ten*
*miles from my ranch."*

Killing all but five of them was not said outright, Pedro noticed. He found no fault with the accuracy, but it had holes in it. It told of the men camping,

> "150 yards from my house. Myself, wife and others out to bury a member of the family deceased and previous to leaving the ground, I was informed the party of men were at the house about to kill the Indians there."

No mention of Pedro. So far so good. Sheldon continued reading,

> "... the 'Captain of the Company' requested a beef, and 'I refused.'"

He continued to read about the shooting at the grave in a rather bland way, giving the correct number of dead and injured. But did the brazenness come though? Men asking to be given a beef while lying in wait to kill the ranch workers?

> "... The next morning I was called by my wife to see two men who were riding rapidly to the south, in a few moments they wheeled and galloped hard back. Then I saw Indians running to take shelter in the brush."

Pedro replayed the scene in his mind, his role unmentioned, and Sheldon ended with a sentence about the mass burial. "Signed Wm Daylor." Slowly the patrón folded the newspaper.

Pedro looked toward the river behind the cottonwoods, the birth hut about twenty yards from the bank. He spoke in Spanish, a language better suited to intimacy. "When the men from North America read about this, will they not whisper that it is a coward who fails to shoot murderers who camp on his property and kill his workmen?"

The silence between them had a sharp edge, Sheldon looking into the distance with the point of his jaw moving. He then looked at Pedro and said, "Mr. Daylor is a smart man even if he can't read. He knows this is a damned war of extermination, and a lone white man can't make a dent in it with a gun."

At that moment Pedro was certain that Sheldon knew about the grave, and wanted Pedro to think well of his friend, brother-in-law and partner.

He didn't.

Sheldon got to his feet, speaking Spanish. "Many stories in these wretched newspapers," he smacked it with the back of his hand, "tell of white heroes killing Indians, hanging them, torturing them. The bastards print every dirty lie from the mines." His wolf eyes pierced Pedro as he shook the paper again. "Our letter is the only one, amigo, the only one among hundreds of articles that tells the truth, that the Indians are murdered whether they are guilty or innocent! And they are not allowed to testify in a trial." He stared at the paper. "This letter will do more good than a gunman going after two men."

*For sure he knows.*

"Wait here." Sheldon strode into the house and returned with another paper, whipping it open. "Listen to this in the *Alta Californian*. A 'correspondent' writes that the California Indians are 'a degraded and brutish class … the nearest link, of the sort, to the quadrupeds of any on the continent of North America.'"

"Quadru—"

"Four-legged animals." Sheldon's eyes flashed across the page. "Here's another. 'The Diggers graze in the fields like cattle, and their tough, cold, oily skin evokes a feeling of repulsion just as if one had put a hand on a toad, tortoise, or huge lizard.'" He looked hard at Pedro.

Pedro closed his eyes. María's softness came to mind. Listening to these lies tormented him. "The padres came to Alta California to save the souls of the natives," he said. "They cared for them. They touched them and…" His voice cracked and he swallowed what he couldn't find words for.

"To miners they're a blight, competition for the gold, predators to be hunted. They write this trash to mollify the investors and justify the slaughter." He looked down at Pedro with a sorrowful expression. "Not long ago I read an editorial crowing happily that within a few years not one Indian will be left. I'm afraid it might be correct."

Pedro scowled at the newsprint, half expecting his anger to scorch it. "I'm glad I cannot read." He went down the steps to his waiting horse.

"Odds are that part about the skin," Sheldon said, "comes from the pen of a man in some fancy hotel in San Francisco. They hope to clear the Indians out of the mining areas so the water ditches they're selling shares in won't be, as they say, infested with vermin. Understand, Pedro. This is much bigger than we are. And there's nothing we can do about it. It took courage for a merchant like Mr. Daylor—" He stopped himself and swept his eyes over the trees, giving out a long sigh. Then he said, "A man has to hope when this is over, there'll be a few Indians left."

"I will never—" It exploded harshly, and Pedro lowered his voice. "María and Isabella will live!"

The patrón looked at him with weary respect.

"I'll go break that bay stallion for you," Pedro said, heading for the corral. That four-legged lightning bolt would wring out some of this anger. And very soon Pedro would be a clear-eyed warrior again.

# 72

The first time Ben Wilder saw Elitha McCoon up close, it was late August. She was sitting in the shade before her little adobe house reading the *Placer Times*. Already that put her on the uphill side of the great divide separating females—those who could read and those who could not. Lord knows, a man didn't need schooling to succeed; plenty went on to make their fortunes and marry refined ladies. Oh yes, men with schooling, like Ben, might romp with the downhill females, but he had a whole different set of feelers out for girls who could read. And he hadn't expected to find one here, not after what he'd heard of Perry McCoon—a gambler who spent his few sober hours practicing rope tricks.

In heavy block letters the backside of the paper proclaimed: "Indian Murderer Dies Like a Man"—a hanging Ben had read about this morning. As her dark, neatly parted head lifted over the newspaper, he connected with the biggest, saddest brown eyes he'd ever seen.

He was tongue-tied. Not since a long time ago in Rhode Island did a girl affect him like that.

"May I help you?" she asked in a rich contralto. Was that breeding or natural grace, the way she laid the paper on her lap?

He remembered his hat and dislodged his tongue. "No thank you, ma'am. Just paying a neighborly call. Resting from what you might call the most peculiar way to earn a living man ever invented. Sorry to startle you." He nearly drowned in those eyes. What secrets dwelled there? He finger-combed the rooster tail his shadow told him stood on his head.

"I'm a married woman." Out of the blue! She'd read his mind.

"I know that," he stammered—not his smooth self at all—and I surely didn't mean to unsettle you, ma'am." She didn't wear a ring, and speculation had it....

She smiled, that is her full lips did. The dark eyes kept their secrets as she spoke. "I don't make this a habit, but you look like you could use some shade." Folding the paper she nodded at a stump near the fire pit, indicating he should sit on it. "How long you been in California?"

Not Californy—the only way he'd heard it pronounced in months. *Good family.* "Two weeks come Sunday, and they tell me I'm a native for being here so long."

Her lower lip widened in a little smile, and he saw that she liked his joke. "Come by ship?"

"Nope. Hoofed it the whole way."

Her brows lifted a notch. "But it's only August."

He appreciated the opening. "My brothers and I had a notion to beat everybody to the gold. And we did a pretty good job of leaving that whole mess of wagon trains in our dust—a man can outdistance any four-legged critter hitched to a load—so we weren't prepared for the mob of humanity that got here first."

"Did you cross over at the Truckee Pass?"

That puzzled him until he remembered it bore the name Donner now. "No ma'am. I doubt anybody'll use that trail after what happened to those starvin fools." Maybe she didn't know that every paper in the East had run the gruesome details of the Donner Party, and though nothing of the sort could happen in August, most overland emigrants agreed the route was jinxed. Her fascinating eyes seemed to reflect the whole suffering world, yet she was so young!

"We came over the Carson Pass," he said. "Ran into a bunch of Mormons going the other way. They said it was a good road. My hunch is all the emigrants will use that trail now."

"Sounds like you might have met Mr. Rhoads."

"That was it, by thunder! Rhoads was the name." Marveling at this coincidence—a link between them—he recalled the meeting in the sagebrush. The Rhoads wagon had creaked about as slow as any Ben had seen.

"They're friends of mine."

That stopped him cold, and his voice betrayed it. "You Mormon?"

She grinned and shook her head.

He cocked his head sharply to the side, dismissing with a chuckle the barbaric images that had crossed his mind, then took a turn at the questioning, which is what he'd come for. "How long have you been in California?"

She hesitated. "Let's see. Forty-seven, March. I guess that makes it two years and about six months."

Before the gold. Rarely did you meet anybody who'd been here that long. "Married a while?" The direct approach, an intrusion, but a fifty-dollar bet said she was leaving McCoon, and Ben had been delegated to investigate, which was the story of his life. When anything needed to be checked on, figured out, or explained, Ben Wilder was appointed. This time it was a pleasure.

"Since June of forty-seven."

He calculated. Married soon after arrival. Couldn't be much over sixteen now. He waited for contingencies, caveats, a wedge to get a toehold in. Hearing none, and seeing her struggle to avoid his face—did she find him attractive?—words drained from him. Firmly married. Not what he'd dared hope.

A prairie grouse, that ubiquitous gray bird pecking all over the gold country, called a three-syllable cry. He turned his hat between his knees, realizing that after two thousand miles in the company of argonauts, he was overdue to see any girl, never mind which side of the divide, never mind how married. When he finally found his tongue, he said, "Got family hereabouts?"

She swallowed and murmured, "The family's back in Illinois." Something sad there.

He followed her gaze as it swept down the swale away from the house. Motion caught his eye near the river ford. Her cheeks went slack. She stood up, tall and slender, the folded paper in her hand mutely screaming: *Joaquín Strikes Again!*

She said, "My husband is coming. I don't mean to be unneighborly." A rider was heading up the hill.

He jumped up. "Didn't mean to impose. Those brothers of mine'll be riled, being left with the digging." Seeing the dust rapidly advancing, its source soon to emerge from under the hill, he put his hat on his head.

She was saying, "I enjoyed the company, but I don't—"

"Make it a habit," he finished.

Her smile showed apprehension, as if she wished he'd drop down a deep hole.

He turned and left for the Wilder claim, which was half a mile upstream and across the river, reasoning that Mr. McCoon might have seen him but was too far away to recognize him. Jealous husband. He passed an interesting split boulder and walked swiftly up what he judged to be an old Indian trail.

A shout froze him in his tracks. A man's voice, words running together. Looking back, he saw only the slabs of slate on the adobe roof, the house beneath the fall of the land. More shouts. McCoon's. Something crashed. A washtub against a tree? The Englishman was crazy, everyone said. She might need help. Then the shouting quieted and he continued walking. It could be worse for her if he showed his face. You didn't get between a man and his wife, especially if you were the cause. Maybe she had denied having company. It would have taken an eagle to see much. Just leave it alone, he said to himself, continuing up the path.

But when night came and he lay in the tent with his brothers—three tall men laid out like fish in a tin, tent flap open to a triangle of bright stars—he imagined those brown eyes looking at him in a more than neighborly way.

# 73

María sat at the cave entrance nursing the baby and gazing over the warm brown hills and the dry gulch called French Creek. The cave cooled her back while the sun warmed her front and the baby's back. She couldn't see the place where the trickle called Big Creek joined French Creek, nor could she see the little town called Spanish Camp. If she went down the trail, just around the hump of the hill she could see the white tents and frame houses tiny in the distance. For three moons she'd lived in this cave with the survivors of the massacre. There wasn't enough water nearby to submerge wholly, and this inability to bathe sapped some of her power. Often she felt lost, without the umne around her.

Isabella released the nipple and smiled big, letting the pooled milk slide off her tongue. María smiled back and lifted the baby to her shoulder. She was plump and growing fast. Pedro had named her too soon, just as Perrimacoo had named Billy the day he was born. Burping the baby she reflected that Pedro had changed, being more secretive about his activities. For a moon he'd lived in the cave, but now he left for days at a time, trusting that she'd be safe with the others. He always returned with food and skin pouches of gold for buying beans and rice in Spanish Camp. He's been gone for three sleeps but would be back tonight, and she longed to hold him in her arms.

Below the mouth of the cave the children played—Billy, Bent-Willow-Reflected-in-Pond's two boys, and Hummingbird Tailfeather's daughter. They liked to take turns pretending to be a baby. It amazed her how they could find fun in everything. They didn't think about the past or the future, or care where they lived. They had each other and their mothers. Often she worried about what the future held for Billy and Isabella.

Grizzly Hair appeared around the hump on the trail with a cottontail rabbit hanging in each hand. The low sun on the west ridge illuminated his painful limp—the lead ball continuing to hurt his back—but she also saw his satisfaction in supplying meat for his little group. He laid the rabbits beside María, and then slowly stepped up into the cave and settled himself against his place on the wall.

Soon after, Broken Salmon returned with her gathering basket partly filled with greens and bulbs. Her husband and only child lay in the mass grave. Often she and Grizzly Hair sat on opposite sides of the cave staring across the fire pit past one another. Coyote Man and the other four surviving men of the Omuchumne were hiding somewhere near the deserted Wapumne village.

Isabella burped and María put her to the other breast, hoping she'd get a belly full before—

A pop in the distance cut through the birdcalls and children's prattle.

Two more pops. The baby looked up, questioning María's rigid posture. Grizzly Hair stepped outside the cave, listening. "Maybe shooting birds," he murmured unconvincingly. He stood in the golden sunlight looking toward Spanish Camp, where he'd recently made friends with men who spoke Spanish. Pedro had said they were friendly but cautioned everyone to stay in hiding, and if they had to trade in town, to be vigilant.

Three more pops. Her breasts quivered with every beat of her laboring heart. Sometimes the men of Spanish Camp held gatherings and shot their guns into the air. But these shots came from a different direction. East, up French Creek. A ranchería was up there.

Bad power swooped throughout the land as the pops continued, and continued.

🐝

In the quiet of midday, with the children napping, María went out to catch some of the newly arrived grasshoppers. She cupped her hand over them, cracked their necks, and tossed them in her basket. The heat of the long dry had brought large numbers of hoppers, but no round-up could be held with so few people. The hoppers in her basket would only whet appetites.

She heard footsteps, and hid behind a toyon bush.

It was the hunters, Spear Thrower and Stalking Egret, coming up the hill without any game. She went to greet them. When they emerged from behind a manzanita bush she saw something small between them. A child. They were holding the hands of a little girl, one man on each side. The child's hair hung halfway down her slender back—too young to have it singed, possibly she'd seen seven rainy seasons. As María approached, the girl suddenly backed up and tried to break free. Gently, the men pulled her forward as though they'd done this many times. The girl kept jerking and pulling back, looking over her shoulder. At last Stalking Egret lifted her to his shoulder. Throughout, the child made no sound whatsoever.

"Where are her people?" María asked.

Stone-faced, Spear Thrower gazed away and said, "All dead."

Horror tore through her. She nearly vomited. But then she gathered up her power and said, "I will care for her."

Clearly relieved, her cousin-brother set the girl down and went on with Spear Thrower toward the cave.

María kneeled beside the slim girl with a chubby baby face, dry eyes open too wide, her mouth also open in a silent scream. María started to hug her, but the girl jerked away and ran back down the trail.

She wanted her mother and her umne. Dashing after her, María understood Pedro's passion to make the killers suffer and die. Did the men from Spanish Camp do this? Broken Salmon had recently gone to the town to exchange gold for beans. She said Indians walked about freely there. But that could have changed like everything else.

María overtook and grabbed the girl. "You must come with me," she said, carrying the kicking child back to where she'd left her basket. "Here," she said, "a grasshopper for you."

The girl turned her head away.

"I want one!" came the cries of the other children, now awake and running from the cave.

"Okay, one for each of you now, but we must save the rest for roasting on the supper fire. Won't that taste good?" The children seemed unconvinced, but by now had shifted their attention to a strange child in their midst, one a little older than they were.

"She will live with us now. You see, she lost her family and forgot how to talk. Will you help her? Take her hand and show her where we live. That's right. Show her the way up." Disappointment over the grasshopper treats faded as the children brightened to the task of leading an older child up the trail, as a mother would walk a toddler. They cocked their heads solicitously toward her as if she were the most precious thing in the world.

And she was. A tender survivor in a world of scrambled power. The hair on María's scalp moved to think of what that child must have witnessed, and to know that all the children padding up the path were in grave danger.

Much of the twilight had gone from the cave entrance by the time supper steamed in the baskets. The litte girl stood upright in the cave, as only children could, gazing into the dark outside world. Bent-Willow-Reflected-in-Pond handed her man the nu-pah basket and tilted her head quizzically at him. Neither of the hunters had yet said anything about what happened. They sat cross-legged in their places, eyes of polished obsidian catching the firelight. Not ready to talk.

Supper had been prepared in a limbo of cautious respect, and though the hunters surely would have advised the people to leave if there had been immediate danger, María wondered if they should flee anyway and leave a scent trail of skunk for Pedro to follow.

Grizzly Hair broke the silence. "Los Españoles, maybe they are the shooters."

Stalking Egret shook his head. "No." He spoke in a detached monotone. "It was North Americans with fast-shooting guns. They kill the grown people. Then they put the children in a wagon, but not the babies. They shoot them. They haul the children to the north. This one ran away." He nodded at the girl.

María touched the girl, gesturing to a place where she could sit and eat. But the child made no acknowledgement of being spoken to. She continued to stand.

María sat down and patted the dirt. "Come. Sit down." She did not. The flickering shadows of the fire, however, seemed to soften the silent scream.

"Eat," Hummingbird Tailfeather told Stalking Egret, pointing at the rabbit nu-pah.

He blinked back moisture. "No food tonight."

Grizzly Hair spoke in the singsong of a headman's oration. "You are welcome here, child. You are welcome. We are your new family."

She neither moved nor ate. Much later she finally sat down at the cave entrance and stayed there all night, refusing kindnesses and never making a sound. Watching to make sure she didn't run away, María slept little herself. She heard the muted whispers of the two married couples and listened to the coyotes yipping across the hills. Sinister owls hooted from the trees, and she longed for Pedro.

When morning grayed the cave mouth, the girl remained sitting, facing the trees. Spear Thrower and Stalking Egret squat-walked toward the doorway, bows and quivers across their backs. As they trotted down the trail, María took last night's nu-pah to the girl, sprinkling it with roasted, crushed grasshoppers she'd saved for her.

With a trembling hand, the child scooped two fingers-full and placed it on her tongue. *She will live,* María thought. A sharp moan came from behind. Broken Salmon twisting her head from side to side, trying to shake away her memory, María knew. Sometimes it took more strength than people had to refrain from thinking the names of the dead and all the things they'd done when they were alive. So many dead! The little girl's presence reminded everyone in the cave that the killing of Indians had not stopped.

"We need a Cry," Grizzly Hair declared before leaving on his morning trap rounds.

Puzzled, María watched him go. A Cry must be held in a dancehouse or an outdoor consecrated circle. But proper wailing and singing could be heard a long distance, so it didn't seem possible.

The young girl left the cave to make water. María stood a moment watching her and the flight of a flicker, the bright coral of its underwings flashing as it swooped from pine to oak.

"Little Flicker," María said aloud, naming her.

The girl had good ears. She looked at María as if the word had meaning to her. "Little Flicker," María repeated, pleased to have drawn a response.

Then suddenly, when Little Flicker came back to the cave, her chin quivered and tears flowed down her baby face. First tears. María pulled her close, wishing to wring the bad memory from her, as she sometimes wished Pedro could squeeze her own memories away. And if María were to be killed, she hoped someone would care for Little Flicker as well as for Billy and Isabella.

☙

That afternoon when María was outside pounding acorns in the portable mortar stone, she heard the jingle of spurs. Looking up she was thrilled to see Pedro hurrying to her, bolero flapping, his face stretched in a big smile beneath his black hat.

She flew into his arms and buried her face in him. Tears of joy and relief flooded her eyes. Billy darted from the trees, hugging their four knees while his three playmates watched in a polite row. Quapata came up the trail with a large leather bag.

Every time they returned, always without warning, her heart overflowed with sudden happiness. Each time they left their horses in a different place and came by secret routes to the cave. The other people were glad to see

Pedro too. In some ways he had become their headman.

When she and Pedro entered the cave, bent over, Grizzly Hair nodded a greeting, but Little Flicker shrank back.

"She is afraid," María explained. "Her people are dead."

Quapata crawled, pushing a leather bag ahead of him to the dark tail of the cave—the gold Pedro was storing for a safer time. The women who had been outside came in and assumed their places. Ready to listen. Pedro asked them, "Where are your men?"

Bent-Willow-Reflected-in-Pond said, "Not back from hunting."

María sat tight against Pedro. How did one tell of such horror? She started, "Before the sleep—"

His face gave him away. He knew. He glanced at Little Flicker, her eyes wide with terror as she looked at him. "We were building a brush corral when we heard shots," he said. "By the time we got there it was done. We followed the wagon tracks—did you know they took the children?" Seeing nods, he continued. "We followed them to Hangtown. I asked questions."

The women edged closer to hear, for his tone was low and grave. María knew that when he went among North Americans he removed his black wig and left Quapata in hiding. Still, she feared for him constantly.

"They sold the children," he said. "To a barber, a merchant, a banker, a whorehouse and several saloons. Young mothers of the murdered babies they sold as wet nurses to the wives of ranchers."

"Sold them?" María had never heard of selling people.

"Two-hundred dollars for pretty girls and boys old enough to work, down to twenty dollars for girls not so pretty and boys too young to work much." He looked at Little Flicker. "She was lucky. Does she speak Spanish?" Pedro knew some words of the umne, but usually spoke Spanish.

"She does not talk."

Grizzly Hair cleared his throat and sat taller. He had a hint of renewed power in his mien. He said, "I take my people to the home place. We will hold a Cry."

She caught her breath. Grizzly Hair meant what he'd said, but Pedro had previously made it clear that they must stay in the cave. A choice between husband and father would feel like lariats pulling her in opposite directions.

Pedro looked him in the eye. "No. You cannot. North Americans continue to pan for gold at your old ranchería. It is dangerous there." It came so like a parent to a child, or a mother quail watching over foolish chicks, that María cringed inwardly.

Grizzly Hair's eyes sparked as in old times. "North Americans come here now. Shoot Inyos."

"There you would need to hide all the time," Pedro said.

"Here we hide all the time." That was true.

"I have amigos in Spanish Camp." Pedro traded gold for goods in their stores.

"I also have friends in Spanish Camp," Grizzly Hair sparred. "They tell me store man give Inyos bad trade." That was also true.

"You have gone down there." Pedro had told them not to, except in an extreme emergency.

Grizzly Hair sat taller. "Every man must find his own way." That was true.

"It is the same everywhere," Pedro said in a softer tone, "not just here. Storekeepers have two sets of weights. Indians get little for their gold. Let me buy all the food. There is no need for you men to hunt and expose yourselves. I'll get what you need."

"Hunt makes men strong," Grizzly Hair said.

Pedro leaned back, closed his eyes and exhaled. He said nothing more. Neither did Grizzly Hair.

María felt sure that Stalking Egret and Spear Thrower would follow Grizzly Hair, their old hy-apo, and their women would follow. Fearless in her bereavement, Broken Salmon didn't care where she lived as long as it was with others. But if everyone else left, surely Pedro wouldn't ask María to live in the cave alone with the children. A sudden longing for the scenes of her childhood filled her mind—the village center as it had been, the u-machas and cha'kas standing about, the roundhouse and river-baby spirit singing in its green channel, and the plant people whose growing places she knew as well as Isabella's face.

Pedro crawled to the entrance and in his special way glanced back at María.

She handed Isabella to Broken Salmon and joined him. The children knew not to disturb them. The setting sun tinted all things the color of red clover blossoms—the hills, his pale shirt, and the lichen-splotched boulders. In their secluded place the dry grass lay flat.

He kneeled in the circle of boulders and removed his hat. Damp auburn curls stuck to his forehead. She kneeled before him, looking into his gray eyes, and touched a curl on his collar. Isabella had such hair.

"Amapolita," he said, cupping her cheek. "Have you been well?"

"Sí, but my heart needed you."

He wrapped her in his arms. "My heart missed you too. But it is full now. We talk later." They rolled over together and rocked back and forth, his smoky aroma mixing with the clean smell of the straw beneath them. His clothing fell away and they connected—two halves of a lightning bolt. Afterwards she lay with tears in her eyes, never wanting to separate.

Pensively he stroked her back. She would never tire of his hand sending magic through her skin. Coyotes yipped, out hunting for supper, and small animals rustled as they stepped into the twilight, careless of the whispering grass.

Free of the hot sun, Mother Earth released whiffs of fragrant moisture from deep within. María inhaled it, and it seemed to restore the world's harmony.

His hand stopped moving. "He is determined, no?"

It broke the spell. She became aware of the absence of a running stream, the poverty of a communal bucket for washing. "Father's luck is returning," she said.

"His suerte?" It came quiet, disbelieving. After a while his hand resumed stroking her and he murmured, "Once you said a woman lives in her man's house, in the place of his choosing."

"In the home place of her man's people," she corrected. But Españoles wandered far from their homes. Breaking the connection, she rolled to the side and nestled her head on his shoulder. Was he asking her to stay in this place? Even if the others left? It felt like a snare and she couldn't say more.

His hand circled absently on her shoulder and after a while he spoke as if to himself. "My home is where I put my helmet." Rising on an elbow, he kissed the tip of her nose, his eyes dark in the fading twilight. "And, Amapolita, my helmet will be where you are, wherever that might be."

Joyful for that concession, she rose on an elbow and rubbed his furry chest in longer and longer ovals. None of the old ways applied in these changing times. All was in flux, all power scrambled, hers hibernating since they'd moved to the cave. But Father's sudden strength gave her a sense of awakening.

"The good spirits of the home place might give us luck," she said. "And we hide well. We can bathe at night when no one sees."

"Often they kill the men, and take the women for themselves."

"We are wary as mountain lions," she assured him, loving the contours of him. "And Perrimacoo is there. He and Elitha might help us."

"Don't count on it." The undertone of acceptance came through the whisper.

The first stars winked in a deep purple sky. She leaned down and kissed his thickening, lengthening man's part. His groan sounded in her depths. In his trembling and her hunger for him, the future floated away.

# 74

M rs. McCoon. A letter for you!" It was Mr. Packwood's voice.
Elitha put down her knife, wiped her hands on her apron, and hurried outside. Sure as shooting, a dollop of civilization had come to Rancho Sacayak. Every other day Mr. Packwood carried letters from the gold camps to Sacramento, then rode back the other way. And every five days a teamster came with supplies.

She reached up for the letter, executing a reflexive curtsy with her "Thank you."

He touched his hat, his smile lingering longer than necessary, and kicked the horse up the trail. Tearing open the envelope she sat on a stump. It was from Catherine Sheldon.

*Dear Elitha, March 20, 1850*
*Just a note to say I'm still planning to come with Mr. Sheldon on Easter*
*day! That's April 3. Remember? We said we'd have tea like real ladies?*
*Well let's do it! The Mister says there's a new eating house over in Cook's*
*Bar! Sally and Elizabeth want to come too. So don't forget! I'll be there*
*helping Mr. Sheldon decide where to build our new cabin—someplace*
*on that 300 acres across from you. The Mister does not want to leave me*
*and the babies alone with all these bad men roaming the countryside.*

Elitha looked up. Not in a hundred years would Perry build a place so she could be near him while he worked away from home. Heaven knew, it might be a hundred years before he got around to working at all. No. That wasn't fair. On his better days he went down to the river and charged for helping men get their animals and supplies across the river. But the Indians had spoiled him for hard work, and now they were gone. She looked back at the slanted handwriting.

*We know you have to cook breakfast for the miners, so we'll be there*
*mid-morning! Love, Catey*
*Post Script: Isn't it dandy about Mary Murphy!*

All she knew was that Mary Murphy had run off with a Frenchman, who bought a ranch up on the Yuba River. She had done the unthinkable, yet by all accounts was contented as could be. Where was the pain? The everlasting suffering that befell such women? You stayed with a man until death....

She shoved back the weight crashing down from the attic of her mind and penned a happy note to Catherine, saying how much she looked forward to the tea, and how glad she would be if Sarah and Elizabeth also came.

❧

## EASTER DAY, 1850

One by one the miners pushed back from the table or, if they were eating outside, stood up and held out their pokes. From each little bag Elitha took a pinch of gold and dropped it in her can. Twelve men this morning. The last said "Good-day," jammed on his hat and headed for the diggings.

She transferred half the dust to her secret can, and then stacked the plates. Taking the leftover biscuits and a pan of clabbered milk into the oak forest, she laid them on the flat rock for Indian Mary. A chunk of a boulder had split off and fallen before the mother rock. It reminded her of the stone tablets of Moses, one leaf upright and the other flat as an altar.

Yellow and purple flowers bobbed on either side of this wilderness table.

She admired the spring beauty all around, half expecting Indian Mary to step from the trees. A ground squirrel piped his alarm from another boulder. "It's only me," she told him, loving the way they notified their friends and family about intruders.

The food seemed an offering on this Easter morning, and suddenly she heard in her mind the voices in the tent under the snow: Low in the gravy lay, Jesus my Savior—The wrong words to an Easter hymn. But a grave it had been. And it was about this time of year when Ma and Pa died. *Spring death.* She shivered, though the warm breeze portended summer around the corner. When would she see her little sisters again? Not very soon if Perry could help it. Lately he'd lost all self-respect and lay in bed most of the time. He didn't even ride much. The adobe was an unfriendly place, no place for children.

Elitha returned to it, knowing that Indian Mary would leave her pan on the rock after she'd taken the food. She still didn't dare come to the house. Indians hid like deer. How did they eat, now that the river plants had been demolished by the miners, and relentless commercial hunters had cleared out all the game to sell to eating houses like hers? Their old village was full of bad women, the roundhouse their hotel, with blankets partitioning the spaces. What dark things transpired within those walls she didn't want to imagine. Sometimes Perry took the unhidden can of gold and came back smelling of rose water. But it didn't matter anymore.

Back in the adobe she lifted the drape. Asleep, he lay half off the bed, one leg on the floor. Odors of spilled liquor and his unwashed body were strong. He'd gambled in Cook's Bar until late and hadn't been home even in the wee hours when, by moonlight, she'd finished preparing some of today's dinner and hoisted it into the oak.

The dishes could wait. It was almost mid-morning and Cook's Bar was a quarter of a mile away. What fun it would be to see Catherine, Sarah, and Elizabeth! As she undressed to wash herself, she recalled the last time she'd seen them, at Mr. Keyser's burial in February. A burial was no time for a proper visit, but now the timing was perfect.

Washing herself from the bucket she heard snuffling sounds behind the curtain. She held her breath, hoping Perry would not wake up. Snoring followed. Good. But when she lifted the corner of the curtain and reached for her new brown frock, his eyes opened. She whisked the dress from the peg and dropped the curtain.

"Goin someplace be ye?"

"I told you. To the Eating House, with the Rhoads sisters." She slipped the frock over her knickers and camisole.

"That were Easter."

"Today's Easter."

He groaned.

She buttoned her bodice.

"Expect me to cook dinner for the rascals do ye?" A threatening tone.

She had two kettles of stew already simmering over a very low fire. "I'll be back in time."

"Ye better, or I'll smack yer backside."

Swallowing humiliation, she combed her hair, ducking and bobbing to see in the small mirror. Some of the hair evaded her as she tried to turn it into neat rolls around her ears. Haste makes waste.

"Bring me the morning take!" he yelled.

She jumped, dropped the hair. Now she'd have to start over. Hurrying in with the can, she gave it to him and turned back.

He grabbed her hand. "Kiss fer yer man." He puckered his lips, now surrounded by a scraggly beard since he hadn't shaved for two months.

Lightly kissing the bristles, the stench of his breath turning her stomach, she tried to pull free.

"Not so fast, lassie mine. Me thinks a little pokin would feel good about now."

"Oh Perry, please not now. I gotta hurry, so I can get back and wash the tins in time for the noon meal."

But he was stubborn and his physical state was such that it took him an eternity to satisfy himself.

＊

Angrily she made her way over the half-dug ditch, which was intended to divert the river from its channel. Gummy clay stuck to her shoes. She was late. She'd had to sponge off again and redo her hair. Furious at Perry, though she had no right to be—it was her duty—she threaded her way through pits and clay mounds.

Men doffed their hats, "Howdy, Miz McCoon." They watched her struggle to lift her shoes, which grew heavier with each step. How they dug in this muck she'd never know. It didn't fall from the shovel. They had to scrape a boot down the face of it and then scrape the boot on the shovel to remove it again. She wished for a bridge to get over the mud.

"Top o' the day," said the grinning red-headed boy named Vyries Brown. His name rhymed with diaries. "Fine vittles they was this mornin."

Preoccupied by the fear that her friends would think she'd forgotten them, she forced a smile and made her way around Vyries' rocker and between the staring men. Wasn't there flesh enough in the old roundhouse to go around? They acted like they'd never seen a female.

The river ran brown now. It amazed her how quickly all the trees had been cut and burned. Scraping her shoes so she wouldn't stick to the planks, she crossed the water on a teetery, makeshift bridge balanced on boulders. On the opposite shore, equally barren of vegetation, she made her way around pits, long toms, and cradles manned by miners who suspended their digging as she passed.

"Hello, hello, hello," she repeated as she slogged by, trying to hurry. As she climbed the bank, the footing improved, but her shoes seemed to weigh forty pounds apiece. Between the densely grouped tents, long underwear hung over guide ropes. What had been a meadow less than a year ago was now a town pockmarked with hoof holes to trip the unwary. The town backed up to the oaks, which continued to recede as new wooden structures were built.

She arrived at a plank building that bore a large cloth banner across its front COOK'S BAR EATING HOUSE. As she scraped a shoe on the bottom step, she almost didn't see the tall man smiling at her, the corners of his blue eyes slanting downward across generous cheekbones. Ben Wilder. She caught her breath.

He removed his hat. "Good day to you, Mrs. McCoon."

"Why, Mr. Wilder, I haven't seen you in the longest time." The surroundings came into focus—the precise lines of the tents against the blue sky, the oaks with pale green haloes. The Goddess of Spring was touching the world with her wand.

He stood before the steps gazing down at her. "I been gone since November."

A tall girl, she liked looking straight into his eyes though standing on a step. Few men were that tall. During his brief visits she'd appreciated his gentlemanly manner. Schooled, she recalled, in Rhode Island. Twenty-eight years old, ten years younger than Perry. Suddenly uncomfortable in his gaze, she went back to adding curls of clay to the pile beneath the step. "Tried your luck someplace else?"

"Luck?" He threw back his head and woofed a laugh. "Why I'd think Lady Fortune had retired altogether if it weren't for the beneficence she bestows on others." The corners of his wide lips lifted in a very friendly manner.

Forgetting her hurry, she asked, "Where was it that Lady Fortune failed to bless you?"

"Downriver. Near Daylor's ranch." He continued to look at her, but not rudely. "Truth is, I didn't have much time to prospect for all the politicking."

She smiled, realizing that he was just the kind of man who could speak easily to crowds. Abe Lincoln. That's who came to mind—Pa's young friend. Ben Wilder was handsomer, but he had that same loose-jointed lankiness and amused confidence. But California wasn't yet a state, and no counties had been organized. "What is there to politick about?"

"Keeping the masses from rising up." His easy manner invited questions.

Looking anxiously at the door, she forced herself to end the conversation. "I'm having tea with my friends this morning. Good to see you again. Maybe you'll... stop by? Like you did? I'm cookin' meals now." Feeling her ears burn, she nodded good-bye, lifted the patterned brown fabric, and hurried through the door, hearing: "Be a privilege." She turned and smiled.

Inside, her steps echoed on the wooden floor. The room was empty except for the Rhoads sisters sitting near the kitchen in the back. Sarah raised a hand in greeting. Catherine twisted around. Walking between the rows of tables and benches, Elitha heard her heart thudding. She'd been anxious to see her friends, but that had nothing to do with a delayed surge of excitement coursing through her.

"We thought you'd fallen in a mud pit," Catey said, her familiar grin helping quell Elitha's unthinkable thought.

"Sorry. Perry was sick." She felt as rattled as the dishes clattering behind the eating-house kitchen door. "Did I ruin our tea?"

Catey's lips blurred in an exasperated buzz. "Silly goose. Course not." She pointed to the bench across the table. "We're just glad you could come at all, with all that cookin yer doin."

Settling next to Sarah, she felt her cheeks redden. A woman cooking for a living was to be pitied. Sheldon and Daylor's Indians were gone too, but those two men got by without their wives selling meals. Nicely dressed, the three women smelled of good soap, and as usual every hair of Sarah's dark bun was in its place. The three regarded her with obvious pleasure. Elizabeth had a delicate attractiveness. Her husband had drowned two months ago ferrying men and animals across the river near Slough House. At the funeral Elitha noticed the Rhoads family hadn't taken the Austrian's death terribly hard, perhaps because of his Indian wives and nobody knew how many "pickaninnies." The thought brought Johnson's ranch to mind.

She leaned forward on her elbows. "What's this about Mary Murphy?"

Catherine beamed a grin. "You didn't see it in the *Times*?" Seeing the shake of her head, she continued, "Her Mr. Covillaud is dividing his ranch into a town and it's to be named Marysville. Isn't that grand!" Her smile was infectious.

"He must love her very much."

"Ever so much," Elizabeth agreed. "Good thing she up and left that lowdown excuse for a man she married the first time! The only problem is, Mr. Covillaud's a Catholic and they're saying she won't be accepted in that church."

Watching the kitchen door open Elitha realized she'd never met Mrs. Gordon, the proprietress. Out came a frightfully skinny woman with a face like an ancient lava flow. Her eyes sparked beneath apelike brows, much like Elitha had pictured the witch in Pa's Hansel and Gretel story. The line of her mouth widened in a lipless smile. "You girls ready for my famous brandied peach cobbler?" A younger version of Mrs. Gordon came from the kitchen.

Everyone nodded for cobbler and told Mrs. Gordon how they wanted their coffee and tea. The two women whisked their black skirts back to the kitchen and shut the door.

Amusement flashed in the three pairs of eyes and Catherine's gold watch bumped on the table as she leaned her bosom into it, her whisper threatening to explode into laughter. "Mr. Sheldon says," she nodded at the kitchen door, "she brought six daughters to California to find husbands." She pressed her lips together until they quit quivering. "They all, even the youngest, is—" she paused to gain control, "WAY past marrying age."

Feeling fortunate to hail from a family of somewhat comely women, Elitha learned that the Gordon women had come from Missouri, having spent the winter in Drytown and Amador. "Do they all work here?"

"Most of 'em work up at Willow Creek and Forest Home." The best hotels around, Elitha knew. Musicians played there and she longed to go hear them.

Elizabeth whispered, "I'll bet ever one of 'em gits a man afore summer." A sudden flush rose on her neck and she looked down.

Catherine and Sarah stared at their sister, her pink cheeks flanked by twists of honey-hued hair. With men outnumbering white women so heavily, she'd likely had offers during her two months as a widow, living as she did near Daylor's busy store. And the shopkeeper, young Mr. Grimshaw, was a looker. Ben Wilder had been in that area too, which brought to mind his puzzling statement about trying to keep the masses from rising up.

The homely women returned and set flowered china around the table. Straightening, smoothing her apron, Mrs. Gordon announced, "I gotta meet the supply wagon. Lorena here'll take care of you."

As the older woman went out the front door, Lorena fetched plates of cobbler and poured clotted cream over each serving. "Is there anything else you'd like?" Schooled accents, Elitha noticed. Hearing "No thanks," Lorena Gordon picked up a broom and began sweeping around the other tables.

Elitha lifted her tea and looked at Sarah over it. "One of the miners said you had trouble down near your place."

"You haven't heard?"

She shook her head and sipped.

Catherine jumped in. "Squatters are running rampant, burnin' everything in sight for firewood, even planks off the outhouse! They butcher the cattle and hold big feeds at our expense. Steal horses too. The Mister had the worst of the thieves hung and sent a petition down to the sheriff. It declares we hafta protect our property." She shook her head, the impish grin replaced by a troubled look, "There's too dog-gone many miners."

Elitha knew of the hangings, and was surprised they hadn't served as a lesson.

Sarah continued. "A couple weeks ago there was a showdown. Mr. Sheldon ordered the squatters off. We was afraid there'd be shooting."

Glancing at Lorena Gordon, who now swept vigorously, Elizabeth lowered her voice. "The ringleader's here." She pointed to the floor. "Right here in Cook's Bar! Him and his brothers."

"Ben Wilder," Sarah filled in before forking the dessert in her mouth.

Elitha's cup rattled into the saucer and she realized she'd elevated Mr. Wilder in her mind, imagined him as a civilizing influence.

"It's bad for Captain Sutter too, up at his Hock Farm," Sarah said. "The Mister says the Captain's lost thousands of horses and cattle. Havin' a conniption fit about the squatters too, when he's not drunk." She and Catherine exchanged a glance.

Mr. Sutter had been at his so-called Hock Farm since the arrival of his wife and family. Elitha heard the jokes from Perry, the gist being that the befuddled gentleman was firmly under the thumb of a shrill "fish wife" who slammed the door in the faces of his drinking cronies. And young Indian girls were not seen anywhere near him.

Lorena Gordon brought her broom to the table. "Can I bring you anything more?"

"Not me," Elitha murmured, knowing she should invite Lorena to call on her, but was of no mind to given Perry's unpredictable behavior.

Lorena's craggy face brightened. "You can't imagine how AGREEABLE it is to meet young women of GOOD character. My sisters and I are starting a Christian morality group to discuss how best to bring the PURIFYING female influence upon this WICKED country. We'd be obliged if you all could join us."

The Rhoads sisters exchanged a glance.

She continued, "We might invite the Reverend Fish here to Cook's Bar. He HAS been preaching temperance in the southern mines. Men WILL listen to a speaker of such persuasion." She pursed her lips and furrowed her prominent brows. "This community needs a man of his character."

"We'll think on it," Catherine said reaching into her pocket.

Elitha displayed her thimble of gold dust, wrapped tightly in a length of cloth. "Yes. I'll think on it too. What do we owe?"

It was decided that each of them would pay two pinches—the brandied peaches being dear. Lorena headed for the kitchen to fetch her pay can.

A nerve-shattering scream shocked Elitha to her feet. The benches toppled back as all four rushed toward the kitchen where the scream emanated.

There stood Captain Juan between the work tables, wearing castoff trousers, fear stamped on his dusky face. His arms hung limply from his hunched frame. Lorena swayed, then slowly sank to the floor.

# 75

María had been waiting for some time behind an oak tree. The bikoos weighed her down, Isabella being nine moons now. Father had allowed plenty of time after the last male eater left before he entered the wooden house. She had come with him hoping for a glimpse of the kind Bad Face, who filled Father's basket with potatoes, fresh vegetables and bread.

Every three sleeps he went to the house and returned to the boulder hideout with a full basket. "The new people are many," he had said. "We must make friends with those who live in the place of our ancestors."

"How?" Broken Salmon had asked.

"The same way we befriend wild dogs. One at a time." María was proud of the way he adapted to the changing times. Not all Americanos were bad. Many smiled at Indians, and she never forgot the admiring way they looked at her in Sutter's camp. Spear Thrower reported that he'd been approached by friendly Americanos talking with hand signs. But Stalking Egret had been fired at by white hunters as though he were game.

She felt torn. By conquering fear, Father was healing his soul. Pedro warned him every day, but Grizzly Hair insisted that bringing supplies to the hiding people made him more of a headman, no matter how much food Pedro brought in his saddlebags. A spirit had directed Father to return to the home place. He was courageous and wise, but Pedro looked at him with tight lips. The tension between them upset her.

A scream jerked her back to the present. Isabella whimpered. Grizzly Hair lurched out the door he'd gone in, and came toward her faster than she'd seen him move since the lead ball lodged in his back. He limped along in his torn trousers, which he wore in deference to Americano ways. She couldn't imagine what had gone wrong.

In a short time a fringe of shovels and picks spiked the air, then hats as a swarm of miners came up from the river. Diggers, she called them, enjoying the joke that Americans called her people Diggers because the women dug for bulbs. Any fool could see which group did more digging. They thrust their heads into the eating-house, and then, to her shock, stampeded after Grizzly Hair. He lurched toward her, not knowing she was there.

Fearfully she stepped back from tree to tree. She must protect Isabella. Father started to run then stumbled and fell. A gun exploded. Her heart skipped a beat and she squatted with her back against a tree, hurriedly shrugging out of the bikoos to quiet Isabella.

The shouting came no closer. Terrified, preparing to see Father dead, she rolled to her hands and knees and peered around the tree. He was alive! On his feet, being herded by the Diggers. Señora Daylor and Señora Keyser walked behind him. Then she saw Elitha and Señora Sarah coming. They would help. Where was Bad Face? She would help too. Pedro had ridden away this morning. He wouldn't return until late in the night.

The crowd stopped beneath a tree. "Git a rope," she heard.

"Hang the Digger! Hit'll be a lesson to others."

"Hangin's too good! I say whup im to death."

*The blackbird men!* Her bowels felt loose.

"He didn't do anything," Elitha said, but the shouting drowned her out.

María touched her amulet, trying to find her calm.

A narrow-faced woman, skirts gathered above her high shoes, ran toward the men. Her hair was pulled tightly back from prominent brows. Bad Face. "Let that pathetic Indian be!" She had a voice like a screech owl, elbowing her way through the crowd.

Every man turned.

"I give that old beggar scraps all the time," Bad Face said. "Why he's tame as a pussycat. Lorena just didn't know. She fainted to see him in the kitchen, is all."

A jumble of overlapping talk combined to make a roar. A tall man spoke calmly. People listened, then the blackbird men started again. María made out: "Not on yer life… rope… Injuns'll cut him down." Again they were herding him, back toward another building.

Bad Face yelled. "Leave that Indian be, I tell you!"

They took him inside. After a long time Bad Face, Elitha, and Señora Sarah came out and disappeared behind the tents. Most of the Americanos went back to the riverbottom with their shovels and picks. Feeling as if she were nothing more than skin stretched over a huge beating heart, María waited. She heard nothing.

❧

"Perry, please go and have them cut that Indian down!" Unable to watch as they strung the chief up by the thumbs—the "lenient" punishment they'd settled on—she had rushed back to the adobe. Perry knew these men. He gambled with them. Surely he'd made friends despite the fact that he, as he jokingly said, was a "Mexican rancher."

He sat on the bed and finger-combed his dirty hair, which was beginning to be flecked with grey. "Expect me to risk me neck, do ye, fer that 'eathen what shot me pigs? Forgot that, did ye?"

"But he—"

"I'll tell you what he did. Refused to wash gold for me—his whole bleedin tribe. Wye, if I ent had to pay Jared that fifty cents a day extra fer every Indian, we'd a had a pretty penny by now."

"Perry, it's Easter. Where's your pity? His people were massacred. Everything they eat is trampled under the mud or killed by white hunters. He only wanted a few biscuits."

"Hangin by the thumbs ent so bad, not fer an Indian. They don't feel pain like whites do. Hit's done all the time—five days at a stretch." He looked up at her. "Yer Easter miracle is they didn't kill him, on the spot, or cut off his balls." In the shaft of sunlight his eyes were red, white and blue with pinpoints of black. No help there.

Did he ever think how many times she'd looked into his eyes for help only to know it wasn't to be found? Did he remember Mary Murphy divorcing her husband? But Captain Juan was the important thing now. After serving the noon meal, she must do something—she'd locate Ben Wilder. He'd turned miners around before, and maybe could do it again.

🌿

A freckle-faced boy stepped partway down the bank, boot sliding in the mud. "Mr. Wilder, Miz McCoon's looking for you." Like a happy terrier he pointed up the bank.

Ben scattered his shovelful of gravel into the upper end of the Wilder rocker and followed the finger. There stood the angel of the adobe cabin, seeking him out personally. To Asa and John he said, "Be a minute," and hurried up the bank.

Her voice was demure. "I'm ever so sorry to disturb you, Mr. Wilder, but, well, I couldn't help but notice how the men listened to you over there." She pointed across the river. "And I—" She stared at her clasped hands, a flush creeping up her cheeks.

"Did you think we should have killed the Indian?"

"Oh no!" She looked up sharply, confusion falling away. "He's a poor old man with a bad injury in his back. And it was true what Mrs. Gordon said. He couldn't possibly have hurt Lorena. He wasn't in there long enough. I was there the moment she screamed. He must be cut down immediately."

"But what if no one else had been there, and Lorena hadn't been able to scream for help? That's what worries the men. They feel responsible for protecting you women." He gazed into her eyes and remembered somebody had said eyes were the portal to the soul. He wanted to know what lay behind them, but she was married and reason must prevail. "I had the feeling Lorena wanted him killed."

"You won't try to get him cut down?"

Disagreeable sensations crawled up his spine. Lack of conviction rarely afflicted him, and he'd felt certain until this minute that justice had been done in the matter of the Indian. The savage could have raped Lorena, but even if he was only begging, Cook's Bar was a growing community. That kind of behavior wasn't to be tolerated. "What do you care about a Digger?"

"He was the chief of the village that used to be here."

"Chief?" He couldn't help but smile. Men claimed to have spied naked Indians living in underground dens and eating bugs. Such primitive beings didn't have the organizational sense to designate chiefs. They weren't like the warriors of the plains.

"Yes. And he was grand, like Chief Delaware."

"That skinny old wretch?" He recalled the beautifully beaded and befeathered Sioux. Was it possible that tattered hand-me-down trousers denoted authority among beings as naked as jays? Her interest in the Digger interested him.

"His people were all killed, and," her cheeks colored, "his daughter is a friend of mine." She looked at her muddy shoes.

Such a girl admitting such a thing! His heart went out to her. Before the gold discovery no one else lived around here. She must have been lonely beyond reckoning, with that gambler husband of hers riding off to distant card games. Now this young and vulnerable girl possessed a certain stubborn dignity. Strange, the way the courage of her admission attracted him all the more. He found himself saying what he wouldn't have believed five minutes ago. "I'll go over and see what I can do."

A heavenly smile rewarded him. The sight of her standing there hit him like liquor hits a drunk, every fiber craving more.

She curtsied. "I'm obliged, ever so much. I'd come with you but—" She looked back over her shoulder. "I gotta get back."

To McCoon, he knew. "I'll do my best."

A few minutes later he was glad he hadn't made any promises. Looking through the open boardinghouse door, he saw Jared Sheldon, that son-of-a-bitch who'd thrown him off the Slough House digs. Ben had nearly smashed his flinty jaw. Now, assaying the drift of the conversation in the building, he realized Sheldon also wanted the Digger cut down.

The proprietor retorted, "You'd better git on outa here, Mister Sheldon. Who d'ya think you are anyhow? Tellin us to go soft on Diggers! We got ladies to protect, and businesses too."

A plump young girl stood beside Sheldon, gripping his arm. What was the man doing here in Cook's Bar anyway? It was just like those highfalutin so-called Mexican ranchers to think they owned the whole damned countryside. This one had the nerve to point to a distant peak and claim it was his property line. Not an inch fenced! Why, he'd even hung white men. By thunder, these throwbacks to the Spanish Empire lived like kings, and contrary to United States law too. Not till hell froze over would a United States court allow those huge land tracts to stay intact. This grandee would have been dead if Ben hadn't calmed the mob of miners staking claims on what Sheldon claimed to be his property, and no thanks had come Ben's way either. So now, was he about to jump into this argument on Jared Sheldon's side? Damned if he would!

He was out of there before the ass turned around.

Again María watched Bad Face leave the building. Then Señora Sarah and Elitha left. A tall man left. Next Catherine and Señor Sheldon walked away. But Grizzly Hair remained inside. She would wait for dark before looking in. The first coyote howled. Isabella fussed. María put her daughter to her breast.

No gunshots had sounded. No cries came from the building. No sounds of whipping. They could have cut his throat. They didn't care that he was a man of knowledge. Her milk didn't flow, though the baby was pulling hard.

Later, a dampness descended and she shivered. Loose spirits moved about in the dark. A warm trickle ran down her back from the bikoos, the baby wetting through the oak moss. She got to her feet and walked quietly toward the wooden building, careful to avoid the dried holes that horses had punched into the clay in the time of rain. A squashed moon had risen over the tents and houses and hung awkwardly at the side of the sky. Coyotes yipped near and far. Oil lamps glowed inside most of the tents and winked from the windows of the wooden houses. Occasional shouts of muted laughter came from throughout the town.

Squares of light glowed through the windows on both sides of the building. She crouch-walked along the moonless side, only about two body lengths from a neighboring tent. Fortunately the miners in the tent were busy. She saw their shadowy figures playing cards and lifting bottles to their mouths. Beneath the window of the building she slowly raised up until her eyes were over the sill. Men there also played cards and smoked. Others slept. She swept her gaze around the lumps of blankets, to the shadows in the back.

Her heart jumped. There he was! Strung up by his thumbs, stretched thin, toes just off the floor. His ribs jutted above the concavity of his belly, the ratty trousers hanging loose on his hipbones. He looked dead, thumbs big and black and round, head forward, long hair over his face. Then his head lifted, hair parting. Alive! Their eyes locked, and she felt his absolute helplessness. He had felt her spirit. Her vision swam with tears.

She sent her thought. *Pedro can help.* But how late would he return?

Go quietly, father said in his thoughts. Now.

She circled through the dark forest upstream of the town, shadows startling her. Grizzly bears and mountain lions hunted at night, as did Bohemkulla. She stepped across the Sacayak boulder and swam across the stream above the boulder falls, paddling like a dog to keep Isabella's head above water. The river-baby spirit touched her and she began to feel the pull of Grandmother Howchia calling to her.

Ashore in the moon-shadow of the oaks, her feet recognized the familiar path to the old village, a ridged boulder cresting the trail like a turtleback. Danger lurked about, not only from unpredictable spirits. Americanos camped in the old village. She could smell them. In a torment of conflict, wanting to hurry to the boulder hideout in hopes Pedro had returned, but knowing he would be very late tonight, she stood still. The safest route was straight back into the forest. But when she looked up through the tracery of branches, Moon Woman told her to heed Howchia's call. She moved toward the mother oak growing out of the mound into which the dancehouse was excavated.

Gone were the u-machas and cha'kas. Americano tents stood in their places. Light spilled from the dancehouse, flooding the small amphitheater before the doorway. It beamed up from the smokehole into the branches of Grandmother Howchia's tree. As she approached the light, all else darkened around her and she bumped her toes on the tongue of a wagon.

Laughter stopped her in her tracks. A man and woman came to the dancehouse door. Naked. Chalky white. The man was prepared to couple. She hunched down into the semblance of a rock. The river had awakened Isabella, but she was quiet. *Stay silent.* Men's voices muttered, and she saw the red tip of a cigarrito moving in the darkness, back in the trees. *Blackbird men.* Waiting to take turns with the women who lived in the house of spirits. The woman pushed the eager man away and squatted to urinate. They didn't know this was a place of sacredness, that their actions placed them in danger.

They went back inside, embracing as they walked. The erratic spark scribbled in the darkness, and she continued her careful steps to the rear of the dancehouse, one foot before the other, already beneath the outstretched arms of the tree that flourished in the mound. Out of view of the blackbird men, she stepped up the familiar soft earth, toes sinking, the pull of Grandmother intensifying. She stopped at the trunk and let herself merge with the tree. Fear dropped from her shoulders. She embraced the healer she had never seen in life. Her arms reached only partway around, but she pressed her cheek and breasts into the furrowed bark and sensed Grandmother's healing spirit.

Father hangs helplessly, she said without words, though he went in friendship to the strangers. They could kill him. My strength has waned and I cannot help him. I will send Pedro, but I fear for him too, Grandmother. They could both be killed. I am ashamed that my first man stole the condor robe. We suffer much because of it.

The tree-spirit spoke. *Molok's robe cannot be retrieved. Do not be sad over it in this time of upheaval. You have power, Granddaughter, but follow your man. He is a warrior. He faces danger for you. Trust him now. Keep your children under his protection as long as possible. Learn from my son. Keep the knowledge of our people. Pass it to your children. Better times will come.*

Trust Pedro. Gratefully she leaned against the sculpted bark. She had done right to follow both Pedro and Father, though their ways were different. This cataclysm would end. "Thank you, Grandmother," she whispered aloud.

Feeling rested, she left for the boulders where she would wait for Pedro.

# 76

Pedro considered himself a soldier with a holy mission. On his way to the boulder hideout long after dark, he recapitulated. Three of the killers of the Omuchumne remained alive. But dispatching them wasn't his sole mission. He stole gold from the miners who destroyed everything the Indians ate. He stole from miners from all lands, except those who spoke Spanish. Some of them were bastards too, but he had limited daylight hours, and plenty of others were willing to part with the gold in exchange for their lives. Single-handedly Pedro was keeping large numbers of Indians alive.

Not only Captain Juan's group, but he made the rounds of others in hiding—starving, filthy women with singed hair reduced to prostitution in exchange for crusts of bread, and once-proud men, now walking skeletons brave enough to beg from those who had destroyed the waterways and annihilated fish, game and food plants. Indians were routinely shot for begging. Men who had once hunted deer by stealth and cunning now stole food in the night, though the massacre of their people was the common punishment. They were dying of disease and privation, but considered of no more consequence than insects.

Ay, ay, ay. A bandit now. Not long ago he'd been a good soldier, if a little more independent than most. But he couldn't help but think as he picked his way through the dark, that if Mexico hadn't lost California, he would be heading for his hacienda and some of the Indians dying in the hills would be his grooms and herders. The sons and grandsons of Spain held the souls of the Indians as beloved by the Virgin, equal in the Church. One harmed them with trepidation. Spanish law was the sword of the Church. But in this barbaric land Pedro was the sword—a bandido living a dangerous life, one who would have taken his family to Mexico long ago except that every day he saw more pobrecitos who needed help.

A crooked moon provided little light as he approached the boulder-crowned hill. He let Chocolate find his way. As he dismounted, María surprised him. Not asleep. She told him Captain Juan was hanging by his thumbs in a big sleeping house! Ay madre, why wouldn't that man stay in hiding?

"Por favor, go cut him down and bring him home," his María said.

"You think I have magic, Amapolita, to walk into a lion's den and ask the beasts to hand him over?" He threw off his black wig.

"You are a good warrior, mi hombre."

No man could refuse that. He kissed her full warm lips, then woke Quapata and the two other Indians, and rode toward the boardinghouse, still wearing his North American clothing. His auburn hair differed from the black bandido wig. He would scout the place and figure out a plan. Quapata,

Spear Thrower and Stalking Egret trotted alongside, bows in hand, quivers full. Each of them could take two men before anybody knew what happened, and with his new Springfield rifle, Pedro could hit a running rabbit through the eye. But that was only a start on the twenty to thirty men in the boardinghouse. You never knew how many. When they were "flush," miners paid to sleep inside. He would use cunning, and the Indians would serve as backup.

He waved them into the moon-shadows of the trees, draped Chocolate's reins over the limb of an oak and crouch-ran to the building. Peeping through the window he saw a floor strewn with men. Four groups sat hunched over cards under four oil lamps. Haloes of smoke tied the groups together. He made out the shadowy mounds where the hips of sleeping men pushed up. Barely visible all the way in back hung Captain Juan—skin-sheathed bones, but clearly alive. What had gotten into him anyway, to walk into the Eating House kitchen?

He studied the card players, silently thanking God there were no familiar nose and beard combinations. The color, curl and trim of beards made men easy to remember. However, like flies to horse dung, miners moved around after gold strikes and he had to be careful that his former victims didn't recognize him. Señor Cuidadoso, other bandidos called him. Nothing wrong with being careful, the two full pouches of dust pressing on his belly told him. That gold was the mainstay of the plan forming in his mind. Among miners, greed could be counted on. Now he would stake his life on that.

He returned to his horse and took three monte cards from his saddlebags and slipped them into his sleeve. Swinging the bedroll over his shoulder he walked toward the front door and pushed it open.

Heads jerked up. Bueno. No familiar faces.

He smiled and glanced around, and when he located the proprietor, said in his North American accent, talking as though cornmeal mush filled his mouth, "Howdy. Got room for one more?" His eyes met Captain Juan's. The Indian looked down, motionless as a crucifix. Seeing his swollen, blackened thumbs, Pedro cringed inwardly, but Mother of God, the man was lucky to be alive. Maybe this would teach him.

A rough-complexioned man of middle years, who had been reclining with his jaw cupped in his hand, pushed to his feet and sauntered toward Pedro. "One pinch, up front. No vittles."

Pedro untied a purse. The man extracted a huge pinch, then nodded toward the wall. "Drop your roll over there."

The card players watched from hooded eyes as Pedro stepped over and around sleeping men and lowered his bedroll beneath the window. Rifles lay scattered around the room, and most of the gamblers had handguns in their belts.

A big blond card player spoke in singsong, "You dona talk alike a Yankee." "Transylvanian parents," Pedro responded without hesitation. He remembered a hair-raising ghost story Captain Sutter told about that place, and hadn't met anyone who knew the accent. "I play monte," he said brightly as though just thinking of it.

Men beckoned from all four groups.

He joined the nearest game, and with a great show of concentration made foolish mistakes. Miming the stunned greenhorn who couldn't believe what was happening, he lost steadily. One by one players from other games drifted to his circle, dragging their blanket rolls.

"You find a goot vein, ya?" asked a man offering a bottle of whisky.

Pedro took a small swallow and almost saw their ears perk up when he said, "Yup." He knew that game. Get him drunk and pry the location out of him.

Two men removed their boots and happily wiggled their toes. The stench of unwashed feet thickened with the smoke.

Briefly lifting the corners of his cards, Pedro glanced around with an expression of one who thinks himself wise, and emptied his purse onto the pile of gold dust, turning it inside out, shaking it and patting the dust from the folds.

A needle-nosed man with rat's eyes in a scooped-out face turned over his downed cards and revealed a matched pair.

Angrily Pedro threw in his cards and exploded, "Thunder weather!" A comical oath Captain Sutter used—Transylvania being somewhere near Switzerland.

Needlenose laid down the edge of a newspaper and swept gold onto it with tender strokes of his little finger. Finishing he said, "Guess I'll turn in." He got to his feet and hitched his pants up.

A grizzled older man offered Pedro a bottle of brandy, asking, "Your claim in the neighborhood?" He stretched out a leg, bending it as if to see if it still worked.

"Yup." Pedro said, taking a taste and handing back the bottle with a pained smile. "Hoped to double today's take." He sighed and jerked a thumb at Captain Juan. "What's he done?"

"Skeered a decent woman half to death," said the proprietor.

"Beggin pervert," muttered the old one, rising painfully. He cocked his head at Captain Juan and said, "Ain't they sum'm. Don't never make a peep. Whup em, hang em, don't make no never mind. Nary a peep."

Pedro shrugged and smiled, then drew out his other purse, the big one, opened it, yawned and said, "Men, I'm tuckered, so all this stands on the next hand." He tilted it so all could see what he'd lifted from Big Bar this afternoon—maybe ten thousand dollars. As they settled in their former places, all of them suddenly wide awake, he set the rules:

"If any of you wins, the winner gets half, the rest split the other half. But if I win—" He glanced tiredly around the room, stopping at Captain Juan.

"If I win, you cut him down. He walks out, and I get the gold." Looking at the surprised mouth holes in the array of beards, he shrugged. "I can use him in my digs. Besides, it's Easter."

Men bolted from their blankets to join the game. The proprietor shuffled and dealt, and now Pedro played monte in earnest. Those tedious years at the Presidio hadn't been entirely wasted. Perhaps Lady Fortuna would smile on him as she sometimes had done then, and he wouldn't need the trick.

The Swede shuffled, setting his bottle before Pedro. Needlenose cut. The proprietor dealt four down, one up. Needlenose checked his hand and squeezed out a handful of gold on the floor, where the cracks between planks were packed with sparkling dust. Pedro leaned down to the floor and peeked under his card. Cabrón! No luck tonight. Slipping cards past these hawks would be tricky.

Something, he didn't know what, made him turn around. He looked up and met Captain Juan's gaze for a stunned instant. It almost seemed he was trying to speak without words—María said they talked "from head to head" all the time. Pedro heard nothing, but read intensity in those dark eyes. Men were making little thinking noises as they considered their cards, and he turned back to the pensive faces around him, several sucking on cigarritos.

"Mebbee the Digger won't walk," said a man eyeing the card he had just drawn from the bottom of the pile.

Pedro took a card from the top of the pile. With his breath coming shallow, he reclined on his elbow, jiggling the hidden cards down in his sleeve, and looked at the worthless card while positioning his wrist for a quick transfer. A muscle twitched in his eyelid. Dios del Cielo, the things he did for María!

A piercing, inhuman cry reverberated in the room. He jerked his head up. Everyone was looking at Captain Juan. With a single move he swept the cards into his sleeve and replaced them with a new set. His heart kicked like a horse in his ribs and he looked calmly at the men as they turned back to the game.

"He done peeped," Needlenose observed.

"Yup," the old one admitted, smiling at his cards.

But Pedro was not smiling. Perspiration felt clammy on his forehead. His cards lay badly askew. Casually he pushed a corner of the worst one, straightening it a little. Did they suspect? Poker faces were part of the game, and not even a maddened grizzly was more dangerous than a roomful of cheated gamblers.

But the proprietor added gold to the pile and Needlenose dumped half his poke on the heap and guzzled brandy. Pedro slowly released his breath. Gracias a la Virgen! In the aftermath, his arm felt shaky as he extended his heavy purse to the center of the circle and plopped it on the plank with the loose gold.

Their eyes slid over the gold, and over Pedro. Willing his runaway heart to quiet, he slowly turned over his cards. Otra vez cabrón! The colors were faded! Deciding whom to shoot first and second and third, by then the arrows of the Indians would be flying, he forced a surprised smile.

"Hit cain't be," said a man who had until now been quiet. Hostile stares lifted to him.

Pedro's accent came ragged. "At last I get good luck."

Alert to every move in the room, he put his feet under him, squatting, concentrating on the exact locations of his Allen pepperbox four-shooter and his skinning knife, beneath his belt on either side. "Now we cut the Indian down," he said, reaching for the gold.

"The hell with the Injun, I say som'm stinks." Nobody moved, including Pedro.

The old one squinted at Pedro, his eyes hidden beneath tangled brows, "This here worked out jest right fer ye, didn't it, Transylvanian."

He withdrew his hand. "Most of you finished better than I. No?" He spread his hands, trying to look reasonable. The accent sounded wrong. His eyelid twitched.

Needlenose said, "This here sounds like a Mexican to me."

A knot tightened in his innards. Blood tingled in his legs, telling him to run. About this time he'd normally be leaning over Chocolate's mane, hooves digging distance between him and his adversaries. But normally he had their gold. Now they had his. And Captain Juan.

The proprietor eyed him. "I don't do business with Mexicans."

"Thunder weather!" Pedro exploded, leaping to his feet. "I'm no Mexican." He was a lion mid-spring, not knowing where to land. Ay ay ay, soon he'd be hanging beside Captain Juan, and not by the thumbs.

Something moved. He turned to see a Colt in the proprietor's hand, aimed at him. The men on the floor reached for his poke. In the poor light the proprietor's pitted complexion added menace to his voice. "Why don't we all jest loosen up a mite and play us another hand."

The miners sat back, leaving the gold where it was. "Sounds fair to me."

"Me too."

"Yup."

"Ya iss goot."

But it was not good. Ignoring the gun, Pedro gestured dramatically around the room and the lion in him roared, "Another hand! I thought you were gentlemen!" Raising his nose and bracing his feet, he welcomed the torrent of rage that broke the dam and let him speak with passion. "I am an honorable man. I came as a friend, to patronize this establishment and maybe find an honorable partner for my rich claim." Several faces relaxed into eyebrow-cocked interest. *Greed.*

His words echoed within the plank walls, resonating with the force of a practiced singer able to project to a thousand head of cattle. "You won a big purse from me." He looked the proprietor in the eye, lowered his gaze to the Colt, "And now you pull a gun on me because I win one lousy hand. Now cut that Injun down!" He pointed like the accusing finger of God.

The Colt nosed into its home under the belt. Outside the haloes of the oil lamps men sat up in their blankets, rubbed their eyes and grumbled obscenities. A number of gamblers stepped back from Pedro, exchanging glances. No one moved for a weapon.

Seeing the calming effect of his outrage, he roared one last volley. "You men have no honor!" Reaching down, he snatched up his poke and jammed it in his shirt, silently praying to the Virgin that the cards would not dislodge and fall. No one moved. He pointed at the piles of gold dust on the floor. "Keep your own filthy gold. I would not touch it."

From the blankets came a sound like a wounded bear followed by: "Fer Crissake, cut that ugly Digger down and let me sleep or I'll carve somebody's liver out!"

The proprietor hurried to the corner, whisked a chair beside Captain Juan and stood on it. He slashed a strap, Captain Juan's weight swinging to one thumb. The Indian winced, trying to stand on the tips of his toes.

The Swede drew the chair to the other side and sliced through the other thong. Captain Juan's knees buckled as he hit the floor, but he regained his balance and stood working the nooses from the stems of his ballooned thumbs.

He seemed taller. His eyes spoke to Pedro: Gracias. Pedro acknowledged the look and nodded toward the door.

"Here," said the proprietor to Pedro while taking a pinch from the pile of gold the squatting men were dividing. "This is for your trouble. Stay here tonight, on me."

"I have no wish to stay here," he said, proudly turning his back to the outstretched hand. With Captain Juan he walked swiftly toward the door, keenly aware of rapid footsteps scurrying in the room, following him. Not breathing, he continued without turning—feeling his back like a target.

"You'll need this," said Needlenose.

He whirled, took a breath, and cuffed his own head with the heel of his hand, then accepted his bedroll and rifle. "Thank you."

"I can dig with the best of 'em. Make ya a damned good pardner." The rat eyes pleaded from the dished-out face.

Captain Juan went out the door and Pedro looked over the men in the room, their easy posture. He smiled at the ugly man. "Maybe I come back. Maybe we talk tomorrow." He swung the roll over his shoulder and gripped his Springfield.

Crouch-running along the moonless side of the building, afraid they'd come for the gold, as he would have, he and Grizzly Hair joined the three shadows. Not until they crossed the river did he breathe freely. Captain Juan sat behind him in the saddle, the Indians trotting alongside.

Turning over his shoulder, Pedro said, "It must have been very painful."

Captain Juan hesitated only a moment. "First time in many moons back no hurt."

# 77

Pedro pulled María to him. Her lips moved with his, the sweetness of her breath feeding his appetite, making him want to stay. He shut his eyes, wondering what Joaquín Murieta wanted with him. Jesús Gonzáles hadn't said what the meeting was about, only that Murieta's closest associates would be there. He pushed her away, holding her by the shoulders. "I will be back in two days, Amapolita."

Her black eyes glistened in the morning sun. "I will wait for my warrior."

He loved that. This child wife of his was a diamond in the gravel of his life, and, no señor, he was not too proud to bask in her adoration. He had finally learned how to read past her mask. Last night he'd seen her joy when he brought Captain Juan to the hideout.

Kissing her one more time, he mounted and waved at Quapata, who was staying here to see that Captain Juan didn't try anything foolish in his absence. In the high grass before the cathedral-like boulders crowning the hill, the children, the strangely silent Little Flicker among them, waved to him. Indians didn't believe in saying good-bye; they'd learned it from him. He reined the horse and rode away.

The day was warm but pleasant along the flank of the hills, big swathes of yellow and purple flowers streaking the greens. Giving wide berth to the mining camps and the trails to his prime "hunting" grounds, he made his way through thickets of live oak, a hawk circling and crying high overhead, and reflected that Murieta must have a joint raid in mind, something really big. Pedro's own reputation had grown and some said he rivaled Murieta for the title of the "real Joaquín." Other "Joaquíns" tried, but didn't measure up in horsemanship, or careful planning. He loved nothing more than leaning against a porch in some boomtown listening to stories of his own raids, his machismo wonderfully exaggerated.

The wisp of an old story followed him, lurking at the edge of his memory. Something about a young man being drawn into a forest and the ground opening up and swallowing him. No fire or devils greeted him, but instead pleasant men whose skills he admired. They taught him their tricks and secrets. He couldn't recall how the story ended, and wondered why it came to him now.

Puzzling over it as Chocolate picked his way around rocks and fallen limbs, it suddenly occurred to him that Murieta was an antiquated word for death. An omen? Death for all who stood in his way? The real Murieta taunted death and was young and brave enough to get away with it. A Castillian, bonito in the way a flattering artist would paint a young man—and light-haired, almost blond. An angel of death. He dressed liked a true caballero, and he had more machismo than any twenty-year-old ought to have. Pedro thought back over Murieta's exploits. Actually it was warfare, like in the forests of old Spain.

Many North Americans coming to the so-called gold fields didn't seem to realize the war with Mexico was over. Nowhere had the trouble been more heated than around the hills of the mining camp called Sonora. Murieta and his brothers had been among the thousands of Sonorans to come north to try their luck. They had staked a family claim not far from where Pedro rode now. Experience gave the Sonorans a big advantage over farm boys and bankers. They knew how to read color and trace it to its source. It was they who removed most of the millions from this area. Jealous North Americans whipped, hung, and shot them, even passed a law that "Mexicans"—by that they meant anyone who spoke Spanish—could not own mining claims. Pedro smiled to recall the furious merchants having the law repealed because they could no longer gouge the "greasers." But North Americans trailed the Mexicans and jumped their claims like eggers following quail to their nests. That was why, on that fateful night, they attacked Murieta's camp.

Rumor had it that Murieta had been lashed to a tree and forced at gunpoint to watch his woman raped. That was one reason Pedro didn't want María traveling with him. She and the children were safer with the Indians. Quapata had the Allen pepperbox and knew how to use it.

It was evening when he rode into the secluded camp, open on all sides beyond the copse of trees. Good visibility and escape routes in all directions. He dismounted and hobbled Chocolate near the other horses. Murieta came across the inner clearing to pound Pedro on the shoulders, his dark blond hair luxuriant on his shoulders. "Bienvenida, Señor Cuidadoso," he said, not hiding his pleasure. "Gracias for coming to my humble camp." He even smelled young, beaming his hundred-candle smile at the other men as though to have them admire his prize.

Six men came forward to greet him. He already knew Jesús Gonzáles. The other five spoke on cue, signaled by Murieta's subtle nods. Most of them were even younger than the young lion. Pedro unloaded his bedroll and positioned it by the fire as a backrest, and made himself comfortable while the two women, disguised as men, offered meat and beans from a still-warm pot and a stack of tortillas wrapped in muslin. Rosita and Teresa.

The food was piquant and sabrosa. Gonzáles playfully pinched Teresa as she stacked wood by the fire. Her black eyes snapped with fun and she slapped him and ran away. Pedro liked her, liked the fire he saw in both women. The feel in the air was expectant and fresh, men on a dangerous mission, and he realized that El Cid and his men many centuries ago probably camped at such fires with such a feeling in the air.

Across from him, Murieta reclined with catlike grace, his eyes somehow directing everything that happened—the serving of food, the placement of the men, even the storytelling. Everything fit into his scheme except Pedro. It had been a long time since he'd fit anybody's mold. But it pleased him to be here, and he was happy biding his time until the lion revealed his purpose. As the spring night dampened and chilled around the friendly fire, he realized he was the primo guest, the one whose presence in the lair pleased Murieta the most.

Murieta nodded at Valenzuela, a Chilieño with an Aztec nose torqued to one side. "Tell my friends about your escape near Hornítas."

Valenzuela pushed up his hat, hanks of inky hair hanging under it, and told of a night attack by a posse. His eyes glinted as he described how he had jumped into the branches of a tree and swung out over a cliff to get away. He and two compadres found themselves barely able to stand on a narrow ledge high above the steep declivity.

"The North Americans searched for us and we heard one say, 'Look, the branches are broken. Let's go get them.' They were braver than we thought, muchachos. We heard the branches crack and knew they were coming. So we shot at them in the dark and tried to hurry along the ledge. They shot back— four times as many of them. I was hit. We all were. Bullets flew around us like bees, and tree bark, and chips of rock from the cliff. We lay down and slid down the steep gorge, praying we would not die. I almost did. Doña de Guadalupe! It was the closest I ever came to heaven." He hoisted his pants to show a scar on his calf. "I gashed that on the way down. Cracked my skull so hard I didn't wake up until morning." Murmurs of appreciation circled the fire.

Murieta all but whispered, "Ah, but you had a hundred horses stashed in the next canyon." With a smile on his lips, he narrowed his eyes at Pedro. Pay attention to my man, he was saying.

Pedro told how he'd gambled for Captain Juan's release, and what the Indian said about it being the only time his back didn't hurt. The men slapped their knees and chortled. Gonzáles tipped up a bottle of whisky, ahhed as it went down, and said, "You never know what is funny to Indians. Once I heard Apaches laugh while they slowly cooked the brains of a man hung upside-down over a small fire." Back in the shadows the women paused, listening as they prepared bedrolls, only their eyes reflecting firelight. Gonzáles continued, "To the Indians it was funny, like a rabbit caught by an eagle. 'He was careless,' they say. 'He offered himself. And now the joke is on him.'"

After a silence, Joaquín Murieta raised his head and the fire highlighted the streaks in his mane. "Did I tell you about my friend who fought with General Santana?" Hats wagged and lips turned up in pleasant anticipation.

"My friend he was very brave and much admired by the women." Everything about Murieta was soft like the paw of a mountain lion. He stalked his enemies with the same concentration as he charmed the pants off women. Now he all but purred and Pedro struggled to hear him over the crackling fire.

"One night my friend was on his way to Texas. He and his men camped near the Río Grande to wait for ammunition. It was about nightfall and they looked down the hill over a small village. My friend saw some señoritas walking to the cantina." His lips curled up at the corners and he glanced around the fire. "My friend, he can see a señorita five leagues away."

Smiling, Pedro leaned back on his saddle and sipped the cup of whisky-spiked chocolate that Rosita had made for him. The fire felt good and he enjoyed Murieta flattering him with solicitous looks.

"About twenty soldiers slipped away and went down to the cantina to make the acquaintance of the beauteous flowers of the desert. Before long my friend had the prettiest one, and she took him to her house." He surveyed the expectant faces. "That is true, amigos. My friend, he always has the prettiest girl. And what I tell you next is true also."

The purr softened and everyone breathed quietly so as to hear, Murieta extracting subordination from his disciples. Or was it only that he didn't want the women to hear?

"Suddenly shots rang out. North Americans shooting in the plaza. For my amigo this happened at a most embarrassing moment and he could not find his pants. So he ran outside in his shirt. He was outraged at the bad manners of the dogs who stole Texas. His friends joined him, but the bad men were already galloping away. My friend, he says, 'These are worse cowards than I thought!' His compadres looked down at his naked front and said, 'No amigo, they fear your cannon.'"

Laughing, Pedro realized how much he missed the company of men who'd learned Spanish at their mother's knee. He'd been something of a loner at Sutter's Fort and at Sheldon's rancho, straddling different worlds. But in childhood he had run with a lively group of boys. He saw that same closeness around this fire. It touched him, tempted him.

Murieta's brother-in-law Claudio was telling about some men who got into a fight in an old adobe in Mexico. "They threw each other against the wall and the plaster broke, and Spanish coins fell out, very old. The kind of gold brought over on the galleons from Spain." Eyes gleamed around the fire and Pedro recalled that Grandfather Valdez had sailed to Mexico on such a ship. Anything from old Spain fascinated him, maybe because he'd always felt like a far-flung son, a seed trying to root in these hostile rocks. Claudio leaned forward.

"Let me tell you what else was found behind the plaster of a wall. This happened at Alamos, an old silver mine not far from La Colorada." He told of a brother and sister separated when they were very young. The girl grew up far away, but returned to Alamos. Not knowing one another, the two fell passionately in love, and when their father found out, he put her in the wall and sealed it, because they were brother and sister. For many days the people of the pueblo heard her cries, muffled and strange. "It was her bones those miners found. And it is true. Her bones are there to this day. No one will go near that old house." Claudio looked around at the men. "Every night her ghost moans and shrieks. You will hear it if you go there."

Wood shifted on the coals and the glow from the waning fire barely lit the shadowed men. Pedro was contemplating the sin of incest when Valenzuela said, "I thought you said the mines around Sonora were closed because of fighting and revolution."

"Some vecinos remain there," Claudio said. "They scratch around in the slag left from centuries of mining." He looked at Joaquín Murieta. "Some of them are my kin."

"Señores," said Murieta, sitting up, "I have been thinking."

Now it comes.

"You are all brave bandidos, and our enemies ride stiff-legged on mules. They cannot shoot straight." He glanced around at the smiles. "Every one of you can ride circles around them." He told of his home in Mexico, and said that working as a disciplined army they could drive large caballadas down there, and his family would sell the horses at a big profit, and convert gold dust to coin. "In a short time we could have a million dollars each. For the rest of our lives we would live like Spanish grandees."

"Kings," Valenzuela amended.

Pedro realized how tired he was of riding alone and how much he enjoyed this brotherhood. Though he often felt close to Quapata, Indian language and superstition divided them. With María it was different. A man enjoyed mystery in a woman. But mostly he was tired of hiding her and the baby. He no longer wanted land in Alta California, where he wasn't wanted, and he knew that he could grow old stealing gold for the Indians and still not come close to what they needed. The thought of ending this dangerous and frustrating life thrilled him. He could just as well have his rancho grande and beautiful hacienda in Mexico, and put María in it. And he wouldn't need to look over his shoulder every time he stooped for a drink of water. He dipped his hat at Murieta and said, "We would live like kings."

The young lion lounged back on an elbow with his mane caressing a shoulder. He smiled, eyes slit in contentment.

But there was a limit. "Each man keeps his own gold," Pedro added, doubting if any of these men did as well as he did.

Valenzuela's back stiffened in the shadows. "No Señor Valdez. We divide our profits equally. We always do." The other five nodded vigorous agreement. Somebody said, "Share and share alike."

Before he could respond, Joaquín Murieta beamed a smile at Valenzuela. "Of course. You are right, my friend, about the horses, the ones we help each other herd. That is natural. Our friend Señor Valdez speaks only of the gold that we take from the obliging miners, no?" His hundred-candle-power smile turned on Pedro.

The supreme confidence was fascinating, disarming. "Sí," Pedro said, "And if four of us cooperate, those four divide the gold."

Murieta nodded at the reluctant men and extended his hand toward Pedro. "We have much to learn from Señor Valdez."

The men exchanged glances but grunted approval.

Silently chuckling, Pedro couldn't help but give Joaquín Murieta an admiring snort and wag of his head. Later as he sank toward sleep, rustles and moans of lovemaking came from Murieta's blankets across the coals. He reflected on the oddity that a man so young and vigorous would bear the name Death.

With coyotes laughing across the hills, he floated into dream and rode with shadow men through the underworld. Weaving among the hooting owls and shrieking night birds, he suddenly found himself apart from his fellows, imprisoned in a strange crystal palace. People peered in but he could not see out. Terrified, he opened his mouth to yell for help, but no sound came out.

# 78

### LATE SEPTEMBER, 1850

Summer still blew across the destroyed land and up the hill to the adobe. It could have saved its hot breath, Elitha thought as she dipped beans from the sack. Everything withered six months ago, including her young apple tree. She looked up at the oblivious vultures gliding across the blue, apparently deaf to the clank of picks and shovels in the riverbottom. The incessant sound of digging grated on her nerves. And that wasn't all.

Ben Wilder had been avoiding her. He hadn't eaten at her table even once, and she knew it was because she had been forward. He hadn't done the favor she'd asked either. Hadn't said a word on Captain Juan's behalf, a customer told her. Well, he was nothing but a selfish Forty-niner out for himself. Yet she dreamed about him, long sensuous dreams that left her stunned.

Angrily she dashed half a bucket of water into the bean pot, then singed her rolled-up sleeves, her eyes narrowed against the wind of the flames, as she struggled to lift the pot shoulder high, finally pushing the handle over the tripod hook. She went inside. It was cooler, the only good thing about adobe. She unwound the newspaper from the seven-dollar-a-pound beef she'd bought from a teamster. And to think she'd once been surrounded by cattle! But she had to offer more than wild game if she expected to compete with the other eating-houses. The four-pound slab of meat stuck to the paper, quivering as she pulled it off. Her stomach bucked. Gulping hard, she took the honed knife and cut the flesh.

The maroon halves parted smoothly behind the blade. A warm animal odor rose from it, a smell deeper and fuller than blood alone. She dropped the knife and ran outside, bent forward, spewing the salt pork and biscuits of breakfast. Connected by strings of mucus, it draped over the parched grass. Again and again she heaved, crying from her mouth, retching from her soul, sick of the scorch of fires, the clank of shovels, Perry gambling away the gold, sick of knowing, yes, knowing she was pregnant again. Knowing she couldn't leave him and that she had been stupid and piteously self-deceitful to think Ben Wilder would whisk her away like Mary Murphy's Frenchman had. She heaved out the truth with the last strings of spit. Even if he had, she wouldn't leave a husband and run away, because Donner women didn't do that.

Feeling weak and quivery, she wiped her mouth with her apron. The bean pot hung too low in the flames. Straightening the tripod, she headed inside, but the meat-smell turned her back. She went to the shelter of the split rock where, three years ago, she had buried a gold nugget, and sank to her knees. The boulders stopped the worst of the Devil Wind.

As a little girl she'd never imagined life would look this bleak, hadn't imagined being pregnant would feel like this—the birthing fearful yes, but not the sickness of wanting a man to know her secret heart. She scraped back a rich accumulation of decaying vegetation. Perry was oblivious. She knew he would laugh at the girl she'd once been, sitting among apple blossoms, and she believed, clawing in the dirt, that he had deliberately stood between her and her little sisters. Two years had elapsed without a word from them, the house as crude as ever. She pulled the nugget from the earth, exactly where she'd buried it.

It lay heavy in her palm. She brushed off the encrusted earth until rich glints of gold shone through. Someday when she found her sisters, she would have lockets made for them, with Donner inscribed on the inside, and they could carry a lock of hair or some other small treasure in them.

Horses approached. She looked out and saw Perry, who had shaved and combed for the first time in weeks and ridden away early. He and another man dismounted. Perry stuck his head in the house, then yelled around the yard, "Elitha, hit's company."

She dropped the gold in the hole and patted the earth in place. Wiping her hands on her apron, she walked dutifully to the house. The meat was teeming with layers of small yellow and black striped bees, so thick they held the smell in.

Perry pointed at it. "Seein how much the yellow jackets can eat, be ye?" It was a tone meant to amuse a guest, but it perturbed her to have him talk to her like that in front of a stranger. Perry looked old. Not just weathered like a woodsman, but aged. His eyes swam in a permanent film and his nose had grown lumpy and purple-veined. The missing tooth made him look ruined and simple-minded.

The other man removed his hat, displaying reddish hair on a thinning pate, and she recognized him as one of the men at the fort; he'd been there when she and Perry returned from San Francisco. Embarrassed to forget his name, she looked at the insects.

"George McKinstry," said the man. "We've met before."

"Elitha McCoon." She gave him a hint of a curtsy. "At Captain Sutter's table." In rough clothes then, he now wore dark broadcloth like an Illinois banker. "You still the sheriff?" He didn't wear a badge, and she hoped Perry wasn't in trouble.

"No. I prefer to get paid for working." He smiled. "A pleasure to see you again. Perry and I been talking about the news." As if seeing her confusion, he continued, "You haven't heard? California's a state now."

"Is that a fact!" She was truly surprised. The papers said Congress had been stymied for more than a year debating the slavery question.

"That's right. We're in the Union now. The thirty-first state. Word came yesterday. Like I was telling Perry, the newspapers came on the New World. She's a paddle-wheeler, come out of New York only two weeks ago. Can you believe? Cut the record in half I heard. You should have seen it! Men running all over town and galloping around on their horses waving the papers and hollering, 'California's admitted and Queen Victoria has a baby!'" He chuckled. "Shootin off firearms to beat the band."

"Are we free or slave?" she asked. The South had many supporters in California.

"Free."

She released her breath. "I'm so glad for the Indians!"

He looked at her funny. "It has nothing to do with them. Just Negroes."

"I don't under—" A glance at Perry ended the conversation—very peeved. He didn't like her speaking up about men's affairs.

"Indians are a different situation," Mr. McKinstry was saying. He looked at Perry. "Mrs. McCoon takes to politics I see. You tell her what the Legislature decided?"

With his eyes on McKinstry, Perry wrinkled his nose her way like this was too complex for her poor mind and said, "She don't need to know. Clean up the table, lass. We got important business."

That vexed her. "Perry, I've heard Indians are bought and sold all the time and I want to know if ours are still in that kind of danger, that's all I was going to ask."

Perry started to open his mouth but the ex-sheriff was saying to her, "The only time Indians can be auctioned is if they're found to be loitering and strolling around or being immoral, you know, unemployed. Then they're arrested as vagrants. But they're not bought and sold outright, so the laws of slavery don't apply."

Seeing that Perry looked resigned, she continued, "Who auctions them?"

"Towns, counties, after they're in custody."

"Do they get paid for their work? Can they leave if they want?"

With a look at Perry, McKinstry assumed a concluding tone, "Well now, they're getting their keep and learning the arts of civilization and that's pay of a kind, and no man wants his workers to up and leave. So no, and no." He looked to Perry as if to say, let's get on with business.

Giving the man a grateful glance for talking to her, she took the broad side of the knife and scraped the meat, insects and all, onto the newspaper, carrying it at arm's length with yellow jackets swarming all over and bouncing off her wrists. But she was thinking about the Indians. They could all be called vagrants, except those who were employed by white men. And most people thought they were immoral. So it sounded like an excuse to get free labor and for towns to make money. Why didn't the anti-slavery laws apply? Glad not to be stung, she placed the meat on the stump by the fire pit. The black men she'd seen mining didn't seem to worry about being captured and forced to work for somebody else, but Indian Mary and her father did.

She took the pot to the ditch for water, deciding to boil the meat whole and cube it when it was done. Neither insects nor muddiness mattered. The grit sank and nobody would know. She'd learned not to scrape the bottom of the gravy. And there was something else she wasn't scraping the bottom of either. Free. What did it mean? She sat down and waited for the water to simmer, then dipped the floating insects out. Was she free? She worked hard and felt trapped, even though her customers paid her. Perry took what gold she couldn't hide, and played with it. That's what gambling was, playing. He didn't gather wood or fix the house, and of course men didn't cook or wash the plates. In the beginning he'd worked with cattle and mined gold. But not since he lost the Indians. Yet he wouldn't be arrested as a vagrant or be auctioned like a workhorse. He was white.

Perry came outside with Mr. McKinstry and they shook hands. Putting on his bowler hat, Mr. McKinstry nodded at Elitha, mounted, and rode away. Something flew into her eye and she was rubbing it when Perry said happily, "Lass, it's on the road to riches we be headed now!" He extended a poke filled with gold for her to see. "Twenty-five thousand dollars, it tis! And a fraction of what I'll win when the speculatin's done." It was the first time in weeks she'd seen his dimple.

She blinked at the gold dust. What on earth had he sold? What did he have to sell? Then like a slap, she knew. She couldn't bring herself to speak, knowing he'd lose the gold quickly and soon she wouldn't even have a house to cook in, to make a living in, never mind how crude.

"Well ent ye going to congratulate yer man?"

"You sold the ranch."

"Not too feebleminded, ye be!" He held the purse before him, admiring it. "But only the ground up there at the road."

"Not the house?"

"Not daft entirely is this man o' yours." Despite his pleased expression, she detected a certain heaviness behind it, like even he didn't believe in future riches any more.

Relief didn't cancel the despair or the hot wind. She wilted, sank down on a stump in the shade. "Oh Perry, I was so afraid for us, and—" she made herself say it, "our child. We need a place to live."

With a sudden "Wahoo!" he threw up the purse and caught it. "A babe is it!"

She couldn't even smile, and at that moment caught sight of Indian Mary in the trees, holding up a bundle of herbs. For the retching.

❧

Several months later Perry slid off his horse, dragged himself into the adobe and announced that Bill Daylor had died. He threw himself on the bed with a cup of whisky.

Stunned, Elitha stood by the bed despite a yard full of men waiting to eat outside. Perry hadn't been nearly this dejected when he'd lost the gold. But then, he'd lost it by stages. The trip to San Francisco to speculate with the "big boys" finished it. Now he looked nearly dead himself. "What of?" Elitha asked. It didn't seem possible anything could fell a man so full of life.

Perry turned toward the wall. "Cholera morbus."

*Cholera.* Brought on the very steamship carrying the news of statehood. The newspapers screamed with stories about rampant sickness in Sacramento City, the scarcity of doctors and the lack of hospitals. Disease was reported in the mining regions too. Poor Sarah!

Early the next morning she drank Indian Mary's tea, which stopped the nausea, hung out her No EATING TODAY sign and pulled the brown frock over her head for the first time since Easter. The waist buttons couldn't be coaxed together. With a sigh she counted. July, August, September, October. Four months pregnant, going on five. She slipped a clean apron over the gap and sadly tied the strings behind. At the funeral she'd look like a woman who had to cook for a living.

Perry gulped the last of his whisky and went for the horses. He'd been drinking more since he'd lost the money from Mr. McKinstry. She ducked to see herself in the tiny mirror, pinning her hair, and heard his call, "Elitha, damn it to hell." As if Daylor's death were her fault.

"I'll be right there." She must be careful with him today. Daylor had been his best friend.

He muttered as she rushed to mount her mare, and didn't get off Paint to give her a hand up. It was a bright autumn morning, the last cottonwood left standing flashing yellow leaves against a blue sky. Soon it too would be cut down for wood. As they rode past Mr. McKinstry's new plank store and house, which he'd built near his bridge, Perry grumped, "Taiks me land for a song 'e does, then builds a bridge to steal me customers!" *Ferry customers.*

Mr. McKinstry's bridge spanned the river at the narrowest place, and every time a heavy supply wagon rolled across, the timbers bounced. On the opposite bluff stood Mr. Sherwood's store, on Mr. Sheldon's new ground, and come spring Mr. Sheldon would build a cabin over there. Civilization was springing up all around, yet it seemed to Elitha that she would live in that crude adobe forever.

The eight miles to Rancho Omuchumne were long, Daylor Road crowded with wagons and teams and riders, most of them with picks and shovels jutting at odd angles from their saddles. Many men tramped past on foot with pans dangling on their backs. Perry barely nodded to them. Celestials in peaked straw hats and cloth slippers trotted tirelessly along the road. His road was busy, but Daylor was dead. The first time she'd seen this road, it was nothing but a faint pair of wagon tracks leading to what seemed the end of the world. Only three years ago.

And it didn't seem fair that Mr. Daylor died twenty-four hours after acting the Good Samaritan. He had gone to Sutter's Embarcadero for supplies for his mercantile, and on his way back stayed the night at the old fort, which was nothing but a derelict sleeping place now. Hearing a moan, he discovered a sick man on a pile of old straw. He gave him a drink from his cup and tried to make him comfortable, but the man died during the night. At his store the next day, Mr. Daylor felt ill as he unloaded the supplies. Sarah put him to bed, and he was dead in two days. By a fluke Perry had been there.

Now as they approached Daylor's store, Elitha saw the long wooden box in a wagon. Sarah stood beside it, tall and elegant even in grief. Not pregnant. How many times had Elitha thought that as she looked at her? Now she would never have a child, at least not by Mr. Daylor.

Mr. Sheldon raised a hand in greeting. He looked older, stricken. At his side stood Catherine, visibly pregnant again, with toddler Will at her knee and little Sarah in her arms. Dismounting, Elitha nodded a greeting to John and Matilda Rhoads, who were working to keep their children in tow. Also in the yard were the new neighbors—the big Wilson family who had built a bridge and Wilson's Exchange on the other side of the river in Slough House. She saw the Pattersons, Elders, Cummings and many others. Old Rancho Omuchumne was well populated—a settlement around the Daylors' expanded store and a big blacksmith shop across the road. A new and bigger mercantile store had been built. And John Rhoads was building a school over by his house. The very last remaining Indians of the original people stood by the trees, two boys and a man. The new Indian workers from down-river lived nearby but weren't present. Perry and Elitha tied the horses to the porch rail.

Mr. Grimshaw, the young storekeeper came over, his slicked, side-parted hair so straight and blunt below his ears it seemed a shiny brown fabric. Mr. Daylor had made him a partner in the store. "You're the last," he said, "so we'll head down to the grave in a minute." He and Sarah were partners now.

Poor Sarah. She'd loved Mr. Daylor. Elitha went over and hugged her. Struggling visibly to keep from crying, Sarah patted Elitha's belly, her swollen eyes betraying envy. It wasn't fair at all. With a stab of guilt Elitha stopped the thought and said, "Please let me know if there is anything I can do."

Elizabeth brought a man over on her arm. "Elitha, this here is Mr. Gunn." Both sisters were widows now. In two years.

"Sorry to have to meet you at such a sad time," Elitha said with a curtsy.

Catey looked over at her middle. "You too." They shared a commiserating look.

Mr. Sheldon called, "Let's go."

Elitha returned to Perry, still sitting on Paint. She mounted Gay-Gay.

Women loaded their families into wagons and Mr. Sheldon helped Sarah and Catherine to get up beside the coffin. Mr. Sheldon stepped up to the driver's seat and flicked the reins, starting the procession. Elitha and Perry rode in the middle, behind the Cummings' horses, in front of the Wilson's wagon. All proceeded slowly toward Slough House. Elitha leaned toward Perry and asked, "Where's the grave?"

"At the old Indian ranchería."

She knew the place. She had searched for grass nuts with the women and girls of that village. All dead now. She'd been pregnant then too. Maybe this baby would die too. Maybe she would. The Grim Reaper pointed his bony finger at random. Unless you were Indian; then it was much worse.

The procession stalled at the foot of the mound into which the vanished roundhouse had been dug. People stopped the wagons and climbed out. People ahead on horseback were riding up the mound, Perry and Elitha waiting their turn. She looked up the road at the town of Slough House, the Inn's shed roof arching over the road at the far end. Mr. and Mrs. Quiggle, who managed the Inn, walked toward them.

They ran the Inn profitably, though it was a rowdy place, drawing from the heavy travel between Sacramento City and the southern mines, and they paid the Sheldons good rent. Over a shop this side of town stretched a limb of the hanging tree, where Sheldon had been judge and executioner to horse thieves. The grass beneath it and along the road was green again now, with the recent rains, the air musty with fallen, rotting leaves. It seemed a particularly eerie time for a burying, the day after Halloween.

Gay-Gay pushed up the hill on strong haunches. Elitha dismounted and tied her to a tree with other horses, and walked to the pile of dirt in which shovels bristled, marking the open grave. The aroma of earth was strong. The Hicks family and others were waiting. She stood beside Perry while about fifty people gathered, the cheerful birds sounding disrespectful. Then the men slipped ropes around the coffin and lowered it into the hole.

Mr. Sheldon started to speak in a voice slightly frayed: "Mr. Daylor's the first white man to be laid in this Indian burial ground. No man was more beloved by the Indians than William Daylor." Glancing at the two Indian boys, Mr. Sheldon said, "No man was more respected by any of us." He swallowed and looked at the sky, blinking. He paused long, and Elitha heard Sarah and Catey softly weeping.

Elitha glimpsed Señor Valdez through the trees on his magnificent dark horse. He sat tall in the saddle, his dark hair full of rich glints of auburn in the sunlight coming through the branches. His sombrero hung over his saddle horn. Paying respects to Mr. Daylor.

Mr. Sheldon resumed: "Mr. Daylor was born in England about 1810. Didn't get any schooling. Except on board a commercial brig, an education of sorts, and he was smart as a whip. He built the first trading post east of Sutter's Fort right here on this land. He was brave," he swallowed. "and honest." Moisture appeared in Perry's eyes, and he rolled the brim of his hat.

"He was the first to see this beautiful Cosumnes valley and convinced me it was the place I'd been looking for. And he was right about that. I gave him half of it, and we, we always, always—" He gained control of his voice, "worked it together."

Sarah sobbed openly beside Catey, who supported her on one side while Elizabeth held her on the other. Mr. Sheldon pulled out a piece of paper, unfolded it and read:

"*Last Will and Testament.*
*Daylor's Ranch, October 31st, 1850.*
*Know all men by these presents, that I, William Daylor, being attacked with cholera, as my friends think, and to carry out, and to fulfill my last wishes, I hereby appoint Jared Sheldon, my only administrator...*
*as I wish him to arrange and settle all of my affairs truly and honestly.*

*I, therefore, leave him in possession of my effects and property to administer—"*

"And a pretty penney 'e 'ad too," Perry whispered, too loud.

People turned to look. Sheldon shot him a glare and continued to read,

*"My wife is to have a provision made for her first.... My two Indian boys are to be taken care of by Mr. Sheldon according to his judgment. I being in my right mind and senses approve of the above and do so by my signature.*
*Signed William Daylor, his mark.*
*Witness to the above: the signatures of John Connack, Perry McCoon, Thomas Coburn."*

Mr. Sheldon folded the paper, slipped it in his pocket, looked up at the blue autumn sky, and said, "Lord, help us fathom your ways." He grabbed a spade and jammed it in the dirt and threw the first dirt in the hole. It sounded hollow on the box. "Ashes to ashes," somebody said. Other men picked up shovels.

Elitha went to Gay-Gay and leaned her forehead on the young horse's back, the strong, warm smell of horse life in her nose, and pressed her hands over her ears to stop the sound of dirt hitting the coffin, men trying to cover up the hole of death. Death fooled a person. Before she'd left the tent under the snow, she'd thought life was tougher, more tenacious. But Mr. Daylor breathed a miasma too thin for the eye to see, and even he, the strongest of men, was gone. She must not waste time pining after fantasies. She would walk this trail. With all her heart she would love this baby growing inside her, and maybe Perry would become a man more like Pa.

# 79

One more Indian-killer lay dead. Punished. As Pedro aimed the flat of his hat into the rainstorm, trusting the horse to pick his way to the boulder hideout, he thought back to morning when he'd roped the man's arms to his sides and run him behind the horse. He had turned in the saddle and said:

"Now it's time to think of the little children you killed. And women, and unarmed men. You remember them?" Running hard with his mouth open, the man gasped. Pedro continued, "Remember their faces when you shot them? Talk to me, Goat. Or maybe you want to run faster?"

"No, no," the man coughed, wheezed and said, "I 'member. But they was only Injuns."

Nudging Chocolate a bit faster, hearing the man's breath growing raspier, he turned back and said, "And you are only a dead piece of goat shit."

He'd used his spurs. Chocolate dug into a run, dragging the man half a league across a rocky slope. Pedro left what remained of him for the vultures.

He'd been lucky to find the man, he thought as rain lashed his knuckles and trickled down his neck. Only two of those eight killers still drew breath.

He was wet to the skin. Mother of God, it was cold, and coming from the southeast again. At this angle rain drove beneath the overhanging boulder where he and María normally slept. Tonight they'd have to crowd in with the Indians under the lintel boulder. His guitar had been ruined long ago. He envied Joaquín Murieta and his men, who now wintered in the dry cave above Spanish Camp where he had formerly camped with the Indians.

Still, his purse was full. The German outside Bedbug had promptly handed over his take. That plus the sack he and Valenzuela removed from the store made Pedro flush. And satisfied, getting the killer. He felt invincible, almost bored with danger.

Near McCoon's cabin, half a mile from the hideout, he smelled cooking meat. Pulling on the reins, he sat looking at the drenched adobe. The fire outside steamed and smoldered beneath a metal tripod, a pot over it. Señora McCoon did well to keep the fire going in this weather. She needed money, he knew. Everyone knew. Everybody pitied her for being married to McCoon.

The aroma was mouth-watering. On a whim he headed for the adobe.

Seven months along now, Elitha stared out the window at the brimming brown river, wondering how she would ever get money ahead to fix the house. They still used the same door, and the cross section of an oak still teetered on its stump and served as a table. At least she had four nice chairs now—a skilled miner made them in exchange for food. But with supplies so dear, she needed more customers, and with the weather and the high water so bad, most of the miners were wintering in Sacramento City, or San Francisco.

Perry was back from the river. With his drinking curtailed by the inflated cost of liquor, thank the Lord for that, he ferried a few men across the water and made a trickle of money. Mr. McKinstry's bridge had washed out, and Perry had acquired the raft Mr. Keyser had been using when he drowned. Perry wasn't a swimmer either, but she knew he wouldn't take chances with cattle after what happened to Mr. Keyser—the animals shifting all to one side, the man's body never found.

Perry yanked off a boot. "Neptune's bones, a gully washer she is!" He rubbed his foot. "What's fer dinner?"

He knew perfectly well. "The usual."

"No potatoes?"

"Ten dollars apiece." She gave him a level look. She couldn't even afford a newspaper. For all she knew the people in Sacramento City were still dying from cholera. Five had died in the Slough House area. Not having a newspaper made her feel isolated and poor.

Over the drumming of the rain, she heard a horse whinny. Peering through the veils of moisture moving crosswise over the window, she saw a man in dark clothing tying his horse.

Perry joined her at the window. "Well if it ent the greaser."

Pedro Valdez walked boldly to the door and knocked. "Buenos dias, señora," he said when she opened it, "and Señor McCoon." Perry's eyes widened. In fear? Anger? There was still bad blood between them, but the Spaniard smiled and bowed. She was sure he meant no trouble, and it wasn't civilized to leave a man standing in the rain.

"Come in," she said.

He entered like a king, smelling of wet wool. His black hat nearly touched the damp ceiling. He seemed to fill the room, the tails of his red and white sarape streaming water. Sometimes she wondered if Mr. Valdez was Joaquín, the dashing gentleman bandit. The outlaw never struck Cook's Bar, Michigan Bar, Slough House, or any of the nearby camps. A possible sign that he lived around here.

"I hope you are well?" Valdez asked warmly, carefully removing his hat and balancing the water until he pushed it out the door to shake it off.

"Git to the point," Perry said.

Elitha cringed, but Valdez merely elevated his somewhat hawk-like nose and said, "I understand you serve food to travelers. Perhaps I could buy a plate."

Perry exhaled, and she hoped he'd treat Señor Valdez like any other customer. "We'd be obliged, sir," she said.

"SIR!" Perry glared at her then snapped at the Spaniard. "Five pinches to ye." He reached for the pay can.

"Perry—"

He thrust the can at the man. "I said five pinches." Normally a meal cost one pinch.

"Está bien." Mr. Valdez pulled a fat poke past his Colt revolver and opened it to Elitha. "Go ahead, señora. Take five."

She took one and didn't want more.

The Spaniard acted fast, placing five more pinches into the can. Then he smiled and said, "And one extra, for the señora."

Maybe he was the bandit. The one that paid over-generously for meals and was gracious toward women. She set a plate and cup before him and lit the spermaceti lamp, it being dark with the weather so bad. Perry hooked back the divider curtain and sat on the bed as if to keep the man under surveillance. Pulling her cloak over her head, she went outside for the stew.

When she returned, Mr. Valdez had removed his sarape and folded it over a chair. "That smells *sabrosa*," he said with a smile, eyeing the steaming pot. "Men say you cook very good. Taste good."

She shrugged and asked after Mary's health. He answered politely, dipping out a plateful and not mentioning the baby.

After several minutes of eating, he twisted in his chair and looked back at Perry. "I will be pleased to buy this rancho."

Stunned, Elitha stared at him. The aftermath of the sale to Mr. McKinstry had been disastrous and Perry had sunk to a new low. But he rose from the bed and came to the table where he could see Mr. Valdez' face.

"Sold part of it, I did."

"Sí, and I will buy the rest."

Dread crawled through her veins as Perry seated himself across from the Spaniard. Gold flew from his hands faster than birds flushed from a bush.

Pedro was having fun. He'd planned none of this, but rumor had it McCoon wanted to sell land at inflated prices. Pedro didn't believe he owned a proper title to sell. Moreover his sights had shifted to Mexico, where he would live with honor. But this was too amusing to pass by. While McCoon's fortunes had gone sour, his own had blossomed. He had helped drive another five hundred horses across the border and buried a hundred thousand North American dollars in a secret place in Mexico. Indians talked of power. Gold was power when you had it to play with.

He told McCoon, "I will pay thirty-thousand dollars for the remainder of your rancho." That and McKinstry's money would give the *desgraciado* a total of fifty-five thousand dollars for land he'd acquired for nothing. He bit into a warm, flaky biscuit dripping with butter and stifled a smile as Mc-Coon labored visibly with his emotions. He would hate doing business with a "greaser," but temptation showed in his eyes and he licked his lips. He was sober and out of liquor or he'd be drinking. Once he had dressed like a grandee, but now his clothes were worn out and the soles of the boots in the corner gaped like the mouths of dead men.

McCoon looked up and narrowed an eye at him. "Come next Sunday we'll have ourselves that ridin' competition, we will. Or has ye forgot?"

Long ago Pedro had concluded that McCoon was too much of a coward. He'd never set a date. Filling his lungs, he said, "I do not forget nada."

"Ride then we will by Jove! Up behind the Bridge House store, where all can see and ye can't cheat. If I wins, I gits yer thirty thousand and keeps me land. If you wins, ye gits title to me ground."

As if any real vaquero would cheat, or need to, to defeat the likes of him! Pedro gave back, "I think you have no land title, señor, and I win nothing."

"Yer afraid to lose, is all." He went to the bed and pulled a leather bag from underneath. "Show ye the front end of a 'orse, I will." As he fumbled through the bag, Pedro filled his stomach. Elitha stared out the window, tall, with child, dark hair swept back from a pretty face. She would appeal to any man. After a few minutes McCoon came back and sat in the chair across the table, extending a yellowed sheet of paper.

Pedro put down his fork and took the paper. Documents from Mexican governors had an eagle stamped into a glob of wax. Only Captain Sutter's swirling scrawl marked the bottom of this one. Knowing McCoon couldn't read either, he pretended to follow the writing from side to side, while Mc-Coon looked one way and then the other, glancing between the paper and Pedro's eyes.

He held the paper at arm's length and said, "Capitán Sutter wrote this, not the Mexican governor."

McCoon jumped to his feet. "Callin me a liar in me own 'ouse is ye!" He jerked his head southward. "Mexico ent worth a hill of beans, or 'as ye forgot? Cap'n Sutter's an official in the new gov'ment and a damned sight more consequential than a beggared Mexican!" His defensiveness gave him away. He owned nothing and he knew it.

After he disgraced this bastard on the field, maybe he would throw the supposed land title back at him and inform him how worthless it was.

McCoon put the paper on the table and slapped his hand down on it. "If it's good enough fer me and McKinstry, it's damn well good enough fer a greaser!" He glowered like a tomcat.

"Está bien." Suddenly he was impatient to show McCoon how to ride a horse. "The Sunday that comes, when the sun is high." By then the ground would be drier. Rubbing his full belly, he smiled at Elitha, pitying her as much as he despised McCoon. "Sabrosa," he said. Delicious.

# 80

**JANUARY 5, 1851**

It was a sunny spell between the winter rains. Elitha went outside, tugging her cloak around her shoulders. Perry stood leaning toward the small mirror that was tacked on the doorframe, the stretched wool of his longjohns sagging badly at the knees and drooping between the two rear buttons.

The ground was damp, the packed clay of the yard firm underfoot. "Looks like a good day for riding," she said. Droplets of moisture sparkled on the new grass. The sun and breeze would dry out the footing even more.

"Aye, lass." With his face stretched to the razor, his voice was distorted, but happy.

She headed down the path, getting an early start on the quarter-mile to

Bridge House. He said cheerfully,"Ent seemly fer me wife to walk in like that, big in the hold 'n all."

She turned to him, his face soaped white. He grinned a mouthful of teeth, except for the one that was missing. "If ye don't be wantin' to saddle the mare, wait. I'll give ye a ride up." His dark hair gleamed in the sun. She had helped him wash it—and his clothes, the shirt hanging over a branch with its empty arms waving. With each passing day his humor had improved until he now seemed as saucy as the day she met him.

She nodded that she would wait. Not for a long time had he shown off his riding, and nothing pleased him more than being the center of attention. If he won the money, he'd be drunk and dangerous for weeks. If he lost .... She wouldn't think about it. For now he was the old Perry, an attractive man proud of his abilities, a man who could charm the birds out of the trees. Despite everything, she felt something like happiness for him. She would enjoy the moment and cheer for him.

He cocked his elbows, pushed out his rear, and bent toward the mirror. How he could disdain the Spaniards and yet desire to be hailed as a great vaquero was a mystery to her. But he didn't seem to notice the contradiction. Men were like that; they admired the fancy-riding of the Californios and, like them, accepted riding competitions as a test of manhood.

"Howdy do, neighbors!" came a call.

She turned to see fifteen to twenty men, the remnant of Cook's Bar, diehards who panned in winter swinging down the old Indian trail on foot.

One sang out, "Looky thar. He's gittin all prettied up."

Perry splashed water over his face and, chin dripping, beamed a dimpled grin. "On your way to Bridge House be ye?" He reached for the towel.

"Ain't a man fer miles around would miss this here buckaroo contest."

"Female neither," chirped Vyries Brown with a freckled smile. They stood a respectful distance from Perry as others appeared on the trail, including the tall figure of Ben Wilder.

"At's right," said another of Elitha's customers. "Even the Ladies of the Roundhouse'll be there."

She watched Ben Wilder's loose-jointed walk and something about his smile raised her spirits a notch. He would see Perry at his best, maybe wouldn't think her entirely daft to be his wife. Somebody was saying: "Mrs. Gordon and Lorena went on up with the Hays women in their wagon."

Mr. McKinstry had repaired the bridge for the event. He'd make a pretty penny today, even if he didn't charge for single riders and pedestrians. The crowd would be large, and he'd stocked several kegs of beer. Earlier the Gaffneys, a family Perry permitted to build on his land, had waved as they rattled by in their wagon. Perry invited everyone he knew. He'd posted a handbill at Daylor's, now called the Cosumne Store. She lettered it for him.

Elitha received a note from Catherine saying all the Rancho Omuchumne folks were coming. She hadn't seen them since Daylor's funeral. Today she would hold up her head. Perry was the star attraction.

"Go on ahead," Perry told the miners with thrilling authority. "Taik a minute 'ere, I will. Go get yerselves good places to gander from." He was a changed man.

The men started down the swale, one calling over his shoulder, "Ever one of us's got a bundle ridin on ya, McCoon."

"Good lads! Ent plannin' to disappoint ye." His clean cheeks glowed in the high sun.

She couldn't help but smile.

Pedro combed Chocolate's mane with a salmon-rib comb, smoothing in bear grease between strokes. The mane and tail glistened, as black as the eyes of the watching children. They stood to one side, their brown skin a shade lighter than the horse's coat. He saw them admiring his new clothing, the best from Mexico. His black trousers were decorated with silver brads. His Spanish hat was new. He'd let his hair grow long because it was auburn, different from the black wig of his bandit disguise, even though he doubted any of the men from the boarding house remained from last Easter. But no matter the risk, a vaquero answered a challenge. This one was long overdue.

"We want to go watch," said the seven-year-old daughter of Bent-Willow-Reflected-in-Pond. The children nodded in unison, including Little Flicker, who never talked.

He glanced at María, sitting on a small boulder holding the baby. She was upset because she wanted to go too. All the Indians did, the children parroting the adults. María said he was being too careful. Hardly a day went by without her saying, one way or another, that times were changing, that it was safer now for Indians.

Five-year-old Billy said, "My father rides with you, señor. Por favor. I go too." His light eyes marked him as McCoon's.

Pedro reconsidered. In his own way the Englishman loved his son. Every once in a while Pedro still heard the boy practicing his name in English. With him there, McCoon wouldn't want trouble. In truth, it would probably be safe. Word of the contest had generated a fiesta mood. All Pedro's friends were coming, Murieta and his men in disguise, the Sonoran miners from the Río Calaveras, and the vaqueros from Don Andrés Pico's rancho, every Californio, every Chilieño and Mexican within twenty miles. The North Americans would be matched, maybe outnumbered. That in itself was security. Maybe five thousand people in all would attend, vaquero contests being a favorite pastime, especially when the streams were swollen and mining difficult. Men put aside their quarrels at entertainments. Many times he had seen that. And when he and McCoon were finished, others would show off their skills. No one would want the fun spoiled by violence. Least of all the merchants, who had set up tent stores near the arena—one selling cloth, buttons, and sundries for women.

Women were another assurance. The wives of Pedro's friends were coming, the Gaffney women, Señoras Gordon and Hays and their grown daughters would be there. Ramón had sent word that the women and children of Rancho Omuchumne were coming with Mr. Sheldon. If North Americans shared one trait with all other men, it was the protection of their women. And yes, Pedro had to admit, he rarely heard of Indian massacres any more. The killings tended to be random and isolated. Maybe the sheriffs were putting more pressure on the slave traders. Those maggots crawled in the dark and would not raise their filthy snouts in this crowd.

María's gaze weighed on him as he anointed and combed Chocolate's hock-length tail. He had to chuckle at himself. Fearless in encounters with desperate men, he never could say no to her.

He turned to the children and gruffed his voice. "Está bien, but you stand exactly where I tell you, and stay there." He would put the Indians with Joaquín Murieta and his men, who would know what to do if trouble started, or if a bucking horse came too close.

The children's eyes widened. Then they squealed with delight, joined hands and jumped up and down. The pobrecitos, he realized, had been holed up under terrible conditions, living more like foxes than people. He threw back his head and laughed at the jubilation.

María came over with shining eyes. She embraced him from the back and kissed his neck, her breasts soft through his shirt and bolero. "Gracias," she murmured. To her father she called, "Come to the big time."

Captain Juan had been watching from the other side of the boulders. Now he stiffly made his way through the rocks and green grass. "It is well, my son-in-law," he said approaching. "Big time make friends."

Speaking to the children and anyone else within earshot he pointed to his genitals and added, "Cover up, wear cloth, American way."

❧

Self-conscious to be pregnant in front of the huge crowd, Elitha rode side-saddle before Perry as Paint walked into the arena defined only by the crowd. A roar of approval resonated. A one-sided blizzard of hats flew skyward. Men yelled, "Show him, Perry! Give him hell!" Bottles flew high and plummeted.

Perry turned back to Elitha and said, "About to see an old tar trounce a Spaniard at his own game, they is." Even he didn't know all the events that would be performed. Mr. Valdez would start every other one. But Elitha knew Perry would do standing rope tricks. He'd been practicing.

The quiet side of the arena was crowded with more Spaniards than she knew lived nearby. Many stood in miner's clothing and sombreros. Others sat astride fine animals, the men attired in the Mexican manner. A few of their women sat on horseback too, lace mantillas draped over high combs, but mostly they stayed with their children in wagons. Among the Spaniards, Indians stood wrapped in blankets—mothers and children, men in tattered shirts. She saw Indian Mary's brown face, the straight cut of her shoulder-length hair slick and shining under her grass cap, the baby in her arms, Billy at her side. Elitha raised a hand. Mary waved back.

Perry reined Paint to a halt before the Sheldon wagon, where Elitha was to watch. Catherine's impish grin welcomed her as Mr. Sheldon stood in the wagon to guide her transfer, Mr. Grimshaw helping. She felt big and awkward stepping into the crowded wagon.

Catey patted the boards beside her, bubbling, "Oh, this is such fun!" Beyond her, Elizabeth leaned forward and smiled an excited welcome, as did Mr. Gunn, her new husband. Mr. Sheldon sat little Will on his lap. Beyond him, Sarah Daylor held her plump niece. Not quite three months since Mr. Daylor's death, Sarah and Mr. Grimshaw were betrothed; working together in the store had acquainted them.

Flouncing her frock she whispered in Catherine's ear, "We're both ladies in waiting." Catherine giggled at that, and Elitha smiled toward Perry, who was riding around the arena.

He looked grand in his white shirt and dark trousers tucked inside his blackened boots. A coiled reata hung from the saddle in the Spanish manner and his hair glistened in the sun, not grayed or receding. He was proud of that, and hadn't wanted to cover it with his stained hat.

She caught the eye of John and Matilda Rhoads in the next wagon, and smiled at them and their numerous children, including twin boys named for presidents—Andrew Jackson Rhoads and James K. Polk Rhoads. With them was Sarah's twin, Billy Rhoads, two Indian boys and a man Elitha didn't know, all clapping and shouting for Perry. The eldest Rhoads boy stood and raised both fists. "Go git'em," he shouted. She saw they all admired the way Perry rode. Not a soul gave her a pitying look, and she felt happier than she had in ages.

She looked around the crowd—men on horse and muleback, but mostly standing in joshing groups already liquored up. She located Ben Wilder, taller than most. He was listening to the men of Cook's Bar, who were talking up at him. She turned away before he saw her looking.

Beyond the American miners stood about fifty Chinamen in peaked straw hats, long black pigtails down their backs. "Look at all the Celestials," she said to Catherine.

"Pourin' off the boats, the Mister says. The only ones who'll take the time to sift out the flour gold after the others move on." Her voice rose in excitement as she pointed toward the Bridge House toll station and waved. "There's Kate."

Fifteen-year-old Kate Beale had come from Illinois with her parents, and before you could shake a stick she married Mr. Sherwood, who had built a store called Bridge House on the opposite side of the river from McKinstry. Elitha had attended the wedding about a month ago. Now Kate was teaching in the school her husband built for her. Having organized it, he named the community Katesville—the second town named for a girlfriend. Kate sat waving from her chair on the porch. By the looks of the miners tramping in front of her, streaming in and out of the store, Mr. Sherwood's sales were brisk. Waving back, Elitha sensed Kate's admiration for Perry's riding. Newcomers were quick to catch on to California traditions.

A flock of women in beribboned frocks and pushed-up breasts sashayed across the arena before the crowd. Their glances lingered on the men as they lifted their skirts, showing calf.

"Brazen," Catey breathed.

"Advertising," Elitha said. Perry would know their names. But he didn't even look at them as he floated around the arena in a graceful sitting trot, proud as any Spaniard. She could tell Paint felt the tension too. A sheen of moisture rippled on his large brown spots, and his eyes were wild in his controlled head.

On the opposite side, a thunderous cheer exploded—Señor Valdez entering the arena. He sat straight-backed and motionless on his magnificent dark brown horse. Neck arched, the horse slowly pranced around the circle, stepping high, its long black tail gently flouncing. The silver gear winked in the sunlight. The perfection of horse and rider sent chills up Elitha's spine. Californios were all but born on horseback, and Perry hadn't learned to ride until he was full grown. Still, even lacking the Spanish clothes and silver trim, he was the best trick rider most men had seen. She knew he would give his all to keep the Spaniard from winning.

While the two men circled the arena half a lap behind one another, an eerie thought entered her mind. Perry was like a man rising from a long sleep. Seeing the starch in his posture, she somehow knew the ranch and the gold had nothing to do with it. He had slipped beyond caring about such things. Even when he wasn't drunk he sometimes lay in bed for days. And now, from this low state, he had risen and readied himself to compete with a youthful vigor he no longer possessed. It was a miracle. Did anyone else see it?

Valdez stopped his horse before the Spanish section, removed his stiff-brimmed hat—red-banded, red-tasseled—and bowed to his audience. The roar deepened. "Vaquero! Vaquero! Caballero!" Sombreros sailed up and down, up and down. The Celestials were cheering too.

Isolated in the quiet American section, Jared Sheldon clapped his hands—a dry sound. Heads turned toward him. Feeling hurt, Elitha looked away toward the wild horses and cattle being driven into a brush pen. Had

Mr. Sheldon clapped for Perry? It seemed to her that this newly risen Perry McCoon deserved everyone's applause.

The Spaniard donned his hat and his horse stretched into a smooth lope. Perry watched from the side, sitting on Paint. With an economy of movement Valdez took his lariat from the rear fender of his big saddle and began feeding it upward into the air where it opened into a larger and larger loop. He turned the loop vertical before the horse and ran the graceful animal through it. Again and again he repeated the trick as the horse cantered in even strides. Cheering from the Spanish section never let up as he completed two laps. A few admiring oohs came from the Americans.

Stopping the horse, Valdez coiled the rope and nodded at Perry.

Perry spurred Paint into an even stride. He took his lariat, which he had oiled with bear grease, and swung it overhead. Effortlessly he ran the horse through the loop. Twice around the arena. Once the rope touched the back hooves and she held her breath, but Paint recovered without breaking stride. Perry finished to tumultuous clapping and shouting. Elitha and Catherine stood and stamping their heels on the boards. Bottles sailed as high as men could throw. Perry had done well, and Elitha felt mild surprise at how good he really was.

Señor Valdez tipped his hat at Perry. Perry galloped Paint and drew himself up in the saddle, kneeling, then standing, balancing a moment before he began whirling the lariat. Elitha had seen this before, but it never ceased to amaze her. He again tilted the whirling loop and ran the horse through it. Knees flexing with the gait, he regained his balance and brought the huge loop overhead. On the second lap he repeated the trick without a flaw. The yelling and stamping hurt her ears. Perry retrieved the lariat, sat down in the saddle and reined Paint to the side. Running his fingers through his hair, he smiled to the boisterous crowd, then nodded at Valdez.

The Spaniard's dark horse galloped until its tail drew a black line and its hooves only ticked the ground and tucked beneath its belly as it circled the arena, the rider still and straight-backed. Spectators stepped back. Señor Valdez was keeping the area open. Then in a graceful move he was on his feet standing proudly, chest out, one boot before the other. The lariat was in his hand and he fed it upward where it lifted and widened and tilted, and with the fluidity and timing of a dancer he ran the horse through the loop again and again without pause, the harmony of the rope keeping time with the drumroll of hooves. Perry had run the horse through only twice. On the second lap, without altering the rhythm, Valdez raised a hand toward the Spanish crowd.

The crowd responded with a report like close lightning. Even on the near side she heard clapping and, "Never saw the likes!" Mr. Sheldon stood and shouted, "Bravo caballero! Bravo vaquero!" Maybe he shouldn't be blamed, she realized, for cheering for the man who had once been his mayordomo.

At the end of the lap, Valdez sprang to the ground, coiling his lariat and bowing to the spectators as his riderless horse slowed, circled and stopped beside him. Señor Valdez bowed toward Mr. Sheldon.

No one would mistake the winner of that event. Even Perry nodded graciously toward the Spaniard. Valdez beckoned a group of Mexicans. They ran into the arena and positioned themselves about three horse lengths apart, their sombreros like pale mushrooms in a row.

With a handspring into the saddle, Señor Valdez melded with the horse and flew to the end of the line. Then he wheeled and rode hard in and out between the men, digging sharply into each turn, sliding a little in the damp ground. He circled and repeated the dodging course on the way back. At the end of the line he ran the horse full tilt at the Rhoads wagon. The animal never flinched or slowed, but slid to a sitting stop inches away. Cheers drowned the screams and the relieved laughter of the women and children.

The sombreros remained in place as Perry ran the same course. The pinto lunged and strained and slid at the sharp turns. At the end Perry ran Paint full tilt to the wagons, sliding and sitting him perfectly. Who would guess Perry had been a sailor? He was superb.

He trotted the horse back to the center of the arena where the mushrooms were scattering to the sidelines. Perry reached for his lariat and was circling it as he sprang out of the saddle. Beneath the whirling loop he slapped the horse away and stood alone, starting his rope tricks. He excelled at this. He traced a series of figure eights—overhead, side to side, dancing through it. He added twists and flourishes she hadn't seen before. She watched in silent awe. Ooohs and aahhhs sounded around her, and sporadic clapping before he was finished. Then Perry bowed and applause boomed. It was Señor Valdez' turn.

María had never seen Billy in such a trance. As Pedro danced with his reata, the boy's mouth fell open. He had yelled and clapped with the Españoles, then cheered for Perrimacoo.

Longhorns were driven across the field. First Pedro, then Perrimacoo lassoed a flying hoof, expertly tripping the huge animals then, after they thumped to the ground, deftly tying their thrashing feet. Both men made it look easy, but she knew the souls of cows—powerful, vicious when they were restrained. A careless man could be gored, or get his head kicked off.

"Bravo! Bravo!" people cheered, and María wondered about the strange magic that had made both these men her husbands. But her heart was swollen with love for Pedro.

Then Pedro and a crowd of men went to the brush corral. Many people stood between her and them, and for a time she saw only moving hats, Pedro's red band and tassel distinctive among them. She knew they were struggling with a dangerous animal, jerking back from it, and then approaching it again.

Suddenly Pedro burst into the clearing on the back of a leaping horse. It kicked and twisted like it would break itself in two, but he held on.

She held her breath. Beside her, Joaquín Murieta murmured, "Ah, que bronco!" His companion said, "Muy bruto!" Her heart beat rapidly. It would be nothing for that horse to kill him.

Holding the saddle horn with one hand, Pedro flapped violently up and down, the attached coil of the lariat waving with his spread legs. In the silence of the crowd she heard the horse's gasping, snorting, grunting breath and the trumpeting farts with each leap, and the deep punk punk of its landing.

He flew loose! Somersaulting over the animal's lowered neck with his legs following his shoulders, hat flying away. She stepped forward, winced at the thump of his landing. In a twinkling he rolled away from the crushing hooves, and jumped to his feet. Hands up, smiling. Uninjured! The horse continued to buck away from him.

Her voice caught in her throat as she squeezed Billy's shoulders and said, "He defeated the horse." The crowd screamed its relief and appreciation as mounted vaqueros swung their lassoes and chased the bucking animal. Men, women and children stood in the wagons stamping. "Bravo, caballero!"

Pedro waved his hat at the spectators, his private smile locating María across the distance. "Bravo!" she called, but her voice was lost in the roar.

Another horse was being prepared. Hats seethed in the corral.

❧

Perry flew into the open on the back of another bucking devil. Elitha stood in the wagon. Catherine, standing beside her, took her hand. The crowd quieted. Where did they find such animals? The horse hovered airborne like it weighed nothing, twisting as it kicked out one side, then the other, then landed—ears laid back, eyes white, teeth bared, snorting like a dragon in old-time stories. The furious horse was bent on murder and Perry held the saddle with one hand as it humped high, mane flying. A big swath of daylight showed between him and the saddle, his legs wide over the neck. The horse wrenched away and Perry fell to the ground. She heard the thud and saw his legs up in a V. The hooves thrashed down, around and around. Perry writhed as if trying to curl himself, but one foot stayed up, caught somehow. He was under the hooves. She held her breath. Not a sound came from the crowd.

The horse continued to buck, Perry jerking with it. Oooh pushed like a monster's breath from a thousand throats. Her heart banged on her ribs. Señor Valdez was running on foot across the field, circling his lariat.

Men converged. Valdez lassoed the animal's neck. It sat on its haunches, then reared and flailed its front hooves at the onrushing men. They shrank back. The horse wheeled up and dug into a furious run, jerking Pedro Valdez and pulling Perry. Valdez let go of the rope. Mounted men came whirling ropes, but the horse had parted the Celestials and was digging for open ground, dragging Perry behind. Riders galloped after.

She scrambled down from the wagon and hurried with the crowd after the runaway horse. A shout came. "They got him!"

She pushed through the people, pleading, "Let me pass, please. I'm his wife. Please."

The horse was being led away, kicking and fighting a dozen ropes. Perry lay on his back surrounded by men. She squeezed between them, excusing herself, and knelt at his side.

His eyes were open, his cheek torn and bloody. He looked up at her and his old sidewise smile formed on his lips, the dimple almost in his cheek. "Caught me damned boot in the lariat, I did." A thin line of blood trickled from the corner of his mouth and he made no attempt to move.

Her hand trembled as she smoothed back his hair, barely aware of all the people peering down. "You hurt bad?"

His voice came whispery. "Knocked the wind out 'o me sails." He started to smile, but winced.

Above, a familiar voice said, "I wanted to trip the horse with la riata, but he might fall on heem." Señor Valdez, looked troubled.

Voices yammered. Is he dead? Back broken? Reg'lar thrashin! Poor girl. Bout to burst. Tongues clucked and heads wagged. She didn't know what to do. Suddenly Ben Wilder was saying, "Better get him off the ground. Asa and I'll carry him to a wagon." They reached down, almost took his arms and legs.

"No. Let me...." Perry's voice trailed off. The tall men stood back.

Alarm jumped through her, followed by an odd calm. She knew what was important. "Perry, you were splendid. I've never seen such riding in my whole life. Honest, I never have."

The wrinkles on his brow smoothed and the corners of his mouth twitched into a faint smile. He closed his eyes.

"You were wonderful!" She said, taking his hand. His head fell to the side. Pink bubbles slid off his tongue and out the side of his mouth. A man knelt, took his wrist.

"He's hurt bad," she said to Ben Wilder. "Please take him to the Sheldon wagon." She stood with her knees trembling and pointed the way, but the man with Perry's wrist said, "He's a goner," and removed his hat.

She stared at Perry and kneeled awkwardly beside him, leaning over her belly to put an ear on his chest. It caved in with sickening ease. She jerked back. Then listened again. Silence.

# 81

M aría and Pedro followed the crowd, Pedro leading his horse. Ahead, about three twenties of people walked down the swale and up the curving path behind the small wagon in which Perrimacoo lay dead. They were planning to bury him near his bad luck house.

"His roping was good," Pedro said. Until now he'd been quiet, silently acknowledging the compliments of people passing by.

"You won," she said as quietly.

By his face she saw that he was more sorry than proud. She understood. A man preferred his opponent to live. It made winning sweeter.

"You won the land paper," she reminded him. This was what they'd wanted for so long, a paper that gave them the right to live on the land of the umne. Yet there was a problem and she had to speak truth. "You must destroy the bad house without touching it in any way."

"María, her husband is dead and that house is Elitha's only shelter. She needs a rest. I'm not going to ask for the papers for a while."

"The house will kill her. It killed her unborn baby, it killed my cousin-brothers who helped build it, it killed her husband, it killed Mr. Daylo after only one short visit, and it will kill her and the second baby. I'll explain it to her and I'm sure she'll move away." Some unearthly power had kept Elitha alive this long.

He expelled air from his nose, which meant he was impatient. "That is pure superstition." He spoke under his breath so the people around them wouldn't hear. "It was the horse, and my failure to trip the animal, that killed him, not a cabin or a condor skin. Mother of God!"

They arrived at a place in the bottomland of the river where people stood around while the grave was being dug. She held Billy and Little Flicker back from where Perrimacoo lay. Unpurified Americanas knelt around him, dabbing cloths on his face, hands, and clothing. Touching the dead. Most of the crowd had gone elsewhere. Joaquín Murieta had told Pedro his group wouldn't stay for the burial.

She and all the people who lived between the boulders watched Americanos take turns digging. She held Billy's little hand while he stared at his real father. A rattle of harnesses announced the arrival of the Sheldon wagon with Catherine, Sarah and Elizabeth. After they stepped down, Mr. Sheldon and Mr. Gunn drove the wagon away again. "He's bringing wood," Pedro explained, "to make a coffin. He has a pile of lumber a short distance away—he's building a cabin."

People were not purifying themselves in the river, though a dangerous spirit could be springing about among the onlookers. The river itself was brown; nevertheless María took the children there to bathe. Others from the boulder group followed. After bathing, they found a few sprigs of purifying herbs scattered among the lumps of clay. They picked only a small piece of each, careful to leave some in each location. It worried her that no pine tea could be made. Not a single gray pine was left.

The gravedigger stood up to his waist throwing dirt out of the hole, the earth here water-softened. Back with a wagonload of wood, Señor Sheldon made a wooden box. Americanos and Españoles sat in their wagons, some of them perilously close to the dead.

Billy asked, "Did the spirit come out?"

"I have not seen it yet." Until it lifted from the body and floated up into the sky, danger abounded. Anyone might become the host of a lost and angry soul. "We must sing the ghost on its way," María told him in the tongue of the umne.

"When?" Billy wanted to know.

"When they put him in the ground," she said, recalling the Americano death rite.

Pedro said in Spanish, "I will tell Elitha to remain in the house as long as she wants."

Elitha felt as though a rope binding her to a post had been cut.

Many people had left, but a lot of them sat on downed river logs or stood in the winter sun. Perry lay dead in the open coffin. It had been neighborly of Mr. Sheldon to provide the pinewood. She kept expecting Perry to move, but the hands stacked on his chest were like stone. She glanced around at the people. Not seeing Ben Wilder, she remembered the trouble between him and Mr. Sheldon, who was conspicuously present. Ben and his brothers hadn't stayed for the burying.

"We thought you'd like to say your farewell first," said Sarah, stepping back to give her privacy.

Elitha stood alone before Perry. The blood and mud had been washed from his face, and his hair was combed. He still wore his best clothes and the new boots he'd bought at the Cosumne Store. Mud discolored his trousers and his muslin shirt and smeared his boots.

She knelt beside the coffin. "Well, Perry," she murmured, truly saddened by his sudden death and not wanting anyone to hear, "it's good-bye. I'm sorry you didn't live to see our baby, and I'm afraid you won't go to heaven, unless God takes pity, so I hope it's not too terribly bad where you end up." Aware of her bulk and clumsiness, she began to get to her feet.

An arm shot around her, helping. Vyries Brown's freckled young face creased with concern. Thanking him, she stepped back beside Catherine.

Mr. Sheldon put the boards over the coffin, and loud hollow bangs rang across the hills as he hammered the nails. Afterwards, John Rhoads, Billy Rhoads, Mr. Grimshaw and Mr. Sheldon lowered the box into the grave.

The silence was awkward. No one had a Bible. The Gaffneys offered to go home for theirs. "No, that's all right," Elitha said. "Perry didn't believe in it anyway."

Mr. Sheldon stepped forward and removed his hat. All the men's hats came off. He cleared his throat and spoke. "William Perry McCoon will be remembered as one of the first California pioneers. He and I came up from Monterey with John Sutter, and he helped build the fort. We didn't always see eye to eye. But Perry, for a sailor you were one damned fine buckaroo. We lay you to rest here on your own rancho."

He stepped back next to Catherine and their little Will.

No one else spoke, but strange singing started in the trees. The Indians! Singing a death dirge, Elitha realized. Mournful but soothing tones rose in long progressions across the quiet hillside and up the riverbottom. The singing felt exactly right. The tones and harmonies floated heavenward. Maybe God would hear it and forgive the soul of this wayward sheep.

When the singing stopped, in the silence that followed, Perry's little half-Indian boy, about five years old now, stepped to the edge of the grave—naked except for a small leather loin cloth. He looked down at the box and said, "Me nime is Billy McCoon."

# 82

After two weeks with the Daylors, Elitha was restless to go home to the adobe and give it a good cleaning. She also wanted to start saving gold. She caught a ride with Mr. Sheldon, who was taking more lumber to his cabin at Bridge House. He had the Yankee knack for neat construction, and would put in a plank floor today.

The first thing she did in the adobe was pull off the blankets and haul them to the river for a good scrubbing. They weren't perfectly dry when dark fell, but she slept well anyway. Even with the baby kicking inside her. The next morning she was sweeping out the spider webs and packrat debris when a man's voice called, "Howdy neighbor."

She pulled back the leather drape. Ben Wilder stood there, tall, lanky, and smiling. "Howdy," she said back, noticing that his eyes sloped a tad bit downward at the outer corners.

He was dressed in typical miners' garb, suspenders over a red flannel shirt tucked into brown trousers, which were tucked into knee-high boots. His shapeless hat made a wavy frame for the top of his face, the lower half hidden in a bushy black beard. "Thought I'd pay my respects."

She led him to the grave down in the riverbottom. The only marker was a grave-shaped mound between clay slicks.

He removed his hat and stood silently, then replaced the hat. "There's a marble quarry some twenty miles south, I'm told," he said. "If you'd like I'll get you a marble block delivered here."

"I'd like that very much."

He stood looking at her. She felt embarrassed about being so very pregnant. "I'll be serving food again," she said, "starting tomorrow morning, and I'd be obliged if you spread the word in Cook's Bar."

He raised his brows. Surprise or admiration, she couldn't tell.

The next morning he and ten other miners ate on the tamped soil of her front yard. It was his first time. As she took a pinch of his gold dust, he said, "I've made arrangements for the stone to be delivered."

Two days later he arrived, pulling a mule with the stone strapped on its back. It had been nicely squared, about a foot long, eight inches wide, and four inches thick. With a comfortable smile he said, "I'd be happy to letter it for you."

"Could you?" She heard her own enthusiasm.

From his pocket he took a crevice tool, a tough little implement for prying gold from rocks. Squatting, he scratched one of the rough sides. "Yup, this'll do the trick."

"First let me think what to put on it," she said.

"Think till tomorrow afternoon." He touched his hat and left.

The next day he sat at the table inside the adobe and told her the gossip of Cook's Bar as he scratched at the marble. "Won't do to rush this," he said nodding at the stone.

She was glad to have him come for an hour or two each afternoon. He said it rested him after shoveling mud. The next afternoon as he etched, she sat across the table and penned a letter to her three youngest sisters, Leanna having written that she was hired out to a farmer in Calaveras County.

*January 20, 1851*
*Dear Georgia, Frances and Ellie,*
*How are you? Are you going to school? I hope so. I have sad news and happy news. Perry died of a bad accident and I am about to have a baby. I am cooking meals for money and my house isn't any better than when Ellie was here. Still, I would like you all to come visit, if you would. I am the more lonely since Perry died, and would so like to have our family back together.*

*Do you get my letters? Please write. It would be such a welcome sight to be handed a letter from you. Did I tell you that mail is delivered by*

*stage every day to the Bridge House Post Office? I'll be checking for a
letter from you.*
*Love as always, your big sister, Elitha*

Several days later it was pouring again, but supper was cooked. At the
table Ben worked the marble, the scratching sound oddly soothing to Elitha.
The clouds made it so dark outside that she lit a spermaceti lamp.

Sorting through the things in Perry's big leather bag, she came across
the letter from Captain John Sutter and suddenly realized Mr. Valdez hadn't
come by for it. She opened her mouth to ask Ben's advice, but then recalled
that he believed in squatters' rights. And if Perry's ownership were in doubt,
as Mr. Valdez seemed to think, it wouldn't do to advertise that to the miners.

She lined up her words. "How would I go about transferring Perry's land
to Mr. Valdez?" Everyone knew about the bargain. If Perry lost, the land went
to Pedro.

Ben stopped scratching. "Well, since the State Constitutional Convention
of forty-nine, women can own property in this state, so I'd say you inherited
Perry's title. You could just sign it over, right on the front side of the paper.
Get three witnesses to sign." He scowled, looking at the marble. "He didn't
come for it then? The Mexican?"

"Nope."

"If I were you I wouldn't be too quick to hand it over."

"I haven't exactly been quick, have I?" she grinned.

Ben resumed scratching.

"I heard you Forty-niners don't think the Mexican ranch titles will stand
up in court." In no uncertain terms Sarah had told her as much and advised
her to keep all squatters away.

He raised his brows at the RIP, the P of which he'd been lengthening.
"Way I understand it, anyone living on a piece of land can challenge title,
so it's up to the ranchers to prove their property is legal. They gotta prove a
proper survey was conducted according to Mexican law." He looked up, his
eyes kindly. "Maybe he won't come for it."

"You think my title would be challenged?" Perry had let miners camp everywhere, the Gaffneys, for instance, down near the old Indian village. She
knew Mr. Sheldon had told the Wilder brothers to get off his Cook's Bar land.

Ben seemed well informed. "First, the U.S. Land Commission has to rule
on your title. If the Mexican government granted legal title, the U.S. is supposed to honor it. But I've heard of cases where Sutter gave land he didn't
own, and didn't have the authority to grant. That's the kind of thing the U.S.
commission looks for."

Elitha sat heavily on a chair next to Ben, the baby kicking inside her.
"Why would Captain Sutter do such a thing? I mean give away land he doesn't
have the right to."

His lips twisted in a wry smile. "Power."

Indian Mary's favorite word. "It doesn't seem powerful to me, just dishonest. Or stupid. People would find out he hadn't the authority."

"That's how the feudal lords of Europe operated."

"You mean in the Middle Ages."

"Uh-huh. A man consolidated power by making the surrounding knights beholden to him. He rewarded them with land, and in exchange they swore to defend him in battle." He glanced up at her. "Empires were established that way."

"Surely the Mexican governor would have stopped Captain Sutter from doing that. Wouldn't he?"

He blew away marble dust and stood the block on its four-inch–wide edge, examining his work. "In a fort bristling with cannons, surrounded by wilderness, and all those men ready to fight for their supposed property?"

Suddenly she didn't want to hear any more. What did he know? Captain Sutter had gone to war for a Mexican governor, Perry told her. Ben was just a Forty-niner, a greenhorn with notions. Anyway Mrs. Sutter was turning the Captain's old friends away at the door. He was no feudal lord, more like a pathetic old man. She wouldn't mention it to Ben again.

But one thing he'd said she agreed with. She would wait to hear from Señor Valdez, and keep it quiet that all she had for a land deed was Captain Sutter's letter to Perry, a document he'd never been able to read.

On a cloudy afternoon in early February, Ben finished the last numeral on the stone. He took it to the grave, set it on edge at the head of the grave, and packed dirt around it. Elitha stood back to see the effect.

William Perry McCoon
RIP
Native of England
Died January 5, 1851

She said, "I wish there'd been room for 'California's Best Vaquero.'"

He gave her a funny look. "I can't spell it."

That made her chuckle. "Me neither." They laughed together.

Seriousness crossed his face and he looked over the green hills. "Maybe it isn't my place, but I've been worrying about you. Out here alone and all." He glanced at her belly.

She looked down, felt heat in her ears.

"I heard of a doctor in San Francisco. Maybe I could get him up here."

Astonished that he would suggest such an expensive and doubtful thing, she stared at him. That was something a good husband would say, a husband unlike Perry. Again her face burned. She'd often caught herself wanting to hold Ben or wondering how he would feel against her, but such thoughts were unseemly in her condition, and she couldn't imagine that any man would find her attractive. Yet if she could choose a man, it would be Ben Wilder. Embarrassment tangled her tongue.

"You ought to have a midwife or a doctor." He spoke with the self-confidence she so admired. "When will your time come?"

"A few weeks," she murmured.

"Few?"

Her face was so hot she turned away. "Maybe two or three." The baby had dropped. That was a sign. What she couldn't say was that she'd arranged to put herself into Indian Mary's care. Indians had an easier time with birth, but she couldn't say that either. Forty-niners thought Indians were animals, and being part Indian herself she didn't want to talk about it.

He laid a hand on her shoulder. "I'll see what I can do."

"Oh, please don't trouble yourself. I'll be fine."

"By thunder, you're a brave girl." His look melted her. "Mind if I ask how old you are?"

"Eighteen."

"How old are you?"

"Twenty-eight."

🌺

Elitha felt like a player in a strange fairy tale. After four days in a tiny brush hut made for her by the Indians, she now lay on her own bed, her sweet baby girl beside her. Very much alive. Her coming to light hadn't been anything like the painful birth of the dead baby boy.

Elizabeth, she named her, after Aunt Betsy. The baby had Perry's long lashes and a thin wash of dark hair on a perfectly round head. She never tired of staring at the sweet little face. Perry would have loved her.

"Anybody home?" It was Ben, standing out in the rain.

"Just a minute." She finger-combed her hair and straightened the blankets, making a neat fold below her chin and the baby's. "Come in."

Too tall for the house, he ducked inside, wet hat in hand, and came to the bed. He stared at Elizabeth. "Well I'll be! Look at that little rosebud! What a miracle life is!"

"Told you I'd be fine. Pull up a stool."

Without taking his eyes off the baby, he reached back and pulled the stool to him. "What is it, I mean a boy or—"

"Girl."

"Well, I don't believe I've ever seen two more beautiful young ladies. I thought you'd dropped off the face of the earth!"

"Went to a friend for help." She looked away from his steady gaze and hoped he wouldn't probe.

He didn't. It was one of the things she liked about him—quick to pick up on her feelings. Discreetly he inquired after her health, then told her about the Wilder claim. He and his brothers had been trying to tunnel into the riverbank, finding gold that had been deposited there centuries before. "Coyoting it's called bec…" The sound of a horse distracted him.

They both listened. A man's voice called, "Hola, señora."

"Come in, Mr. Valdez," she called.

Pedro Valdez opened the door, removed his hat and dumped the rain out of it, and stepped inside. "Señora McCoon," he said nodding a greeting to Ben, "You have company. I return later." He made no move toward the bed.

"Nonsense. Come and see my baby." She shifted the infant to face the men.

Valdez stepped hesitantly toward her, eyes on Elizabeth. "Muy bonita, like my wife said."

Ben echoed, "Wife?"

Elitha cut in, "They live nearby. She helped with the birth." She jumped to the point. "Did you come for your land title?"

Mr. Valdez bowed slightly. "I return later."

"Good idea," Ben said.

"Señora, have no fear," Valdez said while backing out the door, "The house I do not want. Stay here all the time if you wish. A mother needs a roof over the head."

"I appreciate that."

"Other thing. I will pay for the land."

"That wasn't the agreement. You won it fair and square."

He looked at her a moment longer, then vanished into the pouring rain. Ben seated himself at the bedside, and suddenly she didn't want to hold anything back from him. She would tell him who she really was, Indian blood and all. And if he didn't like it, better to find out now. But first the title.

"Ben, I'm afraid Perry was one of those who got his land from Captain Sutter, not the governor. All I have is his letter. But whatever it's worth, I'm going to sign it over to Mr. Valdez. I want you and your brothers to witness it."

His down-sloping eyes looked friendly in the dim light of the adobe. "River property is valuable, even more so when it's not raining cats and dogs. If I'd've thought you had a chance in Hades of proving up on this place, I'd help take this to court, but—"

"A bargain's a bargain." That much she'd learned from Pa.

"Yes, but these Mexicans…." He trailed off and started again. "There are bandit gangs around, and I'd sure hate to see you give anything of value to criminals." He glanced at the baby.

"It doesn't sound like I'm giving up a thing. Not a handful of dirt."

"You never know. Possession is sometimes nine-tenths of the law. I hear squatters are getting big blocks of land that used to be John Sutter's, down in Sacramento City."

She smiled. "Well then, I'm squatting here in this house, then maybe I'll own it someday." Soon she could cook again and keep all her wages. She would save for improvements and collect her sisters. They could help with the baby. It didn't matter who lived on the rest of the land.

Ben seemed troubled, but she knew it was the right decision. She would wait and see what developed around her.

He reached out and petted the baby's head, then shook his head. "Most young ladies I know would be headed straight for home. Did you say your folks were in Illinois?"

Nobody around Cook's Bar knew her story. That had been clear for a long time. The miners were transients. They knew her only as Mrs. McCoon. "There's another thing I gotta say, Ben."

Playfully he said, "You weren't married to Perry McCoon?"

She chuckled, but then took a breath. "My maiden name was Donner."

His eyes flew open. "You don't mean the—"

"I'm the daughter of George Donner."

"The mountain tragedy?" He looked flabbergasted. "Why didn't you say? All that time I was carving on the—"

"Why do you think? With me cooking meals and all?"

Comprehension spread slowly across his face. "But Mr. McCoon... I don't mean to speak ill of the departed, but he didn't seem the kind to keep a secret from the whole damn—forgive me, I've been around men too long."

"Guess he got tired of the jokes too, like well, 'Be careful what goes in the dinner pot.'" Immediately she regretted that.

"People say such—?"

Tears clouded her eyes and she turned her head away, appalled that time, which was supposed to heal all wounds, didn't.

He touched her shoulder through the blanket. "By thunder, I said you were the bravest girl I knew, and I didn't know the half!"

She dabbed her eyes with the edge of the blanket and turned back to him. Not a trace of disgust showed in his face. She waited, but he didn't say Pa was stupid for taking the cutoff, or that the Party was foolish for not knowing how to live off the land. All he did was look at her like she was the most precious thing on earth, the way Mr. Sheldon looked at Catherine, the way Mr. Daylor used to look at Sarah. Tears blinded her again, but they had nothing to do with the past. It was as plain to her as this crumbling adobe that he cared very much for her, and that made her so happy she couldn't speak.

Indian Mary had said strong power lodged in this house. And power could mean good luck as well as bad. To Elitha, Ben Wilder was the luckiest thing that ever happened to her. She reached for his hand and squeezed it, brazen as that was. Then out of the blue and not so happily, she recalled the trouble between him and Mr. Sheldon. She slowly removed her hand. Why did things have to be so convoluted?

Being cozy with someone the Sheldons didn't like would be difficult.

*Oh it rained, rained, rained forty days and forty nights,*
*And the animals in the Ark swayed to and fro,*
*But it rained no more after forty days and nights,*
*And old Noah told 'em, now we're going home.*
*Goin' ho-o-ome! Goin' ho-o-ome!...*

Elitha couldn't get that song out of her head. It was mid-February, Elizabeth thriving, but there weren't enough dry days to take her out to see the world. Nor were miners eating in her yard. Mostly gone to Sacramento City for the winter, except the Wilder men. For some reason they stayed here despite rain and high water.

One day there was a knock on the door. Elitha opened it and found Indian Mary standing outside with a deerskin over her head, shoulders, and baby in its cradleboard, little Billy at her side. "Come and see," she said in a disturbing tone.

Elitha threw a cloak around her shoulders and a blanket around Elizabeth, and followed Mary into the rain. Mary led her down the hill and across the slippery old planks spanning the worst of the mud, in the direction of Perry's grave.

The grave was submerged! The violent current seemed to be pounding on something large, wagging it back and forth.

The coffin! Before long it would lose its moorings and float down river. They'd dug the grave in river silt. They should have put it up near the adobe. She must get help.

It seemed to take forever, but she finally made it to the Wilder camp and told Ben.

"Well," he said, pulling on his rubber boots and Macintosh, "let's go see about that."

Asa came too, John having gone with friends to Hangtown.

Mary took a different route back to her people, who lived in a makeshift place under two giant boulders, and Elitha accompanied the Wilder brothers back to the coffin.

The brothers waded into the current up to their waists and dislodged the coffin from the grip of snags, where it was about to pop free. They wrestled the waterlogged thing up on the bank and across the slippery mud bridge. Then they shouldered it, one on each side behind the coffin, digging in their boots to push it up the hill toward the cabin. It gouged out a wide trail. With both admiration and revulsion, Elitha watched.

"That's far enough," she said when she knew it wouldn't slide back.

Exhausted after their strenuous work, the two strong men sprawled on their backs to rest, obviously enjoying the rain on their faces. Meanwhile Elitha realized what an awkward situation she'd put herself in—Perry a month and a half dead in a moldering, blackened pine box with some of the boards warped away from the nails. In truth he ought to be buried up here where the ground was rocky and the digging difficult, but Ben had already done so much for her, she couldn't ask him to dig a grave too. She also couldn't stay here—not for a night, not even an hour, and if she were alone, not for a minute—with Perry's coffin emitting the distinct odor of death so near to the house. No man in his right mind would stop here to eat either, even next summer, if he walked past now seeing and smelling this rotting horror.

Ben groaned, turned over, got on all fours, and then jumped to his feet. He joined her on the downed tree trunk next to her watery fire pit. Elizabeth, on her lap, seemed to enjoy the rain.

With a half-joking, half-disbelieving, all-loving look, Ben said, "Do you have a shovel?"

She did. And she knew that he and Asa had shovels in their camp, which they could fetch; but she also knew that Ben understood that she didn't want to sit here alone with the daylight ebbing, waiting for them to return. He was willing to use Perry's shovel to save her from that, and she loved him for it.

Asa said, "I'll go get a pick and a shovel. Ben, you dig 'til I get back, and I'll be ready to spell you." He took off at a fast stride.

These were both remarkable men, Elitha realized. From a good family.

By now, Elizabeth was fussy.

Ben said, "Why don't you go inside and forget about this. I'll find a good place for the new grave, back a ways from the adobe."

"Oh, the headstone!" she suddenly remembered.

"I saw it there down in the river, tight between some big rocks. Don't worry about it. We'll put it up at the new gravesite."

# 83

*June 20, 1851*
*c/o Mr. and Mrs. Brunner, Sonoma*
*Dear Frances, Georgia and Ellie,*
*Do you get my letters? I would ever so much like to hear from you.*
*Leanna writes often. She is betrothed to Mr. App in Jamestown. If you were here we could all go to the wedding on the stage. What fun that would be!*

*I think of you often and wish you would come and live with me. I could arrange to have you picked up. I am making enough money now to rebuild the house. The school in Katesville is only a mile away, and the teacher is very nice. You could attend school there. I hope you are attending school somewhere.*

*Tomorrow I am going to a dance in Fiddletown. My best friend, Catey Sheldon, will care for Baby Elizabeth. Catey's husband built her a cabin very near my place, so she could be with him for the summer while he's building a dam in the river. She has a new baby too. Please write. Love to each of you,*

*Your Big Sister,*
*Elitha Cumi*

To show them how fine the dance would be, she enclosed one of the many invitations she'd received from an assortment of men—this one embossed with pale pink roses. Ben said the men who organized the dance had all the printing done in Sacramento City.

Folding the letter, she sat a moment staring across the table and out the open door. Jared Sheldon had ordered Ben off his land and said he would round up a posse to throw him off if he and his brothers didn't leave immediately. Ben was riled. Elitha hadn't known what to say, except she declined to attend the dance with him—she needed Catey to care for Elizabeth while she was gone.

Catherine had moved into the cabin Jared built a short walk from Elitha's cabin, which deepened their friendship, also being neighbors. But Catherine was Mrs. Jared Sheldon. So Elitha arranged to go with Sarah and Mr. Grimshaw, and if Ben happened to be at the dance, per their arrangement, she would dance with him. Before that she'd have a good long buggy ride to tell Sarah and her new husband, Mr. Grimshaw, Ben's side of things.

Deep down she doubted it would help. Sarah and Catey had a tight bond. Nevertheless she floated around her house and yard imagining the music as she danced in Ben's arms.

🐾

Elitha peered into the mirror—heavy black hair securely pinned, lace collar on her brown frock fresh. She pulled up her skirt to check the shine of her shoes, bear grease a marvel. Then she danced through the door tying on her brown bonnet, as carefree and silly as the woodpeckers that swooped and cackled in the oak trees. Her sign proclaimed: No MEALS SERVED TO-DAY OR TOMORROW. That by itself lightened her feet. She was ready to take Elizabeth to Catherine, but the baby was taking an unexpected morning nap and Elitha wanted her to rest as much as possible before going to a strange place.

With her skirts billowing, she whirled to the conjured beat of a waltz played on violins—the chink and scrape of shovels from the riverbottom adding percussion. The baby cried.

She hurried in. Elizabeth's face was twisted, and she writhed on the bed. "Poor little sugar," she said, reaching for a fresh square of muslin. "You didn't eat much this morning. What's the matter?" Her diaper was stained with pale green liquid. Colic. Most babies had it sooner or later.

Quickly she tied on a clean diaper, then took a blanket and made a handy sling like Indian Mary did. The walk quieted the baby.

As she crossed the bridge, Mr. Sherwood rose from a chair on his porch and said, "My but we're in fine feather today, Miz McCoon. Headin to the dance are you?" The new sign on his porch said Bridge House Station & Post Office.

"Yup. Going with the Grimshaws. Looks like they got here already." She nodded toward the buggy in front of the Sheldon cabin.

"Come up about half an hour ago."

"You and Kate going to the dance?"

Mr. Sherwood petted back the few hairs on his pate. "Aw, she's been needlin me nigh onto a month now. Even hired a boy to take toll. I'm startin' to weaken."

She laughed. "See you there." She adjusted the blanket and hurried on as a six-mule team crossed the bridge, the planks bouncing and creaking. "Six bits," she heard Sherwood call at the teamster.

The door was open and Catherine waved her in, the scent of the new walls and floor like walking into a pine forest. In her rocking chair from the main house, Catherine was nursing her newborn daughter, whose tiny face made four-month-old Elizabeth appear huge by comparison. Sarah and Mr. Grimshaw perched on the extra chairs, Sarah pregnant at last, but not showing much yet. She looked angelic in a blue satin frock, eyes shining and every hair of her dark bun in place as always. Mr. Grimshaw's brown suit matched his hair and his coffee-colored eyes. He rose, nodding formally.

Elitha complimented Sarah on her dress and said how much she appreciated being driven to the Fiddletown dance. "Where are little Will and little Sarah?" she asked Catey.

"With their pa. He's workin on the dam."

Glad that Catherine wouldn't have the older children to care for in addition, at least not right away, Elitha said, "The baby's got a loose stool this morning. Sure you want to take her?" A whisker of hesitation and she'd stay home.

"Silly goose! Just lay her on the bed."

That done, she leaned down and kissed Elizabeth's forehead. "Give yer ma a big smile now, precious. Come on." Elitha tickled the fat under her chin, but the baby seemed listless. "Her dimples are so darling when she smiles," she tossed over her shoulder.

"From Perry," said Catherine, like she tasted something sour.

Perry had been uncommonly handsome and Elizabeth was lucky to have his looks, but Elitha let that pass. "Does she feel warm to you?" She asked, knowing Catherine's three children gave her a world more experience.

With her newborn over her shoulder she got to her feet, stepped to the bed and felt Elizabeth's brow. "Feels fine to me."

Relieved, Elitha looked into Catey's hazel eyes and said, "How can I ever thank you."

"Easy. Next time, I go to the dance and you watch my THREE. Now go on, git! Have a good time." She shooed Elitha, Sarah and Mr. Grimshaw out the door.

Elitha sat in the backseat of the buggy behind Sarah while Mr. Grimshaw checked the horse's gear. Mr. Sheldon rode up on a horse with his little son and daughter. Dismounting, he plucked them from the saddle and stood with his hands on his waist staring at nothing while the children went around the house holding hands. His jaw twitched beneath his whiskers.

Timidly Sarah asked out her window, "Something wrong, Jared?"

"Those damned Wilder boys like to git their derned heads blown off, that's what." He looked like a starved wolf eyeing prey. Elitha closed her eyes and inhaled quietly.

"What'ov they done now?" Sarah asked.

"For starters, built a fence around their gol derned claim. Right there on my property! Can you believe that? Like they owned it." He breathed like a winded horse, through his nose, his eyes fierce. "And that tall one!" He turned toward the trees as though afraid his eyes might scorch somebody. "He's got together a so-called Miners Committee!" He shook his head, turned toward them, and drew a piece of paper from his pocket "Gave me this. From the damned committee. Pardon my language, ladies."

Catey came out with a baby on each shoulder asking, "What's wrong, Jared?"

"Later. Better send these people on their way. They got a three-, four-hour drive."

Mr. Grimshaw stepped into his seat and shut the door, looking out the window. "Jared, if there's anything I can do ...."

"Thanks, but this here's my fight." His hard jawline showed through the whiskers. A tremor edged Elitha's stomach.

Mr. Grimshaw gentled the reins over the brown rump and the buggy lurched over the lumpy ground back to the road. Wishing men could get along better, Elitha held onto the backseat rail. The Grimshaws said nothing, but that was normal. They were quiet people.

The buggy creaked eastward with the ruts, past what looked like a funeral at St. Joseph's Church and past the shanties and hovels of Live Oak. The reminder of death ignited Elitha's resolve. She would explain her friendship with Ben Wilder.

Mr. Grimshaw was a calm, reasonable sort of man, not swashbuckling and colorful like Sarah's former husband, or ingenious and hardheaded like Mr. Sheldon, but a born mercantile proprietor. His prosperous business depended entirely on the patronage of miners, so Elitha thought he might be a little more sympathetic to a Forty-niner than a rancher would be.

"Oh," Sarah said twisting around in the seat, "before I forget." She handed Elitha the teardrop earrings she'd ordered. "They're pretty, huh?"

"Yes they are, and I'm so glad they got here in time for the dance." Thanking Sarah, she slipped them into her pocket. A few minutes later she found herself thinking momentarily of Tamsen and how she would have liked to paint these golden hills dotted with oak trees, all of them pruned straight across the underside by deer. But the pigments were lost in the snow, and so was Tamsen. Life was tenuous enough without men fighting each other.

She took a deep breath. "You know, I am acquainted with Ben Wilder. He was the one that bought the marble block for Perry's grave, and carved on it. He was so nice about it."

Sarah briefly turned her head, her prim nose slightly downturned. Mr. Grimshaw kept his eyes on the road.

She continued, "He's an educated man." That drew a glance from Mr. Grimshaw, an educated man himself. "And there's something more about him," she paused trying to put words to it. "Men listen to him. Sarah, remember when Captain Juan was about to be hanged, out back of the Eating House?" Sarah turned sideways and nodded. "Well, Ben Wilder was the one who calmed everybody down, and got them to settle for hanging by the thumbs."

"Mmm," Sarah said noncommittally.

"I think he's a good man, at heart," Elitha soldiered on, "and if he's at the dance, I guess I'll dance with him." There. She'd said it.

The Grimshaws were quiet for a time before Sarah said, "You sweet on him?"

She felt herself blushing. It had been only four months since Perry's death. "Maybe," she admitted.

The Grimshaws were quiet. Every mile or so they passed a road stop—some with huge hay barns and watering troughs catering to teamsters, others small eating houses sized for riders and men on foot. But no matter what they passed, the golden grass stretched out in a seemingly endless tapestry in every direction, the white-capped mountains in the distance. Mountains of death.

Mr. Grimshaw cleared his throat and started a new subject, or so it seemed at first. "You know, I heard there are more than six hundred men for every white female in the mining regions. Some calculate more like a thousand to one. Isn't that something?" It was like him to think in numbers.

"Is that a fact!" Sarah exclaimed, slapping her satin-sheathed knee. Elitha could almost hear: So why pick Ben Wilder?

Innocently she said, "I don't think that's surprising. Ladies don't want to risk everything coming across the plains or walking through that pestilence in Panama. I don't think they like to leave their homes the way men do." Pa had been the one bound and determined to come to California.

"Mmm," said Mr. Grimshaw.

Then the Grimshaws were quiet, the late morning air heating up unpleasantly. At Forest Home, the large rock hotel built by the Castles of Michigan, they stopped for water—horse and people. She and Sarah visited the four-seater. Miles later they ate noon dinner at Willow Creek House, a place as busy and almost as elegant as Forest Home.

The closer they came to the Fiddletown turn, the more men they saw heading for the dance on mules, horseback and foot. The buggy had joined a parade of rigs coming from the junction of Bedbug—the sign crossed out, Ione written above it—then from Drytown, Sutter's Creek and Jackson, then China Camp and Pokerville. The dust seemed almost as bad as on the great migration across the plains. Then at last they were climbing a steep grade, pine trees mixing with the oaks the higher they got, until the trees were dense enough to shade them from the heat of the late afternoon. At the first huts and shanties of Fiddletown, most of the trees were cut.

Fiddletown straddled a stream in a mountain gorge. The Chinese section came first, some of their buildings resembling adobes, the squiggly lines of their signs colorful. In the doorways stood men with long black pigtails and stacks of peaked straw hats at their feet, sides of pork hanging in front. After that came large buildings, many brick, with upper-story balconies. Fiddletown certainly looked like the commercial hub Mr. Grimshaw said it was.

They stopped before the Sign of the Star Hotel. A large white star blazed on a blue placard, and a groom opened the buggy door. Blue bunting draped the upper-story balcony. Mr. Grimshaw ushered Elitha and Sarah into the dining area while the horse was led to a hostelry up the road.

Inside, a mob of people, mostly men, milled around the half-filled tables, which were set with white linen, stemmed glasses and silverware. Tinsel and ribbon hung from the stairs and the upstairs balcony that over looked the main floor. Along one wall stood a table heaped with platters of steaming food. Elitha hadn't seen such a grand place since Springfield. She didn't see Ben, but with a couple hundred people in the place and new arrivals coming every minute, that wasn't surprising.

They joined a table with two men, who stood and helped with Elitha's chair while Mr. Grimshaw held one for Sarah. Everyone was in a festive mood, and it infected Elitha.

As Mr. Grimshaw went to pay, Elitha followed Sarah in search of a woman who could tell them where the privy was. "Mr Grimshaw is such a gentle-man," Elitha said as they wended their way through the buzz and press of bodies. She looked for Ben, realizing it was possible he'd brought somebody else, or hadn't come.

"He's from a real good family in New York," Sarah replied, clearly pleased Elitha had noticed. "His father's in shipping." A beaded dowager with clown-red cheeks told them the privy was upstairs on a bridge.

They exchanged a shrugging look—on a bridge?—and pushed their way through the crowd. With queenly posture, Sarah led up the stairs. Near the top Elitha turned and looked down at the crowd. There, in line well behind Mr. Grimshaw, she saw Ben, taller than anyone else. He had come! And the way he smiled at her, raising his poke in greeting! He'd been watching her. The night opened like a blooming flower.

She caught up with Sarah, who was down a short hallway opening a door. They stepped outside onto a long narrow span of rope and wood, which connected with the rest of the hotel across the stream. The bridge swayed beneath them, and she looked down, waiting for Sarah to finish inside the canvas cubicle marked "ladies." She had the odd sensation that if she didn't hold the rope handrail, she might float away. Maybe it came from being away from the baby for the first time, or the thought of dancing with Ben, or just the heat lifting. It was late June and the days were long—probably about eight-thirty now, guessing from the red sunset in the gorge. The dust suspended in the air looked like spun gold.

When Sarah lifted the canvas and came out, Elitha avoided the eyes of the men who were waiting for the cubicle marked "Gents," and went in. An oak seat teetered on a bottomless wooden box, the stream moving below, and she felt the sway of people walking on the bridge. After a good inspection, she concluded that no men were below in the stream, though the possibility was unnerving.

Later, on their way to the Powder Room, Elitha said to Sarah, "That was an adventure." Sarah raised her brows over a tight smile. In the Powder Room they studied themselves in a large brass-framed mirror, a profusion of red wallpaper roses behind them, and they fixed the hair that had jarred loose on the journey. Pouring water from the ornate pitcher into the matching basin, they washed and used an embroidered cloth smelling of lavender. After three years in the adobe, Elitha felt like Cinderella in Prince Charming's palace.

This was the only quiet time they would have to talk, so she said, "I saw Ben Wilder downstairs."

In the mirror Sarah glanced at her and continued screwing on her earrings.

"I'm going to talk to him, and tell him how ranchers feel about men moving onto their property and putting up fences," Elitha said while putting on her new eardrops.

Sarah said nothing.

Back at the table Mr. Grimshaw handed them each a folded card with a pink ribbon threaded through it and a tiny pencil dangling from a string. The front said, The Walker Cotillion. Embossed in the upper corner were three pink roses. The numbered lines puzzled Elitha, having danced only in barns and in the front rooms of houses. She was glad Sarah asked what the cards were for.

"Like this," Mr. Grimshaw said, holding the ribbon to her wrist. It hung like a bracelet. He pointed at the lines and said, "Your dance partners write their names there." He wrote his name on Sarah's card and said, "I'd like the first dance, and the last, and every other dance you want me to have." He didn't seem disturbed that Elitha wasn't familiar with the manners of a ball. Men were gathering, and he whispered loud enough for them both to hear, "Ladies are in short supply, so the polite thing is to dance with plenty of men."

"May I have a dance?" blurted both men at the table, ignoring their filled plates. Men with water-slicked hair and trimmed whiskers formed a line at the table. She saw Ben come over and stand at the end of the line, looking at her in that solid, easy way she liked so much.

She excused herself and went to him, the face of each man she passed brightening before falling with disappointment. She felt like the princess in the fairy tale who had to choose between the lined-up men outside the palace gates, all hoping to marry her. That princess married the only man who could make her cry. But with Ben smiling down at her with his sloping blue eyes, crying was the last thing on her mind.

"May I have a dance," he asked.

She handed him her card. "The first one."

"Honored, ma'am." He used the proffered back of another man to write his name, asking, "Any more? It's a long night."

She wanted to dance every dance with him, but thought he might like to dance with others too. But then she saw the mob around every female, never mind how old or ugly or married, and said, "How about every fourth dance?"

"Including the last?"

She smiled a yes, and within five minutes her entire night was planned, "Ben W." on every fourth line. Other men wrote in their names until she got to the bottom, and the crestfallen line melted away. Ben disappeared into the crowd.

Feeling like singing, Elitha picked up her plate and followed Sarah and Mr. Grimshaw to the food line, where the breaded oysters made her mouth water.

"Griz," a man called, craning his neck around the line. A man digging into the scalloped potatoes looked up.

"Didja hear bout the Joaquín gang strikin here?"

"Warn't that som'm!"

Elitha took a roll and thought about Pedro Valdez. But that wasn't fair of her, just because he was the only Spaniard she knew. She dipped brandied peaches on her ham and went back to the table, feeling added excitement to know Fiddletown had been struck by the famous outlaw. She couldn't wait to tell Ben.

A waiter poured champagne and she spread the linen napkin, suddenly recalling the mouse suppers in the mountains. *God reminding me to give thanks for this feast.* She closed her eyes and was halfway finished with her prayer when Mr. Grimshaw said, "You men hear about the Joaquín attack?"

The one with a large bony nose forked in an oyster and talked through it. "First thing we heard when we come to town, wadn't it Zeke?" Bobbing his head, Zeke chewed enthusiastically. She had read about those bandits stealing tens of thousands in gold dust from miners in far-flung mining regions. She couldn't believe that the same men got around so fast.

The two men competed to tell another story, raising their voices to curious listeners at the next tables. One would finish and the other would start the next part. A gang of bandits had been playing monte in the card room at the back of Mr. Erauw's mercantile, when somebody recognized the leader and accused him of being Joaquín. The fancy Mexican threw down his cards and jumped up on the table, "spurs ajinglin." He brandished his gun over his head and yelled, "I am Joaquín!"

Then he leaped from the table and raced through the mercantile, where ladies screamed. Men followed the gang as they ran out the door to get on their horses, but the pursuing card players yelled for help from the men on the street, one of whom grabbed the bit of a horse and shot a bandit "dead between the eyes." By this time the whole town was chasing after them, but the superb Mexican horsemen dodged a hail of bullets. Then they jumped off their horses and wriggled into the brambles west of town, "jist like a bunch of snakes."

"Why, no white man could git though thet stuff!" Zeke supplied.

"What color was Joaquín's hair?" Elitha asked.

"Black as midnight, is my guess," said the man with the big nose.

"No one mentioned the color?"

"No ma'am. But Mexicans all have black hair."

No they don't, she thought. People at the surrounding tables had gone back to eating. In the middle of the room the candelabra was lowered by a system of ropes. With the heavy wheel suspended over the heads of diners, a man lit tiers of candles, maybe forty altogether, and the huge fixture was pulleyed up. Elitha joined the cheering as the room brightened. She longed to be dancing in Ben's arms.

More champagne was poured, and by the time everyone had finished eating, she felt-lightheaded. Words tumbled easily from her mouth. She felt she was floating as she carried dishes to the kitchen, the men taking the chairs and tables out to the yard. She and Sarah visited the bridge again—it was twilight now—and in the Powder Room ladies chattered and patted their hair. One told the story of the town's founding by the Walker family, Forty-niners from Missouri who drove down the mountain from the Kit Carson Pass and broke an axle. Instead of repairing it they sat and fiddled, the story went. They found "color" in the stream and called the place home, right where they'd broken down. They built their hotel business on that very spot, and the town sprang up around it. By the time Elitha and Sarah returned to the dining hall, it was cleared for the dance.

The four Walker men, three grown sons and their father, climbed up on a table with violins in hand. They helped their sister up with her Irish tin flute. Beside the table stood the dowager Mrs. Walker with a washtub made into a drum and a scrub board bordered with bells and metal cups. Bringing their fiddles to their chins, the men moved their shoulders in silent rhythm, and then delivered a spritely waltz.

A hand touched Elitha's waist.

She turned and looked into Ben's blue eyes. Before she could introduce him, he swept her across the floor. It was thrilling. Enchanted. She was transported to a ball in Vienna exactly as she had imagined. She whirled in Ben's arms to a fast one-two-three one-two-three, skimming the floor with her toes, whirling like a star in the heavens, her spirit sparkling with the tinsel. He was tall enough to look over her head, but he looked down, only at her. And she looked up, locked in his gaze, loving the feel of his arms and the warmth of his breath.

She almost moaned in disappointment when the waltz ended. A smiling man appeared at her elbow. Consulting the card, she saw it was Mr. Tom Richards. The music began and they both struggled to recall the steps of the gavotte. Stumbling through it, she asked all the obligatory questions, "Where are you from?"

"Cornwall." "Where is that?" "Not far from Wales." An accent. "What did you do there?" "Me two brothers'n me was miners." "It's lucky you knew something about mining before you got here." "That it tis." "Havin any luck?" "Fair." A careful tone. Probably finding good color. "Where's your digs?" "Amador, over by Drytown."

The next man was a lawyer from Massachusetts who said with a twinkle that he could make more money shoveling sand in San Francisco. "Why don't you then?" "And miss this? Not on our life!" He said he was on the dance committee and similar events were to be held on a regular basis. "A civilizing influence, don't you think?" "Sure is," Elitha agreed.

Back in Ben's arms for a quadrille, she had a strong feeling that she'd come home. With him teaching her the steps, she twirled easily and paraded up a corridor of dancers, noticing Kate Sherwood, Miss Orten and the Hays girl in the arms of smiling men. Even Mrs. Hays had a beau. Most of the men danced with each other. Then she connected with Sarah's icy eyes, and lost a beat.

"Would you like to go out for a breath of air?" asked Ben, reading her mind.

The street was dark, oil lamps glowing from windows high and low. Pine scent wafted down the mountain. The little breeze cooled her cheeks. From the open door came perky music and the rasp and stomp of shoes. Ben went to a pump on the boardwalk and cranked the handle up and down until water flowed from the spout into the tin cup chained to the pump. Offering it to her, he asked, "Something on your mind?"

"Yes." But first she took the cup from him and drank.

"Well, I guess we got till the next man comes for you." He worked the pump and guzzled two full cups while she sorted her thoughts. "Is it something I did?"

"Oh no!" Then she realized in a way it was. "Do you know Sarah Daylor?"

"No."

"Mr. Grimshaw?"

"The proprietor of the Cosumne Store?"

"Yes. Well they're married now, and she's one of my best friends. They gave me a ride to the dance."

"Pretty brunette in a blue frock?" His tone was cautious. She winced to see dark spots on the front of her dress, her breasts leaking, visible even in the half-light. She had missed two feedings. She told Ben about the Daylor-Sheldon partnership and explained that Sarah and Catherine Sheldon were sisters.

The music ended. Immediately an older couple came out the door, the woman fanning her dance card as Ben said, "I think I'm getting the gist. You feel traitorous being seen with me."

"Well, they've done so much for me." Embarrassment tied her in knots. She couldn't see his face, couldn't tell if he was nettled.

A man appeared at the door speaking in the gentlest, humblest tone she'd ever heard. "Ma'am, I guess this is dance number five."

"I'm coming." Turning to Ben, she whispered. "I don't mean to be rude, but I guess I had to tell you." She hoped he would dance with her again.

He put his large warm hand on her shoulder and said, "Three dances from now we'll talk some more."

The night whirled by in disjointed chunks—chatter with strangers about their digs and occupations, interspersed with increasingly personal talk with Ben, conversation softened by the excellent music and the warm embrace of this long loose wonderful man.

First she explained that Catherine was minding the baby, and that Ben and his brothers were considered the ringleaders of the squatters who had threatened Mr. Sheldon down at Cosumne about a year ago. Three dances later she described the difficulties Mr. Sheldon was having raising cattle, now that the Indian herders were gone and so many outlaw miners were stealing horses and butchering cattle. She had to wait three more dances to tell him how angry Mr. Sheldon had been this morning about the fence and the Miners Committee. It was a slow waltz and Ben held her closer than ever. It seemed unreal, feeling that good while telling him what a nuisance he was.

His breath was warm on the part of her hair. "There's a few things that need to be straightened out, that's all," he said. "Let's us have a talk with the Grimshaws during the intermission." His tone resonated with the confidence she loved.

Relieved, she looked up. With his mouth so near, his breath so fine, she would have kissed him if he'd wanted. Surely a gentleman like this would win anyone over. And maybe, through him, she could help stop the awful conflict in the riverbottom.

# 84

Ben's long arm stayed around her as they drove down the mountain in a little spring wagon he had rented. Dawn spread across the immense valley, tinting the distant coastal mountains. In the big valley a silver stream twinkled like a diamond necklace that had been carelessly laid down. The cheeping of awakening birds might just as well have been wedding bells. She and Ben were moving toward a shiny new future. Despite dancing all night and eating a wonderful breakfast, she didn't feel one bit drowsy. He had asked her to marry him!

The way she'd smiled, he must have seen the yes in her eyes, but she was a proper girl, and said she'd give him her answer before the week was out.

He had handled the talk with Sarah and Mr. Grimshaw like a diplomat, erasing her worries. They had surely seen him for the gentleman he was. She couldn't wait for him to speak to Catherine and Mr. Sheldon and explain to them that he'd actually stopped the squatter mob, and that if he hadn't, Mr. Sheldon could be dead now. In the confusion, nobody had realized that. Far from a hothead, Ben Wilder was the most reasonable and kind-hearted man she'd ever known. She would be proud to call herself Mrs. Wilder. The thought made her believe in miracles.

She chattered about Fiddletown. "They sure hauled a lot of brick up there to make all those buildings. Must have been Mr. Zins' bricks."

He tugged her closer. "Mr. Zins?"

She explained that he had married Mrs. Wolfinger, who had been rescued with Elitha, and that he had started a brick kiln in the clay pits of Sutterville.

He grinned down at her. "I sure do admire the way you know all the old-timers."

"Old-timers!" she said with a playful jab of her elbow. "Just cause I got here two years before you!"

"Two and a half," he corrected with a crinkle-eyed grin.

She snuggled into him and said, "It's a wonder they built Fiddletown so fast."

"Don't ever underestimate the argonauts, or the power of Manifest Destiny. The optimism I heard crossing the plains would float an anvil. Nothing can stop these men."

Other wagons and riders traveled the road, many leaving the dance. Elitha waved at Mr. Richards and his brothers on their way back to Amador. She felt married already, her earrings in her pocket, her loosened hair on her neck as the rig bounced forward. She didn't even mind Ben's glance at her front, where rings of white had dried on the brown fabric. A married man needed to know about such things.

At the thought of the milk, a powerful surge swelled her already engorged breasts. The thought of the baby hungrily sucking and relieving the pressure made the milk well up like unstopped geysers. The frock was too tight. The pain cut clear up under her armpits.

Too slowly the wheels ate up the rutted miles, and it became harder to enjoy Ben's arm around her. She squirmed on the seat until he asked after her comfort. As if it were a small thing she joked, "I hope I can last till we get to the Sheldons." The bumps nearly tore her apart.

He was quiet for a time, then said, "Mind if I ask you a question?"

"Go ahead." Anything to take her mind off the pain.

"Well, maybe since you understand how ranchers think, you can explain why a man who purports to own more than," he paused, then emphasized each syllable, "eighteen thousand acres down at Slough House, would come nine miles up to Cook's Bar to grow vegetables where he can't even irrigate without flooding the place with this—dam thing! And that's not profanity, though it tempts me sorely." Something hard and masculine in his tone alerted her to the depths of his feelings, and though she worried about the frightful quarrel in the river, it interested her to see this new side of the man she would marry.

As to the why, she had asked the same question the first time Mr. Sheldon mentioned it, so it was to be expected from a Forty-niner. "Well, like I said, it's real hard to make a living from cattle now, with almost no Indians left to herd them. Some of the miners think the stock is there for the taking, just because there aren't any fences. I know for a fact Mr. Sheldon has lost many thousands of animals. So I guess he decided to try his hand at crops."

"By thunder, then why the devil doesn't he grow his beans or whatever it is down on the land he threw us off of the first time? A bee gets under his bonnet and he takes a notion to waltz up to Cook's Bar and throw us off again!" He took back his arm and held the reins with both hands.

She realized it might seem like Mr. Sheldon was trying to bedevil him. She tried again. "Catey says there's too many brambles near the slough to grow vegetables down there, and with no Indians to help clear brush, I guess he thought it was easier to buy Mr. Hartnell's land across from me and—"

"Back where I come from, a man clears his own land." A voice like granite.

She had to understand him if they were to be married. She must try to see things the way he did. "What is your Miner's Committee doing?"

"Held a meeting yesterday." He turned to her. "See, Sheldon claims he owns the riverbed. Showed us a property deed from the Mexican government. It's like if your pa and his neighbors were growing crops on their homesteads in Illinois, when all of a sudden somebody comes along and says: I can make money by running cows over your land, so sorry boys." He waved a flippant hand. "Backed up by nothing more than foreign writing on a piece of paper! From a foreign country we just defeated. And like we talked before, it's not likely to stand up in the U.S. courts."

"Would your claims be honored by the courts?" She had an interest in the Wilder claim now, which would be underneath the backed-up water after the dam was built.

He dipped his head in sharp agreement. "Seems like Mr. Sheldon's got the notion he can part men from their gold." With a dry laugh he looked over at her, "men who walked across the continent to get it. He's planning to flood the claims of about a hundred men. Course at the moment, with the water diverted into the ditch, everybody's happy scraping up color from the main channel; but the minute he shuts down the sluice gate, the water'll back up. And not a man on the river believes he has the right."

"Including you?"

"Correct. A couple of the boys read law in the states." She felt the futility of trying to push the two sides together, and began to feel tired.

He turned to her. "Every day men are killed for less than that."

"Killed!"

"I'm not saying it's right, just a fact. Those of us on the Committee had our hands full trying to keep order."

*Killed.* She sort of changed the subject. "It's been nice having Catherine at Bridge House."

He sighed, reached his long arm around her, and pulled her to him. "That's enough of that. We'll get it all settled. Don't you worry about it." The confident, reasonable, fully in-charge tone was back. She didn't let on that the squeeze hurt her tight breasts.

An hour later when the buggy stopped before the Sheldon cabin, she was crazy with pain. Climbing down with Ben's help, the entire front of her dress soaked, she prayed the baby was hungry. No doubt she would be, Catherine having had too little milk for both babies. Elizabeth would suck hard and pull out the pain, and restore her to her former cheerful self. Nothing else mattered as she approached the door, not even Ben beside her ready to face up to Mr. Sheldon.

The door opened before she lifted the latch. Catherine stood there with a blank expression, hair straggling from her bun, little Sarah gripping her wrinkled skirt. She seemed ill. Behind her, Mr. Sheldon stared at Ben.

"Catey," she said, "I'm about to burst. Ben here talked to Sarah and Mr. Grimshaw up at the dance, and he'd like to talk to you, Mr. Sheldon. I hope you don't mind if I come in and get the baby fed while you're all talking. Maybe you could go outside?"

Hollow stares.

She laid a hand across her breast and added, "It's REAL bad."

Mr. Sheldon came forward and gently moved Catherine from the door. "Come in, Elitha." To Ben he said, "You stay outside," and closed the door.

She looked at the bed, her pale green blanket laid over a lump. "Where…" She reached.

Catherine grabbed her hand and said, "We did all we could."

Mr. Sheldon added, "Musta been cholera."

She jerked her hand free and threw back the cover. Elizabeth lay perfectly still, eyes closed. Collapsing at the bedside, she drew the baby to her aching bosom and pressed her nose into her cool sweet neck and said quietly, "Mama's come back to you, precious. Wake up, Lizzie." What was the matter with these people! Milk flooded from her nipples. Elizabeth felt cool, but not … I was having fun while …

Catherine tried to pull her up.

Violently she shook her off and hugged Elizabeth.

"Breathed her last a little while ago," Mr. Sheldon was saying.

"Don't say that!" Panic and anger blinded her as she jumped to her feet with the baby and threw open the door and ran to the rig. Ben joined her with a surprised look on his face.

"Take me home," she said, missing the foothold and nearly falling on Elizabeth. Ben caught her. A cry sounded. But not from Elizabeth.

❧

Ben stayed the night, rocking her in his arms as she rocked the baby. Blazing color bursts exploded in her mind whenever she allowed herself to step toward the black void, then she would lurch into angry refusal. In her embrace the baby also refused. All night she refused to nurse, refused to move, refused to make a sound. Her little arms and hands grew cold and firm, though Elitha warmed her with her body. Outside, bitter gray light outlined the trees. Daylight. Something nudged her toward the void, and at last, trancelike, her mind made the leap. A harsh scream scraped her throat.

Implacable silence responded. The first sob boiled up and exploded from her, then long wails. Water poured from her eyes and nose, milk from her breasts, anguish from her heart. Her baby was dead. Oh God no! Ben held her tightly as the sobs rocked her, and over and over she told Elizabeth, "I wasn't there to hold you when you cried." Then she cried like a baby.

After what seemed hours, her strength waned and dissolved into whimpers. Slowly Ben disentangled the baby from her arms, laid the small body on the bed, and covered it with the green blanket. Taking another blanket, he led Elitha from the adobe and, beneath the oak tree, spread it and lay down holding her length to him, petting her hair and murmuring, "There's nothing you could have done. Cholera's bad now. Lots of men have died. Whole tribes of Indians. It's a blessing she went so fast. She's in God's arms now. Sleep, dear Elitha. You must rest."

Closing her eyes seemed a betrayal of Elizabeth, but she finally forced her lids down. Brilliant orange and yellow shapes careened at her from her throbbing head, shocking her to alertness. Thoughtless birds chirped as if Elizabeth had never existed.

Much later, how long she had no idea, Ben took the old slats from the door she had made, telling her he'd make a better one, and fashioned a little coffin from them. Then he dug a grave, and together they buried Elizabeth next to Perry.

"She was so sweet," Elitha said.

"Would you like me to get another marble block?"

Kneeling, touching Perry's block, Elitha said, "No. Just carve Elizabeth's name on the bottom. Here." The hot sun stabbed her swollen eyes and she felt like she was going to faint. Her breasts still cried for Elizabeth, but her eyes had dried. Ben helped her up and supported her.

Asa Wilder appeared on the path, hat in hand. "My condolences, Mrs. McCoon." He had to have been watching.

She couldn't speak.

He cleared his throat apologetically, "Ben, I gotta talk to you a minute. Something's come up."

"I'll see her back inside. Wait by that split rock."

As Ben steered her across the threshold of the adobe, a sensation pressed into her, something formless, dark and sinister. She made a frightened sound, and backed out. He looked her a question.

"I can't go in." Everyone that went in there died.

"What do you mean?"

"I'll lie down over there."

He helped her to a flat spot. She lay straight and still, hands over her womb, her thoughts compacting like a clock wound tighter and tighter. She had known the baby was sick when she went to the dance. She had enjoyed herself while her baby was dying. She had neglected her.

"Elitha," Ben called after a minute or two, "I've got to go over to Cook's Bar. There's a problem. Will you be all right?"

She sat up. A shiver passed through her though the day was warm. Her head was muddled and she couldn't answer.

He kneeled beside her. "I'm sorry to say this now, but Asa says the men are up in arms down at the dam."

"I'll come with you."

He looked at her for a long time with his sloping blue eyes, and then took her in his arms and said, "I'm sorry but you can't. It wouldn't be safe."

Men thought they were immortal. They fought over unimportant things. "I'm all right here."

As his lanky frame disappeared up the path, Indian Mary stepped from the trees holding a handful of vegetation. She had been waiting. At her knee, Little Billy's dimples cut into his chubby cheeks when he looked past Elitha. Mary looked up, heard something.

Elitha looked too. Coming up the trail from Bridge House were Catherine and her new baby with little Will helping little Sarah toddle alongside.

Remembering how rude she'd been, she staggered to her feet.

They met in an embrace, the live baby between. Elitha's voice shook. "Forgive me, Catey." Her cheek felt plump and smooth, and wet.

Catherine sniffed back tears. "I was afraid you'd blame me. Oh, Elitha, I'm so grieved. We tried so hard. Did everything we could think of." She swallowed hard, the baby squirming in her arms.

"I never should have gone to the dance," Elitha sobbed. "But I'm ever so grateful for all you did." All words were pathetic. She hugged this best friend with every ounce of feeling she had.

Indian Mary's voice came from behind. "I bring sleep tea."

They both turned. Mary laid her hand on Elitha's shoulder and seemed to see into her, although, in the Indian way, her gaze missed its mark. They formed a three-way embrace, a huddle, the newborn in the middle, the older baby on Mary's back, Billy and Sarah and little Will embracing their mothers' knees.

# 85

Joaquín Sheldon stood before his Bridge House cabin with his wolf eyes leveled at Pedro. "Gracias for coming so fast."

Pedro dipped his hat. The Indian runner had found him in Spanish Camp, and he had not hesitated.

"I need you to help get this cannon into position." Sheldon tilted his sombreroed head toward the wagon bed where heaps of moth-eaten old mission blankets covered a big lump.

"A cannon? From the fort?"

Sheldon nodded. "There's a dozen of 'em left down there, no use to anybody. Figured I might as well help myself. It'll show those miners I mean business."

He had a team hitched to the wagon, but Pedro and Sheldon sat on the stoop smoking and talking about what was going on until a man rode up. Sheldon introduced him as James Johnson, a friend from the Slough House area.

They all positioned planks around the cannon to better disguise it. Then Pedro and Mr. Johnson rode ahead of Sheldon's wagon up through Cook's Bar just as cool as you please, Mr. Sheldon clucking his team and nodding to acquaintances as if he were hauling nothing more than the next load of lumber for his dam. Men seemed accustomed to the sight.

They passed the Eating House and the thickest bunch of tents and started up a hill through the live oaks. Mr. Johnson looked over at Pedro and said, "You working fer Jared?" He had an amicable smile, blue eyes and a pale complexion—an ordinary North American face like the men Pedro routinely relieved of their gold.

"He is an amigo. And you, señor? You work for him?"

"Jared's gonna cut me in on the vegetables for my work on the dam. I wrote home for the missus and the boys to come out and join me. Plan to make a new start in California, maybe buy some Sheldon land down around Slough House."

They left the trail and headed up an incline, the ground rough with rocks and scrub trees, easy for the saddle horses but difficult for the team. In only a few minutes Sheldon called ahead to stop. They had arrived near a rocky bluff overlooking the mud of the river channel and the dam, another marvel of Yankee ingenuity, an amazing structure with two walls sixteen feet high made of horizontally laid split oak trunks fitted between uprights. The space between the big walls had been filled with large boulders. The sluice gate in the middle would back the river up to a height where it would flow into Sheldon's channel just upstream of this outcropping—a natural ravine. It would water his row crops. Miners on both sides of the dam were still working their pans and long toms.

Pedro helped slide the disassembled cannon down a wooden ramp, and they unloaded the wheels and tongue piece. Sheldon set to reassembling the old fieldpiece while Pedro and Mr. Johnson stood lookout. No man showed his face. It took all the strength the three had to pull the heavy brass piece up the tiered rocks to the wide, flat top, like pulling it up stairs. When they positioned it, they saw men down below looking up.

"Good," Sheldon said. "Give 'em something to think about."

They went back for the canisters of grapeshot, carrying armloads from the wagon, and stacked them beside the cannon. Still no one came up. Johnson mopped his face with a bandana and said, "Well, that's about it."

"Yup," Sheldon agreed.

Pedro was looking at the cannon, realizing it was the same type as La Pulga Vieja, as they had called her, the eight-pounder General Vallejo had used in the Indian war. Captain Sutter collected it along with many other unused field pieces.

"Which one of you wants the first watch?" Sheldon asked. "I gotta go down to a meeting at the Eating House." He had a number of men lined up to keep a round-the-clock vigil.

"I will guard the old lady," Pedro said in Spanish.

Señor Johnson stuck out his hand. "Peers we're pardners."

As Pedro shook the friendly North American hand, he felt a peculiar sensation, like sand shifting under his feet.

Then after both men rode away, he felt an even stranger feeling when he examined the brass nozzle and found the foundry mark. He knelt there staring at it, stunned to learn that he'd fought against Captain Juan with this very weapon. He well remembered going to the shop with his fellow soldiers and checking the marks to be sure they used the one that had been repaired. This very cannon had given the presidios their so-called victory over the Valley Indians. And here he was, twenty-two years later, positioning it to kill North Americans. How quickly things shifted! Missions in decay, the war with the United States lost, the rush for gold sweeping all before it. His former enemy was now his father-in-law. He shook his head in disbelief at the tricks life played. María would call it a Coyote trick.

Ben Wilder stood on a crate and banged two shovel blades together over his head. The packed Eating House quieted as the agitated men looked up at him. Handing the shovels to his brother Asa, he slipped Sheldon's proposal from his pocket and read aloud:

> *July 6, 1851. Proposition of Jared D. Sheldon.*
> *I wish to use the water upon my farm long enough suffi-*
> *ciently to irrigate it—which will probably require from 6*
> *to 10 days, after which I expect to leave the water run, as*
> *usual, and pledge myself through my Committee that the*
> *river shall not be interfered with, under this arrangement.*
>
> *Second, it may be necessary to use the water once in 2 or*
> *3 weeks after this, if so, I shall use the water but one day*
> *in the week and that on Sundays. The miners reaping*
> *the benefit all the rest of the week. [Committee: James*

*Breen, Henry Waddilove, A. W. Lewis] This proposition to
be accepted or rejected before 6 o'clock this evening.*

Talk erupted. Pointing to the wall, Ben raised his voice and cut off the clamor with: "For those who can read, I'm nailing it over there. For those who can't, here's the gist: Mr. Sheldon," he waved the paper toward the window where Sheldon and his dozen men stood, will finish out the dam with a sluice, a four-foot gate."

He chose his words carefully. This was no time for inflaming the men. "Then he'll back the river up for six to ten days, or as long as it takes to give his ground a good soaking. After that he'll pull up the sluice and let the water run. He doesn't think the vegetables will need but two or three more soakings after that, depending on the heat. And at those times he'll lower the sluice at sundown Saturday and let the water rise till it reaches his race, then raise the gate Sunday night. Most of you souse yourselves on Sundays anyway.

He glanced at Sheldon's intense stare. "Is that fairly stated?"

Sheldon dipped his hat.

Ben concluded, "Now we'll discuss whether to sign this proposal. We on the Miner's Committee want to hear all sides—whether your claims are down under the dam or back behind it. Who'll speak first?"

As the Counselor came forward, Ben stepped down, gesturing toward the crate. He felt torn. Much as he despised Sheldon's attitude and felt that no man had the right to flood mining claims, never mind how long, his love for Elitha had moderated his sense of justice. Through her, he now had a personal link with the Sheldons, and he had to admit that in presenting this written proposal, the rancher had shown a measure of self-imposed restraint. Ben would listen carefully and weigh what others had to say.

Balancing on the crate with an almost comical show of caution, the heavy, gray-haired speaker leaned back on his heels and made himself comfortable before the crowd. Then flowed the stentorian tones:

"Gentlemen, verily I say unto you, the granting of this proposition will set a dangerous precedent for years to come. As many of you know, my claim is below the dam and I stand to benefit for a time from the absence of water. But the Interests of Justice for the Majority must, in this case, override personal gain. I warn you against the placement of signatures upon any document penned by a California man of agriculture, and hereby set forth my reasoning." He moved his feet farther apart. Ben listened attentively, though he'd heard the Counselor speak on this subject before.

"At this juncture, we in California find ourselves hoisted on the horns of a dilemma. As we speak, the Legislature has commenced to consider disputes arising between the interests of mining and those of agriculture. Farmers claim to own the streams and riverbeds and that means, my good friends, if it be found to be true, they control all the water in this dry territory—the very substance of life, the crucial element in mining. Yet they are few and we are many. The Majority possesses the right to divert water as befits its needs, when and where it wishes. This is the American way. Furthermore, our Creator endows each of us with the inalienable right to work our claims without interference!" A cheer exploded, the Counselor waiting.

"And so, gentlemen, you miners stand on the profoundly opposite pole from the so-called ranchers, who are the direct beneficiaries of the defunct Mexican government." He made eye contact around the room, finishing with a look at Ben. "If you sign any document that can be construed as granting Mr. Sheldon the right to control the river, as sure as day follows night, it will weigh on the rancher's side of the scales when the Legislature acts. Do not wait until it is too late to recognize your folly."

Ben thought through the complexity of that as, beneath the Counselor's furrowed gray brows, his glance shifted around the crowd. Then the man cocked an eye to the ceiling and proceeded like a storyteller. "Two men are wrestling." He turned to one side, put his heels together and bowed slightly. "The smaller of the two asks the other: If you would be so good, sir, please allow me to lock my arm around your neck before the whistle is blown."

He raised his voice. "That, gentlemen, is the request before you today. If you wish to continue mining in California, do not kowtow to Mr. Sheldon. Insist on the dam's removal. We, my friends, are the Majority."

As the older man stepped down amidst shouts of approval, Ben raised an arm, pointing at James Gallogly, known as Corky, who was coming forward. In the moments before Corky spoke, Ben reviewed the merit of the Counselor's argument. It differed from his usual: the United States government owns the nation's streams, not the Mexican ranchers. And he had a flash that the resolution of this dispute could affect all areas of the arid West, which would no doubt follow California as settled territories of the United States.

Corky, a spokesman for the hoards of Irishmen who had flocked to the mines, observed in bemused humility: "Would that we were all blessed with tongue such as that!" He bowed low toward the Counselor, drawing a laugh. Many regarded the potato famine refugees as little more than monkeys. But they constituted about a third of the mining population in this area, and that was a measure of power. Ben wanted their opinion.

"In me County Cork homeland, ye understand, I had me perfect fill of the outrageous claims of the landed. And a wonder it tis to come to America, all these distant fathoms away, only to find that ilk bedevilin the mines of Californy. I, for one, will swim back before I sign that paper." A roar came from the Irish, supported by claps from others. "As for the dam: Laddies, take up yer axes!"

More than the Irish yelled approval. "Axes to the dam!" "Axes to the dam!" It came from many throats. Mr. Sheldon looked from one to another, mouth slightly parted, wolf-like. It was good for him to hear this, Ben thought.

Others spoke in succession. Jim Breen, Sheldon's man, also an Irishman, tried to speak, though miners interrupted with shouts, especially when he declared, "A perfect gentleman is Mr. Sheldon, and a better friend we couldn't find to represent us in the Legislature." Breen's claim was beneath the dam, so few took him seriously.

"Give him the floor," shouted Cody. "We need to hear all sides of this." Had Cody changed his mind?

Breen continued and then Ben called on Cody, a tough breed of man with a good education.

"We've heard Mr. Sheldon called an imperious and callous landowner," said Cody. "Yet I've been standing here amazed to see a landowner willing to curtail his self-perceived rights to satisfy men who might be termed squatters." An angry rumble reared up, and Cody raised his voice to be heard over it.

"Men, men, you have every right to establish claims along the river, you know I believe that. All I'm saying is, put yourselves in this man's place." He pointed to Sheldon. "Give him credit for backing down from where he started."

As the man spoke, Ben handed Asa the paper and pantomimed nailing it to the wall. Cody's points were well considered. Sheldon had, indeed, come in the spirit of compromise. Cody finished:

"Most of you take the day off on Sundays anyway—sewing on buttons, reading Scripture and—" Laughter stopped him and he smiled, then resumed. "So go prospect somewhere else during the first flooding, then, when the water recedes, it'll do some of your work for you, washing out dirt you'd have to dig otherwise. Sign the paper, I say. Mr. Sheldon proposes a fair deal."

Ben respected Cody, and he noticed by the nodding heads in the audience that others did too. But young hotheads who relished violence were peppered among them. "Ain't fair," they shouted.

"We'll lose more'n a week's take!" Another yelled.

Jared Sheldon came forward without waiting to be invited. When he stepped on the crate, the hooting and shouting seemed about to lift the roof. Ben raised his arms. "Let him talk, boys."

"That cannon don't look like no negotiatin!" Somebody yelled. Ben had been notified about the cannon, Sheldon's backup strategy. The rancher stood hard-jawed, taking in the men's reactions. Angry shouts continued, and it looked like the meeting might splinter into a fight. Men's hands hovered near the guns in their holsters. Sheldon started speaking, but the shouts didn't stop.

The word "compensate" stood out from Sheldon's drowned statement. It softened the faces of those in the front. They turned to those behind. "Listen to him!" "… pay you…" "Compensate" hissed back through the crowd.

At last even those in the back quieted, all men looking at Sheldon. He narrowed his eyes around the crowd. "I will compensate every man in the backwater for every lost day of mining."

Shouts: "How much?"

"I've been told the average take here is fifteen dollars a day." He continued through a growing rumble, "I'm prepared to pay twenty." That would make the vegetables dear, Ben thought.

Silence. Then a shout: "To each man in every claim?"

"Ayuh." A clipped, New England sound. Reading the mood-shift of the crowd, Ben recalled Cody's words, a fair deal. It was the most they could have hoped for, a deal to prevent violence.

Ben climbed the crate Sheldon vacated, and the crowd silenced. "Men, I've heard enough. As Committee Chairman I think we'd better take this offer. Do I hear a motion?"

"So move," Cody called.

Ben was quick. "All in favor say aye."

A chorus responded.

"All opposed say no." The hotheads shouted no.

"Ayes have it."

Sheldon and his men beelined through the parting crowd. Ben reached for the shovels, clanking them overhead. As men looked back over their shoulders, he said, "If Mr. Sheldon doesn't honor the agreement we meet here and talk." But he hoped Sheldon was an honorable man.

The outcome of the meeting seemed too pat, too easy. The ornery cusses in the corner gave him cocked-eyebrow skepticism.

# 86

SUNDAY MORNING, JULY 12, 1851

Señor Sheldon had been in his field since dawn, clearing the little ditches from the main channel to the crop rows. The corn had begun to wilt; however, the river had backed up all night and the water was starting to flow. Sheldon's son worked with his own little hoe, which the patrón had made for him. Three años now. Pedro smiled at little Will from Chocolate's back, hoping someday he too would have a son working beside him.

But his heart was not smiling. This morning, waking up to the flooding for the first time, the miners had demanded more compensation. Sheldon had refused. That was an hour ago, and the bastards had been drinking ever since.

"Will you still pay twenty dollars a day?" Pedro asked the patrón.

"They terminated the deal." His lips pressed shut and he turned on his heel.

He rode back to where he could see the cannon and check on the guard. Downstream, the other scout waved his hat, the signal that all was well. But it was not. Trouble could erupt at any time. All of Pedro's senses felt honed.

॰ॐ

Feeling disconnected, like she'd been dismissed from the earth's gravity, Elitha finished washing the breakfast tins. Since Elizabeth's death, the only thing she looked forward to was driving through the southern mines with Ben and planning their wedding. They were supposed to leave after the noon meal. But it was frightening, the things the miners had muttered over biscuits and gravy this morning. Some seemed to hate Mr. Sheldon, despite his agreement to pay them for lost time. She looked out over the full ditch and the empty river channel, all of it too muddy to cross, and felt drawn to Ben and his side of the river. She walked up to the bridge and around toward Cook's Bar.

Fifteen minutes later she saw Ben in a circle of tents, standing in the midst of a noisy crowd of men, many putting bottles to their lips. He saw her and tried to pull himself away, but every time he did, a man would shout something and he would turn back and speak to the crowd. With a look of desperation, he looked over their heads—like it pained him to tear his gaze from her—and finally waved her on. He'd talk to her later.

Knowing Ben was sorely needed there, glad—oh so glad he was there to make these rowdy men stick to their agreement—she went beyond the town to the high rocks. She found Vyries Brown sitting beside the cannon with a rifle over his knees. He raised a hand in greeting. "What brings you out here, Miz McCoon?" His voice still cracked.

"Nerves, I guess." Never having seen a cannon, she gathered her skirts and climbed up the rocks. Beside the little cannon stood a keg stamped: GUN-POWDER, McCallister & Co.

"Makes the skin prickle don't it?" Vyries' pug nose and red hair made him look even younger than his fifteen years. Worry showed in his eyes when he looked at the group of men in the riverbed.

But she had faith in Ben. "Do you know how to fire it?" Catey had said it was only to show the men Mr. Sheldon meant business, and it certainly had garnered their attention.

"Sure. Mr. Sheldon showed me. One shot of these'll level a crowd of men." He patted the stack of open canisters filled with round gray balls.

"Well, I hope it won't come to that." She changed the subject. "Did you come out to California by yourself?"

"Me and me big brother came round through Panama," he said, chewing on a long yellow straw. "But dead he is now, lying up yonder." He jerked his head up river.

"I'm so sorry."

"There be a lot of dyin in those lonely hills, missus. Many a poor man lyin down before his Maker without so much as a proper prayer said o'er him." His red hair flamed in the sunlight. He knew about Elizabeth because he often took his meals at Elitha's, but they had never really talked.

"Some are afraid to help the ill," she said. "Did you know Mr. Daylor was stricken after he helped a dying man?"

"Aye. And that's a story comin round. T'would make a man feel forsaken to be shunned at his own dyin." Looking over the dam, he worked on his straw.

"I wish men wouldn't fight. Why are you doing this, Vyries?" She touched the tarnished brass muzzle, hot already in the sun.

The straw wiggled and he shrugged.

"If you end up firing it, you'll kill your friends. Have you thought of that?"

He sighed and gazed down at the river channel, empty below the dam, full above. "Me friends is all back in the old country."

"I know better than that. You've got friends here all right, and it'd be a terrible sin to kill them."

He blinked his glistening eyes. "Me dear old mither woulda said such a thing." Pensively he added, "And t'would be a wonder if she's eatin atall, over there!" He let out a sigh.

"Do you believe in sin?"

He crossed himself. "Aye." It came out a man's voice.

"Then how could you fire at living men?" She touched the neat bunches of iron balls, like big seeds in open pods.

He threw down his straw. "Sure and tis what I've been thinkin since sunup!" He stood up with his gun, his voice cracking high. "And me own dear mither limpin down to Saint Paddy's to pray fer me soul all those many miles away." He wiped a sleeve across his peeling nose and walked away, his tattered trousers disappearing into the brush.

She stayed there, feeling the intensifying heat, expecting him to return from a call of nature. Below the weeping dam, a few miners shoveled madly in the mud. Others hurriedly rocked sand and gravel in their cradles, as if expecting the river would soon spill back into its bed. She heard drunken shouts. Perhaps Lorena Gordon was right that Temperance was the answer to the wickedness of mankind. Liquor had certainly made Perry nasty, and a lot of it was being consumed this morning. But that was no different than other Sundays. Fights were common on Sunday. Fortunately, most men appreciated Mr. Sheldon's deal.

She heard footsteps and looked up, but it wasn't Vyries. Three men came up the rocks, her regular dinner customers. They returned her nod and smile, but she felt awkward beside the cannon, so she stood up and brushed her skirts and was leaving as they opened a little lid on top and positioned something in it. One of the men pounded with the side of his pick. They had to be Sheldon's men, no doubt sent to spell Vyries and fix the cannon.

She walked all the way around, passing Ben, who remained occupied, crossed the bridge, and returned to the adobe. But she couldn't let it rest. She walked up the path to where she could see the dam from her side of the river and was about to sit on a rock, when she saw a large rattlesnake coiled on it. She backed up and tossed a stone. When the snake's tail buzzed, she found a different rock. Shuddering—rattlesnakes were so thick—she sat down tentatively and hadn't been there more than a few seconds when Indian Mary stepped beside her, Isabella on her back, Billy alongside. "My man says maybe trouble." Mary's face showed worry. "Your tall friend too?"

"Maybe." Their men would be on opposite sides. She patted the big rock beside her.

Sitting down, Indian Mary looked toward the cannon. "Big gun break big walls in war of black hats," she said. "Many people die."

"It's only to scare the miners. They won't need to fire it."

Then she noticed men descending the riverbank to join those already in the muddy riverbed. Other groups of men joined them too. She watched in sudden comprehension and shock as they converged and headed up the channel toward the dam, extracting their feet slowly from the mud, like men in a bad dream, axes and guns in hand. Three tall men were among them. Oh God, no! Would Vyries fire at them? She looked toward the high outcropping, but couldn't see the cannon. And though the miners arrived at the dam and raised their axes to it, no explosion sounded. Her stomach tightened in anticipation; but then with sudden and absolute clarity she knew that the men working on the cannon had not been on Mr. Sheldon's side. Had her talk with Vyries upset the balance?

A rider appeared on the crest of the opposite bluff—Señor Valdez looking down at the miners. He turned his horse and galloped away, dust rising. Mary stood up, staring after him.

❧

Pedro spurred Chocolate through the corn. He and the other scout arrived simultaneously. "Jared," Señor Lewis yelled, "they're axing the dam!" Sheldon threw down his shovel and looked toward the river, which couldn't be seen from there.

"It is true, patrón," Pedro said.

Sheldon's wolf eyes drilled him. "Then why don't I hear the cannon?" Instructions were to fire it if anyone touched the dam. To Señor Lewis, he ordered, "Ride to Sacramento, get the Sheriff." It would take hours.

Nodding, the man held out his rifle. "Here, Jared. I won't need this. You'd better take it."

Sheldon took the gun, picked up Little Will and ran for his horse, which was tied to an oak limb. He put Will in the saddle, mounted behind him and rode smoothly toward the river. He called Pedro to his side, and as they galloped together he said, "I thought that boy on the cannon was a good kid."

They rode beside the freshly dug ditch, past scattered tents, Sheldon shouting to his friends to drop what they were doing and join him. When they pulled the horses up at the bluff, about a hundred armed men stood below the sluice, many with picks and axes, all looking up at them. Sheldon's nostrils flared in angry disbelief.

To his left, the cannon dozed in the sun with its top open. The boy was nowhere to be seen. Across the river María and Elitha sat at safe distance downstream. From the riverbottom came a thunk. Then more thunks. Axes on wood.

Señores Johnson, Cody and the others arrived, panting, rifles in hand. "Why ain't that cannon blasting 'em all to hell?" Cody asked.

"Yeah! What the dev—"

"I will go see, patrón," Pedro said. He started to dismount.

"No," Sheldon said, "Tex, you do it." As Tex dismounted, Sheldon turned to Pedro and said, "Por favor, I trust you with what is mas importante, most important. Keep my son safe." He lifted Will from the saddle and held him, short legs walking in the air.

The child would hamper his ability to help. He sidestepped Chocolate and took the boy to his lap, but spoke from his heart. "Those men look dangerous, señor. The dam, he is not so important as your life."

"A man's gotta draw a line, Pedro. This here is my property. If I back down now, pretty soon I'll have nothing left."

Pedro glanced down at the angry mob and felt as if the grapeshot, which should have been felling these disgracers of God, was churning in his stomach.

Tex peered into the cannon port with the posture of a man discovering a broken axle. Looking up, he said, "Spiked." More thunks came from below.

Sheldon dismounted and gestured with his rifle. "Come on boys, follow me." He strode down the bank, boots skidding, gravel rolling ahead. His men followed, rifles in hand.

"Virgin help him," Pedro murmured, crossing himself.

The boy looked up asking, "What did you say?"

"It was a prayer, muchacho."

Outnumbered ten to one, Sheldon walked toward the miners. It flashed in Pedro's mind that he could leave the child and help, but no. The boy might follow, and Jared had said his boy was mas importante.

Pedro could see the patrón standing face to face with the miners. His clear voice carried up the bank: "You men are trespassing. The next one touches that dam dies!" In a line behind him, his friends raised their rifles, maybe twelve of them.

A shot exploded. The boy flinched.

A man collapsed and fell over a rock. A shout: "Give it to Sheldon." Pedro held his breath.

Multiple gun reports echoed up the river. Men fell, Sheldon face down in the mud. Sick to his stomach and gripping the child's hand, Pedro watched helplessly as men scrambled into the rocks. Shots rang off boulders and thudded into the wooden dam. Men ducked in and out as they fired. The boy was urgently asking a question, indistinct as if underwater.

"Hold your fire!" somebody yelled.

Slowly men crept into the open. Some of the miners toed up the bank, guns in hand, hat brims down over their faces. It had happened in less than a minute. The shooting was over.

Sheldon's men squatted and turned Sheldon onto his back.

Pedro said to the young child, "Can you sit on those rocks by yourself? And not move?" The boy nodded. Pedro dismounted, quickly hobbled the horse, and sat the boy down, giving him a stern finger. Little Will looked like he'd never move again.

Pedro went down. The patrón's eyes were open but blood ran from a large hole in his right breast and from his left armpit, a single ball having torn through him and come out. Señor Johnson was badly wounded, blood pumping through his shirt from an opening over his heart. Señor Cody writhed and moaned, bleeding from the abdomen. Others gripped their wounds and clenched their teeth. No miner that Pedro could see was dead or wounded.

Armed miners remained in the riverbottom; men with axes watched from the sluice on top of the dam. They had won. Pedro's heart boomed with pent-up, futile pain, wishing he could turn back time. What had gone wrong? So terribly and irreparably wrong?

Looking down at Sheldon, he could hardly see him for the moisture in his eyes.

Weakly the patrón whispered, "My son?"

"He is well, señor, up there." He pointed, blinking tears. "Now I take you to your house." Only a miracle could save a man losing that much blood, but Señora Catherine would want him near her. As he lifted Sheldon's feet and another man took his arms, a splintering thunk came from the dam. And another, and another.

"You bastards!" a man yelled. "At least wait until we git the wounded outa here." The hacking stopped.

When they had Sheldon halfway up the bank, the sounds resumed. Pedro rode with the boy alongside Jared Sheldon, who hung face down over his own saddle. A friend of Jared's led his horse by the reins. Others took Johnson and Cody to their tents. The ride from the dam to the cabin, which had always seemed short, now seemed long, but they couldn't rush it with the patrón bleeding so badly.

Still trembling with shock and rage and the need to turn back time, Pedro helped carry Joaquín Sheldon into his new cabin and laid him gently on the pine floor at the feet of his wife. She stared down, her infant in her arms, and then kneeled beside her husband, blood pooling around both of them.

Sheldon's eyes were rolled back in his head and his lids fluttered. "Is Pa dead?" asked Will, his innocent face troubled.

"No," Pedro said, turning around, gulping back emotion. *Más importante.*

The señora laid the baby on a chair, then she tore strips of the infant's blanket and pressed them into the wounds. Hands trembling, she took her husband's hand and put it between hers, leaned down and kissed his lips. An eighteen-year-old widow with three children.

Pedro said, "I will ride for María. She knows herb medicine." But he knew it was hopeless. On the floor lay the most honorable man he had ever known, killed by gold miners. He knew as he went out the door that his last link to the so-called civilized world had been severed.

Watching for snakes, Elitha stepped down through the rocks, the dam drawing her like a magnet in a nightmare. María was running up the path toward Bridge House looking for Pedro Valdez. They had been too far away to see the shooting, and it happened too fast. Men were being carried out. Who? Mr. Sheldon? "Couldn't be." Ben? "Couldn't be." These words kept time with her steps and competed with the gunshots still ringing in her ears.

The mud was deep in the riverbottom so she made her way along the side, over humps of clay and around coyote holes. She couldn't distinguish her heartbeat from the thuds of axes. Questions jumped to mind. Had men died because Vyries left the cannon? Who fired first? Was it her fault?

When she got there, Ben wasn't among the men chopping at the dam. No men lay among the rocks, though some blood-covered boulders resembled bloodied heads poking out of the mud. A man cried, "Stand back!" The men with axes dashed for the south bank. She climbed the bank, realizing she should have crossed the river when she had the chance.

Water spouted from an opening in the sluice as if from a giant faucet. Then with a noisy crack, a timber broke and the rush of water widened, breaking loose another timber until it flowed easily, washing the blood down the river and rising up around the bald red rocks, smooth fingers of water rapidly probing their way downstream. Miners wrestled their rockers back from the rising flow.

Elitha gathered her skirts and broke into a run back toward the bridge. She had to find Ben.

But the sight of lathered horses outside the Sheldon cabin brought her feet to a halt. One of those horses belonged to Pedro Valdez, and the saddle on Jared Sheldon's horse was bloody. Gasping for breath, and with a gathering sense of dread, she knocked.

Catherine opened the door and stared as if blind, the white of her face as shocking as the huge red pool of blood on the floor. Mr. Sheldon lay in the middle of it, still as a statue, mouth open, face blank. The brightness of the blood dulled all else in the room—the baby fussing in the chair, little Will sobbing and little Sarah staring. Three babies. Two miners squatted beside Mr. Sheldon with their hats off in prayer.

Indian Mary and Mr. Valdez passed Elitha, going out the door she stood in.

"Oh Catey!" Elitha stepped toward her friend.

"You'd better go," Catherine said in the distant voice of a stranger. "Ben Wilder did this."

Slowly Elitha backed out as Catherine shut the door. Feeling as though her body were melting apart, she stood numbly outside the door. Oh dear God in heaven, no. Jared Sheldon was dead or Indian Mary wouldn't be leaving. She had to sit, out of sight of the cabin. Out of sight of Mr. Valdez and Indian Mary, who were mounting his horse, out of sight of the ogling driver clucking his team across the bridge, and the Chinese miners trotting behind, out of sight of the curious men coming down from Cook's Bar. She couldn't talk to Ben or anyone until she could breathe again. Until the pieces of her firmed up and came back together.

Shakily she went down the steep rocky incline and sat under the bridge watching the recently pent-up river hurl itself through the boulders. The splash of it swirled with the tempest in her mind. Overhead, the rumble of wagons and hollow tattoo of hooves and boots drummed along with her confused heart. The cursed adobe and condor feathers hung over her. The world had gone crazy. She was responsible for Jared Sheldon's death. She had neglected Elizabeth in her time of need. She had been blinded by her love for Ben, and now her best friend had shut her out, a girl with three babies and no husband. For all she knew Ben was dead too, but she hadn't the strength to go see. She felt paralyzed in the shade of the noisy bridge.

Later, unaware of the passage of time, Pa's words came to her. You got the Donner blood. Nothing can stop you. Just go down the trail. But Pa, she heard herself sob in disagreement, it is a path littered with death. Heads like signposts along a road, beloved people buried to the neck stared at her as she passed by. How many? She didn't know. But she had to find out if Ben was among them.

Slowly picking up one foot and then the other she climbed up through the boulders under the bridge. The horses were gone from the Sheldon cabin, the wagon gone too. No doubt they'd taken him back to the mill house and would bury him in the Indian mound beside Mr. Daylor. Sheldon and Daylor together again. In the space of two years she and the Rhoads sisters, Elizabeth, Sarah and Catherine, were all widows. She yearned to be included in the circle of their forgiving arms, to ease the guilt scraping through her, and to help Catey with her babies. But the door had shut in her face. Perhaps deservedly so.

The sun had moved across the sky and the river quieted to its normal summer flow, miners washing dirt as if nothing had happened. She arrived at the

Cook's Bar Eating House and looked over the heads of the eating men, Ben not among them. She then headed toward the Wilder claim, beyond the dam.

She came over a rise and saw the crude fence, but no tent. A square of packed earth marked where it had been. The Wilder long tom lay on its side. Her heart pounded as she approached the river's edge where a man was rocking a cradle. He looked up, touched his hat and smiled. "Ma'am?"

"Howdy. Would you know where I might find Ben Wilder?"

"Nope. Them Wilder boys abandoned their claim. Looked awful keen to clear out, I'd say." Watching that hit her—every man in Cook's Bar knew she and Ben were to be married—he pushed the upper box back and forth over the lower box, sand and gravel dropping to roll down the screen, dirty water leaking from the spout at the bottom.

"Thank you," she managed, much of her leaking out too. Cleared out. Alive. Maybe he had tried to find her, but she'd been under the bridge. She returned to the Cook's Bar Eating House, walked up the aisle between men who stared at her, opened the door and went into the kitchen. *Cleared out like a guilty man.*

Three women turned from the counter, Mrs. Gordon and her daughters, their sleeves rolled up on hairy arms. Elitha collapsed on a chair.

Mrs. Gordon furrowed her heavy brow. "You're not cooking supper over at your place tonight?"

"No. I was wondering if you knew where Ben Wilder went." It hurt her pride to admit she didn't know.

Mrs. Gordon wiped her hands on her apron and pulled up a chair. Lorena went out the door with a stack of plates and a steaming pot hanging at her knees, "All I know is what I'm about to say." Her manner, sympathetic and motherly, increased Elitha's alarm.

"I got dinner done and set out by noon, but the men came in late. By then the grease was skinned over. And my, what a sorry lot they were!" She glanced away, frowning at the memory. "Their chins hung right down to their chests. You could just see the—" She stopped as if searching for a word, and settled on, "remorse."

Narrowing a dark eye, she continued, "Ben Wilder took one look at the food and ran outside. He retched good and long out there. In the meantime his brothers said, over and over, 'If only we hadn't done it. If only we hadn't done any of it.' Just like that. Over and over. Finally Ben comes back in and says to me, 'Mrs. Gordon, I can't eat.' He slumped down on one of the benches for the longest time with his head on the table. Then, when most of the men had gone, I came over and ladled the stew so he could see all the goodness in it, but he shook his head. Then he settled his bill and says to me, 'I'm done with mining, for good.' Just like that. He went out the door, and I haven't seen hide nor hair of him since. Would've asked about you, but he was heading out so fast—" She gave Elitha a pinched expression of sorrow—a woman who had brought six daughters to California to find husbands. "He didn't talk to you?"

"I wasn't home." She needed to escape the pitying eyes. He had to be guilty.

"Mr. Johnson and Mr. Cody died too," Mrs. Gordon said, adding to the horror, "and more bad wounded."

"Any miners hurt?"

"One that I know of."

One-sided. She forced a thank you and left.

Outside, men were talking to a young man in a nice gray suit. He was scratching notes in a tablet. He raised his chin and said, "Excuse me, miss. I'm with *The Sacramento Union*. Did you happen to see the riot this morning?"

"No." She hurried toward the bridge, knowing the reporter had gotten an earful. *Riot.* Would all of California soon read that Ben Wilder had led a murderous mob? And that Elitha Donner had been his intended?

Dread slowed her steps as she crossed the bridge. Ben could be hiding at her place, expecting her to protect him. Could she tell him to get out? Catey's face kept coming at her, the way she'd looked shutting the door. It brought to mind the expressions of certain people when they had called her a cannibal, expressions that said she occupied the unwanted side of the world. Passing by, she saw the door of the Sheldon cabin gaping open, a place as empty as its owner's heart.

Her adobe was also empty. She searched, but found no note. The sun was going down. Elizabeth was dead. Perry was dead, Pa and Tamsen, Uncle Jacob and Aunt Betsy, her cousins, and all the others taken from her. And now Mr. Sheldon. People picked themselves up after a barn burned or a loved one died, but this was more. She was alone on the trail and had no place to go.

# 87

Long hours of work and talks with Indian Mary kept Elitha going. She hauled water up from the river and brought in loads of oak limbs, chopped wood, dickered with professional hunters who sold her strings of birds. She singed and plucked feathers and cooked meals for larger and larger crowds. She spoke little with her customers and declined many invitations to sings, stage performances and other events. At night she slept in the adobe with a knife and Perry's gun.

Then the Bridge House Dance Hall was completed and she began accepting invitations. Music and dancing helped put Ben out of her mind, and she was glad she hadn't married him. She was also glad the turnover of miners was so great that most of them had never heard of him. Nevertheless, she couldn't forget the "horrible riot in the Cosumne," as *The Sacramento Union* had called it. She felt driven to learn every detail of what had happened.

On the shelf with her dishes she kept the folded newspaper containing the lengthy article, re-reading it often. Forty to a hundred miners had been involved. Then the words she couldn't stop reading:

> *... we are informed that a man by the name of Wilder, who had settled upon and built a sort of brush fence around a small piece of land in the immediate neighborhood of the selected location of the dam, objected to his (Sheldon) building the dam at that point, and claimed, by settlement, the property. Mr. Sheldon took immediate steps to eject the man... and commenced preparation to go on with the work. In a short time, however, he was informed by a body of miners who were working in the river some distance above and with whom Wilder was engaged, that he could not construct a dam at the point alluded to....*

The story told of the event in bloody detail, but the account seemed one-sided. It named twelve men who worked for Mr. Sheldon or were his friends; clearly they had provided most of the information. And the writer did not directly accuse Ben.

> *We have since been told that the mining party charged Mr. Sheldon's men with having first fired. Sheriff Harris has informed us that the miners engaged in the riot are willing to put themselves into the hands of the law, and abide by the results of the trial. We forbear to express any opinion in regard to these scenes of blood and inhuman conflict as far as the respective parties are concerned, because we know that an adjudication of the case by law will be the only true guide that can be used in forming a conclusion, and because our feelings are too deeply and profoundly affected by the strong prejudices of friendship towards some of the parties on one side to speak with impartiality.*

Six weeks passed without mention of a trial, in the newspaper or from anyone's mouth. Neither did she hear word from Ben. She thought it for the best. Perhaps he had gone back to Rhode Island. But it cut terribly that she could not help Catherine, who would be grieving so, and tell her how sorry she was.

One day a bespectacled stranger appeared in Elitha's yard, a young man with an air of unusual vitality. She judged him to be in his early thirties. "They say the fare is good here," he said in a schooled Southern accent, doffing an elegant gray top hat in one hand and gripping a carpetbag in the other.

"Room for one more," she said ladling out beans. She pointed at the ground. "If you don't mind sitting there in your fine clothing." It was noon. Sweat soaked the upper half of her dress and trickled from her temples.

He pulled a handkerchief from his pocket and dabbed his face. "Maybe I can squeeze in over there, if those gentlemen in the shade don't mind."

Within a few minutes she noticed half her regular customers were listening to the stranger and answering his questions. As she cut squares in the pan of corn bread, she heard snatches about the prospects around here and mining techniques. Stepping carefully through the seated men, she extended the pan toward him, asking, "Where you from?" The first time in weeks she'd roused herself to wonder about any of them.

His face was smooth, oval, and alert, his spectacles thick. "Louisiana. Name's Oliver Wozencraft. Lately of Washington, District of Columbia."

The Capitol. What was he doing here dressed in a gray pinstriped suit, asking men about mining? "I am Elitha McCoon," she told him. At his gentlemanly acknowledgement, she turned to start another pan of coffee.

"I've talked to some people down in Slough House and Cosumne who say you've been here a long time, Miz McCoon," he said. She turned. He continued, "They say you know the local Indians. I'd like to speak to them, if you could arrange it. I understand they are in hiding."

It was a link with Catherine and Sarah, no matter how fragile. But what was this about Indians? The surrounding men seemed equally amazed to hear this from a man in an expensive suit and top hat.

"I'm a federal Indian Agent," he continued, eyeing her through his thick lenses, "setting up reservations for the California Indians."

She didn't know what that meant, and began to wonder if he was one of the unscrupulous men swarming all over the hills looking for Indian "vagrants" to sell as "apprentices." It was a brisk underhanded business that made some men rich. She told him she'd talk with him when she was through serving dinner. He ate, probing the other men the whole time about the frequency of the rains and other topics. Then after everybody else left, she suggested they take a walk up the path to the old Indian village.

He put on his hat and they strolled in that direction while she told him about the people who once inhabited Rancho Sacayak, a name that had been all but forgotten. She told about the massacre, but withheld the fact that some Indians still lived nearby.

Mr. Wozencraft shook his head sadly, and said he had come to negotiate treaties with the surviving Indians, to provide them with reservations where they would be safe. So far, he had been north to Mount Shasta and all through the valley. He and two other agents were arranging more than four hundred separate treaties, but he was hindered by the fact that so many Indians were in hiding.

This was, she thought, too elaborate a ruse for an Indian trader. As they ambled toward the remains of Sheldon's dam—he claiming to be a trained medical doctor and personal friend of President Fillmore—she realized that what he proposed would be a blessing to the Indians. But something about him bothered her. Why would such a man settle for work with Indians? "Would they be put on good land?" she asked, thinking to draw him out on the details.

"I'd see to it. The President means to tame the West in every respect, and that starts with the Indians. They must learn to farm, and farming means good ground. They must learn to plough and sew and—" he broke off and stood staring at the river. "Say, that looks like the remains of a dam down there." He pointed at the protruding uprights and horizontal oak planks, water eddying and swirling around the broken sides.

Briefly she explained what had happened.

"Well, I'll be." He stood admiring the dam's construction, the backs of his hands on his waist, topcoat threaded through an arm. "Just what this country needs! The first time I came out West, in forty-nine, I traveled the Santa Fe Trail. Ever since, I've been telling Congress they must invest in dams, water being the most critical element to the development of the West—that and railroads." He slung his coat over a shoulder and pointed at the dam. "And here I find somebody else had the same idea." He wagged his head in pleased wonderment, perspiration trickling into his sideburns.

It occurred to her he was a builder looking for free labor. "You've spoken to Congress about dams and railroads?" she said. *It didn't fit.*

A smile pushed his glasses up on his cheeks. "They haven't responded."

Not wanting to challenge him directly, she said. "I'm right worried about the Indians, and I can't help but be surprised an Indian agent would be speaking to Congress about dams."

He studied her through the thick lenses, but showed no anger. "And I wouldn't have thought the lovely young proprietress of an eating establishment would take such an interest in Indians. I have papers."

"I'd like to see them." She led the way back to the adobe where he'd left his bag. Inside, where it was cooler, she sat him on "Ben's stool," sat down herself at the table, and studied the stack of papers he fished from his carpetbag—all related to treaties with Indians, including some that chiefs had signed with Xs. Two letters addressed to Mr. O. M. Wozencraft were signed by President Fillmore and bore the seal of the United States government.

"Looks all right," she said as he returned the papers to the bag and buckled the clasp. "But a bag like that could be stolen."

He smiled like he admired her for being so cautious. "I invite you, Mrs. Mc-

Coon, to write to the President of the Mechanics Institute of San Francisco—a friend of mine and a man of excellent character, known by everybody from Sam Brannan on down. He'll vouch for me. Meantime, I'll stay at Forest Home till I hear from you. Word is, that hotel is as fine as any in these United States."

Only three days later Elitha received her reply: a letter redolent in praise of Mr. Wozencraft, attesting to his veracity as a federal Indian Agent. What surprised her most was the speed of the mail. Steamboat side-wheelers churned from San Francisco to Sacramento in six to ten hours now—a voyage that had taken her and Perry over a week one way. Times were changing fast. Maybe the Indians would finally get some help.

She sent a note to Forest Home, offering to arrange a meeting between Mr. Wozencraft and Captain Juan.

# 88

Beneath the unfamiliar but friendly yellow pines, María Howchia sat in the talk circle beside Grizzly Hair, covertly looking at the smooth face of Mr. Wozencraft. She noticed that the round lenses balanced on his nose enlarged his eyes as he turned this way or that. Baby Isabella, who stood upright in her staked bikoos, stared openly at him. He had met them at this place, where he wanted the peoples of the six remnant bands to live. She and Father had left at dawn with Pedro, who rode ahead and watched for bad men. They arrived in late afternoon. The five other hy-apos in the circle spoke the same tongue, and she could tell by their questions that they were suspicious of this Americano despite the good things Elitha said about him.

Pedro repeated each of Wozencraft's English utterances in Spanish, and María repeated it in the tongue of umne. Wozencraft had brought three Americano "witnesses," including Billy Rhoads, the brother of Catherine and Sarah, who also sat in the talk circle although they didn't talk. The rest of Grizzly Hair's remnant band, including little Billy, had stayed in the boulder house, but the wives and children of the other hy-apos had accompanied their men to this meeting place. Not wanting to listen to the talk, they were exploring the place to see what they could find for supper.

"When you sign the treaty," Mr. Wozencraft said, "you promise to be under the control of the United States government. You promise not to steal or kill, or injure United States citizens, and you promise not to return to your old lands. In return, you will live here in safety." He opened his arms to the beautiful valley, saying it was only a small part of the "reservation."

"Would Americanos hunt and fish and wash gold here?" They had seen miners shoveling and panning all the way along the river.

"No," Mr. Wozencraft answered. "Only the Indians of the six bands here represented would be allowed on this property."

Grizzly Hair lifted his brows just enough to let his doubt show, then turned to talk quietly with Mi-ony-quish. During this pause in translation, María recalled Pedro's scorn about reservations. Nevertheless, he had agreed to escort them here, ready to protect them with his guns if necessary. During the long walk he had spotted a group of miners that had interested him, though he kept himself and his horse out of sight.

"They believe miners never will leave this place," María explained to Pedro, who explained to Wozencraft. Grizzly Hair had briefly told Mi-ony-quish what had happened to Señor Sheldon when he interfered with gold washing in the home place.

Wozencraft said. "I speak for the big chief President Fillmore who lives in Washington. He will make them all leave."

She feared that he lacked wisdom. Grizzly Hair voiced a discrepancy. "Captain Sutter is Inyo agent. He speaks for the big chief."

The oval face remained calm. "The State appointed Mr. Sutter to count Indians. He only…." He changed directions, "I am from Washington Dee Cee." Many times he had mentioned that place, clearly a place of power.

"This place is good," Grizzly Hair said glancing around. "Water clear." The other chiefs nodded. They too liked this land where the river cascaded over the rocks but also slowed down near some flat granite slabs that collected the sun's heat. The desperate survivors of the six bands hoped for food and safety. Clearly this place was the home of deer and many food plants. Too good to be true, Pedro had said beneath his breath before the talk started.

Poltuk of the Loclumne leaned forward, meaning she should translate: "We need guns. Will the Big Hy-apo give us guns?" Sadness showed in Father's gaze at the mention of guns. When Mr. Wozencraft heard it he stiffened.

"Absolutely no guns. That's the whole point. There will be no hostility toward the people of the United States."

The sad look lingered in Grizzly Hair's face. He wanted no killing. He hated guns. Now he changed the subject, asking to hear exactly what goods would be received in exchange for the people moving here for all time.

Mr. Wozencraft reached inside his cloth bag and drew out a paper. After each item Pedro and then María translated:

500 head of cattle, averaging 500 pounds apiece
200 sacks of flour weighing 100 pounds each
75 brood mares and 3 stallions
300 milk cows and 18 bulls
12 yoke of work cattle
12 work mules or horses
25 plows, assorted sizes.

This last item drew questions. "What is plow?" Pedro explained it and María explained it again—a tool pulled by an ox or a horse that rips big grooves in the earth. All the hy-apos looked amused.

Mi-ony-quish asked, "Why tear the earth when plants know how to grow in the earth as she is?" Hearing the answer, that plowing makes corn and wheat grow more abundantly, Poltuk asked, "Why should we grow strange plants when our own food is already abundant?"

Appearing unfazed, Wozencraft continued his list without answering those questions.

200 garden hoes
80 spades
12 grindstones
1 pair of strong pantaloons and 1 flannel shirt to each man
1 linsey gown for each woman and girl
4000 yards of calico and 1000 yards of sheeting
40 pounds of Scotch thread
2 dozen pairs of scissors.

From his bag he pulled out a snapping instrument with sharp blades and used it to cut a thin curl from the bottom of his paper. María and all the headmen stared in wonderment at the clever device.

8 dozen thimbles
3000 needles
1 Mackinaw blanket for each man and woman over 15 years old
4000 pounds of iron
4000 pounds of steel

Santiago said quietly in Spanish. "In the mission I learned to bend iron. What is steel?"

Pedro answered, "It is like iron but harder."

Wozencraft leaned forward and said, "None of the stock—that means horses, mules, and cows—are to be killed, sold or exchanged without the consent of the agent. That's me."

"You have many animals." Grizzly Hair said.

"Well, uh, the government owns them, but you would have use of them. Big Chief Fillmore wants the animals to bear many young for you. You take care of them."

Hin-co-ye, a doctor who'd been leading his remnant group since their hy-apo died said, "We like to eat animals."

"Only with my permission," said Wozencraft. "Milk the cows. Use the mules and horses to pull the plows. Don't eat them. This is the beginning of a big Indian farm."

"Rancho," Pedro translated.

"I am asking you to sign these lines to agree with this good and generous offer." Looking around the circle, Wozencraft added: "You must learn to live like white men."

María pictured the homeless, dirty, hungry men who wandered around with tents on their backs and wondered why they should live like that. She saw the same question in the faces of the hy-apos, but instead they asked about the goods, each question answered by Wozencraft in a friendly, straightforward manner. She could tell that the others shared her opinion of the man: He had good intentions but they doubted his knowledge.

The golden light from the low sun filtered through the dark pines, highlighting clusters of reddening toyon berries. The spirits of the place were peaceful. She glanced at Pedro, and saw in his aloof manner that he disdained the agreement. Others wouldn't see it. They didn't know him like she did.

Grizzly Hair spoke in the tongue of the People. "I will mark the paper. I see no harm in that. If too many Americanos come, Wozencraft and Headman Fillmore will ask them to leave. Maybe they cannot make them go, but we will hunt and fish better here than where we are now. Many deer, many rabbits, many birds and food plants live here. This land paper means respect and good luck. I will mark it."

María knew he was right. She felt the power of the earth here, not destroyed or weakened by intruders. She told Wozencraft, "He will mark paper." The other men nodded agreement.

A smile pushed up the strange man's glasses. Opening his bag, he brought out a feather and a bottle of dark fluid. He gave the quill to Billy Rhoads and the other witnesses, who dipped the quill and made squiggly marks on the paper.

Grizzly Hair took the quill next and Wozencraft, with his finger, showed him what the mark should be. Father drew a big strong X on his line. When the other five had marked their lines, Mr. Wozencraft said, "Now, each Indian must tell me his name." He dipped the quill and held it expectantly on the line beside the first X.

The men were prepared for this rudeness. Each one gave the next man's name—Hin-co-ye carefully pronounced Grizzly Hair's name in the tongue of the umne, Mi-ony-quish presented Hin-co-ye's name, and so on. When Wozencraft finished scratching, he grabbed the paper with a pinching device that left a round mark with many tiny indentations, the mark of Headman Fillmore, he explained. Then he produced an identical paper, and the ritual was repeated, each step exactly the same. The second paper he presented to Grizzly Hair.

With a dignified nod, Father accepted it, and then pushed slowly to his feet—his back still hurting, the torn trousers loose on his hips—and shook his land paper in each of the four directions, each time declaring: "Our new home place."

To María he said, "Tell Señor Valdez to ride back for Spear Thrower and the others. You and I stay in our new place." He then extended his hand to Mr. Wozencraft, who seemed surprised, perhaps not knowing that Indians had seen this custom. After they shook hands, Grizzly Hair told María to ask when the listed goods would arrive.

Wozencraft answered, "After President Fillmore and the Senate ratify, that is, mark the paper." Pedro and María translated.

Grizzly Hair pointed to the paper and said, "Mark already here."

"Yes, but they must see your names first," Wozencraft said. "Then they write their names on the paper too." After the translation, while the others watched Wozencraft show where the mark of the man named Senate would be, Pedro rolled his eyes skyward.

The other five hy-apos talked it over, and she was proud they agreed that the second land paper should remain in Grizzly Hair's possession. As his gaze swept over the new home place, she realized he'd been right about making friends among the new people, and she was proud of him. Americanos had honored the People.

And Pedro no longer needed to go to Mexico. He would live here in a new u-macha.

Mr. Wozencraft stood up and retired to his own fire, where the witnesses were preparing his supper. Tomorrow he would leave on the long journey to his home in Washington Dee Cee.

On the way here, Pedro had spotted one of the two Omuchumne killers left living. This morning the faces of the killers' companions had been hidden as they squatted over gold pans, but if Lady Fortuna smiled, both of Pedro's prey would be camped at the same place. Captain Juan had asked him to go and bring the people from the boulder house. Gladly, he agreed. He'd leave at the first light, which would put him in that killer's camp about breakfast time.

He looked at his Little Poppy, nursing Isabella, her silence conveying disappointment that he lacked faith in the North American paper. All along he'd seen her hope and therefore hid his distrust, but now that the meeting was over he needed to speak truth. The other Indias, back from their exploration, were preparing supper, so when the baby finished her supper, he asked María to walk with him down to the river. She shrugged the bikoos on her back.

As they walked through the low coyote brush she said in a heart-melting tone, "You are not happy for us."

That required a little thought. Watching for rattlesnakes, he said, "If I trusted North Americans I would be very happy for you. I am afraid your people will expect too much from that paper, and be sad later."

She didn't reply for some time, but then said, "The land paper is all my people have. It has given us something to look forward to. The North Americans have shown respect, giving us a place to live where we can hunt and gather."

"I have a land paper too, but it is worthless." Pedro referred to the paper Elitha had given him. "But there is much more. We Californios hear many stories about our countrymen who went to court with lawyers only to have their land papers declared worthless." Looking over, seeing her displeasure, he explained, "North Americans do not honor the land papers of Español grandees, even though their Senate and the Big hy-apo in Washington put their marks on the end-of-war paper—a paper that said they could keep the lands the Mexican government had given them. I believe they will honor your land paper even less. I am sorry to say this, but you know that most North Americans have no respect for Indians, and they will be angry to learn that beautiful land with gold has been promised to your people."

María said, "When the horses and cows and all the other things come, you will see. You won't need to go to Mexico. You can build your hacienda right here."

He had recently returned from another trip to Mexico where he had helped take a big caballada of horses and a large bag of gold—a fifth of it his. He felt that Mexico was his home now, but he loved his little wife so much that he spoke truth when he replied, "I will wait with you, mi amor, and I will see what I see. But do not forget how happy we could be in Mexico, where North Americans are very few."

On their way back to the supper fire, which beckoned more brightly in the twilight, María's tone also brightened. "Show your land paper to Señor Wozencraft," she said. "He can mark it with the power of the Headman in Washington Dee Cee."

Suppressing a mocking remark Pedro noticed that, in fact, the tall-hatted Mr. Wozencraft had left the Americano fire and seemed to be waiting for him.

Pedro faced him, alert and ready when Señor Wozencraft said, "Mr. Valdez, wasn't it?"

"Sí, señor."

"Are you aware what an Indian reservation is?"

"I believe so."

"I must inform you, Mr. Valdez, that no Mexicans may dwell upon these grounds, or benefit in any way from the largesse of the United States."

Pedro narrowed his eyes at the man, the round lenses blank in the twilight. "I am a native Californian. I was born in this country and this is my wife." He put his hand on María's shoulder.

"Californios are excluded from the reservation."

"Are you telling me to leave?"

"Not this minute. But I must advise you that if you are seen here with the Indians, I'll be getting letters of protest. It could ruin the ratification process. It would be advisable for you to take your wife to your hacienda." He seemed pleased to know a Spanish word. *Que cabrón!*

Holding back a furious retort, Pedro glanced over at the Indians around the fire, polite in their silence. The last thing he wanted to do was destroy their "good luck," however slim its chances. "No one will see me live here," he told the man. "I give you my word."

Mr. Wozencraft stared at him through the round glasses, and then finally dipped his head in seeming approval, and returned to his fire.

María sounded hurt. "You told him you will not live here with me."

"I said no one will see me living here. We talk later, Amapolita, when we are alone."

Captain Juan spoke in the home tongue. María explained. "Father says we will hold a big time when all the other peoples have arrived. Everyone is happy."

"Good," Pedro said with a yawn. "I will eat quickly and go to sleep early tonight, so I can get up very early tomorrow."

# 89

The Indians were asleep when Pedro rode out. Later Wozencraft would lead them around, pointing out distant landmarks defining their supposed new territory. Meanwhile Pedro rode downstream past the fork in the river, and found the camp. He waited in the willows, positioned to see the five sleeping men.

Color spilled over the ridge top where the sun would rise, and birds rioted in the cottonwoods and willows. A noisy company. A man crawled from his blankets, unbuttoned his long underwear and urinated. Not the right one. At the fort Pedro had met men from every land, and knew such underwear was not worn beneath buckskins. Trappers wore leather next to their skin, and slept in it. He waited.

A man in buckskin rolled to his knees and staggered to his feet, wiping sleep from his eyes. The fringe hung motionless as he shot an arc of water into the willows. Chocolate stepped nervously, sensing Pedro's alertness. Patting his neck, he whispered, "He is my man, but El Bandido Cuidadoso, he is patient." The man's friends slept with their guns.

The North American's return woke up the other four. Their horses grazed so far away they didn't whinny or pay any attention to Chocolate. After eating, the miners went down to the stream and began shoveling. But all men had to shit. Pedro nudged Chocolate to a spot where he could see the tops of their hats. About an hour later, he saw Buckskin trudging up the bank alone, heading into the willows.

With a light touch of the sides of his boots, he walked the horse slowly toward the willows. Gravel rolled. The miners in the river looked up. He dipped his hat in casual greeting and proceeded behind a wall of brambles as they refocused on their work. The babbling of the stream and the cacophony of birds covered the soft hoof sounds up to a point. He stopped a short distance away.

So far he'd had good luck. Through an opening in the willows he saw the goat squatting, facing the other away. Pedro took his lariat, realizing this would test his skill. The clearing was narrow. Trees and bushes were the enemy of a lasso. It would be like threading a needle. Está bien. He could do that.

With a glance to be sure the others hadn't followed, he snaked out a small loop, circling, feeling the weight of the rope, judging the distance. "Son of a whore," he called softly as he let fly.

The man's head jerked toward him as the loop settled around his neck. He and Chocolate were one, backing and tightening the noose. "Remember the little Indian children you killed, and the women."

Then he let Chocolate feel the spurs. The horse bounded into a gallop, the rope snapping tight across his thigh. He turned back to see the man dragging behind, gritting his teeth, trying to dig his fingers in between his beard and the horsehair rope. His pants trailed from his boots. Pedro called back to him, "Now you can shit, mister."

Shots whistled by. He leaned down to the mane, spurring southward, and the shots stopped very soon. They didn't want to risk their lives for this one, he realized. Besides, he was flying away on the fastest horse in California. He didn't look back.

Later as he reined down a boulder-strewn cañon and picked his way through poison oak and piled rocks, the lariat suddenly tightened on his thigh. He looked back. The head had come through the rocks, but not the shoulders. He touched Chocolate. The horse pulled, then stopped and turned a questioning eye on him.

"Go muchacho," Pedro urged without looking back. The big animal threw his weight into it. He felt the rope cut into his thigh, then pop slack.

He rode on, waiting for the anger to lift and relief to replace it, as it always had before. He coiled the lariat, hung it on the saddle pin, and considered going back to see the faces of the other men, but this time he felt no such relief or joy. He was finished killing.

# 90

For five moons the People had lived in the new home place given to them by Wozencraft from Washington Dee Cee. Not trusting the gold diggers, who became more numerous all the time, the men had built the u-machas on the hill where intruders could been seen from every direction. María and the children slept in the house with Grizzly Hair and Broken Salmon, Pedro visiting at night. Not a day went by without someone wondering aloud when the goods and animals would come from the big hy-apo, President Fillmore.

One morning María left Isabella in Salmon Woman's care and took Billy and Little Flicker to gather mushrooms in the pine forest. The intermittent rain had stopped and the shimmering pines smelled unusually fragrant under the partly cloudy blue sky.

Little Flicker, who still didn't talk, pointed to a large cream-colored fungus. María pronounced its name and tore the heavy prize in half. Billy pointed at a stand of hooded gray fungi pushing out of a rotten log. Delighted, she plucked all but four and tossed them in her burden basket. "Always leave some of the mushroom people, so we can have more next time."

"They come again in time of rain," Billy filled in. She smiled at him.

As María and Little Flicker skirted the hillside, Billy called and pointed. "Grandfather is going to the river."

María went to Billy and looked down. Grizzly Hair, Stalking Egret and Spear Thrower were walking toward several Americanos who stood beside a wagon piled with goods. She noticed Grizzly Hair's stride—not as bent and halting as usual. Hope soared in María.

"Children," she said, "I'm going down there to talk for Grandfather. Go to the u-macha." She positioned her carrying basket.

"I want to stay and hunt mushroom people," Billy said.

She shook her head at the little man. "Remember, children do not collect mushrooms alone. Go to Salmon Woman."

Before she reached the little meadow beside the river where the strangers had stopped, she detected disrespect in the North American faces. Then she heard it in their talk as they looked at Grizzly Hair. He took two steps backward, and fear punched her stomach. Meanwhile two of the Americanos had taken a long, toothed implement from the wagon, and now stood on opposite sides of a generous pine and began pulling the blade back and forth between them, chewing into the soft flesh.

At the home place she had seen many tree friends cut down. In an alarmed impulse she stepped from the manzanita bushes and went to the tree. Touching the cold metal and said, "No. Not to cut. This good tree."

One of the sawyers shoved her so hard she fell back to the ground on her carrying basket. Slowly she rose to her feet, leaving the basket and the mushrooms on the ground. They didn't understand.

She said, "This tree is strong healer. He gives medicine."

Grizzly Hair added in English, which he had been learning, "Tree helps Americans too." They continued pushing and pulling, the flakes flying.

The tree cried shrilly and María felt the cut as if it were her flesh. It took her voice away. Grizzly Hair gestured around at the boundaries of the new home place. "Inyo home place. Inyo tree. Big chief in Washington give to Inyo."

"Jed," said one of the men, "What's that Digger yammerin bout?"

"Land paper," Grizzly Hair said, pulling the tightly folded square from his loincloth thong, where he always carried it. "We sit. We talk." She saw that he avoided looking at the suffering tree and tried to ignore the wet squeak of the saw and pine essence spilling around them as the men continued sawing. She would never understand why Americanos burned the best medicine trees for firewood.

The man nearest Grizzly Hair yanked the paper from his hand, shaking it open. "Well, I'll be. Whar'd this old buck Digger git a thing like this. Got the President's mark on it! Looky here." The others looked.

Relieved that they recognized the mark of the Big Hy-apo in Washington, she saw Grizzly Hair's dignity as he opened his hands at the new place. "Inyo share land," he said. "We talk." Many times he had stated his belief that the gold diggers would not leave, as Wozencraft said they would, and the People must befriend them. All must share, he liked to say. Power was realigning itself.

The North Americans eyed him with apparent amusement, except for those cutting the tree. They never stopped sawing.

Father sat down, folded his legs, and patted the earth.

María explained: "He says, our people will share this land with you. Please sit down and talk."

One man erupted in laughter, slapping his thigh. The others laughed and chuckled with him, but the sawyers continued their work. Then the man who started the laughing wiped a finger across his cheek and said, "Rich, ain't it? He'll share the land with us." His hand went to his belt.

Stalking Egret whipped an arrow from his quiver.

Two bangs cracked the air, caused her to jump. Stalking Egret folded at the knees and fell forward.

A smoking hole opened in Father's chest, red froth oozing out. He sat stiffly, his face unchanged, and then slowly toppled.

With four men pointing guns at him, Spear Thrower gradually released the tension on his bow. An Americano walked over and yanked it from him.

Another gunshot made her jump. Grizzly Hair jerked on the ground. Pink matter pushed up through his shining black hair. A strange low-pitched wail came from the bottom of her soul as María reached for him.

The shooter shoved her back saying, "Now let that be a lesson. You Diggers stay outa our way. Hear?"

She stared into the small black circle of his gun barrel.

A ripping shriek came from the tree, followed by a swishing sound as the branches swept through the air, and a deep boom shook the ground and traveled up María's bones. A second boom shook her as the tree bounced on the resilient beast of Earth.

# 91

During the long autumn, the population of Cook's Bar turned over two or three times—a thousand men, Mrs. Gordon estimated at the peak. Now it seemed in decline, though the business at Bridge House held steady as travelers came checking on the average gold take per day. Few of the men who courted Elitha had heard of Ben Wilder, and none knew where he was. They eagerly sought her promise to let them squire her to dances at the new Bridge House dance hall and all over the Mother Lode. This reminded her of the way men stood in line at the Fiddletown dance, here in a different way. The only dance halls she wouldn't go to were Sander's Hall at Sheldon's Mill Ranch and the Slough House Inn. Sarah and Catherine could be there, and Elitha didn't want to upset them. Men spoke gallantly of protecting Elitha's honor, and claimed she needed only say the word and they would "take care of" any man who bothered her. They watched the adobe when she was away. They tussled with each other to do little favors for her, and she felt safe.

In the Counselor's company she went to Volcano to see Shakespeare's Richard III, laughing with the audience when, well loaded with "ammunition," they hooted at the overwrought King Henry dying from stab wounds and pelted him with rotten cabbages, pumpkins, potatoes, a sack of soot and a dead goose. The next week Counselor took her to an all-night dance in the Gaffneys' barn and asked her to marry him. But he seemed more like a pompous uncle than a husband.

A South Carolina gentleman took her by stagecoach to see Lola Montez in Sacramento City. The theater tickets cost a hundred dollars apiece, and the spider dance intrigued her. Afterwards an actor named Edwin Booth, from the famous Booth family of actors, recited from Hamlet. During the entire eight-hour round trip, she parried the southerner's syrupy compliments and rejected his marriage proposals.

Vyries Brown invited her on a horseback ride up and around the little Sugar Loaf peak. He explained that he'd been captured, "gagged and tied by the men who spiked the cannon." Grateful to him for telling her, she felt easier knowing she hadn't contributed to Mr. Sheldon's death. But when they stopped to rest in a grassy place, he too asked her to marry him. She was no more interested in Vyries than the boys in Kate's school.

At every dance men held her too tightly. They pulled her to them on the homeward drives, and she pushed them away, saying, "No, please. Have you heard of Ben Wilder?" That usually worked. They would twist their whiskers and mumble, "Can't say as I have."

The "forthcoming trial" mentioned by *The Sacramento Union* never occurred, or, if it did, wasn't mentioned in print. But though she constantly wondered where Ben had gone, she was glad she hadn't married the man accused of killing Jared Sheldon. Someday, she hoped, Catherine would come to her to heal the rift, which stung like an open sore.

Ben visited her dreams—his easy manner, his length lying with her as he never had in life. She would awaken with a sensuous desire for him. Sometimes it took three hours of cooking and serving meals to banish it, and she worried about her mind.

In December she caught the stage to Jamestown, a booming camp town in the southern mines. There she hugged Leanna, praised her fine good looks—she'd been so skinny—and witnessed her wedding to Mister John App, a good and decent farmer who prospected on the side. When the newlyweds climbed aboard the stage for a San Francisco honeymoon, Elitha felt a piece of her life disappearing. She wiped tears and waved until she could no longer see the bouncing coach.

Back home she wrote more letters to the Brunners in Sonoma County asking why her letters to her little sisters went unanswered. She also made an effort to socialize with the local women. With Lorena Gordon, who had indeed married quickly, she heard a lecture in Ione City on the Water Cure for Females. In Michigan Bar she heard a woman from the National Temperance Union speak on the Evils of Drink. One Sunday she accompanied Lorena to her church in Ione, but though Lorena tried to get her to come again, Elitha wouldn't return. "I have to cook," she said. Nothing in church roused the sense of God she felt in an unspoiled place. A pink streak on the horizon of a winter's sunset brought her closer to prayer than Reverend Fish in a building filled with judgmental people.

In Amador she and the Hays sisters heard a female speaker in blowzy pantaloons denounce the Male Principle as the cause of all corruption and praised the power of the True Woman. But these outings failed to deepen friendships. The women were inclined to talk in exaggerated accents about trifles. They made Elitha yearn for the old ease with Catherine, Sarah and her hundred-percent sister Leanna. However she corresponded with Leanna and enjoyed reading what was going on in Jamestown.

A steady stream of women flowed into California. St. Joseph's Catholic

Church at Live Oak turned out Irish brides and grooms every Sunday, many of the men settling on open land. There were plenty of funerals too. Ten thousand people were said to live, at least temporarily, between Michigan Bar and Slough House. Men came and went in waves, following the latest rumors of "color" found in some stream. But everyone knew the easy gold was gone. The growing number of small weekly or monthly newspapers bemoaned the increasing lawlessness, called for more schools, and praised the beautiful countryside.

In this stew of strangers, Elitha hardened herself when they bantered in her somewhat remodeled eating house about the cannibals of the Donner Party, and she was glad when they shifted to the only other story known to everyone in California, the dashing exploits of Joaquín Murieta. It came back to her that she was called "the quiet McCoon widow." Fondly she recalled tracking animals for the enjoyment. It didn't seem possible that was only four years ago. The wilderness was gone now, and at eighteen, she felt old.

She missed Indian Mary too. But the reservation was a blessing, especially now that a crew of men was blasting away the hillsides with water cannons and silting the river so no fish could survive. Prospectors at her board had been replaced by teams of company men. The water was so bad that Elitha let it settle for days before cooking with it, and even then customers complained of grit and alkaline taste. Despite the nice reservation, she heard mention of Indians still living in the hills—the brunt of jokes and cruel treatment deemed to be amusing.

Why, she often asked herself, when righteous people lectured about wickedness, did they fail to see the evil of their actions toward the Indians? At the very mention, most women's faces wizened like they'd sucked a lemon. But injustice didn't happen only to Indians, as she learned from a man named Jimmy Buetler.

Buetler worked on the hydraulic crew in Michigan Bar. When he mentioned having been a carpenter in Delaware, Elitha gave him a can of gold to buy lumber and other supplies, which were very dear. He had agreed to add two bedrooms to the house, a wooden roof, and a porch across the front.

Two weeks later he came to dinner without the lumber, but said he was "in line" for it. Instead he asked her to accompany him to a fiddler's contest at Willow Creek. "The Walker boys'll be there," he said, sweetening the pot.

She smiled. "Pick me up at noon." Music was balm to her soul. Sometimes it made her feel better for two whole days.

The next day she hung out her NO EATING SIGN and climbed in his little rig. At the Willow Creek hotel, fiddles flew. Like puppets on strings, men hopped around the room dancing jigs, all elbows and knees and beards, until they became drunk and a fight escalated into bottle throwing. When the ruckus was over, Elitha crawled out from behind the bar and joined the singing of "Old Dan Tucker" and "Get Along Home Cindy." Jimmy tried to kiss her, but she pushed him away hard and he stayed pushed.

A miner with a sweet Irish tenor all but made her cry with, "When the Work's all Done this Fall"—a song about a man working on a rancho in the southwest, longing to return to his mother in the East, and being murdered on the way home. Had Ben gone home to Rhode Island? Did he have another name there? As the popular ditty went: Oh what was your name in the States? Was it Johnson or Simpson or Bates? Did you kill with a knife and fly for your life? Oh what was your name in the States? California was part of the states now, but that didn't seem to make much difference. People said California had its own rules.

They left the hotel at dawn, Jimmy clucking the horse to a trot. "They say you're sweet on a man what hasn't been seed in these parts nigh onto six months." No mention of the shoot-out. It was like it never happened.

She felt exhausted. "Ever hear of Ben Wilder?"

He scratched under his hat. "Tall string bean?"

Fatigue vanished and she bolted up straight, staring at him with the rising sun at his back. "That's him. Where is he?" At first she hardly noticed Indians coming down the road at the Dry Creek junction.

"Last I heard, haulin freight on the Stockton-Sacramento Road. Does business outa Sacramento."

So near. Yet no word, no explanation. Relieved that Jimmy asked no more questions, she sat quietly as the horse trotted past a lengthening line of Indians. What was wrong with her? She'd told herself a thousand times she didn't care a fig about Ben Wilder. She looked at the Indians, not having seen so many in one place since before the massacres. Men and women and a few children walking in twos and threes. They all seemed to be headed her way. It was like a dream. Maybe she would wake up and they would be gone along with Jimmy Buetler and what he'd said about Ben. Maybe knowing that Ben was in Sacramento City would exorcise him from her mind.

Passing the camp of Chinamen who worked for the hydraulic company, they met Indians coming toward them from Bridge House, all converging and heading down the road to Michigan Bar.

"What the devil!" Jimmy pulled the horse to a stop. "We got Injuns crawlin outa the rocks. And ain't they the funny bunch!"

Elitha caught sight of a young woman's back with a big baby in a cradleboard, a light-haired boy at her side—her head was a black ball, singed in mourning. But her body looked like Mary. "Wait here," she said, and jumped down from the buckboard.

She made her way past Indians of every description wearing cast-off clothing, a few in torn top hats, men in tattered jackets and no pants, some in loincloths. Around their necks hung strings of buttons, shells and the bottoms of glass bottles with holes drilled through.

"Mary, Mary," she called, hiking her skirts and running up the rutted wagon trail past something long and shrouded, carried by Indians. On both sides the denuded hills had been reshaped into eerie angles and ugly gashes. The girl turned.

Seeing the pitch and ash on her face, fear needled her. "It's really you, isn't it, Mary?"

The girl nodded yes.

"Who died?"

The black eyes surrounded by the startling whites looked up from a black face, while a baby with an auburn tint to her curls grinned peek-a-boo—the child whose birth Elitha had witnessed. "Father died," Mary said.

Captain Juan! She watched the shroud passing by, "How did he die?" He'd been terribly crippled, maybe mortally.

"North Americans shoot him with guns."

Elitha sucked in breath. "Where did it happen?"

"New home place."

Outrage and anger hit her. "Mr. Wozencraft said it would be safe there!"

"My father want Americanos share land."

"No. It wasn't to be shared. It was for you Indians alone!"

A tremor quivered through Mary's reddish lower lip. "Señor Wozencraft go. No come back." Her gaze followed the men with the load.

Guilt gripped Elitha. She'd been too trusting, too hopeful. She should have left them hiding in the boulders. And now they were having a funeral for a fine chief, and all she could think to say was, "I didn't know so many Indians were left."

"Come far away—many peoples." Mary swallowed hard.

Elitha touched her shoulder, wanting to comfort her, but not knowing how. She felt out of place and full of blame. "Why is everyone coming here?" Michigan Bar was a tent town about a mile from the old ranchería, and the busy headquarters of the hydraulic mining company.

"Dancehouse here, close bym home place. Put ashes in old home place."

"Then you're going back to the reservation?"

Her black ball head turned from side to side. "Bad place." She laid her hand on Elitha's forearm. "You are friend. Come cry with us. Honor to Father." She conveyed no accusation.

Elitha blinked back tears, remembering the supply wagon she had to meet this afternoon. "It might take me a day, but Mary, I will come and honor your father." Indian ceremonies sometimes lasted four days.

As Mary continued up the road, Elitha turned back to Jimmy's rig, her thoughts racing. Yes, she would return, but she would ask Catherine to come. They had shared an intimate time in the birth hut with Indian Mary, and though Catherine had shut the door in Elitha's face, nothing in the world said Elitha couldn't re-open it.

# 92

That afternoon Elitha bought flour, sugar, pork and a quarter slab of beef. The young distributor was about to flick the reins when she had the thought that haulers might know each other, and she'd never seen this one before. She asked, "Do you happen to know Ben Wilder? He has a freight route from Sacramento to Stockton."

"Yes ma'am, ran into him yesterdee."

Her heart turned over and found a different beat.

"Want I should give 'im a message?"

"No." She turned to the house hearing the "hah!" and the creak and rattle of the wagon. Putting the beef and pork in a "cheese house" some of the men had dug for her, she tidied up, hung out her NO EATING sign, and walked up to Bridge House in time for the evening stage. "Slough House," she told the driver, giving him half a half-pinch.

She wedged in between smelly miners and looked across at more of them, one with a splinted leg that made her sit a little sideways. All doffed their hats and stared unabashedly, as she'd grown to expect. "Slough House did I hear?" the splinted man asked.

She nodded. They spoke all at once. "At's where I'm headed." "Goin thar myself." "to the dance."

"Mill Ranch," she clarified, "Sheldon's place." They looked puzzled, not knowing the name. And he'd been in the ground only seven months. "It's near the roadhouse." She felt again the groundlessness of a world overrun with people entirely ignorant of what came before them.

"Well, a looker like you orter shake a leg. Heared the Walker boys'll be there. Be right proud to squire you, ma'am."

"Alla us," another man chimed in.

Serving meals these three years had made her feel easy among men. "I expected you'd be headed for Sacramento City," she said.

"Fer a chance like this, we'd frolic a spell and catch tomorry's stage." Their hairy mouths spread in smiles as they nodded to each other.

"I thank you kindly, but my friend is expecting me." Knowing they would think "male friend," she looked out the open window, overcast sky, the short day ending.

The stage stopped before the enlarged Cosumne Store and Post Office— barrels and crates neatly stacked in the yard. Elitha kept her eyes down, not ready to see Sarah and Mr. Grimshaw. Last time they'd met, Ben had acted the peacemaker only to be accused later of murdering Sarah's brother-in-law and partner.

She felt again the unwelcome sensation—part pain, part aching emptiness.

Time was supposed to heal it. Out the other window the blacksmith shop was closing its big doors. Men thumped onto the roof, boots scrambling up over the window, the wood bowing under their weight. The coach rolled forward. A mile beyond the driver called, "Slough House—supper, spirits, and team change."

Lamps glowed beneath the shed roof built over the road. Hostlers rose from chairs where they'd been tipped back against the wall. The coach door opened, and faintly, she heard fiddles, laughter and stomping feet. Horses neighed from the big commercial barn and the horses of the stage neighed back. The driver made a beeline for the roadhouse door while she hurried into the gathering dark in the opposite direction.

Passing the "hanging tree" and a new mercantile store, she slipped in the mud and skated before catching her balance. Her shoes echoed on the much-improved plank bridge across Deer Creek. Lost in the darkness ahead was the large and ancient mound where Mr. Sheldon and Mr. Daylor lay buried with centuries of Indians. She shivered, realizing she'd neglected to bring her cloak. The day had been fairly warm, as many February days were in California, but the nights turned cold.

Leaving the lamp-lit windows of the town of Slough House, she hugged her arms and continued up the narrow road flanked by tall trees. An owl glided close to her head, startling her. Dogs barked. Indian dogs now feral? Did they feel the spirits of their dead masters lurking about?

The stars gave little light. She stumbled on a root and fell, hands into cold mud. As she pulled herself up and straightened her frock, she saw the millhouse looming blacker than the night, and light spilled from the familiar house across the yard. She picked her way toward it.

Quietly she scraped the mud from her shoes on the bottom stair and stepped up to the door. Now, she thought, I will end this one way or the other. But first she wiped her hands on her petticoat then brushed down her outer skirt, hoping to clean off any mud, and patted her hair into place. Memories of this place surrounded her like ground fog—Catherine's impish grin, their talk beneath the walnut tree, the outhouse, the cookout with the Rhoads family, Mr. Valdez playing his guitar, the excitement over gold, the New Year's dinner in forty-nine when the baby was stillborn. Catherine had said *You're not alone, you know that, you always got us Rhoadses.*

Bawling wouldn't do. Again she pulled up her underskirt and this time used the warm tears to wipe off any lingering mud on her face. The door opened.

She threw down her skirt and faced the dark shape of a man. Liquor breath came with, "Well, now we know what them dogs been abarken at."

Catherine's plump silhouette joined him, lamplight at their backs. Unable to see, Elitha felt the absence of smiles. Who was this man? She'd hoped to see Catherine alone. Sarah appeared in the light behind, tall and very pregnant, and there was little Will, grown taller. Inwardly she groaned. Too many people. Sarah's white face and small downturned nose seemed—what, haughty? angry? cold? She must look a sight and almost wished she could drop through the porch floor. But she'd come to do this, never mind who else would hear. She took a deep breath and said it all.

"Catey, I'm just plumb tuckered at our not being friends. I don't know if Ben Wilder killed Mr. Sheldon, but I haven't seen him since before it happened. And I've never felt so down in my life as I've been thinking I almost married a man that, well, helped kill Jared. Now you can shut me out again if you like, but I came to say my piece." Her voice betrayed her, turning into gravel and whine. "I've been sorely missing you and Sarah." She willed the tears to stay in her eyes. All she could see was Sarah's strange expression and Catherine's shadow-dark form.

Catherine said quietly, "Well you sure pick yer times."

What did that mean? And who was this man?

"Sorry to bother you," she said, feeling unwanted. It was pointless to mention the Indian funeral. Maybe the Quiggles had room for her at Slough House. Then tomorrow she'd talk to Billy Rhoads about the Indian treaty he had witnessed. She turned to leave. A hand stopped her.

She turned round, bumping into Catherine. With a rush of relief and joy she felt herself being hugged. She laid her cheek on Catherine's head, squeezing back. Tears spilled over the dam. "Oh Catey, I'm so, so grieved about Jared. He was the best man in California."

Catherine nodded, but the amount of her crying alarmed Elitha. This wasn't joy over a reunion. She seemed about to collapse. She took Catherine by the shoulders and turned her toward the light. Puffy red eyes told her Catey had been crying for hours, and now she sobbed like her heart was breaking.

The unknown man circled an arm around Catherine's waist and helped her back through the door. Over his shoulder he said, "We pulled her little girl outa the river this mornin'." He hooked an armful of air. "Come on in."

The scythe of the Grim Reaper loomed in Elitha's mind, Indians and whites cut down left and right. Recalling her own pain after Elizabeth's death, she stepped gingerly into the house. The man sat down with Catherine on his lap, rocking her like a baby. That started to answer who he was, but which little girl had drowned? Catey had just given birth to a baby girl when Jared died.

With Catherine occupied, she went to Sarah and touched her arm. The poor woman looked in terrible distress—not only about to give birth, but seemingly unconcerned that some of her hair hung loose from her frayed bun.

"It was my fault," Sarah said with tight lips and red-rimmed eyes.

"Stop it, Sally, that's not true," Mr. Grimshaw said, rising from a chair. "It was an accident." He took Elitha's elbow and guided her to the kitchen.

"Sally and I are living in Sacramento now. Yesterday we came to visit.

Today, Will and little Sarah went out to play. Will said her foot slipped ... and the river's right there. We all thought someone else was watching. Sally loved the little tyke, named after her, you know." He looked down, shaking his head.

Imagining how that could happen, Elitha whispered, "Have you had the burial?"

"In the morning. She's laid out in the back room."

Sarah entered the room rolling from side to side in her pregnancy, a woman with all the color washed out except for her red eyes. "Elitha, we had no idea you wasn't seeing Ben Wilder." Reaching an arm around Mr. Grimshaw, she sighed like it was too complicated, and leaned on him.

"I think you got enough on your minds. I'll stay the night at Slough House." Elitha nodded toward the front room whispering, "Who is that man?"

"John Mahone," Mr. Grimshaw said. "Catherine's friend. Came up here with the Mormon Battalion some time ago." The three returned to the parlor where Catherine continued to weep, her head in her knees.

"You shouldn't have to sleep at a roadhouse," Mr. Grimshaw said in a low voice. "I'll drive you on over to John's. We're staying the night here with Catey so there's no extra bed."

"I hate to put you to any trouble."

Mr. Grimshaw was already reaching for a coat, which he gave to Elitha.

❦

Mr. Grimshaw let the horses pick their way in the dark.

"Is Mr. Mahone a good man?"

"I think he is. A good builder. Built the new bridge across the creek. Did you notice?" Before she could answer he added, "She needs a man around."

"I noticed it was a nice bridge." She sat quietly thinking about Catherine, who had always been so full of spunk. The poor girl! Nothing tore you apart like losing a child. And Mr. Mahone could never take Jared Sheldon's place. Elitha felt sure that no man could. When she had a chance, she'd tell Catherine not to marry any man unless she was sure of him. She'd tell her that living alone was easier than people thought in this strange new world with few women, a lot easier than living with a bad-tempered drinker.

Dogs barked a ruckus when they stopped before the Rhoads house, and she felt bad to rouse everybody. Mr. Grimshaw felt his way up to the porch, Elitha following. A couple minutes later she saw, through the window, a tiny flame illumine a long-fingered hand. Then a lamp wick burst to life, lighting a sundries table and Billy Rhoads in his nightshirt, straightening the lamp glass.

He opened the door, clearly surprised to see her. From back in the house came loud coughing and then a tortured croak: "Who's there?"

Billy called over his shoulder, "Stay abed, Brother John. It's WR and Elitha McCoon." He lowered his voice. "Bad ague and chills. Pneumonia, the doctor calls it. Water on the lungs." Ushering them in, he shook his dark head of hair. "Gits it every winter when the rain starts up. I vow it hangs on longer every year."

As WR Grimshaw explained her need for a place to stay, she saw herself again pleading with John to go back up the mountains for Pa and Tamsen. Supposing that scene would follow her to her grave, she felt the magnetic pull of the robust man who had rescued her, who had kept everybody moving when the food caches were found plundered. It seemed three lifetimes ago that she had joked with Mary Murphy about becoming his second wife. But John hadn't been a polygamist after all. He was a good solid man devoted to one wife, a man who provided for so many children she couldn't keep track.

Meeting Billy's pale eyes, she said, "I don't mean to put Matty out, with John sick and all."

"You don't know?" He glanced at Mr. Grimshaw, whose downcast eyes announced he was only an in-law.

"Know what?"

"Matty passed away, long about two weeks ago."

*The Grim Reaper.* People were dropping on every side, and with John so poorly! "Who's caring for all those youngsters?" Surely these two men couldn't do it.

"We sent 'em down to Brother Dan and Amanda, in Gilroy. Matilda made her wishes known before she went. Sent the girls down there too so they'd be help raising the boys. So all we got here is Thomas and Jonathan. Big strong boys, good help on the farm."

Relieved that they hadn't been fussing with little children, she asked, "Who gets your meals?"

Billy shrugged. "Oh, we throw on beans in the mornin' and pry the crust off 'em at night. John feeds the stove when we're out, though I vow he oughta stay abed. We're still cogitatin' on how to make biscuits. Catey sends a few over, but she's got the babies and Sally's gone."

God sent her here! Besides cooking, these men had clothes to wash, mending to do, cows to milk, and chickens to tend to. No farm could run without a woman, and there weren't nearly enough to go around these days.

"Well now," she said, "I can make biscuits with my eyes closed. John saved my life and now I'm going to take care of him and the rest of you 'til you throw me out. And that's final." She pointed at the sofa bed in the parlor. "I'll sleep there."

Mr. Grimshaw's glance said he'd hoped for this. Billy stood grinning like he'd never heard anything so fine. "No need for that. Two upstairs rooms is empty. You're heaven-sent, Miz McCoon."

"Tomorrow I'll tidy up here and cook enough for two days, then go back for my things. And I have something else to do, too." She removed the coat and handed it to Mr. Grimshaw, looking Billy in the eye. "I'll talk to you about that in the morning."

# 93

In the morning she rose before dawn as usual, lit the stove, dipped two buckets of water from the settling barrel, set them to heat on the stove, made up a batch of biscuits and had them in the oven before the amazed boys came from the back bedroom. As they pulled up their suspenders, she explained why she was in their kitchen.

They exchanged a happy look. "Mighty bliged, ma'am," said one of the strong-looking boys. After she got them to say which was Jonathan and which was Thomas, they headed for the outhouse. Billy came in combed and clean.

"Mornin," he said, reaching for the steaming coffeepot.

With a smile she removed his hand from it, sat him at the table and poured him a cup. "What do you think women are for anyhow?"

She turned back to the stove and peeked in the oven. The biscuits needed a couple more minutes. "I've got to go up to an Indian funeral this afternoon, up at Michigan Bar. For Captain Juan. Remember him?" She turned around. "Maybe you didn't know he was shot by Americans up at that place where they were supposed to be safe." She couldn't keep the bitterness from her voice.

He looked at her with water-colored eyes. "Lord that's a shame!" A witness to the treaty, he might be feeling guilty too.

"I mean to write to Mr. Wozencraft, and I hoped you'd help me find him."

"Heard he's hung out a shingle in San Francisco. Don't work for the government anymore."

He really had abandoned them! "Well, who else has taken responsibility for those poor Indians?"

He sighed. "It just wasn't to be, that's all."

The two boys came back in and sat at the table. "I'll drive you up to the funeral," Billy said.

"I can take the stage."

"No sense paying fare. Sides, I mean to give my condolences to that Indian girl."

He did feel guilty.

❧

Billy and the boys had gone out to the field when the sound of coughing came from John's room. Elitha pushed open the door.

His dark eyes were dull, sunken. His cheeks were hollow, and the corners of his lips pulled down like Father Rhoads. He bore no resemblance to the bear of a man she had known. Struggling to keep the shock from her face, she brought the chair closer to the bed, explaining that she was here for as long as they could use her.

His eyes came to life in the bottom of their pits, a kindly, intelligent look transporting her back to that afternoon when he had appeared at the Donner tent to take all who could walk to the fort. "You're an angel of—" He broke into a fit of coughing, rising on an elbow, and when he was through, blood-streaked sputum lay in his hand.

She glanced around for a cloth, but he wiped it on the bedclothes. "There now," she said. "You rest. No need to talk. But I'm warning you, I'll wash every stitch on that bed and make you a pile of handkerchiefs."

His lips stretched in a smile. "Angel of mercy," he said.

"What do you think YOU were? Up there in the mountains? It's the least I can do, and I don't want to hear one more word about it."

Did she imagine more than gratitude in that craggy face? Four years ago she would have rejoiced to see it. Now she wasn't sure, but it surely felt good to help the man who had saved her life.

That afternoon she traveled on the buckboard beside Billy, heading past the Cosumne Store and up Daylor Road. They talked about the reservation.

"I shoulda known politics would interfere," Billy said.

"What do you mean politics?"

In profile his small nose resembled Sarah's, and he squinted at the road ahead where a line of jackasses swayed under huge burdens. "Well, John says a passel of drunks in the California Legislature got riled up about not bein' consulted and sent a smoking resolution to Washington DC. Right high and mighty it was, full of whereases about how our miners got the right to pan wherever they da ... good and well please, and no redskins should be allowed in the Mother Lode." He looked over at her. "Had strong words for Mr. Wozencraft too."

"But the President wanted the reservation. Isn't the federal government more powerful than the state?"

Billy shrugged. "California's the richest state in the Union now. Maybe they don't want to tangle with us."

Fresh anger fired her. "Well, I read the Legislature is meeting in Sacramento City now, and I'm going to give them a piece of my mind!" The Indians had been deceived, pure and simple.

Billy looked at her skeptically, and then dipped his hat to the trader on a good-looking horse, leading the line of jackasses.

She was already making plans. She would catch a stage in a week or so, when John and Billy could spare her. The anger wouldn't quiet down until she'd done her best to get to the bottom of what had gone wrong, and try to rectify it. The certainty of that quieted her mind, and they fell into silence, seated far apart on the buckboard—passing Chinamen shouldering poles with huge baskets hanging from both ends.

Billy was a puzzle. She'd never felt the slightest spark of male interest from him, though most men seemed ready to swoon at her feet. Nevertheless, she was glad for it. He lived with John, and her work there was easier without that complication. A tall handsome man of twenty-two years, Billy held himself with spinsterish dignity.

And John. Poor John, weakened in the lungs because of rescuing the Donner Party. Come hell or high water she would bring him back to health. Maybe her woman's touch would help with his grief over Matilda too. She'd been pleased to learn of his relief that her standoff with Catherine and Sarah was over. "Never did cotton to it," he'd blurted out this morning between coughs. She'd made him a mustard plaster from seed Matty must have gathered in the field, mashed the seeds in an Indian mortar in the kitchen, mixed with vinegar and water. Indian Mary knew a tea that loosened phlegm but she couldn't remember the herbs. If the right moment presented itself at the funeral, she'd ask.

"Mind stopping at my house first?" They were approaching the tents and buildings of Bridge House and she needed to make a Closed sign. She also had to leave a note for Vyries Brown asking him to watch over her place. Billy was turning the horses up the old McCoon road along the north side of the river.

A saddled sorrel mare, one she didn't recognize, stood grazing near the buildings, tugging a rope tied to an oak branch. Thinking Vyries must be there, she jumped off the wheel and started toward the door of the old adobe now much bigger and covered with wood siding. Then her heart jumped to her throat to see the lanky frame of Ben Wilder sauntering toward her from the back side of the house.

The sloping blue eyes crinkled in a smile across his cheeks, the easy manner straight out of her forbidden dreams. As he looked back and forth between her and Billy Rhoads, she felt the spark flaming across time, across the chasm of betrayal and violence. And Billy would think she had lied about not seeing him. Her voice stuck in her throat.

"Howdy," Ben said, a little scratchy. "Heard you asked after me. Thought maybe...." He studied her face, did he see the wild confusion? He changed direction, "A teamster...." What stopped him? Maybe her unvoiced question about his killing Jared Sheldon.

He swallowed and looked across the hills, turning his hat in his hands. A tuft of dark hair fell over his nose. She used to love that, a part of him never under control. She'd learned there were other parts.

At last she found her voice, but it came out rusty. "I didn't think I'd see you again." She remembered her manners. "This is Billy Rhoads, Sarah's brother. You met Sarah with Mr. Grimshaw at the dance in Fiddletown. Billy, this is

Ben Wilder." Billy seemed unfazed. Ben displayed the gentlemanly warmth she had loved. "Your sister is a fine lady, Mr. Rhoads. I can see you favor her."

"She's my twin," Billy said.

Elitha saw a question flicker in Ben's eye as he glanced from Billy to her. Part of her would have been glad to say, *sorry Ben, maybe I'll see you around sometime*. But she didn't really want to dismiss him. He seemed to be digging in his heels, adjusting his long legs. Looking her in the eye, he said in a level voice, "I'm glad if you found happiness, Elitha. I'll rest easier knowing you're taken care of." He nodded approvingly at Billy, the breeze moving the tuft of hair across his forehead.

Before she could speak, Billy was saying, "It's not what it looks to be." He held his hat toward the adobe door. "Why don't we set a spell and make a pot of coffee. I'll get water and start the fire."

Gratefully, she nodded. Billy was right. They needed to talk. He went inside, found the buckets and headed for the settling barrel. Ben's puzzlement was obvious. "You mean you're not..."

She shook her head. "I'll make something to eat." Michigan Bar was only a mile or so upriver, but Indian fare didn't appeal to her.

He set his hat on the new table and pulled up a bent-willow chair. "You're not married yet, or promised?"

Reaching into her cupboard she shook her head. Was he? Now that they were alone again, the other question was trying to take shape on her tongue. He spared her the trouble.

"I left to save you heartache, Elitha. After all you'd been through, the last thing you needed was to be hitched to an accused killer. Hitched in any way, even being friends."

Unable to look at him, she sliced salt pork. "You didn't send word."

"I shot Mr. Johnson. It was self-defense pure and simple. Then all hell broke loose, but I never fired again. I knew how you'd feel, your friendship with Mrs. Sheldon and all. But by thunder, I've been waiting all this time to get my name cleared, not wanting to see you till it was. You see, I couldn't ask you to take my word for it." The last came out so rough, he cleared his throat.

She didn't look up. "You could have told me."

He swallowed. "I wanted you to take me without reservation. I knew I'd stand between you and your friends until I was cleared. So I went directly to Sacramento City and gave myself up, told the deputy sheriff my whereabouts and kept hoping for a trial. Every day I expected it. But time went by and I needed work, so I started a hauling business. Got real busy, but not busy enough to stop wondering if you forgot about me, maybe found somebody more suited, somebody not implicated in—"

"You went down to the dam with a gun."

Their eyes locked. "That I did." He looked down so all she saw was the top of his dark hair. When he looked up he pushed aside the tuft of hair between his eyes and said, "I'd probably do it again. Things were hot that day, in more ways than one. The deal blew up. Sheldon said he'd flood claims without compensating the men. Tempers were high, some saying it was my fault for trying to negotiate, and well, I don't think any man would'ov been without a firearm that day. I felt like I'd brought the men that far and I'd better stick with them. I suppose I even imagined I could stop the trouble."

"You said Mr. Johnson was going to shoot?"

"Had me in his sights. I saw the muscle move in his hand." He blew out air and looked away.

The cold thing in her kept pushing out questions. "Why didn't the sheriff put you on trial?"

"Now there's a good question. First off, the widow, Mrs. Sheldon, didn't accuse me of murder. And I've spent some time thinking about this. Back where I come from, things are set up to clear a man of false charges. I get the feeling out here nobody cares. Everybody's heading for the next bonanza, the sheriff right along with the rest. And the miners I made go to town with me?" He shook his head. "To a man they said, forget it. I think what this state needs is good men to see that courts of justice are established. Without that, there can't be a real civilization." His eyes pleaded.

Did she trust him? That's what it came down to. The trial was happening right here in her house.

"You musta had a million offers." His tone told her he still cared.

Thrill and suspicion mixed badly. She managed a careless shrug and said, "Now I'm cooking for the Rhoads men down at Slough House."

While Billy got the fire started, she palmed flour into the bread pan. "We're on our way to an Indian funeral over in Michigan Bar. Remember my Indian friend's father? Shot and killed by white men in a reservation that was supposed to protect Indians." It felt like a test.

He frowned, made a clucking sound in his cheek as he shook his head.

She added a pinch of salt, three pinches of saleratus and a splash of water from the bucket, stirring with her hand. Blindfolded she could whip up a light batch of biscuits. Lord in Heaven, what was this sensation inside her? It felt wonderful to have him sitting here. She liked the way he watched her hands fly as she pinched out dough, folded it, and swiped the balls through the grease in the old coffee can. Why did her heart race so?

The three ate in the eating house, and she watched him charm Billy, talking about how Sacramento City was booming with all kinds of interesting people. She wanted to trust this man. His education showed in the way he talked, and she knew for sure he hadn't made up the part about going down to the sheriff. That much had been reported in the newspaper.

"I'd like to go to the Indian funeral with the two of you, if you don't mind," Ben said when Elitha was cleaning up.

Pleased about that, she took her roll of paper and made her sign. She also wrote a note for Vyries. Jimmy Buetler she'd given up on. He stole her gold clear and simple. Then she climbed up onto the buckboard between the men. What was Billy thinking? What would he say to his brother John?

With Ben beside her, she sat up tall. The sun was low when Billy pulled the team to a stop overlooking Michigan Bar. At least fifty campfires were strewn across the destroyed hills. Indians didn't look extinct here, though the morning paper had predicted the "imbecilic race" would be gone in seven years, "crushed beneath the iron heel of progress."

How would Ben see the Indians? The trial she started in her house would continue.

# 94

"Eat. Eat before we dance," urged Hin-co-ye, the Temayasa dance-doctor. "You will need strength. Eat before we cry."

María had eaten her fill. At the fire of Grizzly Hair's remnant People, she looked around at the large assembly that had gathered in the former home place of the Wapumne. It still amazed her how widely respected Father had been. Bent-Willow-Reflected-in-Pond, Spear Thrower and their children sat at the fire with Hummingbird Tailfeather, her face and bald head blackened as so many were. On all sides people ate oolah, which María and the other women had made from the acorns packed on their backs. The ceremonial food would keep them dancing all night.

Father would have been proud. From as far away as Monterey and the home place of Ts'noma they were still arriving, though tonight would be the second night. All were dressed for the celebration, many in the cast-off skirts and trousers of North Americans. Shell money hung around their necks with other glass and metal trinkets they had found and honed. Feathers decorated their hair, the few who had hair.

Most of the gold diggers had disappeared, because the water cannons were eating the hills and muddying the water. However, a few of them sat leaning against the old roundhouse. She controlled her fear as they tipped up bottles and laughed coarsely—men apparently drawn from upriver by last night's ceremonies. With them sat a few men from the big house of the water cannon. She hoped the rituals of the Cry would snuff out her awareness of all of them.

Last night at the orations Hin-co-ye had said that if the people were meant to die, nothing could be done about it. If they were to be captured and forced to labor, it was not important. More important was the proper conduct of the Cry—purification, wormwood in the nostrils, the right food. For those prepared for death, the time of dying didn't matter. "Eat. Eat. Eat. Eat," he called now as he walked among the fires stamping the bottom end of his plumed walking staff. "So that you are ready to cry."

Several fires away, María saw one of the men who had orated so well about Father. She'd thought she knew everything about him, but last night she learned he was the most admired headman in the wide place called California. She heard details of how he'd gathered warriors from many villages in far flung areas to fight the combined Mexican presidios. Coordinating with Estanislao, who led hundreds of mission people to join the battle, he organized arrow runners, food suppliers and medicine women to use a network of underground trenches leading to a three-tiered stockade. She knew Father had been a war chief back then, but as the orations progressed, she appreciated for the first time how eloquent he must have been to persuade two thousand men to leave their villages and fight side by side with strangers. No such thing had been done before.

"Except for the Departed," one of the speakers had said, "all of us would have been forced from our homes and into mission labor. The Departed, who now goes to the Happy Land, helped assure that no missions were built in the big valley. He helped stop the black hats from coming to our home places and herding us away. Some people say it was a bad thing the missions withered, but I say they did not suffer the azote on their backs. They were not locked in the wooden trap to stand in their own water and defecation."

As María listened to the orations, she imagined her father as a brave young warrior, so different from the father she had known, a man convinced that the sorrows of killing-war could not stop the changes in the world, and that Indians should make friends with the new people. She realized now that he could have chosen a path no Indian had walked—war chief of many peoples fighting to expel the gold diggers. All the speakers made it clear they would have followed him. But Father had defeated that temptation, the most seductive of enemies, and had become a man of wisdom instead.

She noticed a line of pale-robed people just arriving. Their shoulder-length hair indicated they were women, but their bare faces looked male. What did the costumes mean? They looked like spirits. Leaving Pedro, she threaded her way through the campfires, walking toward the robed people, exchanging greetings with the people from the Lake of the Tulares, and from Estanislao's River.

The robed men came to a halt before her, maybe twelve or thirteen. "Where do you come from and where are you going?" she asked of the first—clearly a man, and not young. His dark skin stretched tightly across wide cheekbones. Creases fanned outward from his eyes. Even his feet and hands, which protruded from the woolen robe, looked emaciated. The man said, "We come from Mission San José. We come to cry for our friend, and we will return to the mission."

That surprised her. His way of speaking was precisely like the umne.

"We are hungry." A ritual statement of the umne.

"Come and eat," she responded, intrigued and looking from one robed man to the other, making sure she didn't know them.

They followed her to where women dipped out baskets of oolah and peppermint tea. As they received the ritual food, the robed spokesman said in the warm and wonderful accents of a cousin-brother: "We will sing at the Cry and play our flutes."

"Your talk sounds familiar."

"Your home place is mine." Stunned again, she saw a ripple in his wide, mobile lips as he said, "The Deceased went to the mission with me. I stayed. He was the best friend of my childhood."

Bowstring! The long-lost Bowstring whom Father had praised as the best flute player in the world, the one who married a mission woman and played Español instruments under the direction of Padre Duran. Bowstring's mother had never given up hope of seeing him again, and now she was dead—killed by North Americans. Honored by his presence, María extended the traditional: "Thank you for coming to cry for my father. It was along walk."

"Your father!" He stared too long at her char-blackened face. "You are my cousin-sister then." He glanced around at the peoples preparing themselves to dance. "Is your mother here?"

Closing her eyes, she looked down and shook her head. "All gone. Your mother too. We dance for everyone." Politely she looked past the shock in his eyes and saw a wagon pulling to a stop. On its bench sat Elitha and Señor Rhoads, the one who had been a witness, with them the tall Americano who had been good to Elitha at the time of her baby's death. María must greet them too, and offer food.

"Eat," she said to Bowstring and his men. "And bathe. Soon we will cry." She gestured to the barren river banks and silt-choked water. Leaving Bowstring, she threaded her way through people adorning themselves with beads and dance feathers, and heard Hin-co-ye announce in ceremonial tones: "All here are sad. All cry. Last time to be sad."

That landed like a thunderbolt. María stopped for a moment. *Last time to be sad.* The traditional statement meant "until the next Cry." But this might actually be the last time. Her umne were all but dead except for a small group. It was the same with the other peoples. When Hin-co-ye died, no one would know the right words. Could anyone else rouse the spirits of the dead? Those camping here would leave when the Cry was over. They would creep back into their hiding places in rocks and caves, many to die of disease and shootings, some to starve in the plundered land. Bowstring would return to San José.

Those who had believed in the reservation now needed a new hiding place. They were as homeless as bears, sleeping in different places each night. She could not imagine organizing another Cry.

Strength drained down from her shoulders and out the tips of her fingers. Last time to be sad. She might never again freely picture Father's eyes as he looked lovingly at her, or remember the strength of his body before he was injured, or recall the lines of wisdom in his face. She might never again commune with his soul or the souls of Etumu and Dishi and all the dead loved ones. *Last time to be sad.* A spiritual desert stretched before her. But Grandmother Howchia still lived in the oak tree. The fire that destroyed the roundhouse burned the leaves off the strong oak, but could not kill it. The thought moved her forward. She would visit Grandmother Howchia when there was a break in the Cry. Now she would welcome her American double.

After a brief visit with Indian Mary, Elitha remained on the buckboard between Ben Wilder and Billy Rhoads, looking across the twilight expanse of Indian campfires. Mary had said that earlier in the day the Indians had tamped out a dance floor—a huge rectangle—and swept it clean. In its center stood a platform of dry brush upon which the body of Captain Juan had been placed. Last night there had been speeches about him. Tonight, besides the burning, only dancing and singing were planned.

Four Indians with flaming sticks moved across the open ground and knelt to ignite the brush. Another, wearing a torn top hat and cape, walked with ramrod posture around all sides of the rectangle calling out Cry messages. From the corner of her eye she saw Ben smile and realized how clownish that man must have looked to him and the drunken miners, who laughed coarsely within earshot of the ceremonies.

Indians from all sides began to walk onto the dance floor. They threw baskets, blankets, hats, and smaller things on the funeral pyre. Then suddenly a piercing female-sounding wail came from the top-hatted Indian. Eerie, mournful beyond anything Elitha had ever heard. The miners stopped laughing and watched.

Silence followed. Then the top-hatted Indian tilted back his head and emitted a second unearthly wail. Another voice joined him, and another, and another until slowly the wailing rolled into her and teased out every sorrowful emotion she had ever felt—all the deaths that she had suffered. The sound of sorrow entered her soul. It rose in pitch, even the dogs howling, until it seemed to come from the very landscape, the lacerated hills, the upside-down earth, the dead fish and animals, the dead Indians who once populated this region. Goose bumps prickled her arms. Then suddenly the wailing ceased.

The death-like silence stood her hair on end. She glanced at Ben, whose expression had changed to awe, and whispered, "I'll bet that lasted half an hour." He nodded, and for a moment she thought he would take her hand, but felt relief that he didn't. She wanted to feel this funeral without distraction.

Another wail started, followed by a new piling-on of cries as penetrating and lengthy as the first. Then again the sudden, more terrifying silence. As if Hell had swallowed everything.

The Indian with the flapping high hat strode around the dance floor gravely orating, the feathers on his staff flouncing each time he pounded the butt end on the ground. Elitha could tell he repeated phrases three and four times. After about twenty minutes of this, he stopped.

Shadowy Indians moved onto the tamped ground, young women form-ing a circle nearest the fire, men standing in a large group nearby. It looked like Indian Mary went out to dance, though it was hard to see at that distance, the firelight and shadow making them all look alike, so many without hair.

Wooden flutes were raised. Eerie, hollow music floated across the hills, joined at intervals by a dirge-like chorus of men. Beneath, steady as a heart, thumped the drumbeat. Wails and wild ululations interrupted the chorus as the Indian women leapt around the fire, pouncing twice on one foot, then twice on the other. Their high leaps forced air from their lungs as they landed causing a rasping heh, heh, heh, heh like one monstrous grinding voice. Blood tingled in Elitha's veins, and a nameless terror infused her along with the stench of burning flesh and the sight of the frenzy of elbows, knees, feet, and flying hair black against the orange firelight. It seemed a likeness of Hell.

"A savage spectacle. *Walpurgisnacht*," Ben said.

Grandma Donner had used that term for the night the earth belched up witches, some riding on farting goats, others on flying brooms. But it was more than a "spectacle." Elitha knew that such violent dancing would have helped her pour out grief for her own dead. Maybe Ben thought it was more like a circus. But why care what he thought? She didn't really know him. He could be a murderer.

☙

The first hour of the wild dancing held Pedro entranced. Then he thought ahead. Tomorrow he and Murieta's men would leave to herd the last of the huge caballadas down to Mexico. He had told María and made her sad. Ay, but he worried about her and the baby while he was gone. It could be two months. But he had seen a wagon arrive and it looked like Señora McCoon with two men, one of whom looked like Señor Rhoads. They might help.

It was out of the question to take her with him. The dangers had quadrupled. The state lawmakers had hired a desperado named Harry Love and twenty of the most vicious killers in Norteamerica to end the career of the "Joaquín gang." Paid to hunt for five "Joaquíns," the rangers were now combing the hills and streams, and bribing the weak. Pedro couldn't expose María to that.

He had convinced Joaquín Murieta they should bypass the big valley, take the herd through San José, thence down through Santa Barbara and Los Angeles. Don Cristóbal and other rancheros would hide them at night.

In the half-light he could see the wagon still there. He left Isabella in Spear Thrower's arms and, in the flashes of firelight spaced by lurching dancers, stepped carefully around masses of clay that had been dislocated by a water cannon. Then suddenly the singing and dancing ceased.

He looked back and saw María and other young women collapsing where they stood. He shook his head. Ay madre, where did she get the strength? He couldn't jump up and down like that for two hours straight. The medicine man was making an announcement, speaking in the stiff way of Indians. Then he shifted to Spanish: "The men of the mission now sing to Dios and María, Mother of God."

Without the dancers, the fire provided more light. A pure voice cut through the night like an angel. Other voices joined the first—sweet, interwoven, a sound as ancient and sacred as the cathedrals of Spain. The Latin Requiem! He knew it from his boyhood. He looked back at the robed singers, and from habit picked out a few words that sounded Spanish.

*Dona eis Requiem.* Give us rest.

"Yes God," he said aloud. "Grant the pobrecitos rest." But do not wait until they join you in heaven. Pedro wouldn't be here much longer to help them.

*❦*

The musical tones threaded around one another like the knitting needles of angels shaping a heavenly fabric. It transported Elitha to another realm.

Ben exclaimed, "Well I'll be hornswoggled. Latin! They don't sound like monkeys now."

That brought her back to earth. She knew perfectly well that people commonly called Indians monkeys, but she didn't want to hear it from him.

Billy Rhoads leaned past Elitha to speak to Ben. "Do you know Latin?"

"My schoolmaster gave me a little credit for poking through all those books of Cicero and Herodotus. Listen."

In exquisite harmony, the voices hung suspended, and then one by one peeled away and tripped down a delicate ladder regrouping at the bottom in new, enchanted harmonies. Like disembodied spirits moving through the night, neither male nor female, they repeated phrases, each time flowing in reshaped harmony. Ben translated:

"Lamb of God, who taketh away the sins of the world, give us rest." Staring intently at the singing Indians, he echoed the Latin as they sang: *"Agnus Dei, qui tollis pecatta mundi, dona eis requiem."*

He knew these were no monkeys, she could tell. And she had to admire his education. Far beyond hers. This was an exceptional Forty-niner.

A man's voice startled her. "Señora McCoon. Por favor, may I talk with you?"

It came from beside the wagon in the resonant accents of Mr. Valdez. She hadn't seen him since she'd given him Captain Sutter's letter about land ownership.

She started to rise, but Ben put his hand on her. "Do you know who he is?"

"Pedro Valdez," she said standing up.

Ben whispered, "Careful, don't get out of the wagon."

For months she'd yearned to be cared for and looked after, but now his solicitous attitude annoyed her. After leaving her alone in the world for seven months, Ben Wilder was telling her what to do. "Señor Valdez is an honorable man," she said more coldly than intended. Pushing past Ben's knees, she climbed down the wagon wheel.

"I only mean to keep you safe, Elitha. It must be midnight," Ben said.

It was indeed dark. Indians continually tossed fresh branches into the flames, but the fire was too distant to illuminate the Spaniard's features. She sensed him drawing himself up.

"I must go away for a leetle while, señora. My wife and her children need a safe place to stay for two months. I am sorry but I must ask if you can help them find a place."

"Gladly. I'm staying at the Rhoads place now. Maybe they wouldn't mind." She raised her voice toward the dark figures on the buckboard, "Billy, Indian Mary needs a place to stay, and I could use help with chores. Do you suppose she could stay at your farm?"

"Sure," Billy said. "And we could use a couple of bucks to clear brush in the new field."

"Señor Rhoads?" Valdez said. "I thought maybe it was you. Buenas noches. I hope your family is healthy."

"John's under the weather, but Elitha here'll bring him back. Say. Stop by sometime and tell us what you're up to. We lost track of you."

"I have been working and saving money for a rancho far away. I will return and take María with me in two months. We talk then, no?"

"A pleasure."

"Muchas gracias for taking her. I will find men to clear the brush. Go with God and say hello to your family."

Elitha said to Señor Valdez, "Tell Indian Mary to come when the funeral's over."

"A thousand times gracias, señora." With a bow in the dark, he was gone.

❦

First light grayed the sky, and María's legs wobbled to the drumbeat. She had been dancing since Bowstring and his troupe finished singing. All night she had pounded her grief down through the soles of her feet and wrung her spirit inside out, indulging her sorrows together with the hundreds who had known Father. She had shouted his name and pictured him. She had remembered and remembered and remembered, and she had wailed out her last spark of strength. Now, sleeping people littered the spectator circle and the dance floor. Her legs moved erratically as she staggered past them toward Pedro's bedroll. Like a dying animal too exhausted to think, she struggled to reach that destination, though it was only a few steps away.

She lifted the cover and fell in beside him. Heavy sleep rose up from the earth and sucked her down.

# 95

"María. María." It was Pedro, kneeling beside her.

Gradually she surfaced, disentangled herself from her dream and realized the sun was bright and high, Isabella crying, dogs barking, people stirring all around.

Pedro peered down at her. "Are you well, Little Poppy? I am afraid you danced too long." Despite the sunlight, a haze sat on his head and shoulders.

She blinked and rubbed her eyes. "I am well. Did Isabella eat?" Pushing hair from her face, she sat up. She felt stiff and sore.

"Sí, the little girl ate acorn mush. I don't know why she is crying." The strange fog around his head defied the sunshine. Nowhere else did she see such fog.

She blinked again and looked at the surrounding people in the large, sunny encampment. Her vision was crisp except when she looked at Pedro. Passing a hand over his face she felt nothing. And then with heart-stopping certainty, she knew.

No! She closed her eyes and trembled, unable to accept it. Too many had died. She couldn't lose Pedro. She wanted to shout *peligro!* But he was speaking.

"Señora McCoon says you can stay with her at the rancho of Señor Rhoads while I am gone." He scowled with concern. "You are shaking, Amapolita."

"Stay, Pedro." She looked at him in the direct Español manner, repeating that he should stay, not caring that she sometimes chided him for repeating things and now was doing it herself.

He put his hands on her shoulders and spoke forcefully, "María, te amo. I love you. You are la dueña de mi corazón, the owner of my heart. Understand? I promise you, this is my last ride with Joaquín Murieta. I will return in two moons with horses enough for all your people who want to come to Mexico with us. We will travel by a secret route. I have hidden four hundred thousand dollars in the knot of a tree down there." After evil struck Father she'd been ready to go, and now it would strike Pedro while he continued to dream. "It will buy us beautiful land and build us a comfortable hacienda. Our children will wear fine clothing. Our mayordomo will escort them to church and school. They will read books. Picture that life, my little poppy, and stay safe with your friend Elitha until my return. I ask this from my heart."

Absently, she glanced to where Elitha's wagon had been.

"They will send Ramón for you and the others when the dance is over." He took her hands and forced a smile, the haze remaining, and explained that Señor Rhoads needed the help of two men.

Hardly able to breathe, much less feel gratitude about having a temporary home, she said, "Do not leave before the Cry is finished." If he would stay just one more sleep, she could live a lifetime cherishing each additional moment.

He made a vexed noise in his throat. "Joaquín says we leave today from the hotel of Señor Simas. I have already delayed our departure, Little Poppy, and Joaquín is restless. He is afraid Captain Love is coming north." He shrugged. "I must go, now."

Señor Simas dwelled a short ride away, the "Portegee" having left his wife and four young boys to ride with Murieta, never to return. Pedro had told the story in disbelieving tones, and now María knew Pedro wouldn't return either, not because he didn't want to, but because of the men who hunted him—circling, sniffing like wolves. She couldn't warn him about the aura of death because he would call it superstition. She rose to her knees and started to say, "No. Por fav—"

He pulled her to him, pressing his face into her breast, his voice cracking as if he might cry. "Amapolita, this one time I must say no to you, and I will not change my mind."

She laid her cheek on the top of his head, the black curls with reddish tints that he had given Isabella. Their last embrace. Her last taste of his leathery, smoky scent. Gently she lifted his chin and rubbed his face with her tears, his mustache, his nose, but she could not look at his eyes. She murmured, "I wish I had the power to shrink to cricket size and ride in your pocket."

"I cherish you, te quiero," he breathed, closing his eyes.

"Te amo," she said back. She had begged him to stay. No more could be done. She ran a finger across his cheek, collected a tear, and put it in her mouth, repeating his sentiment. "You are el dueño de mi corazón."

He pushed up to his feet and stood looking down a moment, the gray facets of his eyes blurred by the haze. Quapata was in the saddle nearby, holding Chocolate's rein. People moved about them, but all faded as she reached out and ran her hand down Pedro's buttoned trouser-leg, down the soft goatskin around his calf and ankle. Sitting beneath him, she left her hand there, the last touch.

She heard his effort to lighten his leaving. "They will not catch el Bandido Cuidadoso, my love. I will hold the memory of your beautiful face and black eyes here." He closed his fist over his heart. "Hasta la vista." He turned, the goatskin pulling from her hand, and walked toward Chocolate, his hips shifting in his black trousers.

"Vaya con Dios," she managed to say as he mounted in a fluid move. Great Spirit of the Españoles, protect him! Maybe the aura was in fact superstition. Fervently she hoped so as she watched the horses gallop away and disappear behind the deformed hills. Then her ears and eyes opened. She heard the baby cry, saw Little Flicker and Billy staring at her, the nearby people politely averting their eyes. The Español custom of saying good-bye cut to the heart.

Father's death had weakened her. She must go to Grandmother Howchia. Maybe she would say the fog around him was not Death.

❧

Spear Thrower agreed to accompany her to the home place, and to leave immediately in order to return before the afternoon ceremonies. As she put the children in the care of Bent-Willow-Reflected-in-Pond, he slung his bow and quiver over his torso, and they headed up the old Wapumne path.

Every step stretched the distance between her and Pedro, and hurt more—she walked downriver, he rode upriver to the Simas place. Without the willows and cottonwoods, birds lacked perches and had flown away. The sun was naked, the breeze unfriendly. She had walked this trail often as a child on the way to the Wapumne big times, skipping beside Grizzly Hair, Etumu, Crying Fox, and her cousin-sisters and -brothers. But now the landscape was unrecognizable. The silt-choked river ran straight where it had turned. Pits and trenches scarred the shores. Noticing that Spear Thrower walked like Crying Fox, she choked back a sudden sob. At the dance tonight she would let her mind dwell on her brother, eaten by Americanos. A bad sound buzzed in her ears. His angry soul. Yes, she must call it out and speak to him tonight.

Only a few hairy-faced gold diggers squatted alongside the river. When they glanced up, María held her gaze forward. The buzzing sound grew louder as they neared the village center. Now and again violent shudders racked her at the thought of Pedro being caught by Captain Love. I will return, he had said. She would cling to that and remember that she owned his heart, the place where his love came from. Rounding the river bend near the old walnut grove, she and Spear Thrower stopped in their tracks.

The once-wooded hillside where she had played as a child and gathered as a young woman gaped open. At the top, three men controlled the long snout of a water cannon, which ejected a powerful stream. Pale clay and rocks crashed down in a torrent, the big hill fast eroding. Only two trees were left in the deepening muck, soon to be buried. Below, mud boiled into a wooden trough bisecting the trail, numerous men poking shovels into it. At the end of the trough, thick tan-colored water made a waterfall into the river.

Spear Thrower signaled María. She backtracked with him and they headed around the other side of the hill. Maybe Grandmother's tree been buried too. Maybe Howchia had gone to the happy land at last, her soul released from the tree. The tiny remnant of Howchia's people were in

constant mourning. Few babies were born. The dance places gone. Pedro ...
Her spirit buckled and her feet moved as though in a dream

Approaching the home place from the north hills, the village center was
barren. The gold diggers were gone. Nothing remained of the dancehouse,
not even ash. But the mound still rose behind the wide excavation that had
been the entrance to the house of spirits, and on it stood the magnificent oak,
taller than the two other oaks on the denuded creek bank. The tree spread
her arms over the area where the u-machas and cha'kas had been, green buds
swelling on her flourishing twigs. Grandmother was here!

Spear Thrower went and stood at the river's edge watching the pale torrent, perhaps speaking to his own spirit ally, perhaps respecting María's privacy. Looking at his strong back and sloping shoulders, his acorn brownness,
his hip slung to one side, she realized he was the last man of the umne, and
she the last woman.

She climbed up the mound, toes sinking into the softness, a cloud of
yellow finches scattering from the twigs above. At the wide trunk she closed
her eyes, inhaling the tannic aroma of the bark, and emptied her mind of
everything else. *Grandmother, I come in fear and sorrow. Once, I slept here
without noticing the smiles of my uncles and aunties and cousins, the caring
of my parents, the sounds of children playing and women pounding. I went to
Señor Sutter's place. I married men not of our people. I wanted them, Grandmother. I liked their different ways. I said I will go to Mexico with Pedro, but...*
She moaned and clung to the trunk with outstretched arms, trembling, not
daring to ask if Pedro would die.

A rumble came from deep in the ground and reverberated up the trunk:
*I am rooted. In time of rain I wear the mist rising from the earth. In the long
dry I wear the dust. I do not ask if there is a better place. I am what is. Older
than the finches, younger than the rocks, I am not immortal. Granddaughter.
Where are you going?*

Her soul quieted. That question had the same weight as the answer she'd
sought.

# 96

Elitha stood in the doorway feeling a pang of guilt as she looked at Indian
Mary washing the breakfast dishes. Mary had refused to wear Matilda
Rhoads' clothing, insisting that bad spirits would kill her for touching the
belongings of the dead, and now she wore Catherine's once-green frock,
faded to gray. The oft-mended underarms revealed Mary's brown skin, and
the frayed hem hung like fringe about her calves. The rags of civilization had

transformed a lovely wild girl into a barefoot scullery maid.

About to leave for Sacramento City, Elitha said, "Mary, you've been working hard these two months. Let the other girls wash the bedclothes. Take time with Billy and Isabella. Go for a walk."

Two other Indian women, Mary's cousin-sisters, had come with her to the Rhoads farm. They also wore rags. If she hadn't given Jimmy Buetler all her gold she'd have been able to buy material to sew them all new frocks. But working for board and room didn't give her any extra.

Mary turned and looked at her, black hair framing a face no longer plump, cheeks flat beneath prominent bones. "Work makes wait short," she said. "Work makes forgetting. Billy is happy with men. Go. I do washing." She turned back to the dishes.

"I mean to do what I can to get the reservation back."

"No matter. Bad place." She didn't look up.

That was Mary's attitude. She would go to Mexico with Mr. Valdez, but all the other Indians needed a safe place. It made Elitha furious the way they'd been tricked. They had let down their guard. And yes, work made forgetting. How well Elitha knew that! Mary's wait for Señor Valdez had made her withdrawn, hard to talk to. Elitha turned and left, hoping Señor Valdez would arrive today. The girl deserved a little happiness.

She climbed aboard the seven A.M. stage, immediately making it clear to the men inside that she didn't wish to talk to them. Not only would she speak to the lawmakers, but she intended to locate Ben Wilder's place of business. This could be the most important day of her life, and she needed a clear head.

Last evening after the supper dishes were put away, she'd gone to the porch for a breath of cooler air. John Rhoads joined her, the hot dry air having healed his lungs. He was fleshing out again and working a little in the wheat field, almost his old self, except for his eyes, which looked thirty years older than when she'd met him five years ago. "When you gonna cook us some bad grub?" he had asked.

She'd replied, "Well now, maybe you'd like some rock biscuits. I used to do those up pretty good. Or maybe some hornet grubs, fried just enough to stop the wiggling." She turned a sisterly smile at him, but he was standing very close by. He laid a bear paw on her shoulder.

"You've brought this household back together, Elitha. Made us a family again." His voice was thick and she knew where that was leading. Reason said she should grab him while she could. It also said her cooking days at the Rhoads farm were over. She would not mislead this man, this greatest of California heroes.

"I appreciate that, John," she'd tried to explain, "but I've been thinking. About Ben Wilder." She struggled onward, stumbling over words and unformed thoughts. Since the Indian funeral Ben had visited once, but after a strained buggy drive, she told him she needed to think alone. Everyone said he'd been the ringleader in Mr. Sheldon's death, even if he hadn't pulled the trigger. For two months he'd stayed away. It boiled down to trust. And somehow over the months of helping the Rhoads men, disentangling dreams of Ben from the daylight world, and appreciating his respect for her feelings, she had decided to trust Ben. It was like the "leap of faith" Reverend Fish talked about.

During that fumbled explanation John had stepped back, listening quietly. Only the slightest crack in his voice betrayed his feelings. "'Preciate your tellin me." A vise tightened on her heart. Never had it felt so bad to speak her mind. And now, as Perry used to say, the die was cast.

The driver cried, "Walsh Station!" She went to the outhouse while the four-horse team was watered, and soon they were racing full tilt down the road to Sutter's Fort, bouncing over the ruts. The occupants of the coach continued to leave her alone, and silently she practiced her speech: Gentlemen, my name is Elitha McCoon. I have lived at Rancho Sacayak since before the discovery of gold and am here to object to… No. A friendly touch would work better, like the way Abe Lincoln opened when he spoke to the farmers in the Donner yard. Good afternoon, gentlemen, esteemed Legislators. I feel privileged to speak to you, and I must say I applaud your great wisdom in deciding that the heat in the fair city of Sacramento is insufficient to… No. She couldn't joke like a man, and besides she'd just read that the majority of Legislators wanted the capitol in Vallejo or Benicia or San José. Gentlemen. My name is Elitha McCoon and I feel honored to speak to you today about the plight of the Indians, the wise and wonderful people… No, even the Spaniards from the coast thought Indians had childish minds and were born horse thieves.

How could she explain the Indians as she knew them? Slow to anger, at home with nature. She looked out the window at the grasslands, the large oaks standing every fifty yards or so. But thoughts of Ben intruded. She hadn't been very nice to him that last time. The coach slowed and stopped at Perkins Station. It felt good to stretch her legs and join the other passengers with a bowl of soup while fresh horses were hitched.

Back in the coach she could almost feel the miners' spirits lifting the nearer they came to the steam-driven floating palaces that plied the waterways between Sacramento City and San Francisco.

"Where'd ye say you was headed?" one man asked another.

"New York," the man smiled. "Older and wiser."

BRIGHTON, a sign announced as the coach passed through a small town at the junction of roads: Sutter's Fort to the north, Stockton to the south. She glimpsed the racetrack where the paper said two thousand people had watched "thrilling combat" between a bull and a grizzly bear. The coach rattled and bounced westward down a new road bypassing the old fort. These days everything bypassed the fort. It seemed sad, the adobe walls crumbling, people hauling off the good bricks. In her mind she saw it as it had once stood, substantial and isolated on the plain, the end of the trail for weary travelers, none wearier than she. Now Captain Sutter was in disrepair too, occasionally brought down from his farm on the Feather River to march in a parade, or sit in the front row of an entertainment. A relic of another time. "Disgracefully drunk," one reporter wrote.

Tables, chairs and pitched tents began to appear beneath the oaks, which were leafed out despite cavities burned in their trunks. People used them as windbreaks and fireplaces. She'd seen that six months ago, on her trip to the theater with the Counselor. Blackened spires stood as reminders that even these large trees would eventually burn through. Frame houses flanked the road. She craned her neck to see flowers behind a whitewashed fence, but jerked back as a wagonload of men whizzed by, too near, too fast, about fifteen men gripping rifles.

At regular intervals, roads intersected J Street, down which the coach flew. Square blocks had been laid out far beyond the actual town, she recalled, but now houses had sprouted on them. The growth was startling. Then two-story places of business stood between the houses, and all manner of buggies and rigs passed by in clouds of dust. The driver slowed the horses to a more stately pace. Some of the houses were as grand as Springfield's best. She tried to see the names of the commercial establishments, but before she knew it, the stage stopped in a confusion of men and conveyances.

The driver opened the door. Across the transportation yard, over the heads of the milling men towered a three-story structure with Union Hotel painted on it. Two-story buildings lined all the surrounding streets, many sharing walls.

"After you," said the New Yorker.

Stepping out, she turned and asked, "If you please, have you the time?"

He pulled out a watch, flicked it open. "Eleven o'clock."

The twenty-mile trip had taken only four hours. "Thank you, sir. Have a pleasant journey. Your wife and children will surely be glad to see you." He touched his hat.

Stepping into the dust, she jumped in her skin as a heraldic voice yelled, "Leaving for Marysville. Five minutes." A few feet away the man pointed a finger at a freight-sized wagon where men sat on rows of benches. *Marysville.* She felt a pang of desire to go see Mary, but realized as she made her way through the melee that the return ticket to Slough House would cost all her remaining coins.

Hawkers yelled over the blare of voices and the rattle of harnesses: "Departin fer the southern mines. Big strikes in the Calaveras." "All points to Nevada City. Make your fortune." "Stockton, Sonora, Columbia. Ten minutes." "Bound for thc famous Folsom mines. Don't git left behind."

She dodged men with rifles and bedrolls scurrying uncertainly from one wagon to the other. A driver reached down and grabbed a man's elbow, a hawker boosting him from below. They plunked him down in a bus, deciding for the undecided. Six-bit teams stamped impatiently, jangling their harnesses as they shook off flies. A man in a passenger wagon yelled, "Git the hell on the road! We been sitting on these benches for an hour." Guns rested over shoulders.

The driver drawled back, "Not rollin till I gits four more."

"Yer on my foot," yelled a passenger, shoving the man next to him and causing the others to lean like angry dominoes.

It was the oppressive heat, Elitha decided, that made the men so surly, the transportation yard so unpleasant—that and the stench of human waste clinging to the city air. Too many cesspools, too many people using outhouses too close together.

She stepped inside the cool, quiet lobby of a hotel. An old clerk put his finger on a line in a leather-bound volume and looked up as she asked where the Legislature met. "Go up Fifth to China Slough, that's I Street, then take a right to the Court House. You can't miss it. About the size of a twelve-horse livery stable, Greek pillars and a dome like St. Peter's." Almost smiling, he went back to Shakespeare.

She passed many people. Nodding at a woman in a calico bonnet waiting on the buckboard of a covered wagon, she nearly collided with a man staggering from the Miner's Supply with a heavy box. The flies and stench thickened the nearer she came to I Street. Then it opened before her, the Chinese sector on her left, a string of crowded stores backed up to a marshy, filthy slough— clearly the city dump. Celestials bustled around the stores featuring plucked chickens and meat hanging outside the doorways, and stacks of pointed straw hats stood with pans, boots, shovels and picks. Behind the stores the brown spikes of cattails poked at odd angles through the garbage and she could almost see the rank odors rising in the heat waves.

On her right, beyond the huts and Chinese men tending green leafy vegetables, she saw the unlikely dome, an enormous red-white-and-blue flag draped tiredly over it. Hoping the Legislature was in session, she went up the stairs between the pillars and pushed the lettering on the door: SACRAMENTO CITY AND COUNTY COURT HOUSE.

With relief she found the chamber benches filled with men. At a table in front, a white-haired gentleman with mutton-chop side-whiskers fondled a mallet and gazed at her as she entered, and a speaker orated about rampant crime. Men of all descriptions stood crowded against the back wall, all turning to look curiously at her as she shut the door.

The air was close, warm, and smelled of unwashed bodies. She was the only female. Her heart raced at the thought of speaking. Where would she stand? At the front? How would she signal her desire to be recognized? Would she fall in a faint? She squeezed in beside two men, one in a top hat and tails, apparently a banker, and leaned against the wall as others did.

After paying twenty dollars to come all this way, she would say her piece, just as she had at Catherine's. But first she'd watch how others did it. A legislator stood beside his bench gesturing broadly, his stentorian tones overwhelming the chatter of the spectators. He finished with: "I propose we amend the bill to expel every Mexican from the interior of the state." Men shouted and stamped approval, others clapped. Some sat stonily.

The chairman recognized Assemblyman Philemon Herbert from Mariposa County. In common trousers and shirt, the young man leaped on the bench. He pivoted often as he spoke, so all could see his face. His speech was clipped, slightly southern, his vocabulary large—he mentioned he'd come from Texas. With a flourish he whipped a newspaper from his pocket and read a list of crimes committed by the bandit Joaquín.

"My fellow lawmakers," he shouted, "Are we going to take these outrages lying down? Or are we men? The time for action is long past! Captain Harry Love and his twenty rangers have done nothing but dispatch a few common horse thieves. Meanwhile the five Joaquíns listed in this petition run free. It's high time to support Governor Bigler's resolution and post a five-thousand-dollar reward for any person or persons who capture the robber leader. Dead or alive. I move we send the Governor's resolution to my committee. From there, I promise you it will be approved and signed before the sun sets."

"Second," came a shout as cheers exploded. Hats hit the ceiling. Elitha's heart pounded all the louder. How could she match such fervor? These men had no fear of public speaking. Would they laugh at her? Behind her fear niggled an old disquiet. Was Señor Valdez one of the five Joaquíns? His means of support remained mysterious.

Assemblyman Catlin was recognized. "Mr. Speaker, my fellow lawmakers," he said as he rose to his feet, "there's another bunch of thieves you should be worrying about. At this very moment they are pilfering the State Treasury. I speak of none other than Captain Love and his gang of rangers. They are no doubt laughing through their teeth, to be put up at nice hotels and fed fine meals while they pocket a hundred and fifty dollars apiece each and every month. I ask you, why should they ever catch Joaquín? Any Joaquín? Why, that would be downright contrary to human nature. Now I don't mean to denigrate their abilities. We all know of their fame as bounty hunters, scalp collectors, Texas border fighters, and the like, but my fellow legislators, if we're going to catch Joaquín, we've got to stop spending public revenue to keep those twenty men in spending money. Support our colleague from Mariposa County. Issue an honest reward. Then see how fast the villain is caught!" More clapping and stamping.

The chairman recognized Señor José Cavabarrubias, a tall, dignified Spaniard with a face as white as any European. He spoke in the distinctive accents of a Californio. "The bandidos must be stopped. All honest men are in agreement. But none of the five Joaquíns named in the petition are known to be criminals." He went on to say that Carillo and the other listed names were common Spanish surnames, and Joaquín was an extremely common given name. Furthermore, no daguerreotype or tintype of the bandit existed.

"Gentlemen," he said, "my Military Affairs Committee rejected a reward, and properly so, because it is an invitation to murder. A reward would tempt unprincipled men to attack innocent men. Native Californians would be in great danger. If a Mexican is brought to this chamber, who among you would know if he is the bandido?" He paused only a moment. "We do not even know his full name! We do not know if he is one man or five, or ten men. Gentlemen, for the sake of humanity and civilization, join me in defeating this bad measure." Polite clapping followed as he resumed his seat. No doubt he came from the coast or the southern part of the state, Elitha thought. Californios still out-voted American emigrants in those regions.

A legislator stood rattling a newspaper. When recognized, he read from an editorial in the *Los Angeles Star*: "Many men of veracity assert positively that Joaquín Murieta and his band are now somewhere between San Juan Capistrano and San Diego, bound for Lower California." He let the paper drop to his side and turned around, looking nonplussed. "That was two weeks ago, gentlemen. I could read from a string of papers from Santa Barbara south, men asserting they saw the bandit, OUR bandit, passing through, helped out by his countrymen. A regular newspaper trail." He shook the paper in the air. "These men know his name. They know his face. He was well known in Los Angeles before he ever came to the mines. He was wanted for murdering General Bean." He twisted his face into a mask of wry amazement. "Esteemed colleagues, the whereabouts of Joaquín is no state secret. So what in heaven's name are the California Rangers doing on their posteriors in Mariposa County? The representative from Sacramento is correct. Only a substantial reward will net us the robber chief." Much clapping followed, men stamping as they sat, some mopping their brows.

She felt the arms of men on both sides dampening her all the way through their broadcloth and her gingham. So far, only legislators had spoken and the subject of debate hadn't changed. No one standing in the back had raised a hand. She knew nothing about procedures, and what she had to say seemed out of place. Light-headed from the heat and odors, she knew she must wait and observe longer.

"Dinner break," shouted a legislator from the floor. A rumble of agreement followed. Another shouted, "Men can't think starved." Meanwhile a man struggled with a window, grumbling, "White men can't think in this heat!"

"Order!" The chairman's mallet rang like a pile driver. When the room quieted, he said in a reasonable tone, "Somebody pass those men a drink." Bottles appeared, passing overhead, hand to hand along the benches with frequent stops. As the liquor was imbibed, the debate continued until a crash and the sound of falling glass silenced all. A man had kicked out the window. He growled in a threatening tone, "This is the worst damned hellhole I ever got trapped in. I move we go back to Benicia."

"Out of order," thundered the chairman, banging his mallet. "There's a motion on the floor, and we're not leaving the room until the matter's settled. Do I have to remind you that men all over this state demand an end to the reign of Mexican terror? I'll accept a motion on the question."

Immediately a vote was underway, men circulating bottles and calling aye or no after each name was read. The chairman banged again. "The ayes have it. Thirty to nineteen. Do pass. Meet back in chamber when you're done eating. Session adjourned." He tapped the mallet lightly on the table, whisked his top hat to his head and pressed forward into the rising crowd of men.

Elitha floated out the door and across the porch like a boat on a tide, shoes barely touching. The air smelled worse outside, but she was relieved when the pressing bodies dispersed. She almost welcomed the broiling sun drying her damp frock and was glad for her poke bonnet. She hurried up the dusty street overtaking the banker. "How much time do they take to eat?" she asked.

He was rushing after the legislators who were already turning down J Street. He stepped aside to let a spray wagon pass, Down with Dust, City of Sacramento, gaily painted on a huge perforated barrel. He looked at her like a fond uncle and said, "They get back to work whenever we can get them rounded up." He touched his hat and waddled across the dampened street, elbows pumping, long coattails flapping.

Wondering where she should eat, she fell in behind him and watched until the flock of dark-suited legislators disappeared into a building. She looked to where J ended at the riverbank, the tops of paddle-wheelers and sail tips of sloops and fishing boats visible over the bank. Men were unloading heavy bundles on the levee, though it had to be over a hundred degrees.

Then it came to her. She should go find the chairman in his eating house. She hurried to the corner of J and Third Street. A simple wooden sign read: KESEBERG'S RESTAURANT: Inquire about Hotel within.

It kicked her stomach, forcing up the image of the man's scraggly beard ticking denial. She had attacked him, and then endured the long river trip by looking past him as if he didn't exist. He had done likewise. Would that happen here? Or would he tell people she was a Donner and make a sideshow of her—a cannibal in a cannibal's restaurant. A man in tails stepped around her to hold the door for his fellows. One of the men quipped, "Good eating here, if you like brains." They all guffawed.

The jokes never stopped. She turned to find a shady place to calm herself. Maybe she should forget about the Legislature. But that would give that vile man a victory. No, his name on a sign wouldn't stop her from trying to help the Indians. If she saw him, she would ignore him like the offal he was. If he told people her name, she would face it.

She stepped into the cave-like interior, much cooler than the courthouse. Glancing warily around the dim room, the only windows in front, she removed her bonnet, heard the clink of dishes and the hum of conversation. As her eyes adjusted to the dark, she saw a long table in the back filled with legislators. A dark-suited waiter, too short for Keseberg, was setting stemmed glasses before them. In the light of the oil lamps she picked out the mutton chop whiskers of the chairman at the head of the table, took a deep breath and went to him. The banker, she was surprised to see, sat at the opposite end of the table.

"Well, well," the chairman said as she stopped near him. "Here's the pretty little thing I saw in chambers." He reached, encircled her waist and drew her to the side of his chair, glancing at the other diners like he'd caught a large fish.

She hadn't anticipated feeling like a child, men chuckling at her. She tried to step back but he secured his grip. A man was joking, "That's why I want your job. Better view of the back of the room." Men howled.

The chairman sipped from his glass and gave her a squeeze, asking juicily, "What can I do for you, my sweet little dear?" With a nod he dismissed the waiter with a white towel over his sleeve.

She cleared her throat to dislodge her voice. "I came to bring your attention, that is, the attention of the Legislature to a matter, and I was wondering how to go about it. I'd like to speak this afternoon, if I could." It seemed incongruous, embarrassing, to be standing in this man's embrace while asking a serious question.

Within the brackets of his whiskers, his pudgy cheeks tightened into a big-lipped smile. "Depends on what it's about." His grip never lessened.

Not wanting to be drawn into the particulars within the hearing of only a few legislators, she kept it simple. "About an Indian reservation."

"Which one?"

A man came from a swinging door behind the table, a flash of light from the steamy kitchen briefly illuminating his face—filled out now, the blond hair neatly tied behind, the beard still long and stringy. Lewis Keseberg stood three feet away, eyes registering recognition. The chairman was saying, "Which reservation, little lady?"

Her voice shook. "Ah, up around Spanish Camp." Without thinking, aware only of an instinctive need for freedom and mobility, she jerked out of the chairman's grasp.

"Spanish Camp," he frowned, clearly disliking the way she'd pulled away. "Must be a dozen by that name. Be specific."

Under Keseberg's glare she was trying to think when a sandy-haired legislator at the side of the table said, "Up on the Cosumnes River?"

"Yes," she said weakly, knowing she didn't sound like a girl who could address an assembly of men. But Keseberg towered in the shadows like a ghoul, opening his hairy mouth to speak. Heart drumming, she gave him her fiercest look and willed him to silence. He swallowed back the words.

The sandy-haired legislator was explaining to the chairman, "She must mean that idiotic Wozencraft scheme to give half my district away."

Keseberg cut in, "If you will, gentlemen. May I tell vhat we haff for eating today?" She released her breath. He was sticking to business.

"Yes, by all means," the chairman said.

"Liver and onions," Keseberg began.

Men tittered. She backed up, bumping a chair. Men at another table looked quizzically at her. "Sorry," she murmured, seeing Pa's empty breast in her mind, and Tamsen hanging upside down like an animal being bled. Keseberg continued, "Fried chicken and meatloaf."

"No brains today?" asked a smirking legislator. Obviously they loved eating at the famous cannibal's table, and even with his back turned, she saw that Keseberg welcomed the notoriety. It probably gave him an edge over other eating-houses. She felt unstable, like she was standing in a boat. But, thankfully, he kept his mouth shut.

After what seemed an eternity he returned to the kitchen. She stepped to the chairman's side, weak with relief but feeling better for having faced down Keseberg. The chairman buttered his roll. She waited. After a long time he jerked his head at her like he was dismissing a bothersome bug, and bit into his bread. Rude. Or was she rude to interfere with his dinner? Or was it that she had pulled away from him?

She stammered, "About my speaking to—"

"No Indian reservation is subject to debate." He looked ahead, the flesh of his eyelids flat across marble eyes.

"I only meant to—"

"Miss," the sandy-haired legislator said, "you're talkin about gold country. Hasn't been any Indian trouble there. No need for a reservation."

"But the Indians—"

"Take a tip," snapped the chairman still looking ahead. "You'd rile the members." He leaned toward the banker at the other end of the long table, "Now about those securities…"

Hot with humiliation, she turned and walked to the door. No need for a reservation! There was a great need, and she'd spoiled her chance to tell them. If one location wasn't good, another could be found. How could she get them to listen?

Sunshine slammed into her. Tying on her bonnet she walked the two blocks to the busy riverbank. A steamer blasted. She should have played it coquettishly, kept her subject a secret. Keseberg had thrown her off. No, she decided on second thought, she had failed to ignore him. There was a difference, something to do with the kind of power Indian Mary talked about.

Her breathing returned to normal as she watched an auctioneer among the piled goods on the docks, rattling out numbers and stabbing his finger at the gathered men. Two young women dressed in lovely frocks and modern face-framing bonnets chattered beneath parasols as they entered the high-arched SACRAMENTO CITY MARKET. Horse-drawn rigs of all kinds rattled up and down the dusty levee, Front Street the sign said. She had done her best and failed. Now she would find Ben. Maybe he could suggest what to do next. After all, he had worked in Sacramento for a year and might be familiar with the procedures.

A Wells Fargo stage left the boardwalk at the corner-building where J Street met Front. Three men in tails and high hats stood talking beneath the sign: PAGE, BACON & CO. BANKERS. Waiting for a pause, she asked for directions to Wilder's Transport Company, and felt a pleasant thrill that these distinguished gentlemen, the first she asked, knew of Ben's place of business.

# 97

Seventh and M was a long, hot walk. The Sacramento Iron Works disgorged black smoke, adding dark haze to the outhouse smell. But the air cleared a little as Elitha passed a row of hotels and the Stanford Brothers Wholesale Provision House, where a freight wagon backed up to a landing and iron doors stood open against brick. One man handed crates down to another man standing in the wagon. Then came modest houses with gardens and barking dogs, and Rowe's Olympic Amphitheater and Circus. She stopped to read the posted bill:

MASTER RAFAEL
Little Rising Star
To Perform Daring Equestrian Feats:
Leaping Whip, Garters and Hoops,
Riding upon his Head with Horse at Full Speed.

Not even Señor Valdez rode upon his head.

She turned up M Street past intermingled houses and commercial establishments. Weedy empty lots appeared between unpainted buildings made of fresh lumber, some half built. Several blocks farther she stopped.

A hostelry and foundry stood beside a small frame building with a sign painted over the door: WILDER TRANSPORT AND HAULING COMPANY. Behind the structure lay a freight wagon on its side. Sensing Ben's nearness, she took a deep breath. *Wilder.* What she needed was Tamer. But she had told John she would tell Ben he could come calling, if he wasn't spoken for. Then they'd decide if they were meant for one another. This was serious business, and she wouldn't play with John Rhoads. She was here for a purpose.

The unnaturalness weighed on her. Only a bad woman went to a man. He could turn her away on that account. No matter what else he was, Ben was a gentleman when it came to manners. The door was open a crack. She pushed it inward, peering inside from her poke bonnet. A young clerk looked up from a table stacked with paper.

"I was looking for Mr. Wilder."

"He's out." He removed his pinched spectacles, twin indentations marking the bridge of his nose, side-parted hair hanging in brown sheets like Mr. Grimshaw's.

"Out of town?"

"No ma'am. If you'd take a seat?" He nodded at two wooden chairs against the wall. "Your name please?"

She told him and he went out a back door. She lowered herself to the edge of a chair, hands folded, telling her heart to slow down.

Moments later the door opened and Ben ducked through it. He stood staring at her as if thunderstruck, dark beard shaved back from his mouth, red shirtsleeves rolled up on grease-streaked arms, a towel in his hands. Perspiration glistened on his forehead and streamed down into his substantial black sideburns, which linked his unruly hair with a wide bushy beard. The only thing that moved was a lock of dark hair falling over his nose.

She swallowed and stood up, aware of the clerk waiting at the doorway in the sun. "Ben," she managed, "I'm sorry to bother you at your work. Could we talk?"

He stared at her left hand and her right, and then lifted his gaze to her eyes, his wide mouth twitching into a ghost of a smile. He wiped his hands on the towel, and she caught the scent of tar, perspiration, and excitement, mixed with memories—dancing with him, sitting beside him on the long ride home, the way he looked at her when he asked for a shovel to re-bury Perry, and the way he held her when Elizabeth died. No matter how married he might be, she would never forget.

The clerk cleared his throat. "Excuse me, sir." Ben was blocking the door.

His electrifying gaze never left hers as he stepped to the center of the small office, the clerk shutting the door behind him and resuming his seat behind the little table. Elitha couldn't stop looking into Ben's eyes.

"You're not married?" he asked.

That was her question. "No, Ben. I ... came to talk to you."

Suddenly he sparked to life, whirling to the clerk. "Tell Leland Stanford an urgent matter came up. I'll see them—" he turned to Elitha asking, "in two hours? …three?"

She smiled and shrugged.

"Two and a half," he boomed, telling her to sit and wait a minute while he washed up. He walked briskly out the back door.

Tickled it had been so easy, and he was pleased as any fool could see, she couldn't sit still. She went out the front door and peered around the side of the building. Ben stood at a horse trough by the hostelry, shirtless, backside to her. He widened his stance, bent his knees and dunked head, shoulders and half his lanky torso under water. In a few seconds he popped up in a brilliant sunburst of spraying water. Furiously rubbing the towel over his hair, face and armpits, and scrubbing hard on his blackened arms, he saw her and froze, and then stepped to an open lean-to, threw in the towel and pulled out a pale shirt. He flung it over his head, thrust his arms into the sleeves and walked toward her, smiling. His wet hair stood up like Indian feathers and his beard dripped.

"My toilette," he said jabbing the muslin shirttail into his trousers, shifting from hip to hip. "How 'bout wetting our whistles on some soda water?" Smiling into her unabashed grin he came to her in his loose-jointed way and said something about a hat, took a giant stride up both steps to the front door of his place, and in two seconds was back, combing his hair, the hat under the other arm. "Seen J Street?"

"A little. I came in on the Amador Stage."

He stopped mid-comb. "What time?"

"Eleven this morning."

He resumed combing. "Didja see my passenger wagon, Stockton bound?"

"Yes," she sang out, overjoyed to recall that. This was a respectable businessman, not a murderer. She liked seeing dirt and grease on him. She understood work.

Looking pleased, he tilted his head and extended an elbow. "Ma'am?" He led her into the hostelry—straps, barrels, tools and harnesses all arranged neatly, several rigs parked close behind one another—and helped her into the seat of a small trap, more like a bench and a footrest between two large wheels. It was cunning, with its seat and wheel rims newly painted black and its spokes red. He shouldered it outside, and hitched a horse.

Soon they were clopping down Seventh Street with the sun frying them and Ben finger-combing his damp beard. His hat hung loose and wavy around his face and he turned every other second as if to see whether she still sat beside him. Or was he waiting for her to say her piece?

Happiness pushed it out of her. "You got a sweetheart?"

He squinted ahead, his sloped nose pointing to the horse, the silence unhitching her heart. The sun seemed to melt her words and they slid down around her feet and dripped behind in the dust. At last he answered, "Maybe."

That meant yes. She tried to swallow the darning knob in her throat, and it hurt. He reined left on J Street. Visions of women loomed before her like dust devils—young beauties touring with their families, captivated by this man of the Golden West. Brazen actresses of the entertainment stages. Painted lips, whale-boned waists. Maybe a fine lady like one of those she'd seen entering the Sacramento City Market. SHE wouldn't know of the trouble on the Cosumney, and Ben would like that. No doubt he'd been a man about town since she last saw him, and women weren't in such short supply here. With his tall good looks, enterprise and education, Ben would attract anything in skirts. She blinked tears, felt the hot air drying them in her eyes. He didn't look at her the way he had done at the beginning of the ride.

The road was crowded. He reined to a stop, waited behind several other rigs, then steered the horse around an enormous pit in the middle of the road. "They dug out a big oak tree here," he explained as if she were a mere acquaintance. "J Street's got to be straight and clear." A little farther up the road he pulled to a stop at a hitching ring.

All the excitement and anticipation she'd brought to Sacramento City had oozed out with the perspiration. Feeling dried up, she stepped down. He lifted his elbow to her, and she clung to his arm, damp and sinewy beneath the muslin, a muscle twitching as they walked beneath the porch overhang with the sign JENSENS SODA PARLOR. The most she'd ever seen of his body was at the water trough—except in dreams. And now those dreams must stop.

It was much cooler inside. Several groups of men and three young women sat at tiny round tables. Ben removed his hat, hung it on a rack and pulled an iron filigree chair for her. Then he went to a man behind the counter, spoke to him and produced money from his pocket. The man went into action at an elaborate machine, pumping a handle up and down. It hissed as he held a glass beneath the spout.

Ben returned and sat opposite her, his knees jutting out both sides of a table designed for shorter people. She could hardly look at him for the darning knob, the pinch in her chest, and the disappointment. But she forced a smile. "I'm glad for you, Ben." She'd always been a poor liar.

Elbows on the table, he leaned forward, interlocking his long fingers and resting his bearded chin on the platform. "You wanted to talk to me." His eyes were a foot away.

She looked down. The door banged as others entered. People at other tables spoke quietly over drinks. She told him the easier thing, how she'd fared so miserably with the Legislature. The proprietor brought two shapely glasses of pink, fizzing liquid, ice clinking. *Ice.* An icehouse must be near. Ice from the lake now called Donner. That's where she'd heard people got it.

She wrapped her hands around the cold glass and explained about Keseberg. She held nothing back. Ben knew her secrets. Most of them. The berry-flavored soda cooled a path to her stomach and cleared her head. The confession loosened her, gave her heart to face Ben as nothing more than a friend.

He guzzled his entire drink, set the empty glass down with an ahhh, and called to the proprietor to bring another. "Tell you what," he said, his blue eyes lively, "I know Assemblyman Catlin. Helped pay for his flyers when he got elected. The stage for Slough House leaves too early. Why don't you stay in town tonight, and I'll get us an appointment with Catlin in the morning."

She realized it was his vitality that attracted her so powerfully. No doubt his lady friend liked it too. Still, he had said *us*. She savored it like the crumbs of that first biscuit up in the mountains. "How would that help?"

"Well, he's your representative. Mine too. He's bound to pay some attention to us. We'll go talk to him."

*We*. And he was right. A woman wasn't viewed as having important ideas. But it would be excruciating to spend the night in the same town, knowing he might be around the next corner escorting his lady friend to the theater, or visiting her…

"Would you like that?"

"Yes. I'll stay. I appreciate your help, Ben."

"The least I can do. We'll go by his office when we leave here, and see about an appointment." The soda man removed Ben's empty glass and set down a full one, pink bubbles foaming over the top and sliding down the side.

She took a cooling swallow of hers and said, "Ben, I don't think for one minute you did more than defend yourself, back at the dam." It graveled her voice, but relieved her to get it out.

He sucked down more soda, set the clinking glass on the table and gazed at her in his unsmiling, direct manner. "Thank you, Elitha. I appreciate that." He moved a finger down the damp glass, pushing beads of moisture. "But I'll go to my grave thinking if I'd done something different, Mr. Sheldon would be alive. He had some admirable qualities."

Men got up and walked out the door, the soda parlor emptying like her heart. Ben was in pain too, she could see, but for a different reason. Wanting to reach across the table and take his hand, she said, "Terrible things happen all the time, and it's not to be explained. Sometimes I think the Indians are right about their Coyote. Do you know about him?" He looked blank. "It's sort of a god that mixes everybody up and laughs at us when we're trying to do our best and everything goes sour. I guess he's supposed to teach us to laugh at ourselves. I know you did what seemed right, but things got out of hand. Not because of you, in spite of you."

His gaze shifted from her left eye to her right, then back. "You really don't hold it against me?"

She shook her head. "No. And I think we gotta go forward in life. Just like I can't dwell on Mr. Keseberg. I'll never excuse what I think he did, but still, I don't really know he did it, do I? And I guess I'm proud of myself for not letting that stop me from trying today, with what I wanted to do for the Indians. Maybe it's a little like the Bible says. Turning the other cheek." It was a poor comparison.

The corners of Ben's wide mouth twitched upward. "Now there's one fellow I'd keep all my cheeks turned away from." His tone was soft, amused.

She found herself grinning, half embarrassed, smiling at a Keseberg joke! No other man could do that to her. And the way he looked! Lord in heaven, she must have been in hibernation two months ago not to know her feelings for him went all the way down to her roots. It hurt to keep swallowing back the knowing that he belonged to another.

He reached across the table and suddenly her hand was inside his warm hand. "You asked if I have a sweetheart." Something clamped in her chest. She couldn't hide her feelings. Was he deliberately torturing her? She started to pull her hand back.

He squeezed it. "I hope so, Elitha. I've hoped it for a long time. But I didn't want to rush you."

*You.* She stared at him, wondering if she'd heard right. The pained smile on his face confused her, but if she'd heard right, she wanted to jump up and hug him. "Me?" She couldn't keep the surprise and joy from her face.

With a scrape of his chair he came to her and pulled her up, wrapping her in his arms, his big hand pressing her head against his shirt. Her lips touched the crisp, damp hair in the open V of his shirt and through the muslin his heart thudded rapidly. For her! Her tears wet his shirt and she didn't care who was looking. This was how it was supposed to feel.

His voice rumbled from the muscle-padded chamber of his ribs. "You want me then?" He still didn't know.

She pulled back an inch and looked up past his beard, swallowing, blinking. It squeaked out. "I want you, Ben." She'd meant only to have him court her, but her heart had spoken. It smashed through the dam and the darning knob, and she wept, clinging to the beat of his urgent heart. She felt a tremor, a slight earthquake in his bones.

"I need you, Elitha." His voice cracked. "There are women. But it's you I think about." He swallowed. "Dream about."

She wrapped her arms around his neck, hugging him, wanting to care for him as one would a child. She knew now why the princess in the fairy tale married the only man who could make her cry.

He pushed her back to arm's length, the blue of his eyes pooled with tears, the folds at the corners crinkled all the way across his face. His voice reverberated in the soda parlor. "By thunder, this calls for a celebration!"

# 98

After all these months of wanting her, Ben couldn't let go. He pulled her to the counter and dug in his pocket for coins. Jumpin Jensen wiped a tear off his cheek and said, "Git on outa here, Ben Wilder. Ain't ever day a man sees sum'm 'ike 'at."

"You're a gentleman. This here's going to be my missus." As if he didn't know! Ben thought he would burst with happiness.

He couldn't stop looking into those beautiful dark brown eyes weeping with joy for him. Never mind Jumpin Jensen, he pulled her to him—full-bosomed beneath the blue gingham, tall for a girl, slender, the satin cushions of her lips tentative at first, then eager for him. The hunger of pent-up love thundered in his ears. "Come," he said forcing himself to put air between them, "we've got places to go."

Time flew in a happy whirl. Leaving the rig in front of Jensen's, he escorted Elitha to the first of three stores offering ready-made women's clothing, and refused her protests. "It's for our meeting with Assemblyman Catlin," he lied. It was for her from him.

Viewing her in a variety of gowns, he grabbed his beard and leaned back, considering how this or that color set off her fresh complexion and dark beauty. A goddess. It was all he could do to keep from dancing a jig and yelling, Elitha McCoon will marry me!

Viewing her in an aqua-colored, drop-waisted frock with embroidered roses all over it, the unctuous proprietress said, "Ahhh, she has a midriff like a wasp." She grabbed a handful of loose material at the small of Elitha's back. "See, the style shows it so beautifully! I can stitch this up in minutes." But the frock was excessively ornate, unharmonious with Elitha's natural dignity.

He thanked the woman and escorted Elitha up J toward the City of Paris, a place women crowed about. But passing the cluttered front of Warren's New England Seed Store: Everything for the Farm and City Garden, she wanted to go in. He liked that.

Bags of all kinds were stacked high. Ox yokes and hay rakes hung from the rafters. A planting machine stood beside a barrel of seed potatoes. She felt the shiny leaves on a row of unfamiliar potted plants. A voice came from the back of the store, "Camellia Japonica." A youngish man of obvious energy appeared. "Bought those right off a boat from China. My guess is they'll grow in this climate."

The smell of dirt and seed affected Ben in an interesting way. He felt nostalgic, sentimental, and loved the man's New England accent. He introduced himself and complimented Mr. Warren on his store while wondering about his sudden desire to cut and plant potatoes. Farming was in his blood.

"This camellia," she was saying, "does it bloom?"

Mr. Warren made his hands into a large circle. "Pink blossoms this size. He grabbed a flyer off a shelf, "Grows to the size of a small tree." He handed it to her.

Back out on the boardwalk, she said she wanted an ornamental garden to work in some day. He loved that. Too many women viewed dirt as a disease.

In the City of Paris she tried on a gown beribboned in every possible place with small green bows. Looking down at it she murmured, "I can see this at a dance, but I think something more suitable for day wear would be better."

"Hmm," said the vampirish proprietress, a woman of indistinct age and false eyeteeth of a darker hue. She dashed to the back of the room and disappeared through a curtain. Moments later she reemerged shaking out a cloud of dark brown and white taffeta, thrusting it to Elitha's neck. "What do you think?" She bared her teeth at Ben.

The deep brown matched Elitha's eyes, the checkered pattern big and bold. No gewgaws or froufrou, yet dramatic. "Good," he said.

After several minutes behind the curtain with the vampire, Elitha emerged in the frock, floating toward him with the dignity he loved so much, more beautiful than ever. Pleasure showed in the natural sadness of her eyes, the crisp white of the blouse setting off the peach glow of her cheeks. At the sleeves the pattern slanted at a graceful bias, hanging wide at the wrist. The front opened in a V to the waist, revealing the white blouse.

"Do you have a brooch?" Ben asked the woman, "and half-gloves in the same brown?"

She flew behind the back curtain.

Elitha whispered, "It'd be dear, Ben."

"What do you think money's for?" He saw she liked the dress. Everything he'd ever worked for was standing here before him. Without a doubt he was the luckiest man in California. For once in his life he had done the right thing to wait and hope. By thunder, the number of times he'd stopped himself from riding out there! The many wadded letters! "A parasol too," he called to the woman. "Same brown if you have it. Oh, and one of those little white bonnets that just frames the face and hair." He smiled at his goddess.

"Ben, the cost!" She gave the taffeta a friendly shake.

He liked her frugality, a virtue plenty of women lacked. "Elitha, this is the grandest moment of my life, and my business is booming." He could have hired men to do it all, but needed to work with his hands and wasn't the kind to sit speculating in hotel lobbies and saloons while the sun was up. He winked down at her. "This is an engagement present." Later he would pick out a ring and surprise her with a diamond set in pure California gold.

Before long he was parading up J Street with parasoled Elitha on his arm, and a box with her old dress under his spare arm. She had insisted on taking it back to her Indian friend. Most people just tossed their worn clothes on the boardwalk for the Indians. Passing men tipped their hats, getting an eyeful before their gazes slid enviously to Ben. She was magnificent.

"Oh Ben, look!" She stopped at Nahl's Art Shop—a narrow space roofed over between two buildings. The artist, a slight acquaintance whom he greeted with a nod, sat before an upright canvas within his open doorway, reaching out, tickling the canvas with the tip of his brush.

"Such lively work!" she said. "Look at the color, the faces!" Nahl smiled at her and continued working.

"I didn't know you appreciated the arts," Ben said, guiding her inside. But of course she liked the arts. She was a goddess.

"Tamsen was good at it," she said, surveying tiers of canvasses and standing before a likeness of a Mexican dandy galloping a black horse up a steep trail with a knife raised in defiance.

Ben liked the paintings along the floor. He didn't share the popular taste for languid scenes. "Look at this," he chuckled. "Charlie, I see you been in a gold camp."

She came to look. The more he examined the details of "A Live Woman at the Mines," the funnier it got. A man was leading a demure woman from a tent, gesturing proudly at her. A large crowd of miners faced them, hair and beards askew as they jumped, trying to see over heads to get a glimpse of a woman. They stamped their boots, threw up their hats and fired pistols in the air, one being boosted by another who made a stirrup of his hands. In the background men raced down a hillside, skidding and sliding toward the viewing. "You ever feel like that?" he asked, recalling the first time he'd gone to see her.

She shot him a secret smile. Charles Nahl asked, "You are an artist, madam?"

"No. But I'd like to take lessons."

"I giff you lessons." He smiled at Ben.

Suddenly awkward, Ben was still seeing those potatoes. Marrying Elitha somehow went with farming. He didn't understand it entirely but maybe it had to do with children.

She seemed to understand his dilemma. "But first we need to talk about where we're going to live."

"Charlie," Ben hurried to say, remembering his manners. "This is my betrothed, Elitha McCoon. I'll contact you about art instruction." The German nodded and went back to his canvas.

On their way out she asked Nahl, "Did you name that oil of the Spaniard, the one with the knife?"

"Joaquín."

"Is that really what Joaquín Murieta looks like?" She opened her parasol and twirled it prettily behind her head.

Nahl grinned like a schoolboy caught copying. "Well, Mexicans haff Indian bloodt. So I paint him wit black hairs, black eyes." He smiled. "Very white teeth."

"I know a Mexican with auburn hair and gray eyes."

"I paint da image dot folks carry here," he tapped his temple.

Ben steered her up the boardwalk.

She glanced at the Placer Times building and said, "I can hardly believe this is such a big city. Only five years ago it was nothing but cattails, oak trees, and ducks."

"Didn't I tell you?" He loved the opening. "Never underestimate the men who come for gold." Slyly he added, "Or the men who haul their supplies." He turned back and opened his arms to the city. "This town is a huge capital T, the top of it along that levee. J Street here is the stem. Some of us are fattening the stem." Continuing up the boardwalk he added, "I agree with those who say it was a brilliant stroke of democracy to give the streets numbers and letters instead of naming them after highfalutin men. Here we are." He pointed up a staircase over a hattery and followed the rustle of taffeta up the dark stairs.

He knocked at the door that said: AMOS CATLIN, ATTORNEY, MINING AND WATER LAW.

"Enter," a man's voice called.

Catlin was alone, the clerk's desk closed for the day. The legislator rocked forward to all four chair legs, smiled across his table and rose to his feet. He had once assured Ben that Jared Sheldon shouldn't have dammed the river, even if laws were not in place yet. Now, any structure impeding the flow of a stream had to be proven for the public good.

They shook hands across the table and pushed-up chairs.

"This is Elitha McCoon, from Bridge House." Catlin conducted a surreptitious survey. "We're to be married," Ben quickly added.

Elitha curtseyed like a princess.

"You lucky old bloke. So that's where the light in your eye comes from. Take a seat."

After perfunctory questions about the transportation business, Catlin signaled with his eyes and Ben told him about the problem of the Indian reservation. "I thought you might be able to help." Feeling the intensity of her eyes on him, he added, "A reservation sure looks to be needed." Women often devoted themselves to society's unfortunates and though it was out of the ordinary to care about Diggers, this was no ordinary girl.

"Well now," Catlin said, leaning back on his chair's hind legs, hands behind his head, "as I recall, the boundary of that reservation was to go from the Sacramento County line out the Cosumnes River to Yoemet on the river forks, then south, taking in twenty square miles, including Drytown, Amador and Sutter's Creek. That your recollection?"

Elitha said she didn't know the boundaries, but Ben had heard all he needed. He was glad it was Catlin explaining instead of him.

"Miz McCoon, wasn't it?" She nodded. He rocked to the level, hands folded on the table. "You're talking about proven mining regions. The commercial segment of this state is laying the groundwork to break that area into a new county—Amador it's to be called. Pushing El Dorado north, Calaveras south. Now these Amador mines are going to be extremely important for a long time. You see, that federal reserve would have gobbled up the best half of it." He wagged his head in dismay. "That Wozen-something left his brains at home when he wrote that up. Of course the Indians won't like it. But you'd just as well try to get New York City back." It interested Ben that Catlin talked to her almost as if she were a man.

Elitha sat tall, her opaque half-gloves folded in her lap, her voice low and ladylike. "If the federal government can't locate a reservation, perhaps the state should." Not only did she speak well, she knew government was conducted at different levels. Ben was bursting with pride.

Catlin put his elbows on the table and knuckled an eye and then looked at her and Ben. "I'll say this. The locals understand the economic potentials better. But I doubt—" He looked away, the window illuminating the curve of his cranium through the thin hair. "How many Indians you worried about?"

Ben said, "Not many."

Catlin leaned forward. "Take 'em in as apprentices. Train them to tend your horses. Fix your wagons."

A flicker of consternation skittered across Elitha's face. "Those people used to eat plenty well living along the rivers and streams," she said. "They took care of themselves. Miners killed them. They don't need employment, they need protection."

"Times have changed, my dear. They've got to change with it." Hearing the shift to indulgence, Ben knew it was time to go.

But she continued, "Do you think it would do any good for my friends in the Slough House area to write up a petition? The Rhoadses, Grimshaws, Mahones might help. They see the plight of the Indians. Maybe we could find an out-of-the-way place for a reservation and bring it to the Legislature to consider." Magnificent, Ben thought. Legislators needed to have solutions pointed out.

Catlin scowled and nodded. "I'll think on it. Those are fine people you mention." He rose to his feet. So did Ben.

She stood immediately. "I appreciate your taking the time."

On a sudden impulse, Ben put his arm around her and said, "Amos, I've got to say it: would you believe she survived the Donner Party?" As surprise registered on the man's face, her shoulders stiffened slightly. Maybe he shouldn't have said that, but now he had to plow on, "In fact she's the eldest daughter of George Donner."

"CAPTAIN George Donner!" he exclaimed. Elitha nodded meekly and Catlin said, "Well, I'll be. What a courageous pioneer your father was! And your sainted mother. Ma'am, I am honored to make your acquaintance, and it would be my privilege to help you in any way I can." He extended his hand. She lifted hers, but he took her in his arms and patted her back. He pushed to arm's length, looking into her eyes, his own glistening. Ben saw her bewilderment and wished he'd kept a clamp on his tongue.

Showing them to the door, Catlin slapped Ben on the shoulder and said, "You ugly old bounder! I should've known you'd pick a famous girl, and it's about time you settled down." Opening the door, he added, "Stop by sometime and tell me what's going on in Stockton." The Natomas Company being his major client, Catlin had his ears cocked for anything related to water supply for the mines. He looked at her. "Come in any time, my dear, any time, and we'll see what we can do."

Then they were back on the street and Ben was thinking about a place to eat—he needed a quiet setting to find out if she was peeved at him. But unfortunately the best food was in brothels. She was working her parasol open, the sun blazing hot though it had to be well after six o'clock.

Remembering the Bay State Oyster House, he asked, "Could you eat now?"

"Well yes, but Ben, don't you have some men to see?"

God Almighty! He touched his forehead as if to restore his mind. The Stanford account! It had been over three hours. She would think him a dolt! The shock in his face must have been as plain as the house-sized cut-out of a beer pitcher across the street—he'd meant to take her in the Zins and Weiser Brewery, her being acquainted with Zins.

Pleased how fast she hurried and scrambled into the trap, barely holding him back, he snapped the reins on the rump of the startled horse. The animal stretched into a full gallop and they bounced up the rutted street, Elitha hugging the frock box and laughing like a happy child. And a funny sight it had to be, him grimly leaning forward with the reins, clearing man and beast from the road. Worried as he was about the account, he was worrying more about being too quick to tell Catlin she was a Donner.

Elitha had waited patiently, and now sharp angles of sunlight slanted across the floor of the Oyster House and laid a bright wash over her dark hair, the linen tablecloth, the flower in the vase, and the dish of oysters on the shell between them. It was hot as Hades. The waiter had propped the door open with spittoons, trying to catch the delta breeze if it happened to come up the river. So far, not a breath stirred the lace curtains at the windows. Ben leaned forward and spoke softly, though the other tables had few occupants.

"About my mentioning your being a Donner. It just fell out, before I remembered you like to keep it secret. I'm sorry. Will you forgive me?" He'd lost her once and that was one time too many.

Her sad eyes were moist, her voice soft. "He spoke of Pa with respect."

That startled him. "He doesn't grow wool between his ears. The better element holds your father in high esteem. His story, yours, will be told and retold as the great tragedy of this state. You ought to be proud of your part in it."

She looked down. "A lot of people blame him, and they think I ate—"

"Like I said, Amos Catlin's among the better element. Are you grieved with me?"

"No. I wouldn't have done it myself. But now that it's done, I'm glad. I'm proud to be the daughter of George Donner. I just don't like to be in a position of defending him. He doesn't need defending. But knowing your friends see him the way I do, I can hold my head up even if people make jokes. I have you to thank for that, Ben." Her eyes brimmed.

Suddenly afraid he'd get teary-eyed in a public place, he reached, patted her hand and changed the subject. "Did I tell you my people were farmers?"

She nodded.

It was time to get this out. "Well, I miss farming. Oh, there's a certain verve here in the city. Nice for a single man, but I like the way the sun looks in the morning when it comes across a tended field." He couldn't read her face.

Something bothered her. With a pronged tool she pried an oyster off the shell. "I thought you liked the transportation business." She slipped the oyster into her luscious mouth.

He swallowed. Oysters were supposed to be an aphrodisiac. "I like the money," he admitted, "but I guess I've seen it as a way to get by until my actual life starts." He looked at her through the steam from the potatoes, onions, carrots and kale, which the waiter was spooning on their plates, unfortunately adding to the heat. "At first, when I came to California, I figured I'd make a fortune picking gold nuggets off the ground like hen's eggs." He loved her little smile.

"Then came the trouble over the dam." Not one to pussyfoot around, he said, "I'd like to buy a farm." He noted her equanimity and remembered what she'd said at the soda parlor about going forward in life. He liked that. "What do you think about farming? We're to be a team, Elitha." He picked up his prong and worked at an oyster. He'd live in Hell if she wanted.

"Ben?"

He looked up to see her put the prong down as if about to make a confession. A fire-bell rang inside him. Women were notorious for changing their minds. He'd better make himself good and clear. He squeezed her hand beside the bud vase. "To me, where I live isn't half as important as who I live with. Understand? I just want to be with you. Go ahead, sweetheart." Her word, she'd used it at that dance in Fiddletown. If only he could fathom those eyes!

"I made a promise to Ma and Pa, up in the mountains." He held his breath. "When my little sisters got to Sutter's Fort, they told me again, I was to care for them until my folks got through. Well, that meant forever." She looked him in the eyes. "I promised God. I want to find them and care for them."

He had feared much worse. "Where are they?"

Clearly she was fighting to control her emotions. "I don't know. Sonoma I think. I write to Mrs. Brunner in care of the post office, but nobody writes back. They're getting along in years, and I guess the girls are helping with the farm work."

"But Sonoma. How—"

"The Brunners were at Sutter's Fort, then over in Rancho del Paso, and then they went to Sonoma." Her eyes told him this was more important than farm versus city. "You see, Perry didn't want them."

She hadn't changed her mind, and he could have whooped for joy, but restrained himself to match her mood. "I insist they live with us." It gave him a deep feeling of satisfaction to say it, because he meant it.

She started to sob, strange little laughing, crying noises, and covered her face with the spread fingers of her half-gloved hand. He felt something coming up from the basement of his soul. He was thirty. He wanted children around him, wanted a son to carry his name, wanted to right some of the wrongs life had handed those poor orphans. He envisioned all of this on a farm with milk cows, clover on dewy summer mornings, and a dog named Bowser. She looked so grave he feared there was something else. "I mean it, Elitha. I want you and your sisters."

He reached for her other hand and held it in his. "I can hardly believe this but I love you even more now than I did five minutes ago. I admire your convictions, about your sisters, and the Indians, and helping John Rhoads though it like to've killed me." His own eyes were filling up. "We'll go get your sisters. You and I. The two of us." The people at the next table were looking so he smiled to let them know this was private.

"Thank you, thank you, Ben." She gave him a look close to reverence.

That bothered him. Any decent man would take those girls in.

The lace at the windows lifted slightly, and the meal passed in animated discussion about the Donner girls, their names, their traits, the way they'd come through the ordeal and Tamsen's high hopes for them. They discussed the fact that Sacramento City had no school yet, though at least fifty children were roaming the streets, and those who could afford it sent their girls down to the Dominican nunnery in Benicia via paddle-wheeler.

"The girls come back Friday night, I hear. And having them gone Monday through Friday means..."

"There's Rhoads School near Slough House and Katesville, but they're primary. I could teach as much. The girls need more. Benicia sounds right, that is, ah, if we—"

"Speaking of the Cosumney," he jumped in, rescuing her, "what's going on at your place now? Is Valdez settled out there on your place?"

"Oh no. He's going to Mexico. Vyries Brown is living in the house, with a mining partner named Delaney. They're watching over things for me."

The rocky hillsides came to mind, passable for grazing, but useless for real farming, except for the bottomland claimed by the Gaffneys. And those titles could be clouded. Ben intended to purchase surveyed land, and it was funny how the thought of a farm turned him around on the squatter question. In fact, it would be prudent to charge Brown and Delaney rent, but that could wait.

She was saying, "I paid a lot of gold dust to a man to rebuild the house, but never saw him again."

"Wouldn't you know! Sometimes I doubt if there's a thief left in the rest of the world. California sucks 'em all in. The only thing for it is to elect good men to run the government."

The future was taking shape, and he wasn't one to stall once things came clear.

"Elitha. Here's what I think we should do. You go back and settle your affairs with Rhoads. Write to the Brunners and say you're coming for the girls. Then come back to Sacramento and we'll get married. By then, I'll have some time cleared and we'll go to Sonoma and find your sisters. Just take them if we have to." He gave her a look she wouldn't mistake. It infuriated him that those people hadn't written back.

"Would we live in your building, here?"

The narrow cot and miniature stove came to mind, a room designed for a midget. "No. I'll rent a place, maybe out around 18th and K. Pretty cottages are going up there. Your sisters can start the fall term in Benicia." He felt enlivened, the hauling business a key to paying for the future. "Unless you don't want me to, I'm going to look for a farm to buy. I don't see any reason why we can't have both places, town and country. What do you say?"

"I'd like that. I'm a farm girl at heart." Her smile was succulent, her dark eyes suddenly sparkling with mischief. "But I'm warning you, I've got to have an apple tree."

"Apple tree! I'll plant an orchard. We'll have apple pan dowdy, apple strudel, apple pie, apple cobbler, apple cider, apple—"

Her laughter bubbled full and rich, then her head tilted. "You'd leave me to live in town while you're gone?"

Alarm shot through him. She thought him uncaring. "I wouldn't be far, close enough to get back in a couple hours. See, the river land near town is spoken for." Could he explain it? "You're not like the hothouse flowers from the East, or the girls that fall over the traces at the first setback. You've cooked for a living in a gold camp. Alone. In a mud shack. So while I'm getting the farm going, a day or two in a nice house in Sacramento City would be nothing. In no time you'd have friends among the better women, go to church if you wanted." With sudden inspiration he added, "You could take regular art instruction. Then when the girls finish with school, or a good school is built near the farm, we'll be together all the time on our prosperous rancho."

She looked at him with those wondrous yes.

"Want another reason why I love you?"

She covered her smile.

"Perry McCoon, may he rest in peace. Every man in Cook's Bar knew what kind of a man he was. But you stuck by him and earned the living, with grace and dignity." Ben would never tell her about the deep fingernail scratches on the inside of Perry's coffin lid. Maybe he and Asa shouldn't have looked, but no woman needed to know about that.

"I didn't always want to stay with him," she was saying.

"That's the point. You stayed anyhow. You're a natural-born pioneer." She had no idea how well she would be cared for. Oh sure, life on a farm was work and you had to expect setbacks, but by thunder, this girl was a survivor! That's the kind of mother he wanted for his sons. And she also had a dignified bearing to impart to the girls. But the main thing was the way he felt when she looked at him.

The waiter came to light the candle, but he was helping Elitha from the chair, anxious to show her the city at night. His California gold was on his arm.

# 99

Father Sun came through the windows of the Rhoads kitchen. Elitha had been back for two sleeps with a ring on her finger, a beautiful crystal on a golden band. It sparkled as she sat at the table reading the paper that talks. María saw her new strength. She would soon marry the tall Americano and move to an unknown place—understanding at last that the house of Perrimacoo was bad luck. But María also noticed that when she was happy and lucky, Elitha had little power. And now that Elitha's luck was improving it seemed María's was waning. Magic doubles.

María would go to a strange new home too, when Pedro came back. She clung to that hope despite the aura. She was waiting for Pedro, and if he came to get her, she would joyfully go with him to Mexico, a place so strange that the plants had long, sharp spines.

She stirred the heavy clothing in the boiling pot and waited, feeling like a leaf circling in a backwater, waiting to be swept away. Every move she made, she waited and listened. All day, all night she listened for the sound of his horse. Her ears felt sore from listening. She longed for his touch. She looked up at Elitha, who was looking at her over the paper.

"Have you heard from Señor Valdez?" she asked.

María wiped her sleeve across her brow, the sleeve of the old blue dress Elitha had given her. "A runner says he comes soon." Remembering how joyful she'd been to hear he was alive and how disappointed to learn he was still far away, she started to heave the huge pot off the stove.

Elitha rushed to her side and pushed her hands away. "Just leave it be. Let it cool on the stove." With a puzzled look, she asked, "Where was he when he sent the message?"

"In the southern mountains."

"Coming this way?"

"Yes."

She picked up the paper and stared at it. "It says here Captain Love killed Joaquín Murieta. About a week ago."

María's breath caught. "Where?" Her heart beat no, no, no, no. She could hardly hear Elitha's reply.

"Cantua Canyon. In the mountains, down at the far end of the valley."

The messenger had come from there. "Did they kill other men too?" María asked.

"Murieta and Three-Fingered Jack. No one else is mentioned. They've pickled Murieta's head and the other man's hand in brandy."

María steadied herself on a chair back. Men who would cut off a head would do anything. "Did any of the men escape from Captain Love?"

"Yes, most of them escaped, the way this reads. And it says that many people believe they killed the wrong man. That these were innocent Mexican horse herders that got ambushed on their way to Mexico."

*Wrong man. Head cut off.* These thoughts scrambled her mind as she stared out the window over the spent corn stalks. But horse herders on their way to Mexico helped her breathe. Pedro would have been coming the other way. "What color is the hair on the head?"

Elitha scanned the paper, pursing her lips. "It doesn't say. Only that Captain Love will display it in Stockton next week—preserved in a pickle jar. He wants anyone who knew Joaquín Murieta to come and identify him. He's positive he got the right man." She looked at María. "You said you met him. Maybe you should go. I could arrange for you to ride on one of Ben's freight wagons."

"Go see a head?" Bone-deep dread chased her out the door and across the packed yard. Big danger would lurk around a severed body part. She stopped beneath the black walnut tree, hoping the babble of the river-baby spirit would calm her. Americanos had no understanding. They played with strong power. No calm came. She remembered the aura.

More sleeps passed and she lay awake listening. When Father Sun was high, her eyes felt like they had been rubbed with sand. Isabella's fussing bothered her, though it was rare, and she felt grateful to Ramón and the two boys, young men now, for taking Billy with them when they worked. The little man rode well and helped to herd cattle. "I will be a vaquero like Pedro and my father," he had said in English better than María's.

To take her mind from Pedro, she lay remembering happy days. Being Grandmother Dishi's eyes, telling her the exact shade of the sky and river. She remembered hot days when all the umne swam together contented as lazy fish, and the excitement of sliding down the Sacayak boulder for the first time with her cousins. She remembered Father's fine orations and the way people looked up to him as he stood on the dancehouse roof.

Since then, she had lived in Sutter's Fort, Pedro's room above Sheldon's mill, the cave near Spanish Camp, the hideout in the boulders, the reservation, and the Rhoads rancho. Mexico would come next, she hoped. And yet the home place pulled her. She decided to go back and visit it. The clarity helped her sleep.

The next day as they kneaded big lumps of dough, Elitha asked, "How long will you be gone?"

"I say good-bye to my home place. Maybe one sleep."

"I thought Indians didn't believe in saying good-bye."

María folded the dough and pressed the heels of her hands into the softness. "In old time Inyo no say good-bye." Bent-Willow-Reflected-in-Pond, who was learning English, looked up then went back to kneading at her end of the table.

"That's fine. You go. But do me a favor. "Remember my gold nugget, this big?" She held up her flour-white fingers. María remembered, dipping her head. "I buried it in the dirt between the two sides of the split rock, near my adobe house. Would you dig it up and bring it back to me?"

Later, during the men's meal, the sound of horses clattered outside. María set down a pan of rolls and hurried to the window. But it was only Ben Wilder in a small rig. Elitha ran outside and down the steps and into his arms. They kissed in the sunshine.

Hand in hand Elitha brought the man into the house, her aura glowing with energy and power. María put a plate and fork on the table for him. Maybe today he would take Elitha away. The Rhoads men ate in strained silence, Elitha hardly eating at all. Mr. Wilder rarely took his eyes from her. "Heard from the Brunners?" he asked.

Elitha shook her head.

"Well, I've got some news." He slathered his steaming bread with butter, closed his eyes at the first bite and made a mmmm noise. "John," he said, "I smelled this bread all the way to Sacramento. Wouldn't blame you for chaining that woman to the bread pan, but I'm afraid you'll lose her real soon now. I've found a place, my brothers and I, out by Katesville. Rancho de los Cazaderos. Heard of it?"

John Rhoads nodded thoughtfully. "Sold to a conglomerate, wasn't it?"

"Yep. Think we might buy it from them, my brothers and I. Thought I'd go on up there and take a gander. You heard anything about the title?"

"Nope." John forked a piece of meat and chewed, holding bread in his other hand. "Thought you was plannin' to live in town a spell."

"Oh, I got us a little cottage lined up too, at 18th and K."

"Ben," Elitha said suddenly, "Mary needs a ride up to Bridge House, if you're going that way." She nodded at María. "Could you give her a ride?"

"Be glad to." He went back to eating.

She began collecting the dishes as Ben said, "One of my teamsters went to see Murieta's head, down in Stockton." María froze.

The men began standing up, holding their hands over their bellies as if in pain. John Rhoads said, "I hear it isn't Murieta."

Elitha's man cocked his head like he'd heard something very strange. "They got sixteen signed affidavits to prove it was. Musta been hundreds lined up to see it. Captain Love'll get the state reward all right."

In fear of missing something, María barely breathed.

Mr. Rhoads spoke in a restrained tone. "Well, I heard the mining camps are refusing the rewards, saying they got the wrong Mexican. There'll be another showing. In San Francisco."

*Another showing.* They weren't burying the head! The horror and ignorance continued. While the men ambled into the front room like nothing was wrong, María could almost hear the whir of air, the click of a condor beak. Where was Pedro?

⁂

She walked the old, familiar path from Bridge House, and easily located Elitha's gold nugget in the split rock near the adobe house. Feeling the weight in her pocket, she walked the ancient trail down into the gully, then up the hill to the place where Pedro had sat on his horse so long ago looking down on the umne. Now she looked upon a very different place. The playing field was a fenced pasture for strange, hornless cows with white faces. The trees and vines along Berry Creek were gone, the village center vacant. Grandmother's oak still flourished but with no dancehouse beneath it. The river still flowed, the color of yellow clay, with a fringe of sick gray-green willows growing unhappily alongside—hardy, deep-rooted souls.

Near the Gaffney house and barn marked the far end of the playing field. Two mules stood there heads to tails, flicking flies. White cloth hung at the windows of the wooden house, and a young child in a yellow frock stood in the yard with chickens pecking around her.

María walked down the hill and went to the tree, slipping the bikoos from her shoulders and leaning the sleeping child against the wide trunk. Big green acorns studded the branches. No people to harvest them. She pulled the frock off over her head, and then pressed herself against the warm acrid-scented bark. I am here, Grandmother. Silence.

She sat at the base of the tree, glad for the shade. Soon it would be Cos time, but how would salmon find their way through this murky water? They must. They always had. Isabella fussed and María released her from the bikoos. She stood on her chubby legs smiling in Grandmother's shade.

Suddenly wanting her daughter to know the home place, María took her to the old bathing place. A small sprig of peppermint grew near the water's edge. "See," María said pointing, "Some of the plant people live yet." She swam with the baby, pointing out the familiar rocks and finding more brave plant survivors. For the first time in more than two moons she forgot to notice the sun's movement across the sky, and Pedro's face never haunted her.

When she took Isabella back to the tree, her dress and the bikoos were gone! Strange. But she felt no fear as she sat in the eastward slanting shadows, enjoying the warm air. Beside her, Isabella poked twigs in the soft black earth where generations of her ancestors had played and been buried. She extended a little acorn cap to María.

"A gift of Eagle Woman," María explained. "Your great-grandmother lives here. See?" She patted the bark.

"Home," Isabella said with a twinkly smile.

The earth rolled beneath them. Leaves rattled overhead, the giant turtles awakening beneath the tree roots. María tingled. Hair bristled at the base of her neck as in a lightning storm. She stood up, felt power enter the soles of her feet, travel up through her body. It sizzled in the oak-smelling air and shimmered over the hillsides. She stretched her open arms to gather it and hold the power in her body.

"Home," Isabella repeated.

She swept her daughter up, hugging her. "Home," she said, her voice cracking with emotion.

A small voice said, "What did you say?"

Turning to see the young girl in the yellow frock, María spoke English. "You finish your supper?" Many times she had heard Americanas say that to children when the sun was sliding into his western house.

"Cleaned my plate," the child said sweetly, running her gaze over María's naked body. Then she arranged her unlined face into a scowl. "Did the ground move?"

"Yes," María said, setting Isabella down, her little feet moving toward the little girl before they made contact with the earth.

The rosy-cheeked little girl stroked Isabella's hair and looked up at María and said, "Was that your tattered frock?"

"Yes."

"Don't you have another?"

She shook her head.

"I didn't know it was yours." She beckoned María to follow, adding, "You ought not to be naked outside."

At the Gaffney house lamplight glowed through the lace curtains and spilled through the open door. In her power, María entered, amazed to see a man jab his fist into another man's jaw. The two men, with hands wrapped thickly in cloth, stared at her as two women jumped out of their chairs in surprise. Strangely, the men didn't seem angry with one another.

"Saint Paddy save us!" said a woman with no eyelashes or eyebrows and hair the color of iron rust, "What have you brought us, Mary?" The other woman had hair the color of a mountain lion.

"She wants her old frock back," the child said, taking María's hand and pulling her into the kitchen. The dress hung on a peg behind the door, the bikoos on the floor beneath.

As she slipped the dress over her head feeling the weight of the nugget in the pocket and the strength of earth within her. All four people came into the kitchen, their eyes very blue. One of the women helped María fasten the buttons on her back and then gently pushed her down into a chair at the table. "Sure and we're awondrin where you come from."

"My home place is here," she said, gesturing toward the river.

"A wonder it tis, a body niver laid eyes on you then." Turning to the others, the rust-haired woman said, "And it's fine English she speaks." She cocked her head at María much like the child had. María saw that she had lashes and brows after all, but they were extremely pale.

The other woman said, "Have ye family hereabouts then?"

"My people are dead."

The women exchanged glances. "And you, my dear, how be ye keepin flesh to the bone? And with a babe to boot?"

She had to think about the meaning.

Before she could tell them about the Rhoads ranch, one of the men said, "Mither, ye been aprayin after a hired geerl." He gestured at María. "Methinks the Lord provides."

The rust-haired woman crossed her arms beneath her bosom, narrowed her eyes and laid a finger on her jaw. "Wouldja be willin to work here fer us then?"

"Maybe," she said, surprising herself. "But maybe my man comes."

"And it's a man she's got!" She opened her mouth and turned to the others.

The woman with honey-colored hair said, "You boys could use the help of a strong young Indian." They nodded, their wrapped hands hanging loose at their sides.

Pedro had a land paper for this place, but it lay with a bag of gold coins under her bed at the Rhoads ranch. It seemed a Coyote joke, these people inviting him to work here. Not speaking for him, she accepted the offer of tea and had a stray thought that someday she would make them other kinds of tea.

She and Isabella stayed the night in the warm Gaffney barn, nesting in hay. She slept well with bats whirring about, picking mosquitoes from the air. Friends from home.

# 100

Seven sleeps later, still feeling her power and waiting for Pedro, María entered the Rhoads kitchen and was surprised to see Elitha up so early. Her packed bags stood at the door, and she wore her new brown and white checkered gown with an apron over it. She had a fire in the stove and was making coffee and biscuits.

"You leave now," she said to Elitha. To meet Mr. Wilder, she knew. The two of them would find Elitha's sisters.

"Yes," Elitha said with a glance at Isabella, who gripped María's frayed skirt and stepped flat-footed on chubby feet.

They had talked. Elitha wanted María to live with her in the white "cottage" in Sacramento City, where she and Little Flicker would wash the clothes of Elitha's sisters. María had said no. She would wait where her man could find her. Besides, Billy would be sad to leave Ramón.

But now, seeing Elitha ready to go, María thought about the men who displayed the severed head and hand in the jars, and decided her power might be strong enough to repel the bad power. "Captain Love," she said, "Is he in San Francisco with the head of Joaquín Murieta?"

Elitha cracked open the oven door and peeked at the biscuits. Shutting it, she said, "I don't know. Maybe. Why?"

"Maybe I go ask how many men killed." Sixteen people had sworn that Captain Love and his men had killed Joaquín Murieta and Three-Fingered Jack, but had they also killed Pedro?

Elitha came around the table and put her hands on María's shoulders, her face filled with kindness. "Mary, I know how worried you've been about Mr. Valdez. Sometimes we have to force ourselves to do what we don't want to do, so we won't be wondering forever. I think you'd be doing the right thing to go there and ask questions."

"You show me how go on boat?"

"Maybe Ben and I can go with you. We're heading to Sonoma, and that's a stop along the way. But hurry. The Sacramento stage leaves in a half hour."

"I go talk to Billy and Little Flicker. How many sleeps to San Francisco?"

Elitha looked at the ceiling then back at her and said, "Better figure one night in San Francisco, and another night in Sacramento City on the way back. Two nights."

She continued to feel her power. Billy was glad she wouldn't take him from what he called his work. Hurrying to the river for herbs, she packed them with dried meat and nu-pah in the bottom of the bikoos, along with a purse of gold coins.

She hardly had time to realize, as a Rhoads boy drove her and Elitha to Slough House, that she would see a new world.

On the hurtling ride to Sacramento City, Elitha looked stronger than María had ever seen her. Color glowed in her cheeks. She mentioned everything they passed. But María kept her strength inward. As the distance from the home place lengthened, she unfocused her eyes. Isabella seemed to understand. Sitting quietly on her lap, the child stared out the window before taking a long nap.

When Mr. Wilder helped them from the coach, María hardened the shell around her strength to protect against the shouting and quick movements of strangers. She was shocked to see structures encrusting the earth like fungus. Only a few large trees remained in an area where many would have grown old. Too many people—she could smell their excretions—lived where sedge and redbud would have grown. The walls of the new people reached out to capture earth, changing outdoor space to indoor space. Only small dusty lanes remained between the buildings.

Elitha spoke to Mr. Wilder. María saw in his manner that he didn't want to go to San Francisco. Elitha whispered, "She's been like this the whole way." They didn't know her senses were keener than ever, that she heard Elitha's words as well as the words of people across the road.

She followed Elitha and her man down a canyon of buildings, then up a man-made slope to a wide brown river crowded with huge boats, some with tooth-like railings. The shore had been made straight and sterile. At a big ticket house, more crowds made her heart race, everyone staring rudely at her. But she stood with Elitha and Mr. Wilder and regained her calm.

With it came clarity. As Mr. Wilder extended a handful of coins toward a man in a cage, she touched the elbow of his shirt and said, "I go alone." Their presence, their love for each other, his yearning to be with Elitha alone, and Elitha's hurry to get quickly to her sisters would tug at María's power. He pulled his hand from the cage.

Elitha leaned her head around him and said, "You might get lost, Mary." Her brow was creased with worry.

"Many people go. I ask the way."

They exchanged a look. Elitha asked, "You sure?"

"I be alone in San Francisco." It had once been called Yerba Buena and that gave some comfort.

A man behind said, "Hurry it up, up there in front." Others in the line muttered.

Mr. Wilder thrust his hand into the cage and said, "One round-trip ticket to San Francisco. Two one-way tickets to Vallejo." He turned to María and explained that they would travel on the same boat, but he and Elitha would get off before she did.

They walked on a wooden pathway, a bridge laid from the man-made bank to the mid level of an enormous floating structure with two layers of toothed railings. Beneath her dry feet she felt the movement of the water and marveled again at the cleverness of the new people. Father would have enjoyed this.

The boat filled with people and the wooden pathway was withdrawn. The boat shuddered and roared, belching black smoke from a tall, fat pipe. A gigantic wheel at the side turned, slap, slap, slapping the water, faster and faster, the spray flying to the rail where she stood. It startled her at first, but seeing that it made the boat move, she welcomed the cooling spray.

A blast screeched. In fright she lurched toward the benches where Elitha and Ben sat. They smiled and called it a "whistle."

Recovering, she realized she must expect the unexpected and control all fear. She must retreat deeper into herself. Digging a coin from the bikoos, she handed it to Mr. Wilder. "It is the gold of Señor Valdez," she explained. "He tells me use it for travel. You take."

He looked at her oddly, then, seeing Elitha's nod, accepted the coin, but handed another back.

"No, you take," she repeated, refusing it.

"I already did. The fare was only two dollars," he said. "Put that back in your purse." He smiled kindly.

Wondering if she would ever learn the secret language of coins, she put the gold beneath Isabella's feet. The baby wriggled and thrashed, not wanting to be laced up.

With a happy look Elitha said, "Let me walk her around."

She gave the baby to Elitha and returned to the rail at the front of the boat. The sun was high and the trees along the banks of the big river stood motionless as she cut through the breeze, racing through the wooded river channel on the giant grinning fish. Here the miners hadn't destroyed the huge sycamores and oaks, the ripening vines hanging in great veils from green heights. Clouds of birds flitted through them. Life remained abundant. Around her and on the deck below, people talked and laughed.

Seven hours, Elitha had said the journey would take. Many channels ran outward, the driver skillfully guiding the boat through the watery maze. Sometimes, rounding a bend she saw a fence, a house, or waving children running toward the water. The boat whistle screeched its greeting. She inhaled the fecund aroma of the backwaters, her power intact, and flew toward Father Sun.

The roar and vibration stopped. The whistle blew, a bell clanged, and a man yelled, "All out for Vallejo."

Elitha came to the rail with toddling Isabella gripping her finger. She had eaten. Bits of food clung to her smiling cheeks. "María," Elitha said, "I'm going to miss you terribly." She hugged her, her breath smelling of coffee, her hair of American soap. "I'll send things for you and the children." Mr. Wilder added, "When I finalize our agreement at Rancho de los Cazaderos, we want you to come live with us there. If you're still in California."

"Maybe I go to Mexico," she said, sorry tears prickling her eyes at the maybe. "Good-bye," she said, glad that Elitha would soon be reunited with her sisters.

Elitha picked up Isabella. "You sweet thing, I gotta go now. Take care of your mother now, hear?" She kissed the child's cheek and handed her to María. "She's so beautiful. I love those auburn curls." She fluffed them. "She's got Pedro's eyes too." She smiled wistfully at Isabella, then rustled away after Mr. Wilder—a bag in each of his hands. The checkered fabric of her gown soon melted into the throng on the wooden pathway

María sank back into her power.

The boat erupted into life. She picked up Isabella. "See. Father Sun goes to his house in the west." The water was streaked with fiery gold. Isabella fussed to return to the bikoos, having had a tiring day. María laced her in and hung her on her back. Then, she continued to stand at the front of the boat, racing toward the sun, toward knowledge. The trees and water were dusted with gold, the sun bloated and red. But after a while the colors faded and the shores moved apart.

A salty aroma permeated the wind as the boat churned into a wide, flat, silvery world. This was how it was before the creation of land—Raven, Coyote and Turtle on a boat drifting endlessly in a watery world. Turtle conquered his fear of the depths and dove all the way to the bottom, bringing up mud in his claws. Raven shaped the mud into earth. María knew how Turtle felt, alone and fearful in the deep water.

An island loomed indistinctly in the darkening mist, then fell rapidly into the dusk behind. She heard only the slap, slap, slap and the roar of boat.

Ancient and new times lived together. Turtle had conquered fear and brought land. What would come of her journey?

She hardly noticed that most of the passengers had gone below and the air had turned chilly. A man moved from lamp to lamp along the rail, lifting glass shells and lighting wicks. Like a many-eyed monster, the boat forged through the young night, the lamp glass protecting the flames from the wind.

Ahead, a mountainous silhouette became visible, black against the twilight lingering in the sky, a mass of twinkling lights along the shoreline. As the boat approached, the pinpoints of light separated and shadowy buildings appeared. The roar in the boat's bowels stopped abruptly, as did the slapping. The silence jolted Isabella awake. People emerged on deck. A woman pointed, holding back her blowing hair. "There it is. The City!" *San Francisco.*

The grinning fish monster glided silently through the black water. With a thud that threw her forward, it stopped. Her head spun with the lack of motion. Voices shouted. People thronged toward the wooden pathway. The journey was over. After the sleep she would conquer fear rising like mist from uncongealed thought, a nameless horror lurking like a dark island apart.

⚘

All night she huddled in an unlocked portion of a sprawling waterfront building, lying between pieces of iron that smelled of rust, grease and salt. Rodents scurried in the dark. Dawn jabbed slivers of light through the walls, but she ate none of the food she had packed. Like a young man on his quest, she would hold onto her power and enhance it by fasting.

San Francisco was like Sacramento, but without sunshine. Men and animals rushed up and down roads lined with brick and wooden structures. She shivered—not expecting cold in this season—and glanced both ways at an intersection. She saw many men, but no women or children. Three men in tall black hats stepped from a coach, the driver whipping the horses onward.

Approaching, she asked, "Where is head of Joaquín Murieta?" She gazed politely past them.

"Well, I'll be damned," said one. "First squaw I've seen since the mines!" He smiled down at her torn blue frock and bare feet as one would smile at the antics of a child. "Even they're flocking in to gawk at that atrocity."

Not understanding, María repeated. "Where is head?"

The man pointed to a building higher than the intervening buildings. Turning to leave, she heard: "Amusing the way they ape the whites." She didn't understand ape, but it didn't matter. She knew where she was going.

A hill rose vertically behind the town, the peaks concealed by clouds. Shivering, she realized the truth of the old wisdom, that clothing provided little warmth. Only acceptance warmed. In time of rain she could stand naked in sleet and frost with less discomfort, because she expected and welcomed the cold. Now as she walked beneath the overhanging porches of the stores with wind blowing her hair and plastering her skirt on her legs, she thought of the home place. Father Sun would be heating the morning air. The sky would be blue.

Approaching the building, she slowed. About four or five twenties of people, men, women and children, crowded around the door. But they parted as she passed through them, staring at her and at Isabella in the bikoos.

Talk crackled. "Filthy feet" hissed on their tongues. "Hooves." But nothing mattered except talking to the men who had killed Joaquín Murieta.

The cold metal doorknob moved in her hand, but the door held fast. Turning to a woman hugging herself in a woolen shawl, María said, "I come to see men who show head of Joaquín Murieta."

The woman lifted her nose and said, "This show ain't fer Injuns."

"Squaw, you got a dollar?" said a man standing stiffly near the door, a ring of keys rattling in his hand.

"Yes."

People within earshot turned to repeat what she'd said to those behind, and stared with eyes like fried quail eggs. But she was prepared for anything, glad to be alone, and glad for the strength that fasting had enhanced. "You can see the show," he said, "but git to the back of the line." He flicked his hand the way Elitha shooed chickens.

Relieved not to be excluded, she asked, "You ride with Captain Love?"

"I ain't gabbin with no squaw."

From the back of the crowd she watched the line slowly move, boots and shoes shuffling forward. The door had been opened. As new people arrived, she nodded for them to go before her. In a strange place one followed the rules of courtesy. People who had viewed the head hurried the other direction, speaking in excited tones: "Grotesque... vicious... Joaquín for sure... loathsome hand."

Warming to the spirits swirling off the waters of San Francisco, she waited. Isabella seemed to enjoy the brisk wind and strange sights. María prepared to face the fearful possibility that the men had not seen Pedro, and that she would never see him again and would never know why. Yet an even darker island lingered in the mist.

At last the viewers moved faster, the sun slipping in and out of the clouds. It blazed brilliantly as she stepped over the threshold, and slanted through the windows inside a cavernous room. The people ahead of her bunched before two tables, a large jar on one, a smaller jar on the other. "Lord amercy!" "Ooooh!" echoed within the walls. Beside the large jar sat two men in chairs. Men she had come to talk with.

"One dollar," said one of the men.

She handed him a gold coin, unsure if it was a two-dollar or five-dollar piece. He dropped it in a metal box and waved her inside.

The room went dark, the sun hiding. She calmed herself as she drew nearer to the jars—the air prickling with angry, hovering spirits. She grew taller in her power.

The place lacked air, all houses did, but this was worse. The smells of many people mingled. The room grew darker yet, the door being shut, new people being kept out. Periodic flashes of light washed across the room as the door opened and closed, viewers leaving.

Without looking she saw the amber fluid in the jar. She didn't want to see Joaquín Murieta, who had been a vibrant man in life, reduced to a head. Instead she focused on the men in the chairs. Both wore white shirts and dark jackets, their faces shadowy in the gloom. The one nearest the table held a sheaf of papers on his crossed thigh, and a pencil. He asked the people in front, "Did you know Joaquín?" They shook their heads. He waved them on. María stepped before him, trying not to see the floating hair.

He asked, "Did you know Joaquín Murieta?"

"Yes."

"Where are you from?"

"Río Cosumney." He scribbled on the paper.

"Your name?" He looked at her.

She stood thinking, as light briefly washed across his cheek and nose, the last of the viewers leaving. She had hoped to cloister her strength. Still, she had come to ask this man a question, and couldn't afford to upset him. Looking over his head at the framed likeness of a white-haired man hanging on the wall, she murmured, "Mary." Life was balance.

He scratched on the paper and nodded at the jar. "Say if it's him."

Not intending to look, she asked, "Captain Love, he kill other men too?"

"Nope. Just Joaquín Murieta and Three-Fingered Jack there." He rose from his chair and accidentally bumped the table. At that instant Father Sun blazed brightly through the wall of windows, brilliant light sparking off the glass jars, clearly illuminating the reddish brown hair moving like moss at the bottom of a river. It drew her unwilling eyes.

Pedro stared blindly at her through the brandy, his mouth a silent scream. The tails of his mustache waved in gentle synchrony with his hair and shreds of pale flesh on his neck. Below that flared the flat shoulders of the table. Stiff. Dry. Dusty.

Giant wings whumped into the room. Concussive beats, pulling her inside out. The air shrieked. She barely heard: "Holy Jesus, we ain't got all night. Say and git on outa here, squaw."

Power suffocated and blinded her. Her legs collapsed and she slumped to the floor. Men's voices howled in the maelstrom. Rough hands yanked her. The room whirled in chaos. Through the crackling wind she heard Isabella cry, a voice demand: "It's him, ain't it. It's him!"

"Yes." She managed, struggling to her feet to face Condor. Yes. She had known it would be Pedro.

The fractured air aligned itself as the bird settled on the jar and gripped the wide lid with its talons. Molok thrust his naked pinkish head at her, scowling, red eyes unblinking. His wings stretched from one side of the room to the other—wings slashed with white, the tip feathers apart as if grasping the air. Below him, Pedro's gray eyes stared. Next to Pedro, Quapata's claw of a hand curled, the scar on the stub of the finger exactly where she had applied the herbs. The men in suits stood motionless as rocks.

Molok asked the courteous question, "Where are you going?"

A yipping howl came from behind her. She turned to see Coyote, tongue draped over his incisors. "Give her a peck," he said. "She wants to die."

But the power of Condor flowed into her and filled all the hollow spaces. She expanded until she was tall as the building and broad as the bird's wingspan. Her voice came quiet and steady within the wooden walls:

"I go to the home place. In time of rain I will wear the mist rising from the river. In the long dry I will wear the dust of the earth. I will sing and dance to celebrate the spirit that lives in all things—life rising from the ashes, the living feeding upon the dead, the eternal cycle. I will help the plant and animal people to repopulate the shores and teach the new people to know them. I am old, Molok, in decay. I am food for the new people to root in, and someday they too will talk to birds. They too will hear spirits in the boulders and the river and the trees. Someday they will listen."

# Endnotes

# Endnotes

**Pedro Valdez** is a fictionalized, fleshed-out representative of the handful of Mexican pioneer soldiers who went to the Sacramento Valley with John Sutter to help him "pacify the frontier." The Sheldon family has forgotten the name of the "Spanish friend" to whom Jared Sheldon is said to have handed his son during the shootout with miners, so Pedro became that man. For personal background he became the son of old Pepe. Dmitry Zavalishin, a Russian scientist, linguist and diplomat who in the early 1820s attempted to lay the groundwork for a Russian takeover of California, wrote later from Siberia (where he was exiled and jailed for being part of an attempted coup) that he had met a man called Pepe near San José who constantly talked about rich sites of gold far east of where he lived. Pepe was considered mad. Zavalishin writes, "…he was a tall, lean old man with wild, roving eyes … almost naked and barefoot, in a threadbare cloak … but he gave very definite answers to my questions and displayed no insanity at all." During the gold rush Californios like Pedro were sometimes flogged and hanged in the mining regions. Ethnic violence was common and well documented.

**Mary.** In the early 1990s local old timers shared a sketchy memory of an Indian woman named Mary who lived to old age in the vicinity of Bridge House. "Indian Mary" was not married, but had a daughter with "reddish" hair who sometimes worked with her. Indian Mary treated the sick with herbal remedies, and for many years delivered most of the ranchers' babies. According to Hilda Granlees, Mary (then about 70) delivered her father Arthur (1898). When Art grew up, he built the house that was later bought by the author and her husband, the house where these words are being typed. Another historical record of Mary is in the memoir of Heinrich Lienhard, who was at the Fort during the time of this story. He mentions that in December 1844, Perry McCoon took his Indian wife, "Mary" to the Fort to have the name of their baby, William Perry McCoon, recorded in Sutter's New Helvetia Journal (the portion before September 9, 1845 was lost in a fire). The baby, known for the rest of his life as Billy, is a major character in *Rest for the Wicked*, this book's sequel. Lienhard tells of other incidents involving "McCoon's mistress," a beautiful Indian girl named Mary, including her bamboozling Sutter out of two-thousand of dollars when he was camped with his Indian and Kanaka miners. In a humorous tone Lienhard mentions Sutter trying but failing to bed Mary. Readers will find Lienhard as a bit player in the story, in Sutter's Fort and the mining camp that became Sutter Creek.

**John Augustus Sutter** (Johann Augustus Suter), part vainglorious pretender to rank, part chronic debtor, part visionary, entrepreneur and self-promoter, part generous host and booster of California's interior. Born in Germany, he moved with his family to a small town in Switzerland when he was a young teen. There he apprenticed and worked during his 20s as a store clerk for his father-in-law. His portrayal here was shaped by many diaries and historical references, and the following books: Richard Dillion, *Fool's Gold* (1967), Kenneth Owen, ed, *John Sutter and the Wider West* (1994), William Breault, SJ, *John A. Sutter in Hawaii* (1998), and excerpts of Heinrich Lienhard's notes and memoirs about Sutter's Fort in the 1840s (pub in German 1860s, part of an enormous autobiography, extracted and trans from German by Marguerite Eyer, *A Pioneer in Sutter's Fort* (1941). Escaping a mountain of debt and a warrant for his arrest, he left his wife and 5 children in Switzerland and sailed to the U.S. In Missouri he acquired more debt, dodged creditors, and trekked to Oregon with mountain men, where he boarded a ship for Hawaii. There he socialized with international financiers who bought up debt as a means of making money. He admired them, and one imagines it was there he picked up his tendency to think large and present himself as a man of affairs. Somehow acquiring a ship, he manned it with Kanakas and sailors, one of them apparently Perry McCoon, and sailed to California. Posing as a European military officer he became a Mexican citizen and received a large grant of land, which he named "New Helvetia," on the confluence of the American and Sacramento rivers. This place was, and is, called Sutter's Fort. Lienhard and others wrote of Sutter's use of young Indian girls. Leinhard describes the fight at the fort when Sutter learns of Wm Daylor's advances on Manu-wiki. The Micheltorena War is variously interpreted. Dillon describes an outfoxed and incompetent Sutter trying to succeed on the battlefield. The present book simplifies the movements of that campaign. Exactly why a decapitated mule was the only casualty remains uncertain. Sutter's treatment of Indian workers at the fort was arguably better than they received in the missions—he paid for labor, if sparingly. Wm Daylor did indeed loan the money that brought Sutter's wife and family to California, changing Sutter's life dramatically. Sutter gave his son power of attorney, seemingly to dodge debt, and Sutter Jr. paid off some of his father's debt by selling pieces of Sutter's land to the men who developed the City of Sacramento, much to the elder Sutter's dismay—he never spoke to his son again. Buried in Lititz, PA, Sutter died in 1880, having spent his last years in a futile attempt to lobby the U.S. government into compensating him for his fort, livestock, and supplies when the U.S. Army took possession during the Mexican War. Sutter's life demonstrates the opportunity presented by the Old West to an ambitious man. Sober and less prodigal, he might indeed have become the King of California, as a plaque on his birth house in Kandern, Germany hails him.

**William Perry Mccoon**, an English sailor hired by John Sutter to help with the cattle and pilot the riverboats. A scatter of records tell of McCoon stealing calves, drinking too much, being vain about his appearance, and deserting during the march to war. In the New Helvetia Journal John Sutter records McCoon's receipt of title for the pig farm on the Cosumnes River (no title was granted). On February 5, 1846 Sutter mentions McCoon's marriage to widow Lewis in the New Helvetia Journal, and 4 months later, he mentioned her burial at the Fort. The memoir of Dr. Duval, visiting doctor at the Fort, suggests to those who have read it that Mc-Coon (Mr. Perry in Duval's memoir) beat her badly and then hauled her to the Fort because he'd heard a doctor had come there to visit. The doctor feels sorry for the 18-year-old with youth and beauty being badly injured from the waist up. She miscarried before she died. Dr. Duval omits the cause of her wounds; men in those days often beat their wives without consequence or shame. On June 1, 1847 Sutter records Perry McCoon's marriage to "Mis Donner." The Houghton memoir describes the wedding feast. The cattle drive of Sheldon, Daylor, Mc-Coon, Charles Weber and others to Coloma in 1848, which led to their discovery of gold in Weber Creek (Placerville), is well documented. "Dry Diggings" yielded up to $17,000 per week, one source states. This continued until the Indian workers were massacred. In 1943 the author of *Early Day Romances* writes that Mc-Coon wasted his wealth drinking and gambling, losing self-respect and pride in his appearance. His sale of mining claims is speculative, but County records say he sold George McKinstry all or part of his ranch for $25,000. McCoon died at Bridge House in a riding demonstration witnessed by a large number of people. One diarist said he was buried at his home. The author believes he is likely to lie under the white quartz rectangle emerging from the old asphalt near the author's lawn, but that could be his second grave. In 1997 in Reno, while attending a conference about the West, the author met a man who was also interested in the Donner Party. He said he'd run across a gold-rush diarist who had been called upon to help Elitha rescue her husband's coffin from the rising river. He and a companion did so, and in the process noticed that the pine lid had been scratched on the inside with fingernails, indicating that Perry had been buried alive. The author inquired about the name of the diarist, but the informant could not recall it. He'd been researching something else at the time and didn't write it down. Someday, someone will find it.

**Elitha Cumi Donner McCoon Wilder**, the eldest daughter of George Donner who accompanied him on the ill-fated journey to California. To reduce confusion with Elitha's name, the author called the youngest sister "Ellie," though her real name was Eliza. The stories of the baby nailed to the wall, the $10,000 inside the quilt, the

Brunners' failure to answer Elitha's letters, and the happy day in which the Indian women feasted on hornet grubs are from Eliza's published memoirs 65 years later, assisted by Elitha—the first break in the Donners' long silence. By Eliza's account, Frances remained at the Brunners with her sisters until removed by Elitha and Ben. (Other accounts place her with the James Reeds in San Jose. This author chose to tell it the way the girls recalled it). According to Eliza's memoir, Ben and Elitha whisked the little girls away from the Brunner place in Sonoma and settled them to live in a rented house in Sacramento at 18th and K Streets. Soon afterward, Mr. Brunner was convicted of murdering his nephew and was incarcerated in San Quentin. Most people today would be surprised at the extent to which the survivors were blamed and, especially the females, made sport of on account of the cannibalism. During the Donner Party rescue, George McKinstry penned a lewd, unprintable note to Lt. Kern about "man eating women," which is preserved in the California State Library. Regarding the San Francisco property, the earthquake and fire of 1906 destroyed records, but a *San Francisco Chronicle* story in 1928 told of the town "doing itself proud" by giving lots to the "Donner orphans" (names omitted) in 1847. The timing fits with the Houghton account of Elitha accompanying McCoon to San Francisco and not returning for a couple of months. In an undocumented endnote to his revised edition of *Winter of Entrapment,* the late Joseph King says that James Reed orchestrated the property gift for Elitha's cousins Mary and George, whom he adopted, and that they subsequently lost it in court battles with squatters. Mc-Glashan's history is the apparent source for this interpretation. Except for her cooking for miners, nothing is known about Elitha's life after McCoon's death and before she married Wilder. She is not known to have spoken on behalf of Indians or to have worked for John Rhoads, and there is no evidence of a romance with Rhoads.

At a 1997 book-signing when the 1st edition of this book was published, an elderly descendeant of a neighbor of the Ben Wilder family in Galt, California said his father had attended a one-room school with the Wilder children, and that each year when the teacher presented the Donner Party story, Elitha would come to the school in her long black dress and sit quietly in the back of the room. She never spoke but it was understood that she was there to nip any sensationalism in the bud. Elitha's grandchildren remembered her as a dignified old woman sitting quietly on the porch overlooking the fields. In 1923, at nearly 91, she died and was buried in the Elk Grove Masonic Cemetery next to her husband. As recently as the 1960s her great-great grandchildren hesitated in school to identify themselves as descendants, because of jokes about cannibalism.

**Elitha's Baby, Elizabeth McCoon.** When the 2013 edition of this book was in the editing process, Kristin Johnson, the author of the Donner Party blog, wrote to say she located a death notice for Elizabeth in the obscure *Daily Alta California* (San Francisco, April 27, 1852, p. 2, c 6). This is the first time any modern person knew the exact age of the baby or the date and cause of her death. In her memoir Eliza

Donner Houghten mentions the baby's death in passing, and this reader came away with the impression that Elizabeth was younger. It was too late to change the date, the season, and the cause of death, as everything affects everything else in a novel. Still, perhaps the reader will be interested the contemporary news report: *"DIED. At Cook's Bar, on the Cosumnes River, April 21st, of measles, ELIZABETH, only daughter of Mrs. E.C. McCoon, aged two years and three months."* This means Elizabeth was probably born in January, 1850. A cholera epidemic had been raging through the mining camps, and the author made a guess.

**The Forlorn Hope**, the name given to the 15 snowshoers who left the Donner Party lake camp on Dec 15, 1846, to seek help for the starving party. Until recently it was assumed that this moniker was used by the emigrants themselves however recent and ongoing research of the letters of survivors prove that this name was first used after the tragedy. Therefore that name was deleted from this 3rd edition of this novel. Kristin Johnson, http://user.xmission.com/~octa/DonnerParty.

**John Pierce Rhoads,** a giant of the Donner Party rescue, was truly a man to match the mountains—one wonders if he and Reasin P. Tucker, the other "giant" rescuer, were the real-life models for Irving Stone's novel, *Men to Match My Mountains.* John Rhoads and his family are represented as faithfully as possible, including their rich "Rhoads Diggings" near in the present town of Folsom. Their removal of gold from Dry Creek nine months prior to the usual gold-discovery date is Rhoads family history, as is Father Thomas Rhoads' scouting for Zion in California to help Brigham Young, and the Rhoads family's return to nascent Salt Lake City with a barrel of gold. Family legend claims that the golden Angel Moroni atop the Mormon Temple in Salt Lake was made from that barrel of gold. Thomas married again (plural wives) and founded the Utah branch of the family, which spells the name Rhoades or Rhodes. After his first wife Matilda died, John Rhoads married Mary Murray in 1854, a year after Elitha married Ben Wilder. John Rhoads served in the California Legislature. In 1866 at age 48, he died of pneumonia and was buried in the Slough House Pioneer Cemetery. His raft ride on belted logs down the raging rivers to alert Sutter's Fort of the stranded Donner Party is family legacy—the Bear River portion noted by other sources. His descendants meet annually to maintain his grave in the Slough House Pioneer Cemetery. The Daughters of the Utah Pioneers also keep the cemetery neat. They have recently erected an interpretive sign that shows the graves-map.

**Salvador** and **Luis** are historical Indians who worked for John Sutter. In his fort Journal Sutter calls them "good boys" from the "tribe of Cosumne." They were in fact killed by their white companions. They are the only members of the Donner Party known to have been murdered to be eaten.

**Lewis Keseberg,** his cannibalism, his trial at the fort, the morbid jokes and the contention that he developed a taste for human flesh, are the subject of ongoing speculation. The Donner money—estimated at over $14,000—was never found by anyone who admitted it. An educated and intelligent man, Keseberg bought a hotel, restaurant and brewery in Sacramento, but was plagued by business failure and the care of two epileptic, uncontrollable daughters, one mentally retarded. Phillipine Keseberg, said to have been a buxom woman with an eye for other men, bore him seven other daughters, most of whom died young. A friend wrote that Keseberg was loathe to talk about his Donner Party ordeals, which had become something of a fixation bordering on "derangement of mind." Poverty-ridden in his last years, he died in 1877 and is buried either in the Old Sacramento City Cemetery or, more likely, in the pauper's cemetery near the old County hospital.

**Mary Murphy** and her abuse by William Johnson are from Mary's letters. She is buried in the town her rancher-developer husband, Charles Covillaud, named for her: Marysville. William Johnson left California and went to Hawaii.

**Grizzly Hair** is patterned after an impressive Miwok leader who organized his people into a gold-panning cooperative and whose funeral drew hundreds of Indians from miles around—mentioned by Steven Powers in *Tribes of California* (1871).

**Jared Dixon Sheldon,** an educated and skilled millwright from Vermont, narrowly escaped death after being left alone on the early Santa Fe Trail. Sheldon arrived in California in the 1830s and became in effect California's first English-speaking contract engineer. Fluent in Spanish and more than one native language, he built water-powered mills in Los Angeles, Marin, Bodega Bay (for the Russians), Contra Costa (for José Amador) and Mission San José (on Mill Creek) before building one on his own land grant. His life in California with his ranch partner Bill Daylor, is well documented. Sheldon and Daylor lie side by side in the Slough House Pioneer Cemetery, formerly the Omuchumne burial mound. During the gold rush Sheldon did indeed hang horse thieves on his property, for the reasons given. His death in the violent struggle over damming the Cosumnes River was the first of California's unending "water wars." Not until 1878 did the California constitution clarify that the public has the right to access the streams and rivers. The news article and Sheldon's written proposal to the miners are verbatim. Hydraulic mining, which is just beginning at book's end, deposited at least 16 feet of silt in the riverbed, covering all but the top of Sheldon's damaged dam. Sometimes the top edge can still be seen underwater in the riverbed. Recently, a memorial plaque was erected on the south bank, overlooking the dam site. In the gold rush community of Bridge House, Jared Sheldon's cabin stood until it rotted with the large bloodstain on the pine floor. Remnants of his gristmill can be seen at the river's edge today, when not silted over or underwater. The remarkable oak-trunk mill spindles still exist, but need a permanent home. The spiked cannon was repaired by the Grimshaw family and fired by the men every Fourth of July until one year, when overloaded with powder, it exploded. No one was injured. Son William Chauncey Sheldon (little Will) prospered, fathered a family and maintained his father's papers.

**Catherine Sheldon "Catey,"** daughter of Thomas Rhoads and sister to John and Sarah Rhoads, was Jared Sheldon's wife. She lived a long life and her grave is marked by the largest, most elaborate headstone in the Slough House Pioneer Cemetry. Her marriages to two men after Jared was killed were not happy. She became a noted midwife, and made a success of the Slough House Inn, which now serves spirits and meals after a hiatus during the Great Recession. She visited Mahone when he was dying, and then married Dennis Dalton. Catherine died in 1905 at the age of 73. While standing in the Slough House Pioneer Cemetery, one can see the backside of the Greek-revival house her second husband, Mr. Mahone, built for her a short walk from the Inn.

**William Daylor** was a tall, strong English sailor saved by Jared Sheldon when he was forced to walk the plank far out in Monterey Bay. Lienhard describes the fight in Sutter's Fort, with Daylor pitted against a large number of Indians and Kanakas. Sheldon rescued him from deportation, and for the rest of his life Daylor was Sheldon's partner. Daylor did indeed become a very wealthy man during the gold rush, and he did loan Sutter Jr. the money for the passage of Sutter's wife and daughter, but the amount was $7000; another man loaned a similar amount. Daylor's motive was suggested by Lienhard's colorful description of Frau Sutter.

**Sarah Rhoads Daylor Grimshaw**, sister of Catherine and John Rhoads, had no children by her first husband, William Daylor. With her second husband, William Robinson Grimshaw, she founded a large clan. The circumstances of Mr. Daylor's death and the advent of Mr. Grimshaw as shown in this novel are historically correct. The old Indian trading post became the prosperous Cosumne Store of the gold rush, and now stands a bit derelict next to the locally famous "corn stand" of the Davis Ranch. The old boarded-up store still faces Daylor Road, now State Highway 16. Sarah is buried beside her husband William R Grimshaw and her numerous children and grandchildren in the Slough House Pioneer Cemetery. W.R.Grimshaw, who arrived in California on a commercial vessel at the start of the gold rush, penned an engrossing personal memoir. *Grimshaw's Narrative,* with a photograph of him as a young man, was published by the Sacramento Book Collectors Club in 1964. The watch on the back cover of this book is made of the gold Sarah found in the roots of spring grass while pulling them up to make a garden. She sent the gold to a goldsmith in England and commissioned him to inscribe the image of a jaunty gold miner, and gave the watch to her husband, WR Grimshaw, as a gift. The gold is "red gold," the variety found in the California Mother Lode. The watch was photographed by Sarah's great, great-grandson Rick Grimshaw, who continues to be involved in the roadside business at the site of Daylor's trading post, which the locals refer to as the Sloughhouse corn stand.

**Ben Wilder** is represented as faithfully as historical records allow, including his role in the miners' shoot-out with Jared Sheldon. *The Sacramento Union* quotes are verbatim. Wilder's words and actions after the shooting were orally reported by Mrs. Marguerite Gordon of the Eating House, who later worked for the Sheldon family. Shortly after they were married in 1853, Ben and Elitha took the Donner girls from the Brunner's yard in Sonoma and cared for them in their rented Sacramento cottage on 18th and K streets. Via paddlewheeler, the little girls journeyed to school in the Dominican nunnery in Benicia. Wilder and his brothers acquired Rancho de los Cazadores near today's Rancho Murieta, but lost it when the U.S. Lands Commission ruled the title invalid. After a brief return to mining, he bought a farm in Galt, a few miles south of Sacramento, where he and Elitha lived for 50 years and had six children. Wilder became a conservative pillar of Sacramento County's GOP. Their eldest son, George Donner Wilder, hung himself after his wife and three children burned to death in their house on the Wilder ranch. Their other son, was thrown from a horse and died of a fractured skull. The daughters continued the family.

**Joaquin Murieta** is and always was a blend of historical fact and gold rush mythology. The legislative debate about the reward occurred. A maimed hand was displayed along with the head, but historians believe the villainous "Three-fingered Jack" was a fiction of the bounty hunters—a sort of bonus offering (See Remi Nadeau, 1974). Many old-timers who claim their forebears were acquainted with the real Murieta say his hair was blondish. Aided by the head and hand, which he exhibited in Stockton and San Francisco, Captain Love succeeded in getting the State reward. The grisly display later made the rounds of gold rush towns. In the 1890s the head came to rest in a San Francisco museum of medical curiosities. Some historians believe the earthquake of 1906 threw it off the shelf where it lay in broken glass and alcohol and was quickly consumed by fire, while others believe it was rescued and is the same head that sits today on a TV in Santa Rosa, property of a Mr. Johnson, who inherited the relic from his grandfather (colorfully described by Richard Rodriguez, 1992). Many descendants of pioneers tell family stories of Murieta's long and peaceful life after his purported death.

**Oliver Wozencraft** wrote the reservation treaty with the Indians, the goods listed quoted verbatim. Unfortunately for the native people, Wozencraft resigned from government service and is remembered as a persuasive advocate for federal dams and subsidies for railroads to the West. The story of Indian reservations in California is one of the sorriest episodes in U.S. history.

**Many Minor Characters** with European names are historical—including William Tecumseh Sherman, who surveyed Jared Sheldon's land grant, acquired land in the Slough House area during the Gold Rush and a decade later played a key role in the Civil War; General Mariano Vallejo, Edward Ord, John Frémont; William Leidesdorff, from whose rancho the town of Folsom sprang; and Leland Stanford, who sold dry goods in Sacramento and Stockton when Wilder was hauling. Stanford is remembered for the university he founded for his son and for being one of the Big Four who built the first transcontinental railway. George Donner did in fact know Abraham Lincoln. They had served together in the Black Hawk War.

**First Wagons Over the Sierra.** The Stephens-Townsend-Young-Murphy party, the first wagon train to cross from the east, found it necessary to leave all their wagons behind. Having no maps, they broke up into three groups and went different directions; all of them eventually found their way to Sutter's Fort. Fortunately, the snow wasn't deep enough to stop them, as it stopped the Donner Party the next winter. Sutter dispatched Indians to fetch the wagons and take food to the stragglers. A widow of the S-T-Y-M party married Perry McCoon, as shown here.

**Gold Rush Towns.** Marysville is a thriving city. Katesville and Cook's Bar vanished with the 49ers. Michigan Bar lasted longer, then withered after 1920. Sutter Creek, Amador City (smallest incorporated California city) and Drytown are quaint Amador County towns on Highway 49. Ione (formerly Bedbug) is a rural town best known as a state prison site. The little that remains of Fiddletown's commercial center is virtually unchanged since 1852, including the Erauw's brick mercantile that may well be the site of Murieta's interrupted card game, and a Chinese apothecary (Dr. Yee's) locked since the Gold Rush with herbs and cures still on the shelves, recently reopened as a museum. At Sloughhouse (modern spelling) a couple of businesses besides the Inn remain, but the old town of Cosumne is entirely agricultural, though the store, rebuilt in 1862, still stands. The surviving structures of Bridge House were torn down by the developers of Rancho Murieta in the early 1970s.

**The Omuchumne** were indeed massacred while panning gold for their employers and then running toward their home. Daylor's letter was published as quoted, excerpted in this novel because of its length. The episode is also described by killer-participant M. Case in the Oregon Historical Quarterly (1900). A preface by the Quarterly's editor states: The "… conflict was between a system of peon and contract labor and free labor" and the Oregonians, representing free labor, employed the only method available—"brute force." In other words, disliking the labor system, they exterminated the labor force. Pedro's retaliation is fiction. Quapata was a child at the time, one of the two Omuchumne orphans provided for in Daylor's will, and was not a bandit. He is buried in the historic Slough House Cemetery.

**Spelling and Pronunciation.** Anthropologist James A. Bennyhof states that Amuchumne is the correct spelling of the Slough House area natives. The author chose to use Jared Sheldon's spelling to honor the linguistic ability of the area's first Euro-American settler, a man fluent in English, Spanish, a native southwestern language (Comanche or Apache), and who learned fluent Plains Miwok from his workers. To him "O" in the first syllable more closely renders the native sound, and u in the second syllable, the short u of "muck", represents the native sound.

**The Cosumnes River.** When Padre Duran of Mission San José enticed or abducted a Delta village to the mission and asked them their tribal name, they said Cosum-umne, deemed by anthropologists to mean the people of Cosum, Salmon. Padre Narciso Duran wrote the shorter version on his map and not realizing that the word was already plural he added an "s": Río de los Cosumnes. The name and spelling stuck. His is the first written mention of the river. The spelling of the river varies in this book, just as the pronunciation of the word varies by the speaker. It is clear that the descendants of the first English-speaking pioneers pronounced the river Cosumney, accent on middle syllable. This matches the Miwok suffix umne, meaning "the people of" and pronounced um-ney. Early Spanish speakers used the long u, rhyming with loom.

**Rancho Sacayak** is noted in the earliest Sacramento County histories, though not having been surveyed (a requirement of a Mexican land grant), it had no official boundaries. About the time Elitha left her adobe, an Irish miner named John Driscoll built a rock-lined dugout nearby. Over the next 53 years Driscoll expanded his holdings for stock-raising, purchasing adjacent land from departing miners, as did his descendants for another 50 years. Unknowingly they were piecing the old rancho back together. In the 1930s grandson Art Granlees acquired the property of Vyries Brown, an old prospector living alone in his dilapidated frame cabin, and built a new house a few yards away. It is not known what happened to Maria's people at Rancho Sacayak. They might well have been massacred, as were other whole villages, as shown in this novel. They also might have left their destroyed home, and it is possible that the people whom maps of California natives show with various spellings of Sacayakumne or Sagayakimne, were a remnant of the relocated people.

**The Condor-Skin Robe** was stolen after the Indians refused to sell it to John Sutter. He "acquired it" and gave it to Russian collector I.G. Voznesensky, who wrote in his diary that the natives who saw the robe were "terrified" of it, as if seeing Satan, and "astonished that I could keep such a thing in my room" (without dying). Russian scholars see an ancient link between Miwok and Siberian-native bird animism (See Okladnikova on Voznesensky, translated by M.W. Kostruba, *Journal of California and Great Basin Anthropology*, 1983, Vol 5, Nos 1 and 2. In a lengthy endnote, California anthropologist Craig D. Bates probes the range of the Molok dance and regalia in California, noting that a similar robe displayed in that museum might have originated in Sek (visited by Voznesensky, approximate modern location CalExpo, Sacramento, see map in author's *Eye of the Bear*). The identity of the thief on the Cosumnes River is unknown, so McCoon became that man in this novel; he had opportunity and motive. By 1917, the Tsar's private collection housed a large number of Miwok artifacts, including the condor-skin robe(s). Communists broke in and executed the last Tsar's entire family. Today the robe(s) can be seen in the St. Petersburg Museum of Archeology and Ethnography, and on its website. Imbued with spiritual significance, the Molok regalia was rare in the 1840s, and the Miwok people would like it back.

**The Miwok People**, Maria's people, were so-named by anthropologists who categorized California natives by language — miwo means human being in the northern range (Cosumnes River south and east of Sacramento), mewuk in the southern range (Yosemite area). The entirely autonomous Miwok tribelets, like thousands of other tribelets in California (speakers of 50-300 languages depending on the cataloger), identified themselves as x-umne, the people of x, often, a headman. No ties bound them to distant tribelets of the same language. Peaceful people, they prided themselves on speaking the languages of neighboring peoples—a mosaic of 8 linguistic groups in the San Francisco Bay Area alone. (Randall Milliken, *Time of Little Choice* (Ballena Press 1995). The disintegration of tribal culture began with colonization from Mexico—missions and military, which spread new diseases that flashed throughout California as well as policies and attitudes that stirred up rebellion against the colonizers. (see *Eye of the Bear*, set 1825-1829.) In starting *River of Red Gold* in 1844, the author chose to skip 15 years of pestilence, massive Indian die-out, and polyglot bands of Horse-thief Indians. See epilog of *Bear* for consequences of Indian victory in war, and also George Harwood Phillips, *Indians and Indian Agents* (1997) for an understanding of California history during those important years. A much larger village site downstream from Maria's place had been deserted by the time of the first settlers, likely due to disease. Those who wish to see these sites should visit www.bridgehousebooks and sign up for one of the author's history-nature walks.

**The Derisive Term Nigger.** During the time period of this novel it was not uncommon to hear it applied to the California native peoples, and sometimes the Californios, as well as people of African descent.

**Californios,** also called Native Californians, gave themselves this name, possibly so as not to be confused with Native People, or Natives. They were the Spanish speaking people who colonized California from New Spain (later to become Mexico). The military and political elite prided themselves for having Spanish blood—many sought to acquire certificates of "pure blood" from Spain. However, most Californios were a mix of Spanish, indigenous people of Mexico and/or California, African or all three. They developed a distinctive culture based on the skills of cattle-raising and horsemanship, and evolved unique dances, social traditions, and music. By the 1840s their leadership was shifting to those who had been born in Alta California.

**Californio Vaquero Songs** were often sung while watching herds of cattle. They were sung, remembered, and shared, but the authors of the compositions and lyrics were lost to time. During the "Spanish Revival" period in California, a few of these songs were collected, translated and arranged by William J. McCoy and published with guitar arrangements in 1926 by Sherman, Clay & Co in San Francisco. The title of the collection is: *Folk Songs of the Spanish Californians.* This is the source of the song Pedro Valdez sings in this novel. In Part I: *El Tormento D'Amor, The Torment of Love*

**Hymn Sung By the Donner Family In Part II.** *Christ Arose.* It might be a stretch, but not a long one, to have put this song in the mouths of the Donner family while they were under the snow in December, 1846. The prolific composer Robert Lowry (1826–1899) probably wrote the song after 1846.

**Turkeys and Bees.** Because the California Department of Fish and Wildlife (DFW) "introduced" turkeys in California in 1906, many readers contacted the author to say that no turkeys existed in California prior to that. It would be unique to California if the early Spanish colonists did not bring turkeys with them (1775–1820). Most extant inventory lists of priest-led migrations north from New Spain (Mexico) included turkeys. In addition to overland migrations, settlers depended upon regular shiploads of supplies from Mexico, which included live poultry. Turkeys were prolific and prized by the natives of Mexico, as Cortez learned, and Spaniards loved to eat them. Wild turkeys are easily domesticated, but the cactus fences of mission and pueblo compounds couldn't contain them. San Jose is a short distance from the central valley. Turkeys fly well and are suited to California terrains. If they were not in California prior to 1700—the native people maintain they were—they arrived soon afterward and were exterminated before the DFW existed. Dozens of bird species went extinct in California from 1848-1870 due to hunting by tens of thousands of hungry gold seekers and by professional hunters supplying the eating houses. The bigger and slower the bird, the faster they disappeared. A number of articles in California newspapers 1860s-1880s describe weddings or other celebrations for ordinary people in which turkey was the main course. That they would serve an expensive import as the main course is highly unlikely. It bears mention that until the mid-1950s wild and domesticated turkeys were indistinguishable; the big–breasted white variety not yet bred.

Many beekeeping readers insisted there were no bees in California prior to 1856, because in that year a farmer imported the first European Honeybees. However, it is well known that scores of species of bees are native to California, including 20 species of bumblebees in the area of this book's setting, some of which nest in trees or the ground and produce honey and wax. H.H. Bancroft (1888) mentions that in pueblo San Jose in the 1820s, ragged arguardiente producers living in hovels spiked their product with honey. One assumes this delicacy was not imported.

**Ending.** This book was first published and distributed in 1996. In 1999 HarperCollins issued a novel by Isabelle Allende with much the same ending.

## About The Author

Author Naida West and her husband live in an old farmhouse on a small ranch bounded on the south by the Cosumnes River and the north and west by Rancho Murieta, a distant suburb of Sacramento. A poet with a Ph.D., in 1990 Naida quit teaching and lobbying to be a full time novelist. During her 20 years of researching and writing about the people who walked the land before her, large new houses have altered the area but artifacts from the ground and the unchanged river landscape were a constant inspiration.

### Other books by Naida West
*Eye of the Bear: a History Novel of Early California* (book 1)
*Rest for the Wicked* (book 3)

*Murder on the Middle Fork* (with her uncle Don Ian Smith, set in Idaho, not part of the California series).